THE AFFAIR OF THE

BLOODSTAINED
EGG COSY

MUTILATED
M I N K

THIRTY-NINE
CUFFLINKS

AN OMNIBUS EDITION

JAMES ANDERSON

This omnibus first published in Great Britain in 2010 by
Allison & Busby Limited
13 Charlotte Mews
London W1T 4EJ
www.allisonandbusby.com

The Affair of the Bloodstained Egg Cosy © 1975 by JAMES ANDERSON
The Affair of the Mutilated Mink © 1981 by JAMES ANDERSON
The Affair of the Thirty-Nine Cufflinks © 2003 by JAMES ANDERSON

The moral right of the author has been asserted.

A CIP catalogue record for this book is available from
the British Library.

All titles published by arrangement with Poisoned Pen Press,
Scottsdale, Arizona, USA.

10 9 8 7 6 5 4 3 2 1

ISBN 978-0-7490-0915-1

Typeset in 10.5/15 pt Sabon by
Allison & Busby Ltd.

The paper used for this Allison & Busby publication
has been produced from trees that have been legally sourced
from well-managed and credibly certified forests.

Printed and bound in the UK by
CPI Mackays, Chatham ME5 8TD

THE AFFAIR OF THE
BLOODSTAINED
EGG COSY

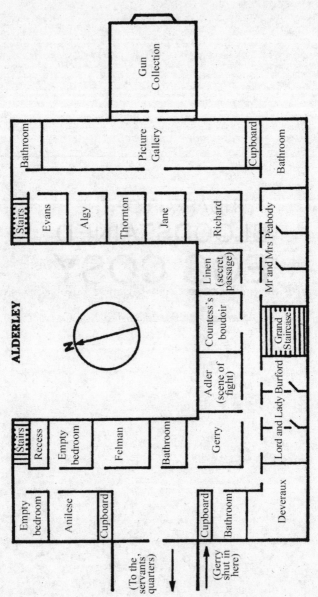

ALDERLEY

N

Plan of First Floor

Gun Collection

Bathroom

Picture Gallery

Cupboard

Bathroom

Stairs

Evans

Algy

Thornton

Jane

Richard

Linen (secret passage)

Countess's boudoir

Mr and Mrs Peabody

Adler (scene of fight)

Grand Staircase

Stairs

Recess

Empty bedroom

Felman

Bathroom

Gerry

Lord and Lady Burford

Empty bedroom

Anilese

Cupboard

Cupboard

Bathroom

Deveraux

(To the servants' quarters)

(Gerry shut in here)

The author wished to acknowledge with
thanks the contribution made by Ewan W Wilson
towards the publication of this Allison & Busby edition of
The Affair of the Bloodstained Egg Cosy.

PROLOGUE

PROLOGUE

'How well do you know Adolf Hitler?'

The man who asked the question was short and dapper and wore a military uniform heavy with insignia. He turned away from the window of his office as he spoke and surveyed the only other occupant of the room with a look of slight distaste.

This was an older, somewhat seedy-looking man in a blue serge suit and a dirty collar. He was smoking a cigarette and lazily blowing smoke rings towards the ceiling.

'Not well at all,' he said. 'I've met him twice. Why do you ask?'

'Last week your department supplied me with the transcript of a speech he had just made to a secret meeting of Nazi party officials.'

'Concerning the Duchy?'

'Yes.'

'What about it?'

'I just wondered if you were able to read between the lines of that speech.'

'Well, it's obvious he wants the Duchy.'

'That has been obvious for a long time. On this occasion, however, he laid considerable stress on her strategic importance – and on her military weakness.'

'Indicating that he intends to act soon – to annexe her?'

'We believe so. Which would, of course, be disastrous to our interests.'

'Would it? Well, if you say so.'

'I do. It was decided many months ago that if any country was to annexe the Duchy, it had to be ourselves. But there was no great urgency. Because there is an obstacle.'

The older man sucked at his cigarette and puffed three or four smoke rings upwards. 'England,' he said.

'Precisely. Or Britain, to be more accurate. Britain recognises the importance of keeping the Grand Duke on the throne and the Duchy, to put it crudely, on her side. She will certainly be prepared to act to ensure this. Just how much she will be willing to do we've never known. However, Hitler's speech has changed the situation entirely. Now it is essential we act quickly. As the American cowboy films so quaintly put it, we must beat him to the draw. But first of all we have got to find out just how far Britain is prepared to go in the Duchy's defence.'

'Which, I suppose, is why I was so peremptorily summoned here this morning.'

The short man sat down in a chair near the other, leant forward, and spoke in a low voice. 'There is shortly to be a secret meeting between a representative of the Grand Duke – probably Martin Adler himself – and a British government minister. Can you discover where and when that meeting is to take place – and what is decided at it?'

The older man's eyes narrowed and he eased himself slowly upright in his chair. 'That,' he said, 'will not be simple.'

'Of course it won't be *simple*. But can you do it?'

'Perhaps.' The older man was silent for a moment, then added: 'There is one agent – and one agent only – in the world who might succeed. Not one of my own people – a freelance. If this agent is available, then the answer is probably yes. But it will cost a great deal of money.'

'The cost is immaterial. Just find out what we want to know.'

'Which is – precisely?'

'Exactly what arms and equipment Britain agrees to supply, and – most important – how soon she can deliver: we must know how quickly we have to act. Also, what Britain would do in the event of the Duchy being invaded: would she intervene directly by sending troops? On the answer to these questions depends our course of action. It is entirely up to your department to get them.'

The civilian was still for a few seconds. Then he stubbed out his cigarette and got to his feet. He brushed a few specks of ash from his waistcoat, and ambled towards the door. 'I'll be in touch,' he said, and went out.

CHAPTER ONE

A Resignation

Jane Clifton was fuming. Some customers were absolutely intolerable. And Mrs. Amelia Bottway just about took the cake. Jane replaced the red dress on the hanger, took down a green one, and returned to Mrs. Bottway.

'Perhaps you would care to try this one, madam.'

'Oh, really, you are the most stupid girl! I told you distinctly not green.' She had a piercing voice.

Jane reddened, then swallowed hard. 'I'm sorry, madam. I didn't hear you. I'm afraid this is the last one of your size in a bright-coloured satin.'

'Well it's no good to me at all. None of them 'ave been. You've been wasting my time. It's disgraceful.'

'I've shown you nine gowns, madam. I'm sorry if none of them is suitable, but—'

'I shall 'ave to try h'elsewhere. Somewhere where they keep a adequate stock – and employ some h'intelligent girls.' Mrs. Bottway struggled to her feet and fixed Jane with what was plainly meant to be a withering glance.

Jane looked back at her with revulsion, her face fixed in what she called her painted-doll expression. The foul-mannered, ugly old barrel, she thought to herself. How dare she speak to me like that?

'You foul-mannered, ugly old barrel,' she said loudly and distinctly, 'how dare you speak to me like that!'

She hadn't meant to say this: the words had just come. But they were out now, and Jane suddenly felt very much better.

For several seconds Mrs. Bottway did not react at all. Then slowly her face started to go purple. Jane suddenly realised that she was the centre of attention. There were three or four other customers in the shop, and, together with the assistants, they were all staring at her speechlessly.

Mrs. Bottway, whose complexion by now resembled an overripe plum, at last got her mouth open. 'You—' she said, 'you – you – you 'ussy.'

Jane watched her with a cool and curiously detached air. She marshalled her thoughts: might as well be hung for a sheep as a lamb.

'Mrs. Bottway,' she said, 'you and your sort sicken me. You are insolent, bad-tempered, and arrogant. You've got pots of money and not the first idea how to spend it. You ask for a satin dress in a bright colour. I ask you – with your figure! You'd look even more grotesque than you do now.'

She got no further. For from behind her came a voice raised in a screech. 'Clifton!'

Jane swung round to confront the proprietor of Mayfair Modes, Monsieur Anton. 'Clifton – you wicked, wicked girl. You will apologise to madam this instant.' He was almost hopping with rage.

Jane interrupted quietly. 'I shall apologise to nobody. I

meant every word of it. Don't bother to say any more. It's too late. You can't fire me. I resign!'

And she strode to her cubicle, jammed her hat on her head, grabbed up her coat and handbag, and made for the door. Just inside it, she turned.

'Mr. Anton,' she said loudly, 'I have a week's wages due to me – three pounds, seven shillings and sixpence exactly. But don't bother to send it on. Put it towards the cost of a new wig.' And with her head held high, Jane marched out into Bond Street.

She walked off briskly, struggling into her coat as she did so, and cursing herself for a prize idiot. Fancy throwing up a steady job, walking out without a reference – and no hope of getting one now! – not even claiming what was rightfully hers; when she had just £9 18s 7d in her bank account and 11s 3 1/4d in her purse.

But it had been worth it. Their faces! Jane suddenly laughed out loud – greatly to the surprise of a plump, bowler-hatted little man she happened to be passing.

'Jane – wait!' The voice came from behind her and Jane spun round to see a small, red-haired girl darting along the pavement towards her.

'Gerry!' she exclaimed.

Lady Geraldine Saunders, only daughter of the twelfth Earl of Burford, rushed up to Jane and caught her by both hands. 'Jane – darling – what a simply devastating performance!'

Jane stared. 'You were there?'

'You bet I was there. I called in to ask you to lunch. I was just waiting quietly for you to finish with that ghastly person when you suddenly blew up. It was magnificent. Jane, tell me, does that funny little man really wear a wig?'

'Not that I know of. But everyone will think he does now, won't they?'

Gerry gurgled happily. 'Oh, how priceless. Jane, you must come and lunch with me at the Ritz. It's ages since I saw you. I've got tons to talk about.'

'You'll have to treat me, Gerry, if you really want the honour of my company. I'm absolutely stony broke.'

'Who isn't, darling? But I can just run to it. Come on. Let's hail a cab.'

In the taxi Jane reflected ruefully that her friend's idea of stoniness was quite a different thing from her own. To Gerry it meant trying to stretch to the end of the year an annual allowance of fifteen hundred pounds. It was ironic that there should be such a contrast between the situations of two girls whose families a few generations previously had been of about equal standing – two girls who had gone to the same school, been 'finished', and come out together. But whereas the present Earl of Burford was still the proprietor of estates in the West Country and Scotland, a series of disasters and blunders over a period of sixty or seventy years had gradually eroded the Clifton fortune. So that Jane had to fend for herself.

She sighed. 'Oh, Gerry, why am I such an ass? Why do I keep throwing over all these jobs? I know it's irresponsible, but I can't seem to help it.'

'Well, nobody could put up with being spoken to like that. You had no alternative.'

'Oh, but I did. To bite my lip, keep smiling, and say I was very sorry if I hadn't given satisfaction. That's what any of the other girls would have done. It's what I've done – often.'

'I don't know how you stood it for so long.'

'Because I wanted to eat. It's as simple as that.'

A minute later the taxi pulled up outside the Ritz. 'Come along,' Gerry said, 'you'll feel better after a good lunch. No banting today. Let's forget our figures and have a real blow-out.'

It was while they were drinking their after-lunch coffee that Gerry suddenly said: 'I say, I've just realised you're a free woman. You can come down to Alderley for a bit.'

'Oh, it would be heavenly. But I must start job-hunting again.'

'Bunkum! You needn't begin straight away. You need a breather first.'

'But, Gerry, I explained, I'm practically on my beam ends. I can't afford—'

'You're not going to be any worse off by spending a few days with us. It won't cost you anything to live while you're there. Look, I'm motoring down in the Hispano-Suiza tomorrow – oh, of course, you haven't seen her, have you? She's absolutely my pride and joy. She's got a nine and a half litre V12 engine. Does over a hundred miles an hour. Pushrod ohv, two twin-choke carbs – sorry, I'm being a bore. Where was I? Oh, yes, you must come with me, you must, you must.'

Jane laughed. 'All right. It's terribly sweet of you. Thanks awfully. But I can't come tomorrow, really. I must put in a few days job-hunting first. Next Thursday OK?'

'Lovely.'

'Actually, it's just what I need. Who else is going to be there?'

'Oh, some Americans called Peabody. He's a fabulously rich Texan. Oil, I think. We've never met them, but he's got one of the biggest collections of old guns in the States and he wants to see Daddy's. No doubt they'll both be excruciatingly boring the whole time about frizzens and multiple matchlocks and things. Then Richard's bringing down a couple of foreign diplomats, and a man called Thornton from the Foreign Office. I gather they're all going to be engaged in some sort of governmental talks. Richard asked if it would be all right and of course Daddy agreed, though why they've got to use Alderley, I don't know.'

'How – er, how is Richard?'

'Fine. He comes down about every fourth or fifth week on average. It must be quite a long time since you've seen him.'

'Over two years.'

'Really? Yes, of course, the two last times you came he was abroad. He'll be thinking you've been avoiding him.'

'Anyone else expected?'

'Well, I'm afraid – and you must brace yourself, darling – that Algy is.'

'Algy Fotheringay? Oh, Gerry, no! What on earth possessed you?'

'Not me – Daddy. Algy buttonholed him at the Eton and Harrow match. You know how he's always trying to cadge invitations. Daddy swears he couldn't get out of it. I've just about forgiven him. But I'm afraid we're all going to have to spend merry hours listening to Algy talk about himself, his rich and fashionable friends – and food.'

'If you go on like this,' said Jane, 'I may well change my mind.'

CHAPTER TWO

Ten Downing Street

The Honourable Richard Saunders sat in the ante-room to the Prime Minister's private study and wondered again why the Old Man had picked him, a junior minister, for this job.

It had happened just two weeks ago. He had been unexpectedly summoned into the Presence and given a surprising little lecture.

'It is highly important that a stable democratic state friendly to Britain be maintained in central Europe as a bulwark against both Fascism and Bolshevism,' the Prime Minister had ended. 'The Duchy fills that rôle admirably. Now, however, she is extremely weak military and is threatened by invasion from several directions. The Grand Duke has approached us for assistance. We want to help; it will be in our interest to do so. However, in the present political climate we cannot be seen wantonly distributing British arms to small states, or committing British troops to war in Europe, without something tangible to show in return. The Grand Duke has indicated his willingness to cede to the British crown certain so far unspecified colonial territory, where rich mineral deposits have recently been discovered, but which the Duchy herself is not in a position to exploit. He is sending an envoy to negotiate a treaty whereby we will supply military aid in exchange for this territory. What has to be determined is precisely what aid we supply – and how soon – and exactly what land is given in return. Until we can announce full agreement, the negotiations must remain secret. Clearly, neither the Foreign Secretary nor I can be involved. We want you to handle them. Think you can manage?'

Richard, of course, had said yes. But still he wondered – why him? Today he was determined to find out.

'The Prime Minister will see you now, sir.'

Richard rose and entered the private study.

'Ah, come in, Saunders.'

The Prime Minister got to his feet and held out his hand as Richard went forward. 'Do sit down.'

Richard sank into a deep leather chair and waited silently as the Prime Minister lit his pipe, leant back and eyed him keenly from under bushy eyebrows. 'All set?'

'I think so, Prime Minister.'

'The Foreign Secretary and the War Minister have briefed you fully?'

'They have.'

'Splendid. There are just one or two points I want to emphasise. Firstly, the importance of speed: this matter must be settled quickly. Intelligence sources tell us that the threat the Duchy faces is very real, and growing. Fortunately, we are in broad agreement with the Grand Duke. Naturally, their envoy will try to obtain from you more than we are able to give, earlier delivery of the equipment, and so on; and to keep the extent of the territory they hand over to us to a minimum. They may also want British troops stationed permanently within their borders. But we wish to avoid this: you must keep it in reserve as an ultimate concession. Your task is really going to be extremely delicate: obtaining the best possible deal for Britain consistent with assuring the security of the Duchy.'

The Prime Minister reached into his drawer and took out a large envelope, which he handed to Richard. 'Here are the blanks for the draft treaty. Simply fill in the details in accordance with the agreement you reach. The final terms are entirely your responsibility: we will stand by whatever arrangements you make. You'll have Thornton from the FO present as your adviser throughout, of course. You've met him?'

'Yesterday for the first time. He seems very able.'

'He is extremely able. Highly experienced, and with a full knowledge of our capabilities.'

'Which is something I conspicuously lack, I'm afraid. Needless to say, I'm deeply honoured, but I cannot help wondering why you asked *me* to undertake these negotiations.'

'Why do you think I asked you?'

'Well, obviously if outsiders weren't to realise the importance of the talks, you had to pick somebody fairly junior; yet it's patently too important a matter to be handled at Embassy level. But I can't help feeling there are others better qualified than I to deal with it. The only real asset I have seems to be—' He broke off.

'Seems to be what?'

'Alderley.'

'How do you mean, Saunders?'

'Well, I do spend a certain amount of time there with my brother and his family. My sister-in-law gives frequent house parties. Then there are the Alderley collections – foreign visitors do call now and again to examine them. So the visit of two men from a small European country, at the same time as I'm there myself, will cause no talk; while at the same time they will be well out of sight of the press and the diplomatic corps. In addition, the house is extremely secure. From the moment the Foreign Secretary asked if my brother would be willing to entertain a couple of strangers for a few days, I had in mind that that might have been the reason I was chosen.'

The Prime Minister shook his head firmly. 'No. Those factors did enter into our calculations and Alderley did seem an eminently suitable venue. However, there were others equally suitable. I did not select you because your brother happens to be Earl of Burford, but because you are the best junior minister for the job. All right?'

'Very much so. Thank you.'

'Please convey to the Earl and Countess our gratitude for their cooperation. I shall, of course, write when the talks are concluded. There are to be some other guests present, I understand?'

'Yes, an American couple by the name of Peabody. He's in oil, I believe.'

'They are the only ones?'

'The only ones I know of. My niece, Geraldine, may have some friends of her own down. Why – do you think she ought to be asked to put them off?'

'By no means. We do not want to give the impression that anything out of the ordinary is taking place there. By the way, how much do you know about your opposite number?'

'Adler? Only that he's been very much the power behind the throne in the Duchy in recent years.'

'Comparatively few people know even that much. The general public have barely heard of him. Have you realised how rarely you see his picture in the papers?'

'No, I hadn't. But, of course, it's quite true.'

'He's an American, you know.'

'Really?'

'Well, half-American. His mother was American and he lived there most of his life until about ten years ago. He met the present Grand Duke at Harvard and returned to the Duchy with him. Since then he's never looked back – even though he's reported to be a highly unconventional kind of diplomat. Apparently he's the one man in the country who's got all the facts necessary to conduct the negotiations at his finger tips – without even having to consult notes.'

'Remarkable. Who is this man Felman who is accompanying him?'

'Oh, just a young aide or secretary of some kind. We are not, at their request, laying on any official welcome. We do not even know by what means they are travelling to this country. They will make their own way to Alderley.'

The Prime Minister rose. 'Now I must wish you luck – and assure you that if you succeed in bringing these negotiations to a satisfactory and speedy conclusion, I will not let the fact go unrecognised.'

CHAPTER THREE

Guests

'I'd just like to see any doggone jewel thief try to lift my Carrie's diamonds. Even this guy they call the Wraith.' And Mr. Hiram S. Peabody looked pugnaciously up from the magazine out of which the faces of himself and his wife stared at him.

His secretary, John Evans, who had been the one to bring the magazine to him, gave a sigh. 'I'm afraid you might get your wish, HS.'

'Let him. I'll be ready. My daddy didn't make half a million bucks, and I didn't turn it into fifty million, by backing down to cheap crooks.'

The two men were in the sitting-room of Mr. Peabody's suite at the Savoy Hotel in London. Evans, a thin young man, with hornrimmed glasses and a small toothbrush moustache, was looking harassed. 'The Wraith is hardly a cheap crook, sir. And I'm not suggesting you should back down to anybody.'

'Tell me, John, how long have you been with us?'

Evans looked surprised. 'Nearly twelve months.'

'For the last four of those we've been travelling all over

Europe – Athens, Rome, Venice, Paris, and a whole lot more. All that time Mrs. Peabody has had her necklace with her. You've never worried about it before. Why start now?'

'Well, for one thing, your exact movements – and the facts about the necklace – have never been so publicised in advance before.'

'But if this Wraith character moves in society, as he's reputed to, he doesn't need a newspaper to tell him where the wealthy are, does he?'

'There's more to it than that. This magazine lays down a definite challenge. It's not the sort of thing the Wraith will want to ignore. He's been inactive for some time now and he's probably ready for a comeback. This is thoroughly irresponsible journalism, if you ask me.'

'I'm with you there. Guess I was a mite foolish to speak so freely to that reporter.'

Just then the door opened and Mrs. Peabody sailed in. A smart woman of about fifty, with a round, good-natured face, she was followed by four package-laden page boys. They put down their burdens, were lavishly tipped, and departed. Carrie Peabody turned a beaming face towards her husband. 'Hiram, you really should have come. I've had a dandy morning. And I don't suppose I've spent more than two thousand dollars, either.'

'That's swell, Carrie. Come and look at this.' He held out the magazine to her.

Carrie took it and gave an exclamation of pleasure. 'My, isn't that nice? You look truly distinguished, honey.'

'Read what it says.'

'Read it to me, will you? Save me putting my eyeglasses on.' She passed the magazine back.

Peabody read aloud: 'Mr. and Mrs. Hiram S. Peabody, who arrived in London this week on the final stages of a European tour. Mr. Peabody is the well-known Texas oil millionaire, and the owner of one of America's largest collections of antique firearms. Mr. and Mrs. Peabody will be staying for some days at Alderley, the country seat of the Earl and Countess of Burford. His lordship is, of course, well known as the foremost collector of old weapons in England, and Mr. Peabody is anxious to inspect the Alderley collection – and to show Lord Burford one of his own prize possessions, which he recently purchased in Rome.

'Mrs. Peabody is here seen wearing her famous diamond necklace, which is insured for five hundred thousand dollars. It is perhaps fortunate that Alderley has one of the most elaborate burglar-alarm systems in Britain. Otherwise, we feel the necklace might make an almost irresistible target for the notorious Wraith!'

'The Wraith?' Carrie Peabody said sharply. 'That's that society jewel thief, isn't it – the one who always leaves a calling card?'

'That's it. A drawing of a sheeted ghost. John figures we should deposit the necklace in the bank before we go to Alderley – just to be on the safe side. What do you think?'

Mrs. Peabody shook her head firmly. 'Oh no. Definitely not. I've never stayed with the English aristocracy before. Our hosts may have a title going back hundreds of years and a famous stately home full of art treasures and antiques. But they don't have a diamond necklace worth half a million bucks. I must have something to keep Uncle

Sam's end up. I'm taking my necklace – and wearing it.'

Her husband chuckled. 'Good for you, Carrie. That's just what I figured you'd say. Something else our hosts lack, too, is a unique, personally-engraved Bergman Bayard 1910/21 semi-automatic pistol, custom-made as a gift for Tzar Nicholas II just before his assassination. I'm sure looking forward to seeing the Earl's face when I produce it.'

In the smoking-room of his club, Algernon Fotheringay was talking.

'Then, of course, next week I'm toddling off down to jolly old Alderley for a few days. You ever stayed at Alderley?'

His listener, the laziest member, and the only one who hadn't made a hasty withdrawal within moments of Algy's appearance, yawned and shook his head.

'Oh, it's an absolutely topping place. The Earl and Countess are ripping people. So's Gerry, their daughter. I met the Earl at Lord's the other day. He almost begged me to go down. They're having quite an exclusive party, and he said that it wouldn't be the same without me at all.'

'I'm sure that's true.'

'I had several other invitations outstanding, of course, including one to Cliveden. I was tempted, but when it came to making a decision, Alderley won. The grub there's ripping. The cook does a perfectly spiffing steak and kidney pie – and she's a dab hand at soufflés, too, don't you know. The only possible fly in the ointment is that a little bird tells me there are going to be a brace of foreigners there. Some Americans, too, but I don't bar Americans. No

these are a couple of *real* foreigners. Of course, if they turn
out to be too hairy at the heel, one can steer clear of them.
It's a pretty big place. But the danger is that Lady Burford
might be tempted to dish them up some of their national
dishes. I was staying once at a place in Norfolk, don't you
know. Of all things they had a bally Arab staying there. A
sheikh or something. Well, you know, the chief delicacy
among those johnnies are sheep's eyes. Well, would you
believe it – I say, old man, are you all right?'

But the laziest member was asleep.

CHAPTER FOUR

The Richest Man in Europe

In a large house on the outskirts of Paris, in a big curtained room lit only by a flickering log fire, a little wizened, bald old man sat in a high-backed armchair. He was holding an open atlas and studying a map of Africa. Eventually he raised his head, revealing a hooked nose and deep set eyes, which burnt with a fierce light. His lips were thin and his jaw long and pointed. His hand, which now moved slowly to press an electric buzzer set into the low table beside his chair, was scrawny, like a claw. The old man looked frail, almost lost in the big chair, dwarfed further by the high vaulted room, and by the huge old-fashioned grate, the flickering light from which barely reached the distant recesses of the room. Yet in spite of his frail appearance, there was strength in the old man – strength in the talon-like hand, strength in the jaw, above all strength in those dark and darting eyes. The old man dominated his surroundings, as for forty years he had dominated the lives of thousands of people all over the world – people who had never even heard his name.

That name was Jacob Zapopulous. It was a name which

was spoken of with something like awe in the financial centres of the world; the name of a man who, through a combination of financial genius, treachery, graft and blackmail, had made himself the richest man in Europe.

Jacob Zapopulous had no friends and no partners, for he trusted nobody. There were, however, half a dozen men in his employ in whose efficiency and sense of self-interest he had confidence, and it was one of these who now entered the room in response to the buzzer. He was a man of about forty, with a pale face, light blue eyes, and blond, short-cropped hair. He was a Dane and his name was Bergsen. He crossed the room silently, his feet sinking into the sumptuous Persian carpet, stopped in front of his master, and stood waiting impassively. Thirty seconds passed. Then in a high-pitched, cracked voice, Zapopulous spoke – slowly, quietly, and distinctly.

'I have a task for you. It is for you alone. Succeed in it and you will become a rich man.' He held out the open atlas. 'Take this.'

Bergsen did so.

'Look at the territories shaded blue.'

'May I switch on a light?'

'Yes, yes.'

Bergsen crossed to the mantelpiece, switched on a lamp, and stood under it with the atlas in his hands. 'Yes?'

'How many are there?'

Bergsen was silent for a few seconds. Then he said: 'Thirteen.'

'Yes, thirteen – scattered throughout the entire length and breadth of the continent. An absurd empire! Each individual colony isolated, not one of them large enough ever to be of any importance. The fools in the Duchy could never even afford to develop them slightly, to exploit them in any way. Not one of those colonies has any industry to speak of, no large-scale commerce, no great city. They are peopled almost exclusively by primitive native tribes and poor white farmers. A few of the people are tolerably prosperous, most of them just scratch a living. The territories are backward, moribund, useless. Or they have been until now.'

Bergsen looked up, but said nothing.

'In one of those primitive, useless colonies, something has been discovered,' Zapopulous said, and his voice was harsh. 'What it is, I don't know: gold, diamonds, oil. And I don't know in which one. But I do know that the Duchy is quite unable to take advantage of the discovery. She is weak, threatened from all sides, desperate for military aid. And in return for this she is prepared to cede that entire territory, her only negotiable asset, to the British.'

Zapopulous sat up. His voice grew higher. 'Some people in one of those little blue patches are sitting on a fortune. And they do not know it. Their land will shortly become immensely valuable. Whereas now – now, most of those people could be bought out for a comparative pittance.'

Bergsen nodded. 'If we knew who they were. You want me to find out?'

'You are quick, Bergsen. That is just what I want: ascertain what mineral has been discovered and the precise location of it. Bring me the information when you have it; later you can handle the actual purchasing of the land on my behalf.'

'You don't think that there might be a risk? If the whole

colony – whichever it is – is going to change hands, might not individual landowners lose their holdings?'

'Pah! Nonsense!' Zapopulous made a gesture of contempt. 'Whatever government is in control of the territory, it will not affect the legal standing of individuals. The British government are not Bolsheviks. They will respect the rights of landowners. I intend to be the biggest landowner. And the first essential is to discover which land is involved. Find out – and ten per cent of everything I make will be yours.'

He was being offered the chance of a fortune, but Bergsen displayed no emotion – and offered no thanks. He waited, aware that there was more to come.

'Very shortly,' Zapopulous continued, 'a representative of the Grand Duke, a man named Martin Adler, is going to England to discuss the deal with a British government minister. Who this minister is to be and where the meeting is to take place, I do not know. How you make use of this information is entirely up to you. But obviously if by some means you can learn what is said at the meeting, your job will be done. Now go. Do not come again until you have all the information I require. Turn the light out before you leave.'

CHAPTER FIVE

Misgivings

'What's the matter, Nick? You look worried.'

Martin Adler's companion in the first class compartment of the Orient Express looked up and gave a smile. 'Why do you speak in English, Martin?'

'Good practice for you, pal. Frankly, yours sounded a bit rusty when you were speaking with those Britishers at the reception the other day. So I think we'll stick to English for the rest of this trip. Nothing makes an Englishman feel more superior than to hear another guy talking broken English.'

Nicholas Felman hesitated for a moment; then: 'OK, you are the boss,' he said carefully. 'How did that sound?'

'Not bad. Keep trying. But you didn't answer my question: why the anxious visage?'

Felman shrugged. 'Just nervousness. I have never had experience of anything so important as this. I cannot help wishing that you had not asked for *me* to accompany you, Martin. You need someone older – someone more practised at negotiations of this nature.'

'Don't be such a hick. I didn't want one of the old

guard of stuffed shirt diplomats – all hot air and protocol. I wanted someone I could talk to, who understands me, and whom I understand. You know just as much about the situation as any of those old buffers.'

'Yes, I believe I do, and I do not want you to think I am not grateful for your confidence. It is merely that I cannot bear the thought that I might fail my country. The situation is so perilous—'

'You don't need to tell me that, old buddy. But I don't see in what way you *could* let the country down. If we should fail, I'd be to blame. But the British aren't our enemies. They want to help. These are just going to be cosy, informal talks to decide the precise details of how best they can help – and how we can best repay them.'

'You make it sound very easy. But I have this feeling that things are not going to proceed quite as smoothly as you anticipate.'

'You're a natural-born pessimist,' said Adler.

'Blasted foreigners.' George Henry Aylwin Saunders, twelfth Earl of Burford, muttered the words as he sat in a wicker chair on the terrace at Alderley, gazing out across the tree-dotted parkland, baking under the summer sun.

A few yards from him, a hammock had been slung from a hook on the wall of the house to the spreading branch of a nearby tree. At that moment the only indication that Lord Burford was not simply soliloquising was a bulge in the underside of the hammock; but after a quarter of a minute his daughter's voice from inside it murmured: 'Which ones? Richard's? What's wrong with them?'

Ten seconds passed before Lord Burford said: 'Coming

here. Disturbin' things. Having to be entertained. Shown round. Talked to. Not understandin' English all over the place. Deuced unsportin' of Rich to foist 'em on us. I blame your mother, I'd have said no.'

'You wouldn't – any more than you did to Algy.'

'Well, no, p'raps I wouldn't. But I'd have said yes in a grumblin' manner. Algy Fotheringay's different. No one can keep him away when he decides to pay a visit. He's like a 'flu germ.'

'Well, what about the Peabodys? You invited them, too.'

'Couldn't very well get out of it. Been correspondin' with the feller for donkey's years. When he wrote saying they were coming to England and he'd like an opportunity of examinin' me collection I had no choice. But I didn't *want* 'em here.'

'You'll thoroughly enjoy having them. You love showing off your guns.'

'Not to Peabody. I know these Americans. He'll keep insistin' how much better his stuff is, and crowing over this new piece he's picked up in Italy. Yankees!'

'I thought he was a Texan.'

'He is. Why?'

'I don't think he'd take very kindly to being called a Yankee.'

'Why not?'

'A Yankee's an American from the northern states. Even you must know Texas is in the south.'

'Oh, I can't be bothered with these fine distinctions. Americans – Yankees – foreigners: they're all the same. I don't mind entertainin', but I like to choose me guests.

And I like 'em to be English. But when the party consists of two central Europeans, two Yankees, and the only two Englishmen are some septic civil servant and Algy Fotheringay, it makes a chap feel like emigratin'.'

'Perk up. Jane's coming too, remember? You like her.'

'Course I do. Charming gal. Wish all your chums were as presentable. She doesn't make up for the others, though. I think we're in for a ghastly few days; and you know one of the worst things about it? However gruesome things get, I won't be able to blame your mother. She didn't invite one of 'em.'

'Perhaps she'll meet somebody up in town today and ask them down.'

'If she does, it'll be somebody absolutely charming, who'll be personally responsible for saving the weekend from complete disaster. You mark my words.'

'Excuse me, but it is Lady Burford, isn't it?'

The Countess of Burford paused in her leisurely examination of Messrs Harrod's furnishing fabrics and surveyed the speaker through her lorgnette. He was a tall, bronzed young man with deep-set blue eyes, and he was smiling at her engagingly.

'It is.' She looked for a few seconds, then her face cleared. 'Of course. You're Lucy Arbuthnot's nephew.'

'My word, you've a good memory.'

'For faces. I can never remember names.'

'Giles Deveraux.'

'Of course. We met at her Yorkshire place about three years ago.'

'That's right. How are you, Lady Burford?'

'I'm very well, thank you.'

'And the Earl – and Lady Geraldine?'

'They're both in excellent health, I'm thankful to say. You're looking extremely fit. Been abroad?'

'Yes, for several months.'

'Lucky you.'

'It was far from pure pleasure. My work keeps me on the move.'

'Oh, of course, you're in the Navy, aren't you?'

'Was. I left a couple of years ago. I'm by way of being a writer now.'

'Indeed? What sort of things do you write?'

'All sorts. Bit of freelance journalism. Travel books. Guide books.'

'And what is the current project?'

Deveraux hesitated. 'Um, well, I'm about to start on a hectic series of country house visits in connection with a commission I've received.'

'Oh?' Lady Burford fixed him with an enquiring gaze.

Deveraux seemed a little embarrassed. 'Actually, I've been asked to write a book on famous British houses – one of a series. Each one will cover a different period – Elizabethan, Queen Anne, Georgian, and so on.'

'And which period are you dealing with?'

Deveraux cleared his throat. 'Er, late Stuart.'

'I see.' Lady Burford looked at him somewhat grimly. 'And why isn't Alderley being included? It's the finest smaller Carolean mansion in England.'

'Unfortunately, the houses have been more or less selected by now—'

'Which ones?'

'Well, Eltham Lodge, Ramsbury, Honington, Belton—'

Lady Burford interrupted with a snort. 'You must be out of your mind! Some of those places aren't in the same class as Alderley.'

'Well, that's a matter of opinion—'

'Fiddlesticks! It's not a matter of opinion: it's a matter of fact. You ever been to Alderley?'

'No, I've seen pictures of it.'

Lady Burford dismissed pictures with a gesture of contempt. 'You definitely committed to include certain houses and no others?'

'Not really. There's nothing about it in the contract.'

'Then you must come and see Alderley. Don't make up your mind until you've been. I guarantee that afterwards you'll agree Alderley's got to be included. How about it?'

'It's very kind of you. But I'm afraid my time has been very carefully allocated. At the end of next week I'm off to Eltham, and from then on it's a different house every few days until the end of October – and my publishers want the manuscript by the New Year.'

'I see.' Lady Burford thought for a few seconds. Then she said: 'What about this coming weekend?'

Deveraux hesitated again. 'I haven't made any firm arrangements. I was hoping to do some sailing...'

'You must come to us. Now don't argue. You'll be under no obligation to include Alderley afterwards if you don't want to. But you must see the place and talk to my husband before you make up your mind. Will you?'

'Well,' Deveraux smiled, 'if you insist.'

'That's settled, then. We are giving a small house party, anyway, so it'll fit in quite nicely. Thursday suit you? That's when most of the others are arriving.'

'Thursday will be admirable.'

'Trains at quarter-past ten, twelve, two, and four from Paddington. Takes about two hours. Tell the guard to stop at Alderley Halt. It's an old right we've got.'

'Actually, I shall probably motor down.'

'Well, it's easy enough to find. Look forward to seeing you. 'Bye.'

'Good-bye, Lady Burford. And many thanks.'

Deveraux watched Lady Burford walk briskly away. Then he strolled off in the other direction. He gave a little smile to himself. 'Well, my boy,' he muttered under his breath, 'congratulations, I must say you arranged that very nicely indeed.'

Richard Saunders eyed the man who was sitting opposite him, fastidiously sipping coffee out of a Crown Derby cup. Then he pushed an open box of cigarettes across his desk. 'Cigarette, Thornton?'

'Thank you, no, Minister. I do not smoke.'

Richard took one himself and lit it before saying: 'I asked you here this morning because I thought it would be a good thing if we got together for a chat about the weekend. I wondered if you have any advance thoughts about these talks.'

Edward Thornton put down his cup, took out a white linen handkerchief and carefully wiped his lips. Then he said: 'None of any importance, I'm afraid, Minister.'

He was a tall, thin individual, wearing pince-nez and a wing collar. There was little in his personality to impress. Yet Richard knew him to have a reputation as one of the

Foreign Office's best negotiators – a man of icy logic, decisive speech, and prodigious memory.

Thornton said: 'As I see it, the negotiations should be relatively straightforward. After all, there is no clash of interests involved. HMG and the Grand Duke want basically the same thing.'

'The details may be tricky, though. That's where you're going to come in especially.'

'I feel confident I am adequately prepared and can advise you with a high degree of accuracy.'

'Good man. Just talking to you makes me feel happier. As you know, I'm very much a new boy at this sort of thing. But I don't think you'll let me make too many floaters.'

Thornton smiled thinly. 'I do flatter myself that I have saved the reputation of more than one minister in the past. But I do not expect to be called upon to do so on this occasion.'

'I hope you're right,' said Richard.

Merryweather, Lord Burford's venerable and stately butler, sat in his pantry and ticked names off his list. Mr. and Mrs. Peabody, the Royal Suite; the European gentlemen, the Cedar and the Blue bedrooms; Miss Jane her usual; Mr. Fotheringay, the Green; Mr. Deveraux, the Grey; Mr. Thornton, the Regency; and Mr. Evans, the Dutch. All the rooms ready. Everything done.

Merryweather read through the list once more, and suddenly a strange feeling of uneasiness smote him. There was something wrong with this house party. It was in a way different from any of the others, the many, many others, which he had supervised at Alderley. The guests were too diverse, too disparate. Most of them were strangers to each other, and even to the Family. There weren't enough ladies, either, which made the seating at table awkward. And speaking of that...

Merryweather made a quick count of the guests. Yes, there would be thirteen to dinner. It was the last-minute addition of this Mr. Deveraux that had caused it. The Family wouldn't mind; but it was to be hoped none of the guests was superstitious. Had her ladyship realised? Perhaps he should point it out to her.

Merryweather got to his feet. He found himself hoping her ladyship *would* find an additional guest. For thirteen to sit down this evening would somehow set the party off on quite the wrong foot. And he couldn't help feeling that the weekend was handicapped enough already, without further troubles being added to it...

CHAPTER SIX

Jane's Journey

It always gave Jane a kind of thrill to tip the guard and loftily instruct him to have the train stopped at Alderley Halt. It seemed so delightfully feudal and anachronistic. So it was with a slight disappointment that she heard him reply cheerfully: 'That's all right, miss. We're stopping there anyway. There are some other passengers for Alderley on the train.'

But he took her hard-earned shilling nonetheless. Jane found an empty compartment and leant back in a corner seat, reflecting that it was a pity she'd mentioned it. On the other hand, she was forewarned now. For one of the other passengers for Alderley might well be Algy Fotheringay, and it would be ghastly if he spotted her and she was stuck with his company all the way. But she probably didn't need to worry: Algy would certainly be travelling first class and wouldn't deign to enter her humble third class compartment. In fact, she thought, with a momentary and uncharacteristic twinge of bitterness, it was probably rare for any but first class passengers to have the train stopped at Alderley.

It was horrible to be poor. Especially when your family had once been rich and influential. It had been in her grandfather's day that things had really started to go wrong. It was almost frightening, looking back, to see how quickly a family fortune could shrink. Her father, an only child, might have been able to retrieve the situation. But he had been a charming and impractical dilettante, who had never really woken up to the fact that he was becoming poor. His wife and family had not realised it, but the cost of giving Jane and her younger sister Jennifer a good education, and enabling them to do the London season, had almost bankrupted him. He had died suddenly, almost penniless and uninsured.

Mrs. Clifton and her daughters, then twenty and eighteen, had found themselves in great difficulties. They had raised some capital by selling both the country home near Bath and the town house, and had rented a smaller one just outside London. But it had been clear that they would not be able to live on this money for long, and that at least one of the girls would have to get a job.

Jennifer had been fortunate. She had been the beauty of the season the previous year, and at school had shone in theatricals. She had decided to try her luck on the stage. She could afford no formal training, but her looks and a natural talent had stood her in good stead. After a few months in provincial repertory, and a cameo part in a talkie by the promising young director Alfred Hitchcock, she had got her big break: the chance of going on a long tour of the United States with a leading Shakespearian company. Jennifer had jumped at the opportunity.

With the tour half over, she had died suddenly.

It had fallen to Jane to break the news to her mother that Jennifer had succumbed to a rare disease and been buried in the mid-west of America.

Mrs. Clifton had never really recovered from her husband's death, and the new shock had been too much for her. She suffered an immediate heart attack and died eight weeks later.

A distraught Jane, who in at little over eighteen months had seen her whole world collapse, had tried to drown her grief with gaiety. She had joined up with a set of the so-called bright young things and had lived wildly for twelve months.

She had gone through about half her money when, one day, on a visit to Somerset, she had run into one of her father's ex-gardeners. He had told her that his young son was dangerously ill. There was no hope for him – unless by a miracle he could be taken to Vienna for a new operation perfected by an Austrian surgeon.

Jane had seen the family's doctor, checked with her bank, and agreed to pay all the expenses.

The operation was completely successful. But Jane had been cleaned out: she had no choice but to get a job.

This, however, had not turned out to be so easy. She was without qualifications, and she shied away from the usual sort of position taken up by girls of her class in similar circumstances – nursery governess or paid companion. Eventually she had obtained a post as a hotel receptionist – only to walk out after one week when the manager made a pass at her. Then she had moved to the country to become an instructress at a riding school. This had gone well until one day she had seen a pupil, the seventeen-year-old daughter of a rich company promoter with a large family of potential clients, viciously beating a troublesome horse. Jane had snatched the whip and used it to give three or four vigorous thwacks across the back of the girl's riding jacket.

In London again, Jane had got work with an antique dealer. This had lasted until she had discovered she was expected to ask certain customers to pay with two cheques – but to enter only one in the books. Finally had come Mayfair Modes. It was not the sort of job Jane had ever imagined herself doing – but she had been getting desperate. Almost from the first, however, she had known she wouldn't stick it long. In a way the blow-up with Bottway had come as a relief – even though she had put herself in a terrible stew financially.

But she wouldn't think of that this weekend. She was going to enjoy herself, pretend she was accustomed to ease and plenty and forget that in a few days she'd have to start looking for a job again.

It would be good to be back at Alderley. Like going home. Her visits there, and her friendship with the family, had been the one unchanging feature of her life. And, thank heaven, the weather had cleared up. After a long hot spell it had rained heavily that morning and Jane had feared that a wet period had set in; but now it was lovely again, and all the fresher for the rain. Jane stared out of the window and watched the city give way to suburbs, and the suburbs in their turn to soft green meadows.

When at last the train puffed into Alderley Halt, Jane heaved her two small cases down from the rack, jumped out, and, without waiting for a porter, ran awkwardly with them to the barrier. She stopped, and glanced back; she wanted to see who else alighted. Two men were getting down from a first class compartment. Jane gave a puzzled frown, then her face changed, as from another compartment the figure of Algernon Fotheringay emerged. He was wearing a blazer in two-inch wide red and yellow stripes and the most voluminous plus-fours Jane had ever seen. She turned and hurried out to the sleepy station yard.

Lord Burford's Rolls Royce was waiting there, the liveried figure of the chauffeur Hawkins, an old ally of Jane from her schoolgirl days, standing beside it. Jane walked across. 'Hullo, Hawkins.'

Hawkins touched his cap and permitted himself a discreet smile of welcome. 'Good afternoon, Miss Jane.' He came forward and took her cases from her.

'How are you, Hawkins?'

'Nicely, thank you, miss.'

'Hawkins, who were you expecting to meet?'

'Yourself and three gentlemen, miss: two foreign gentlemen – Mr. Adler and Mr. Felman – and Mr. Fotheringay.'

'They'll be out in a minute. I think I'd prefer to walk. I'll take the short cut. Tell her ladyship I'm on my way, will you?'

'Very good, miss.'

Carrying just her bag, Jane started off briskly. The station was about a quarter of a mile from the quaint, old-world village of Alderley itself. Jane walked along the single street, passing the Rose & Crown, Jenkins's Garage, and the half dozen shops, and out the other side onto a quiet country lane. Shortly she came to a stile on the left. She clambered over it and set out across the field along a footpath – just as the Rolls passed along the lane behind her.

Five minutes later Jane topped a rise, climbed over a low wall that marked the boundary of the Burford estate, and looked down on one of her favourite sights – Alderley itself, solid and serene, flanked by its outbuildings and surrounded by the tree-dotted park, the lake, which at one point came within thirty yards of the house, the beech copse, and the home farm half a mile beyond. All was spread out below her like a perfect miniature model, and Jane just stood looking down in sheer pleasure.

From here the house, which was built basically in the form of three sides of a rectangle, looked like a reversed capital E with the centre bar missing. It was three storeys tall, but outwards from both top and bottom bars of the E – the east and west wings – a two-storey extension projected.

Jane started down the slope. Another ten minutes' brisk walking and she came to the higher wall which flanked the park. Somewhere the other side of the wall she could hear the sound of a car engine, getting closer. It was noisier than the Rolls, and Jane wondered if it was Gerry in the Hispano-Suiza. She followed the wall until she came to a small door. She stopped, opened her bag, and took from it an old key. This had been given to her by Lord Burford many years previously – an act considered a special mark of esteem – and had been treasured by Jane ever since. She opened the door, passed through, and locked it after her. As she did so, she realised the sound of the car engine had stopped. Just in front of her stood a row of trees, flanking the drive. Jane passed between two of them – and was instantly splattered from head to foot by a thick spray of cold, dirty water.

She stood gasping, rubbing the water from her eyes. She heard a squeal of brakes, got her vision cleared, and looked up to see a bright red two-seater open car, which had pulled up a few yards along the drive, facing the house. The young man in the driving seat was looking back over his shoulder, an expression of dismay on his face. He hurriedly put the car into reverse and backed down the drive until he was level with her. In spite of herself, Jane could not help noticing that he had blue eyes and very brown skin.

'I say, I'm most terribly sorry,' he said, in a pleasant voice. 'I didn't see you until it was too late. Are you in a frightful mess?' He broke off. 'Oh dear, you are, aren't you?'

For five seconds Jane was speechless. Then she let fly. 'You blithering idiot! Do you always dash along private drives at ninety miles an hour in complete silence?'

'Well, no. Actually, I was only doing about thirty. And it was so beautifully peaceful I just switched off the engine to coast a little way and enjoy the quietness.'

'Not caring two hoots that you might knock down some poor footbound pheasant—'

'Footbound pheasant? Is there one of those around here? How very sad. What's the trouble? Rheumatism of the wings?'

Jane breathed deeply and clenched her fists at her sides. 'I meant peasant,' she hissed. 'You didn't care what footbound peasant you knocked down.'

'Oh, I assure you there was never any danger of that. I could have stopped very quickly if anybody'd stepped out. I mean, I didn't hit you—'

'Thanks for that, anyway.'

'Everything would have been all right but for an unfortunate combination of circumstances. There's a hollow in the road just here, you see, and it's right in the shadow. Also it was full of water. It must have been left from the heavy rain this morning—'

'I didn't think it had been left from last January's snow!'

'I'm trying to say that I'm not really all to blame. I was simply cruising quietly along. I couldn't see the hollow or the water or you. And you know, you did step straight onto the drive without pausing.'

'Oh, that's right. Motor like a lunatic, half-drown me, and then blame me.'

'I was not motoring like a lunatic and I am not blaming you. I'm merely exonerating myself. It was an accident.' He was starting to sound cross.

'I sincerely hope it was an accident! Because if I thought you did it on purpose—'

'Oh, don't be such an idiot.' He swallowed and apparently with something of an effort, said quietly: 'Are you going up to the house? If so, can I give you a lift?'

'No thank you. I think I'll be safer if I stay a considerable distance from you.'

'Just as you wish.' He slammed the car into gear, accelerated, and let in the clutch – just a little too rapidly.

Now, while they had been talking, the water from the puddle, having spread itself over a larger area when the car

first passed through it, had been soaking into the surface
of the drive around the rear wheels. The result could have
been anticipated: as the wheels spun fiercely Jane was
comprehensively sprayed by a fine cloud of muddy specks.

The young man looked round, realised what he had
done, made as if to stop again, seemed to think better of it,
and roared away.

Jane stood quite still. The only word she managed to
get out was a long drawn out 'O-oh.' Then she started
to march up the drive, muttering imprecations against all
motorists. After a few minutes, however, her anger gave
way to misery, and she found herself blinking back tears.
Absurd to get so upset. And she'd made a bit of a fool of
herself, too, by flying out at him like that. But she hadn't
been able to help it. She was going to arrive at Alderley
looking like a drowned rat. Moreover, her feet and legs
had taken the worst of the deluge, and in her traps, now
presumably at the house, reposed the only other pair of
silk stockings she possessed in the world. She would have
to change into them as soon as she arrived; and if they
should ladder before she had a chance to get the ones she
was now wearing washed and dried, she would have to
borrow a pair from Gerry. Humiliating.

Before Jane got in sight of the house she stopped,
cleaned her face as best she could with her handkerchief,
applied some powder and lipstick, and ran a comb through
her hair. Having done this, she felt a little better. But not
a lot.

When she approached the house she was tempted to
avoid the front and to enter by a rear door. But this would
entail a long march, round the stables and orangery and

through the kitchen garden – and then she would have to find a servant to notify her hosts of her arrival. So she strode up the shallow steps, past the huge Doric columns, to the great front doors, and rang the bell.

The door was opened almost immediately by the pontifical Merryweather. 'Good afternoon, miss.'

'Hullo, Merryweather,' Jane said, going into the big, oak-pannelled hall. 'How are you?'

'I am in my usual excellent health, thank you, miss. May I take the liberty of enquiring after your own?'

'Oh, I'm pretty fit, but as you can see wet and dirty. I had a contretemps with a – a –' Jane gulped, 'a *gentleman* in a red tourer.'

'Yes, miss. Mr. Deveraux explained there had been a slight accident.'

'Oh dear,' Jane said. 'Tell me, Merryweather – is he a guest here?'

'Yes, miss.'

'Crumbs. I hoped he was just calling about the drains or something. Do you know if he's a great friend of the family?'

'I believe not, miss. He is here professionally rather than socially. I understand he is writing a book on the stately homes of England and is considering including Alderley in it.'

'I see. That's something, anyway. I'd like to go straight up to my room now.'

'Certainly, miss. If you will just follow me.'

'Is it my old room?'

'Yes, miss.'

'Then don't bother to take me. I know my way. Have my traps been taken up?'

'Yes, miss. You should find Marie unpacking.'

'Fine. Tell Lady Geraldine I've arrived, will you, Merryweather?'

'Certainly, miss.'

'Thank you.' Jane made her way up the grand staircase. At the top she turned right along the main corridor, and at the end left into the east wing. She opened the second door on the left and went in. This was a small but pleasant room, overlooking the courtyard. Gerry's maid, Marie, a pretty, dark girl, had just completed the not very arduous task of unpacking. She gave a shriek of horror upon seeing Jane.

'*Mille tonnerres, mademoiselle!* What 'ave they done to you?'

'Not they, Marie. One man in one car.'

She took off her tweed coat and skirt and gave it to Marie for sponging and pressing. Then she removed her precious stockings and handed them to her too, with a request to have them laundered with the greatest possible care. After Marie had left, Jane washed her face and hands, and gingerly put on her other stockings. This operation completed without mishap, she was just struggling into her dress, when Gerry burst in.

By the time she had given an account of her misadventure with Deveraux, Jane felt more cheerful. Gerry proved a most satisfactorily sympathetic audience, exhibiting just the right amount of indignation on Jane's behalf. When they'd talked the subject out, she said: 'Now, tell me: have you got a job yet?'

Jane shook her head.

'Good. Then you can stay as long as you like.'

'I wish I could, but honestly I must get fixed up soon.'

'Jane, darling, can't you marry money?'

'Lead me to it.'

'Perhaps I have. Perhaps there's somebody here. Pity you got off on the wrong foot with Giles Deveraux. He's not exactly good looking, but he's rather attractive. And I should imagine he's pretty well-heeled. His car looks expensive.'

'Probably stolen.'

'Then how about one of our mittel Europeans? I don't know anything about them financially, but these continental diplomats usually come from ancient aristocratic families.'

'Somehow the idea of being married to an ancient European diplomat doesn't really appeal to me.'

'No, honestly, they're not at all bad. I was very agreeably surprised. I was expecting terribly stiff and formal old buffers with thick accents and monocles and little imperials, bowing and kissing my hand all over the place. But actually they're both quite young. They speak very good English – in fact one of them could be an American. The secondary one – Felman, I think – is a bit quiet, but the chief one, Adler, has really got a lot of charm – and SA.'

'Sorry, darling, but I'm not keen. What about this oil millionaire? Any chance for me there?'

'I don't know. He hasn't arrived yet. He is bringing his wife with him, though.'

'Perhaps I can entice him away from her. Alternatively they might have an eligible son.'

'If they have, he's not coming with them. Just a secretary. Name of Evans.'

Jane applied lipstick. 'I'm not interested in secretaries

unless they've got double-barrelled surnames if English, or have "Van" in front of them if American. Is that the lot?'

'There's somebody Richard brought. From the FO. I don't know if he's married. Nice enough, but a bit of a stick. Then there's Algy—'

'Stop. There's no need to be obscene. I must say, none of them sound awfully promising. It seems likely that in the immortal words of Amelia Bottway, I shall 'ave to try h'elsewhere – somewhere where they keep an adequate stock. However, I will inspect what you have.'

'Then if madam will follow me to the terrace, she can do so at her leisure while taking tea.'

CHAPTER SEVEN

Tea on the Terrace

The two girls went downstairs and onto the terrace. After Lord and Lady Burford had greeted Jane, the Countess started on introductions.

'May I present Mr. Adler? Miss Clifton, a very dear friend of the family.'

Adler smiled easily, stood up and held out his hand. He was pleasant-looking in a quiet, inconspicuous way, slightly below average height, slim yet nonetheless with a look of latent strength.

'Miss Clifton, I'm very glad to make your acquaintance.'

Jane suddenly knew what Gerry had meant by charm. Adler had oodles of it and, without meaning to, Jane found herself smiling more broadly than she usually did on meeting anyone new.

'Mr. Felman,' said Lady Burford.

Mr. Felman was tall, fair-haired, with finely-moulded sensitive features; he was also plainly ill at ease. He murmured a few words of greeting as he shook hands, then backed away quickly, glancing at Adler as he did so;

it was almost as though he were seeking approval.

Lady Burford moved on. 'Mr. Thornton.'

Thornton gave a severe little bow of the head and shook hands with stiff, cold fingers.

'And Mr. Deveraux,' Lady Burford said.

Jane turned towards the fourth man. She had decided to be very magnanimous, to make no mention of the incident on the drive. She was all ready, therefore, to be extremely pleasant to Mr. Deveraux. But as he looked at her, she clearly saw his lips twitch and she knew at once that he was remembering her as he'd seen her last, standing, dripping and furious, on the drive. At that second all her good intentions went to the wall.

So as Deveraux stepped forward, she extended her hand, smiled sweetly, and said: 'Mr. Deveraux and I are acquainted, Lady Burford. How are you, Mr. Deveraux? Have you assaulted any other young women since last we met?'

And as Lady Burford stared blankly, Jane turned away to where Algy Fotheringay was still sitting, a cup of tea in one hand and a chocolate éclair in the other, and greeted him in a tone of great warmth. 'Hullo, Algy. How delightful to see you. How are you?'

Algy got hurriedly to his feet, knocking over his chair as he did so, held out half an éclair to Jane, tried to transfer it to his left hand, couldn't do so because of the cup, popped the éclair into his mouth, swallowed, and gave Jane limp and sticky fingers.

'I'm in topping form, thanks, Jane. How's yourself?'

'Very well, thank—'

'I've had a really ripping year, Jane. In January I went

to Le Pinet as a guest of Lady Masters. Do you know her? Charming woman. She said I was the most unforgettable guest she'd—'

'You must tell me all about it, sometime,' Jane interrupted firmly. 'I shall look forward to it.' And she moved away towards the last member of the party. This was a tall, slim man, impeccably dressed, with a moustache and dark hair touched with grey at the temples; he was twinkling at her out of deep-set eyes.

'Hullo, Jane. It's been a long time.'

Jane held out her hand. 'It has, hasn't it?'

'I've been here often enough, but you never seem to have come then.'

'I am a working girl, you know. Anyway, it's very nice to see you again Unc— er, Rich—' She smiled. 'What do I call you now?'

'I think you should follow Gerry's lead, and call me Richard. Come and sit by me and let's have a chat.'

He pulled forward a chair for her. She sat down. Richard looked at her with pleasure. He saw a tall girl, very slim, with raven-black hair, a generous mouth, clear grey eyes, and a straight, steady gaze.

'It was Gerry who started me calling you uncle,' Jane said. 'We were at the share-everything stage – and that had to include you.'

'I insisted on her dropping the uncle part a long time ago. It's nice to be called it by a schoolgirl, or even by a debutante; but once she'd grown up it just drew attention to my advanced age.'

'Advanced age my foot!' Jane accepted a cup of tea from a footman, added milk, and selected a cucumber sandwich from a laden trolley wheeled up by a maid. 'You are sixteen years older than me. I know that because when I was sixteen Gerry and I worked out that you were twice my age. I am now twenty-four, so you are forty.'

'You are superbly diplomatic, Miss Clifton. Actually, I'm forty-one.'

'All right, forty-one. And a future Prime Minister, according to at least one paper.'

'Oh, that. They talk a lot of rot. But you didn't come to Alderley to talk politics. Tell me, what was the meaning of that cryptic remark you made to Deveraux?'

'Oh, don't let's talk about it now. I'll explain later.'

'As you wish, madam.'

Jane gave a mock groan. 'Why does every conversation I have today remind me irresistibly of Mayfair Modes?'

'Ah yes, the job from which you so magnificently departed. Gerry told us about it. Have you got another one yet?'

Jane shook her head.

Richard frowned. 'I wonder if I could help to fix you up. What sort of thing do you want to do?'

'Anything at all. But I've no qualifications.'

'There must be jobs going where you don't need formal qualifications.'

'Do tell me what. I can't type or do shorthand, I've got no academic degrees or certificates, no artistic or acting talent. I talk in the right sort of accent, know the right sort of people, wear the right sort of clothes. I speak passable French and good German, ride moderately well and play a reasonable game of tennis. And there are thousands of girls who can say exactly the same thing. So what do you suggest?'

Richard pursed his lips. 'Nursery governess?'

'Can you honestly see—'

He interrupted with a laugh. 'All right. I wasn't serious. Doctor's receptionist?'

'No thanks. I don't want anything to do with medicine or illness.'

'Some other sort of receptionist?'

'I've already tried it at an hotel – without great success.'

'Hm, you're a problem, aren't you? A nice problem, but a problem nonetheless.'

'I'm a problem to myself. It's no good. I shall have to become an adventuress.'

'Well, I'll keep my eyes and ears open for something else all the same – just in case you don't take to it.'

'Thank you. But enough of me. Tell me about your foreign friends.' She nodded towards Adler and Felman, who were talking to Lord Burford and Geraldine. (She noticed with satisfaction that Deveraux had been cornered by Algy.)

'Oh, they're not really friends. They're over here on official business and the PM thought it would be nice to give them a taste of a typical English country house party.'

'I see. And what about Mr. Thornton?'

'Oh, he's just a chap from the FO I've got friendly with lately. Nice fellow. We're all going to take the opportunity to do a bit of work, actually. Just some routine business.'

'Is this your first visit to England, Mr. Adler?' Gerry asked. By dint of some complicated conversational manoeuvres, she had at last managed to divert her father and Felman into one channel of discussion and had then gently detached Adler from it.

'Yes, Lady Geraldine, it is.'

'Too soon to ask how you like it, I suppose?'

'What I've seen so far I've liked very much. Particularly your charming house.'

'It is nice, isn't it?'

'When was it built?'

'Commenced 1670. One of the genuine, if smaller, stately homes of England. Complete with secret passage.'

'Really?'

'Yes, I'll show you later, if you're interested.'

'I'd be fascinated. I've never seen one. They're such wonderfully romantic things.'

'After dinner tonight, then. I'll take you to the room where one end of it comes out, and I bet you half a crown you can't find the entrance.'

'You're on.'

'There are quite a lot of interesting things here, actually – if you can afford the time off from your talks.'

He smiled. 'Don't you have a proverb in this country: something about all work and no play being a bad thing?'

'Something like that.'

'Then I'll certainly find time for as many conducted tours as you're able to give me, Lady Geraldine.'

He looked steadily at her. Gerry seemed to find this disconcerting. 'Er, another cup of tea, Mr. Adler?' she said hurriedly.

'Thank you.'

Gerry signalled to the footman, then watched Adler

surreptitiously as he took a fresh cup and added lemon. Strange; his features were quite ordinary really. But he certainly had something. And she felt sure he could tell a few stories. She was starting to look forward to the next few days...

'Personally,' said Lord Burford, 'I'm very attached to the good old-fashioned cesspit.'

He had been finding Nicholas Felman a most admirable listener. The young man did not initiate much conversation himself, but he was splendidly attentive and sympathetic to the trials and tribulations of an English landed proprietor: the iniquities of county council and government, and the insatiable demands of tenants – the latest of these being for modern sewage disposal.

His last remark, however, was overheard by the Countess, who interrupted firmly: 'George! I'm sure Mr. Felman has no desire to converse about such a matter. Kindly desist.'

'Oh. Sorry, m'dear.'

'It's clearly time to change the subject. Tell me, Mr. Felman, is this your first visit to England?'

Felman gave a little start. 'I beg your pardon? Oh – yes, it is.'

'Have you been long in the diplomatic service?'

'Yes. Since I left University.'

'Always stationed at home?'

'No. I did – let me see – two, yes, two years in Stockholm.'

'That must have been enjoyable. A delightful city.'

'Yes, very pleasant.'

'We were there ten years ago. Tell me, do you know a charming little restaurant called Olsen's in Storkyrkobrinken?'

'No, I'm afraid not.'

'Oh.' Lady Burford fell silent. Strange that a professional diplomat, good-looking and presumably intelligent, should seem so gauche, so ill at ease, so, frankly, dull. Still, the Countess was not a person to give in so soon.

'I expect your family have been in the diplomatic service for generations, have they?' she asked next.

'What? Oh no. Actually, I'm the first.'

It was hard work but the Countess persevered, gradually eliciting from Felman the information that he was unmarried and that his only close relative was a younger sister, Anna, a medical student. Then he appeared to make a great effort.

'You have a wonderful home, Lady Burford.'

'I'm glad you like it.'

'You seem to have quite large stables.'

'Fairly. Do you ride?'

'A little.'

'Then you must talk to my daughter. She's the keenest these days. Geraldine!'

'Yes, Mummy.'

'Come and talk horses to Mr. Felman. Excuse me, Mr. Felman. I must go and speak to cook about dinner.'

She got up and walked away. Gerry, who'd been getting on famously with Adler, looked a trifle put out, but she made her apologies and went across. Lord Burford, who had been listening to her conversation, leant over and tapped Adler on the shoulder. 'Tell me all about this country of yours,' he said.

'That's quite a tall order, sir. What exactly do you want me to tell you?'

'I don't know anything about it hardly. Tell me what I ought to know.'

'Well, we're small, peaceful, and prosperous. The people are free and on the whole happy. We have what I suppose you'd figure was a pretty measly little empire, but which we're kind of proud of. I guess our main aim is just to keep things pretty much as they are.'

'And you think Britain can help, is that it?' Lord Burford spoke in a quieter voice. 'And you needn't worry,' he added. 'I know this is all hush-hush. Me brother got the OK to give me an outline of what'll be going on. I do sit in the House of Lords and I have taken the oath of allegiance.'

'Oh, I'm well aware nothing needs to be kept from you, Lord Burford.'

'Keep as much from me as you like, my dear feller. This sort of thing's not my cup of tea at all. Good luck to you, though.'

'Thank you.'

'You've spent most of your life in America, I understand.'

'A good part of it.'

'Would it be bad form to call you a Yankee?'

'On the contrary, I'd be honoured.'

'Oh, capital. You must tell my daughter.'

Adler looked a shade puzzled at this somewhat enigmatic remark, but he got no enlightenment, Lord Burford then asking: 'How did you come to take up a political career in another country?'

'Well, I was born in the Duchy, of course. But my mother was American, and after my father died when I was eight, she returned to the States. The only connection I retained with the old country was a knowledge of the language. Then when I was at Harvard, the then Grand Duke, the present one's father, sent his son there to finish his education. Shortly after he arrived, he discovered that there was a solitary compatriot of his there also. He invited me to visit him. The short of it was we struck up a friendship, and when we finished he asked me to go back with him and become his aide. My mother had died about a year before and my best girl had just jilted me. I had nothing to keep me in the States. So I went. Over the years I've worked my way up. That's just about it. Rather a boring story, isn't it?'

'Have we ever met? Your face looks definitely familiar to me.'

It was Edward Thornton who spoke, and Giles Deveraux turned with relief towards the source of the precisely enunciated words. He had been listening for what seemed like hours to a lengthy discussion on some of the More Memorable Meals served to Algy Fotheringay by his aristocratic hosts, and the interruption had come opportunely in one of Algy's few pauses for breath.

'Is that so?' Deveraux said. 'I fear that it's merely that I've got that sort of face. I can't say I reciprocate.'

'In the war, perhaps? I was with the Somerset Light Infantry.'

'I'm sorry to say I missed the show – by about two months. I was in the Navy afterwards, but not until after all the shooting had stopped. Frustrating. Still, I've seen a fair amount of the world since – both in and out of the service.'

'You've travelled extensively?'

'I've got around.'

'Whereas I have never been farther than four or five European capitals.'

'And you with the FO!'

'That is the precise reason. I am attached to the European section.'

'Ah, then it's unlikely we met abroad, anyway. Probably we've just sat next to each other at Wimbledon or Twickenham.'

'I think not. I have little interest in games. You are a writer, I understand.'

'Of a sort.'

'I have to admit never recalling having seen any of your books.'

'Probably because I write under various pseudonyms.'

'May I ask what names?'

'Oh, G. K. Chesterton, Ernest Hemingway, Virginia Woolf.'

For a split second Thornton looked startled. Then he smiled icily. 'I'm sorry. You think I'm being too inquisitive.'

'Not at all. Merely a feeble joke. No, I'm not a best-selling author. Mine are mostly travel and guide books. And I write magazine articles. I use the names Jonathan George and Andrew Lewis mainly.'

'Oh, I am familiar with the name Jonathan George. A work on Malaya, I believe?'

'One of my slightly better-known efforts.'

'Surely a far cry from the stately homes of England, is it not?'

'I believe in casting my net wide.'

'Who are to publish this book?'

'It's for the American market, actually. A New York firm. I doubt that the name would mean much to you.'

'What other houses are to be included apart from Alderley?'

'I'm not quite sure Alderley is to be included yet,' Deveraux said. He listed some of the other houses.

'I see,' Thornton said. 'Your plans seem to be far advanced.'

'Far enough, I think,' said Deveraux. 'Far enough.'

CHAPTER EIGHT

The Secret Passage

Mr. and Mrs. Peabody and Evans arrived about six. Jane, who'd had vague expectations of meeting the caricatured Texans of fiction, was pleased to find the Peabodys pleasant, unassuming people. She took to them at once.

The only person, in fact, who seemed not to like them, was Lord Burford himself. This puzzled Jane until Gerry explained the Earl's fears and suspicions about the guns. 'He'll be all right in a few hours, though,' she added, 'when he realises how nice they are.'

However, this wasn't to be. During the pre-dinner drinks, Gerry found her father standing alone, looking glum.

She poked him in the ribs. 'What's wrong?'

'Don't. Him.' He gave a jerk of his head.

'Peabody?' Gerry glanced towards the millionaire – a squarely-built man of about fifty-five, with a pugnacious jaw and rimless glasses. 'I thought you'd be happier now you'd seen how pleasant and quiet and intelligent he is.'

'That's the trouble. I was hoping he'd be a brash, self-opinionated fool, who'd just used his money to buy blindly. But I've got a horrible feeling he's going to turn out to know more about guns than me.'

'Oh really, Daddy, don't be ridiculous. I'm sure you'll get on like a house on fire when you really know him. Now go and talk to him.'

'Oh, all right.' Lord Burford squared his shoulders and ambled across. He tapped Peabody on the shoulder. 'Tell me all about Texas' he said.

In spite of Merryweather's forebodings, dinner that evening was a very successful occasion.

The food – clear soup, dover sole, saddle of lamb with garden peas, strawberries and cream, and a fine Cheddar cheese – was superb. Lord Burford, having talked to Peabody, had, temporarily at least, got over his apprehensions and was a jovial host. Lady Burford, who, after Merryweather's warning, had spent a hectic time trying to find an unaccompanied lady to invite at short notice, had at long last succeeded in getting hold of a Mrs. Carpenter, the relict of a former bishop of the diocese, who usually dined at Alderley a couple of times a year. So the Countess was happy, and determined not yet to worry about the same problem at future meals.

The guests seemed to get on well together. Mrs. Peabody wore her famous necklace, and the magnificent stones were an immediate talking-point. Peabody and Adler found a common interest in baseball. Felman seemed less ill at ease than earlier. Algy was eating too eagerly to bore anybody greatly. And Jane and Deveraux, finding themselves seated side by side, had caught each other's eye, hesitated, then both smiled tentatively. Thereafter – much to the relief of Gerry, who had arranged the pairing – they talked, formally at first, but later more cordially.

So the atmosphere was in every way thoroughly satisfactory, and as Merryweather supervised he wondered why he had earlier felt so uneasy. The house party was clearly going to proceed swimmingly.

After dinner, when the men joined the ladies in the drawing-room, Lord Burford made a short speech. 'While everybody's here I'd like to explain something about our security system. As you know, there's a lot of very valuable stuff here – paintings, silver and personal jewellery, as well as quite famous collections of stamps, first editions, and coins. In addition, of course, there are my firearms and ammunition, which mustn't fall into the wrong hands. So to be on the safe side we've had a unique and, we think, foolproof burglar alarm installed. The drawback is that not only can nobody get in without setting it off, but nobody can get out either. Your bedroom windows will open six inches only. If you should force them wider – and, of course, you can do that quite easily in an emergency – or open or break any other window, unlock or force a door, you'll trigger the alarm off. Merryweather switches it on – or if we're having a late night, I do – last thing after locking up, so I'm afraid that it's just not possible to go for a stroll in the grounds after that. Sorry.'

Peabody said: 'You can turn it off, I suppose, Earl? There is a master switch?'

'No. We wanted to be as secure as they could make us, and we had to think of the possibility of a really serious burglar—'

'Like this Wraith guy, huh?'

'Exactly. We had to think of the possibility of a thief like that bribing a servant to turn it off. So the thing's on a time switch. After it's primed it stays on until the morning, when it switches off automatically – at six-thirty this time of year.'

'What would happen if a door had to be opened at night?' Adler asked. 'To let a doctor in, say, if someone was taken ill.'

'We'd just have to put up with the alarm bells for five minutes or so. Actually, they wouldn't cause too much of a disturbance. There's one in my bedroom, one in the butler's, and one in the hall. Unless you were a very light sleeper or left your door open, I doubt if you'd hear it in your room. Now, who's for bridge?'

Two games were soon started, one involving Lord Burford, Peabody, Felman, and Thornton; and the other Carrie Peabody, Richard, Algy, and Evans. Lady Burford sat with Mrs. Carpenter, who did not play.

Meanwhile, Gerry took Adler off to hunt for the entrance to the secret passage. Deveraux also expressed an interest in seeing it and went along too. Jane made up the fourth.

Gerry led the way across the great hall to the breakfast-room, which was at the eastern end of the main block. She went in, switching on the lights. The room was oak panelled and had french windows leading onto the front terrace. Heavy velvet curtains were at present drawn across them.

Gerry perched herself on the edge of the mahogany table and smiled at Adler. 'Right. It's all yours.'

He stared round. 'I don't know where to start.'

Deveraux said: 'Can I help?'

'Sure. I figure I'm going to need it.'

'If we find it, I'll expect a half-share of your winnings.'

'I'm not at all sure that's fair,' Jane said. 'Mr. Deveraux is an authority on English country houses. He'll know just where to look. I think they're out to break you, Gerry.'

'I'm no authority, I assure you,' said Deveraux. 'I haven't started to write the bally book yet. My entire knowledge of secret passages is drawn from the storybooks of my misspent boyhood.'

The room itself was sparsely furnished. Apart from the table, there was only a large sideboard and a dozen or so upright chairs placed round the walls. A large cupboard was built into one wall. For over ten minutes, while Gerry and Jane sat on the table, smoking and making unhelpful remarks, Deveraux and Adler examined the room. They tapped at panels, twisted, pulled and pushed at each small protuberance, and stamped on every accessible inch of the floor. Eventually they were forced to give up.

Gerry stubbed out her cigarette, got off the table, and crossed to the cupboard. She opened it wide, then twisted the knob twice in each direction. Suddenly there was a click, and to the right of the fireplace one whole panel slid silently aside, revealing a black square, just large enough for a man bending low to pass through.

Adler stared. 'Holy smoke.'

'Well, well, well.' Deveraux shook his head. 'Most remarkable.'

'It only works,' Gerry told them, 'when the cupboard door is wide open and the knob turned right-left-right-left.

We think the cupboard was only put in as a sort of *raison d'être* for the knob.'

'Fascinating.' Deveraux walked across to the hole in the wall and peered in. 'Can't see a thing.'

'Allow me.' Gerry pushed past him, stuck an arm into the blackness, fumbled for a moment, and withdrew it, holding an electric torch. 'Don't let it be said that the Saunders are unprepared. Coming?'

'Where does it lead?'

'Wait and see. Mr. Adler?'

'Oh, sure. I'm not backing out at this stage – whatever terrors are in store.'

'Then I'll lead the way. Are you coming, Jane?'

'Not this time, darling, thanks. Not in the only evening dress I've brought with me.'

'I think it's pretty clean in there, actually. It's completely enclosed, so it can't get very dirty. Still, perhaps it would be a bit risky in white.'

'Have a lovely time,' said Jane.

Gerry disappeared into the opening, saying as she did so: 'Keep your heads down.'

Deveraux and Adler followed her. Jane heard Gerry's voice, muffled: 'Mr. Adler, if you reach upward with your left hand you should feel a sort of handle. Will you pull it downwards?'

There was a slight rumbling sound and the panel slid into place. Jane left the room and made her way upstairs to the first floor, turned right along the main corridor, and then went through a door on the left into another large panelled room. It was filled with shelves, which were stocked with sheets and other household linen. She waited for a few minutes, then heard a bumping sound behind the wall, a panel slid back, and Gerry emerged, followed by the two men. They looked around them, blinking.

'Welcome back to civilisation,' Jane said.

'Where are we?' Adler asked.

Gerry told them. 'Did you both enjoy it?'

'Well,' Deveraux brushed a speck of dust from his cuff. 'As secret passages go, I'm sure this one is one of the most delightful. But, frankly, if I should again have the occasion during my stay to proceed from the breakfast-room to here, I shall ask Miss Clifton to guide me by the overland trail – no matter what dangers we may face from hostile natives.'

'I think you're a soulless beast,' Gerry said. 'I'm sure Mr. Adler appreciated the romance and mystery of it.'

'Indeed yes, Lady Geraldine. In spite of having banged my head at least a dozen times, I consider it to have been one of the most deeply satisfying experiences of my life. And I must congratulate you on never once losing your way.'

'What on earth was the passage built for?' Deveraux asked. 'Isn't the house rather late for a thing like that?'

'Yes. Nobody really knows. My great-grandfather's chaplain is reputed to have said that it was to be assumed it had been installed in order to facilitate an irregular liaison, but as Alderley was built by the first Earl, and it must have been included at his instructions, that theory hardly holds water.'

'Something of a puritan, was he?' Adler asked.

'Precisely the opposite. He was the most notorious profligate in the county. And utterly brazen withal. He didn't care who knew about his activities – and the sort of ladies he entertained were hardly likely to have cared either. So a secret passage would have been rather an unnecessary expense. Probably he just wanted a secret passage for prestige, in the same way he wanted a – a lake, say.'

'How does that sliding panel downstairs work?' Deveraux asked. 'It's very ingenious.'

'Oh, it's a highly complicated system of levers and springs and weights. It was added much later, by the fifth Earl, who was very mechanically minded. Before that it was just a matter of sliding the panel aside with your hands – as you still do this end. Incidentally, I hope you're both paying attention. You will be examined on the subject before you leave.'

CHAPTER NINE

Friday Morning

Friday dawned another glorious day.

At ten a.m. the official talks commenced in the small music-room, which was soundproof and had been set aside for the discussions. At the same time Lord Burford finished breakfast and ambled somewhat gloomily out to the terrace, where Hiram Peabody, who'd breakfasted earlier, was reading.

Lord Burford spoke heartily. 'Mornin' Peabody. Lovely day.'

'Good morning, Earl. It sure is.' He folded up his paper.

'Sleep all right?'

'Fine, thank you. Actually Carrie and I are both notoriously heavy sleepers. But who wouldn't sleep well in a place like this?'

'Where's your missus got to?'

'Oh, she's exploring the house. The Countess kindly told her to feel quite free to go anywhere. She'll be happy as a cricket for hours just poking round on her own. It'll be the furnishings chiefly that'll take her attention, I guess.'

'Capital, capital.' Lord Burford coughed. 'I was thinking, p'raps you'd like to come and take a dekko at my little collection now.'

Peabody got to his feet with alacrity. 'Lead me to it, sir. This is something I've been looking forward to ever since we arrived in Europe.'

'Well, I hope it comes up to expectations, that's all. Come along, then. I'll take you up.'

He led the way up the stairs and turned right. They went along the main corridor and at the end turned left into the east corridor; about half-way along it, Lord Burford opened a pair of imposing double doors on the right and went through. Peabody followed. They were in a long gallery, which ran most of the outer side of the east wing. It was lined with paintings.

Lord Burford said: 'These are our pictures. Supposed to be very fine, if you're interested.'

'Oh, I'm sure they are. They certainly look beautiful. But I'm afraid I don't – I'm not...'

'Nor me. Come along.' He crossed the gallery to another door, almost exactly opposite. This was the entrance to the top floor of the eastern extension, the ground floor forming the ballroom. Lord Burford took a bunch of keys from his pocket, unlocked the door and opened it. Four feet beyond this was another door. This was not locked. Lord Burford opened it, then stood back and ushered his guest in. Peabody went through – and stopped dead.

He was at the end of a long, high-ceilinged and delightfully-proportioned room, with tall french doors leading onto a balustraded balcony at the far end. Through these could be seen the beech copse and the lake. The room had a finely-moulded gilded ceiling, elaborately panelled walls, and a highly-polished floor.

But Peabody had eyes for none of this. For the room was crammed from end to end with hundreds of guns. They were of every shape and size, from tiny pistols up to several huge cannon at the far end. He looked round reverently for ten seconds, before turning to his host.

'Earl,' he said. 'During the last four months I've seen most of the sights of Europe – the Parthenon, St Peter's, Notre Dame, the Tower of London – you name it. But this for me is the highlight. Now, where do we start?'

'Well, suppose first we have a quick survey of the whole collection, then later on you can examine the pieces that particularly interest you in greater detail.'

'Lead on,' said Peabody.

While Lord Burford was showing his collection, his wife had begun her task of impressing the glories of Alderley on Giles Deveraux. Determined he should miss none of the finer points, she had swooped on him shortly after breakfast and swept him off on the start of a detailed guided tour.

They commenced in the hall. 'Right,' the Countess said, 'let's first take a look at the staircase. We're quite proud of it. It's an early example of a type introduced at about the time Alderley was built. As you can see, the balustrades are composed of these pierced and carved panels in four-inch pine. The craftsmanship is considered particularly fine. If you look closely at the acanthus foliage...'

* * *

Jane and Gerry had gone riding.

'I was frightfully glad you made it up with Deveraux,' Gerry said. 'It would have been awfully awkward if the two of you had kept up a running feud all over the weekend. He's really much too nice to fight with, anyway, don't you think?'

She spoke casually, but cast a glance sideways as she asked the question, searching her friend's face.

The two girls had dismounted to rest their horses on the extreme southern border of the estate and were sitting on the bank of the little meandering river which eventually fed the Alderley lake.

Jane was lying back with her eyes closed. 'He's nice enough, I suppose, but he's not really my type. And you needn't use that innocent tone with me. I know just what's going through your scheming little mind.'

'It's not a little mind.'

'All right, your scheming big mind. Use it to scheme yourself into getting off with Martin Adler.'

Gerry screwed up her nose. 'I'm not sure I really want to. I could understand someone falling for him in a big way – I think I would have myself three or four years ago. But he's just a little too charming. I'm not sure I don't like Nick Felman better. He's nice I think. Even though he is like a cat on hot bricks most of the time.'

'He's worried about something.'

'Yes. Now and again he manages to throw it off – but he can't keep it up. I wish I knew what was wrong.'

'Why don't you ask him?'

'Oh, I couldn't.'

'Why not? I would.'

'You might get away with it. He'd probably tell me to mind my own business.'

'I don't know why you should think that. He hasn't given the least sign of being interested in me.'

'And, of course, he's not really your type, is he?'

Jane laughed.

'In fact, none of them are, are they? You'll have to try elsewhere, after all.'

Jane hesitated fractionally before saying: 'Looks like it, doesn't it?'

The pause lasted only a second, but it was enough for Gerry. She gave a squeak, grabbed Jane by the shoulders, and stared into her face. 'Jane – there is someone. There is, isn't there?'

'No, don't be silly.' Jane sat up and looked away.

'There is. I can tell. Who? Oh lor' – not Martin Adler – not after what I said?'

'Of course not.'

'Evans, then, the secretary? But you've hardly spoken to him. And it couldn't possibly be Thornton.'

'Oh, Gerry, really!'

'Algy! Not Algy – I just won't believe it. But there isn't anybody else. I don't understand. Apart from them, Daddy, Mr. Peabody and Richard are the only men—' She broke off with a gasp as she noticed Jane's eyes flicker. 'Richard! Not Richard? Darling, you're not in love with Richard?'

Jane didn't answer.

'Jane, I just don't believe it!'

'Nobody's asking you to.' Jane spoke snuffily.

'But he's so much older than you.'

'He is not. He's sixteen years older. Which is nothing.

Not that it would make any difference if it was a hundred and sixteen years. There never has been, and never will be, anything between us, so just shut up.'

'Darling, I'm sorry. I honestly had no idea you felt like that.' Gerry sounded rather dazed. 'How long – I mean, when did you first...' She tailed off.

'When I was about seventeen.' Jane's voice quavered a little.

They both sat silently for a few minutes. Then Gerry said: 'I think it would be ripping.'

'What would?'

'For you and Richard to team up.'

'You didn't sound as though you thought that.'

'Well, it sort of took me on the hop. But now I've had a chance to think about it, I'm beginning to *see* you together.'

'Well, forget it. It's never going to happen.'

'But for heaven's sake, why not?'

'Because he just doesn't think of me that way, that's why not. To him, I'm just his little niece's little friend.'

'Then it's up to you to open his eyes.'

'Never.' Jane shook her head firmly.

'Oh, don't be silly, Jane. I don't mean you've got to *vamp* him.'

'What else would it amount to?'

'You've just got to make him see you for what you are – a fully mature and very attractive woman.'

'Thanks for the compliment, but nothing doing. He's either interested in me, or he's not. I did hope that after such a long break he might see me in a new light. I've avoided him, you know, for over two years. But when we met yesterday, nothing happened. He was pleased to see me, friendly, interested, helpful. And that was all. So let's just leave it at that, shall we, and talk about something else.'

'No, let's not. I think you'd be crazy to let things stop there. Look, why don't I have a word with him—'

She broke off and winced as Jane grabbed her fiercely by the arm. 'You dare, Gerry! I swear I'll never speak to you again if you so much as hint to him how I feel.'

Gerry tried to unwind Jane's fingers from her arm. 'Jane, let go, you're hurting.'

'Promise me you won't ever mention it.'

'All right – I promise.'

'To Richard – or to anybody else.'

'All right.'

Jane let go, dropped down onto her back again and stared at the sky. Gerry rubbed her arm.

'Your trouble, Jane, is that you're just too proud.'

'Maybe. But I will not make myself cheap – for anything or anybody. Besides,' Jane rolled over onto her stomach and spoke a little less vehemently, 'he's probably got a girl already.'

'I don't think so. Not a regular one, anyway. There are women he takes out, of course, but no special one, I'm sure. I believe there was a girl once he was in love with, but that was a long time ago.'

'Oh? When?'

'During the war, when he was in France. I've got an idea there was some sort of tragedy about it. I don't know any details. He's never talked about it. But I vaguely remember hearing him telling Daddy some story when I was quite a little girl.'

'I suppose she died, did she?'

'I honestly don't know. Probably. I just remember him and Daddy sounding rather grim, then seeing me and shutting up. I could try to find out.'

'No don't bother. There's no point in dragging up the past.'

Jane got to her feet and brushed down her jodhpurs. 'Come on, let's give these beauties of yours a really good gallop.'

Richard Saunders was feeling a little worried. The talks were not going quite as he had anticipated. It was not that, so far at least, any real differences had arisen between the sides; but matters were certainly not proceeding as smoothly as they should be.

The trouble, to Richard's mind, lay in the attitude of Adler. He appeared to expect the British to make a number of firm commitments, yet seemed unwilling to reciprocate himself. He repeatedly asked for facts and figures regarding the proposed military aid, but so far had been strangely unwilling even to mention the existence of the land which was to be handed over in return – let alone discuss it in detail. Already Richard had made concessions – had promised the delivery by a certain date of specific equipment. But no corresponding concession had been forthcoming. It was very puzzling. Richard wondered if he had said anything which might have led Adler to distrust him. If so, he would have to find out what it was and put things right as quickly as possible.

Now Adler was giving a long, repetitious and quite unnecessary peroration about the great peril faced by his country. When he eventually stopped, Richard suggested a coffee break. He rang the bell and the coffee arrived a minute or so later. After the footman had left, the two sides drifted to different ends of the room.

Richard cocked an eyebrow at Thornton. 'Well?'

'Odd, Minister. Very odd.'

'I'm glad you agree. I was beginning to think it was *me*!'

Thornton shook his head. 'No, it's Adler. He's behaving very strangely. There's something here I don't understand.'

'It's almost as though they're trying to go back on their government's word – trying to avoid ceding any land.'

'I know.'

'Do you think they could have discovered that these territories are much richer than they originally estimated?'

'I would say there's more to it than that. Something peculiar is going on here. I've never known anyone conduct negotiations in the way Adler is.'

Richard looked at him keenly. 'Then what is the explanation?'

'I don't know – yet.'

'Well, what's our next move? Concede a little more?'

'That would not be my advice.'

'You thought I was wrong to give in just now, didn't you?'

Thornton hesitated. 'Well, frankly, I would not have done so.'

'Maybe you would have been right. I simply thought it was time for somebody to make a gesture of good will.'

'Oh, I appreciate your motive, Minister. And you've certainly put yourself in the right. But I would recommend firmness now – press hard for more details of this territory. That I think is vital.'

Adler said to Felman: 'What do you think?'

'Saunders is worried.'

'I know. I'm getting to feel quite sorry for the guy.'

'Sorry for him!'

'Yes, he seems a decent fellow. I don't want to louse up his career.'

'Then you know what to do.'

'Talk sense. Anyway, if he does strike out over this business, at least you won't have to blame yourself. Because, to be frank, Nicholas, you haven't been a great deal of help this morning.'

'What do you expect? I'm not exactly used to this sort of situation.'

'I'm not used to it myself. I've never handled anything like it before. I'm not enjoying myself, you know. I like these folk – Saunders' brother and his wife, those two girls. Nothing would give me greater pleasure than to spend another two days here, inspecting the old boy's collection, seeing over the house, playing tennis with the chicks, then shake hands all round and go home. But I can't and you can't either. So I'm afraid you're going to have to make the best of it.'

Before Felman could reply to this, Richard spoke from the other side of the room. 'Well, gentlemen, shall we get down to business again?'

* * *

'Here's a rather nice fourteen-barrel volley gun,' said Lord Burford. 'Made by—'

'Dupe & Co, around 1800?'

'Yes, but let me tell you—'

'Remind me to tell you something about Dupe's later on. Now, let's have a look at that case of percussion pistols.'

'Oh, the Devillers.' Lord Burford picked up the case.

'About 1830?'

'Twenty-nine, actually.' He handed the case to Peabody.

'What a beautiful pair of gold-damascened duellers,' Peabody said reverently.

'Calibre point—'

'Point fifty. I know. Multi-groove rifling, right?'

'Right. The two pocket pistols—'

'Point four-four, I think. Folding, single selective triggers. Now, talking of double-barrelled pocket pistols, let me tell you about something I picked up in New Orleans a year or so back.'

Lady Burford flung open a door and went in. Deveraux followed her meekly. 'This is known as the Parlour. Note the bolection moulding of the fireplace. Nothing like black and white marble.'

Deveraux peered at the fireplace. 'Oh, very fine indeed.'

'Also the oak wainscot. And the enriched architraves round the windows. Right, come along. We can examine everything in more detail later. I want to show you the Royal Suite while the Peabodys are out. The bedroom has an Angelica Kauffman ceiling.'

* * *

'Ah,' said Hiram Peabody, 'what's this?' He pounced. 'A French arquebus, eh. Very nice...double crowned muzzle...brass orthoptic sight...about 1600?'

'That's right,' said the Earl.

'I've got a similar one myself. Only mine...'

The morning passed peacefully.

CHAPTER TEN

Friday Afternoon

Since it was uncertain just when Richard and Adler would want to break off the talks, a cold buffet lunch was served that day.

The afternoon proceeded much as the morning. The talks continued in the small music-room. Jane and Gerry played a couple of sets of tennis with Deveraux and Evans. When they'd finished, Jane, prompted by a vague sense of duty, settled down on the terrace and let Algy talk to her. Gerry went to make some adjustments she claimed were necessary to the Hispano. Deveraux and Evans both went to do paper work. The Earl and Peabody spent the entire afternoon with the collection. And Lady Burford took Mrs. Peabody along to her boudoir for a quiet *tête-a-tête*.

'Tell me, Lady Burford, do you like guns?' Carrie Peabody asked the question a trifle diffidently.

'Like them? Let us say I've learnt to live with them.'

'Yes, one has to do that. What I really mean, is do you take an interest in them?'

'Not in the least. Do you?'

'I never have. But I sometimes wonder whether I should try.'

'Well, of course, I don't know your husband well, but I'm sure George would not welcome *my* trying to take an interest in *his*. He would have to keep explaining things to me and answering my questions, and that would make him highly impatient.'

'Oh, Hiram likes talking about his guns – to anybody who will listen. I think he'd enjoy educating me in the finer points. What stops me chiefly is a fear of what it might lead to.'

'How do you mean, my dear?'

'They take up so much of his leisure time already. Naturally I am thankful that he has gotten this hobby. If he didn't, he'd probably spend all the time he now devotes to guns at the office, which wouldn't be good for him. His heart's a little weak—'

'I'm sorry. I didn't know.'

'It's not a serious condition, as long as he takes things fairly easy. Our doctor told him some years ago that he had to learn to relax. Guns were his way. He'd always been interested in them, but it was after that that they really became a passion with him. It's only consideration for me that stops him giving even more time to them. If he thought I was an enthusiast, too, I really don't think we'd get anything else done at all, out of business hours.'

'You might actually *become* an enthusiast – have you thought of that?'

Mrs. Peabody chuckled. 'I hardly think that's likely. I quite like some small ones. They can be very pretty with their ivory or silver inlay.'

'Oh, I don't mind the pistols and things like that. It's the cannon I object to.'

'Cannon?' Mrs. Peabody stared. 'The Earl has cannons up there?'

'Yes. Not many, I'm glad to say, because I managed to talk him out of going in for any more. But he's got half a dozen really big pieces.'

'Oh dear.' A look of consternation appeared on Mrs. Peabody's face.

'What's the matter?'

'Hiram's never gone in for anything like that. I just hope he doesn't get ideas.'

Just at that moment Lord Burford was saying: 'And down this end, as you see, I keep the heavy stuff.'

'Which is where I guess I get a trifle out of my depth. I know very little about artillery.'

'Really?' Lord Burford seemed to perk up a little at these words. 'Then let me try to enlarge your education.' He cleared his throat and took a deep breath.

'Now this first little job is one of the earliest machine guns. Invented in 1718 by James Puckle. Six chamber cylinder. Each chamber has to be primed through the touch hole. Fired by a conventional flintlock mechanism fitted to the barrel. Its weakness was a loose-fitting breech mechanism which allowed a lot of gas to escape. All the same, this type of gun was reported as firing sixty-three rounds in seven minutes under test conditions in 1772. Next is a British 2.75 inch mountain gun. This was the basic weapon of the Indian mountain artillery. Introduced 1914. An improved version of the original ten-pounder "screw" gun. Replaced after the war by the 3.7 inch Howitzer. Next we have a thirty-two-pounder carronade – made at the Carron foundry in Scotland, you know. This one's off HMS *Victory* – Nelson's flagship at Trafalgar. Range about five hundred yards. This next giant's a circus cannon. Used by Burundi the Human Cannonball to set up a world record of 165 feet. The barrel's sixteen feet long. Fired by compressed air. The electrical compressor plugs into the mains. Takes three or four minutes to build up pressure. Triggered by that lever and the barrel elevated by this handle. Now we come to a Maxim Nordenfeldt 75 mm. These were used by the Boers in the South African war. Hydro spring recoil system. They're light and—'

Lord Burford broke off. 'Not boring you, am I, old man?'

Peabody was looking a bit dazed. 'Not at all,' he said.

'Good. Where were we? Oh yes. Next a Becket Semag cannon. This was a forerunner of the Oerlikon gun, and...'

In the music-room Richard got to his feet. 'I think,' he said, 'that it might be a good idea if we called it a day now. I know it's early, but we don't seem to be making a great deal of progress and we may do better if we start fresh tomorrow morning. I don't quite know what's gone wrong today. There must, I think, have been some sort of misunderstanding between our respective superiors, and it might be necessary for one or both of us to take fresh instructions before the morning. I hope now we can forget our differences and spend the rest of the day pleasantly.'

'Oh, I'm sure we can,' Adler said with a smile. 'We don't want to spoil the weekend for your brother's other guests.

And I think, Saunders, that you are tending to exaggerate the differences between us. I'm sure that by tomorrow evening everything will have been settled satisfactorily.'

'I sincerely hope so,' Richard said.

They left the room and walked to the hall. Felman went straight upstairs. Adler paused and seemed to hesitate for a moment. Then as Richard and Thornton walked on, he called out: 'May I make a 'phone call, please?'

Richard turned back. 'Yes, certainly. The telephone room is along here. I'll show you.' He led Adler to the door and asked: 'Is it a trunk call – long distance, that is?'

Adler seemed somewhat surprised by the question. His eyebrows went up. 'Yes – that is, if you don't mind—'

'Of course not. I'm sorry; I wasn't being inquisitive. I was just going to explain the procedure. You ask the operator for "Trunks".'

'Thank you.'

Richard started to move away. Then he stopped and said: 'You're welcome to ring the Grand Duke himself, if you think it'll help.'

Adler smiled. 'I don't think that will be necessary.'

Richard went back to the hall, where Thornton was waiting for him, and said quietly: 'He's making a trunk call.'

'Indeed?' Thornton looked interested. 'His embassy, do you imagine?'

Richard nodded. 'So I would guess – and probably to arrange for them to inform the Grand Duke that the ploy has failed and he's going to have to start giving away some land.'

'I trust you're right. We must find out something about

this territory soon. I hope I may say without disrespect that I think your firmness this afternoon was admirable.'

'My dear chap, I'm sure in no circumstances could you be disrespectful. Thank you for your support. I suspect that certain of your colleagues would have been urging me to give way – anything to avoid a disagreement. Now, how about a drink?'

Jane entered the drawing-room through the french windows at the same time as Martin Adler came in by the door.

'Ah, Miss Clifton.'

'Good afternoon, Mr. Adler. Business finished for the day?'

'Yes, we decided to knock off early. You haven't seen Felman anywhere, have you?'

'I'm afraid not. Mr. Saunders and Mr. Thornton are on the terrace having a drink – they may know.'

'It's of no importance. A drink sounds good, though.'

'I was just going to ring for one myself.'

She rang the bell, then threw herself down onto a settee. 'Whew! I have been acting as captive audience to Algernon Fotheringay for a full ninety minutes and I'm exhausted.'

'Fotheringay likes the sound of his own voice, does he? I've barely spoken to him as yet.'

'You won't get much chance to speak *to* him, either. Algy will speak to you, though, some time. You won't be able to get out of it, I warn you.'

Just then Merryweather entered in answer to the bell. Jane said: 'Merryweather, could I have some lemonade, please?'

'Certainly, miss. And you, sir?'

'I'd like a whisky, please.'

'Yes, sir. With ice, I imagine?'

'Correct.'

Merryweather withdrew. Jane said: 'What did he mean? Oh, of course, all Americans take ice, don't they? You're only partly American, though, aren't you?'

'Half by parentage, wholly by education, but not by birth.'

'And is this your first visit to England?'

'Yes, it is. I feel I know the country quite well, though. I had an English girlfriend once. She was always talking about London, and about the Cotswold hills, where she'd been born. It sounded nice. She wanted me to come back with her and settle here.'

'Why didn't you?'

'Oh, I don't think I'm the type to settle down to domestic bliss.'

'Love 'em and leave 'em is your motto, is it?'

'That's about the size of it.'

Merryweather came back then with the drinks. Jane sipped her lemonade and watched Adler as he poured himself a whisky and added ice. The man had magnetism as well as charm.

Then Jane gave a start just as Gerry suddenly came bounding in through the french windows. She was wearing slacks and an old open-neck shirt and there was oil on her nose.

'That's fixed the brute. Gosh, I'm dying for a gasper.' She took a cigarette from a box and lit it. 'Oh, lemonade. Gorgeous.' She poured herself a glass and sat down by Jane. 'Darling, you look awfully pale. Do you feel all right?'

'I've got a bit of a headache, Gerry. I sat out there in the sun without a hat and without my glare glasses for about an hour and a half, just listening to Algy waffle. I think I'll go and lie down for a bit.' She stood up. 'I'll see you at dinner.'

She went out. Gerry turned to Adler. 'Had a good day, Mr. Adler?'

'Well, Lady Geraldine, not exactly good, but much as expected. Shall we say everything's under control?'

After the tennis, Giles Deveraux settled down in the shade of an oak tree to do some writing. He stayed there an hour, then put away his notebook, got to his feet, and brushed a few loose blades of grass from his flannel bags. He looked up at the grey mass of Alderley, standing timeless and stalwart under the August sun. It was a magnificent sight. Was it so handsome from each side, he wondered. It was time, for professional reasons, anyway, that he had a good look at it from every angle. He began to stroll round. He had nearly completed one circuit when he came upon John Evans, who was leaning against the wall next to the orangery, gazing at the house in silent admiration.

Deveraux jerked his head towards it. 'Nice, isn't it? What's your offer going to be?'

'Oh, I might run to a hundred quid.'

'You won't get it at that price. I'm offering guineas.'

Evans smiled. 'You're writing a book about it, aren't you?'

'I'm not sure yet. I'm writing a book about country houses. Whether Alderley will be included, I don't know.'

'It would be a great pity to leave it out.'

'I know. Unfortunately, that will apply to many places.'

'I suppose so.'

'I'm just going in to tea. Coming?'

They strolled off. Evans said: 'Must be an interesting job, yours.'

Deveraux shrugged. 'I keep moving.'

'I do, too, to a certain extent, with Mr. Peabody. But it's quite hard work. Voluminous correspondence follows him everywhere. I was dealing with it all the morning. Then on a trip like this I have to make all the travel arrangements, reservations, and so on. Anyway, they're going home next month. I'm not sure I shall go with them. I like England—'

'Your first visit?'

'Yes. I'd like to get a job and stay here for a while, if I could find anything suitable. You don't happen to know of a good billet, do you?'

'Not offhand.'

'Well, if you find the owners of any of these stately homes you're intending to write about are in need of a reasonably efficient tame secretary, perhaps you'll bear me in mind.'

'Certainly. Give me an address where I can contact you before we leave.'

CHAPTER ELEVEN

The Baroness De La Roche

'George,' said the Countess, 'you are not looking well.'

'Ain't I, my dear? I feel fine.'

'No you don't, George. You don't feel well at all.'

Lord Burford stared at her. 'But I do, Lavinia.'

'George – you feel a bilious attack coming on. I quite forgot to get another guest for dinner tonight and it's far too late now. Moreover, I've found out that Carrie Peabody is superstitious, so we cannot sit down thirteen to dinner. You, therefore, will have to dine alone.'

Lord Burford gave a groan. 'Oh, Lavinia, no! Why me?'

'Because we cannot conceivably ask one of the guests to absent himself; and for Geraldine or me to stay away would cause still greater imbalance between the sexes.'

'But good gad, I'm the host!'

'Richard is quite capable of acting as host. You can recover and come down and join the men as soon as we've withdrawn. Now please, George, do not be obdurate.' And with this concession Lord Burford had to be satisfied.

Reprieve, however, was to come to him unexpectedly.

At seven-forty-five, the party was beginning to assemble in the drawing-room when Merryweather entered and crossed to Lady Burford. 'Excuse me, my lady.'

'Yes, Merryweather?'

'Bates has been on the telephone from the lodge, my lady. There seems to have been an accident on the road outside.'

'Oh dear! Has anybody been seriously hurt?'

'Reportedly not, your ladyship. The occupants of the vehicle were a French lady and her chauffeur. The chauffeur is unhurt; the lady merely shaken. But it seems the motor car has been extensively damaged. Bates has telephoned to Jenkins in the village and he is sending a break-down vehicle. But the lady will plainly be unable to proceed on her journey this evening. Her name apparently is the Baroness de la Roche. As the only accommodation in the village is the Rose & Crown...' Merryweather paused diplomatically.

'Why, of course. Send Hawkins down to the lodge and instruct Bates to give the Baroness my compliments and tell her his lordship and I shall be delighted if she will join us. Have a bedroom prepared and lay another place at table.'

'Very good, your ladyship.'

Lady Burford lowered her voice. 'And tell his lordship not to count his chickens yet, but he'd better start dressing just in case. Understand?'

'His lordship is counselled to refrain from enumerating poultry, but is recommended to be in a state of preparedness to descend for dinner. Yes, my lady.'

Merryweather went out and Lady Burford turned to Geraldine. 'Baroness de la Roche. Ever heard of her?'

Gerry shook her head. 'French, did Merry say?'

'That was merely Bates's guess, I imagine.'

'I've got a very good friend called the Baroness von Richburg,' Algy said. 'She's German. Charming woman. I stayed at her Schloss in Bavaria a few years ago. Had a spirting time. Her chef produced the most terrific *apfelstrudel*. I used to eat mountains of it. Unfortunately, after a few days the Baroness was called away suddenly to a sick relative and she shut up the place, so I had to leave. However—'

'Has anyone else ever heard of a Baroness de la Roche?' Lady Burford asked loudly and desperately.

Neither the Peabodys nor Thornton, the only others present, had; nor had Jane or Deveraux, who entered a minute later. So there was quite an air of expectancy in the room by the time Merryweather opened the drawing-room door and announced: 'The Baroness de la Roche.'

There was an almost theatrical four-second pause. Then there walked into the room the most beautiful woman Jane had ever seen. She had a flawless complexion, deep limpid eyes of a most remarkable violet, with thick, long natural lashes, a perfectly straight nose, and softly up-curving lips, exactly outlined in the most delicate shade of lipstick. She was wearing a russet sports suit and a Tyrolean hat, decorated with a long feather, perched on the side of her head. At first glance she looked about thirty, though after closer study Lady Burford estimated her age as seven or eight years older than that.

The Baroness took two or three steps forward, conveying at the same moment an impression of being quite assured yet rather shaky on her feet.

Lady Burford went up to her, introduced herself and Geraldine, and said: 'Welcome to Alderley.'

'Oh, Lady Burford, Lady Geraldine, a thousand apologies for gate-crashing your home in this way.' She spoke with the very slightest of French accents. The voice, warm, vibrant, slightly husky, had the barest trace of a tremor.

'Not at all. We're only too glad to be able to help. What a ghastly experience! You must have been terribly shocked. Come and sit down.' She led the Baroness to a chair.

'Really, you are too kind. I am most grateful.'

'Now, I'm sure you need something to drink.'

'Well.' The Baroness gave the ghost of a smile. 'Perhaps a little cognac, if you have some.'

'Of course.' Lady Burford looked at Merryweather and raised one eyebrow. He bowed his head and withdrew.

'Are you sure you're not hurt?' Lady Burford asked.

'Quite sure, thank you. I feel just rather shaken.'

'And your chauffeur,' Gerry put in, 'is he all right?'

The Baroness looked up at her. 'Roberts? Yes, he seems perfectly well.'

'Yet the car is badly wrecked?'

'He seems to think it will require considerable repair work.'

'How did the accident happen?'

'I really couldn't say. I am afraid I was dozing in the back when suddenly there was a swerve and the next thing I knew we were in the ditch.'

At that moment, Merryweather returned with the brandy. The Baroness sipped it gratefully and Lady Burford said: 'Do you feel capable of introductions? It will make it easier to remember everybody if you can meet people in two instalments, as it were.'

'Yes, I am dying to meet all these charming people.'

Lady Burford briskly performed introductions, carefully forestalling Algy from starting a conversation with the Baroness. Then she said: 'That simply leaves my husband, his brother, and two other' – she had been about to say 'foreign,' but with an obscure idea that it sounded vaguely insulting, amended this – 'two other overseas visitors we have with us.'

'I shall look forward to meeting them.'

Deveraux asked: 'Were you intending to travel far tonight?'

She favoured him with a flashing smile. 'To Worcestershire. I am on my way to stay with some friends of mine there: Lord and Lady Darnley. Perhaps you know them?'

'You are a friend of the Darnleys?' There was a subtle but immediate change in Lady Burford's manner. The Baroness was no longer just an unknown stranger: she was a friend of friends – accredited. It made a difference.

The Baroness said: 'Perhaps I might use your telephone later to let them know that I have been delayed. Heaven knows when I shall arrive now.'

'Well, certainly not tonight,' Lady Burford said firmly. 'Tonight you will stay here. Merryweather, have you prepared a room?'

'Yes, my lady. The spangled bedroom.'

'And the Baroness's things have been taken up?'

'Yes, your ladyship.'

The Baroness said: 'Really, your kindness overwhelms

me. I feel I am imposing on you shamelessly.'

'Not at all. We are already entertaining a moderately large party. We will hardly notice one more – at least, not in any inconvenient way. Now, would you care for some more brandy?'

'Oh, no thank you.'

'Then I expect you would like to go to your room and freshen up?'

'That would be nice.'

'Very well, Merryweather will take you up. Or perhaps first to the telephone?'

The Baroness got to her feet. Lady Burford said: 'Merryweather, after you have escorted the Baroness upstairs, send Celeste to her.' She turned back to the Baroness. 'My maid will attend you. I don't know whether you would like to rest in your room, or whether you feel up to joining us for dinner?'

'Oh, I feel quite recovered now, Lady Burford. I should like very much to join you for dinner, if I may, but I have no wish to delay you.'

'There'll be no question of that. We don't dine until eight-thirty. Take your time.'

Merryweather and the Baroness went out. Before anyone could speak Gerry said, 'Oh, excuse me,' and hurried after them. When she got outside, Merryweather and the Baroness were approaching the stairs. 'Oh, Merryweather,' Gerry called.

He turned and came back to her, with a murmured apology to the Baroness. Gerry spoke in a low voice. 'Merry, tell my father the chicks have hatched.'

Merryweather's upper lip shifted about an eighth of an

inch in acknowledgement of this remark. 'Very good, my lady.' He returned to the Baroness and led her upstairs.

Gerry watched till they'd disappeared, then signalled to a nearby footman. He hurried across to her. 'William, find Hawkins and tell him I want to see him straight away, will you? I'll be in the library.'

By eight-thirty the rest of the party had joined the group in the drawing-room – all agog to see the ravishing beauty spoken of by the others. Five more minutes passed. The Baroness still did not appear, and Lady Burford sent Gerry up to bring her down. A few minutes later there were voices outside, the door opened, and the Baroness entered the rotan, Gerry on her heels.

Lord Burford muttered 'By jove!' under his breath, Algy screwed his monocle into his eye, and there was nobody in the room who did not stare shamelessly.

The Baroness was wearing a backless evening gown of shimmering gold marocain, with the skirt very tight to the knees and flaring out round her feet. Her hair was ash blonde and worn in the ultra-modern shoulder length page-boy style. Her complexion was now ivory pale and her lips vivid scarlet. Around her neck she wore a sea-green emerald necklace.

She paused inside the door, smiled, and said in her low voice: 'I do hope I have not kept you all waiting.'

Lady Burford stepped forward. 'Not at all. My husband's only just down. He's been so looking forward to meeting you.'

'I have indeed.' Lord Burford bustled forward. 'Charmed, Baroness, charmed.' They shook hands. The

Earl said: 'May I present my brother—'

He turned towards Richard, then broke off. 'Rich? What's the matter?'

For Richard was standing as though turned to stone. His eyes were fixed on the Baroness in an expression of utter disbelief. He took no notice of his brother's words, but for a full five seconds just stood motionless. Then in a whisper he spoke one word. 'Anilese.'

The Baroness took a step towards him. Her lovely eyes grew even larger. She started to raise her hand as if to reach out and touch him, but froze in mid-movement.

'Richard. No – I don't – I don't—'

She swayed and fell into a crumpled heap on the floor.

'I wonder – would you all mind going in to dinner? Mademoiselle – the Baroness – and I will join you presently.'

Five minutes had passed since the Baroness's dramatic swoon. Richard and Lord Burford had lifted her onto the settee, water had been fetched, and Mrs. Peabody, saying briskly: 'I've had some nursing experience,' had bathed the Baroness's face and wrists.

Within a minute she had opened her eyes and murmured weakly: 'Where am I?' Then she had looked round in bewilderment, until her gaze alighted on Richard again. She had shaken her head, as if to clear it. 'Richard. It is you. I thought it was a dream.' She had taken his hand. 'It is like a miracle.'

Carrie Peabody had said: 'Do you feel all right, my dear?'

'What? Oh yes. Quite all right, thank you. I'm very

sorry. I'm afraid I have been a fool.' She looked and sounded embarrassed.

She sat up, and then Richard made his request for dinner to be started.

Lord Burford nodded. 'Splendid idea. I'm famished. Come along, everybody.'

Slowly they trooped out. While the room emptied, Richard simply stood, staring down at the Baroness, unable to tear his eyes away from her face. Then as a footman closed the doors behind the end of the procession, leaving the two of them alone, he dropped on his knees beside her and took her hand.

'Anilese – I can't believe it. Is it really you – after so long? I thought you were dead.'

'*Oui*, Richard, *chéri. C'est moi.*'

'But what happened to you? You were never seen after that bomb fell.'

'It is a long story, Richard. You know how things were then.'

'But surely you could have got in touch with me after the war – just to let me know you were alive? You knew how I felt. You must have realised what I thought had happened. Why didn't you?'

'There were reasons – good reasons. I will tell you, I promise. Only later.'

'But why did you seek me out now – after all this time?'

Her eyes widened. 'I did not seek you out, Richard. I had no idea you were here. Would I have fainted if I had been expecting to see you?'

He stared at her. 'But you knew this was my brother's house.'

'No. I was told by the lodge-keeper that it was the house of the Earl of Burford. But that meant nothing to me. I knew you as Captain Richard Saunders. I was aware you came from an aristocratic family, that your brother had a title; I did not remember what that title was.'

Richard shook his head in amazement. 'Then you're really here just by chance?'

'My car crashed outside the gates, Richard. That is why I am here.'

'It's incredible.'

'I prefer to think of it as – destiny.'

'Destiny – chance – what does it matter? You're here, that's the important thing. And to think that when they told me the Baroness de la Roche—' He stopped short. 'Of course – you're married.'

She shook her head. 'I am a widow. I married in 1923. The Baron died in 1928 – nearly penniless.'

'Oh, my dear. And – what since then?'

She looked away from him. 'Since then many things, Richard. Many places. Many experiences I would prefer not to remember. Many ways of making a living. Much heartbreak.'

'And – many men?'

'No one who mattered.'

'No one now?'

'No one.'

'Then I – do you mean I've got—'

She put her fingers on his lips. 'We cannot talk now. We must go in to dinner. We will have plenty of time later.'

'You're staying?'

'Overnight, at least. I shall have to go on when my

motor is mended. But, never fear – I shall come back.'

She took a powder compact from her bag, examined her face, and made some minor repairs. As she did so she said: 'Richard, you will, of course, tell them you believed me dead. Will you also tell them I thought the same about you? I can tell *you* the truth, but not strangers.'

'Whatever you wish.'

She put her make-up away and smiled at him. 'I'm ready. Shall we go in?'

The soup course was finishing when they entered the dining-room. The conversation stopped as they went in, and all eyes were on them.

After they'd sat down, Richard said: 'We obviously owe you all an explanation. As will have been plain, Baroness de la Roche and I are acquainted. We knew each other in France during the war. Our surprise just now arose from the fact that we had each thought the other was dead. The Baroness has been married – and widowed – since I knew her, so the name de la Roche meant nothing to me. She likewise knew me only as Saunders, and was not aware the Earl of Burford was my brother. You can imagine how astonished we both were.'

Carrie Peabody said: 'My, isn't that too romantic.'

Algy spoke loudly. 'I say, Saunders, how come you both thought the other was dead? Sounds as though there might be a dashed exciting story behind that. Why don't you blow the gaff, what?'

'It's an exceedingly dull story, Fotheringay, and would bore you immensely. I'm sure we'd all much rather hear about your visit to Lady Masters.'

Algy beamed. 'Oh, really? Righty-ho.'

Jane paid silent tribute to Richard's skill. There'd certainly be no more discussion about Anilese de la Roche during this meal.

When the ladies entered the drawing-room after dinner, Gerry waited some minutes for a good opportunity, then said to the Baroness: 'You know, I'm intrigued by this accident of yours.'

Anilese looked at her coolly. 'Really? I assure you, intriguing is not what I found it. I doubt, too, that you would have found it so had you been in the car.'

Gerry flushed slightly. 'Perhaps "intrigued" is the wrong word. "Puzzled" would be better. What puzzles me is the cause of it. That's a long straight stretch of road outside the gates. The light was good, the sun was behind you, the road was dry and the surface is in first class order. No other vehicle was involved. Yet your car suddenly swerved off the road and into the ditch, being so badly damaged that your chauffeur thinks it'll take a long time to repair it. Can you enlighten me?'

Anilese shook her head and gave a sweet smile. 'I'm afraid not, Lady Geraldine. I have no knowledge of motor cars. But perhaps it was some sudden mechanical failure in the vehicle itself which caused us to crash. That is possible, is it not? You seem to be an expert on these matters.'

'Oh, yes, that's quite possible. You could have burst a tyre, or a wheel could have come off. Except that I've been talking to our chauffeur, who drove you up here. He had a good look at your car while you were supervising Roberts as he transferred your luggage to the Rolls, and he tells me all the wheels of your car are in place and the tyres fully inflated. Your steering could have suddenly failed, I suppose. But it's a very rare thing to happen.'

'I am very unfortunate then, am I not?'

'Not really. I would say you are exceptionally fortunate.'

'Oh?' The Baroness raised her finely-plucked eyebrows.

'Yes. Hawkins tells me the car is at right angles to the road, facing straight into the bank, and the front is very badly smashed in – as though you'd been travelling at a pretty high speed. And that means you were both very lucky to walk away unhurt; quite apart from the fact that, having turned at right angles like that when moving at such a rate, it's almost miraculous your car didn't overturn.'

The Baroness laughed, a delightful tinkling laugh. 'Why, Lady Geraldine, this is fascinating. Quite like your English Sherlock Holmes stories. You really must talk with my chauffeur about it. I'm sure you'd get on famously with him. Unfortunately, nearly all you've said is completely above my head.'

'I may talk to your chauffeur,' Gerry said, 'though I think it would be better if you were to talk to him yourself – for your own safety. However, I shall be more interested in talking to Harry Jenkins at the village garage, to ask exactly what he found wrong with your car.'

The entry of the men at that moment put an end to the conversation before Anilese could reply.

That night the party broke up early, as for many of them it had been in one way or another a wearing day. Only Algy, who had slept most of the afternoon, was fresh and tried to get some dancing going. But he found no takers, and, rather disgruntled, was forced to retire early to bed with a new Ethel M. Dell novel.

After undressing, Jane slipped on a negligee and went along to Gerry's room. She found her having her hair brushed by Marie, and waited a few minutes, making conversation, until the maid was dismissed. Then she said: 'You think Anilese's crash was faked.'

'Precisely.'

'For what reason? Just to provide an excuse to gatecrash this party?'

'I can't think of any other reason.'

'And you think she knew Richard was here – never thought he was dead? But why go through all that? If she did know, why not just turn up, announce herself by her maiden name and ask to see him?'

'Perhaps she wasn't sure of the reception she'd get.'

'Maybe, but that faint looked awfully real – as though she really was staggered to see him. Couldn't the accident have been faked for another reason?'

'Such as?'

'Well, there are two European diplomats and an American millionaire here – due to return to their own countries almost as soon as they leave Alderley. If she wanted to make contact with one of them, this might be her last chance. You know, I was joking with Richard yesterday about my becoming an adventuress. I didn't know a real one was going to turn up.'

'Her title's genuine, by the way. I looked her up in the *Almanac de Gotha*. Baron de la Roche was French. He married a Mademoiselle Anilese Periot in 1923. He died five years later. So she fits the bill all right.'

'That only tells us there is a Baroness of that name, a widow, somewhere in the world; it doesn't prove the woman who arrived here tonight is she – only that she's got the same Christian name as her. There's no doubt she's *the* girl, is there – the one you were telling me about?'

'None at all. I asked Mummy. They got engaged in France in 1917.'

'You couldn't get the whole story, I suppose?'

'Not tonight. I'll worm it out of somebody sooner or later, though.'

'Of course,' Jane said, 'we don't know he's still in love with her now. There was nothing in his behaviour tonight to suggest it.'

'Not publicly, anyway.'

'Still.' Jane went to the door. 'It's immaterial to me either way. As I told you, there can never be anything between Richard and me.'

'Of course not. All the same, you are concerned for his happiness, aren't you – purely as a platonic friend? You don't want him deceived by a beautiful *femme fatale*?'

'I think he can take care of himself.'

'I'm going to watch her like a hawk, all the same.'

'You won't be the only one, Gerry. Good night.'

Jane returned to her room and went to bed. She turned the light out immediately, but it was a long time before she got to sleep.

CHAPTER TWELVE

Double Deadlock

On Saturday morning it was hotter than ever. But now the heat was sultry and there was a threat of thunder in the air; it was not weather for outdoor exercise and the tennis courts remained unoccupied and the horses unsaddled.

Anilese de la Roche slept late. After a light breakfast of coffee and rolls in her bedroom, she came down at ten o'clock. She then made a telephone call, after which she sought out Lady Burford.

'I am told my motor car will not be ready until Monday or Tuesday,' she said.

Lady Burford brightened. An unescorted titled lady, vouched for not only by her brother-in-law, but also by the Darnleys, was a godsend and just what she needed to balance the house party and eliminate the Thirteen to Dinner problem. 'Then of course you will stay here,' she said decidedly.

'You are too kind. But I can easily hire a car. Or go on by train.'

Lady Burford brushed aside these suggestions and

it was arranged that the Baroness should remain until Monday at least. She went to telephone Lady Darnley.

'Peabody,' said Lord Burford, 'you mentioned in your last letter that you'd picked up something rather special in Rome, and you were looking forward to showing it to me.'

'That's right, Earl. I sure did.'

'Well, how about it? Or have you decided it's not quite as special as you first thought?'

'Not at all, sir. I consider it to be one of the most important purchases I have made for a long time.'

'Well, don't sit on it, man. Let's have a look.'

'Very well, I'll get it now.'

'Take it along to the collection-room, will you? You haven't quite seen all my stuff yet. I've got one more piece, actually, that I think you'll appreciate.'

Peabody cast him a surprised glance. 'Oh, have you? OK, then. I'll see you up there in a few minutes.'

He bustled off. Lord Burford chuckled and rubbed his hands. Gerry, who had recently finished a session on the telephone, was sitting nearby, rather a faraway expression in her eyes. Lord Burford got to his feet, bent down near her and said: 'I knew what the blighter was up to: trying to keep his own piece till last – wait till he'd seen everything of mine, then produce this new thing of his and trump me. I was up to him, though. He'll have a job to outshine my *pièce de résistance*.' He toddled off.

But Gerry was miles away.

Peabody entered the sitting-room of the Royal Suite, where his wife was writing a letter. 'Do you know what that old

sooner's done, honey? He deliberately didn't let me see
everything yesterday. He kept one really good piece back,
just so as to have something to top me. I'll show the shyster,
though. He'll have a job to cap what I've got in here.'

He went through the connecting door to dressing-room,
opened a large innovation trunk, took out a flat hard case
about eighteen inches by twelve and four inches deep,
tucked it under his arm, and strode out.

At ten o'clock the four negotiators gathered again in
the music-room. They all settled down and got out their
papers.

Richard lit a cigarette and looked at Adler. 'Well, my
friend, have you got anything to say to us?'

Adler scratched his nose. Then: 'No, I'm sorry,' he said.
'I regret I cannot alter my position. Before anything else
is discussed, I must have a firm understanding as to what
arms and equipment the British government is going to
supply, and an agreed timetable for their delivery; also full
details of your contingency plans in the event that we are
invaded. If I do not get this information, I shall be forced
to withdraw.'

There was utter silence in the room following these
words. Richard didn't react at all, just sat quite still,
looking impassively at Adler.

Thornton's heart was in his mouth. Never in all
his years of diplomacy had he felt quite so tense. He's
overreaching himself, he thought. The Minister cannot
possibly stand for an ultimatum like that, no matter
what his instructions were. It would be too much of a
capitulation. He's going to have to call Adler's bluff.

Because the Duchy *can't* withdraw. They've got to have our help.

Eventually Richard spoke. He displayed no annoyance or disappointment. 'We seem to have reached deadlock, then. I certainly can give no firm commitments or any information such as you require until something is forthcoming from you in return.'

Adler shrugged. He seemed quite unperturbed. 'Then where do we go from here?'

'I don't see we can go anywhere from here. There's little point in continuing the talks.'

'Are you proposing to let me leave here and report to the Grand Duke that after travelling half-way across Europe especially to talk with you, you sent me home with nothing?'

'I am proposing nothing of the sort. All I propose is that you show yourself willing to negotiate – to give something in return; not just to make demands. If not, I'm afraid you'll have to report just that.'

There was silence again for a moment. Adler stared hard at Richard, as though he were trying to read his mind. Then he cast a quick glance at Felman, before looking back at Richard and saying: 'Then I suggest we adjourn now and spend the rest of the morning reconsidering our respective positions. We would both look rather foolish were we to break up now and have to report complete failure to our chiefs. Perhaps we can reconvene after lunch. Would that be acceptable to you?'

'Perfectly.'

'Then now you must excuse us. Felman and I have much to discuss.' And Adler got to his feet and hurriedly left the room, Felman on his heels.

Richard looked at Thornton. 'Whew, I thought we were in real trouble, then.'

'Certainly his last words came as a relief.'

'What the deuce is he up to, Thornton? And what's he going to do now? You try a forecast. Mine don't seem too accurate.'

'I would hazard the hypothesis that when he made that telephone call yesterday he was instructed to have one further attempt to – er, well, to get something for nothing. He has attempted, and failed. I think now he will make another call to report this, and will be told to settle this afternoon. I would suggest, Minister, that in order to help him save face, we prepare to make some small concession – simply to preserve the pretence that we are meeting him half-way.'

'Right. You put your mind to it, will you? Something that means nothing, but seems to.'

'Very well.'

'I think I'll go and stretch my legs. I've spent most of my time indoors the last few days. I'd like to get a little sun before the weather breaks – which looks as though it might be soon.'

Peabody found Lord Burford waiting for him in the collection-room, in his hands a case very similar to the one Peabody himself was carrying. Lord Burford placed his casually down on a table. 'Ah, got it? Right, let's have a look.'

Peabody said: 'I'm sure yours is the more interesting item, Earl. Mine can wait until I've seen that.'

'Oh, come along, my dear chap. I've been spouting

off about my stuff ever since you got here. Time you
entertained me, for a change.'

'Well, say you look at mine while I look at yours?'

'As you wish.'

They exchanged cases. Simultaneously both cases were
opened. Then simultaneously two pairs of eyes bulged, two
jaws dropped, and two ejaculations burst forth.

'Good gad!'

'Holy mackerel!'

For inside the two cases lay two identical guns.

They were large, automatic-shaped pistols, ten inches
long, with an ammunition clip in the form of an oblong
metal box fitted in front of the trigger guard. Both were
in superb condition. They were elaborately engraved, with
ivory butts, and on the side of each were some letters, and
the small figure of a double-headed eagle, carved in relief.

The two men's eyes met. Peabody whispered: 'You've
got the other one. I was sure it was lost for good.'

'So was I. I thought I'd got hold of something unique.'

'Where the heck did you get yours?'

'From a little dealer I've known for years. Always found
him honest. He came all the way from London just to
show me it a month ago. Couldn't – or wouldn't – tell me
its provenance, but assured me he had title to it. Naturally,
I snapped it up on the spot. You're the first person to see it,
outside the family. What about yours?'

'Little guy came to the hotel in Rome. Said he'd heard I
was in town and thought I might be interested in something
rather special. Rather special! I nearly passed out when I
saw it. He wouldn't say where he got it, but he produced
documents that seemed to prove he was the legal owner.'

Lord Burford said: 'Remarkable. May I?' Peabody handed back the Earl's pistol, and Lord Burford took one of them in each hand, balancing and comparing them. 'Seems they belong together, what?' He handed both guns to Peabody.

'Sure does. I guess I don't need to say you can name your own price for yours?'

'No, I, er, guess not. Sorry – no deal. Obviously no use offering *you* money, old man; but you're welcome to choose any comparable weapon from my collection in exchange for yours.'

'No, sir. I'm not about to part with this baby.'

'Looks as if they're destined to stay apart, doesn't it?'

'Unless we can reach a compromise.'

'Such as?'

'Well, for a start, would you consider lending me yours for a few weeks? There's the big exhibition in New York City this fall. All the leading collectors in the States are sending exhibits. I cabled, entering this.' He held up his pistol. 'It would sure give me a big thrill to exhibit the pair. I'd lend you mine in return, later.'

Lord Burford scratched his chin. 'Like to oblige, old man. But frankly I funk letting it out of my possession. Know you'd treasure it and all that. But you've got these gangster johnnies over there, haven't you? Suppose Capone or someone took a fancy to it?'

'He's in jail.'

'Plenty more like him, I hear. And then again the New York exhibition'll be reported over here, the catalogue will be available; even if you lend me yours afterwards, I couldn't exhibit the pair as my own, as you had. But I'll tell you what. There is one fellow in England who's by way of being a rival of mine – a General Trimble Greene. I'd give anything to fool him into believin' I owned this pair. He's a kind of explorer and he's out of the country at present. But he'll be back in September, just for a couple of weeks, before going off to some expedition to South America. If I could hang onto the pair just long enough to make him drool a bit, there'd be a good chance he'd never see the New York exhibition catalogue, and mightn't find out for years, if ever, that I didn't own 'em both.'

'Sorry, Earl, but the exhibition opens September 24th.'

'That's all right: I'll be seeing Trimble Greene by the 15th. I'll send off yours so it'll reach America in time.'

Peabody shook his head. 'I wouldn't want to risk it. On the other hand...'

The conversation dragged on inconclusively for several more minutes, until they both realised they weren't going to get anywhere. Then they fell gloomily silent. Ten minutes before, each had been completely happy in the possession of a single gun; now the knowledge of the existence of a second, unattainable, one had cast a cloud over the day.

At last the Earl said: 'Fired yours?'

'Not yet. I haven't had a chance to get any ammunition.'

'Come along, then. I've got some.' He pointed to a section of the room which he had partitioned off as a small shooting range. They took both guns across, Lord Burford stopping to pick up some cartridges at a large cupboard where he stored ammunition and various accessories. They had twenty minutes target practice, after which Lord

Burford replaced his gun in the display stand near the door, from which he had removed it before Peabody's arrival. Peabody took his pistol back to his room.

Meanwhile, Gerry had finished her think and gone to find Jane.

'News,' she said.

'What?'

'I've been on the 'phone to Pamela Darnley – just after Anilese had rung herself. She told me Anilese is by no means a close friend of theirs. They met her in Monte last year. She told them she lived in Geneva, and she made a few what Pamela thought were purely conventional "you must look me up next time you're in Switzerland" remarks – which Pamela reciprocated. Then just a couple of weeks ago she had a letter from Anilese saying she was going to be in the area shortly and would like very much to take up their kind invitation. Of course, they had no choice but to say yes.'

'She told them she was going to be in the area?'

Gerry nodded smugly. 'Exactly. But she didn't say what for.'

'Very fishy.'

'There's more. I've spoken to Harry Jenkins. He says he can't find anything wrong with the car which would make it suddenly swerve off the road. The bodywork at the front is badly damaged, the radiator's cracked, and the headlight's broken. But all that must have been done *when it crashed* – none of it could have *caused* the accident. He was a bit cagey and wouldn't commit himself; but he did say the damage was "queer", that he'd never seen a car damaged quite like it before – and he could hardly believe it had happened just by going into the ditch.'

'What did the chauffeur tell him?'

'He was evasive, apparently – said he couldn't remember much about it, suddenly lost control, thinks perhaps he hit a patch of oil. But I've checked and the road's as dry as a bone for half a mile in either direction. And there aren't any skid marks, either.'

'Well done. It certainly seems to clinch what you said. But we're no nearer finding out why she did it.'

'I'll find out,' Gerry said.

At that moment the door opened and Lord Burford entered. He grunted: 'Oh, hullo, you two,' pulled the bell for Merryweather, and sank down into a chair.

'Daddy, what on earth's the matter? I haven't seen you look so browned-off in all my puff.'

'It's that confounded Yankee.'

He explained at length about the two pistols. 'I'd give my eye teeth for that gun,' he added.

Gerry made a few sympathetic noises, but her attention was obviously elsewhere, and it was left to Jane to be chief comforter.

Having left Thornton in the music-room, Richard strolled out onto the terrace. Here he found his sister-in-law and Mrs. Peabody, who had just been rejoined by Anilese, after she had made her 'phone call to Lady Darnley. This morning Anilese was strikingly dressed in a dirndl skirt and a white blouse with short puffed sleeves under a black bolero.

'Richard,' said Lady Burford, 'you'll be pleased to

know that the Baroness is staying over the weekend.'

He smiled. 'That's grand.'

Anilese stood up. 'Richard, when are you going to show me something of these lovely grounds?'

'Now if you like.'

'Oh, good. Let's walk round the lake. I adore lakes.'

'*Enchanté, madame*,' said Richard.

Thornton did not see Richard again during the morning, nor at lunch. No time had been fixed for reconvening, but Thornton returned to the music-room at two o'clock. Adler and Felman arrived five minutes later. But it was not until after two-thirty, when Thornton was about to send a servant to look for him, that Richard entered. Thornton stared at him. Richard looked white and drawn. For several seconds he stood inside the door, then walked slowly across to his chair and sat down. Thornton expected him to offer some apology for his lateness, but instead, without any preliminaries, Richard looked at Adler and said: 'What is the position?'

'Unchanged. Are you prepared to give me the information I requested this morning?'

Richard was breathing heavily, almost as though he'd been running. He raised a hand to his face and ran it down his cheek, as though wiping off sweat. Then, not looking at Adler, he said: 'Possibly. I don't know yet. I haven't decided. I need time to think.'

It was all Thornton could do to keep back a gasp of astonishment. He stared at Richard, his face a study.

Adler said quietly: 'How long?'

'I don't know. Till tonight – possibly tomorrow morning.'

'Not later than that?'

'No. I promise.'

'Very well.'

Richard got to his feet with a jerky movement. He looked at Thornton. 'Sorry,' he said. Then he hurried from the room.

For ten seconds none of the men spoke. Then Adler broke the silence. 'Come on, Nicholas. Let's go and have a game of billiards.'

CHAPTER THIRTEEN

Grand Tour

From about noon that day the weather had grown even more humid. Gradually the sky became overcast. After lunch, Jane borrowed a bicycle and rode down to the village to do a little personal shopping. By the time she'd finished, the sky was a dark greeny-grey and it was plain a big storm was brewing. She hurried back, put the bicycle away, and went inside. Everybody except Richard was indoors. Surprisingly, he had gone for a long solitary tramp round the estate. In the house there seemed to be that air of restlessness and edginess that Jane had noticed an impending storm often produced. People were roaming round, picking up books and putting them down again, starting conversations and breaking them off quickly, or just sitting and staring out of the windows at the still and leaden trees.

The most obviously affected was Anilese. She seemed disgruntled at Richard's absence and sat by herself, flicking through magazines and politely but firmly rebuffing every attempt to engage her in conversation.

At the other extreme, Martin Adler seemed on top of

the world and eager to talk. Jane had a long conversation with him, finding him interesting and well-informed.

Tea was served early, and afterwards Lady Burford made an unexpected suggestion: a guided tour of the entire house for the whole party.

'All of you have seen some of it,' she said, 'but nobody has seen everything. It would be a pity to have stayed here and missed something important. It seems an excellent time now to make sure nobody does.'

It was difficult to refuse such an invitation, and although several of those present – including Lord Burford and Gerry – were somewhat reluctant, everybody went along.

To the surprise of all but Lady Burford herself, the tour was a great success. The charm and tranquillity of the old house cast its spell over everyone, seeming somehow to cheer and soothe, and it was a happier group of people who arrived finally in the gun-room – which Lady Burford was careful to make the climax of the tour. Here, his wife having done most of the talking until now, Lord Burford came into his own. Many years of experience had given him a good knowledge of what appealed to the non-expert, and he talked interestingly, with a fund of anecdotes, holding the attention even of the women. Soon he was obviously in high good humour again; so much so that after half an hour he whispered something to Peabody, who left the room. When he returned a few minutes later, the Earl said: 'I'll end with my latest acquisition.' He crossed to the stand where he had put the engraved pistol.

'In 1918 the famous Danish firearm manufacturers, Bergman Industriewerke, produced a semi-automatic 9mm pistol, model 1910/21. It is commonly known as the

Bergman Bayard. It is very unusual in that the rifling inside the barrel is a six-groove left-hand twist – not the more common right-hand twist. Only a thousand of these pistols were made, and they are already valuable collectors' items. Peabody, would you like to carry on?'

'Surely.' Peabody stepped forward. 'Just before the Bayard was put into production, the firm received an unusual order. It was from a man who said he was acting for a very eminent person, wishing to remain anonymous. This person had heard of the new model and wanted to order a special presentation pair. They had to be elaborately engraved, with ivory stocks, and included in the decoration was to be an emblem in relief. He handed over a drawing to be copied. It was of the Romanov two-headed eagle – the emblem of the Russian Tsars – together with the initials of Nicholas II, the last Tsar.

'Well, the pistols were made – the first Bergman Bayards ever produced – and the man took them away, paying cash. The rest is speculation. Nicholas had by then been deposed and was in exile in Siberia with his family. Had he himself ordered the pistols; or had they been intended as a present to be sent to him – his birthday was in May – and if so, from whom?'

'Nicholas, of course, was related to the royal house of Denmark,' Lord Burford put in. 'His mother, the Dowager Empress Marie, was Danish, and the aunt of King Christian. So who was the eminent customer?'

'The gun world has never known,' Peabody continued, 'and the pistols were never seen again. Did Nicholas receive them? I firmly believe he did – and had them during those last months in Siberia. Then, on 16th July, 1918, he and his entire family were – supposedly – assassinated at Ekaterinburg. But did that actually happen? It's been variously reported that one, two, or even all of them escaped. No one knows their fate for sure. Nor does anybody know what happened to the pistols. Were they stolen by the assassins after the Tsar's death? Or did Nicholas carry them with him – perhaps actually use them – during the family's escape? The only certainty is that they disappeared from public view until a few weeks ago – when I bought this one in Rome.'

'And I bought this one here in England.' Lord Burford took his from the stand. 'If the ordinary Bayard is valuable, you can imagine the value of these.'

The others gathered round interestedly. The pistols were passed from hand to hand, and the Earl and Peabody demonstrated how they were loaded and fired.

It was a fine climax to the tour, and the group started to break up. Jane was one of the first to go towards the door, and as she did so, she saw that Richard was standing just inside it. At that second he turned and walked quickly away – but not before she had seen a very strange expression on his face. She frowned. It looked as though he'd been listening to the story. But why hadn't he joined them all openly?

Thoughtfully, Jane went to dress for dinner.

'Richard, can I speak to you for a minute?'

Anilese's voice came from behind Richard in little more than a whisper, and he turned, surprised. He was walking alone at the tail of the short procession of men on their way to the drawing-room after dinner. Anilese should have been already there; instead, she was just emerging from a shadowy corner of the hall.

He frowned. 'What about?'

'You know.'

'I was out all afternoon. I can't desert the party again now.'

'For a few minutes only. It's very important.'

He hesitated. 'All right. In the library. In ten minutes.'

'Very well. Don't say you've seen me. I'm supposed to have a headache and be lying down.'

He nodded, then hurried on towards the drawing-room.

He was able to slip away quite unobtrusively ten minutes later owing to a sudden outbreak of confusion during the serving of the coffee: some people had two cups and others none, while some who wanted black had white and vice versa. The muddle seemed, predictably, to revolve round Algy Fotheringay, but within a short time nearly everyone was on his or her feet, passing and re-passing cups, and while this was happening Richard left the room.

Anilese paused inside the library door and turned. 'Understood?'

'Whatever you say.'

She opened the door and slipped out, closing it after her. Richard sank back in the deep leather armchair and closed his eyes. He felt dazed and utterly spent. There was so much he didn't understand. But the time to speculate would come later. First there was something else to do. He looked at his watch, got to his feet, and returned to the drawing-room. He let a few minutes pass, then caught

Adler's eye and beckoned him to one side. Adler raised his eyebrows. 'You wanted me?'

Richard took a deep breath. 'Yes. I promised you a definite decision by the morning. But there's no point in keeping you in suspense. I've made up my mind.'

Jane noticed Richard re-enter the drawing-room after a fifteen minutes absence, and she watched his face as he talked to Adler. It seemed to her that in some way he looked different. At dinner he had been very quiet and withdrawn. Now he still looked tired – but like a man who had reached a crucial decision.

He moved away from Adler, caught her eye, and to her pleasure came across and sat down by her. He gave her a smile. 'Hullo, stranger. What have you been doing with yourself all day?'

'Brooding, mainly,' Jane said.

'That's bad.'

'And you?'

'Brooding. But I've been doing mine on the move, which is good for the waistline if not for the soul.'

'Oh, for me it's a luxury to be able to sit around and brood. Don't spoil it for me. But what have you got to brood about?'

'Politicians can usually find something.'

'Oh, it's politics, is it? I'm sorry.'

'I believe the conventional thing for me to say is don't worry your pretty little head about that.'

'I don't intend to, but I can still be sorry.' She was silent for a moment, then said: 'Talking of pretty heads, your friend the Baroness is very beautiful.'

He paused fractionally before saying: 'Yes, she is, isn't she?'

'She looks as though she's led an interesting life, I think.'

He glanced at her quizzically. 'Now just how do I take that?'

'Meaning am I being catty? Well, frankly, I could be. Actually, though, I wasn't making any sort of moral judgement. Obviously I know nothing about her character. I meant quite simply that whatever she's been, I'm sure her life has never been boring.'

'You're probably right. But why could you be catty – why don't you like her?'

'I didn't say I didn't like her. She's got a lot of charm and I should imagine could be very good company. I should like to know her better, because if you must know I admire her a lot. She's the sort of woman I'd like to be myself. Except for one thing.'

'Which is?'

'Well, frankly—'

'Frankly again?'

'Sorry; do I sound too much like a politician?'

'*Touché.*'

'To be blunt, then, if you prefer it.' She hesitated.

'Go on: what's the one thing?'

'I don't think you could trust her to pass you the salt.'

CHAPTER FOURTEEN

Storm Over Alderley

It was half-past one the following morning when the storm broke over Alderley. It was still raging half an hour later when, just as the stable clock struck two, Gerry opened the door of her L-shaped bedroom on the inner corner of the main and west corridors. She had a small electric torch in her hand. She slipped out, closed the door quietly behind her and turned right down the west corridor towards the rear of the house. She was wearing a dressing-gown and bedroom slippers. On the right almost at the end of the corridor, just before the stairs, there was a narrow curtained recess, where the maids kept cleaning equipment. Gerry pulled back the curtain, squeezed herself in, and drew the curtain again, leaving just a half-inch gap. She was a little way past the door to the Baroness's bedroom, which was on the other side of the corridor. Gerry flashed her torch once at the door, to get its exact position fixed in her mind, then switched off.

The clouds that night were so thick that even though the curtains on the nearby window at the end of the corridor were not drawn, she could now see virtually nothing. Then a flash of lightning lit the corridor brilliantly for a fraction of a second before plunging it back into what seemed an even deeper darkness.

Gerry settled down to wait.

As it happened, she did not have to wait long. She had been in the recess no more than three minutes when she heard the click of the Baroness's door knob. In vain Gerry strained her eyes. She heard a very slight rustle of clothing, and groaned inwardly. Why did this of all nights have to be so maddeningly dark?

Then there came light. The dim light of a torch. Gerry could just see that it was held by Anilese, and that she was gliding hurriedly away down the corridor. She was dressed in a flowing white negligee and her feet were bare. Gerry slipped from her hiding-place and followed.

Like a white ghost the Baroness flitted silently along. She rounded the corner into the main corridor, Gerry about ten yards behind. Then, as Gerry herself was about to go round, she heard a faint, indefinable sound from somewhere ahead of her. She paused momentarily before peering round the corner. The light from the Baroness's torch had vanished. Gerry swore under her breath. She stood still, biting her lip in frustration. A minute elapsed. Then a particularly vivid flash of lightning shining through a high window lit up the main corridor just long enough for her to see that it was quite empty.

The Baroness might have gone anywhere in the house. Gerry had no means whatsoever of telling where. She'd probably lost her chance of finding out anything of importance. But she wasn't going to admit complete defeat yet – at least she could find out what time Anilese went back.

Gerry returned to her niche.

She had hardly time to settle herself, when she heard another noise in the corridor. This time it was clearly the sound of footsteps – and they were approaching. They grew closer.

They sounded like a man's. Then a torch flashed – on and off, quickly. It was held low, and all Gerry could see was the lower half of a pair of trousered legs. Just outside the Baroness's door the torch flashed again. Then there came the click of the door knob, and silence once more. Gerry withdrew into the recess, pulled the curtain, and flashed on her own torch for a quick look at her wrist watch. It was just coming up to seven minutes past two. She resumed her vigil.

About half a minute after this she saw Anilese's white figure returning. Gerry drew well back until once more she heard the door open and close. Now she faced an awkward decision. She ached to know what was being said inside the room. It was unlikely that, even with her ear to the keyhole, she would be able to hear anything significant. But there was a possibility of hearing *something*. It should be worth a try. Yet, even though originally a gate-crasher, the Baroness was now a guest at Alderley; and both by instinct and training Gerry rebelled violently against the idea of deliberately eavesdropping on anybody, let alone a visitor to her home. So far she'd only spied on what went on in the open corridor.

However, the problem was solved for her, because the next moment the storm, which so far had consisted of heavy rain, lightning, and distant rumblings, now unleashed its full blast. Gerry had rarely heard thunder like it. It would obviously prevent her hearing anything else, however close she got to the door.

Another four or five minutes passed. Then during a momentary break in the thunder, she heard again the click of the Baroness's door. Gerry strained her eyes hopelessly in the darkness. Then, as before, a shaded torch, held low, flashed briefly, showing the man's legs retreating along the corridor. Twice more it flickered, each time revealing the man farther away.

Briefly, Gerry considered following. But it was Anilese she was chiefly interested in, and she stayed where she was.

It was a decision she was bitterly to regret before twenty-four hours had passed.

The probability now was that everything which was going to happen had happened. If so, she'd been wasting her time. Should she pack up? Bed was awfully inviting. She flashed her torch and sneaked another peep at her watch. Not yet quarter-past. She'd stay until half-past, as she'd planned.

'Blast all Baronesses,' Gerry said under her breath.

The alarm clock under Giles Deveraux's pillow went off shrilly. He awoke at once and stopped it. Almost two-twenty. Deveraux swung himself off the bed. He was dressed in dark slacks, a sweater, and rubber-soled shoes. He picked up a torch from the bedside table and left the room.

He turned east along the main corridor, stopping momentarily outside the door of each occupied bedroom that he passed and listening intently for a few seconds during the lulls in the thunder. He walked the full length of the main and east corridors and at the far end of the latter took the stairs to the ground floor.

Deveraux was unaware of it, but ten yards behind, a dark figure followed him down.

For several minutes all was still in the east corridor. Then, very slowly, the door of the picture gallery was opened from the inside.

Jane stood just inside the door of her bedroom, straining her ears, and mentally cursed the thunder and rain that were preventing her hearing properly. What on earth was going on out there?

She had been awake all night so far. Actually, when she had first gone to her room, she hadn't really expected to be able to sleep. However, after reading for a while she had dutifully turned out the light. But she had soon switched it on again and picked up her book.

It had been sultry when she had gone to bed, and she had left the door open an inch in the hope of getting a draught through the room. It was some time later that she had become aware, between thunderclaps, of a lot of movement about the house. She told herself that others, obviously, would be kept awake by the storm and be restless, and it was merely her imagination which made their movements seem somehow furtive.

But then she had heard a sound both strange and alarming: the door of the picture gallery, across the corridor from her room, opening and closing again.

Clearly nobody would be looking at pictures this time of night. On the other hand, the gallery did house a number of valuable paintings. And beyond the gallery were the Earl's guns. So she couldn't just ignore the sound.

Thus it was that Jane, who had put on a dressing-gown and slippers, was now standing with her ear close against her bedroom door, wondering what to do.

Very soon afterwards the noise came again. And following it she was almost certain she heard the sound of footsteps receding.

Jane took a deep breath, grasped the knob, and peeped out. She could see nothing. She waited, quite still and quiet for several seconds, then stepped into the corridor.

Giles Deveraux was walking lightly up the main stairs when he heard the stable clock strike two-thirty. As the chimes ceased, he heard another sound. He froze and extinguished his torch, for the sound was that of footsteps. They were coming along the main corridor, approaching the head of the stairs from the right. Deveraux stood, holding his breath, as the footsteps got closer. He heard them cross the landing and continue along the corridor towards the west wing. He waited until they'd gone about ten yards, then ran quietly up the remaining stairs himself and, hoping against hope he wouldn't run into anything in the dark, turned in the same direction.

He hadn't taken more than half a dozen paces along the corridor when he heard another small noise – this time behind him. He started to swing round, saw a bright beam of light out of the corner of his eye – and felt a glancing blow on the head.

If Deveraux had not started to turn, the blow would undoubtedly have knocked him out. As it was, he avoided the full force of it. However, it was still powerful enough to bring him to his knees, dazed and half-stunned. Before he could begin to recover, he felt hands grab him from behind. He flinched, waiting for another blow, but all that happened was that his assailant tried to pull him sideways. Unable to resist adequately, Deveraux half-fell on his side. The hands took a fresh grip and gave him another heave. Slowly, Deveraux's senses were beginning to come back to him. From the floor he struck out. He had the satisfaction of feeling his fist make contact. But it was a feeble blow and only deterred his attacker for a second. Then he grabbed Deveraux again.

Deveraux was gathering his diminished strength for another punch, when from nearby came a sudden series of bumps and bangs. Although close, they were not particularly loud, and even in his fuddled state, he realised that their source was either Adler's room, or Gerry's. It sounded like some sort of fight. Furniture was being overturned and bodies were crashing about.

The noise stopped as abruptly as it had begun. And at the same instant Deveraux realised that he was alone. He lay still, trying to make his brain work. For a few seconds all was silence. Even the thunder had stopped. Then Deveraux heard hurried footsteps approaching. They blundered past him in the darkness, going east.

It was at that moment he heard the woman's scream.

Gerry heard two-thirty sound from the stable clock, and with a combination of relief and irritation eased herself out of the recess. What a very nasty shape, and how hard and angular carpet sweepers were! She would never feel the same about them again. And all she had discovered was that Anilese had left her room for about four minutes – not the most suspicious of actions – and had received one male visitor, who hadn't even had the indecency to stay long enough to compromise her. What an idiotic waste of time!

Gerry was on the verge of switching on her torch to light herself back to bed, when yet again she heard the muffled sound of footsteps coming along the corridor. She caught her breath and in a panic scrambled back into the recess.

This time the prowler had no torch, so she couldn't even see his legs. She heard him stop outside the Baroness's door. Very, very softly a finger-nail tapped on a panel. A knob turned and there was the almost undetectable sound of the door opening and closing.

Then, in the distance, Gerry heard something else.

She held her breath to hear better. What on earth was it? For a second she'd thought it was thunder. But no: for the moment that had stopped. This was inside the house. It sounded like furniture being knocked about. Though it wasn't in the west wing, and seemed muffled.

Once more Gerry stepped out of her recess. She stood hesitating. Then, her heart in her mouth, she started off along the corridor, switching on her torch.

She had just passed the alcove in which was set the door leading to the western extension, given over to servants' quarters, when the noise stopped short. Gerry stopped too. For a moment there was dead silence. An unnatural silence. Gerry felt hairs prickling at the back of her neck.

Then she gave a violent start as from the floor below came the sound of a woman's scream.

Gerry just couldn't move. The next second she was conscious of somebody approaching. She started to raise her torch, but then it was knocked from her hand and went out as someone crashed into her. She gave a gasp: 'Who's that?' There was no reply. And then Gerry's fright was overcome by sheer anger. She made a blind grab – and found herself clutching a man.

The man tried to pull himself free. She hung on like grim death and the next thing she knew she was lurching silently about the corridor, locked with him in a grotesque parody of a tango. Stupidly, for seconds it didn't occur to her to shout for help. When it did she took a deep breath. But this must have warned the man of her intention, for a hand was at once clapped over her mouth.

Suddenly, Gerry realised that she'd quite lost control of the situation. She was being manoeuvred in the direction the man wanted – and could do nothing about it. Then her back was against the wall. Keeping one hand over her mouth, the man held her still with his body and reached out with his other arm. There was a click of a door catch, the man carefully prised himself loose from her grasp and moved her gently to the side. Then there was nothing behind her. She started to topple backwards, but the man held on to her and prevented her falling. Instead, still keeping one hand over her mouth, he lowered her slowly to the floor and released her. There was a click and all was silence again.

Jane stood quite motionless outside her bedroom door, listening. She could hear no sound, other than the almost non-stop rolling of the thunder. She felt in her dressing-gown pocket, took out a box of matches, and struck one. Its feeble glow showed little, but it did seem that there was nobody in her immediate vicinity.

Jane crossed to the door of the picture gallery and opened it wide. She put her head inside and switched the light on just long enough to see that the gallery was empty, all the pictures were present, and the door to the gun-room closed. She thought to go across and try it, but then changed her mind. She closed the door, turned to her right, and started to make her way slowly along the corridor towards the main block. As she approached the corner, she heard the stable clock chime two-thirty.

At the same moment the clock chimed, the match burnt down to Jane's fingers. She hastily shook it out, struck another one, and started to creep forward again. She turned the corner.

Then her heart leapt and the match fell from her hand as from somewhere in front of her came a sudden eruption of noise. It was a muffled bumping and crashing, and seemed to come from one of the rooms at the farther end of the corridor. Jane stood frozen, wondering what on earth to do. It was no business of hers. If a burglar had somehow broken in, there were plenty of men about to deal with the situation. Any second, surely, lights would come on, doors would open, voices would call out.

But seconds passed and they didn't. And Jane knew that she had to do something. She couldn't possibly just go back to her room. She took a deep breath and started to grope her way forward again.

Then the noise stopped. The storm, too, had abated

and for a few seconds everything was quiet. She must be near the door of Richard's room. The obvious thing would be to wake him. She took a step, reaching forward to her right, and felt the smooth wood of a door. It gave under her pressure. It was ajar. It was the room where the linen was stored. She had passed Richard's door.

Then Jane's blood froze, as out of the blackness came the sound of a woman's scream.

It was a short, sharp scream, apparently quickly muffled, and seemed to originate from the ground floor. Almost at the same instant Jane heard hurrying, stumbling footsteps coming towards her along the corridor. She sensed rather than saw a dark shape looming up; then someone crashed into her, sending her flying.

Jane ended up gasping for breath in an ungainly heap on the floor.

As she lay there the whole house seemed to be full of muted noises: one set of footsteps blundering away behind her; others approaching from the front; somebody breathing heavily quite close; in the distance, somewhere in the west wing, an indefinable scuffling noise; and in the middle distance, ahead of her, the sound of a groan.

It was all too much for Jane. In a way of which she was always afterwards ashamed, she panicked. She scrambled to her feet and felt wildly for the open door. She almost fell in. She just had the presence of mind to close it behind her softly.

Her heart was pounding. They were coming after her. They mustn't find her. What could she do?

It was not more than half a minute later that her panic subsided. Then she stood absolutely still for a few more seconds, deliberately calming herself down.

There was no danger. She was surrounded by friends. Richard's room was next door. The Peabodys were across the corridor, the Earl and Countess not far away. Nobody was going to hurt her. If there was any burglar about, all she had to do was shout for help.

Jane steeled herself and quickly opened the door again. She struck a match and stepped out into the corridor. The light switch was close at hand. She turned it on.

CHAPTER FIFTEEN

Break-Out

The corridor flooded with light. Jane blinked around, fearful of what she was going to see.

In fact, what she saw was not particularly alarming. About thirty yards from her, past the head of the grand staircase, Giles Deveraux was sitting on the floor, leaning up against the wall and rubbing his head. Jane ran up to him.

'What happened?'

'Somebody beaned me.' He stood up, still holding his head.

'He went that way.' Jane pointed towards the east wing. 'He cannoned into me – sent me flying.'

'You didn't see him?'

'No, it was quite dark. Look, you'd better go and lie down. I'll go and get some cold pads – and some brandy.'

'No, I'm all right. I want to find out what caused that noise.'

'What noise?'

'Didn't you hear? Sounded like some sort of scrap.'

Jane stared. 'Wasn't that you?'

'Oh no. My little fracas was very quiet – and the other started later.'

'Where did the sound come from?'

'Adler's room, I think. Yes – the door's ajar. Let's take a look.'

He strode to the door, put his head in and switched on the light. 'Nobody in here,' he said. 'But there's been a scrap in here all right – the furniture's all over the place.'

Jane said: 'Shouldn't we find out who screamed?'

He spun round. 'I thought that was you.'

'No, I think it came from downstairs.'

'Did it? I was a bit too groggy to mark the direction. We'd better investigate.' He turned to the stairs.

Then Jane stopped him. 'Wait – listen.'

He paused, his head cocked. Somewhere in the west wing could be heard a banging sound, as of somebody pounding on a door.

'Come on,' Deveraux said. He started off along the corridor at a brisk stride, Jane trotting meekly at his heels. They turned into the west corridor – and heard a muffled voice calling. Jane paused to switch on the lights. Deveraux pointed. 'It's coming from that cupboard.'

'I know who it is too,' said Jane.

The cupboard in question was on the left and the near side of the alcove in which was the door leading to the western extension and the servants' quarters. A chair, which usually stood near, had been jammed under the cupboard door knob. Deveraux pulled it away and opened the door.

Gerry popped out like an indignant cork. She stared at them. 'What the blue blazes is going on around here?'

'You tell us,' Jane said. 'How did you get in there?'

'Somebody put me there, you chump! Do you think I decided to spend the night in there just for fun?'

'Don't get in such a stew. What happened?'

'I heard a noise, started out to investigate, somebody ran into me in the dark, we wrestled, and he shoved me in here. What was the noise?'

'A fight, we think. In Mr. Adler's room. The other man involved knocked me flying. And somebody else tried to brain Mr. Deveraux.'

'Jiminy cricket.' Gerry's eyes were big.

'Did you scream?' Deveraux asked.

'No. But I heard somebody else scream just before the blister ran into me. It didn't sound like anyone in real danger – just momentarily startled.'

Deveraux pursed his lips. 'It's time we had a look down there. First, though, I just want to see whether by any chance Adler's gone in to talk to Felman.'

Gerry and Jane watched while he walked further down the corridor, quietly opened the door of Felman's room and disappeared inside. He emerged again in a few seconds and came back. 'No. Felman's fast asleep with the light out. Come on.'

They made their way back along the main corridor and down the grand staircase, conversing in low tones. 'Where on earth has Adler gone?' Deveraux muttered.

'Well, obviously an intruder got in,' Jane said. 'Presumably he's gone after him.'

'An intruder could only have got in before the alarm was set,' Gerry whispered. 'So he must still be in the house. Do you think I ought to wake Daddy?'

'Not just yet,' Deveraux said. 'Let's see what we can find out first. We don't know definitely that there is an intruder.'

Before they could ask him to explain this, they reached the foot of the stairs. Deveraux asked Gerry to turn the lights on. She did so. They looked round the hall. There was no sign of anything out of the ordinary.

'Right,' said Deveraux, 'let's do this systematically. You'd both better stay close to me, just in case. I'll lead the way, but you can guide me. Where shall we start?'

At Gerry's suggestion, they went to the rear of the west wing and worked their way back across the house, looking in every room. Nowhere did they find anything wrong. Yet in the minds of all three there was a certainty that something was going to happen. The tension grew, and by the time they'd been searching for twelve or thirteen minutes the two girls at least were getting decidedly jittery.

It was when they were approaching the breakfast-room that Jane stopped dead and grabbed Deveraux's arm.

He turned quickly. 'What's up?'

'Somebody in there.'

'The breakfast-room?'

'Yes, I heard a movement.'

'Sure?'

'Of course!'

Deveraux hesitated, wondering what was best to do.

But Jane had had enough of skulking about in the dark and talking in whispers. Suddenly, she exclaimed: 'Oh, come on!' Then she dashed forward.

'Wait!' Deveraux hissed. He tried to grab her.

But Jane was already reaching for the knob. Perhaps her

palms were sweaty, but her hand slipped as she clutched it and she fumbled for vital seconds before starting to open the door. Then, as she did so, there came from within the room the most tremendous crash and the sound of breaking glass. At the same moment the alarm bell started to clang in the hall.

For two or three seconds Jane stood frozen, her hand on the knob. Then she threw the door wide open and burst into the room. Deveraux and Gerry were on her heels.

The room was in darkness, but light from behind enabled her to see a big jagged, hole in the window. She stared, then gave a shout and pointed towards it. 'There he goes!' She dashed across the room, but just inside the window tripped and fell sprawling.

Avoiding her, Deveraux ran to the window and looked out 'Which way did he go?'

'Towards the lake.'

Deveraux took a torch from his pocket, carefully squeezed himself through the gaping hole and disappeared into the darkness. Gerry put her head out and peered after him.

'It's pitch black out there. I can't see a thing. And it's lashing with rain.'

She turned to see Jane in the act of putting upright a wooden stepladder which had been lying flat on the floor.

'Is that what tripped you?'

'Yes.' She leant it against the wall.

'You couldn't tell who the man was?'

'No, I only saw him for a split second. And only in the light from the hall.'

Gerry said: 'He must have heard us outside and

deliberately smashed the window – probably with that.' She pointed to a chair which was lying on its side.

Before Jane could answer, Deveraux came back in through the window. He was already soaking. 'Hopeless,' he said. 'This torch is quite inadequate. I can't see more than a couple of yards.'

There was a footstep in the hall. They turned to see Merryweather, as dignified as ever in dressing-gown and slippers. 'The alarm went off in my room, your ladyship. Has there been a break-in?'

'No, Merry, a break-out,' said Gerry.

Deveraux went to the doorway and explained the situation in a few words. Then he said: 'Merryweather, I'd like you to organise a thorough search of the servants' quarters and make sure no one is hiding there. At the same time will you check that the women servants are all right and find out if any of them have been up or out of their wing of the house – or if one of them screamed for any reason.'

Merryweather flicked a brief glance at Gerry. She gave an infinitesimal nod, and Merryweather said: 'Very good, sir.' He walked away.

Deveraux turned to Gerry. 'Lady Geraldine, no doubt the alarm has woken your parents. I wonder if you would be so kind as to go up and explain just what has happened. Tell your father there's no need to hurry down, but I'd be obliged if he could meet me in the library in a few minutes. Then rouse your uncle and tell him the same. Also, afterwards check that the Baroness is all right. I'm sorry to treat you like one of your own maids, but it is urgent.'

Gerry grinned. 'Aye, aye, sir.' She ran from the room.

Jane was looking at Deveraux, a somewhat quizzical expression on her face. 'We're very masterful all of a sudden, Mr. Deveraux.'

'Not really, Miss Clifton. Merely efficient.'

'Do you have no errand on which to send me flying, sir?'

'If you wish to co-operate, Miss Clifton – on a basis of equality, of course.'

'Oh, I would not presume to such eminence. Simply issue your orders.'

'Very well. I'd like to know whether the other guests in the east wing are in their rooms. That's Thornton, Fotheringay and Evans. Will you go and see? There's no need to wake them.'

'I tremble and obey.' Jane salaamed, turned away and started to walk off in the direction of the east wing. Over her shoulder, she said: 'I'll go up the back stairs. It'll be quicker.'

Deveraux watched her retreating form for a few seconds. Then he looked at his watch – it showed two-fifty-three – and went back into the breakfast-room. He crossed to the window, looked round on the floor and saw for the first time that among the few fragments of broken glass which had fallen inwards, a pair of wire cutters was lying. A pot plant, normally kept on the window-ledge, had also been put on the floor against the wall. Deveraux went up to the window and shone his torch round the frame. From the top right-hand corner two electric wires ran straight up and disappeared behind the picture rail. Deveraux fetched another chair from against the wall, stood on it, and satisfied himself that the wire was intact. Then he got down, replaced the chair, and left the room.

Lord Burford ran his fingers through his hair. 'Extraordinary. Absolutely extraordinary. One of me guests knocked on the head, me daughter shut up in a cupboard, and someone smashing a window to break out of the house in the middle of the night after trying to put the burglar alarm out of action.'

'I'm only assuming that,' Deveraux said. 'But the stepladder and the wire cutters would indicate that that's what he intended if we hadn't disturbed him.'

'It wouldn't have done the bounder any good, of course,' Lord Burford said. 'Cuttin' the wires would have set the alarm off anyway. The point is, though, what shall I do now?'

'Naturally, George, you must call the police.' Lady Burford, wearing a dressing-gown and shingle-cap, spoke positively.

'I was just wonderin' my dear, as it seems so far that Deveraux here is the only person hurt, whether, if no other harm's done, we ought to leave the decision to him. I'm prepared to forget about the broken window, but naturally, my dear chap, you'll want the johnny who bopped you traced.'

'It's not that, Lord Burford. The thing is that three people must have been involved in what happened. The man who hit me was not one of those who were fighting. One of those men locked up Lady Geraldine and may or may not have been Adler. It may have been Adler who went through the window. Or it may have been an intruder, who got into the house and hid before you locked up. Or it may have been one of the other guests – we should know that any moment. If it was Adler, why did he do it? If it wasn't, where is he? In either case, he's the envoy of a foreign government, and ought to be searched for immediately. Finally, unless there were two intruders, it seems an inevitable conclusion that at least one of your other guests is not what he seems to be.'

Just then Merryweather entered. Lord Burford turned to him a trifle irritably. 'Yes, Merryweather, what is it?'

'Mr. Deveraux instructed me to make some enquiries among the servants, my lord.' He looked at Deveraux. 'I have searched our quarters thoroughly, sir. No one is concealed there. The housekeeper has woken all the maids. None of them has been out of bed tonight and none has screamed or heard a scream.'

'Thank you. Tell me, are all the girls reliable?'

'I have always found them entirely so, sir, and I am confident her ladyship will say the same.' He cast a quick glance at the Countess, who gave a decisive nod. 'Most of them are local,' Merryweather continued, 'the youngest has been in service here for two years, most of the others considerably longer. Likewise the male staff.'

Deveraux nodded. 'Many thanks.'

'Right-ho, Merryweather,' Lord Burford said. 'Better not go back to bed yet, though.'

'Very good, my lord.'

Merryweather turned to leave, and was nearly knocked over by an excited Geraldine. She addressed Deveraux breathlessly. 'The Baroness isn't in her room. Her bed's not been slept in, though most of her things are still scattered around.'

Deveraux swore under his breath.

Lord Burford said: 'Have you told Rich?'

'No, I thought I'd let you. I called him before I went to her room. He should be on his way down any moment.'

Before the Earl could reply, Jane hurried in. She too was out of breath. She said: 'Sorry to interrupt, Lord Burford.' She turned to Deveraux. 'Mr. Thornton was already awake and I woke Mr. Evans accidentally. They're both coming down.'

'And Fotheringay?'

'Well, Algy's asleep—' She broke off.

'Yes?'

'Well, it's awfully odd. He's asleep on the floor with all his clothes on.'

Lord Burford clapped a hand to his brow. 'This is getting like one of those Greek tragedies where messengers keep rushing in with more and more impossible tidings. Is the feller ill?'

'He doesn't seem to be. He's breathing normally and he looks quite stupidly peaceful. But I couldn't wake him.'

'No smell of drink?'

'None at all.'

'Extraordinary. Have to get the chap a doctor, I suppose.' Then, as John Evans appeared in the doorway behind Jane, Lord Burford said: 'Come in, my boy. Tell us what ghastly news you've got.'

Evans came into the room, looking puzzled. He had dressed in slacks and sweater. He said: 'I'm sorry, I'm not quite sure what's been happening.'

Gerry started to explain. Suddenly Evans went pale. He said: 'The alarm's out of action – and a man's got out of the house?'

'Yes, we don't—'

'Holy smoke!' Uncharacteristically, Evans interrupted. 'Mrs. Peabody's diamonds! The Wraith!'

And he spun round and dashed from the room, leaving the rest staring at each other blankly.

CHAPTER SIXTEEN

Robbery

Evans shook Peabody's shoulder and whispered urgently. 'HS, wake up, sir.'

Peabody opened his eyes and blinked. 'John? What's the matter?'

'There's been something going on here, sir. An intruder. He slugged Deveraux and got away. The alarm was set off. I think we ought to check on the diamonds.'

'Jumping jehosophat, yes.' Peabody sat up and got out of bed, switching on the bedside lamp as he did so. Mrs. Peabody murmured in her sleep and turned over, but didn't open her eyes.

Peabody padded barefooted across the room to the dressing-table, and opened a drawer. He lifted out his wife's jewel-case. 'She's left the key in the lock,' he said. He turned the key, lifted the lid – and drew his breath in sharply. 'They've gone!'

'What?'

'And look.'

He pointed into the box. Lying inside was an oblong of glossy white cardboard bearing a picture of a sheeted ghost.

* * *

'Well, that settles it,' Lord Burford said. 'We've got to call the police. Rich – will you?'

Richard, who had joined them during Evans' absence, nodded. 'Right away.' He left the room. Lady Burford, pale and shocked, murmured something about getting dressed and followed him.

Lord Burford said helplessly: 'I just don't know what I ought to do while we wait for them.' He looked hopefully at Deveraux.

'I suggest we have a look for Adler and the Baroness,' Deveraux said.

'Do you think there's much point?' Gerry asked. 'Alderley's pretty big.'

'I know. Obviously if either of them is deliberately hiding we wouldn't have much chance of finding them. I'm only suggesting a quick look in each unoccupied room upstairs, as we did down here, just to make sure neither of them is lying unconscious anywhere. After all, we know there was someone in the house prepared to use violence.'

'Very well,' Lord Burford said, 'we'll do it.'

'You could get some of the servants to do it, if you prefer?'

'No, no. Quicker to do it ourselves. Besides, I want to be doing something – not just sitting around twiddlin' me thumbs. Come on, let's start. You'll lend a hand, Evans?'

Evans, who had come back down to break the news of the robbery, leaving Peabody to rouse and inform Carrie, gave a nod. 'Of course.'

'Good. Geraldine – we ought to get the doctor for Fotheringay. Will you see to it after Richard has phoned the police?'

Gerry nodded, and Lord Burford led the way out, Deveraux, Evans, and Jane following. They started up the stairs. Lord Burford suddenly noticed Jane. 'Oh, I don't know whether you ought to come, my dear. The intruder might still be in the house. Could be dangerous.'

Deveraux said: 'With respect, Lord Burford, I doubt very much if there's any intruder here now.'

'But only one man escaped through the window. You said yourself three people were involved. We don't *know* there was only one outsider here.'

'I agree; but after the breakfast-room window was broken and the alarm set off, anyone could have left the house by any other window or door.'

'My word, I didn't think of that.'

'In fact, afterwards it would be advisable to examine all the downstairs windows and doors to see if any of them are unlocked.'

They went up to the top floor. Lord Burford paused irresolutely. 'Don't quite know how we should set about this.' He glanced at Deveraux, on whom he was every minute coming to place more reliance.

'I think in the same way as the young ladies and I tackled the ground floor – go to the end and work our way back. Only now we can split into two pairs and meet back here. I suggest one of each pair should be someone familiar with the house.'

'Jane knows the house as well as the family, so you go with her and take the west wing; Evans can do the east with me.'

'Right. Nobody sleeps up here, do they?'

'No. There are some empty bedrooms, a couple of

bathrooms, and the rest store rooms. My family's acquired quite a bit of junk over nearly three hundred years. We'll see you back here. Come along, my boy.' And Lord Burford trotted off, Evans at his heels.

'At the double B squad,' Deveraux said, and started off in the opposite direction. Jane hurried after him.

'Mr. Deveraux, may I ask a question?'

'Certainly, Miss Clifton.'

'How was it you came to be involved in this business in the first place?'

'I was hit on the head.'

'But why were you hit on the head? I mean, what were you doing up and about?'

'The storm kept me awake. I decided to go down to the library and get a book.'

'A highly conventional reason. But why dress first?'

'Now I have to let you into a guilty secret. You see, Miss Clifton, I am not a gentleman by birth.'

'Really? I would never have guessed. How wonderful our education system is!'

'For a member of the lower orders, a stay at a place like Alderley is a somewhat daunting experience. I have been anxious to do nothing *infra dig*. Now it seemed to me that to go downstairs in one's dressing-gown might be considered not the action of a pukka sahib. I pondered the problem for some time, and although I thought it unlikely I'd meet anyone, I decided to play safe. Hence the slacks and sweater. I was not quite happy, even then, and seriously considered putting my dress suit back on – after all, it was still nearer evening than morning. Eventually, however, I decided that would be going too far. Right, this seems to be the end of the corridor. Will you take the doors on the right or the left?'

Five minutes after starting the search they were joined by Gerry, who told them the doctor was on his way. They met Lord Burford and Evans as arranged, and went down to the first floor where they met Thornton. The situation was explained to him and he helped with the remainder of the search.

The result of it all was negative.

'Do you think we ought to wake Felman and tell him his boss has disappeared?' Lord Burford said. 'He might be able to throw some light on it.'

Deveraux nodded. 'Yes. I'll go and do it now.' He hurried off.

Jane said: 'I wish someone else would have a look at Algy. I'm a bit worried about the poor mutt.'

Thornton, Evans, and Gerry went with her. They found Algy still sleeping soundly. They lifted him onto the bed, removed his shoes and jacket, covered him with an eiderdown and left him.

Lord Burford meanwhile had gone to dress. The others met Deveraux again at the head of the stairs. 'I've told Felman everything we know,' he said. 'He can't throw any light on it.'

Deveraux and Thornton then went downstairs, while Jane and Gerry retired to their rooms to throw on a few clothes, and Evans went to report to Peabody. The girls joined Deveraux and Thornton a few minutes later for a check of the ground floor windows and doors. None was unlocked.

'Not that that proves much,' Deveraux said. 'Anybody

wanting to get out and leave no trace could have heard the window breaking and gone through it after we left.'

The storm had now passed, the rain had stopped, and while they were making their tour of the ground floor windows they saw the clouds dispersing and the moon beginning to break through.

They went then to the drawing-room. Gerry rang for Merryweather and ordered coffee. 'Bring lots, Merry,' she told him.

Ten minutes later Richard came in again. He looked pale and drawn. Jane hesitated for a few moments, then went to speak to him. She found him bewildered, almost dazed, quite different from his usual decisive self. While she was talking to him, Felman entered the room and came across. Richard seemed to pull himself together. He said: 'My dear fellow, this is a most incredible business. I just don't know what to say.'

Felman shook his head. 'It doesn't make sense, sir. I must say, I wish I'd been woken before.'

'Yes, you should have been. I realise that now. I ought to have called you immediately my niece roused me. But, of course, until we knew for certain that Adler was not in the house there seemed little point.'

Jane said: 'Mr. Deveraux did look in your room a couple of minutes after we found Mr. Adler's room empty, just to see if perhaps he'd gone to you for assistance. But you were asleep and there didn't seem to be any real reason to wake you.'

Thornton, who had approached the group, touched Richard on the sleeve and drew him aside. 'Minister, may I ask if you've notified the PM?'

'Not yet. Frankly, I don't know whether I would be justified in waking him at 4 a.m. with the information I have at present. If Adler's disappearance is voluntary, it may not necessarily be a matter of great concern for the British government. If he's gone off on his own for some private reason, it will be more your government's worry, Felman. Should it turn out he's been kidnapped, by anarchists or Bolsheviks for instance, it'll be a different matter.'

'I'm just wondering whether I should contact my Embassy immediately,' Felman said.

'It's up to you, of course. If you want my advice, however, I should wait a little longer and hope to find out something definite. It's not as if they could do anything at the moment.'

'No doubt you're right.' But Felman's voice and expression made it clear that actually he had grave doubts.

While they had been talking, Lord and Lady Burford, Mr. and Mrs. Peabody, and Evans had come into the room. Mrs. Peabody's eyes were red with weeping. The atmosphere in the room was very grim, with nobody feeling in the mood to keep the conversation alive. Algy Fotheringay's incessant drawl would for once have been welcome.

CHAPTER SEVENTEEN

Enter Inspector Wilkins

It was not long before there came the sound of cars pulling up outside. Lord Burford got to his feet. 'The police. I'll see 'em in the library. You'd better come too, Rich.'

Richard followed him out to the hall just as the front door bell sounded. They waited while Merryweather emerged from his domain and opened the door to admit two men in plain clothes and two uniformed constables. The first man was something of a surprise to both Lord Burford and Richard. He was short, rather plump, had a drooping black moustache, and wore a worried expression. He spoke to Merryweather and came forward looking round him in a lost sort of way. Somehow he did not inspire confidence. The second plain-clothes man was a brown-skinned young giant with an amiable expression.

Merryweather, in a tone which both Lord Burford and Richard recognised as being one of deep dismay, said: 'Detective Inspector Wilkins, my lord; and Detective Sergeant Leather.'

Lord Burford went forward. 'Inspector, I can't say how glad I am to see you.' He held out his hand.

The outstretched hand seemed to disconcert Inspector Wilkins, who as Lord Burford advanced had started, quite noticeably, to bow. He stopped himself suddenly in mid-movement – without, however, fully straightening up. The result was that he shook hands in an awkward half-stoop, as though he were reaching forward as far as he could to prevent Lord Burford coming too close. 'My lord,' he said in a deep sepulchral voice.

'Will you come to the library?' Lord Burford said. 'We can talk there.'

Inspector Wilkins sprang upright. 'Certainly, my lord. Er, will your lordship be requiring the constables as well?'

Lord Burford looked blank. 'I don't know, my dear chap. That's up to you. Do you want 'em?'

'Oh no, your lordship.'

'Then I suggest they wait here.'

'As your lordship pleases.'

'Come along, then.'

'Yes, my lord. Come along, Leather.'

Lord Burford led the two detectives to the library; Richard brought up the rear. Inside, Lord Burford said: 'This is my brother, by the way. Now, as to what happened...' Prompted occasionally by Richard, the Earl, who had received accounts of their activities from Deveraux and the girls, then gave a rather rambling but comprehensive résumé of the events of the night.

When he'd finished, Wilkins sat silently for several moments. Then, very slowly, he started shaking his head from side to side, saying as he did so: 'Oh, dear, dear, dear, dear.'

Lord Burford stared. 'Think it's bad, do you, Inspector?'

'Bad from my point of view, your lordship. Too complicated for me to unravel – and too big. Foreign envoys. International jewel thieves. American millionaires. European aristocracy. It's a job for the Yard. And the Chief Constable won't like that at all. He likes his men to tackle anything and everything that comes along. He won't be happy.' And Inspector Wilkins sighed deeply.

Lord Burford was again looking somewhat blank. 'But you will tackle it, won't you? I mean, until Scotland Yard gets here. You're not going to just go away?'

'Oh no, your lordship. I'll keep the pot boiling. Go through the motions, as it were. But don't expect me to solve anything. I'm not sanguine, not sanguine at all.'

'Then what do you want to do first?'

'Well, sir, I'd better have more detailed descriptions of the two missing persons – and photographs, if they should be available.'

Richard said: 'It's possible their passports, carrying their photos, will be in their rooms. If not, I can probably give you as detailed a description of both of them as anybody. I can take the sergeant up to look, if you like.'

'Thank you, sir. While you're doing that, I suppose I ought to go and have a look at the jewel-case and this visiting-card. And then at the broken window.' The prospect seemed to depress Inspector Wilkins still further.

'Very well, then, come along,' Lord Burford said, 'I'll show you.'

'As your lordship pleases.'

'Incidentally, my dear chap, I'm not a judge.'

'I'm so sorry, my lord. Force of habit, as it were, after spending so much time in court.'

They made for the door. Then Inspector Wilkins stopped short. 'No,' he said.

Lord Burford stared. 'What d'you mean – no?'

'I don't want to see them. There's no point. They wouldn't mean anything to me. Jack' – he spoke to Leather – 'after you've got the photos or the descriptions, give 'em to Smith. He'll know what to do. Afterwards go and have a squint round Mr. and Mrs. Peabody's rooms, and then at the broken window. Just see if anything strikes your eye. Don't touch anything. I may go and have a look later. But first, my lord,' he said to the Earl, 'I'd like to have a word with the rest of your guests and particularly with Mr. and Mrs. Peabody. It won't serve any really useful purpose, but I find it makes people feel better if they talk to the officer in charge of the case. Perhaps I can cheer them up a bit – convince them we're on the ball, as they put it. But then, Americans are always supposed to think English policemen are wonderful anyway, aren't they?'

Anybody less likely to cheer up the Peabodys would, thought Lord Burford, be difficult to find. But while Richard took Sergeant Leather upstairs, he led the inspector to the drawing-room and introduced him all round. This turned out a somewhat lengthy process, as Wilkins kept getting confused about names, and relationships and exactly who or what each person was. To the Peabodys, however, he was surprisingly tactful and soothing. He got from them the statements that both had been sleeping since before midnight and that neither had heard anything until Hiram had been woken by Evans. Carrie Peabody admitted that she had left the key in the lock of her jewel-box. 'I'd been told Alderley was so secure,' she said, 'it just didn't seem necessary to bother.'

'Well, don't blame yourself, madam. No doubt the Wraith would have had a key with him that would open it. If not, he could easily have taken the box itself. The necklace was the only item taken, I gather. I assume there was nothing else of any value in the box?'

'No, it's mostly paste. I brought just the one really good piece to Europe with me for special occasions. I wish I'd chosen anything but my diamonds. It's not only the value – they are insured – but they were Hiram's present to me when he officially made his first ten million.' She dabbed at her eyes. 'They mean more to me than all the rest of my jewellery put together.'

Wilkins nodded sagely. 'Sentimental value. Of course. I know exactly how you feel. A few months ago I lost the truncheon which was issued to me when I first joined the force twenty years ago. I was highly distressed. I found it eventually. The dog had buried it in the garden. Perhaps we'll be as fortunate with your necklace, ma'am.'

He addressed the room at large. 'Ladies and gentlemen, I understand that several of you have had unusual adventures during the night. But I've had a very clear account from his lordship and Mr. Saunders and I don't think I need to question any of you further tonight. So if you want to go back to bed, as far as the police are concerned you can. Thank you. Now, perhaps, your lordship, we could return to the library?'

'Of course.'

They started to move towards the door. Then Wilkins stopped short. 'Whoa,' he said.

Lord Burford turned in surprise.

'Oh, I beg your lordship's pardon. The whoa was for myself.' He turned round again. 'I've changed my mind. I do that a lot, I'm afraid. I would like to speak to Mr. Deveraux tonight, if I may.' He looked at Evans. 'So if you could accompany his lordship and me to the library, sir.'

'I'm not Deveraux.'

'Oh, aren't you? I'm sorry. Then where...? He looked round the room vaguely.

'Here.' Deveraux stepped forward.

Wilkins looked pleased. 'Ah, good. Come along then, sir.'

Evans said: 'Do you want me, too?'

'No, I don't think so, sir. Nothing personal, you understand. Of course, if you'd like to come along, I'd have no objection, personally.'

'No, really, thanks.'

'OK, then. Well, good night, ladies and gentlemen. I'll be speaking to you all tomorrow – or later today, I should say. Right, my lord.'

In the hall, they found Richard, Sergeant Leather, and Merryweather waiting. Leather came forward and spoke to Wilkins.

'We found both passports in the bedrooms, sir. I've given them to Smith. Neither of the rooms looked as though the people had intended to do a flit, by the way. Their things are still scattered around.'

Wilkins nodded. 'We'll make a proper search later. Fingerprints arrived yet?'

'Yes, sir, they're up in Mr. and Mrs. Peabody's rooms.'

'Take 'em to the breakfast-room after. Oh – wait.'

Wilkins clapped a hand to his head. 'Has Smith gone?'

'He just went out a few seconds ago.'

'Stop him, quick.' Wilkins waved his arms about agitatedly. 'Cockerill,' he called to the other constable, who was still standing near the door, 'go after him. Tell him to wait.' Then, to Leather: 'That Wraith card: did you see it?'

'Yes, sir. It looks just like the pictures I've seen of the others.'

'Go and see if they found any prints on it. If not, put it in an envelope and give it to Smith. Tell him I want it sent up to the Yard pronto for comparison. And Jack, as soon as it's light, you and Cockerill take a look round outside.'

'What for, sir?'

'Oh.' Wilkins looked blank. 'Well, footprints chiefly, I suppose. But anything out of the ordinary. Detect, man, detect.'

'Yes, sir.' Leather nodded and hurried away upstairs.

Lord Burford came across from speaking to Merryweather. 'My butler tells me the doctor's arrived. He's gone upstairs to see Fotheringay.'

'Good. Perhaps you'll leave word for the doctor to kindly join us in the library when he's finished.'

Back in the library, Lord Burford said: 'I don't know about anybody else, but I'm having a Scotch.' He crossed to a cabinet. 'Deveraux?'

'Thank you, Lord Burford.'

'Rich?'

'Please, George.'

Lord Burford started pouring. 'I don't suppose you do on duty, Inspector?'

'Oh yes, my lord, I do. All the time.'

'Oh. I see. How do you take it?'

'Neat, my lord.'

They all sat down. There was silence for a few seconds. Then Wilkins leant forward and spoke confidentially. 'Tell me, my lord, just between us, how many millions is Mr. Peabody actually worth?'

'I really have no idea, Inspector.'

'I've never met a real millionaire before,' Wilkins said. 'Makes you feel quite funny inside.'

Richard said: 'Inspector, I'm sure you know your job inside out, but—'

'No, sir.'

'No, what?'

'I don't know my job inside out, Mr. Saunders. In fact, mostly I'm out of my depth. I am now. I consider myself extremely fortunate to have reached the rank of Inspector.' Wilkins looked and sounded the picture of gloom. 'Sergeant, and in the uniformed branch, at that, was the height of my ambition. I'd be more at home in that position, really. I don't rightly know how I came to be doing this sort of work. But there we are. Here I am and mustn't grumble. And I have got one asset – only one, I think.'

'What's that?' Deveraux asked.

'I'm lucky, sir. And I sometimes play that luck. I get an urge to do something. I can't really tell why. But somehow it very often seems to pay off. Oh well, better to be born lucky than rich, they say. And it was just a sudden urge that made me decide to have a word with you tonight, Mr. Deveraux. Because I think you can put me straight on at least some of the odd things that have been happening in this house.'

CHAPTER EIGHTEEN

The Body in the Lake

Deveraux ran his finger round the rim of his glass. 'I can't think why you should pick on me, Inspector. I've already told the Earl here everything I know, and I imagine he's passed it on.'

'He has, sir. But I'd like to hear it from you in your own words.'

'Certainly, if you think it'll help. Well, I was on the landing, a few feet from the top of the grand staircase—'

'Why?'

'Why? Oh, I see what you mean. I was on my way downstairs to get a book from in here.'

'I see. No doubt the storm had prevented you from sleeping.'

'Quite.'

'Fancy – and you an ex-naval officer, I'm told. So you started to make your way downstairs in the dark. Why didn't you switch on the light, by the way?'

'There was no need. I had a pocket torch.'

'Of course.' Wilkins tutted. 'Silly of me. Now where is your bedroom situated exactly, Mr. Deveraux?'

'On the corner of the main block and the west wing.'

'So you were going towards the stairs in an easterly direction?'

'No, actually I was going the opposite way. You see, I'd got a little way down the stairs when I heard somebody crossing the landing from east to west behind me. So I turned round to investigate.'

'Ah, now I understand.' Wilkins gave a satisfied nod. Then he frowned. 'But exactly why did you want to investigate?'

'I thought to creep about in the dark was rather suspicious behaviour.'

'It certainly was. The man didn't hear you?'

'No.'

'And why do you suppose he didn't see the light from your torch?'

'I didn't actually have it on at that time.'

'Creeping about in the dark, were you, sir?'

'Not creeping, Inspector.'

'No, of course not. I'm sorry. He was creeping; you weren't. Yet you heard him and he didn't hear you. There has to be a perfectly logical explanation for that, but unfortunately it escapes me. Could you enlighten me, please?'

Deveraux looked at him silently for a few moments. Then he chuckled. 'Well done, Inspector,' he said. 'You really got me in a corner. Very neat indeed. Looks as if I'm going to have to come clean. Ah well, I feared I'd have to sooner or later.'

He reached into his hip pocket, took out his pocket book, opened it and handed it to Wilkins. The Inspector looked at it without the flicker of an eyebrow, closed it and gave it back. 'Thank you, sir,' he said. 'I thought as much.'

During these exchanges Lord Burford and Richard had been looking more and more puzzled. 'What the deuce is going on?' the Earl said.

'Well, my lord, Mr. Deveraux has just shown me something which proves that he's in a line of work not all that far removed from my own.'

'What are you talking about? Feller's a writer.'

'I'm afraid not, Lord Burford. I owe you an apology.' Deveraux spoke in a quite unapologetic tone of voice. 'I'm under your roof by false pretences, I regret to say. I don't think there would be much point in my showing you this, as it wouldn't mean anything to you. But Mr. Saunders will recognise it, I'm sure.' He held the pocket book out to Richard.

Richard looked at it and nodded briefly. 'It's right enough, George. Every government minister is familiar with these. There's no need to name Deveraux's department, but as the inspector said, it's allied to the police and I imagine often works in conjunction with Scotland Yard. Thornton told me he knew your face, Deveraux. I suppose he's seen you in Whitehall sometime.'

''Pon my soul.' Lord Burford looked at Deveraux with something approaching awe. 'You mean John Buchan stuff, is that it?'

'Well, rarely so heroic, sir, but something like that.'

'And you're not a writer at all?'

'No.'

'And there ain't going to be any book?'

'I feel a frightful cad, but no, I'm sorry.'

'But I heard you talking about a pen-name – something George; naturally I noticed it specially.'

'Jonathan George. He's a friend of mine. Allowed me to use his name. Andrew Lewis doesn't exist.'

'Why are you here?' Richard asked him.

'I'm here on the Prime Minister's instructions.'

'The PM sent you?'

'He ordered my chief to send someone.'

'Why wasn't I informed who you really were?'

'Because it was important nobody else knew. And it is difficult for the average person to behave naturally to somebody in my line of work. If one person knows the truth, usually the others guess it.'

'I understand that. No doubt it's a sensible policy. But I wish I'd known, all the same.'

'I think everybody here will now have to be told that I'm not what I first claimed to be,' Deveraux said. 'But with the approval of you all, we'll let it be thought I'm a Scotland Yard man.'

'Then mind you remember to call everybody "sir" or "madam",' Wilkins said.

'I'll do my best – sir.'

'Are you able to say why the Prime Minister wanted you here?'

'I think I'm bound to, if we're going to make any progress,' Deveraux said. 'I'll tell you everything I know, Wilkins, on the understanding that it's top secret stuff. Mr. Saunders here and Adler, who is a very important man indeed in his own country, have been engaged in highly crucial talks in the last few days. Exactly what the talks are about, I have not been informed myself; but I do know that a successful outcome is considered vital. I don't think Mr. Saunders can tell us more than that, or indeed that we need to know more. But you'll realise it puts a different complexion on Adler's disappearance.'

Wilkins gave a deep sigh. 'Bad,' he said. He looked at Richard. 'Would it be improper to ask if anything took place during these talks which could account for Adler's disappearance?'

Richard shook his head. 'Nothing. I can tell you that the negotiations were not proceeding as smoothly as we could have hoped; we had run into difficulties. But it would have been absurd to suppose that this could be sufficient to cause Adler to cut and run.'

Wilkins drummed on the arm of the chair with his fingers. 'What was your brief, Mr. Deveraux?'

'I was told that a lot of people want to know what's decided here – or perhaps make sure *nothing* is decided. The PM wanted somebody on the premises just to keep an eye on things. My orders were simply to be alert for any unusual occurrence or suspicious circumstance, make sure nobody overheard any part of the talks – and just be here in case of emergency. Which I was – with singular lack of success.'

'Why exactly were you up tonight?'

'I've been making patrols of the whole house at irregular intervals during the nights. There were several reasons. Firstly, my department notified me on Friday that the telephone authorities had informed them that a call had been made from this house to a public kiosk in London at two-twenty-five that morning. This indicated that something fishy was going on here, and if one call had been made around that time, another one might be. So I decided to check the telephone room now and again each night. Secondly, I wanted to keep an eye on the music-room. There was always a chance that if a spy was present, he'd try to plant a microphone there and run a lead to another part of the house. I checked in the room Friday and Saturday morning early, of course; but just finding a microphone wouldn't be enough. I'd have to know who planted it. The only way would be to catch him red-handed. The planting would obviously be done at night, and if I checked the room frequently, there was a remote chance I'd catch him at it. Again, I made a habit of checking up on the guests – going to their doors, listening carefully, watching for lights, occasionally opening a door and peeping in. It was all a waste of time as things turned out.

'Tonight I left my room just before two-twenty. I went along the main and east corridors and down the stairs at the end. I checked in the 'phone room, then went back upstairs. I had intended to have another hunt round up there and then go down again and look in the music-room and 'phone room once more later. But near the top of the stairs I heard footsteps approaching. I decided to follow them. Then – wham. Of course, as soon as I got to my feet I should have raised the alarm and rung the police. I ought to have realised I needed help. My only excuse is that for some time I was still a bit groggy – my mind not working at full effectiveness. And what with releasing Lady Geraldine, investigating the scream, and so on, there always seemed to be other urgent things needing to be done.'

'Quite understandable,' said Wilkins.

Lord Burford, who had begun to look a little restless, said: 'Look, this is no doubt all very important, but shouldn't one of you be doing something now, instead of talking about what's already happened? I'm personally not so much concerned with Adler and the Baroness as with Mrs. Peabody's diamonds. The Peabodys are my guests, and I'd like to see some action taken to try to recover the jewels before it's too late.'

'Oh, my lord, that's all been taken care of.' Wilkins was eager to explain. 'The alert went out within minutes of Mr. Saunders' call. We're already looking for the lady and gentleman – *and* the necklace. All the usual steps for major crimes have been taken – road blocks set up, and so on. I'm sorry I didn't tell you before, but I thought you'd have realised.'

Lord Burford looked a little abashed. 'Oh, I see. Sorry.'

'I'm afraid it will all be a waste of time, though,' Wilkins added.

'Why do you say that?'

'Well, it was half an hour after the alarm was set off that we were called.'

Richard said: 'We 'phoned as soon as we knew definitely what was wrong. Until then it was merely a question of a broken window and a couple of scuffles in the dark. It could have all been misunderstanding – an accident, or a practical joke, say.'

'I appreciate that, sir. I'm merely pointing out that if a getaway from Alderley had been planned for tonight, anyone with a fast car standing by, and with open country roads all round, could have been thirty miles away before we started looking. The other point is that, as regards the necklace, in a rural area like this, no thief is going to carry round something as hot as that when he can bury it and collect it when the hue and cry has died down. So if we were to catch the thief, he'd be unlikely to be in possession of the loot, and we couldn't prove anything. I'm not sanguine, my lord, not sanguine at all.'

'Then what do you propose to do now?' Lord Burford asked.

'I don't really know, my lord. Let me think.'

But Wilkins was saved from having to think very long because then the door opened and Merryweather announced: 'Dr. Ingleby.'

Ingleby was a tall young man with a mass of ginger hair and a cheerful manner. He had been the Alderley medical attendant now for three or four years, and was also the assistant police surgeon; so he needed to be introduced only to Deveraux. He accepted a drink and sat down.

'How's the patient, doctor?' Lord Burford asked him.

'Sleeping like a baby. And likely to continue to do so for some considerable time.'

'Can you tell us what's the matter with him?' Wilkins asked.

'It depends on how precise an answer you want. He's drugged, of course, but I can't say with what. A sedative of some kind – sleeping tablets, say. Do you know if he was in the habit of taking them?'

Lord Burford shook his head. 'I should think it was extremely unlikely.'

'I couldn't find any empty bottle in his room certainly.'

Deveraux said: 'And if he didn't take them himself...'

'Precisely,' said Wilkins.

Lord Burford said: 'Who on earth would want to dope Fotheringay?'

'I doubt if we'll know the answer to that,' Deveraux said, 'until after we've answered a lot of other questions.'

'He will be all right, will he?' Lord Burford asked.

'Oh yes. He's had a pretty big dose, but by no means a lethal one. Though I expect he'll sleep most of the day.'

'That,' said the Earl, 'is the first bit of good news I've had tonight.'

Dr. Ingleby turned to Deveraux. 'Are you the chap who took a blow on the head? Let's have a look.' He did so, then said: 'You'll live. Take a couple of aspirin before you turn in.' He looked at his wrist watch and got to his feet. 'Nearly four-thirty. I must go.'

Lord Burford stood up, moved across to the bell and rang it. 'Good of you to have turned out so promptly, Doctor.'

Then he looked up in surprise as, far too soon to be answering the bell, Merryweather entered. 'Excuse me, my lord,' he said, 'the police sergeant wishes to converse with Inspector Wilkins.'

The next second he was almost elbowed aside by Leather, who hurried into the room without waiting for an invitation. He spoke urgently to Wilkins.

'Could you come at once, please, sir? It's very important.'

Jane let her gaze fall in turn on each of the other occupants of the drawing-room. Strange that nobody had yet taken up that funny-looking policeman's invitation to return to bed. Though both Thornton and Evans looked as if they'd like to. Of the others, Lady Burford was clearly far too indignant at the very idea of such events taking place at Alderley, to consider sleep; Mr. Peabody was annoyed, too, but chiefly, Jane thought, with himself: it must have been a long time since anybody had made a sucker out of Hiram Peabody; Mrs. Peabody was obviously still extremely upset; and Nicholas Felman plainly anxious.

It seemed, in fact, that the only person in the house who was thoroughly enjoying the whole situation was Gerry. In spite of everything, Jane grinned as she looked at her friend's bright eyes and eager expression. There was nobody with a greater capacity for enjoying life than Gerry.

Jane's train of thought was broken by the entry of Lord Burford and Richard. Everybody stared at them expectantly. It was as though they'd all been waiting for this moment, had known that the events of the night were not yet over.

Lord Burford paused inside the door and looked round the ring of faces. At that moment Jane knew what he was going to say.

'I'm afraid I've got bad news.' His voice was grave. His eyes sought out Felman. 'Felman, I'm very sorry to tell you that Mr. Adler is dead.'

Felman got slowly to his feet. His face was blank. He said: 'Dead? But where – how? I don't understand.'

Richard came forward. He said: 'One of the constables has just found his body. He – it – was floating in the lake.'

'In the lake? You mean he's been drowned?' Felman sounded utterly bewildered.

'No, not drowned.'

It was Inspector Wilkins who said this as he came into the room. 'The doctor thinks he was dead when he entered the water,' he said. 'Adler was shot. This is now a murder enquiry, ladies and gentlemen.'

CHAPTER NINETEEN

Murder

The telephone at Alderley had never been used so intensively as it was in the hour following the discovery of Adler's body. Calls from Richard to the Prime Minister, from Deveraux to the head of his department, from Wilkins to his chief constable, followed in quick succession. Then Felman put through a long distance call to the Duchy. Later, came return calls for Deveraux and Wilkins. The instructions were explicit: to avoid undue publicity Scotland Yard was not, at least for the time being, to be called in; Wilkins and his men were to conduct the investigation, with Deveraux's collaboration and advice.

The reactions of the rest of the party to the news of Deveraux's real reason for being at Alderley were mixed, varying from excitement on the part of Gerry, to a decided annoyance on her mother's.

Meanwhile, the routine of murder investigation proceeded: photographs were taken; the Burfords, their guests and servants were fingerprinted; more policemen arrived and began a search of the park; away from Alderley, the hunt for Anilese de la Roche was intensified.

Wilkins left at seven a.m., when most of the house party staggered to bed for a few hours sleep. He returned at eleven, and after spending a quarter of an hour with Leather, who'd remained, met Deveraux in the music-room. With the automatic suspension of the political talks, Lord Burford had told them to use it as an operations room.

'Well?' Deveraux said, 'what have you got?'

'Very little,' Wilkins shook his head glumly. 'First, the Baroness's driver has hooked it. He was staying at the Rose & Crown in the village, but he paid his bill and left late yesterday afternoon. A man answering his description caught the five-forty-two to London. He was alone. The car, of course, is still at the garage. Second, Adler must have died instantly. When Ingleby first saw the body at just four-thirty rigor mortis had already set in. Now, as you probably know, it doesn't normally occur until at least four hours after death; but as Adler didn't retire until one a.m., and was seen alive by several people right up to then, Ingleby says this must be one of those instances – which occur sometimes in cases of violent death – of rigor setting in instantaneously. They call it a cadaveric spasm. He estimates – and he stressed he couldn't be too exact – that when he saw the body, Adler had been dead approximately two hours.'

'With what sort of margin for error?'

'At first he said about twenty minutes. When I pressed him to give an absolute minimum, he said he'd be prepared only to swear Adler was not killed later than three a.m..'

Deveraux looked thoughtful. 'When Miss Clifton first heard the sound in the breakfast room, I'd just glanced at the luminous dial of my watch. It was two-forty-eight and a half. So we can say the alarm went off at two-forty-nine. We do *know* Adler was in the house until then, don't we?'

'Yes; Leather's just told me the alarm has been checked: it had not been tampered with, and it worked perfectly. No one could have left the house before then without setting it off.'

'Therefore, we can pin the time of death down pretty precisely. What else have you got?'

'Something on that Wraith card: there were no prints on it and we rushed it to the Yard. I had a 'phone call at the station just before I started back here. It's genuine.'

'Genuine?'

'In the past, thieves wanting to divert suspicion onto the Wraith have had similar cards done – based on the reproductions in the papers. But this isn't one of those: it's identical in every respect with the cards left at the actual Wraith robberies: same quality cardboard, exactly the same size of card – and the drawing of the ghost run off from the same printer's block: there's a slight flaw in it. Now, nobody other than a few big chiefs at the Yard has ever had access to those cards. They've been described and photographed, but it's quite impossible that anyone could copy them so exactly. So this one has to be from the same batch as the others.'

'Great Scott!' Deveraux looked staggered. 'That means the Wraith was actually in this house last night?'

'Surprise you?'

'It certainly does. I was sure somebody else had seen that magazine article and come here determined to take advantage of it – pinch the necklace and pin the blame on the Wraith.'

'You suspected one of the guests?'

'I did, yes. I imagined either that the other trouble here last night was a coincidence; or that the bogus Wraith used the commotion as a cover to steal the necklace. This puts all my theories back in the melting pot.'

'Would you like to go over everything that happened last night – help me get it straight in my mind? I found the account a little confusing before.'

'I'm not surprised,' Deveraux said.

He carefully ran through all the events of the night as he knew them up to Wilkins' arrival. Then he said: 'Since then I've spoken briefly to everybody and asked them if they can throw light on any of it. But apart from the two girls, nobody admits to doing, seeing, or hearing anything.'

'What about that scream?'

'That must have been the Baroness. Both the girls were on the first floor at the time. Lady Burford and Mrs. Peabody say they were asleep in bed. There's no reason to doubt them. So unless it was one of the servants...'

'Leather's been round with that butler chappie and spoken to each of them. They all swear they were in bed in their quarters all night. He believes 'em.'

'So do I. In fact, old man, I'm quite certain none of the servants was involved in any way in either the murder or the robbery.'

Wilkins was silent for a few moments, digesting all he'd been told. Then he said: 'Isn't it a bit fishy that all these people claim to have gone on sleeping with so much noise going on?'

'Not really. Plainly not everybody's telling the truth about being asleep in bed, but we mustn't assume they're all lying. Alderley is tremendously solidly built, with thick walls and massive close-fitting doors, many of them with curtains behind them. There are deep rugs and heavy hangings everywhere. From the bedrooms you wouldn't hear much unless it was something really loud and happened in a room adjoining yours or in the corridor immediately outside. Last night there was very little noise actually *in* the corridor. When I was attacked, the only sound was a sort of scuffling. Likewise with Jane and Gerry – neither of them screamed or shouted. The three of us who were in the corridor all heard the noise in Adler's room, but I wouldn't expect anybody else to have done – don't forget Gerry's room is one side and Lady Burford's boudoir the other. When the scream came remember the thunder: that could have muffled a lot of other noises.'

Wilkins grunted ruminatively. Then he asked: 'Got any theories at this stage?'

'Not really. It seems to depend on who went out through the window. Let's assume that it was the Wraith. He'd broken in here during the evening, hidden, come out around two or quarter-past, entered the Peabodys' room and taken the necklace. He'd planned to break out through the breakfast-room – either not knowing about the burglar alarm, or thinking he could circumvent it somehow – was interrupted, had to break the window, and got clean away. It may have been he who hit me and made the Baroness scream. If it was, Adler and the Baroness must have left later – after the alarm was set off.'

'Then what happened?'

'Take your pick. They ran into the Wraith, who shot

Adler and kidnapped the Baroness. Or the Baroness was the Wraith's accomplice and went with him freely.'

'The weakness of that theory is that the Wraith has never used violence – and several times he could have made escape much easier for himself if he had. Nor has he ever been known to have an accomplice.'

'Right, let's say that neither Adler nor the Baroness had anything to do with the Wraith, and that she shot Adler herself. Or, that some third person, an outsider, shot him, and that the Baroness left with this man – either willingly or under duress.'

'And suppose it wasn't the Wraith who broke the window?'

'Then it must have been Adler. In which case, the Wraith and Anilese both got out later. That would clearly point to them being accomplices. Perhaps Adler saw them outside and tried to stop them: if the Wraith wouldn't use violence, perhaps the Baroness would. Or the same outsider met him and shot him.'

Deveraux paused. 'Or somebody from the house followed him out, shot him, and came back. In which case the killer's in this house now. And that's the nastiest thought of all.'

He spread his hands. 'Are those enough theories? I could probably go on. There are things I haven't touched on yet. The scrap in Adler's room, for instance – why didn't the innocent party call for help? Who drugged Fotheringay – and why? I haven't even speculated – and I must say I think this is highly commendable of me – on why I was attacked.'

Wilkins managed a wan smile. 'Perhaps,' he said, 'we're

speculating too much. I doubt we're going to get much further without some more facts.'

'Yes, I agree. Such as an identification of the murder weapon.'

'Oh, I'm sorry, I should have told you. We know something about that. The bullet was a 9mm; and there was something rather unusual about it.'

'What's that?'

'Apparently it was fired from a gun with left-hand twist rifling.'

'What?' Deveraux almost shouted this.

'What's the excitement? Do you know of a gun like that?'

'Not *a* gun. Two. Come on. I'll explain as we go.'

They found a somewhat bleary-eyed Lord Burford devouring a late breakfast of devilled kidneys in the dining-room – the break-fast-room window still being out. Richard was with him, drinking black coffee.

'Any news?' Richard asked.

'Not yet, sir,' Wilkins told him.

'Gentlemen, this is a desperately worrying business. I don't mind saying among the four of us that these talks Adler and I were engaged in are extremely urgent. And we were already behind schedule. The draft treaty should have been signed by this time. Now Adler's dead. Heaven knows how long it will be before the Duchy can get an adequate replacement here – and then we'll have to start all over again. The delay could be very grave.' He broke off. 'I'm sorry. What was it you wanted?'

'We've got some information for Lord Burford, sir.

Lord Burford, they've dug the bullet out of Adler.'

'Oh yes.'

'It's a 9mm – fired from a gun with left-hand twist rifling.'

Lord Burford dropped his knife and fork. 'But that's—'

'The same as your Bergman Bayard. Very uncommon, isn't it?'

'It certainly is. You don't think mine was used to shoot Adler?'

'I don't know. But I think it would be advisable to check on it as soon as possible.'

'Yes, of course. I'll take you up.'

He led Deveraux and Wilkins upstairs and through the picture gallery to the gun-room. He opened the door with one of the keys on a ring from his pocket and went in. They followed him, Wilkins staring round in wonder. Lord Burford hurried across to the case where he had displayed the Bergman and gave a sigh of relief. 'It's all right. It's still here.' He opened the case and made to lift it out.

'Don't touch it, please,' said Wilkins. He took a pencil from his pocket, inserted it in the barrel, lifted the pistol to his nose on the pencil, and sniffed. He shook his head. 'Can't smell a thing. You say Mr. Peabody's got one the same?'

Deveraux nodded.

'We'd better go and have a word with him, then.'

Lord Burford, who had had his eye thankfully on the precious firearm, suddenly gave what could only be described as a yelp. 'Wait a minute!'

He made a grab for the gun. Wilkins tried to snatch it away, but was too late. It was in the Earl's hands.

Wilkins gave a groan. 'Oh, my lord! Fingerprints!'

But Lord Burford wasn't listening. He was peering at the pistol with popping eyes, turning it over and over in his hands. Then he lifted a reddening face to Deveraux.

'This ain't mine.'

Deveraux's eyebrows went up. 'Not yours? You mean it's Peabody's?'

'No! This is a replica.'

Deveraux stared at him. 'Are you sure?'

'Of course I'm sure, you blitherin' idiot! Think I can't tell the difference between my own and a blasted copy? And it's not mine, either.'

Deveraux looked bewildered. 'Not your what, Lord Burford?'

'Not my – not my Bergman. It's a replica. Can't you understand? I've never seen it before. The Wraith's stolen my Bergman Bayard Special, blast him.'

He wheeled round on Inspector Wilkins, brandishing the pistol under his nose. 'Wilkins, you'll get it back for me, won't you? Please. I only had it a month. Hardly anyone's seen it yet. It's priceless – practically unique.'

'We'll do our best, my lord. But I shouldn't hold out too much hope. I'm not sanguine. I'm not likely to succeed in tracking down the Wraith when the best detectives in Europe haven't been able to.'

The Earl gave a groan of despair. 'It's a judgement, that's what it is, a judgement.'

'Judgement for what, my lord?'

'What? Oh – things.' He looked at Deveraux. 'Sorry I snapped. Don't take any notice.'

'That's all right, sir. Could you tell us if there's any ammunition missing?'

'I'll see.' Lord Burford went to the ammunition cupboard, rummaged in it, took out a box, and counted. He looked up and said: 'Ten cartridges missing.'

Deveraux looked grim. He said: 'Do you always keep this room locked?'

'Yes, always.'

'How many keys are there?'

'Two.'

'Where is the other one?'

'Peabody's got it.'

'Has he indeed?'

'He's been spending so much time examinin' the collection that frankly I got a bit browned-off having to be with him all the time. So I gave him a spare key so he could come and go as he pleased.'

'And he had the key overnight?'

'Presumably.'

'Where was your key last night?'

'On my dressing-table. I ought to put it in me study safe, really, I suppose – that's got a combination lock. But I don't usually bother.'

'So actually anybody could creep into your dressing-room adjoining your bedroom, pick up the keys, come here, take the gun, and replace the keys after, without you being any the wiser?'

Lord Burford looked guilty. 'Afraid so.'

'Did you take the keys with you when you went down in the night?'

'No.'

'When you picked up that bunch this morning, did you happen to notice if they were in exactly the same place as last night?'

But Lord Burford couldn't say. Deveraux sighed. 'Well, we'd better have a word with Peabody.'

'What – now?' Lord Burford looked a little startled.

'Yes.'

'Oh, I, er, don't think he's up yet.'

'Then I'll have to wake him, I'm afraid.'

Lord Burford bit his lip. 'Are you sure you really want to do that? I mean, I'm sure you've got other things to do. Why not let me talk to him for you?'

'That's very kind of you, but I must speak to him myself – and as quickly as possible. It's important.'

'Oh, all right then. I'll come with you.'

They made their way to the Royal Suite and found Peabody in shirt-sleeves in his dressing-room. His wife, he told them, was still asleep.

'Any news of the necklace?' he asked eagerly.

Wilkins said: 'I'm afraid not, sir. We wanted to ask you about another matter. Have you got the spare key to the gun-room?'

'Why, yes.'

'Where is it?'

'In the pocket of one of my suits. Do you want it?'

'If you please, sir.'

Peabody went to a clothes cupboard, reached in and came back with a key identical to the one on Lord Burford's ring. He handed it to Wilkins.

Deveraux said: 'It was there all night?'

'That's correct.'

'Did many people know you had it?'

'Why, yes. I made a jocular remark about it at tea yesterday. Took it out and said how I really figured I'd made it to the top now I'd got the key to the Burford collection.'

'I remember,' Deveraux said. 'Nothing to stop anyone coming in here last night while you were asleep in the next room, taking it and replacing it later, was there?'

'None, I suppose. Why, gentlemen, don't tell me somebody's robbed the gun-room?'

'In rather a big way,' Deveraux said. 'They've stolen Lord Burford's Bergman pistol and left a replica in its place.'

'You don't say!' Peabody sounded shocked. 'Why, that's terrible. I can hardly believe it. Earl, I'm mighty sorry. I know how I'd feel if I lost mine.'

Deveraux said: 'Yours is still safe, I suppose?'

'Mine? Sure, it's over here.' He went across the room and picked up the case in which he kept the pistol. 'Here we are, gentlemen. The new pride of the Peabody collection.' He opened the case. Then he gave a gasp of horror. 'It's gone!'

Lord Burford gave a squeak. 'What! Don't say the case is empty?'

Peabody turned and held up the empty case for them to see. His face was a blank mask.

In a whisper Lord Burford said: 'The bounder's got 'em both. The Wraith's nabbed the pair.'

'But no replica left in place of this one,' Deveraux said.

'You can see what happened,' Wilkins put in. 'He found out either about his lordship's or Mr. Peabody's gun, decided to try for it at the same time as he went for the necklace, and had a replica made to leave in its place. It wasn't until later, when it was too late to get a second replica made, that he discovered there was a pair of pistols under the same roof.'

Peabody gave a groan. 'The New York exhibition. I cabled, entering mine.'

'Don't worry, sir,' Wilkins said unexpectedly. They all looked at him. He spoke to Deveraux: 'I was wrong. The Wraith didn't take both those guns.'

'I tend to agree with you,' Deveraux said. 'Tell me how your mind is working.'

'Whoever took his lordship's gun took ammunition as well – so he intended to use it. Now the Wraith is not a killer. He'd only want the gun for its value. So although he may have stolen one of the pistols, he didn't steal them both: the other was taken by the murderer to shoot Adler. And if the killer's got an ounce of sense, he isn't going to have hung on to the gun after the shooting. He'll most likely have thrown it away in the grounds – probably in the lake. So I reckon it will turn up.'

Lord Burford frowned. 'But surely it's *my* gun you're suggestin' was taken by the killer. The ammunition was stolen from the same room; on the other hand, we know the Wraith was in this suite, so it must have been him took Peabody's gun.'

'It would seem so, my lord. But there's a weakness in that argument: it would be the Wraith – not the killer – who'd want to stop the gun's absence being discovered until he had a chance to sell it. The killer would realise that as soon as the bullet was removed from the body we'd identify the murder weapon and would spot the substitution. So it was the Wraith who had the replica made. Now the replica was substituted for your gun. Therefore the Wraith has your pistol, and the killer used Mr. Peabody's. My theory is that the Wraith came to this suite, stole the necklace, but didn't know of Mr. Peabody's gun, went to the collection-room and took your lordship's pistol. Then later the killer went there also, after your gun, discovered it missing, remembered that Mr. Peabody had a similar one, so came along and took that, pinching some ammo from the collection-room before he left it.'

Inspector Wilkins looked round with the nearest approach to pleasure on his face that he had yet displayed. But the reaction he received was not encouraging. Peabody seemed to have developed a sudden interest in the catch of his case, while Lord Burford intently studied the pattern on the carpet.

Deveraux said: 'Well, that's an interesting theory, Wilkins.'

'I think so,' said Wilkins. 'It implies quite a coincidence. But I suppose no more coincidence than the one involved in his lordship and Mr. Peabody buying the two pistols independently in the first place, as you were telling me.'

'Actually,' said Lord Burford, 'that's not quite so much a coincidence as you might think.'

'No,' Peabody said, 'we've discussed this. Granted that the pair were only recently discovered, got split up almost immediately, and were then sold separately to dealers – well, then the Earl and I are two of the most obvious people in the world for the dealers to offer them to.'

They left Peabody to finish dressing and Lord Burford

went downstairs to continue his breakfast.

Deveraux said: 'What now?'

'Well,' Wilkins said, 'the butler was asking me about cleaning up the breakfast-room and boarding over the window temporarily. I think I can let them, but I suppose I'd better have a look at it first, just for the sake of form.'

CHAPTER TWENTY

The Bloodstained Egg Cosy

Deveraux and Wilkins went down to the breakfast-room. Glass was still scattered around, the chair lying where it had fallen, the stepladder against the wall, the pair of wire cutters on the floor next to the pot plant.

Wilkins righted the chair, stood on it, and examined the burglar alarm wire where it went behind the picture rail. He got down, picked up the wire cutters aimlessly, and kicked a piece of glass with his foot.

'No interesting prints in here, I suppose?' Deveraux asked.

'Just those you'd expect, where you'd expect them.'

'Have your boys found out where the stepladder comes from?'

'Cupboard outside the butler's pantry. Easy enough to find – the obvious sort of place to look.'

He went to the window and gazed out. 'The bloke turned left, did he?'

'Yes.'

'Well, that ties up with the body being found in the lake.'

'No footprints anywhere?'

'No, but that paved path runs almost straight down to the lake and if he kept to that he wouldn't leave any.' He turned round. 'What's this about a secret passage?'

'Oh, I'll show you.'

Deveraux went to the cupboard door, opened it, and turned the knob as Gerry had demonstrated. The panel slid back.

'My, my, my,' Wilkins said, 'how very romantic.' He put his head through the opening, looked into the darkness, then withdrew and said: 'Do you think it's a coincidence it should be *this* room – the one with the entrance to the passage – that was involved?'

'I'm not sure. Whoever broke the window might have come down through the passage in order to avoid me and the girls. But then he would have had to go and get the stepladder. Why bring it back here? There are other windows nearer that cupboard where it's kept, which he could have escaped through.'

'Unless he had the ladder already here, waiting for him.'

'That means he would have had to come down earlier in the night, put it here ready, and go back up again. Why?'

Wilkins sighed. 'Don't ask me. I'm baffled by the whole affair. One thing I'm getting more and more sure about, though, is that the clue to Adler's behaviour lies in these political talks. Saunders and Felman must know something they haven't told us. Yet we've hardly spoken to them so far. Shall we now?'

'Good idea.'

'How do we set about that, do you know? I mean,

what's the etiquette? Should we go and search for them, or just ring for the butler and ask him to fetch them?'

'A nice point. I think we can certainly go to our ops room, ring for the butler and tell him to ask Felman to join us. As regards Saunders, I'm not so sure. I think I'll wait for inspiration. Let's get Felman over first, though.'

They were about to go out when Sergeant Leather entered. He was carrying a small object, which he handed to Wilkins.

'We've just found this, sir,' he said.

Wilkins held the object up. It was made of wool. At one time it had been white, but was now darkened with dried mud and earth. There was also a small reddish-brown stain, which Wilkins put his finger on. 'Blood?'

'Looks like it, sir.'

'Where was it?'

'One of the men found it caught waist-high on a lavender bush by the side of the path that runs down to the lake.'

'It's quite dry.'

'Yes, sir. So it wasn't out there during the storm. It wouldn't have dried out yet.'

'Anybody know what time the rain stopped?'

'Between about two-fifty and three-forty,' Deveraux said.

Wilkins said: 'Go and find out exactly, will you, Jack?'

'Yes, sir.' Leather left the room.

'Now,' Wilkins said, 'what is this thing? An ear muff? A doll's hat?'

'May I?' Deveraux took the object and examined it. 'I fancy it's what is known as an egg cosy.'

'What – one of those things you put over a boiled egg to keep it hot?'

'That's it.'

'I believe you're right. What the dickens was it doing out there? And where did all this mud and stuff come from? I wonder if it's from the house.'

'We can soon find out.' Deveraux rang the bell.

Just then they heard footsteps in the corridor and Gerry came in. 'Good morning,' she said.

'Ah,' Deveraux said, 'just the person we want. Can you identify this beautiful thing?'

Gerry took it gingerly. 'Ugh! What is it?'

'We believe an egg cosy.'

Gerry frowned. Then her face cleared. 'Oh yes. Mummy bought some at the Sale of Work a couple of years ago – along with a load of other equally useless stuff. We always get lumbered with a lot of junk. No doubt they were crocheted by one of the old pussies in the village. I doubt if they've ever been used. Ghastly things.' She raised it to her nose and sniffed. 'Smells of lavender.'

'Yes, it was found caught on a lavender bush outside. Where was that kept normally?'

'I've no idea. Merry would know.'

The next moment Merryweather arrived.

'Merry, where are our egg cosies kept?' Gerry asked him.

'In the right-hand drawer of the sideboard, your ladyship.'

Deveraux turned round and opened the drawer. Inside, together with various napkin rings and table mats, were a number of white pristine replicas of the bedraggled object in Gerry's hand. He took one out. 'How many here normally?'

'Six, sir.'

'Sure?'

'Yes, sir. Unfortunately, I see them most days.'

'Only five here now.' Deveraux put the clean cosy back and closed the drawer. 'Any idea,' he asked, 'why that particular one her ladyship is holding should have been attached to a lavender bush outside, smeared with earth and stained with blood?'

'None at all, sir.'

'Lady Geraldine?'

'Search me. I can't find it in my heart to grieve over its suffering, either.'

'I don't know why everyone dislikes them so,' Wilkins said, 'I think they're very nice.'

'Mr. Wilkins,' Gerry said, 'you are very welcome to them.' She went to the sideboard, took out the five egg cosies and handed them to him with a ceremonial curtsy. 'Compliments of the management.'

'Why, thank you, your ladyship. That's very kind. I'm extremely partial to boiled eggs and these will be most useful.' He put them in his pocket.

'Well,' Gerry said, 'on this cordial note I leave you.' She tossed the bloodstained egg cosy to Deveraux and went out.

Merryweather said: 'Will that be all, sir?'

'Yes, thank you, Merryweather. But you might ask Mr. Felman if he'd kindly join us in the music-room in ten minutes.'

'Very good, sir.' Merryweather made for the door,

then stood aside to allow Sergeant Leather to enter before withdrawing.

Leather said: 'I've 'phoned the meteorological office. They estimate the rain must have stopped here at between two-fifty and three.'

Deveraux frowned. 'Within minutes, that is, of my coming back in. And as we already know nobody left the house before the window was broken at just before two-fifty, the information doesn't really add anything.'

'I suppose,' said Wilkins, 'that the most likely explanation is that somebody was running carrying it and either threw it away, or it caught accidentally on the bush and he didn't have time to stop for it.'

'And as it was kept in this room, the somebody must have been the man who went through this window – we know he spent some time here; we know he was running in the dark towards the lake. But why in heaven's name would he want to take an egg cosy with him?' Deveraux turned away and started to prowl aimlessly round the room.

'To carry something in?' Wilkins suggested.

'What could you get in it? Not a diamond necklace, certainly. And why would you want to carry *anything* in it?'

Sergeant Leather gave a discreet cough. 'Sir, the man might have been intending to knock or tap something – perhaps using the wire cutters as a makeshift hammer. The egg cosy would be a good thing to muffle the sound.'

Wilkins looked impressed. 'Well thought out, my lad.'

Leather flushed, then emboldened went on: 'He might have had it in his hand when he was disturbed, sir. Then he broke the window and jumped through, cutting his hand and staining the wool. He ran down the path as you say, and either dropped it or threw it away as he was passing the lavender bush. That would explain everything, I think.'

'Not everything,' Deveraux said. 'It's an ingenious theory, but it doesn't explain the earth and mud.'

'He might have tripped and fallen on a muddy patch with it in his hand, sir.'

Deveraux smiled. 'I wish I could agree with you, Leather, I really do. But look at it.' He handed him the cosy. 'If that's what had happened, you'd surely find a great heavy patch of mud on one side, and virtually none on the other. But you don't. The stuff has been lightly and evenly smeared over every part of it. It's been done deliberately and systematically. And I think I can prove it. Look at this.' He picked up the pot plant. 'Examine the surface of the soil. It's been disturbed. It's had something rubbed on it. See all those little marks? And if you look really closely you'll spot lots of tiny scraps of white wool.'

Wilkins took a magnifying glass from his pocket and together he and Leather closely scrutinised the soil. Wilkins said: 'Yes, you're quite right.'

'It doesn't mean your theory's all wrong, Leather.' Deveraux told him. 'Far from it. But it doesn't go far enough. He must have had a reason for deliberately soiling it. What do you think, Wilkins?'

'Nothing.'

'What do you mean – nothing?'

'I've stopped thinking about it. I reckon I've spent quite long enough on a dirty egg cosy. It doesn't mean anything.

If I keep on trying to work it out, I'll go crazy.'

Deveraux laughed.

'Leather,' Wilkins said, 'get it confirmed that that is human blood, and if so, which group. After that I'm going on with this investigation as though it had never been found. And now, Mr. Deveraux, we'd better get along. We mustn't keep Mr. Felman waiting.'

CHAPTER TWENTY-ONE

Mr. Felman's Bombshell

They beat Felman to the music-room by about a minute. He looked pale and tired when he came in, but there was a decisiveness in his manner that Deveraux hadn't seen before. When Wilkins explained what they wanted, he nodded briskly.

'Yes, it's true. I've got a lot to tell. But not to you two alone. Mr. Saunders must be present. I was just going to seek him out when I got your message.'

Wilkins cocked an eyebrow at Deveraux, who nodded and rang the bell again. When Merryweather came Deveraux said: 'We'd be glad of a few words with Mr. Saunders, Merryweather. Would you ask him where would be convenient?'

'I've no doubt he will join you here, sir.'

'Tell him I think he might like to have Mr. Thornton present, too,' Felman added.

'Very good, sir.' Merryweather withdrew.

They sat in silence for a few minutes. Then Richard and Thornton arrived. When everyone was sitting down, Felman said: 'I'm afraid what I'm going to say may be a shock. I hope, though, that it may not be an altogether unpleasant one. The truth is' – he took a deep breath – 'the man killed last night was not Martin Adler.'

A stunned silence greeted these words. It was broken by Wilkins. 'It said on his passport he was,' he remarked calmly.

'His passport was a fake. He was an impostor.'

'Oh no.' Richard breathed the words. He sank his head in his hands and closed his eyes.

'I knew it!' Thornton's normally pale face was flushed and his voice raised. 'He never rang true. Never. I was a fool! I let myself be convinced he was genuine, merely because I thought he had to be.'

'Would you mind telling us who he really was?' Wilkins said.

'I'm afraid – well, he was a spy.' Felman looked at Deveraux. 'You may have heard of him. His real name was Batchev.'

Deveraux drew his breath in with a sharp hiss. 'Not – not Stanislaus Batchev?'

'That's right.'

Deveraux's face was a study. 'I don't believe it!'

Felman shrugged. 'That's what he told me his name was. I have no reason to doubt him.'

Richard raised his head and opened horror-stricken eyes. 'I've been negotiating with a foreign agent.'

'Don't worry,' Felman said, 'he didn't get the information he wanted. His mission failed. His death was the best thing that could have happened, for both our countries.'

'What – what was he after?'

'What he kept demanding during the talks – full details of your government's commitment. I needn't be more specific, I'm sure.'

'Who was he working for?' Thornton asked.

'He didn't say. He was a freelance, apparently, who worked for the highest bidder.'

'I can guess who that was,' Richard said grimly.

'Whoever it was, they knew what they were doing,' Deveraux said. 'Stanislaus Batchev is – was – a legend in my line of work. He was probably the greatest undercover agent in the world.' He stood up suddenly. 'And I lived in the same house as him for nearly three days and didn't spot him!' In frustration he punched his right fist into the palm of his left hand.

'Perhaps it'll be some consolation,' Felman said, 'if I tell you I don't think he spotted you, either.'

'May I ask, sir,' Wilkins said softly, 'if you knew who he was and what he was after, why you co-operated with him?'

'It's very simple. His accomplices are holding my sister Anna a prisoner.'

Richard stared. 'Oh, my dear chap!'

'I think you ought to tell us the whole story, sir,' Wilkins said.

'There's not a great deal to tell. It started on the Orient Express. On the last night as I entered my compartment I was knocked out from behind. When I came round I was bound hand and foot and gagged, lying on the bunk. Batchev and another man were standing over me. Batchev had a gun. He told me Martin Adler was dead, that they'd stripped him of all identifying documents and thrown him out of the train when it was crossing a bridge over a river. Batchev said he himself was going to take Adler's place at the talks, that I had to go along with him to show him the ropes – and that Anna would be held in safety until the talks were over and he was out of England; but that if I didn't co-operate she'd be killed. He then showed me a photograph of her tied to a chair with a masked man holding a gun to her head. I had no choice but to agree. He had a full set of false identity papers, including a passport in the name of Martin Adler, but with his own photo and description. He needed me because I knew all the arrangements, and could brief him and help him along during the talks.'

'What a fantastic risk to take!' Deveraux said.

'Yes; he could only hope to succeed because the negotiations were being held here – in a rural area – and because Martin had been going to meet only two British representatives, neither of whom knew him by sight. If the talks had been arranged for London, where he'd be almost certain to run into politicians, diplomats, and journalists who knew the real Martin, he could never have attempted it.'

He turned to Richard. 'You can see now why the talks went the way they did. You thought he was just being deliberately obstructive in not giving you the information you wanted. But he couldn't: he didn't know it. He was hoping to find some documents which would help him among Martin's things. But I told him all the facts had been in Martin's head. So Batchev had to bluff. He knew he couldn't hope to keep the deception up for long. His only chance was to try to force you to give him what he wanted quickly, without offering anything in return himself. I was in a terrible quandary. I had to think of Anna's safety, but at the same time I couldn't risk letting Batchev get away from here with all that secret information. As long as you held out, it was all right. Thank heaven you didn't give way.'

Richard expelled his breath. 'If you only knew how close I came.'

'I was trying desperately all the time to work something out. He warned me not to attempt to inform our London Embassy, as a very highly-placed official there was in his pay. This may have been bluff, but I couldn't risk it.'

'Was there no way you could have got in touch with the Grand Duke direct?' Deveraux asked.

'How? A letter would have taken too long, a cable isn't private enough. I could have tried to put through a telephone call; but you can't lift the receiver and get the Duchy instantaneously: the operator calls you back. I couldn't be sure Batchev wouldn't be standing by me when it came. He stuck pretty close to me, you know. He actually warned me he'd be checking on me at intervals during the nights, so I couldn't even try to call then.'

Richard said: 'What's the position now? You've been through to the Duchy this morning?'

'Yes, I spoke to the Grand Duke himself and told him the full story. The police are going to start an immediate search for Anna. The only question is, can Batchev's death be kept secret until she's safe? If his men should hear he is dead, I'm afraid they'll carry out the threat and kill her.'

'Well, naturally,' Richard said, 'we ourselves wanted to keep the fact of – as we thought – Adler's murder quiet until all the facts were known and, if possible, the killer apprehended.'

'That's what I anticipated. May I ask who knows about it so far?'

'Apart from the people who've been in the house, only the Prime Minister, the Foreign Secretary, Deveraux's chief, and the Chief Constable of the county. Obviously none of them will have talked.'

'Neither will any of my men,' Wilkins said decidedly, 'nor Dr. Ingleby.'

'And I made Merryweather personally responsible for keeping the servants quiet,' Richard added. 'That leaves just my relatives and the guests. I don't think there are any real dangers there. I can vouch for George, Lavinia, and Gerry. Peabody wouldn't be where he is today if he couldn't keep his own counsel, and Evans is a private secretary – one of a naturally secretive breed of beings. That leaves Mrs. Peabody and Jane. Mrs. Peabody will, I imagine, be too upset about her necklace to be very interested in anything else. Jane's a sensible girl; I'll have a word with her. It's fortunate that the person who would be the biggest security risk is still asleep. We can be fairly confident the news won't leak out.'

'I know you're bound to worry, Felman,' he continued, 'so I won't tell you not to; but I'm sure your police will find your sister very soon.'

'And,' Deveraux added, 'although Batchev was quite ruthless, in matters like this he was strictly a man of his word. He wouldn't have been so successful otherwise. Nor would he employ men who would dare disobey him. If he told you he gave orders for your sister not to be harmed, I'm quite sure she hasn't been.'

Felman bowed his head. 'Thank you.'

Richard said: 'No matter what precautions we take, with all this police activity here, the press are sure to get onto the fact that something's happened.'

'The press will be told that we are investigating a jewel robbery,' Wilkins said. 'In that respect the Wraith will have served a useful purpose.'

Deveraux said: 'Are we going to tell the others about the so-called Adler's real identity?'

Richard considered before saying: 'I think we've got to. And about the fact – if they haven't already guessed – that he and I were engaged in important negotiations. After all, we are asking for their co-operation in keeping silent, and the truth is going to come out eventually, anyway. Besides, having introduced a spy into the house, I'm more or less honour bound to tell George and Lavinia about him. Gerry will undoubtedly worm it out of her father. That would leave only the Peabodys, Evans, and Jane in the dark – which seems both mean and unnecessary.'

Wilkins gave a nod. 'I agree, sir, and you're much more likely to get people's co-operation if you take them into your confidence.'

'Very well. I'll make an announcement at lunch. Now, is there anything else you want of me? If not, I must go and ring the PM and tell him the latest revelation.'

Wilkins looked at Deveraux, Deveraux said: 'What we hoped, Minister, was that you might be able to tell us something about the dead man that would throw light on his murder. Well, Felman's done that for us – with a vengeance. It changes the whole complexion of the case. We're going to have to start looking at it from a quite different angle. Unless, therefore, you've got anything additional to this that you can give us...' He paused expectantly.

'No, I can't think of anything. Can you, Thornton?'

'Nothing material.' Thornton said.

Richard got to his feet. 'Then, if you'll excuse me, I must go and 'phone Chequers.'

Wilkins coughed. 'Actually, Minister, there is something else, if you could kindly oblige: the Baroness de la Roche.'

'What about her?'

'We have so little information about her. Anything you could tell me would be most useful.'

'What – now?'

'Oh no, sir. Any time. After lunch perhaps?'

'Very well. There's little I can tell you about her life in recent years, so don't expect too much.'

'Shall we say two-thirty, then, sir?'

Richard, Thornton, and Felman left together. When the door had closed behind them, Deveraux looked at Wilkins and said: 'Well?'

Wilkins scratched his nose. 'I suppose we've got to check on Felman's story – find out if the police there can confirm that Anna Felman is missing.'

Deveraux nodded. 'I think perhaps my department can handle that most effectively from London.'

'Good. Can you get 'em to send down anything they've got on Batchev? Particularly names of known enemies. Blimey, there'll probably be hundreds. You know, Mr. Deveraux, I'm not—'

'I know, old lad. You're not sanguine, are you?'

CHAPTER TWENTY-TWO

Behind the Sliding Door

Before lunch Richard had a quiet word with his brother, and at the close of the meal – at which everybody except the still slumbering Algy was present – he stood up and made his announcement about the true identity of the man who had been murdered, about Felman's sister, the importance of the talks, and the necessity of secrecy.

Felman, of course, immediately became the focus of attention and sympathy. This did not seem to please him. He looked decidedly ill at ease, until Gerry, seeing his embarrassment, insisted on taking him riding.

Jane meanwhile went out to the terrace where Deveraux was drinking his after-lunch coffee. He smiled as she approached. 'Hail, fellow sleuth.'

Jane's answering smile was somewhat mechanical. She sat down and said: 'This man Batchev: I suppose he was a killer himself?'

'Almost certainly.'

'That makes it seem not so bad – that he should *be* murdered here.'

'It'll certainly be far less embarrassing to the British

government for a notorious spy to have been murdered than a distinguished foreign envoy, under their protection. If it can be put around that sinister bearded Russians or fiendish inscrutable Chinese were seen prowling around the area yesterday, so much the better.'

'What nationality was he?'

'Unknown. Probably from the Balkans originally, but I doubt if he had a home country in the true sense of the word.'

'He sounded just like an American.'

'Oh, he could assume any nationality almost at will. We believe he spent a couple of years in the States quite recently. He was hired by – by somebody to try to co-ordinate some of the dissident and subversive organisations over there. He travelled all over America, doing every sort of different job as a cover – reporter, waiter, actor, public relations man, lumberjack. He was very strong physically, much stronger than he looked. The FBI tracked him down eventually, and he only just got out in time. But he passed as an all-American boy for quite a time first. He had quite a lot of charm and was reputed to be very attractive to women. I don't know whether you felt that.'

'Oh, yes. He wasn't really my type, but I can easily see how a girl could fall for him. You seem to know a lot about him.'

'Well, he's been a bit of a legend for years. Actually, though, I 'phoned London this morning asking for any data we had on him. They rang back before lunch. So I've got it all at my fingertips.'

'I see. Must be interesting work, yours.'

'Police work, do you mean?'

Jane looked at him quizzically. 'If that's what you like to call it. Tell me, Mr. Deveraux, don't all Scotland Yard detectives start as uniformed bobbies? Would I have ever seen you, say, on point duty at Marble Arch?'

'Of course. Every February 29th – except in Leap Years.'

'That's what I thought. Don't worry, I'm not going to press the point. May I ask if you're making progress?'

'Some. But it's all very puzzling.'

'The business of the missing guns is strange, isn't it? Did I mention that I heard someone leaving the gallery just before I left my room in the night?'

'No, you didn't.' Deveraux looked interested.

'Sorry. It didn't seem frightfully important in relation to the other things. Is it?'

'I don't know. What time was this?'

'A few minutes before two-thirty. I suppose it must have been the thief?'

'Very probably. You didn't see anything?'

Jane shook her head regretfully. 'No. I looked in the gallery. Everything seemed OK. Then I made my way to the main corridor with the aid of matches. Suddenly all that bumping and banging started. It stopped, I heard the scream, and someone crashed into me. Then the whole place seemed full of movement and noises – people all round me. I'm afraid I panicked. I dashed blindly through the nearest door. After—'

'Which door was that?'

'The linen-room.'

'Where the secret passage comes out?'

'That's right.'

'There was nobody in there?'

Jane hesitated. 'No.'

'Sure?'

'Well, I didn't see or hear anybody. Mind you, I didn't switch the light on.'

'You said before that there were people all round you?'

'That's an exaggeration, I suppose. What I meant was that I heard several lots of footsteps – some close at hand, some farther away.'

'The close ones being the man who crashed into you?'

'Those first, but others after.'

'How close?'

'Oh, within touching distance – if I'd wanted to touch.'

'Man or woman?'

'I don't know. Certainly quite light enough to have been a woman.'

Deveraux leant forward: 'Jane, tell me – could they have either come out of or gone into the linen-room?'

He seemed quite unconscious of having for the first time addressed her by her Christian name. It didn't escape Jane's attention, however, and to her surprise she felt a sudden stab of pleasure. She had to force herself to concentrate on answering his question. 'I don't think so.'

'Why do you say that?'

'I – I don't know. I didn't hear the noise of the door opening or closing.'

'Would you necessarily have heard it – if it was done carefully?'

'Perhaps not. Is it important?'

'Who can say what's important? If we knew definitely that somebody used the passage last night, it might in the final analysis turn out to be a vital piece of the jigsaw. I'm only clutching at straws really.'

Just then Sergeant Leather approached. 'Excuse me, sir, Inspector Wilkins' compliments and could you spare him a few moments?'

Wilkins was waiting in the music-room. He said: 'I'm expecting Mr. Saunders along in a minute. I wondered if you wanted to be present.'

'Do you want me?'

Wilkins pulled at his ear. 'Frankly, no. You see, there may be aspects of his relationship with the Baroness that he'd find easier to discuss with me, an outsider, than with a social equal.'

'My dear Wilkins, you flatter me. I've got no earls in my family.'

'You know what I mean. You're an educated man, an officer and a gentleman, etcetera; you were staying here as a guest; no doubt you've got mutual friends.'

Deveraux gave a nod. 'I see what you mean. Perhaps it's a point. I'll steer clear.'

'Right.'

'As long as you know I won't be sticking my meddling nose in, you'll be able to be a bit more ruthless, push him a bit hard, eh?'

'We—ll...' Wilkins spread his hands.

Deveraux grinned. 'And you're the geezer who had the bally crust to say you'd be happier in the uniformed branch!'

After Deveraux left her, Jane remained sitting thoughtfully on the terrace for several minutes. She was casting her mind back to those few moments the previous night after she'd been knocked down. She closed her eyes and tried to re-live it all: scrambling to her feet, half-falling into the linen-room, leaning up against the wall, heart pounding, ears straining.

Yes. Jane gave a firm nod to nobody in particular. It might get her into trouble, but she'd do it. It was time she did something, anyway, and didn't just sit back waiting for other people to do things.

She went indoors and upstairs to her room where she collected her handbag. She returned to the main corridor, entered the linen-room, crossed to the wall, put down her handbag, placed her hands on the sliding panel, and pushed sideways. It slid smoothly back. Jane opened her bag, took out a box of matches, and struck one.

'Planning a little arson?'

The voice came quite without warning from behind her. Jane jumped and spun round, dropping the match.

It was Deveraux. He was standing in the doorway holding an electric torch. Jane gave a gasp. 'Oh, you idiot! You scared me half to death.'

He grinned. 'Sorry.' He came across. 'What's up?'

'Well, after I told you I hadn't seen or heard anything in here last night I started thinking. And I suddenly remembered that, although that was quite true, I had *smelt* something.'

'What was that?'

'Scent.'

'Really?'

'Yes, the Baroness's scent. She was wearing it last night. It's quite distinctive. Perhaps you noticed it.'

'I did indeed.'

'This passage is very cramped, as you know. It occurred to me that it's the kind of place where somebody might leave a clue – rub against the side, catch their clothing, drop something. I thought it might be worthwhile having a look.'

'You should leave that sort of thing to the professionals, you know. An amateur blundering in is just as likely to destroy clues as find them.'

Jane flushed. 'Oh, really! I am not an absolute fool and I'm not in the habit of blundering. This strange idea that a reasonably intelligent person can't carry out a perfectly straightforward task just because he or she doesn't do it for a living is beyond me.'

'All right, all right.' Deveraux raised his hands in surrender. 'I accept that you're quite capable of doing anything you set your mind to, and I apologise. Since you got here first I wouldn't dream of trying to stop you now. However, as you can see, I did have the same idea' – he held up the torch – 'so would you graciously allow me to collaborate?'

'You know,' Jane said, 'you've got an absolute genius for getting my back up. OK. May I borrow your torch?'

Deveraux handed it to her. 'If I may suggest: look very carefully round from the outside before you actually step in.'

'Would you believe that actually had occurred to me?'

Jane hung her bag over her arm, switched on the torch, leant in through the gaping black square, and shone the torch downwards – straight onto the dead staring eyes of Anilese de la Roche.

* * *

Jane uttered a half-strangled scream and hurled herself backwards into Deveraux's arms. He gave an exclamation.

'What on earth—?'

She turned and buried her face in his jacket. 'Her – Anilese – in there.'

'What!'

Deveraux grabbed the torch from her hand, strode to the opening and looked in. He gave a long silent whistle. Then he stepped into the opening and for a few seconds was out of her sight.

Jane leant up against the wall, her eyes closed, fighting nausea. She managed to regain her equilibrium, then opened her eyes to see Deveraux emerging from the passage. His face was grim. In one hand he was carrying an object draped in his handkerchief.

He said: 'She's been shot. Through the heart. Some time ago, I should think.' He came up and put his arm round her shoulder. 'Gosh, you poor kid. What an experience. I could kick myself for letting you look first.'

Jane said: 'I'm – I'm all right. It was just the shock – those eyes.'

'I know. Try not to think about it. You need a drink. Come on downstairs.'

Still with his arm around her, he led her out of the room. Jane had to admit to herself that, infuriating man that he was, he was capable of being very comforting.

'What's that you're carrying?' she asked.

He lifted his hand, shaking back the handkerchief to reveal a familiar-looking pistol. He was gripping it near the muzzle.

'One of the missing guns?' He nodded.

'Do you think she committed suicide?'

'In a fit of remorse after shooting Batchev? Be nice to think so, wouldn't it? Very nice.'

They went downstairs to the drawing-room, where they found Lady Burford and Mrs. Peabody. The Countess took one look at Jane's white face and jumped to her feet. 'My dear, what *is* the matter?'

Deveraux said: 'She's had a nasty shock, Lady Burford. I'm sorry to have to tell you that the Baroness de la Roche is dead – shot.'

He interrupted their exclamations by saying: 'Jane found the body. I think she could do with a little brandy. Could you tell me where the Earl is, please?'

'He's lying down. I'll send a servant to wake him.'

'No, don't bother, please. Mrs. Peabody, is your husband around?'

'He's on the terrace, I think.'

'Thank you.' Leaving Jane there, he hurried outside, where he found Peabody sitting, looking broodingly out over the park. Deveraux went up to him. 'Mr. Peabody, we've just found this.' He held the gun out, still holding it by the end of the barrel. 'Could you say if it's yours or Lord Burford's?'

'Holy cow!' Peabody reached for the gun.

'Don't touch it. Can you tell just by looking?'

Peabody put on his spectacles and peered at the pistol while Deveraux twisted it about in accordance with his instructions. Then: 'Yes, it's mine,' Peabody said. His face lit up. 'Gee, that's swell. What a relief! Can I have it now?'

'Not just yet, sir, if you don't mind. Thanks for your help.' Deveraux turned and walked rapidly off.

'Say, where did you find it?' Peabody called. But Deveraux had already disappeared through the french windows. Wilkins was not going to like having his interview with Richard Saunders interrupted, but it couldn't be helped.

CHAPTER TWENTY-THREE

Lady Geraldine's Confession

Like a ghastly re-enactment of the previous night, the fingerprint specialists and photographers, the doctor and the ambulance men came and went. Finally Wilkins went too. Only two constables were left on guard duty, Wilkins having arranged for a continuous patrol of the grounds until the alarm system was operative again.

The house party passed an uneasy evening, and with all of them by now pretty well exhausted, physically and mentally, everyone retired early.

The only significant incident took place quite late, when Deveraux was writing up a few notes in the music-room before going to bed. A knock came at the door and Gerry entered.

'Can you spare a few minutes?' she asked. 'I've got something to tell you.'

She crossed the room and sat down. She looked pale, all her gaiety and sparkle seeming to have gone. 'I want to make a confession,' she said.

'Splendid. To the murders, the robbery, or all three?'

'Just to withholding information.'

'I see. Will it clarify the problems or cloud them still further? Because if the latter, I'm not at all sure I'm strong enough to take it.'

'Look,' she said, 'I know you mean well and you're being flippant to try to make me feel better. Normally I'd play along. I'm a pretty flippant sort of person myself. But I don't really want to be here. I'm not very happy. So could you take me seriously, do you think?'

'Of course. Sorry. What is this information?'

'One thing first.' She lit a cigarette. 'I haven't told anybody else except Jane any of this, and I don't want to, if I can avoid it. I realise you may have to make it public. If so, I'll be sorry, but I won't object.'

'Good enough.'

'Well, as you probably know I was very suspicious of the Baroness from the start. I feel a bit rotten about it now she's dead, but I was sure she'd gatecrashed the party for a definite reason, and I didn't believe for a moment she didn't know Richard was here. I decided to keep an eye on her. Saturday afternoon I heard part of a 'phone call she was making.'

Gerry wriggled awkwardly. 'I know it's not quite – quite right to eavesdrop on one's guests. But the door of the telephone room had swung open – it tends to do that. I didn't hide or walk on tiptoe or anything. I just stood still as soon as I heard her voice. As it turned out, I didn't hear very much and certainly nothing incriminating. But it *was* interesting. The first thing I heard was, "I just thought I ought to warn you". Then "No, not yet: I don't want a certain party to see us together again now. I'm going to ask him to come to my room late tonight – about two-fifteen or two-thirty." Finally she said, "You cannot make me change my mind, so don't try – just send it." Then she rang off and I did a bunk before she came out.'

Gerry drew deeply on her cigarette. 'Of course, I couldn't let things end there. That night I sat up reading until two. Then this is what I did.'

Deveraux listened closely to her story without interrupting. When she finished, he said: 'Let me get all these comings and goings straight.' He picked up a notebook and pencil. 'You left your room exactly at two?'

'Yes. The stable clock was striking.'

'So you were in position not later than one minute past. The Baroness left her room – two – three minutes after that?'

'Not more than three.'

'We'll say at four minutes past. You followed her, lost her, and returned to the recess. You were away until about six minutes past. Then half a minute after that, the man arrived. You definitely couldn't identify him?'

'No: black trousers and black leather shoes was all I could see.'

'The Baroness arrived back about one minute later, having been gone three or four minutes?'

Gerry nodded. 'Just long enough to have pinched the necklace.'

'Oh, that's your theory, is it? Well, the more the merrier. But what about the Wraith?'

'Has it occurred to you he might have a woman accomplice?'

'It has. But he's never been known to have an accomplice in the past: and if he did, I can't somehow imagine him letting her do the actual stealing.'

'Then suppose the Wraith actually was a woman?'

'My, my, that's an interesting thought. If it's a possibility, I don't know. Everybody's always assumed the Wraith is a man. Whether the police – er, whether *we* know that for a fact, is another matter. However, to revert: at about twelve or thirteen minutes past the man left again?'

'That's right.'

'He held the torch low and just flicked it on and off quickly once or twice; finally, there was another arrival, just a few moments after two-thirty. This might have been the same man, or another. He knocked on the door and went in. Then you heard the rumpus in the distance, hurried along to investigate, and the rest is history.'

'That's about it.'

Deveraux was thoughtful for a few moments. Then he said: 'Can we just go through what happened after we released you? I'd like to see if we agree on sequence and times.'

They spent some minutes on this, finding that their recollection was virtually the same. 'I want to do this with Jane in the morning,' Deveraux said.

He studied what he had written for a few moments, tapping his pencil on the arm of his chair. 'You'd be ready to swear to what happened while you were in the recess, would you?' he asked.

Gerry looked startled. 'Yes – if I had to.'

'You may very well have to,' Deveraux said.

CHAPTER TWENTY-FOUR

'There's a Killer in the House'

The following morning Jane spent some considerable time battling with her pride. Eventually she won, and went along to the music-room. She found Deveraux there alone.

He looked up. 'Ah, just the person I wanted to see.'

'Oh?' She raised her eyebrows.

'Can we go over just what took place the night before last? I'm trying to get the order things happened, and the times, clear in my mind. I should have done this yesterday really, but finding the Baroness's body indoors makes it very important.'

'Well, I didn't have a watch, so I'll probably be a bit hazy about times.'

However, they managed eventually to get everything worked out, and in accordance with Gerry's account.

Then Deveraux said: 'Did you want to see me especially?'

Jane didn't speak for a moment. Then, with quite an effort, she said: 'I – I want to apologise.'

'What on earth for?'

'Oh, everything. I've been feeling very guilty about you.

First of all, after finding you half-stunned, instead of calling the Earl and insisting on your lying down, I let you go haring round the house, chasing criminals. Then, when we heard the man in the breakfast-room, I messed everything up – rushing forward like that, making a noise, fumbling with the knob, hesitating with the door part open. If I'd let you go first, you'd have probably caught him.'

'I doubt it.'

'There'd have been a good chance. But you never said a word of blame afterwards. Then again yesterday, I was an utter ass when we found Anilese – insisting on going first, then making a fool of myself, screaming and nearly fainting, like a silly little flapper. You should have told me it was my own stupid fault. But you didn't. So I'd just like to say sorry – and thank you.'

He smiled. 'Well, I won't say it was a pleasure.'

Jane said: 'Phew. I'm glad to have got that off my chest.' She grinned suddenly. 'Mind you, I still haven't forgiven you for nearly drowning me on Thursday afternoon.'

Just then Merryweather entered to tell Deveraux he was wanted on the telephone.

A few minutes after Deveraux came off the 'phone, Wilkins arrived. He was clearly bursting with news, so Deveraux decided to get his in first.

'Just had a call,' he said. 'Felman's story confirmed: his sister *has* been kidnapped. Now, what have you got for me?'

'Hold on to your hat: the bullet that killed the Baroness did not come from the gun you found by the body – *that* was the gun used to shoot Batchev.'

'It was *what*?'

'Used to shoot Batchev.'

'But – that's crazy! It just doesn't make sense.'

'I know. But there's no doubt about it.'

'Heaven help us. No prints, of course?'

'Yes, but they were badly smudged; quite unidentifiable.'

'Well, at least it takes us one step further,' Deveraux said. 'It means Batchev's killer came back indoors afterwards. So we can stop deluding ourselves with comforting theories about the Wraith or another outsider shooting him and getting away. We know beyond doubt that there's a killer in the house now.'

Wilkins sighed. 'I know.'

'At least it narrows the field. Anyone we can eliminate?'

'Not from the second murder. Virtually anybody could have killed the Baroness. We just can't pin the time of death down accurately enough to say who's in the clear. The doc says twelve to eighteen hours before he examined the body – or between ten p.m. and four a.m. the previous night.'

'We can narrow it a bit more than that, I think. Geraldine claims to have seen her just before ten past two, and I believe her. However, that can keep. Obviously, what we've got to do is concentrate on Batchev's death. We know he was killed between two-forty-nine and three am. It ought to be possible to work out who couldn't have done *that*.'

'Let's try. How long do you reckon it would take?'

Deveraux considered. 'Well, it wouldn't just be a

question of sprinting out, shooting Batchev, and dashing back in again. You'd get very wet. Even if the rain had stopped, your feet and legs would be sodden. So you'd either have to put a macintosh, and wellingtons on beforehand (and you couldn't know in advance that the rain was going to stop), or take time after the shooting to clean and dry yourself. Suppose we try a reconstruction?'

The next hour was spent in repeated re-enactments, by Deveraux, Leather, and one of the constables, of every possible permutation of the actions the murderer would have had to perform. Starting and finishing at various points, they went by every conceivable route, including the secret passage, to each possible exit, down to the lake, and back again; they either donned waterproof clothing and rubber boots first and removed them after, or went through the motions of drying and tidying themselves instead. Wilkins timed everything carefully. Afterwards, he dismissed Leather and the constable, and he and Deveraux returned to the music-room.

Deveraux said: 'How long?'

'Ten minutes absolute minimum.'

'And that's assuming you were quite reckless about the chance of meeting somebody – at just about the time people were starting to move about the corridors.'

Wilkins nodded. 'Then assuming Batchev was killed exactly at three, anyone who has a minimum period of ten minutes between two-forty-nine and, say, three-five for which they can't account must at this moment be considered suspect. OK?'

'Agreed.'

'And you've got the times everything happened fixed pretty accurately?'

'I believe so. I've been over the order in which things occurred with both the girls; at the time I looked at my watch frequently, and the stable clock was chiming regularly – I remember, for instance that it struck three just as Merryweather was reporting the result of his enquiries among the servants.'

'Good. So – who can we eliminate?'

'Well, both girls, of course. Neither of them was out of my sight for more than eight or nine minutes – and even that time is fully accounted for: Geraldine went to her parents' room, then to her uncle's, then to the Baroness's before coming down; Jane woke Thornton and Evans, spoke to them both, then found Fotheringay on the floor.'

'Right. Anyone else?'

'The sleeping beauty himself.'

'Is he still asleep?'

'Yes. The doctor had another look at him last night. He says the sedative doesn't seem to have done him any permanent harm, that he'll wake in his own good time, and we've just got to let him sleep it off.'

'Remarkable,' said Wilkins. 'Now, let's go through the rest.' He got out his notebook. 'First, Lord Burford.'

'He's in the clear. I was with him from two-fifty-seven until three-ten when we split up to search.'

'Lady Burford.'

'Oh, Wilkins, really—'

'We can't leave anybody out. Lady Burford strikes me as being a particularly ruthless type.'

'She's in the clear, anyway: came down with the Earl, stayed till well past three.'

'Peabody.'

'Not cleared. Evans is supposed to have woken him at about six or seven minutes past three – but he might have been outside and just that moment got back to bed.'

'And as Evans works for him and could be lying, we don't really know what Peabody was doing at any time before he and his wife entered the drawing-room later. Which means she's not cleared either. What about Evans himself?'

'I'm not sure. He entered the library not later than four minutes past three. Jane roused him as near as she and I can calculate at two-fifty-five. But it might have been a minute or so earlier – so theoretically he could just have had time. But in practical terms – well, I think I'd put down *cleared – query*.'

'Felman.'

'Not cleared. He was apparently asleep in bed at about two-thirty-five and again fifty minutes later when I went to wake him. Between, he could have been anywhere.'

'Thornton.'

'Cleared. Jane went to his room last of the three – after waking Evans and finding Fotheringay and trying to wake him. It must have been two-fifty-eight or fifty-nine by the time she got to Thornton's room. He was in bed. He couldn't possibly have shot Batchev by the lake before three.'

'Saunders.'

Deveraux didn't answer immediately: 'Cleared – I think.'

Wilkins looked dubious. 'Do you?'

'Well, Geraldine called him at roughly two-fifty-five. He arrived in the library at about seven minutes past three.'

'Twelve minutes. Longer than Evans.'

'All right. Put down cleared – query again.'

'I'd sooner put not cleared – query. That extra two minutes is important. On top of that, remember, he knows the house and grounds like the back of his hand, which windows open easily and quietly, and so on. He could get down to the lake and back much more quickly and safely than any of the others.'

'Yes, I can see that. But if he did, it means he knew exactly where to find Batchev – which implies a rendezvous.'

'That could be said of some of the others, too.'

'Only of Evans. Not Peabody or Felman. If one of them had been up to something, he could have been ready to take advantage of the first break-out to leave by another window immediately when the alarm went off. He would have had to know Batchev was out there somewhere, but given that, he would have had up to eleven minutes just to locate him.'

'Same applies to Mrs. Peabody.'

'I'm sorry, Wilkins, but I'm not for one moment prepared to regard Mrs. Peabody as a serious suspect. Peabody is a possibility – but only just. To my mind it's got to be between Felman, Saunders, and Evans.'

'And who's your favourite?'

'It ought to be Felman. Batchev was a man who'd killed Felman's pal, kidnapped his sister – and was in the act of selling out his country. It would almost count as justifiable homicide.'

'The drawback being the very fact that Batchev's men are holding his sister hostage.'

'Precisely. Would he risk harming Batchev, knowing what might happen to her?'

'He might. If he was a particularly fanatical patriot. Or if his sister means very much less to him than he makes out. Perhaps he hates her.'

Deveraux chuckled. 'You are the most dyed-in-the-wool cynic I've ever met. Here am I, a member of what's supposed to be a hard, tough, sophisticated service, and that possibility had never crossed my mind.'

'Got to think of everything,' Wilkins said. 'I don't think he did it, mind you.'

'Who do you fancy, then?'

'Oh, I'm baffled. I've had a good long talk with everyone here and I still can't see any way out.'

They were silent for a few seconds. Then Deveraux said: 'Anything on the Baroness yet?'

'Very little. She had no criminal record either in this country or France. After the Baron died she travelled a lot, all over Europe and America. Her home address was officially Geneva, but she'd only got a tiny flat there and she didn't spend much time in it. She arrived in this country ten days ago, and she's been staying at the Ritz.'

'What did she live on?'

'Her wits, I imagine. The late Baron didn't die a poor man; but nor did he leave her enough to pay for the amount of travelling she's been doing.'

'Did you get anything out of Saunders yesterday?'

'Not much. He knew her in France during the war, but he hadn't seen her since 1917. He thought she was dead.

Apparently a house where she was staying was destroyed by a bomb when he believed she was in it. He says it was a tremendous shock when she turned up here. He had no reason to think her story wasn't genuine. She told him very little about her recent life. They spent most of their time together after she arrived reminiscing.'

'What did you think of his reaction when he heard of her body being found?'

'Natural enough. Perhaps a little too natural.'

'Rehearsed, you mean?'

'I don't know. Politicians do learn to react in proper, set ways; perhaps it would be wrong to read anything into it.'

'Do you think he was hiding something?'

'Of course. Everybody hides something.'

'I mean, something really significant?'

'Yes.'

'Do you think you can get it out of him?'

'Ooh, I doubt it. He's a skilled politician. It would be too much to expect a simple country bobby—'

'Wilkins, you're a humbug. I think you're dying to have another go at him. And I think you should – now.'

'Do you really? Well, if you say so, I'll give it a try. But don't expect too much. I'm not sanguine, not sanguine at all.'

'Well, before you see him, I've got something else to tell you. It might be useful.'

He took out his notebook and, almost word for word, related the story Gerry had told him. When he'd finished he said: 'No conclusions from me – you don't need 'em. I'll leave you to draw your own.'

CHAPTER TWENTY-FIVE

Cross-Questioning of a Minister

Richard came into the music-room where Wilkins was waiting. Sergeant Leather, armed with a shorthand book, sat unobtrusively in the corner.

'Well, Inspector, what is it?'

'I thought you ought to know straightaway, sir, that the Baroness was murdered.'

Richard closed his eyes. 'No – no possibility of suicide?'

'No, sir; not unless someone found her body with the gun lying by it and deliberately replaced the pistol with another.' He explained what the ballistics examination had shown.

Richard looked dazed. 'It's unbelievable,' he said.

'Have you got any idea of who might have wanted to harm her?'

'None at all. I cannot believe anybody in this house could have done it. What motive could anyone have?'

'There you might be able to help, sir. Did the Baroness drop any hint that she might have met one of the other guests before?'

'No.'

'That any of them looked familiar to her – or reminded her of someone else?'

'No.'

'Did she refer to the other ladies and gentlemen at all?'

'Hardly. She said she was delighted to meet my closest relatives; how kind my sister-in-law was; things like that.'

'She didn't mention Batchev?'

Richard shook his head.

'And you never saw them together?'

'Never.'

'What would be your explanation of the Baroness having made a telephone call on Saturday afternoon, during which she said: "I don't want a certain party to see us together again now. I'm going to ask him to come to my room late tonight, about two-fifteen or two-thirty"?'

Richard's eyes widened and for a second he stopped breathing. Then he said: 'How extraordinary. To whom was the call made?'

'I would guess to her driver – the man she called Roberts. He was staying at the Rose & Crown, but he left shortly after the Baroness made the call, and took the five-forty-two to town.'

'I see. And what's *your* explanation?'

'My first thought, sir, was that the "certain party" she mentioned must be you. But who, I wondered, would that make the man she was going to invite to her room?' He paused, then waited, almost forcing Richard to answer the question for him.

'Well, presumably, since she does seem to have had

some connection with him of which I knew nothing, it would be Adler – Batchev, I should say.'

'Exactly how my mind worked, sir. But unfortunately, there's a snag to that.'

'Oh?'

'Yes. The Baroness said: "I don't want a certain party to see us together *again now*." That means the certain party had seen her and this other man together at some time. But you said you never had seen Batchev and her together. Do you follow me, sir?'

Stiff-faced, Richard said: 'I follow you.'

'I then wondered if you had seen her talking privately or in a clandestine or furtive manner to any of the other guests. Er, had you?'

'Definitely not.'

'It doesn't look as though you could have been the certain party at all, does it, sir?'

Richard didn't reply.

'Do you suppose Batchev could have been the certain party?'

'It's patently possible.'

'Then the obvious assumption would be that, er, you were the...' Wilkins broke off, looking embarrassed. 'I suppose the lady didn't by any chance invite you to her room that night, sir?'

Richard looked straight at him. 'Actually, she did.'

'Oh? Did she?' Wilkins nodded very slowly. 'I see.'

'I'm sorry, Inspector. I wasn't attempting to mislead you. Please note that I told you as soon as you asked me. Frankly, earlier I couldn't see that her invitation was germane to your enquiry.'

'Because you didn't go, sir?'

'I – I did go. But I didn't see her. She wasn't in her room.'

'Oh, really? What time was that?'

'Two-thirty struck while I was on my way along the corridor.' Again Wilkins gave his slow nod. 'You may have cleared up one mystery, at least. Mr. Deveraux heard someone crossing the landing going towards the west wing at just about that time. That would have been you, I take it?'

'I imagine so.'

'That was seconds before he was struck on the head from behind. You didn't hear any sound at all?'

'I did hear an indeterminate sort of scuffling noise, and a sound like somebody tripping. Certainly nothing to indicate a man had been attacked or was in any kind of trouble. Had I done so, I would naturally have switched the light on and gone to his aid.'

'What in fact did you do, sir?'

'I went on to the Baroness's room.'

'In the dark?'

'Yes.'

'Forgive my asking, sir; I'm sure you were preoccupied at the time, but didn't it strike you as odd that somebody was moving about behind you in the corridor in the dark? Didn't it occur to you to investigate?'

'Well, no. You see, the Baroness had been very insistent that nobody at all should see us again together that night. She made me promise not to mention it to anybody, and to come in the dark.'

'May I ask what your reaction was to that request, sir?'

'I thought it was a trifle strange. I imagined she was ultra-sensitive about her reputation.'

'Yes, of course. Very natural. And you were prepared to abide by her wishes even to the extent of refusing to risk being seen merely walking along the corridor – even though this entailed ignoring the fact that someone was prowling about in complete darkness in a house full of priceless jewellery and *objets d'art*? I'd like to say, if I may make so bold, that it's a real privilege to meet such a gallant gentleman.'

He didn't give Richard time to answer, but went on: 'Did you have any idea what she wanted to see you about?'

'No.'

'What exactly had she said?'

'Simply that it was very important she speak to me, and would I come to her room late, after everyone was in bed.'

'I'm sure you had a good reason, sir, but would you mind telling me why you didn't suggest to her that you talked down here – in this room or the library? That could not have damaged the reputation of the most susceptible lady.'

Richard didn't answer. Seconds passed. Then he seemed to sag. 'All right, Inspector. I give in. I had guessed there was a link between her and one of the other people in this house and it was this person she wanted kept in ignorance of our meeting.'

'Batchev – Adler as you knew him?'

'I thought it had to be him – or just conceivably Felman.'

'I know you can't tell me what took place at the talks,

but was it something that happened during them that made you think this?'

Richard nodded.

'The Baroness had been blackmailing you, hadn't she, sir?' Richard buried his head in his hands. He said: 'I can't expect you to believe this. She'd threatened to blackmail me. She brought up something that happened many years ago and told me she was going to reveal it if I didn't make certain concessions in the talks.' He looked up. 'But she withdrew the threat, Inspector. She spoke to me after dinner on Saturday. She told me that she couldn't go through with it, that I didn't have to worry any more. She also said that if I went to her room late that night she would explain everything. It was her insistence that I should come secretly which made me realise she was frightened of somebody in the house; it followed logically that it was almost certainly Batchev.'

'You assumed it was he behind you in the corridor when you were on your way to her room?'

'Yes.'

'So you deliberately hurried on?'

'Yes, in case he switched on the light and saw me.'

'What did you do when you found she wasn't in her room?'

'It first occurred to me that as she was mixed up with a blackmailer, she might have come to harm. So I looked quickly round the bedroom – in the wardrobe and under the bed – in case she had been tied up or knocked out – or worse. Then I merely sat and waited.'

'Did you hear anything outside the room?'

'I thought at one time I heard a distant sort of bumping.

It must have been my niece banging to be let out, but at the time I decided it was thunder.'

'You didn't hear the sound of the fight in Batchev's room?'

'No. You must remember that I was at almost the extreme end of the west wing and that sound does not carry easily through the doors and walls of Alderley. And then, of course, there was the storm.'

'How long did you wait there?'

'Six or seven minutes.'

'Then you returned to your own room?'

'Yes.'

'Arriving there at approximately two-thirty-eight?'

'About that.'

'You didn't see or hear anyone on your way back?'

'No.'

'Did you hear the burglar alarm?'

'No, but again I would not expect to. On the first floor it sounds only in my brother's bedroom. The first thing I knew about anything being amiss was when Gerry came to my room. I'd just that moment got back to bed.'

'Then you dressed again and went downstairs?'

'That's right.'

'But not for about twelve or fifteen minutes?'

'A little less I would think.'

'What did you do during that time?'

'After dressing, I just sat and thought – and worried.'

'I see.' Wilkins scanned his notes and tapped his teeth with his pencil. 'Just one more point, sir. On the telephone the Baroness referred to asking someone to come to her room between two-fifteen and two-thirty. You said simply that she asked you to come, er – when, Jack?'

'"Late, after everyone was in bed", sir.'

'That's it,' Wilkins said. 'Did she in fact mention the specific time, sir?'

'Yes, I remember now, she did. She must have thought he would be up until then.'

'You left it till the very last minute, sir, didn't you? In fact, you didn't actually arrive until a few seconds after two-thirty. I would have expected you to be more anxious than that to hear what she had to tell you.'

'I was. But I was sitting up in my room waiting for two-fifteen when I fell asleep in the chair. I didn't wake until nearly half-past two.'

'Ah.' Wilkins nodded in comprehension. 'Very understandable. You must have had a tiring day – with the negotiations and everything. Tell me, do you think Batchev could have known that the Baroness had backed out of the blackmail and that his scheme had failed?'

'Yes. He'd been asking for some quite unreasonable concessions. I played for time and told him I'd let him know later. He must have thought I was on the brink of caving in. Then on Saturday night, after she had told me her decision, I went to Batchev and informed him there was nothing doing. I think he was quite shaken.'

'Thank you, sir. I think that's everything. I appreciate your being so helpful.'

Richard stared. 'Don't you want to know about the blackmail?'

'Not unless you especially want to tell me.'

'I certainly do not.'

'Then I needn't keep you any longer, sir. If the sergeant

types out an account of your movements during the early hours of the night of the murder, you'd have no objection to signing it, I suppose? I'll be asking everyone to do the same.'

'I've no objection.'

'Thank you, sir.'

Richard left the room. Wilkins watched him until the door closed, then turned hastily to Sergeant Leather. 'Quick, my lad – go and find Lady Geraldine. Bring her here, sharp as you can – my compliments, greatly obliged, all that sort of thing. But don't let her talk to Mr. Saunders first. If he should try to speak to her on the way, stop him somehow – tell her I said it's desperately important she comes quickly – anything. We don't want 'em getting together and changing their stories before we've had a chance to get signed statements.'

CHAPTER TWENTY-SIX

Richard's Story

After leaving Deveraux, Jane felt restless and full of suppressed energy. She found it almost impossible to stay in one place, and began prowling aimlessly round the house and grounds, getting in the way of servants and gardeners. At last, feeling she would burst if she didn't do something, she went to look for Gerry. She couldn't find her at first, but eventually Merryweather informed her that Gerry was in the music-room – 'with the constabulary person, miss'.

Jane hung impatiently about outside until Gerry emerged, then pounced and demanded a game of tennis.

'Oh, darling, no.'

'Why not?'

'I don't think we should, with two of our guests just murdered.'

'Tommy-rot. What possible harm can it do them?'

'Nothing. It's just the look of the thing.'

'Who cares about the look of the thing! Come on, don't be mean. I just must have some action or I'll go mad.'

'Why don't you go for a ride?'

'I don't feel like riding. I want to *hit* something.'

Gerry sighed. 'Oh, all right. But I don't like playing you when you're in this sort of mood. You'll make mincemeat of me. I might as well play Helen Wills.'

Jane and Gerry had played four games when Richard strolled up to the court. He sat down on a bench and watched them. At the end of the set, won by Jane 6-0, an exhausted Gerry begged for a breather. They went across and sat by him.

'You seem red-hot today, Jane,' he said.

Gerry said: 'She's all keyed-up and she's taking it out on me.'

'Why's that?' he asked.

Jane shrugged. 'I don't know. All this happening at Alderley, I suppose. Spoiling the party. It's all wrong. Alderley ought to be a haven of peace. It annoys me to see it desecrated like this. I'm angry with the Wraith, and I'm angry with Batchev and with Anilese for bringing their dirt—' She broke off. 'I'm sorry, Richard. I shouldn't have said that. It was inexcusable.'

'That's all right, my dear. It's true. They were both involved in pretty nasty business. I had my eyes opened about Anilese. Which may be the one good thing to come out of this whole schemozzle.' He looked at his niece. 'You were quite right about her, Gerry.'

'She knew you were here all the time?'

'She did.'

'I was sure of it from the very start.'

'Why did she come here?' Jane asked him.

Richard had picked up Jane's racquet and was looking down at it, plucking at the strings. 'She came here to blackmail me,' he said.

Jane stiffened and Gerry's eyes widened. Gerry said: 'Blackmail! But she couldn't. I mean, what grounds – ?' She stopped short. 'Sorry'.

'What grounds would she have – what was she threatening to reveal? Well, it goes back a long way.'

Gerry was red-faced. 'Please, Richard, I didn't mean to pry.'

'I'd like you to know, Gerry. It seems as though it's bound all to come out shortly, and it'll be better if you hear it from me now. Your mother and father know the whole story, so it's only fair you should, too.'

Jane started to stand up. 'I'll leave you then—'

Richard put a hand on her arm. 'No, stay, Jane, please. You're one of the family.'

Jane sat down again, concealing the warm glow of pleasure his words gave her.

Richard said: 'It's not a long story. I first met Anilese in France in 1917. I was a very green lieutenant, only out from England six months. I was stationed at Amiens. We met at party given by the wife of some local dignitary. I thought Anilese was the most beautiful creature I'd ever seen. For the first time in my life I fell madly in love. For weeks I haunted her and eventually she led me to believe she loved me too. Almost immediately I proposed. To my joy, she accepted me. Our romance lasted three months, during which time I was promoted Captain.

'Then one day Anilese came to me frantic with worry. She had just heard that a cousin of hers, a young man called Pierre, with whom she'd been brought up and who had been like a brother to her, had been arrested on a charge of spying for the Germans. He had been tried and condemned to death. He was being held temporarily in a British army guardhouse, the local jail being full. Anilese swore to me that she knew Pierre was innocent. She told me a long story about suppressed evidence which seemed to prove it. She convinced me that a fearful miscarriage of justice was going to take place and she begged me to try to save Pierre's life.'

Richard paused. Then in a curiously flat voice, he said: 'Eventually, after much heart-searching, I agreed to try to help him escape. I need not go into the details. Suffice it to say that I worked out a plan to free him, which succeeded, and very early one morning I myself led him to a *pension* where Anilese was waiting. She had a change of clothes, money, and papers for him. She had obtained a motor car, and the plan was that she was to drive Pierre to Dijon, where he had friends who would get him across the border to Switzerland. I left immediately to return to my quarters, arranging to meet Anilese the next day, after she got back.'

Richard stood Jane's racquet carefully up against the side of the bench. He looked up. 'Five minutes after I left, the house was destroyed by a stray German bomb. They pulled Pierre's body out of the ruins the next day. Anilese was not identified among the victims, but there were a number of unrecognisable women's bodies brought out; and when I discovered the motor car she had borrowed parked a few blocks away from the *pension,* and when she did not turn up for our meeting the next day, I had to assume that she had been killed. She was officially listed as missing. I was the only person left alive who knew she'd been in the building, and as the body of the escaped prisoner had been found there, I could not admit I knew she had been there too – nor take too great an interest in the house or its occupants. There was naturally a lot of talk about the irony of Pierre's escaping the firing squad only to be killed by a German bomb, and about justice having caught up with him after all. I discovered then that he had unquestionably been guilty of spying.

'You can imagine my state of mind: not only had I helped an enemy agent to escape – and it was purely chance that he hadn't got away – but I had been responsible for Anilese's death as well – for had I not agreed to help, she would not have been in that house when the bomb fell. For a time I was absolutely consumed by grief and guilt. However, my part in the escape was never discovered, and I ended the war with an unblemished reputation.

'A year after the armistice I went back to France, to the town where Anilese told me she had been born and brought up. But nobody there remembered anything of her family. There were no records in the town hall, the church, or the school, of her ever having been there. I told myself that I had misunderstood her, and got the name of the town wrong. I went home, resolving, when I had a chance, to make enquiries about any other places with similar-sounding names. But somehow I never did and, for me, until last Friday, Anilese was dead.'

Richard looked from one girl to the other. 'Well, that's my story. Not very edifying, is it?'

'Oh, I think it is,' Gerry said with a sigh. 'I think it's a terrific story. Frightfully exciting and mysterious and sad.'

'Did she tell you over the weekend what had actually happened to her?' Jane asked.

'She said she'd left the house about four minutes after me to fetch the car while Pierre was changing. The bomb fell when she was about twenty metres away. She was knocked unconscious by the blast. When she came to, she was in a complete daze. All she remembered was that she had to get to Dijon. She started off on foot, then got a lift. She was put down at a crossroads about half way there, started walking again, then collapsed. She woke up in hospital – and found she'd lost her memory. That's as far as she got. How she lived for the rest of the war, when it was she recovered her memory, why she never got in touch with me – all this she had been going to tell me later.'

Rather tentatively, Jane said: 'Do you believe her story?'

'I don't know, Jane. Quite possibly some of it's true.'

Gerry said: 'Perhaps I shouldn't ask, but can we know what happened after she arrived here – when you learnt she was intending to blackmail you, and so on?'

'Yes, you can know. There's not much point in my trying to hide anything any more. I first learnt what she was really after on Saturday morning. We adjourned the talks and I took Anilese for a walk round the lake. Then she sprang it on me. She'd known I was here: she'd known about the talks. Her so called accident had been faked. And I had to make certain important concessions in the talks – or else. Obviously Batchev was behind it – though at first, of course, that didn't occur to me, because I believed him to be the real Martin Adler. I imagined some outside agency was trying to influence the negotiations. But even before I learnt his real identity I came to the conclusion, incredible as it seemed, that

"Adler" was behind it. How he found out about Anilese and me in the first place, whether *he* contacted *her*, or she him, I'll never know. Anyway, he must have previously arranged with her to hold herself ready to fake the accident if he gave the word. I think he'd anticipated after our very first session that his initial plan of bluffing and browbeating us into giving way was not going to work, and he 'phoned her on Friday afternoon. It must have been Saturday morning on the terrace, just after we broke off the talks, that he gave her the signal to start applying pressure.'

Gerry was looking puzzled. 'How did Anilese intend to prove you helped Pierre to escape? Wouldn't it have been just her word against yours?'

'Unfortunately, no. She had a letter.'

'What sort of letter?'

'A short note I'd written to her at the time, making the final arrangements for the escape – telling her to be at the *pension* with the fresh clothes for Pierre at a certain hour. It was something I'd naturally assumed she'd burnt within seconds of reading it. But no. Perhaps even then she saw its potential.'

Gerry gave an exclamation. 'While you were actually planning to save her cousin's life!'

'He wasn't her cousin.'

They stared. Gerry said: 'But—'

'I know. But that was one of the other things she casually revealed on Saturday. She'd never even seen the chap; she'd been paid by his associates to feed me the whole story. And there'd be only my word that Anilese ever told me he was her cousin at all. If the affair came to light, it could be argued that I was paid to do it – or was a German sympathiser myself.'

'But that could never be proved,' Gerry said.

'It wouldn't need to be, would it, Richard?' said Jane.

He shook his head. 'There'd be no danger of my being charged. Not now. But simply a public accusation of that sort would be enough to finish my career, if I wasn't able to clear myself absolutely.'

'Where's the letter now?' Gerry asked.

'I've got it.'

'You?' They spoke together.

'Yes. Anilese relented, you see. She told me on Saturday evening after dinner that she wasn't going through with the blackmail. She'd been going to leave here first thing yesterday morning.'

'And she gave you the letter back?' Gerry said.

'No, she told me it was in London. But she promised I'd get it back today. Sure enough, it came by first delivery this morning. It's postmarked 9 p.m. Saturday.'

Gerry looked blank. 'I don't understand.'

'Anilese's driver, this man Roberts, was obviously a close associate of hers. What their precise relationship was I don't know. But it seems that Saturday afternoon she made a telephone call. It must have been to Roberts at the Rose & Crown. I think she told him that the scheme was off, she was backing out, and she advised him to get away. Wilkins tells me that he took the five-forty-two to town. She must have given him instructions to get the letter and send it to me.'

'And you haven't destroyed it?' Jane said.

'No, and I don't intend to yet.'

'But it's the only proof you helped Pierre to escape,' Gerry said incredulously.

'It's also the only proof that I had no motive for killing Anilese. You see, I had to tell Wilkins of her blackmail threat – and that I went to her room in the early hours of Sunday.'

'So that was you—' Gerry stopped.

'What was me?'

She reddened. 'You – you that Mr. Deveraux heard going along the corridor.'

'Yes, it was. She told me to come along when everyone else was in bed, and she would explain everything. Only when I arrived, she wasn't there. The police could argue that I had opportunity and motive for her murder. However, if I can prove that Anilese didn't have the letter at the time she was killed, and that by then it had actually been posted to me – well then, it would be much harder for them to maintain I had reason to kill her.'

Jane was looking puzzled. 'But can you prove you received the letter this morning?'

'Yes. I was waiting for it and I made sure I had a witness. Peabody was with me when Merryweather brought it. He saw me open it. And I got him to initial and date the letter and the envelope there and then. So he can identify it and testify as to when I received it.'

'Would showing the police the letter clear you?' Gerry asked.

'I'm afraid not. It would weaken the case against me. But they might still suspect Anilese was holding other material damaging to me and that killing her was my only means of keeping it dark. So I'm not out of the wood by any means.'

CHAPTER TWENTY-SEVEN

Concealed Weapons

'You want me to do *what*?' Deveraux said.

'Take Mr. Peabody for a walk, and when he's at least fifteen minutes away from the house, ask him if he has any objection to our searching his suite and luggage.'

'But how do I get him to come for a walk?'

'I'm sure you'll think of something,' Wilkins said.

'And what reason do I give for wanting to search their things?'

'I would have thought that fabricating unlikely but convincing lies was much more your line than mine.'

'I hope that's a compliment. Very well: mine not to reason why. When?'

'Now, if possible. If he says yes to the search, bring him straight back and, unless I tip you the wink to the contrary, try to get him to take you straight up to their rooms without speaking to his wife and start right away.'

'What'll I be looking for?'

'You'll know when you find it.'

'And suppose he says no?'

'Don't push it.'

'All right, old man, I'll play along. But I'm not promising success. Why can't you ask him, by the way?'

'Because at the same time I shall be asking Mrs. Peabody precisely the same question. *You* only search if she says no to me.'

Deveraux achieved his end by the simple process of approaching Peabody when the latter was sitting on the terrace reading a copy of *The Wall Street Journal* which had arrived for him that morning, and saying ingenuously: 'Mr. Peabody, would you care to give me your views on this whole affair?'

Peabody was nothing loath. 'Sit down, son,' he said and waved to a chair.

'Well, sir, I've been sitting down most of the day. What do you say to a stroll round the lake while we talk?'

'Suits me.' Peabody got to his feet and they set off across the lawn.

The millionaire seemed positively eager to discuss the case, and was in no doubt that the murders and the theft of necklace and guns were connected. 'It's simply too much of a coincidence for all those things to have happened just about the same time, purely by chance,' he said.

'I tend to agree with you,' Deveraux said.

'Would I be breaching professional etiquette if I asked whether you're satisfied that one of the people presently at Alderley is implicated?'

'It's an inevitable conclusion.'

'And you've no doubt got your own ideas as to who it is?'

'Ideas, yes. Certainty, no.'

'But you won't want to be cluttered up with other guys' theories?'

'If you've got any theories I'd be glad to hear them.'

'Off the record?'

'Certainly.'

'Then if you ask me, Felman's your man.'

'Why do you say so?'

'He's not behaving naturally. He hasn't from the start. He's jumpy – on his guard all the time.'

'He's worried about his sister, of course.'

'Granted. But he's also worried about himself. I can feel it. Then again, what do you really know about him? It seems to me everyone else here has got a well-authenticated background. But nobody here knew a thing about him before last Thursday. He arrived here with Batchev. It seems to me he's the only one likely to have a motive.'

'Our problem is getting evidence. If we could only search his room, now...'

'Why don't you?'

'We don't know how he'd take the suggestion. He might try to claim diplomatic immunity; and the government wouldn't want us to press too hard. I'll tell what, sir: you might be able to help us in this.'

'How?'

'You're in more or less the same position as Felman. You're not a diplomat, but you are a distinguished foreign visitor. If we were to ask you for permission to search your rooms, and you agreed, then it would make it that much more difficult for Felman to refuse. How about it?'

'Say, look at that squirrel,' Peabody exclaimed.

'Deveraux glanced in the direction he was pointing. 'Oh yes.'

'Interesting creatures. You interested in wild life, Deveraux?'

'Not particularly. About this search...?'

'Oh, the search. Er, when would you want to do it?'

'As soon as possible.'

'I see. Well, it's like this. I'd rather you didn't. Not today, anyway. It's Mrs. Peabody – she wouldn't be at all keen to have strangers poking through her things. Of course, if it were really necessary, I could probably talk her into it, but I'd need time. Do you understand?'

'Of course.'

'That's mighty accommodating of you. Shall we start back now? My doctor doesn't like me to walk too far.'

Deveraux glanced at his watch. 'By all means,' he said.

'Why, yes, of course, Mr. Wilkins, you go right ahead and search to your heart's content.'

'Thank you, Mrs. Peabody. That's very obliging of you. I should really obtain your husband's permission, too, but he doesn't seem to be around, and it is rather urgent.'

'That's quite all right. Hiram would say the same as me. I'm sure we've nothing to hide. And you're welcome to do anything which might help get my necklace back.'

'Then shall we go up?'

'Oh, you want me with you?'

'If you please, madam.'

They went upstairs and while Mrs. Peabody stood

placidly by, Wilkins and Leather began a search of the suite.

It was in Peabody's dressing-room that they found it.

Wilkins was standing on tiptoe, trying to feel if there was anything on top of the wardrobe. His groping fingers touched something that moved, but he just wasn't tall enough to get hold of it.

He called: 'Jack.'

Leather came across and easily lifted down a small suitcase.

Carrie Peabody said: 'Those are just souvenirs of our trip – curios we've bought all over Europe. Do open it.'

Leather did so. He lifted out a number of ornaments, and then came to a folded Spanish shawl. Wrapped in it he could feel something hard and bulky. He unfolded it. Resting inside was an engraved Bergman Bayard pistol.

Wilkins gave a sigh of satisfaction, at the same moment casting a sharp glance at Mrs. Peabody. On her face was an expression of blank astonishment.

'Well, madam?' Wilkins said.

She spoke in a whisper. 'That's – that's Lord Burford's gun?'

Wilkins nodded. 'Can you explain how it happens to be here?'

'No.' Her face was white. 'I don't – I can't understand it. I – he must have brought it ba— brought it here.'

'Lord Burford?'

'Yes.'

'You say he planted his own gun in your suitcase?'

She gulped. 'I don't want to say anything else until I've spoken to my husband.'

'I think perhaps you're wise, Mrs. Peabody. I'll want a few words with him myself when he turns up. But now I must go and show this to his lordship.'

'In Peabody's room!' Lord Burford's eyes bulged.

'Yes, my lord.'

'But what the blue blazes was it doing there?'

'I don't know. It is definitely your genuine Bergman, my lord? Not a replica?'

'No doubt about it. But what does Peabody say?'

'I haven't seen him since, my lord. Mrs. Peabody—'

'What about her?'

'She claims you must have put it there yourself, my lord.'

'*What?*'

'Of course, the idea of your lordship hiding one of your guns in the luggage of one of your guests is quite absurd, but I had to put it to you as a matter of form. So if your lordship will kindly give me a formal denial, we can get on.' Wilkins stopped and waited expectantly. Seconds passed. 'Er – my lord?' Still Lord Burford didn't speak. 'Are you all right, my lord?'

'I've got nothing to say.'

'Nothing at all, my lord?'

'Not until I've seen my solicitor.'

'As you wish, my lord. Then I wonder if I could trouble you once more for the key of the collection-room. I want to have another look round in there after I've seen Mr. Peabody.'

Peabody stared. He opened his mouth. Then he closed it again. He gulped. 'I'm not saying anything,' he said.

'Nothing at all, sir?'

'No. I want to see an attorney first.'

'I see, sir. That's your privilege.' Peabody walked off.

'Well, well, well, well, well,' said Wilkins. Then he trotted off to the collection-room.

'Did you expect to find the gun there?' Deveraux asked, after Wilkins had told him everything that had happened.

'I'm always ready for anything, Mr. Deveraux. Now you can do me another favour, if you'll be so kind.'

Deveraux eyed him suspiciously. 'What's that?'

'Search Lord Burford's study.'

'You – you mean without his knowledge?'

'That's right.'

'You're joking.'

'No.'

'I can't do that! Suppose he caught me?'

'Leather will be placed in a strategic position where he can see if his lordship approaches. He will then rush excitedly up and say that I want to see him on a matter of the utmost urgency.'

'What'll you tell him then?'

'Let me worry about that.'

'Why can't I worry about it and *you* search?'

'Because I can't search without either his permission or a warrant. I can't see him giving me permission at present, and a warrant to search an Earl's premises wouldn't be got quickly. But you're not bound by the same regulations as me. And you're a guest here.'

'That makes it worse!'

'Look, Mr. Deveraux, we're trying to solve two murders. We can't afford to be squeamish.'

'You really think there's something in the Earl's study that'll help solve the murders?'

'Not exactly.' Wilkins tugged at his ear. 'Just something that's going to help complete the overall picture.'

'You talk as though the case were nearly over, and that you only had a couple of minor points to clear up.'

'Yes, I think that's true.'

Deveraux gaped at him. 'What on earth do you mean?'

'That you're quite right – there *are* still a few minor points to clear up.'

'A few!'

'Yes. It's been a very complicated business. Even now I can't explain *every* feature of it. I don't expect to. Hercule Poirot always says that when trying to solve a mystery, any theory you evolve must explain each isolated fact and happening: they've all got to fit into a harmonious pattern with no loose ends. Of course, I'm not in the same class as him – though they do say I look a bit like him – and I can never get that far. At the end of a case there's nearly always something left unaccounted for. But as long as I can explain the main outline of the crime and provide proof of guilt, I'm happy. I'm not an ambitious man.'

'Let me get this straight.' Deveraux spoke very slowly. 'Are you telling me you know who the murderer is?'

'I think so. Of course, I may be quite wrong. It wouldn't be the first time. But to me one person seems pretty clearly indicated.'

'But for the love of Mike – who?'

'If you don't mind I'd rather not say until I've got a bit more evidence. I don't want to look silly if I'm wrong.'

'But – I thought you were baffled.' Deveraux sounded quite stunned.

'I was. I still am about certain things. But you can help me towards getting most of it sorted out by a search of Lord Burford's study. So how about it? Will you oblige?'

Deveraux gulped. 'I'll do it,' he said. 'What will I be looking for?'

'You'll know—'

'Don't say it: I'll know when I find it. OK, let's get it over with.'

Twenty minutes later Deveraux entered the music-room, Wilkins looked up. 'Well?'

Deveraux brought a hand from behind his back. In it was a white silk handkerchief and in the handkerchief was an engraved Bergman Bayard pistol.

CHAPTER TWENTY-EIGHT

Inspector Wilkins Turns Poet

Deveraux said: 'Tucked down inside the armchair.'

An expression of pure self-satisfaction spread over Wilkins' face. 'I knew it,' he said. 'Mr. Deveraux, I deduced that that had to be there. That was pure reasoning, that was.'

'Old man, you have my heartiest congratulations. But how many more of these bally things are there hanging around?'

'No more. There were just the four – a pair of originals and a pair of replicas. This is the second replica. And if we find the fingerprints on this one that I expect to, I'll be a happy man. May I have it?' He took the pistol and handkerchief carefully from Deveraux. 'Thank you. I'll return your hanky later. I'm going away now. I've got to dig out a few more facts. I'll be back late this evening, and I hope then we can make an arrest. I'd like you to get everybody gathered in the drawing-room at around nine-thirty. Perhaps you and I can meet here at, say, quarter-to, for a confab?'

'Any instructions for me in the interim, chief?'

'I don't think so. You can spend the time thinking.

Keep an open mind and I'm sure you'll reach the same conclusion as me.'

'Wilkins, you couldn't give me a teeny weeny clue, could you?'

'You know, Mr. Deveraux, I thought you'd ask that. And I was working on a reply while I was waiting for you. All the following factors are important pointers. Ready?'

Deveraux nodded.

'Then listen carefully.' Wilkins cleared his throat, and to Deveraux's amazement declaimed:

> 'Mr. Deveraux's hearing,
> Lady Geraldine's sight,
> Miss Clifton's keen nostril,
> Batchev's sudden flight,
> Lord Burford's collection,
> Mr. Wilkins's height,
> And last but not least,
> The weather that night.

I've written it down for you. Here. See you later. So long.'

After the departure of Wilkins, the rest of the day passed slowly. The most notable event was the awakening of Algy Fotheringay. This, according to the footman who had been detailed to sit with him, took place at four o'clock. Algy opened his eyes, yawned, saw the footman, and said: 'Morning. Would you get me some tea, please?'

But by the time the tea had arrived, he had turned over on his side and gone back to sleep. Shortly after, Dr. Ingleby had called again. This time, after some effort, he managed to keep Algy awake. When Ingleby had gone, and with Algy sitting groggily up in bed drinking cup after cup of tea, Jane and Gerry stayed with him and very carefully and gently tried to explain to him just what had been happening during his coma. Perhaps not surprisingly, he seemed to have difficulty in taking it in, and the effort needed all the girls' patience.

At dinner which, in view of Deveraux's request for a nine-thirty gathering, was taken at eight, the atmosphere was strained; the imminent return of Wilkins hung like a cloud over everyone and conversation was stilted. Algy, up and dressed, still seemed in a half-trance, and kept asking where the Baroness had gone.

Deveraux was waiting in the music-room when Wilkins and Leather got back. Wilkins came in and flopped into a chair. 'My, we've had a hectic few hours, haven't we, Jack?'

'Certainly have, sir.'

'I've been telling him he's a chump not to get a transfer back to uniformed branch, but he seems set on staying in CID.'

'Don't keep me in suspense, old lad. Got the facts you wanted?'

Wilkins nodded silently.

'And?'

'I've confirmed nearly everything I suspected.'

'What about the guns?'

'The Baroness was shot with Lord Burford's – the one we found in Peabody's case.'

'And – you know who's guilty?'

'I believe so. How about you?'

Deveraux was silent for a moment. Then he said: 'I

think I do. Thanks to your verse. Tell me one thing: in more than one line, it's in a way *negative,* isn't it – referring to things absent or lacking?'

'That's it.'

'And the fact that Batchev's body was found in water is important, too, isn't it? The killer *had* to dump it in the lake?'

'Quite right.'

'In that case,' Deveraux said, 'I fancy I know most of what happened.'

Wilkins leant forward. 'Then let's reconstruct it all. Give me the name of the murderer.'

'The murderer? OK; perhaps I'll make a fool of myself, but here goes.'

Forty minutes later Deveraux said: 'Of course, we've got very little concrete evidence.'

'That's why I want to do it this way. It's our best chance of forcing the truth out. We can confirm the theory a step at a time. And Mr. Deveraux, I want you to do all the talking.'

'Oh no! This is your show, Wilkins. You got there first, right on your own; I wouldn't have tumbled to the truth without your clues. You must handle things.'

'But you can do it much better than me. I haven't got the personality to carry it off. I'd probably get muddled and mess it all up. Please do it.'

Deveraux gave a shrug. 'All right, if that's what you want. We'd better go in now: they'll be waiting. You know, one thing still bothers me.'

'What's that?'

'Even now we haven't got any explanation of that blithering egg cosy.'

CHAPTER TWENTY-NINE

Pistols for Two

Jane sat in the big drawing-room and listened with half an ear to the voice of Lady Burford.

The Countess was giving what amounted to a lecture on the history of Alderley from its erection to the present day. It was doubtful if anyone wanted to hear it. But she had been driven to it by the sheer impossibility of getting any normal conversation going. She was determined to give at least a semblance of normality to the evening, and if her family and guests would not co-operate, she'd do it alone.

It was a fine effort, really, and without it the atmosphere in the room would have resembled that of a morgue. Jane only wished she was capable of helping, of interjecting an occasional comment or question. But she felt far too tense. She looked round the room. So, obviously, did everybody else. Except Algy. He seemed on the verge of falling asleep again.

Jane looked at the clock. It was gone nine-thirty. Would that little detective never come? Did he really know who had killed Batchev and the Baroness? Who would he point to?

Jane let her eyes roam around. Almost impossible to believe that one of the people in this room with her was a killer. Yet there could be no doubt about it: two murders had been committed. Jane gave an involuntary shudder as she recalled again the cold dead eyes of Anilese de la Roche staring up at her from the floor of the passage. She told herself that within feet of her now was the person who had put the life out of those eyes.

Who – in heaven's name, who?

The door opened. Jane gave a slight start and the heads of everyone in the room swung, like spectators at a tennis match, to rest on Deveraux. He came into the room, followed by Wilkins and Leather. Jane scanned the faces of the three men. The only impression she got was one of nervousness. Odd – one never imagined that the policemen might be just as edgy as everybody else on an occasion like this.

Sergeant Leather sat down on an upright chair just inside the door and unobtrusively extracted a shorthand notebook and a pencil from his pocket. Wilkins edged himself sideways along the wall until he reached the corner; here his face was in shadow and he stopped and stood motionless.

Deveraux crossed to the centre of the room, just as Lady Burford said: '...and after *that* episode, I need hardly add, Sam Johnson was never invited to Alderley again. Yes, Giles, do you have something to say?'

'I have. Lady Burford. I'm sorry to interrupt.' He addressed the room at large. 'Inspector Wilkins wanted us all here tonight to try to clear up the very distressing events of the last few days.' He reached into an inside pocket, took out a small black notebook, glanced briefly down at it, then looked up and continued: 'During the early hours of Sunday morning two people died from gunshot wounds in this house. That is one of the few undisputed facts of the night – for exactly what else occurred during that period is extremely difficult to determine. One thing, however, is clear: many members of the household were up and about that night. In fact, outside the servants' quarters, it seems that until the time the alarm went off only three people had remained uninterruptedly in their bedrooms. Of the rest, two – Lady Geraldine and Miss Clifton – openly admitted being up. Others have, for various reasons, been less than frank about their movements. But only one of the people in this room committed murder.

'You all know that the man who passed here as Martin Adler was really a foreign agent by the name of Stanislaus Batchev.

'What you do not all know is that the Baroness de la Roche was brought here by him to assist in obtaining secret information from Mr. Saunders.'

Deveraux paused to let this sink in, then went on: 'Batchev's scheme was that the Baroness should make use of certain facts in her possession to exert pressure on Mr. Saunders. Mr. Saunders has confirmed that the Baroness did in fact threaten him with these facts.'

Every eye in the room turned towards Richard. He didn't move, but sat, his arms folded, his face impassive.

'It seemed at one time,' Deveraux said, 'that the only person with a strong motive for killing both Batchev and the Baroness was Mr. Saunders. However, he then informed us that the Baroness had withdrawn her threat – that he had had nothing to fear from her and therefore no motive for killing her. Against that, he admits going to her bedroom during the night.'

'And finding it empty,' Richard said, slowly and decisively.

'That's what you said, sir. You also stated that you arrived there at almost exactly two-thirty. Is that correct?'

'Correct.'

'What perhaps you do not know is that Lady Geraldine, who was concealed in a recess across the corridor, has signed a statement in which she maintains that the Baroness, having earlier left her room, returned to it before two-ten, and *had not left it again by the time you arrived*.'

Gerry gave a gasp. 'Oh no!' She turned a horror-stricken face to Richard. 'Richard – I'm sorry. I just didn't realise.'

'That's all right, my dear.' Richard's voice was very quiet and controlled. 'You were mistaken, that's all.'

'Were you, Lady Geraldine?' Deveraux asked her.

'I – I—' Gerry looked round desperately. 'I don't know. I don't remember now just what I did say.'

For the first time, from the dimness of his corner, Wilkins spoke. 'You said, Lady Geraldine, that the Baroness left her room at four minutes past two; that two to three minutes later a man entered her room, and that she herself arrived back about a minute after that; that the man left alone shortly before two-fifteen, and then nothing happened until another man – whom we now know to have been Mr. Saunders – arrived just after two-thirty.'

'Well, of course, it's obvious what happened.' Gerry spoke excitedly. 'The first man must have been Batchev. He killed Anilese and hid her body in the room somewhere—'

'I'm afraid Mr. Saunders has already stated that he searched the room immediately on entering it. The Baroness's body was not there.'

Gerry faltered. 'Well, perhaps – perhaps he didn't look carefully enough. And what I say would explain Batchev's flight. He had to get away from the house as quickly as possible without anybody knowing. He tried to put the alarm out of action in the breakfast-room. Then, when we disturbed him he panicked, broke the window and jumped out.'

'Then,' Deveraux asked quietly, 'who shot Batchev? And who moved the Baroness's body to the secret passage?'

Gerry sat quite still. She stared at Deveraux, then at Richard, before sinking down into her chair and turning her head away.

'Isn't this a more likely explanation?' Deveraux spoke in a silky smooth voice. 'That the Baroness left her room and stole a gun for protection from Lord Burford's collection. She arrived back to find Batchev waiting for her, wanting to know the outcome of her attempt to blackmail Mr. Saunders. She told him then that she was not going to co-operate with him any more – and that if he didn't leave the house she would expose him as an impostor. She had the gun, so Batchev could do nothing to her. He left hurriedly to try to get out without setting off the alarm. Then Mr. Saunders arrived in the Baroness's room. She told him she had been collaborating with Batchev, but was going to no longer, that she wasn't interested in secret information – *but that she was still going to blackmail him for her own benefit*. Not for information, but for money. There was a quarrel. She did not fear Mr. Saunders, so was off her guard. He managed to grab the gun. It went off. The Baroness was dead. He concealed her body in the secret passage – by that time Lady Geraldine had left her vantage point. Then he went hunting for Batchev: because he knew Batchev had the same damaging information about him as the Baroness had. He was looking for him at the same time as Lady Geraldine, Miss Clifton and I were searching the ground floor. He was perhaps in the next room when Batchev broke the window. He realised at once what had happened. He probably had a torch. He shone it through the window and actually saw Batchev running away. The alarm had already gone off, so he was able to open the window and go after him without being heard. He caught up with him by the lake, shot him, returned immediately and got back to his room before Lady Geraldine arrived to tell him what had happened. After she'd left, and before coming downstairs, he put the gun in the passage near the Baroness's body.'

Deveraux looked straight at Richard. 'What do you think of that reconstruction, Minister?'

Jane watched Richard, her heart in her mouth, and her admiration for him had never been greater as he remained outwardly quite unmoved, an expression of untroubled detachment on his face. Slowly he turned to meet Deveraux's gaze full on. Then a slight smile touched his lips. 'Plausible,' he said, 'except that you know quite well there's not a word of truth in it.'

Before Deveraux could reply the voice of Wilkins came again from the corner. 'No, sir. That's not quite so. There is some truth in it, though it does leave a number of questions unanswered. And although we didn't really think so, it just *might* have been all true. I asked Mr. Deveraux to put it to you like that to gauge your reaction. I'm satisfied now that that reconstruction is largely false.'

Richard closed his eyes and bowed his head. There was a sudden reduction of tension in the room. Jane realised she'd been holding her breath, and she let it out slowly through clenched teeth.

Gerry spoke with a catch in her voice. 'I think you're a couple of beasts.'

To her own surprise, Jane found herself speaking. 'There's something you all ought to know.' She flushed, as she saw every eye turn to her, but carried on: 'Perhaps it isn't my place to say this, but I'm the only person outside the family who knows it, and if I don't nobody will. The grounds for the blackmail were very flimsy. Richard has never been dishonest, or unpatriotic, or immoral. It was just a case of misplaced loyalty – a long time ago.'

'Thank you, Jane.' Richard spoke very softly, without looking up.

Deveraux continued. 'So, if my previous reconstruction is largely false, what really happened? As you all know, Batchev was killed by a bullet from a Bergman Bayard pistol, the property of Mr. Peabody, this gun later being found by the body of the Baroness. There were fingerprints on it, but they were badly smudged and couldn't be identified. The Baroness was shot with a similar gun owned by Lord Burford, which was later discovered concealed in Mr. Peabody's room. Neither Lord Burford nor Mr. Peabody was able to account for the movement of these guns, though Mrs. Peabody claimed that Lord Burford had planted his own gun in her husband's case. Lord Burford refused either to confirm or deny this. However, what his lordship has told nobody is that sometime around two-ten on Sunday morning, he left his bedroom, went silently to Mr. Peabody's dressing-room, *took Mr. Peabody's pistol and replaced it with a replica of his own.* That is so, is it not, my lord?'

Lord Burford did not answer. To Jane, it seemed he was incapable of speaking. He simply stared at Deveraux and slowly went red.

'It would be advisable to tell the truth, Lord Burford.'

At last the Earl managed to reply. 'Course I didn't. Certainly not. Ridiculous idea.'

'I suggest you did, Lord Burford. I further suggest that you took Mr. Peabody's gun to Batchev's room and forced him to go with you. I suggest that you – as you alone could do – have had the alarm system modified, so that there is one way – known only to you – of leaving the building without setting it off. You shot Batchev, returned to the house and killed the Baroness, who had left her room in the darkness unseen by your daughter. You concealed her body in the secret passage and left Peabody's gun lying near the body in order to incriminate him – a man you hate because you know his collection is superior to your own.'

Lord Burford gave a squawk. 'No! I didn't! I didn't. I tell you. I didn't shoot anybody. Why should I? I—'

'Family pride, Lord Burford. You overheard Batchev and the Baroness discussing the blackmail of your brother and you were determined not to let his career be ruined by a pair of foreigners—'

'No, it's not true!' Lord Burford was positively squeaking by now. 'I knew nothing about the blackmail. I thought Anilese was a lovely gal, Adler – Batchev – a delightful feller. I took Peabody's gun – I admit that—'

'Ah!' Deveraux pounced. 'You did?'

'Yes – yes.'

'What for – if not to shoot someone?'

'Just to show to Trimble Greene – another collector. Wanted him to think I owned the pair. Was only going to keep it until September, then send it on to Peabody in the States, in time for the New York exhibition. Chap who sold me my original sold me the replica as well. Said there'd originally been a pair, but they'd got split up and someone had had the replica made so there'd be a pair again. I thought it might be good enough to fool Peabody, so long as he didn't look at it too closely.'

'George!' The horrified exclamation came from Lady Burford. 'George – I can't believe my ears! You took Mr. Peabody's gun? You stole from your own guest! I've never been so ashamed in my life!'

'I'm sorry, my dear. I really don't know what came over me.'

'I should hope temporary insanity, George. It's the kindest explanation.' She turned towards Peabody. 'Mr. Peabody, I don't need to say—'

Deveraux coughed. 'Lady Burford, I'm sorry to interrupt yet again, but that really must keep. This is a murder enquiry. Lord Burford, let me get this straight: you say you left your replica in the carrying-case in Mr. Peabody's dressing-room and took his original away. What did you do with it?'

'Locked it in the safe in my study.'

'Then what did you do?'

'Went back to bed.'

'At what time?'

'I got back in my room just after twelve minutes past two.'

'How can you explain the gun being found by the Baroness's body?'

'I can't. I've been worried stiff about it. I swear to you, Deveraux, that I killed nobody—'

'I know, Lord Burford. We never thought you did. But I had to find some means of persuading you to admit to the – the borrowing of Mr. Peabody's pistol.'

Lord Burford mopped his face with his handkerchief. 'Gad,' he said.

'Now,' Deveraux said, 'we still have to explain how your gun came to be wrapped up in Mr. Peabody's shawl, how another replica found its way into the display stand in the collection-room – and how your own replica got from Mr. Peabody's carrying-case where you left it, to the armchair in your study, where I found it this afternoon.'

Lord Burford stared. 'You found it there?'

'Yes. Have you an explanation, Lord Burford?'

The Earl shook his head blankly.

'Then,' said Deveraux pleasantly, 'I think it would be reasonable to ask if Mr. Peabody has an explanation.' He turned to the Texan. 'Well, Mr. Peabody?'

Jane noticed that whereas Lord Burford had gone red when Deveraux had switched his attention to him, Mr. Peabody was now a pale shade of green. 'I – er—' he said.

'Mr. Peabody.' And this time Deveraux snapped the

name. 'Did you go to the collection-room in the early hours of Sunday, remove Lord Burford's pistol and replace it with a replica of your own?'

Peabody gulped, then gave a single, jerky nod.

'Hiram!' Mrs. Peabody stared at her husband in horror. 'What are you saying?'

'I put it to you,' Deveraux rapped, 'that you took that gun and used it to shoot Stanislaus Batchev.'

'No, sir, I most certainly didn't.'

'You know that it was used for that purpose?'

'Yes, but—'

'How do you explain that?'

'I can't.'

'I recommend that you try, Mr. Peabody. I think you'd be wise to make a clean breast of the whole thing. Why did you take the gun, if not to kill Batchev?'

'I—' Peabody closed his eyes for two seconds. 'I wanted it to put with mine so I could exhibit the pair at the New York exhibition. Naturally, I was intending to send it back immediately after. The guy who sold me the gun sold me the replica, too, as a curiosity. I figure now both replicas must have been made when the two originals were still together as a pair – perhaps for insurance reasons, perhaps by a crook aiming to do a switch. Anyway, sometime, somehow the four got mixed up, and each original got itself paired up with a replica. I'd intended to mention my replica to the Earl, but the shock of seeing his original drove it out of my mind. Then later I got to thinking that maybe my replica would fool him for a few weeks, so long as he didn't examine it too closely. I thought about making the switch during the day time, but I figured if it vanished then, I'd be the chief suspect, as everyone knew I was in and out of the room all the time, and it would be best to do it at night. So during the thunderstorm I just hustled along to the collection room with my replica—'

'What time was that?' Deveraux interjected.

'Just gone five-and-twenty after two.'

'I see. Go on please.'

'There's not much else to tell. I switched the guns, hurried back to my room, and went to bed. I put the pistol under my pillow. I didn't put it in my suitcase till the next morning. To tell the truth, I found I'd taken more out of myself than I'd realised. I suppose I hurried more than I'm accustomed to, and on top of that there was the tension. My heart was beating like a steam-hammer. I don't remember anything else till John woke me.'

'How long were you in the gun room?'

'A matter of seconds – just in and out again.'

Deveraux glanced at Jane. 'Now we know who it was you heard closing the gallery door.' He turned back to Peabody. 'Mrs. Peabody didn't wake up during all this?'

'Er, no, I guess not.'

'Is that right, Mrs. Peabody? You slept right through?'

Carrie Peabody looked flustered. 'Why – er, I, that is—' She took a deep breath. 'No, I didn't.'

'Because you'd already left the room, hadn't you. Mrs. Peabody?'

She nodded.

'I'm sorry,' Peabody said. 'I didn't mean to mislead you, but I figured it wouldn't look so good, Carrie being out of the room at the time of the murders. Truth is, I woke up and saw her leaving the room. I guessed she was going to the bathroom and it occurred to me it would be a good time to get the Earl's gun without her knowing. That's why I hurried so. I got back into bed before she returned. Sorry, honey,' he added to his wife.

'I see,' Deveraux said. 'But you hadn't gone to the bathroom, had you, Mrs. Peabody?'

Carrie glanced sideways at her husband, then shook her head again.

'Where had you gone?'

'Down – downstairs.'

'Where precisely?'

'To the Earl's study.'

'What for?'

She looked up. 'To get rid of the gun I'd seen Lord Burford putting in Hiram's carrying-case.'

Peabody gave a gasp. 'You did *what?*'

'Why?' Deveraux asked.

'Well, heavens to Betsy, why do you think? Listen, the thunderstorm had kept me awake for an hour or more. Hiram had gone to sleep. So I turned on my bedside light and read for a while. Then I started to get drowsy and decided to turn out the light. I looked at the clock first. It was exactly nine minutes after two. I hadn't had the light out for more than a few seconds when I heard the door from the dressing-room to the corridor open. Then I heard footsteps in the dressing-room. I decided to investigate. I got out of bed and crept to the adjoining door, which we'd left ajar. I saw Lord Burford. He had a torch. He took a pistol from the pocket of his robe and put it in the case where Hiram kept his new gun. I must have just missed seeing him *take* Hiram's gun. Then he went out of the room. I was petrified. I couldn't think just what he was up to. I went across to the case and saw that the gun he'd put there was exactly the same as Hiram's own – in fact, it might actually be his own. I was in a complete quandary. For some reason, Lord Burford had either planted his own gun on Hiram or had taken Hiram's gun earlier and had now replaced it. I couldn't think of any ordinary reason Lord Burford would do that.'

'But for Pete's sake, honey, why didn't you wake me?' Her husband stared at her, baffled.

'I didn't want to worry you, Hiram. Not with your cardiac condition. And you were enjoying your time here so much, I didn't want to spoil it for you by getting you suspicious and uneasy, perhaps without cause. Anyway, for about quarter of an hour I just dithered. Then I acted very stupidly. But I've read lots of mystery stories, and when one person plants a gun on another, he's never up to any good. Then we'd been warned about the Wraith coming after my diamonds and we had the Baroness, obviously an adventuress, arriving out of the blue and foreign diplomats and the whole atmosphere of Alderley and some of the Earl's ancestors none too scrupulous about how they treated guests in the old days so I've read and I suppose I'd gotten sort of crime-minded – so I decided I'd just plant the gun back on the Earl and if it turned out the next day it was just a joke or something no harm would have been done but if anything out of the ordinary *had* occurred Hiram would be out of it.'

Mrs. Peabody stopped talking and took a breath. She looked round the room, apparently satisfied herself that everyone was paying attention, and started off again.

'I couldn't decide where to leave the gun. I wanted it to be a room which was specifically the Earl's domain. Hiram had been in and out of the gun-room all the time and had the key, so I didn't want to put it there. Eventually I made up my mind just to put it in Lord Burford's study. I made my way downstairs, lighting my way with matches. I went to the study and pushed the pistol down inside the armchair.'

'What time was that?'

'The clock struck two-thirty just as I was leaving the study. I was going across the hall to the stairs when the match blew out and I found there were no more in the box. I started to grope my way upstairs in the dark. I hadn't gone up more than about six steps when I heard a noise at the top – first a sort of scuffling, then a louder noise like furniture being overturned. Well, I can tell you, I just froze. A few seconds later I had one of the biggest shocks of my life. Somebody came down the stairs quite quietly and brushed against me without any warning.'

'And you screamed,' Deveraux said.

'Why, yes. I was just so startled. If I'd known he had my jewels, though, I wouldn't have just screamed, I'd have gone after him.'

'You think the man who brushed against you was the thief?'

'Why, surely. He must have bided his opportunity until both Hiram and I were out of the room, don't you think?'

'Perhaps. What happened after you screamed?'

'I just blundered up to my bedroom in the dark, tumbled into bed and went straight to sleep. I may have blacked out. The next thing I remember is Hiram waking me and telling me my necklace had gone. I guess that's about everything. Naturally, ever since I learnt of the murders I've felt terrible. I have to admit I've thought the Earl must have done them, but I had no way of proving it and I was sure nobody would believe me if I reported what I saw. Anyway, I'd just like to apologise to everybody: to you, Mr. Deveraux, and you Inspector, if you're still over there, for not telling the truth before and I truly hope I haven't confused you too much. And to Lord and Lady Burford, for the way Hiram and I have both behaved under your roof. I really am very ashamed.'

'My dear, you have no occasion whatsoever to apologise to us,' Lady Burford said decisively. 'I think you behaved quite reasonably in the circumstances. It is we who should apologise to you. The very idea of George skulking into your rooms in the middle of the night...'

'Oh, but Hiram stole his most treasured possession.'

'George stole *his* most treasured possession first.'

Suddenly Lord Burford banged on the arm of his chair and gave a roar. 'Good gad, I've never heard so much nonsense in my life! Nobody stole anything from anybody. Peabody's was a quite legitimate ruse and I don't hold it against him for a moment.'

'Well said, Earl.' Peabody nodded vigorously. 'Ladies just don't understand these things. All's fair in the collecting game. If my wife had only woken me, I'd have known at once what was going on and told her to stop worrying.'

'Peabody, I want—'

'Call me Hiram, Earl.'

'Very well, Hiram. You must call me George. Hiram – I

want to lend you my Bergman Bayard for the New York exhibition.'

'I was going to tell you to keep mine to show General Trimble Greene, George. I'm sure—'

'Gentleman, please.' Deveraux interrupted rather desperately. 'Did either of you – or you, Mrs. Peabody – see, hear, or do anything else other than what you've told me?' He glanced from one to the other and saw three shaking heads. 'Very well,' he said. 'Having got all that out of the way, perhaps we can now start dealing with some real crime.'

CHAPTER THIRTY

Nightmare

'I now want to turn,' Deveraux said, 'to another of the puzzling incidents of the night: the fight in Batchev's room. This was something which seemed quite unaccountable. Why should *both* the men involved have wanted to remain undetected? Why didn't the one who had been attacked call for help? One explanation which occurred to me was that one of the fighters was the murderer – and the other the Wraith, who had somehow gone into Batchev's room by mistake. But he couldn't, at almost the same time, have been taking the diamonds from Mrs. Peabody's room, then running downstairs, brushing against her in the dark. One thing we do know is that a few seconds after the fight stopped, someone cannoned into Lady Geraldine in the west corridor. It was obviously someone who wanted to get away from the scene undetected. No one who wanted actually to get out of the *house* would go that way – he'd turn towards the main stairs; in fact, only someone who had a room in the west wing would have occasion to go that way. And only one man did.'

Deveraux turned to where Felman was sitting. 'Felman, you told Inspector Wilkins that you went early to bed on

Saturday night and slept until I roused you just before three-fifteen. That was a lie. At two-thirty you were fighting in Batchev's room.'

Felman seemed carefully to weigh his reply. Then he gave a shrug. 'Well, if you can call it fighting. It was mostly sound and fury, signifying nothing. No one got hurt.'

'It was you who shut me in the cupboard!' Gerry exclaimed indignantly.

Felman bowed his head in her direction. 'I regret to plead guilty, Lady Geraldine. My humble apologies. I used the minimum force. But it didn't suit my purpose to be discovered just then.'

'Maybe not then,' Deveraux said, and his voice was dangerously soft, 'but I wonder why you've kept quiet until now. More than anybody, you had a good excuse for being there: you knew Batchev to be a ruthless spy, who had killed your superior and friend, who had kidnapped Anna, and who was attempting to obtain secret information endangering the safety of your country. It would be quite reasonable for you to have been in his room – perhaps looking for incriminating evidence. The fact that his men were holding your sister would protect you from suspicion of murdering him yourself, wouldn't it?'

'Yes, but—'

'But for the fact that they are not holding *your* sister at all – because you are not Nicholas Felman. Is that what you were going to say?'

For seconds the man they'd known as Felman didn't move a muscle. Then: 'You're right,' he said. 'I'm not Felman. I'm Martin Adler.'

* * *

'Yesterday morning,' the real Martin Adler said, 'I told you how Martin Adler was killed on the Orient Express by Batchev and his men. That story was true in every particular but one: it was really Nick Felman who died – though Batchev believed he had killed me.

'The idea originally came from our security service back home. There was a fear that an attempt would be made to stop me reaching this country. The Grand Duke and his advisers seemed to think that my presence here was vital to the success of these talks. So it was suggested that Nick and I switch identities for the trip. Special passports were issued to us. Everybody – including Nick – thought it was a good idea. Except me, that is: I agreed to go along with it just to keep them all happy, but only because I didn't for one moment believe there was any real danger. If I had, I wouldn't have let Nick face it instead of me. As it turned out, they were right and I was wrong. Batchev and his men killed Nick, believing they were killing Martin Adler. I was forced to come along here and watch Batchev masquerade as me, and at the same time masquerade as Nick Felman myself. It was a most wearing – and very weird – experience. Every time anybody here asked me a question about my past life, I had to answer as though I were Nick.'

He looked at Lady Burford. 'For instance, I've never been to Stockholm, yet I had to answer as though I were Nick, who had. I'm sure I slipped up. I know Batchev did. He was supposed always to answer as me, and he'd obviously researched my life, but several times I heard him talking about places I'd never been. Naturally, to Batchev that wouldn't matter: the real Adler was unknown here and, he believed, dead anyway. The negotiations were a nightmare. I was scared all the time that Mr. Saunders here would give Batchev the dope he wanted. I knew that as soon as that happened he'd vamoose – probably trying to kill me first, so I couldn't expose him. Worse than that, once she was no longer needed as hostage, I could see no reason for them not to kill Anna Felman. However, luckily, Saunders, you held out. The ironic thing was that while Batchev simply didn't have the information you wanted, and so had to stall you, I did have it. It's all in my head. But he'd been told – correctly – that only Adler, not Felman, had this knowledge, so, believing I was Felman, it never occurred to him to ask me.'

Richard said: 'But why did you keep the pretence up so long?'

'Because,' Deveraux said, 'he knew that *Felman* was in the clear: that as soon as we confirmed Anna's kidnapping, we'd no longer consider him a serious murder suspect. As Martin Adler, on the other hand, he can offer no reason at all why he shouldn't have killed Batchev.'

'Look, for the love of Mike,' Adler said, 'don't you think Anna Felman's safety is important to *me*? I know the kid – I'm very fond of her. I wasn't going to put her life in danger. I agree I kept quiet for just the very reason you said: I knew I wasn't guilty and I didn't want you wasting time trying to pin the murders on me, and letting the real killer get away. But you don't imagine I thought I could keep it up for more than a couple of days, do you? And I didn't attempt to deceive the Duke on the telephone. I told him what had really happened and what I intended to do. I asked him not to announce Felman's death for the time being – and in the event that a request from the British police for photos of Adler or Felman was received either there or at our London embassy, to ensure that my picture was sent for his and his for mine. In fact, I'm not sure yet how you discovered the truth.'

Deveraux said: 'Wilkins simply asked Scotland Yard to get a photo of Martin Adler from the London office of your country's leading newspaper.'

Adler shrugged. 'Well, I couldn't think of everything.'

'What were you doing in Batchev's room that night?' Deveraux asked.

'Like you said, I was hoping to get some dirt on him – something that would give me a lever to use against him, or perhaps some clue as to where Anna was being held. It was a forlorn sort of hope, but I felt I had to take any chance, however slight. And I guess I've got to own up to something. It's due to me Fotheringay got drugged.'

'What do you mean?'

'I slipped a sleeping-draught in Batchev's coffee that night, so as I'd be able to search his room without waking him. Somehow Fotheringay must have got it instead.'

Gerry gave an eager nod. 'Yes, Batchev suddenly changed his mind after the cup was passed to him, and said he'd have black instead. So Algy took his cup.'

'Perhaps he spotted me lacing it,' Adler said, 'though I don't see how he could have. Nor why it made Fotheringay sleep for so long. Anyway' – he looked towards Algy – 'I'm sorry, buddy. I wouldn't have had it happen.'

But there was no reply. Algy's head had dropped and his eyes were closed. Gerry leant over and gave him a poke. He jerked awake and smiled vaguely round.

Deveraux said: 'What happened in Batchev's room?'

'Search me. I left my own room at exactly two-seventeen. I imagined Batchev would be well away by then. I opened his door very quietly and slipped in. I was just going to switch on my torch when I heard a board creak on the far side of the room. I thought Batchev was lying in wait for me. I couldn't understand it when he didn't switch the light on or challenge me. I didn't want to make the first move myself. So I just stood there in the dark, waiting, for over ten minutes. Then I heard two-thirty strike. I couldn't stay there for ever so I started to creep towards the door. The next thing I knew someone had barged into me in the dark. He tried to jump away from me. I figured he was going to put the light on and that idea didn't appeal to me, so I hung on to him. We fairly waltzed around the room, knocking things over right, left and centre. We rolled clear across the bed and he got free of me. He blundered towards the door, but he didn't switch the light on, just ran out. That surprised me, but I wasn't intending to hang around and meditate on the phenomenon. So I high-tailed it out of there at top speed. There seemed to be all sorts of things going on around me in the dark, but I was only concerned with making sure Batchev didn't find out just then that I'd been disobeying orders. I thought it was vital that he carried on thinking he'd got me under his thumb. So I started feeling my way back to my room. Lady Geraldine knows too well what happened next. Fortunately, I'd noticed the cupboard and the chair every time I'd gone to my room, and was able to find them in the dark. Then I hurried on and got into bed pronto. Somebody – you, I guess' – he nodded towards Deveraux – 'came into the room and looked at me a few minutes later, but I just lay doggo and you went away.'

Deveraux said: 'I thought from the first you were the most likely one to have locked up Lady Geraldine, and it occurred to me I might just catch you out of bed.'

'No chance. I stayed there until you came back again later and told me Batchev was missing.'

'Well,' said Deveraux, 'that's another mystery at least partially cleared up. Let's now pass on to the next: the theft of Mrs. Peabody's necklace.'

CHAPTER THIRTY-ONE

Arrest

'We've proved beyond doubt,' Deveraux said, 'that a notorious international jewel thief known by the sobriquet of the Wraith was in this house after the burglar alarm was switched on, on Saturday night, and that Mrs. Peabody's necklace was removed from its box during the same night. But was it the Wraith who escaped through the breakfast-room window, setting off the alarm in the process; or did he simply take advantage of Batchev having set off the alarm to escape quietly himself another way?

'Now, the more I thought about it, the more I found it impossible to believe that a professional thief such as the Wraith would not have known of Alderley's alarm system, or knowing of it, would have chosen to commit the robbery at a time when he would have to set off that alarm in order to escape. It was just inconceivable. You might say that he could not resist the challenge laid down in the magazine. Which, frankly, is nonsense. The Wraith is, above all, a professional. He's not going to risk his freedom and depart from the methods which have stood him in such good stead for so long in order to answer the challenge of some footling magazine. In addition, there is a further difficulty. Mr. and Mrs. Peabody's evidence shows that one or the other of them was awake and in the bedroom until Mr. Peabody left to go to the gun-room a little after two-twenty-five. There was then a space of about three minutes during which their rooms were empty. Mrs. Peabody met somebody she supposed was the Wraith on the stairs just after two-thirty, and this would tie up with the necklace having been taken during those three minutes. *But nobody could have known that the rooms were going to be empty at just that time.* Are we to assume that the Wraith happened to enter the Peabodys' suite at precisely that moment, purely by chance? Or that he was waiting, say in one of the rooms across the corridor, on the off-chance that Mr. and Mrs. Peabody would at some time during the night both leave the room? Each of these alternatives seems equally unlikely.

'At one stage, I must confess, I did seriously suspect Mr. Peabody himself of having faked the theft. But that theory was soon abandoned. For one thing, enquiries in the United States have indicated that his financial position is as sound as a bell, and secondly there is the evidence of the Wraith's calling card. So the question remained: why should the Wraith have behaved in this incredibly reckless way, leaving so much to chance and only avoiding capture through sheer luck? It was an act of insanity.'

Deveraux paused and Gerry spoke. 'It worked though, didn't it?'

'Precisely, Lady Geraldine. It worked. Improbably, the Wraith got away with the necklace. Or was that merely what we were meant to think? For suppose he hadn't got away at all? Suppose he was still in the house?'

Lord Burford looked puzzled. 'You mean hidin' somewhere?'

'No, Lord Burford. We never seriously suspected that, though Inspector Wilkins' men did in fact make quite sure he wasn't. No – I mean still living in the house openly.'

The Countess interjected. 'I trust you're not suggesting that one of the servants—'

'No, no, Lady Burford. They are all cleared. They've all been with you far too long. No – I mean *here as one of the guests*. Suppose the Wraith had come to Alderley hoping to steal the necklace? Suppose he had then faced the obstacle of a foolproof burglar alarm which would prevent him leaving with the necklace, and so would immediately throw suspicion on to one of the guests when the theft was discovered? Suppose he had just been biding his time, hoping to find a way round this obstacle, when he had been woken in the early hours of the morning and told the alarm had gone off and that a mysterious man had escaped from the house? In those circumstances, there'd be one obvious course: to go straight to Mrs. Peabody's room and steal the necklace there and then – knowing that the Wraith would almost certainly be thought to be the man who went through the window.'

Deveraux swung round. 'And you did it actually *after* alerting us all to the possibility that the necklace had been stolen – isn't that right, Mr. Evans?'

For long seconds Evans didn't move or speak. Then he slowly removed his spectacles and rubbed his eyes. 'That's right,' he said. 'I took it – just about five seconds before I woke you, H. S.' He chuckled. 'It was in my pocket all the time. Then when I was searching the east wing with Lord Burford I slipped it inside a vase in one of the lumber rooms on the top floor.'

'Is it – is it still there?' Carrie Peabody asked breathlessly.

'No, Mrs. P. I buried it near the lake yesterday. I'd been intending to come back and dig it up on one of the open days later on, when the heat was off. I shall be pleased to point out the precise spot to Wilkins' rozzers on my way out.' He looked over his shoulder. 'Are you still there, Inspector?'

'I'm here, Mr. Evans,' came Wilkins' voice from the corner.

'Well, I hope you're noticing how co-operative I'm being: admitting my guilt, making no show of resistance, giving the exact location of the stolen property. What with it being a first offence, and my having yielded to sudden temptation, I think I might get off with a couple of years in jug, don't you?'

'First offence! Sudden temptation!' Wilkins gave a snort. 'The Wraith's been operating for years.'

'What makes you think I'm the Wraith?' Evans sounded quite indignant. 'You'll never prove that.'

'What about the visiting-card?' Deveraux asked quietly.

'I've no intention of revealing my defence at this stage, old boy, but take it from me that I've got a perfectly good explanation for having it. It was my chance possession of that card which first tempted me into *pretending* to be the notorious Wraith.'

'Tell that to the judge,' Deveraux said. 'I fully intend to.'

Wilkins nodded to Leather, who opened the door. Two uniformed policemen came in. Leather spoke to them quietly.

Evans said: 'You want me to go with these gentlemen? Right-ho. The good secretary learns unquestioning obedience. Well, good-bye, H. S. It's been a pleasure. Sorry it doesn't look as though I'm going to be able to work out my notice. Good-bye, Mrs. P. Believe me, I really very much regretted robbing you. I seriously considered not stealing your necklace – until my worse self triumphed. Good-bye, my lord, ladies and gentlemen. I'm sorry to leave you all at this stage. I've never been involved in a murder before and I was looking forward to learning who done it. Still, I suppose it'll be in the papers – which no doubt one can consult in the prison library.'

He went out with the two policemen. Lord Burford said: 'By jove, quite a personality, what?'

Mr. Peabody was white-faced. He said: 'I never suspected him for a moment. He actually tried to persuade us not to bring the necklace here.'

'That was a very clever bluff,' Deveraux said. 'He knew that whatever he said, Mrs. Peabody was quite certain to bring it.'

'Land's sakes,' Carrie Peabody murmured. 'Do you think he came to work for Hiram solely to get his hands on my necklace?'

Deveraux nodded. 'Twelve months would be no time to wait for such a prize. Doubtless all through your tour he's just been waiting for an opportunity. But until now you must always have been too careful for him.'

Jane asked: 'How long have you suspected him?'

'I've had my eye on him ever since a conversation I had with him on Friday afternoon. He was very eager to explain that he was thinking of leaving Mr. Peabody and staying in England for a while. He rather dragged it into the conversation. I think he might have already spotted me as a sort of sleuth and was preparing the ground, so that if and when he did the robbery and then immediately left Mr. Peabody's employ, he wouldn't arouse suspicion. Then, he passed himself off as an American on his first visit here, but he came out with the very British slang word "quid" rather glibly. Again, after the robbery, once we'd accepted firstly that the Wraith would never have stolen the necklace while the burglar alarm was set; and secondly that the murders and the robbery were unconnected (indicated by the Wraith's card and his known dislike of violence), so that the Wraith couldn't have known in advance that the window was going to be broken – both these facts indicating that the robbery took place *after* the alarm went off – well, then, Evans was the obvious suspect.'

'Why?' Jane asked.

'Lady Geraldine suggested the Wraith might be a woman. But I checked and found out the police knew this was not so. The Wraith was definitely known to be a man – and fairly young. And at the time the robbery was discovered only two people who fitted that description knew about the broken window and so could have taken advantage of it as I described. They were Evans – and me. I knew I wasn't the Wraith. Therefore...' Deveraux spread his hands. 'Wilkins made some enquiries into his background today and found it extremely hazy, with at least one of the references he gave Mr. Peabody false. So the picture was pretty clear.'

Hiram Peabody gave a sigh. 'And he was just about the best doggone secretary I ever had.'

CHAPTER THIRTY-TWO

The Killer

Giles Deveraux crossed the room, poured himself a glass of water and drank it. Then he went back to his place. He looked round the ring of faces. Every eye was on him. Even Algy Fotheringay at last seemed fully awake.

Deveraux said: 'Assault, impersonation, suppression of evidence, and thefts of various kinds. We've cleared them all out of the way. And now we can deal with murder.'

'Earlier today, Inspector Wilkins gave me a number of pointers to the truth about these murders. I won't repeat them in exactly the same form that he put them, but they were as follows: Lady Geraldine's sight, my hearing, and Miss Clifton's nostril; then, Batchev's flight, Lord Burford's collection. Wilkins' own height, and finally the weather.'

Deveraux went through them a second time, then said: 'I should add that certain of them refer to things lacking or missing. Perhaps we can try to explain them together. Who'd like to start? Lady Geraldine?'

Gerry wrinkled her nose. 'I've no idea what your hearing or my sight have got to do with it. The significance of Daddy's collection is pretty obvious – the gun that killed the Baroness came from it. Batchev's flight? I suppose it means why did he decide to leave the house so suddenly in the middle of the night. Well, I've already put forward one theory about that. As for Miss Clifton's nostril, Jane's probably got more idea about what that means.'

Jane said slowly: 'I smelt the Baroness's scent in the linen-room just after I was knocked down. I remembered it later, and as a result we found her body in the passage. That's the only way my nose has been involved. What else was there?'

'The Inspector's height.'

Jane and Gerry looked at each other. Jane shrugged. Gerry said: 'Pass.'

'The weather.'

Jane said: 'The thunder drowned certain noises – such as what was going on in Anilese's room when Gerry was outside.'

'How did we do?' Gerry asked.

'Fair. Let's go back. Skip my hearing for the moment and concentrate on your sight. You said you saw the Baroness arrive back in her room at about seven minutes past two, and that she had not left it again at two-thirty. This flatly contradicts Mr. Saunders' statement that her room was empty when he arrived.'

Gerry bit her lip. She said: 'I – I thought…'

'You thought I'd forgotten that discrepancy, Lady Geraldine? No.'

In a voice hard with tension, Richard said: 'You agreed that there was no truth in your original reconstruction which cast me as the killer.'

Again from the dark corner, Wilkins' voice cut across

the room. 'Excuse me, sir, but he didn't. *You* said there was no truth in it. I said there was *some* – though the reconstruction was largely false and didn't answer all the questions. But that that particular reconstruction was at fault didn't mean that you were necessarily innocent of the murder.'

Richard closed his eyes. 'Oh no.'

'But,' said Deveraux, 'something else does prove you innocent: the very important element of time. I wonder if anybody noticed one vital fact brought out by Mr. Peabody's evidence: that he took Lord Burford's gun – the one used to shoot the Baroness – from the gun-room *a couple of minutes before two-thirty* – and that thereafter it wasn't out of his possession. He didn't shoot her himself or he would never have admitted that. So the killer must have replaced it in the gun-room after shooting her and before Mr. Peabody took it. Which means that the Baroness was killed several minutes before that. Therefore, Mr. Saunders couldn't have shot her after arriving in her room a few seconds after two-thirty. By then she was already dead.'

Richard let his head fall back. 'Thank heaven,' he said.

Gerry was looking perplexed. 'But when exactly was she killed? I assure you I saw her going into her room minutes before ten past two.'

'I'm not questioning that. I'd say she was killed at about eleven or twelve minutes past.'

'But by whom?'

'You answered that question yourself earlier. The Baroness de la Roche was killed by Stanislaus Batchev.'

He looked round at the blank faces, as if waiting for

some reaction. But it was as if everybody was stunned. Richard spoke first. 'In her room?'

Deveraux nodded.

Gerry said: 'But who moved the body?'

'Batchev himself.'

'He didn't, I tell you. I would have seen him.'

'Now we're back to Lady Geraldine's sight. Will you tell us again exactly what you saw from the time you arrived in the recess?'

'I saw the Baroness leave her room at about four or five minutes past two. Then—'

'Hold it there, please. She went to the gun-room and took Lord Burford's Bergman Bayard and some cartridges. She knew that Batchev would be furious when he learnt she was not, after all, going to blackmail Mr. Saunders, and she wanted protection. We assume she picked the lock – a skill she could quite easily have learnt, given the life she'd been leading. She might even have done it earlier in the evening, in preparation. But of course she wouldn't take the gun until the last moment, in case Lord Burford should go to the gun-room before turning in and notice its absence. Please go on.'

'About six or seven minutes past, Batchev arrived and went in, then she came back a minute after that.'

'And then it must have happened just as you suggested. Batchev accused her of double-crossing him, threatened her, she pulled the gun; then perhaps he grabbed for it, they struggled and she was shot. They were probably locked together. Their bodies would muffle the shot and that, together with the thick heavy door and the thunderstorm, meant you heard nothing. What did you see next?'

'Batchev leaving – alone.'

'You didn't know who it was at the time though, did you?'

'No.'

'Why not?'

'Because the only light was from his torch, which he held low down. So I couldn't see his face.'

'How much of him *could* you see?'

'Well, really only his feet and about half way up his legs.'

'Precisely. What you could not see was that Batchev was *carrying the Baroness's body over his shoulder*.'

Throughout the room there was a slow expelling of breath. Gerry stared at Deveraux, opened her mouth – and closed it again.

Deveraux said: 'You agree – he could have been?'

'I – I suppose so,' she said slowly. 'But he didn't seem to be carrying any weight. He walked quite briskly and light-footed.'

'He was an extremely strong man – her weight would have been nothing to him.'

'But how do you know that's what happened?'

'Given that there is only one door to the room, that the window couldn't be opened more than a few inches without setting off the alarm, and that both you and your uncle are telling the truth, that's the only way it could have happened.'

Jane said: 'And he put the body in the secret passage himself?'

'That's right.'

'Why?'

'We can only surmise, but he must have known that he was going to have to abandon his assignment. His probable intention then was flight as soon as the servants were up and the alarm was switched off – a man of his experience would have a good chance of getting away without being seen – hoping it would be assumed the Baroness had left with him. So it was essential that her body wasn't discovered immediately. I think he thought of the passage simply as a hiding place, and didn't have any intention of using it to take her body downstairs. I believe later he would have collected all her things from her room and dumped them in there with her. But before that he went to replace the pistol in the collection-room.'

'Why bother?' Jane asked again.

'Well, it was obviously important to get rid of the murder weapon quickly, just in case anybody else had been disturbed and got up to investigate. He could have left it with the body; but he knew the Earl and Mr. Peabody were in and out of the collection-room all the time and that its absence would be very quickly noticed. The fact that he and the Baroness were missing would not make anybody necessarily suspect foul play, but if a pistol were gone as well, it might suggest the use of violence and possible murder, and that in turn might lead to a more intensive search being made. Anyway, after hiding the body behind the panel, he made his way to the gun-room. He must have arrived there just about a minute or so before you arrived in his room, Adler.'

Martin Adler nodded.

'Batchev put the gun back,' Deveraux went on, 'and was no doubt intending then to go and pack his own things. But his plan didn't work out. For he in turn was shot by somebody else.'

The tension in the room was mounting again. It was as if nobody wanted even to breathe.

'I mentioned earlier,' Deveraux continued, 'that outside the servants' quarters only three people in this house had remained in bed all the time prior to the alarm being set off. One of those people was Lady Burford. Another was Fotheringay. The third, strangely enough, was Evans. Which means that one person, other than those who have admitted being up, was also out of bed and creeping about in the dark.'

Deveraux stopped, turned, and looked straight at a slight, unobtrusive figure sitting just outside the main circle. 'That person,' he said, 'was Edward Thornton.'

Thornton neither moved nor spoke.

Deveraux pointed at him. 'There's the man you fought, Adler. There's the man who knocked you down, Jane. There's the man who was paid £10,000 to release secret information about your negotiations, Mr. Saunders.'

Thornton looked at him out of cold eyes. 'You're mad,' he said quietly.

'And there's the man,' Deveraux continued remorselessly, 'who shot Stanislaus Batchev.'

'You fool!' Thornton spat out the words. 'Do you think anyone's going to believe that? What motive could I have had?'

'He knew you were a traitor in the pay of a foreign power.'

'It's a lie! Anyway, I couldn't possibly have had time to kill him. Nobody was able to leave the house before ten to three—'

'You didn't leave the house. You shot him in the gun-room at about two-twenty-five, when he went to replace the Bergman.'

'But the body was found in the lake, you imbecile!'

'Agreed. You transferred it to the lake later – after the alarm had gone off.'

'And just when am I supposed to have done that?'

'Between the times Miss Clifton left your room at about a minute to three, and you joined us towards the end of our search.'

'You're not seriously suggesting that I dressed, carried a body from the gun-room downstairs – without being seen – out to the lake, got back to my room, and joined you dry and free from mud – all in about fifteen minutes?'

'Certainly not. That was the cleverest part of the whole plan. In disposing of the body, you never left the gun-room.'

He looked round. 'Remember the pointers: *Lord Burford's collection*; *Batchev's flight*. Did you all assume that *flight* was used in the sense of *fleeing*, *escape*? No: it referred, quite literally, to the act of flying through the air. That was how the body reached the lake. It was shot there.'

The Earl whispered: 'You – you don't mean—'

'Yes, Lord Burford – from the circus gun used by Burundi the Human Cannonball.'

Richard said: 'Great Scott!'

Lady Burford murmured weakly: 'I don't believe it.'

Hiram Peabody exclaimed: 'Jumping jehosaphat!'

The monocle dropped from Algy Fotheringay's eye.

It was at that moment, when Deveraux had the rapt

attention of every person in the room, that Thornton acted. Like lightning he sprang to his feet. A small snub-nosed automatic had appeared in his hand. He took two steps towards the door. 'Everyone stay where they are.'

Wilkins spoke very quietly. 'Now don't be silly, sir. This isn't going to get you anywhere.' He moved towards Thornton.

Thornton swung round and levelled the gun at him. 'I said nobody move. That includes you.'

From behind him, Deveraux said: 'You can't shoot everyone, Thornton.'

Thornton spun round again and pointed the automatic at Deveraux. He licked his lips and cast a quick glance over his shoulder towards Wilkins and Leather. Then his eyes flickered. 'Perhaps not,' he snapped, 'but I can shoot one.'

He was standing behind Jane's chair, and as he spoke he leant forward, grabbed her by the arm and jerked her to her feet.

'If anybody moves an inch, she'll be the first to go.'

He threw his arm round her neck, pulled her backwards against his chest, and pressed the muzzle of the gun against her temple.

The first shock lasted a few seconds. Then Jane felt quite calm. The cold metal against her head worried her less than the pressure of Thornton's arm on her throat. She saw the ring of white horrified faces, etched sharp and still as a photograph. She realised that Wilkins and Deveraux had both drawn back, helpless.

Thornton was backing towards the door, dragging Jane awkwardly with him. Closer and closer they got to it, and the pressure of his arm was making her eyes water.

Thornton said: 'That's stopped you in your tracks, hasn't it?' He gave Jane another jerk backwards, causing her ankle to knock painfully against the leg of a chair. 'Come on, girl. Don't dawdle.'

Then Jane lost her temper.

The humiliation of what was being done to her swept over her. How dare he treat her like this? She wouldn't put up with it for another second.

She raised her hands, yanked Thornton's wrist towards her mouth, and bent her head. Taken quite by surprise, Thornton let the pistol slip away from her head, and at that instant Jane gripped his hand between her teeth and bit as hard as she could.

Thornton gave a howl and snatched his arm away. Jane drove her elbow hard into his stomach, then leapt away from him as his gun arm flailed wildly in the air.

Already Giles Deveraux was moving. He sprang at Thornton. With one hand he grabbed the wrist holding the gun, and with the other he landed a crisp right cross to the point of Thornton's jaw and sent him flying.

One minute later, Edward Thornton was on his feet again – handcuffed and firmly in the grasp of Sergeant Leather.

Gasping, Thornton addressed Deveraux. 'Listen – I admit I took a bribe. The ten thousand was a down payment. I was to receive a further ten when I handed over the details of certain African territory. But I am not in the pay of any foreign power. I was given the money by some Scandinavian. He was acting on behalf of a private individual – a financier who wants to buy up land there in advance, as a commercial venture. It wouldn't harm this country's interests.'

'No,' Richard said coldly, 'only cheat thousands of poor people out of their rights.'

'I'd bet my bottom dollar that old buzzard Zapopulous is behind it,' Peabody said.

'I don't know,' Thornton said. 'I only dealt with this Scandinavian. I thought it would be easy. But Batchev wouldn't part with the information. By Saturday night I was desperate. That's when I decided to search his room to see if I could find any papers giving the information. How was I to know he was bogus and didn't have it himself? I tried to drug him so he wouldn't wake: I slipped several sleeping tablets into his coffee after dinner. I didn't realise till the next day that Fotheringay had drank it instead. And of course I didn't know somebody else had done the same thing.'

Lord Burford gave a long low whistle and stared at Algy with something like awe. 'By jove, no wonder the feller slept.'

'You're very lucky to have escaped with your life, Fotheringay,' Deveraux said.

Algy gave a smirk. 'I've always been jolly tough. Once—'

'Go on, Thornton,' Deveraux said.

'I went to Batchev's room just before two-fifteen. Batchev wasn't there. I couldn't understand it, but I started searching. After about two or three minutes, I heard the door opening. I naturally assumed it was Batchev and I hid behind the wardrobe. Nothing happened and eventually I tried to get to the door. You know what happened then. I managed to get out and ran back to my own room, colliding with her' – he pointed to Jane – 'on the way. I went straight back to bed and stayed there until she roused me about thirty minutes later. And that's all I did. I panicked just now because the case looked so black against me. But I swear I am not a traitor. And I am not a murderer. I did not shoot Batchev.'

Deveraux looked at him, his face expressionless. Then, before he could answer, Inspector Wilkins spoke again.

'I know that,' he said quietly.

An absolutely stunned silence greeted Wilkins' words. It seemed that no one could even gasp. Again it was Richard who produced the first coherent words. 'Wilkins – are you now saying it was *not* Thornton who shot Batchev?'

'That's right, sir.'

'Then just why did you let Deveraux accuse him of it?'

'I'm afraid it's a favourite ruse of mine, sir – to accuse someone of a major crime to get them to confess to a lesser one. I'm sorry to use it twice in one evening. But as we've got very little evidence, we had to get Mr. Thornton to own up to conspiracy and corruption. Unfortunately, I did not anticipate he would be armed.'

He gave a nod to Leather, who opened the door. Two more uniformed policemen came in. 'Take him away,' Wilkins said.

When the door had closed behind a dazed and speechless Thornton, Lord Burford said: 'Are you telling us now Burundi's cannon was *not* used to despatch Batchev's body?'

'Oh, it was used. But not by Thornton.'

'Then by whom, man?'

'And,' Gerry added, 'if it wasn't Batchev, Evans, or Mr. Thornton who went through the breakfast-room window – who was it?'

'Nobody, Lady Geraldine.'

'Oh, come on! I saw him. We all did.'

Wilkins shook his head. 'No. That's what we were meant to think. By Batchev's killer.'

'This has gone on quite long enough.' The authoritative words came from the Countess. 'Mr. Wilkins, please tell us *now* who the murderer really was.'

'Very well, your ladyship. I will.' He turned and looked straight at Jane. 'I'm afraid it was this young lady.' His face was sad. 'Why did you do it, Miss Clifton?'

Jane met his gaze. For a moment her eyes wavered and dropped. But then she took a deep breath and lifted her head proudly.

'Because he drove my sister to suicide,' she said.

CHAPTER THIRTY-THREE

The Reason Why

'As some of you here know,' Jane said, 'my sister was an actress. Her name was Jenny Howard – she changed it officially by deed-poll when she entered the profession and found there was another actress called, I think, Jenny Clinton.

'Jenny died three years ago in the United States. How she died was never made public. She was on tour with a theatrical company when she met a man who called himself Stewart Baldwin. All I ever knew about him was what I learnt from Jenny. He was supposed to be a freelance journalist who was doing a series of articles on the tour, and he travelled with the company for about eight weeks. Jenny fell madly in love with him. Then unexpectedly he told her he had to leave very soon on another assignment. He said he wanted to marry her, and asked her to go away with him. She cleared it with the manager and left a week later. She and Stewart were married by a Justice of the Peace in a little town in New Mexico. She wrote home the day after the wedding, saying she was deliriously happy and had no regrets at giving up her career.'

Jane drew at her cigarette. 'Although my mother and I were both sad that Jenny wouldn't be coming home, we made the best of it. Mother, however, had a strong feeling that the marriage wasn't going to work out, and she asked me to agree not to tell any of our friends about it, for the time being, just in case.

'For about six months Jenny travelled all over America with Stewart, staying in hotels and rooming-houses. During this time she had very little to do, and she used to write to us two or three times a week. She seemed absolutely crazy about Stewart, and she told us practically everything there was to know about him – all his likes and dislikes and habits and ways of talking. She also sent one blurred snapshot of him, which she'd managed to take without his knowledge, as she said he hated to be photographed. Meanwhile, the theatrical company had come home. When people asked about Jenny we simply told them she was staying on in the States for a bit. Of course, the stage people knew about her marriage, but they didn't come in contact with our circle at all.'

Jane stubbed out her cigarette. 'Then, during March, I came to stay here at Alderley. I'd told Jenny in one of my letters that I was coming, and while I was here I got a letter from her. She sent it here because she hadn't wanted Mother to know, but she was terribly worried and unhappy. They were moving round more and more, and sometimes Stewart would go away for days on end, leaving her in some poky rooming-house. He wouldn't talk about his work, and she couldn't understand what his assignment was supposed to be – he told her it was for some magazine she'd never heard of. Occasionally he'd take her to cocktail parties or receptions and introduce her to lots of people, but they'd never stay long and she wouldn't meet the people again. She said Stewart didn't ever seem actually to write anything and simply told her he was gathering copy. She said she'd just had to tell somebody, as she felt utterly alone and had no friends in America at all. She told me not to take too much notice of the letters she sent to Mother and me at home, but that she'd keep me informed of what was really happening by sending me letters to be called for at the post office.'

Jane looked at Gerry. 'I got that letter on the day of the Hunt Ball, do you remember? You couldn't understand what was wrong with me.'

Gerry nodded, but didn't speak.

'In May,' Jane went on, 'Jenny discovered she was going to have a baby. She was terribly excited, thinking it might make Stewart settle down. But when she told him he was furious. They had a blazing row and he stormed out. She never saw him again.

'She had practically no money, no home, and no one to turn to. She was frantic. Then two men arrived, looking for Stewart. They were Federal agents – G-men. They told her that Stewart was wanted for subversive activities. Baldwin wasn't his real name; he wasn't a journalist; he wasn't even an American citizen. He'd entered the country illegally eighteen months before. They also informed her gently that a year previously he'd married a woman in Illinois. She was still alive and the marriage had never been dissolved. So Jenny wasn't even legally married to him.'

Jane looked at Deveraux. 'I realise now what he'd done. He must have been impersonating someone who was known to be married, and for some reason he needed a real wife to produce sometimes for authenticity. Presumably the woman in Illinois had been unsuitable, or perhaps she'd found out the truth and told the authorities about him. He left her before the FBI arrived and got himself a cover by going round with the theatrical company. Probably he realised there might be a good chance of picking up another wife among the young actresses. He took up with Jenny, and then when the time came to renew his espionage work, he married her. When she told him about the baby, he knew she was going to be too tied down to be any further use to him.'

Deveraux nodded slowly and Jane continued. 'Jenny, I imagine, put on a very good act of being extremely calm and casual about it all. The G-men left, promising to inform the nearest British Consul about her plight.'

Jane took another cigarette with a hand that shook slightly. Richard lit it for her.

'Jenny was a very proud person,' she said. 'We all were. Perhaps too proud. Gerry tells me I am; I don't know. But Jenny was more sensitive than me and more highly strung. After the men had left, she wrote and told me the whole story. She said she couldn't bear the humiliation of coming home with an illegitimate baby, and not even knowing the father's real name. And especially she couldn't face Mother. She went out, mailed the letter, returned to her room and gassed herself.'

Jane looked up. Her eyes were moist, but her voice was steady as she continued. 'I told Mummy Jennifer had been taken ill and died of a very rare disease. The officials I dealt with were all very good and kept the secret. There were a few lines about her in some of the papers, but none of them said more than that she'd died suddenly. None of our friends ever knew the truth.

'I've carried Stewart Baldwin's photo with me ever since. Just so I never could forget. I had a feeling always that sometime, somewhere, I'd meet him. The very first time I saw him getting off the train last Thursday, I thought he looked vaguely familiar. Then when I was introduced to him on the terrace and heard that phony American accent, the sense of familiarity grew. I puzzled over it most of the next day. I think it was only a kind of subconscious rejection of the possibility of it being him that prevented me connecting him with Baldwin. It didn't really come to me until I was talking to him on Friday afternoon. He was obviously talking as himself, not as Mr. Adler, and he mentioned once having had an English girlfriend who'd lived in the Cotswolds. That was almost certainly Jenny, because we used to live there. I was on the point of mentioning it when he took a drink. Now Jenny had told me that Stewart had the unusual mannerism of closing his eyes momentarily whenever he drank. *Batchev did that very thing*.

'It gave me a terrible jolt. I went up to my room and studied Baldwin's photo. I couldn't be sure even then that Baldwin was him. In the photo he had fair hair and a moustache, and, as I said, the picture was rather blurred and several years old. I didn't then even have the similarity of initials – SB – as an indication. You, Richard, and everybody else, accepted him as Martin Adler, a well-known European diplomat, and I couldn't see how it was possible for him to be Baldwin. So I set myself to finding out. I talked to him as much as I could and I watched him like a hawk. I know all Jenny's letters by heart, of course, and gradually I began to recognise in Batchev little things she had told me about Stewart. I won't go into them all now. They were things like preferences in food and drink, turns of phrase in speech, taste in clothes – Stewart always wore plain neckties, for instance, as Batchev did – smoking habits – always using cork-tipped cigarettes – and so on. Eventually I spotted about ten similarities. Then I was sure.'

'An incredible coincidence,' Richard murmured.

'Or fate,' Jane said. 'I did wonder whether he would identify me as Jenny's sister. But of course the surname was different. Whether Jenny told him her original surname I don't know, but if she did there'd be no reason for him to remember it. He must have known she had a sister called Jane, but that's a common enough name.

'Once I knew who he really was, I could have reported to you, Richard, that he was bogus. But I wanted to be sure he was punished for what he'd done to Jenny and I doubted if they'd be able to bring it home to him after all this time. Besides, prison would be too good for him. He had to die. I decided to kill him myself.'

CHAPTER THIRTY-FOUR

Execution

'I quite enjoyed planning the execution,' Jane said quietly. 'It was the three facts of the alarm system, the circus cannon, and the nearness of the lake which were the basis for my plan. I thought that if Batchev's body was found some distance from the house, and he was thought to have been killed at a time when the burglar alarm would prove everybody else to have been in the house, then nobody here would be suspected. I knew how to operate the cannon. I was staying here when Lord Burford bought it, and he tested it by firing lengths of timber from the balcony. Fortunately, after that it was only moved back a few feet – not shifted to the side – so that it was still aimed straight towards the french doors. Of course, I couldn't have done it if the lake hadn't been there: if the body had landed on dry ground, it would have been obvious it had fallen from a height – and then the police would have probably thought of the cannon and put two and two together. If it hadn't been for all the other complications, which I couldn't have foreseen, I think I'd have fooled you – you would have thought he'd gone out to meet somebody and been shot by him. The only part of my plan that went wrong was the business of the pistol. I planned to take one of Lord Burford's from the collection, use it to shoot Batchev, put his fingerprints on it, hide it somewhere in the house, and then the next day go and drop it near where the body had been found. I was hoping to make the police think that Batchev had taken it himself for protection, had met and fought with somebody in the grounds, had been shot with it in the struggle, and that the murderer had dropped it while getting away. I'll explain what went wrong in a minute.

'On Saturday after lunch I went down to the village and bought a small reel of black cobbler's thread. In the afternoon Lord Burford showed us all his collection and I decided that as it was one of the few modern style repeating-guns, with cartridges available, the Bergman would be best for me. I went to bed that night normally and tried to read for a bit. I got up at half-past one. I put on a dressing-gown and a pair of cotton gloves, crept along to Lord Burford's room and took the keys to the gun-room from his dressing-table. Then I went downstairs. I fetched the stepladder, and also a pair of wire cutters from the tool-box that was kept in the same place. I took them along to the breakfast-room and put the stepladder up by the window. Then I stood on a chair, jammed one end of the thread in the crack of the door, fastened the other end to the top of the stepladder, and slowly tilted it until it was very finely balanced – just held up by the thread. As soon as the thread was released the stepladder would crash through the window. I moved the pot plant, put a chair on its side near the window, and threw the wire cutters down on the floor.

'I couldn't, obviously, open the door, so I went upstairs by the secret passage. I went straight to the collection-room to get Lord Burford's Bergman. But it wasn't there. The Baroness must have just taken it. I was absolutely stymied; all the other small guns there seemed terribly old-fashioned and I didn't know how to operate them. It looked as though I'd have to abandon the whole plan. Then I remembered Mr. Peabody's gun, which was identical. I took four cartridges from the cupboard and crept back along the corridor. Then, when I was nearly there, I saw the light of a torch and someone emerging from the Peabody's suite. A second later I saw it was Lord Burford and he had the gun in his hand. He'd said how much he wanted that pistol, so I guessed at once what he was doing. It was vital I found out what he did with the gun. I followed him downstairs to the study and watched him put it in the safe. I hid when he came out, then when he'd gone back upstairs I went in to get it. I learnt the combination of the safe years ago – I sometimes fetched papers and things from it for the Earl when I stayed here as a schoolgirl. But I couldn't remember it exactly at first: it took me two or three minutes to get it. Then I took out the gun, loaded it, and made my way back upstairs.

'My plan then had been to go to Batchev's room and force him to go with me to the gun-room. But just as I got to the top of the stairs I heard a footstep and saw the faint flash of a torch to my right. I thought it had to be Lord Burford again, but then there was a very vivid flash of lightning and I saw quite clearly that it was Batchev. He was walking away from me towards the east wing. I followed him. I watched him go into the collection-room.

I could hardly believe my good luck – he was playing right into my hands.

'I didn't see him replace Lord Burford's pistol, because I took a few seconds to pluck up courage to follow him in. I've believed ever since that he'd gone there to *take* a gun. Eventually I went in, closed the doors behind me, and switched on the light. I must have given him a terrific shock, but he didn't show it too much. I kept Mr. Peabody's pistol behind my back and asked him casually what he was doing. He must have thought I'd seen him replacing Lord Burford's pistol, because he pointed to it and said something about finding it in the corridor and deciding to put it back. I walked across as if I was just going to look at it more closely. Then when I got near him I brought Mr. Peabody's gun from behind my back and told him to put his hands up. I believe he thought then that I suspected him of being a thief, was just concerned for the safety of the collection, and that given time he could talk me round. So he decided to humour me for a bit, and when I told him to walk down to the far end of the room, he did so. When we got near the cannon I said I wanted to have a look round to make sure nothing was missing, and I told him to lie down on the floor against the wall in the corner, where I could keep an eye on him. He seemed quite relieved at this, because obviously he knew nothing was missing and no doubt he thought that when I realised this I'd apologise, and go back to bed. So it would clearly pay him to co-operate with me.

'Then, when he was lying in the corner, I just suddenly sprang it on him that I was Jenny Howard's sister, and I was going to execute him for causing her death. I've never seen anyone so shaken as he was then. It must have come like a bolt from the blue. Any doubts I might have had about him being Baldwin were removed. In fact, he didn't try to deny it, and when he'd recovered a bit from the first shock, he just tried to convince me I didn't know the full truth about Jenny and that he wasn't to blame. I must say he kept his head quite well.

'I told him nothing he could say would make any difference, and that I was going to give him roughly two minutes and then kill him. I counted off what I guessed were quarter minutes. Towards the end he did get really scared, but there was nothing he could do: I was very careful to stand too far away to give him any chance of grabbing me, yet near enough so that my shot couldn't miss; in that position he couldn't duck or dodge, and if he'd rolled, he could only have rolled towards me.

'When I estimated two minutes were up, I said "That's it," and I shot him dead.'

Jane looked around at the spellbound circle of faces. She said: 'Could I have some water, do you think?'

Gerry jumped to her feet and fetched a glass. Everyone was silent while Jane drank. She put it down and went on. 'I knew the shot wouldn't be heard: the gun-room is so isolated from any of the occupied rooms. In the past I've been in my bedroom when Lord Burford was using the range, and I haven't heard a thing. I was quite calm. First of all I went across, plugged in the lead running to the cannon's air compressor and switched it on. Then I lowered the barrel right down till it was nearly touching the floor. I went back and dragged Batchev across to it. I was amazed to find that the body was already rigid, as

I'd always thought it was hours before rigor mortis set in; but I've looked it up since and found that in cases of violent death it sometimes starts immediately. Actually, it was very lucky for me it did set in so quickly, because I've since remembered Lord Burford telling Gerry and me years ago that it was necessary for a human cannonball to keep completely stiff or he might only fly a few feet. Also, I think the rigidity of the body made it easier to get it into the barrel, even though I still had a bit of a struggle. Luckily, he was quite slightly-built, so I managed it eventually. Oh, before that I held the pistol by the barrel and tried to press Batchev's fingers against it. But their being so stiff made it very difficult and I must have smudged the prints.

'All I had to do after I'd got the body in was to turn the handle until the barrel was about level as it had been before. Then I went quietly out, turning off the light and locking the door.

'My plan then had been to hide the pistol in one of the lumber-rooms on the top floor, then come down and wake you, Richard, and tell you that I'd seen Adler – as we were then calling him – creep downstairs, take a stepladder into the breakfast-room, and shut the door. You would have come down with me to investigate. But that plan was spoilt straight away. I'd no sooner closed the door to the picture gallery behind me than I heard footsteps coming along the corridor. It was you, of course, Mr. Peabody, but I didn't know that then. I darted across to my own room and waited just inside. I heard the gallery door open, and I guessed somebody was going to the gun-room. I was terrified in case they found the body. But it was all right, for a minute or so later I heard the gallery door open and close again and the footsteps go away. I went back out to the corridor. I looked in the gallery, but I decided not to go across to the gun-room again. If anybody *had* found Batchev's body, I couldn't do anything about it – and they might raise the alarm and come back and find me there. Besides, I was pretty sure whoever it was was up to no good, and so wouldn't have turned the light on; again, to find the body they would have needed to go right down to the far end and look into the barrel, and I just didn't think they'd had enough time to do that. So I carried on with my original plan. The gun was burning a hole in my pocket and I knew the bulge would be pretty conspicuous if anybody did see me. So I couldn't turn a light on.

'I made my way towards the front of the house. I heard two-thirty strike – and you all know what happened then. Luckily, when I got up after Thornton had knocked me over, the gun was still in my pocket. But I panicked a bit. There were so many people about that any moment somebody was going to switch on the lights. I had to get rid of the gun before that happened. I was near the linen-room and I thought of the secret passage. I dashed in, opened the panel, dropped the gun inside, and took off my gloves. Naturally, I had no idea that Anilese's body was already there. I went back out, turned on the lights, and found Mr. Deveraux.'

She looked at him. 'I decided on the spur of the moment to use you instead of Richard for the next part of my plan. But I didn't say anything about seeing Batchev behave suspiciously in the breakfast-room: for one thing you'd just seen me coming from the direction of my own room; and for another you might have been downstairs yourself and know I was lying. Except for that, however, I followed my plan. After we released Gerry, I was going to suggest we searched downstairs, but luckily you suggested it yourself. Everything worked like a dream. When we got near the breakfast-room I pretended to hear a noise inside. I rushed forward and opened the door. The thread was released and the stepladder crashed through the window, setting off the alarm. I froze for a second, so that you couldn't rush straight in and see the room was empty. Then I dashed in myself and yelled that somebody was just disappearing outside. You went after him. While Gerry was looking out after you, I stood the ladder up and managed to unhook the thread, bundle it up and put it in my pocket.

'Shortly after you sent me upstairs, I put my gloves on, slipped into the gun-room, opened the window, raised the barrel, and fired the cannon. I was on tenterhooks in case it wouldn't work. But it did. Batchev's body went flying into the darkness. I heard the splash of it landing in the lake. I closed the window, unplugged the compressor, and went out, locking the door. It didn't take more than two minutes altogether. Then I went and checked on Evans, Thornton, and Algy, as you'd asked me to, dropped my gloves off in my room, and came back downstairs. Later on, when everybody was down here after Inspector Wilkins arrived, I pretended to want something from my room, went up and replaced the gun-room key on Lord Burford's dressing-table.

'The only other thing to be done was take the pistol from behind the panel and hide it in the park somewhere the next day. I hadn't meant to go and get it just when I did, but when we were talking on the terrace' – she was addressing Deveraux continually now – 'you showed altogether too much interest in the passage, and I thought I ought to remove the gun quickly before you decided to go and search it. Incidentally, I hadn't smelt anything in there: but I had to have some reason for being in the room when you found me, and I'd already said I hadn't *seen* or *heard* anything.

'Then we found the Baroness's body. I think that was the most horrifying moment of my life – and utterly baffling, too. I've been as mystified as everybody about who killed her. I didn't think it could be Batchev, because I knew the murder gun was taken after he was dead; what I didn't know was that it had been taken twice.'

Jane looked hard at Deveraux. 'Was there anything else you wanted to know?'

'Just one thing.' Deveraux took the egg cosy from his pocket. 'It's not vital, but can you throw any light on this?'

The ghost of a smile crossed Jane's features. 'Oh, that. I couldn't get the thread gripped properly in the breakfast-room door: it kept slipping out. I wanted something to fix on the end to stop it – something soft and light which wouldn't make any noise landing. That was the first thing that came to hand. But it was so white I thought that even in dim light it might show up against the dark wood outside. So I rubbed it in the pot plant to darken it. It was still fastened to the end when I put the thread in my pocket. I was nervous we might all be searched, however, and I wanted to get rid of it – it wouldn't be so easy to explain as just a length of thread on its own. So before I raised the barrel, prior to firing the cannon, I reached inside and tried to push the thing into Batchev's pocket. That must have been when it got the blood on it. I thought if it were found there, it would definitely connect him with the breakfast-room and might remove any doubt that it had been he who went through the window – and in addition it would be a good red herring. But I was doing everything so hurriedly I couldn't have put it in the pocket properly. Obviously it fell out as the body flew towards the lake, and landed on that bush.'

Wilkins looked at Deveraux. 'Simple when you know, isn't it?'

Jane stood up. 'And now I suppose you'll want me to come with you, Mr. Wilkins.'

Ten minutes later Jane walked down the grand staircase. She had changed out of her evening dress. She was accompanied by Sergeant Leather, carrying her case. Deveraux and Wilkins were in the hall. Deveraux came forward.

'They want to know in the drawing-room if you'd like to see anybody.'

Jane hesitated. 'No, I don't think—' She broke off and her chin went up. 'Yes. Would you ask Gerry and Richard to come out, please?'

Deveraux nodded and went away. A few moments later Richard and Gerry came into the hall. There was an awkward silence for three or four seconds. Then Jane gave Gerry a grin. 'Cheer up, darling. You look like death. Don't you realise I won't have to worry about job-hunting now?'

Gerry looked at her. Her lips trembled. Then she flung

herself on Jane, threw her arms round her for a second, and turned away, sobbing.

Jane bit her lip sharply, then swung suddenly round on Richard and held out her hand. 'Goodbye, Richard.'

He took her hand in both of his. '*Au revoir*, Jane. Don't worry about the practical side. You'll have the best Counsel in England, never fear.'

'That's sweet of you, Richard, but there's no need, really. I'll plead guilty, of course. Listen, I'm sorry to have put you all through such a ghastly business. Tell the Earl and Countess, will you? Say good-bye and thanks for me, and tell them I'll write if I'm allowed.'

'You didn't put us through any ghastly business, my dear. It would have been even worse but for you. *You* stopped him getting away.'

'Thanks. It was purely personal, though. Say good-bye to everybody else for me – the Peabodys and Mr. Adler and Algy.' She turned to Deveraux, who was standing a few feet away. 'Did you think I'd confess when Mr. Wilkins accused Thornton?'

'We thought you might – rather than let him be falsely charged.'

'I would have, of course. I was just plucking up the courage – when he acted himself.' She paused. 'Are you coming now?'

'Not now.'

'Then good-bye. This morning I rather slyly apologised for hindering you when the imaginary man went through the window. I'd just like you to know that the other apologies and thanks were genuine.'

'I know that.'

'I don't really know why I'm saying this. I knew you spelt trouble for me from that first moment when you practically drowned me through driving like a lunatic up the drive – knocking down footbound pheasants right, left and centre. Very well, Mr. Leather, I'm ready.'

Wilkins opened the front door, and Jane walked through the doorway and down the steps to the waiting car, Leather and another policeman a few paces behind. 'Like a princess and her courtiers,' Richard murmured.

They watched the car drive off into the darkness. Then Wilkins shut the door and went back into the drawing-room.

Very quietly, Richard said: 'I wonder why she asked to see *me*.'

There was a pause before Gerry said. 'Why shouldn't she?'

'She's always seemed rather stiff with me. I got the impression years ago that she didn't like me very much.'

Gerry looked at him sharply, opened her mouth, then seemed to change her mind. Instead, in a voice that shook a little, she said: 'They – they won't hang her, will they?'

Richard put his arm round her shoulder. 'Of course not. Not when they learn of the provocation. Not when they learn what sort of monster she prevented escaping – a murderer, kidnapper, spy, and blackmailer. And they'll learn the truth of that from me – whatever it does to my reputation.'

'She couldn't get off, though, could she?'

'I think she could – with a clever lawyer and a sympathetic jury. She could change her story, claim she was under stress tonight, not responsible for what she was saying, that really she shot Batchev in self-defence – something like that.'

'She won't do that. She'll tell the absolute truth.'

'And in this country we don't approve of people taking the law into their own hands,' Richard said. 'However great a villain the victim. She planned Batchev's murder and carried it out with great efficiency. She'll show no remorse. She's bound to go to prison for a long time.'

'It's not right,' Gerry said in a choking voice, 'for ridding the world of a man like that.'

'Perhaps—' Deveraux said, then broke off.

'Perhaps what?' Richard asked.

'Nothing,' said Deveraux.

CHAPTER THIRTY-FIVE

Inspector Wilkins Explains

In the drawing-room ten minutes later, 'Deveraux,' said Peabody, 'how in tarnation did you get at the truth?'

'I didn't, sir. Wilkins did. I was blundering in the right direction, but I was a long way from the truth when he gave me his list of pointers.'

'Then,' said the Earl, 'I insist that before he leaves he explains his deductive process.'

'Hear, hear,' said Adler.

Looking awkward and embarrassed, Wilkins shuffled forward. He coughed. 'Well, my lord, if your lordship insists. Let me say first that Mr. Deveraux is being far too modest: it was he who spotted Evans as the Wraith. I can't say much about my own deductive process, but I can tell you a few things I thought were rum. And I may add that when I came in here this evening I didn't know everything. I had theories, but not the full picture, and no proof.

'I decided quite early on that nearly everybody was hiding something. It seemed to me the first problem to solve was the matter of the pistols, and when I learnt of the rivalry over the matter of the Bergman Bayards, I suspected that perhaps something a little, er, unconventional might have been going on. When we discovered the gun in the collection-room was a replica, I decided that Mr. Peabody was the most likely, um—'

'Crook,' said Carrie Peabody drily.

'Let's say culprit, ma'am. Then, my lord, after saying that the gun in the collection-room was not yours, but a replica, you added, "And it's not mine either." When questioned you claimed to have meant that it was not your *Bergman*. But, as we'd already established that fact, the remark didn't make sense, and I decided that what you had meant was that *that* replica wasn't *your* replica. As there were a pair of originals, it wasn't unlikely there were also a pair of copies; and if your lordship had one of each, it was on the cards Mr. Peabody had one of each, too. Next, when Mr. Peabody discovered that his pistol was missing from its case your lordship's involuntary exclamation was, "Don't say the case is empty?" – indicating you were extremely surprised not to find *something* in it. Your reaction, sir' – he turned to Peabody – 'both to being told of the theft of Lord Burford's gun, and to the theory I put forward at that time, seemed somewhat unnatural.

'Then there was the matter of the scream on the stairs: both Lady Geraldine and Miss Clifton were upstairs at the time and, once it appeared that the Baroness was by then already dead, barring servants, either her ladyship or Mrs. Peabody had to be the one responsible. And it seemed that Mrs. Peabody, a visitor in a strange house, would be the more likely to be nervous. Considering all these factors, I evolved a tentative theory to account for the matter of the four pistols. Then I played a couple of long shots. First

I searched Mr. Peabody's luggage. Your unwillingness to allow it, Mr. Peabody, and your readiness, ma'am – followed by your genuine amazement when I discovered the pistol – supported my theory that Mr. Peabody had hidden one gun in the room, and you'd taken another one away – the one put there by his lordship. In fact, you started to say something like "He must have brought it back again". I had a good idea you'd want to plant it in a room that was specifically Lord Burford's – which probably meant the collection-room or the study. I had another look in the collection-room myself, then got Mr. Deveraux to search the study. Fortunately, this paid off and my theory was virtually confirmed.'

'Well, I'm exceedingly sorry to have made your job more difficult,' Lord Burford said gruffly.

'That goes for me too,' said Peabody.

'Please don't mention it. It really made the case more interesting – more of a challenge, as it were.'

'I guess I fouled things up for you a bit, didn't I?' said Adler.

'Not really, sir. It always seemed most likely that you were one of the fighters in Batchev's room and the man who had incarcerated Lady Geraldine. Your exact motives were not clear, but you've explained those yourself. The matter of your antagonist was more tricky, but once we'd eliminated Batchev himself – who was already dead – and picked on Evans as the Wraith – who has always been purely a jewel thief and who wouldn't have had occasion to enter Batchev's room – well, then the man you fought had to be either Thornton or Mr. Fotheringay here. I'm sorry to say, Mr. Fotheringay, sir, that I did wonder if you were the Wraith and the drug had been self-administered, but – Mr. Fotheringay?'

'He's just gone to sleep again,' said the Countess.

'Then I can say that Mr. Deveraux assured me that unless Mr. Fotheringay was the most brilliant actor imaginable, he couldn't conceivably be the Wraith. That left Mr. Thornton. There seemed no reason why he should have hidden in Batchev's room, but then I asked the Yard to make some enquiries about him, and they turned up a deposit of ten thousand pounds in £1 notes in his bank account. That brought him right into the centre of the picture. But there was still no way of proving anything. So I decided to try my ruse of frightening him into speaking the truth by accusing him of the murder.'

There was silence for a few moments. Then Richard said quietly: 'And what about the murders?'

'I must admit, sir, that you were the problem there. From the point of view of motive, you were the strongest suspect. Yet I was quite unable to work out a coherent sequence of events with you cast as the murderer. So I changed my approach and decided to assume, at least as an experiment, that you were telling the complete truth. Taking your evidence then in conjunction with Lady Geraldine's – and I could think of no reason why, as she wasn't the killer herself, she should be lying—'

'How did you know I wasn't the killer?' Gerry asked.

'If you were, why should you have admitted being near the Baroness's room? You could have claimed to have been in your room right up to the time you went to investigate the rumpus. Where was I?'

'Comparing my evidence with Geraldine's,' Richard said.

'Ah yes. Assuming you were both telling the truth, Batchev himself was clearly indicated as the murderer of the Baroness. And when I learnt that Lady Geraldine had been able to see only his feet, then I realised how the Baroness's body had left her room. That explained one murder, but left me as much in the dark as ever about the death of Batchev himself. Of the people present, Mr. Felman (as we then thought he was) had the best opportunity and motive, and when we learnt he was really Adler after all, he was a very strong suspect.

'But all the time the main question worrying me was why Batchev had tried to break out at all – and with only a pair of wire cutters to put the alarm out of action. He knew it was an elaborate and virtually foolproof system; he must have known that such an attempt was almost certain to set off the alarm. Having concealed the Baroness's body, with virtually no possibility of it being found during the night, why hadn't he waited until the alarm was switched off at six-thirty, then left quietly by a side door? To try to break out like that was the act of a madman. I just couldn't believe in it, and I started to hunt round for another explanation.

'I told myself that of course he hadn't been meaning to go through the window just then – all he'd actually been doing was work on the alarm. To that end he'd fetched the stepladder to stand on. Then I asked myself *why*? To be sure, Batchev was not a tall man. But neither am I. Yet I could reach the wire quite comfortably by standing on a chair.'

'Inspector Wilkins' height,' Adler murmured.

'Precisely, sir. Or rather *lack* of it. So Batchev could

have reached it, too. Why, then, go to all the trouble of fetching a tall, heavy stepladder? What other use could he have possibly had for it? All the thing had done, apparently, was fall over. That pulled me up short. Was that all it had been *meant* to do? If Batchev had been standing on the chair, and not on the ladder, was it the ladder and not the chair which had smashed the window? The window had broken almost exactly as the door opened. Could it have been the actual opening of the door which had caused it? Had we been intended to think Batchev had gone through the window, when in fact he hadn't? No. Because he *had* gone through the window: Miss Clifton had seen him; and we'd found his body outside.

'Then, after the discovery of the Baroness's body, Mr. Deveraux informed me that Miss Clifton had told him she had smelt the Baroness's scent in the linen-room. That struck me as highly unlikely. I couldn't imagine the Baroness using a powerful perfume, and when I asked Mr. Deveraux he agreed it had been a subtle and elusive scent. I didn't believe that a scent like that would have seeped through an oak panel. That meant that if Miss Clifton were telling the truth, she had smelt a trace left from the Baroness's body being carried through a fairly large room approximately fifteen minutes before. That seemed to me impossible – in view of the fact that Lady Geraldine, who has a good sense of smell (she identified the scent of lavender on the egg cosy), did not identify the Baroness's scent when the body passed within a few feet of her as she stood in the recess. It seemed Miss Clifton had lied. And if she'd lied about that, had she also lied about the incident of the broken window? I checked with Mr. Deveraux and learnt that only Miss Clifton claimed to have seen the man – and that he himself had not even heard the supposed sound in the breakfast-room.'

'Deveraux's hearing, eh?' said Peabody.

'Yes, sir. But again something *not* heard, a sound that was lacking. So I took another closer look at Miss Clifton's evidence. And immediately one question struck me: when, during the night, she'd left her room, supposedly to investigate the sounds she'd heard, *why hadn't she switched on a light?* By then I knew about the movements and motives of everyone else who'd been up, and I realised they'd all had good reasons for not wanting to be seen. But if Miss Clifton were telling the truth, she'd had no such reason. Yet apparently, apart from quickly flashing the gallery light on and off, she'd spent all the time groping about in the dark and striking matches.

'I next asked Mr. Deveraux to go into very precise detail as to their finding of the Baroness's body. Then I learnt something else odd. Miss Clifton had been going to take her handbag into the passage with her. I could think of no reason she should do that – unless it were to put something in it. Which meant she must have known there was something behind the panel. And the only thing – other than the body – was the pistol which had killed Batchev. I was then sure Miss Clifton had set up the business of the breakfast-room window just to fool us.

'I still couldn't understand how she'd managed the actual murder, as it didn't seem she'd had time to leave the house and get back again. I thought of all sorts of things: that she'd had an accomplice; that Batchev wasn't killed instantly and had staggered out to die; even that there might be an underground river leading to the lake with an entrance in the cellars, into which she could have dumped the body. Then, when I was looking in the gun-room again, I saw the circus cannon – and something clicked. We checked and found minute traces of blood inside the barrel. That was it.'

'Lord Burford's collection,' Richard said. 'I thought that simply meant the murder weapon came from it.'

'*One* murder weapon came from it sir. The pistol that killed *Batchev* came from Mr. Peabody's collection. From that aspect, both collections were of equal importance, and I would have mentioned both if that had been what I had in mind.'

'And the pointer about the weather?' Peabody asked.

'Miss Clifton explained that correctly. The weather was important: you had complete darkness followed by vivid flashes of light; dead silence, then loud claps of thunder. So some minor things were seen or heard, while others, normally more noticeable, were not.

'But to revert: my suspicions that Miss Clifton had engineered the business in the breakfast-room were virtually confirmed when, during enquiries in the village, we learnt that a girl answering her description had bought a reel of cobbler's thread there on Saturday afternoon.

'I was then certain there'd been one murderer – and one murderess. When this evening I asked Mr. Deveraux to give me the name of the murderer, and he said Batchev, I knew he'd reached the truth.'

CHAPTER THIRTY-SIX

Future Plans

The next morning Richard and Adler commenced their talks. This time there were no snags, and the desire of each of them for a quick settlement was so great that by five p.m. they had reached full agreement.

Also in the morning, the diamond necklace was dug up by a policeman and restored to a joyful Mrs. Peabody, who immediately insisted on Hiram making out a substantial cheque to the local police benevolent fund.

The Peabodys were to stay on at Alderley for a few more days. Peabody and the Earl decided that Lord Burford should retain both the Bergman Bayards until the return of Trimble Greene, and then take them to New York himself in time for the exhibition. The Countess was to go too, and afterwards the Peabodys were to show them something of America.

Algy had managed to build up a somewhat jumbled picture of the events which had taken place while he was asleep. He came rapidly to the conclusion that two dangerous criminals, recognising in him the chief threat to their nefarious schemes, had both attempted to kill him, and that only his remarkably tough constitution had saved him. This story he was anxious to spread without delay through London society, and by Tuesday lunch-time he had left.

During all this, one person remained downcast. Gerry was very distressed and worried about Jane. She turned down an invitation to accompany the Earl and Countess to the United States, and spent most of the day quietly by herself.

Then came another invitation. The negotiations over, Adler sought her out and, surprisingly diffidently, suggested she visited the Duchy as his guest while her parents were away.

In spite of everything, Gerry was thrilled. But still she regretfully refused.

'It'll be quite safe,' he assured her, 'thanks to the arrangements your uncle and I have completed today.'

'It's not that, really,' she said. 'Normally it would be wonderful. But I couldn't be happy doing anything like that until I know what happens to Jane.'

'I'm sorry,' he said. 'But I'll keep the invitation open.'

It was just after this that Gerry had a long conversation with Deveraux.

Deveraux was dressing for dinner when there was a knock and Richard entered. He sat down on the bed, lit a cigarette, and said: 'Perhaps what?'

Deveraux deftly inserted a cufflink in his dress shirt. He said: 'We're going to be at war before the decade is out.'

'Been listening to Churchill?'

'Yes. Haven't you?'

Slowly Richard nodded. 'Yes. Don't quote me, but I'm afraid he's right. I may say so myself publicly soon.'

'During this war, and in the period leading up to it, my department is going to become more and more important. It's going to expand. I'm lucky enough to have a certain amount of influence in the service, and over the next few years my main task is going to be recruitment. In fact, I've been told that if I find anybody I want, and he's willing, I can have him.'

'Very nice. So?'

Deveraux swung round. 'Last Thursday I met a girl. Since then I've got to know her well, and this evening I made it my business to find out everything I could about her background and history from your niece. I now know that that girl has got every quality and every qualification I'm looking for. She's cool, courageous and resourceful. She's self-confident and highly ingenious. She's intensely loyal, lives by a strict personal code, and I'd swear she's completely trustworthy. She's also pretty ruthless and she's prepared to kill in a good cause. She's strong and fit, and could obviously, even untrained, hold her own in a rough-house. She speaks French and German, and she has no close family. I've no intention of letting a girl like that rot away the best years of her life in penal servitude when she could be doing valuable work for her country.'

'I thought you might mean something like that.'

'Your family has second sight. Lady Geraldine seemed to read my mind quite remarkably.'

'Don't worry: she knows how to keep her mouth shut.'

'Oh, I'm not sorry she guessed – although naturally I couldn't have told her. She cheered up tremendously – then went off to accept some invitation from Adler.'

'How will you get Jane out? If such influence as I have can be any use...'

'Thank you, but I don't think it'll be necessary. First, we'll let her serve six to twelve months of her sentence. It'll do her good. She's a bit too arrogant and self-willed at present. She's got to learn to accept discipline – and control her temper. But after that...'

Deveraux stood up and put on his coat. 'Well,' he said, 'if you read in the papers that Jane Clifton, serving a life sentence for murder, has died in prison, don't grieve for her. It won't be true.' His face went grave. 'Grieve only if years from now you hear from me that somewhere in Europe an unnamed British woman agent has been executed by firing squad.'

Richard drew at his cigarette. 'And supposing she's not shot? Supposing we fight this war and win it, and Jane comes through it? What then?'

'Then,' said Deveraux, 'if I come through it too, I'm going to marry her.'

CHAPTER THIRTY-SEVEN

The Final Mystery

The following morning Richard, Adler and Deveraux left Alderley at the same time. Deveraux and Richard were to drive separately to London, and Adler was to be dropped at the station and from there go home alone, as inconspicuously as he'd come.

The others came out to see the three men off. They were all standing talking, while the servants loaded the luggage into the cars, when another car came up the drive. It stopped and Wilkins got out. 'I thought you'd all be glad to know,' he said, 'that we've just heard Anna Felman's been found safe and well.'

A minute later, while the others were saying good-bye to Adler, Deveraux drew Wilkins aside. 'I was going to call in at your station to say so long,' he said. 'It's been quite an experience working with you, old man. I hope cracking this case will do you some good.'

Wilkins sighed deeply. 'It looks as though it might mean promotion.'

'Isn't that good?'

'I suppose so. But it'll likely mean more cases like

this one. There seem to be hundreds of them among the English upper classes these days. And I don't really enjoy them. I'd be much happier working on the new one-way traffic system. I'm not sanguine, not sanguíne at all. Still, I mustn't bother you with my troubles. What will the case mean to you?'

'Me? Oh, merely memories, Wilkins. I've just got the one memento.' He took from his waistcoat pocket a small woollen object. 'Funny, that's how I'll always think of this business – as the affair of the bloodstained egg cosy.'

'You know, Mr. Deveraux, I suspected you for a while.'

'Did you really? Why?'

'Well, while I believed Batchev had gone through that window, it seemed you'd actually been outside at the same time as him. If you'd had the gun, fitted with a silencer, you'd have had the best chance of anyone to bump him off. You'd have needed an outside accomplice to dump the body in the lake, that's all. But it wasn't long before I ruled you out. Besides, somebody had certainly bopped you on the head—'

'Great Scott!' Deveraux broke in. 'Wilkins – who on earth did it? We were so busy solving the murder, we forgot all about that.'

Wilkins' mouth dropped open. 'Goodness me, so we did. I haven't charged any of them with it.'

'I don't particularly want anyone charged. I've got to know, though. But – I don't see which of them it could have been. Not Thornton. Certainly not Jane. Batchev was dead.'

'Evans, then?'

'It could have been. But why? It doesn't make sense.'

They were standing near Deveraux's car. Nearly everyone else was out of earshot, the sole exception being Merryweather, who had dismissed the footman and was himself strapping Deveraux's luggage onto the rack behind the dickey seat. He turned now and cleared his throat.

'Excuse me, sir. I could not help overhearing your conversation. I am in a position to throw light on the subject.'

Deveraux blinked. 'You, Merryweather? Are you saying you know who hit me?'

'Yes, sir. I regret to say that it was I.'

'*You?*' Deveraux and Wilkins both goggled at him.

'Yes, sir. If I may be permitted to explain. I was suspicious of you. You will appreciate that I had no means of knowing your true standing. There had been that challenge to the Wraith in the magazine. You were a person virtually unknown to the Family, and appeared to have engineered your invitation. It seemed, if I may use a colloquialism, extremely, er, fishy, and I resolved to keep an eye on you. I watched your room on the Friday night and my suspicions were confirmed when you left it and prowled around the house in the dark. I decided not to notify his lordship, as, if you denied it, I would have no proof. I was persuaded that on Friday you had been merely rehearsing and that you intended to steal the necklace on the Saturday night. So I followed you again, hoping to catch you in the act. But you simply continued to walk about the house. I thought that perhaps you were going to postpone the theft yet another night. Then, as you neared the top of the stairs, I heard footsteps approaching, which

I recognised as being Mr. Richard's. You stopped and extinguished your flashlight. But then to my amazement you went rapidly after him. I immediately concluded that you were not a thief, but a hired assassin. My first thought was to save Mr. Richard. I dared not call out, as I was sure you were armed. So I rushed forward and struck you.'

In a weak voice, Deveraux said: 'With what?'

'With a silver salver, I'm afraid, sir.'

'Most – most apt.'

'Thank you, sir. Fortunately I missed striking a direct blow. Then my own torch failed. I endeavoured to reach the light switch at the same time keeping a firm grip on you. But you were too heavy. I was about to call for help, when you struck me a blow in the abdomen which winded me. Then the other commotion started and my nerve fled. Mr. Richard was by then clearly safe. I retreated down the stairs, brushing against the lady whom I later learnt was Mrs. Peabody, and retired to the servants' quarters. The next day I discovered that you were a police officer. I would like to tender my most sincere apologies, sir.'

Deveraux's lips twitched, but he spoke gravely. 'Your apology is accepted, Merryweather.'

'I am gratified, sir. You did, I think, say you did not wish to prefer charges?'

'Quite correct.'

'That, sir, is a great relief to me. Will that be all, sir?'

'Yes,' said Deveraux, 'that will be all. Thank you.'

'Thank you, sir,' said Merryweather.

THE AFFAIR OF THE
MUTILATED
MINK

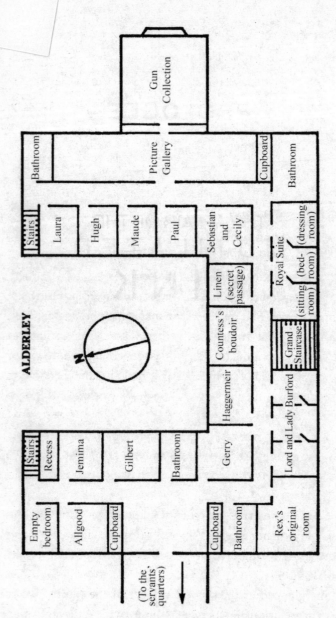

Plan of First Floor

PROLOGUE

'You murdering fiend!'

She hissed the words. Then she hurled the magazine to the floor and kicked it across the room.

This made her feel a little better, and after a minute she calmed down. She retrieved the magazine and again stared at the face that smiled out at her. There was nothing in the features to indicate the ruthlessness lying behind them. Could she possibly be mistaken? It had all happened a long time ago. And they'd only met once. Nevertheless, she was almost certain—

Almost. It wasn't enough. She had to be sure. And to be sure she had to see this face in the flesh – ideally study it at leisure, converse with its owner, lay little traps...

Could she arrange to spend such a time in the company of her suspect – preferably staying under the same roof? It ought to be possible – if not socially, then professionally.

She glanced at the second subject of the photo. What was the relationship between these two? A casual one?

Or were they closer than that? Accomplices? Hunter and victim?

She reread the caption beneath the picture. Then she put the magazine safely away. As she did so, her mind was working furiously.

CHAPTER ONE

'On Guard!'

George Henry Aylwin Saunders, twelfth Earl of Burford, took up a fencing stance and thrust. The ferrule of his umbrella stopped one inch from his butler's waistcoat. 'Yield, villain!' the Earl exclaimed.

'Certainly, my lord.' Merryweather, the butler, relieved his master of the umbrella and his overcoat. 'An enjoyable cinematographic entertainment, my lord.'

'Tophole. Errol Flynn is terrific. You really ought to go and see it.'

'Thank you, my lord, but I prefer to pass my leisure hours with an improving book.'

'I can't honestly believe you need any improvement, Merryweather.'

'Thank you, my lord.' Merryweather vanished into the background.

'You know, Daddy, you'll have to stop doing things like that to Merry. I'm sure he feels it's lowering to his dignity.'

Lady Geraldine Saunders crossed the big oak-panelled

hall and tucked her arm through her father's. She was petite, vivacious, red-haired, with a tip-tilted nose and deceptively innocent large hazel eyes.

'Don't know what you mean, my dear. Never done anything like that before.'

'Maybe, but last month you were calling him an ornery horse stealer and pretending to beat him to the draw, and before that threatening to squeal to the cops about his bootlegging operation in the cellar.'

'Ah, that was during my cowboy and gangster periods. I've gone off those now.'

'Well, can't you go off swashbucklers, too?'

'No fear! Couldn't if I wanted to just now, anyway. The manager of the Bijou's booked the new Rex Ransom for next week – especially for me. Uncommon civil of him.'

'He's just trying to keep you away from the Odeon.'

They went into the drawing-room. Gerry flopped down on the sofa, while Lord Burford poured himself a whisky and soda.

Gerry said, 'I honestly think the talkies have taken the place of guns in your affection.'

'Oh, no. Basically my collection'll always come first. I admit my enthusiasm was dampened a bit after one of 'em was used to commit a murder. But it'll come back. In the meantime I'm very much enjoyin' having something else to do. And I must say, they're remarkably hospitable in these places. Manager meets you in the foyer, shows you to your seat. Pretty little gal brings free coffee in the interval. Amazin' how they can keep up such a service.'

'They only do it for you, Daddy.'

Lord Burford looked surprised. 'Really? You sure?'

'Quite. You wouldn't know. As a rule, most of the other customers are in by the time you get there. But you happen to be a peer of the realm. And they don't get many. It must do wonders for the box office in a little place like Westchester – especially when you turn up in a chauffeur-driven Rolls in full evening dress.'

'Bless my soul.' Lord Burford squared his shoulders. 'You think people still care about that sort of thing in the 1930s?'

'Certainly they do.'

'Well, that reporter chappie certainly seemed interested.'

'Reporter?'

'Yes. Young feller from the *Westshire Advertiser,* waiting for me when I came out. Said they wanted to do a piece about the county's newest film fan. Asked how it was I'd only recently started going to the movies. I explained no one had ever told me how good they'd got. I saw those jumpy old silent things when I was a boy and didn't think much of them. So I never bothered again—'

'Until a few months ago you found yourself with a couple of hours to kill in London, noticed a cinema showing the latest Garbo, felt curious, went in – and were hooked. You told him all that?'

''Course. And he wanted to know all about the pictures I most enjoyed and my favourite stars. Most flatterin'.'

'Well, make the most of it. I don't suppose you'll be going so often once Mummy gets home.'

'Don't see why. Harmless enough hobby. Deuced cheaper than popping off to the Italian Riviera, too.'

'She did want you to go with her.'

'Don't like seaside resorts. Borin' places. Rather watch

Errol Flynn or Rex Ransom any day.' He crossed to the massive fireplace and warmed his hands at the blazing fire.

'Cold out?' Gerry asked.

'Decidedly chilly.'

'I was talking to old Josh earlier. He says we're in for what he calls a 'real shramming winter'.'

'Well, I've never known him wrong about the weather in forty years. Suppose you'll be clearing off to warmer climes before the real winter hits us, will you?'

'No, I'm not going away for a bit.' Gerry suddenly spoke absently.

Her father looked at her closely. 'Oh, lor', don't say you're going off into another brown study. You still ditherin' between those two young fellows?'

She nodded.

'I wish you'd make up your mind and marry one of 'em.'

'*Marry*? Who said anything about marrying?'

Lord Burford frowned. 'But – but that's what it's all about, isn't it? This moonin' all over the house, kickin' things?'

'Not at all. I simply can't decide which of them to become engaged to.'

The Earl raised a hand to his brow in bewilderment. 'Look, forgive me if I'm dense, but doesn't one follow the other?'

'Usually. But not always. Not the first time. Every girl should have one broken engagement these days. All my friends have.'

'Now let me get this straight. You want to get engaged

to one of these boys – Paul or…Hugh, is it? – solely in order to break it off again?'

'Well, not *solely*. It's conceivable I *might* marry him. But that's not the main object of the exercise.'

'Then I can't see what all the fuss is about. If you're not going to get hitched to him, what's it matter which one you choose?

'Daddy, surely you wouldn't want me to get engaged to just *anybody*? This is serious. They've both proposed and I can't keep them waiting much longer. Do advise me.'

'Certainly not! You'd immediately pick the other one and always hold it against me. No, you've got to choose for yourself. Who d'you like best?'

'Oh, that's easy. Paul.'

'Then what's the problem?'

'Just this: I always feel happy with Paul. Relaxed. We get on fine. We can talk about anything. We're jolly good *pals*.'

'But?'

'But perhaps I get on a bit too well with him. He's not really exciting.'

'In spite of careerin' all over the place climbing mountains, running for Britain in the Olympics and so on?'

'In spite of that. Because I'm really not a part of that side of his life at all.'

'But Hugh *is* excitin'?'

'Mm. He fascinates me. But he frightens me rather, too. I'm always sort of on the edge of my seat, wondering what he'll say or do next. And he's thoroughly beastly to me sometimes. But he does make me think – about the only person I know who does. But usually he also makes me unsettled, disturbed or downright angry, too.'

'Sounds thoroughly uncomfortable. He's the painter, isn't he?'

'That's right.'

'Make any money at it?'

'Shouldn't think so; he lives pretty frugally. But he won't discuss it. Or anything about his background. I think he's a bit ashamed of his family, actually.'

'Well, I don't think that's very nice.'

'I'm sure there's a good reason for it.'

'Sounds rather mysterious. Is that part of his appeal?'

'Could be, I suppose. Paul is so open about his background.'

'Yes, I remember, he told me. Rather amusin' actually. "Of course, sir," he said, "I've got no breeding at all; *nouveau riche* you'd call me, I daresay." I quite warmed to him.'

'Yes, that's Paul all over. The *nouveau riche* thing is rubbish, of course; he went to Eton, after all, even though his grandfather did start life as a factory hand.'

'Mill owner eventually, wasn't he?'

'Iron foundry. Paul's mother was his only child. She and Paul's father were killed when Paul was a baby, and his grandfather brought him up. Then, when he died about ten years ago, he left Paul his entire fortune.'

'Well, families like ours can do with a stiffenin' of tough working-class backbone every other generation. Stops us becomin' effete.'

'Daddy, remember we're only talking about an engagement.'

'Sorry. Must admit, though, that I'd rather you got engaged to a chap with a bit of money than a penniless artist. Not that you need it, but I fancy you might always have the uneasy feeling he'd married – er, got engaged to you for your money.'

'I'm certain Hugh wouldn't do that.'

'You've talked to your mother about this, I suppose.'

'Definitely not. As far as Mummy's concerned they're just casual boyfriends, two of the crowd. If she knew I was thinking of becoming engaged to one of them she'd start vetting his background and finances for husband-suitability. And that would be too shaming. I'll tell her as soon as I make up my mind. OK?'

'So long as you promise not to go running off to Gretna Green to get married or somethin'.'

'As if I would!'

'You wouldn't be the first member of the family to try it. Remember your great grandfather Aylwin.'

'I don't want to remember the old scoundrel. I want to think about Paul and Hugh. I've had a sort of idea that might help me decide. I thought I might have them both to stay for a bit.'

'You've had 'em both to stay before. Didn't help much apparently.'

'No, I mean have them at the same time. It occurred to me that if I could see them side by side over several days it would be easier to compare them. What do you think?'

'That it would be highly embarrassin'.'

'Yes, it would be if we had *just* the two of them. It would be pretty obviously a sort of audition. But if we were to throw a little house party, then—'

'No!'

'I don't mean straight away. After Christmas.'

'No, Geraldine! Good gad, I thought after what happened last time you'd have had enough of house parties for the rest of your life. People getting bumped off all over the place, jewel robberies, detectives, spies, secret agents, me nearly being arrested. I never liked having crowds here – stuffin' the place with people, mostly perfect strangers to each other. Always leads to unpleasantness. Your mother and I've agreed: in future we have at most three or four guests at a time. Understood?'

CHAPTER TWO

'Rex, baby, come right in.'

Cyrus S. Haggermeir, head of the Haggermeir Pictures Corporation, strode beamingly across the expanse of deep carpet and gripped the hand of the bronzed, handsome man with the thick blonde hair, who had just been shown into his Hollywood office.

Rex Ransom blinked in surprise at the warmth of his reception and allowed himself to be ensconced in an armchair. Haggermeir went to a cocktail cabinet. 'Scotch on the rocks, isn't it, Rex?'

'That'll be fine, Mr Haggermeir.'

'Cyrus, Rex, Cyrus. Surely we been buddies long enough now for you to call me by my first name?'

'We have? Oh – I mean, yes, I guess we have.'

Haggermeir handed Rex a glass, went behind his huge desk and sat down. He was a big man with a frankly homely face, like an unsuccessful prizefighter's. 'Why I sent for – asked you to stop by, Rex, is to discuss your next starring vehicle.'

Rex breathed a sigh of relief – which did not escape

Haggermeir's shrewd brown eyes. 'Sumpin' wrong?'

'Oh, no. It's just that it's always good to know another one's being planned. I know the box office receipts of my last picture weren't too hot, and—'

'That wasn't your fault. It was a lousy script. A complete change of setting is called for in your next picture. Recently you've played a Corsican pirate, a Spanish conquistador, and an Arabian prince – all with your hair dyed. Time you got back to an Anglo-Saxon type. You're gonna be an Englishman.'

'I did Robin Hood six years ago, so—'

'English Civil War. Cavaliers and Roundheads. You'll be playing a nobleman, the best swordsman at the court of King Charles, who tries to get the king to safety after the Battle of – of...' Haggermeir glanced down at a script lying on his desk. 'Er, one of them battles. But you're also in love with the daughter of a Roundhead boss, the one that's leading the search for Charles. In the end he finds you guarding him and orders you at sword-point to hand him over. You gotta choose between fighting and perhaps killing your girl's pa, or betraying your king.'

'Certainly sounds like a strong storyline. Is that the script you have there?'

'Yeah.' Haggermeir slid the sheaf of oddly yellowing typewritten papers across the desk.

'*The King's Man*,' Rex read aloud, 'a scenario by Arlington Gilbert.' He turned the pages. 'This looks awfully old.'

'It's been hanging round the studio for years. We commissioned it from some English writer. It was back when we were trying to sign Douglas Fairbanks, and this was the bait.'

'I see. But Douglas apparently didn't like it.'

'Sure he did. But then he formed United Artists with Mary and Chaplin, and—'

Rex's eyebrows shot skywards. 'We're talking about Fairbanks *Senior*?'

'That's right.'

'But UA must have been formed fifteen – twenty years ago.'

'Nineteen nineteen.'

'So – this is a *silent* movie script.'

'Sure. But a mighty good one. And it'll adapt just fine for sound. Now, my idea is to make the picture on location – in England.'

'Oh, swell. The exteriors will look far more realistic. What about the interiors, though? Going to rent some studios over there, or shoot them here?'

'Neither.'

'Neither?'

'Nope. I mean to shoot the whole picture in genuine British settings: castles, stately homes and the like.'

'Gee whiz. Is that feasible, technically?'

'Oh, I guess the sound guys'll crab a bit, but I gotta hunch this is going to be the normal thing in a few years.'

'I see. Have you got your stately homes and castles fixed up?'

'Not yet. But I got my eye on several joints. Here.' Haggermeir picked up a large and heavy book, which he passed to Rex. Rex opened it and saw that it consisted of photographs of old English country houses and castles, each accompanied by a page of descriptive text.

Haggermeir said, 'We'll need several places, but the

most important will be the one that serves as your home. Look at page four.'

Rex turned the leaves until he came to several pictures of a lovely house set in tree-dotted parkland. It was built basically in the form of three sides of a rectangle, was three stories tall, but with two-storey extensions projecting from the east and west wings.

He read aloud: 'Alderley, Westshire, home of the Earls of Burford since the late seventeenth century. Alderley houses valuable collections of stamps and first editions, together with the present Earl's famous collection of firearms. Commenced in 1670—'

Haggermeir interrupted, 'It's got everything – including a ballroom, a big oak panelled hall with a grand staircase that'd be swell for a sword-fight, and a secret passage, which'd be just right for the king's hiding place.'

'But what makes you think this Earl would let us shoot there? These English lords are kind of particular about their stately homes, I should imagine.'

'That, Rexy, is where I'm counting on your help. Get a look at that.' Haggermeir took a small piece of paper from his drawer and pushed it across the desk. It was a newspaper clipping. 'As you probably know, the studio subscribes to press clipping agencies in most countries – which means that whenever our pictures or stars are mentioned in any paper, no matter how small, we get a clipping of it. That one was a real stroke of luck. It arrived just when I was gonna start making enquiries about old English houses, so I at once sent for all the dope on this Alderley dive. It's from a paper called the *Westshire Advertiser*.'

Again Rex read, 'One of the newest and most avid patrons of the Westchester cinemas is the Earl of Burford. In an exclusive interview at the Bijou cinema, given before he returned to Alderley, his historic seventeenth-century home, his lordship told me that he had only recently "discovered" the talkies, and is now a most enthusiastic "film fan". The pictures he most enjoys are historical adventures, with plenty of swordplay. His favourite stars are Errol Flynn and Rex Ransom. "I should love to meet them," his lordship added. His lordship hopes that Lady Burford, who does not, incidentally, share his enthusiasm, and is at present holidaying in—'

Haggermeir again broke in, 'You needn't bother with the rest.'

Rex looked up and grinned. 'Well, I'm sure flattered. And you figure the fact that I'm going to be in the picture will persuade his lordship to let you shoot it at Alderley?'

'That's part of it, but there's a bit more to it. We gotta convince her ladyship as well.'

'Who does not share his enthusiasm.'

'Exactly. And I been reading up about her. She sounds a tartar – and real crazy about that house. Then there's a daughter, Lady Geraldine. She's a live wire, always in the gossip columns. Very much a mind of her own, too. That's the first point. Second is that I gotta check the house for suitability before actually committing myself to shooting there: make sure there are no snags – things that don't show up in the photos. So what I thought I'd do is write and ask if I can come and make a feasibility study for a day or two, bringing my leading man, Rex Ransom. That should make sure the Earl don't say no out of hand. Then if the place does turn out to be OK, it'll be your job to put all the famous Ransom charm into persuading the old dame to agree. OK with you?'

'Sure it is. It'd be dandy to stay in a genuine old English country house. Should be real relaxing.'

'Good gad!' Lord Burford goggled at the letter he was holding.

Lady Burford glanced up sharply from *The Tatler*. 'What *is* the matter, George?'

The Earl gazed at her, wide-eyed with excitement. 'Rex Ransom wants to come here?'

'Who?'

'Rex Ransom, Lavinia. The film star!'

'Oh.' The Countess was unimpressed. 'Why?'

'To look over the house.'

'What's to prevent him? Plenty of open days. I suppose he can afford two shillings.'

'You don't understand. He – or rather his producer, this fellow who's written the letter, er, Haggermeir – wants to come here with Rex and go all over it, examine it at length.'

'What on earth for?'

'You'll never guess.' Lord Burford seemed to have swollen visibly with pride. 'It's a tremendous honour.'

'Oh, I suppose he wants to make one of those absurd talkies here. Really, the insolence of these people!'

The Earl's jaw dropped. 'Eh?'

'Naturally, you will write and tell him that it's not convenient.'

Lord Burford gave a squawk of dismay. 'I can't do

that! Turn away Rex Ransom? When I've just been made Honorary President of the Westchester Film Society?'

'Oh, dear. Well, I suppose if you want the man here you'll have to have him. But only him. We can't have this Hog man crawling all over the place, treating it like some second-rate film studio.'

'I can hardly write to the chap and say Ransom can come but not him. It would be most insultin'.'

Lady Burford sighed. 'I suppose you're right. But you must make it clear that filming here is out of the question.'

'Yes, yes, of course, my dear. I will – er, after they arrive.'

The telephone buzzed in Cyrus Haggermeir's suite at the Ritz Hotel in London. He lifted the receiver. 'Yep?'

'This is the desk, sir. There is a – a gentleman wishing to see you. A Mr Arlington Gilbert. His business relates to your forthcoming motion picture.'

'OK, I'll give him five minutes. Send him up.'

Three minutes later there was a loud and peremptory rapping on the door. Haggermeir opened it. Then he blinked. The man standing on the threshold was over six feet tall and of considerable girth. His hair was long. He was wearing a tartan cloak over a black and somewhat grubby polo sweater; black and white check trousers; and on his feet sandals over mauve socks. In his hand he was clutching a newspaper.

For a moment Haggermeir stared at the visitor, then said, 'Er, good day. Mr Arlington Gilbert?'

'I have that honour.'

He had a deep and plummy voice. Then, uninvited,

he stepped into the room, almost forcing Haggermeir to stand aside. With a swirl of his cloak he swung round and gazed at Haggermeir. His expression was of a man looking at some interesting but rather repulsive exhibit in a museum.

Haggermeir said, 'I'm afraid I haven't had the pleasure to know—'

'A pleasure it most certainly ought to be. But I'm afraid you are not going to find it so.'

'Mr Gilbert, if you could kindly state your business—'

'My business, sir, is this.' Gilbert thrust the newspaper under Haggermeir's nose. It was folded to show a photo of a smiling Rex Ransom, surrounded by autograph-hunters. The caption beneath it read:

Rex Ransom, the American film star, who arrived in London yesterday. Mr Ransom and the well-known producer, Mr Cyrus Haggermeir, are in England to make arrangements for their next picture, a Civil War drama to be called 'The King's Man.'

Haggermeir said: 'Yes, I saw that. What about it?'

'*What about it*?' Gilbert cast his eyes heavenwards. 'Jupiter's teeth! It may interest you mildly to know that this film you so blithely announce you are going to make is my property. I own the copyright. I wrote it.'

Haggermeir snapped his fingers. 'Of course! Arlington Gilbert! I thought the name rang a bell.'

Gilbert gave a snort of disgust. 'Absolutely typical. One sweats blood creating a work that they tell you is 'great' or 'the cat's whiskers,' and which is then locked away for years in some vault. When they do eventually deign to produce it they've forgotten your very name.'

'Well, it has been a long time. And I don't think we ever met—'

'True. You sent your underlings to deal with me – assistant producers, associate producers, lawyers – all the faceless men. But I fought them all and I retained the copyright. What's more, I obtained a contract which states that any rewrites necessary shall be done by me.'

Haggermeir scratched his chin. 'Well, it seems our script department may have goofed on this, and I'm sorry you had to read about it in the papers.'

Gilbert waved the apology aside. 'I am interested in only one thing: how much are you going to pay me for adapting the scenario into a talkie?'

'Ah.' Haggermeir looked a little embarrassed. 'Well, that's something that'll have to be discussed. Will you take my word that—'

'No. I won't take your word for anything, Mr Haggermeir. I want everything down in black and white.'

Haggermeir flushed. 'I don't know what you expect to gain by insulting me—'

'Insult you, sir?' Gilbert drew himself up to his full height. 'How is it possible for *me*, a creative artist and therefore one of the noblest of earth's creatures, to insult you who by definition are a villain of the deepest dye?'

'Look here, you've no right to say things like that—'

'I have every right. I have learnt from bitter experience that every film producer – and every theatrical impresario, publisher, editor, literary agent, accountant, lawyer and tax inspector on earth – is a rogue and a vagabond. A bloodsucker. A leech.'

Thoroughly angry by now, Haggermeir stepped forward and jabbed a finger into the other's chest.

'Now, get this, Gilbert—'

'Sir, my friends call me Arlington. Others call me *Mr* Gilbert.'

There was a pause. Then Haggermeir chuckled. 'If your writing's as plagiaristic as your speech, you got a fat chance of doing the script. That was a straight lift from Oscar Wilde.'

For the first time Gilbert looked disconcerted. Haggermeir spotted this. 'Oh, I read sumpin' else besides screenplays and balance sheets.'

'Congratulations. Now to revert: my fee.'

At that moment a knock came at the door. With some relief, Haggermeir called, 'Come in.' Gilbert swore.

The door opened and the head of a middle-aged man peered diffidently into the room.

'Yeah?' Haggermeir barked.

'Oh.' The head's eyes blinked. 'Mr Haggermeir?'

'Yes, yes.' Haggermeir spoke irritably.

'Ah, capital. Er, spare a moment?'

'I'm very busy. What's it about?'

'Well, I wondered if I could talk to you about—'

'Well, come in, man! Don't yell at me from the doorway.'

'Oh, thanks.' An untidily dressed body followed the head into the room. 'Sorry to interrupt, my dear chap, but I wanted a word about *The King's Man*.'

Haggermeir groaned. 'Not another one! I suppose *you* wrote it, too, did you?'

'What's that?' Gilbert gave a roar. He stepped menacingly up to the newcomer. 'Let me tell you that I am the *sole* writer of *The King's Man*, and—'

'Really?' The other beamed and held out his hand. 'I'm delighted to meet you. I suppose that means you'll be coming down to Alderley, too, will you?'

Gilbert stared at him. 'Eh?'

Haggermeir goggled. 'Who – who are you?'

'Oh, sorry. Should have introduced myself. I'm Burford.'

Haggermeir's jaw dropped. '*Earl* Burford?'

'Of, as a matter of fact.'

'Uh?'

'Earl *of* Burford's the correct form. Not that it matters.'

'Oh, my lord, I'm so sorry. I had no idea. Do forgive me.' Haggermeir was red-faced. 'Please, sit down.' He ushered Lord Burford to a chair. 'Will you have a drink, sir?'

'Ah.' Lord Burford thought for a moment. 'I'll have a bourbon old fashioned.'

'Oh, I'll have to send down for that. I only have Scotch.'

'No, no, Scotch and soda will be fine.'

'Sure?'

'Quite. Er, prefer it, actually. No offence. Just thought, you being American...' Lord Burford tailed off.

Gilbert said: 'Whisky'll suit me, too, thanks – Cyrus.'

Haggermeir, crossing to a makeshift bar, cast him a dirty glance.

Gilbert flopped into a chair near the Earl's. 'Why should you expect me at Alderley, Lord Burford?'

'Well, as the producer wants to look over the place to see if it's suitable for filming, I assumed the writer would want to, as well.'

Gilbert nodded, as though a light had dawned. 'Ah, yes, of course – I will want to. I was just surprised you, a non-professional, realising the necessity of that. Cyrus and I were hoping you'd include me in the invitation. That's settled, then. Now, let me see, Cyrus, you're going down when?'

Haggermeir came hack carrying two glasses. He looked grim. He handed one to the Earl and the other to Gilbert, saying, 'Thursday. But on second thought, I'm not sure it's necessary for you to come – until I've decided if the place is suitable.'

'Oh, nonsense. If you do decide on it, the script will need a lot of adaptation. I'll have to start the rewrite as soon as possible.' He downed his whisky and got to his feet. 'So Thursday it will be. I'll make my own way down, Cyrus. See you there. Thanks for the invitation, Lord Burford. I should be there for lunch. Bye.' And Gilbert ambled from the room.

Lord Burford said: 'Interestin' feller.'

Haggermeir grunted grimly.

'Unusual personality. I didn't catch the name.'

'Arlington Gilbert.'

'Oh.'

'Earl, it's an honour to have you here, but is there anything you particularly wanted to talk about?'

'Well, just this: it's my missus. She isn't at all keen on having this picture shot at Alderley. Didn't want you to arrive assumin' everything was cut and dried.'

'Oh, I won't be, my lord. I anticipated that situation. Now, firstly, so her ladyship doesn't object to my looking over the place, I recommend you tell her I want to do it because I'm thinking of building a replica of Alderley in Hollywood. It's quite true. If it turns out it's impractical to shoot at Alderley, I may well do that. Then, if I do find the house is OK, I suggest we leave the next stage to Rex. He has a very persuasive manner.'

'Ah, I see.' The Earl looked knowing. 'Oh, that's splendid. Right ho. Er, he around, by any chance?'

'No, afraid not. He's out seeing the sights. Naturally, we didn't expect you to call...'

'Course you didn't. I'll see him Thursday. Must say it's a real thrill.' He stood up. 'Better be toddlin' off now.'

Haggermeir got up hastily. 'Well, my lord, it's been a real pleasure. And I do apologise for that little misunderstanding.'

'Think nothing of it. Sort of thing that's always happenin' to me. Lavinia says I lack an air of authority. Funny name, that.'

Haggermeir looked blank. 'Lavinia?'

'No, no – Arlington Gilbert. Backwards. Like that singer chappie.'

'Er, I'm afraid I don't—'

'Feller who sings with the MacDonald gal. Always think he ought to be called Eddy Nelson. Well, toodle-oo, my dear chap. Till Thursday.'

CHAPTER THREE

The telephone rang at Alderley. The Countess, who happened to be near, answered it. 'Alderley One.'

A woman's voice said, 'Is Lady Burford there, please?'

'Speaking.'

'Oh, Lavinia. It's Cecily.'

'Cecily?'

'Your cousin. Cecily Bradshaw as was.'

'Good gracious! Cecily! It must be twenty-five years. I can hardly believe it. Where are you?'

'London.'

'I thought you were still in Australia. How long have you been home?'

'Just a few days. We're here for a fortnight, then going on to America.'

'We? Oh, that is you and, and—' Lady Burford groped unsuccessfully for a long-forgotten name, 'and your husband?'

'That's right – Sebastian.'

'How is Sebastian'?'

'Thriving. Lavinia. I was hoping we could get together?'

'That would be very nice. When were you thinking of?'

'Well, we're fully engaged for the next few days, but we're free from Thursday until Monday. Could you come up to town?'

'Unfortunately, that's impossible. We have guests. Next week perhaps?'

'No, we're off to Norfolk to stay with some friends of Sebastian's on Tuesday. Oh, what a shame! I did want to see you again. You're one of the few relatives I have left in England.'

Lady Burford thought rapidly. There was no help for it. 'Would you like to come here?'

'You mean to stay? Oh, I wouldn't want to impose, if you have other guests.'

'Oh, that's no problem. We have plenty of room.'

'That's really very kind.'

'It's settled, then. When will you be arriving?'

'Well, we've hired a station wagon, so we'll be motoring down. We could leave Thursday morning and be there by lunchtime, if that's convenient.'

'Perfectly. Very well, Cecily, we'll look forward to seeing you then. Goodbye.'

'Goodbye, Lavinia, and thank you so much.'

Lady Burford put down the receiver and was turning away when it rang again. She answered it.

'Gilbert here.'

'Who?'

'Arlington Gilbert. Listen, I've got a message for the Earl or his old woman. Tell them I'll be bringing my secretary.'

'I beg your pardon?'

He gave a sigh. 'You deaf? I said I'm bringing my secretary, Maude Fry, for the weekend. I'll need her if I'm to work on this screenplay. She shouldn't be any trouble. She's a big woman, but she doesn't eat much and she's quite respectable – won't dance on the table or anything. Tell him we'll be arriving sometime Thursday morning. Mind you don't forget.'

Gilbert rang off.

'Really, George, the man was insufferably rude.'

'Obviously thought you were a housemaid.'

'That makes it no better.'

'Well, you should have told him no.'

'He didn't give me a chance. And it's getting out of hand. First there were to be two of these film persons, then three, now four.'

'At least they're all friends together. It's you that's turning it into a confounded house party by bringing in outsiders at the same time.'

'My cousin can hardly be referred to as an outsider.'

'She is to Haggermeir and Co. And her husband is to all of us. Even Cecily's virtually a stranger to me; I only met her two or three times.'

Gerry, who was sitting by doing a crossword puzzle, looked up. 'I remember hearing you mention cousin Cecily years ago, but I don't exactly know who she is.'

'She's the daughter of my Aunt Amelia, mother's sister. Aunt Amelia was considered to have married beneath her. She died when Cecily was born. Her father brought her up and she never had much to do with us – her father moved in rather different circles from us. But she came to stay sometimes. Later on she decided to go on the stage. She didn't make much of a success of it, and ended up in a chorus line. Lived a rather fast sort of life, I believe – stage door johnnies, and so on. Which naturally was quite beyond the pale to my mother. She decided we wouldn't have anything more to do with Cecily. But I still met her occasionally in town. Your father and I were engaged by then, and one weekend I brought her to see Alderley. Then a few months later her father died and she told me that as she had nothing to keep her here she was going to try her luck in Australia. I had some letters from her over the next few years. She said she was doing quite well on the stage. Eventually she told me she was getting married – to a sheep farmer. I can't remember his surname, so I don't know what hers is now. She was going to send me her new address, but she didn't do so and I've never heard from her since – until now.'

'You'll certainly have masses to talk about,' Gerry said.

Lord Burford gave a grunt. 'Well, as long as no one expects me to talk to this husband about sheep, I don't mind. I'm going to be fully occupied with Rex and Haggermeir. Stupid creatures.'

Gerry grinned. 'Rex and Haggermeir?'

'No – sheep. Anyone seen my copy of *Photoplay*?' He went to the other side of the room and started vaguely picking up cushions.

Gerry said, 'Mummy, did you remember her husband's *first* name?'

'No; fortunately, Cecily supplied it – Sebastian. I wonder what he'll be like. And what can I do with him all weekend?'

'I don't expect he'll be any trouble: a stable for his kangaroo, an open space to practice his boomerang throwing, plenty of billabongs to eat—'

'Don't be silly, Geraldine. It's just that sort of facetiousness that irritates colonials – quite justifiably.'

'Sorry. You mean you don't want him to be unoccupied all weekend?'

'Well, I can see your father monopolising this Ransom man, and I can't imagine Sebastian having a lot in common with Mr Haggermeir or the Gilbert person.'

'So you'd like there to be additional manpower here?'

'It might be convenient.'

'Mm.' Gerry was silent for a moment. Then she said, 'Excuse me,' and left the room.

She was back in ten minutes. 'Problem solved,' she announced. 'Paul Carter and Hugh Quartus are both willing to help out.'

'Lady Burford jerked her head up. 'You've invited them both – for this weekend?'

'Yes. Wasn't it lucky they were free?'

'Really, Geraldine! That's very naughty of you.'

'But you said you wanted extra manpower.'

'One extra man – not two. And certainly not two who are almost strangers to me.'

'It doesn't matter if they're strangers to you. They're not coming to amuse you. I've made it clear that their main function will be to entertain my wild colonial second-cousin-in-law-once-removed Sebastian. It was necessary to invite both because we don't know what he's like. Now, Paul can discuss lowbrow things like sport and the London shows, and Hugh can talk about literature and art. Paul can play him at billiards, Hugh at chess. You ought to be grateful you have a daughter who can supply a man for every occasion.'

Paul Carter put the receiver down and gave vent to a loud whoop of joy.

It had to be a good sign. It had to be. True, it was short notice to be invited for a weekend – almost as though he was a last-minute addition. But he *had* been invited. It must mean something – other than merely helping with the Australian relative.

He'd been rather uneasy lately about Gerry. At one time things had been hunky-dory between them. Then she'd seemed to cool off and he'd started to have horrible misgivings.

But now this. Glorious Alderley. A long weekend with Gerry. And surely a chance to win her. She must at the very least be meaning to give him that opportunity – an opportunity when she would be free from the presence of that twerp Quartus.

Hugh Quartus hung up and stood gazing at the telephone, a suspicious frown on his pale, slender-featured face. His dark, deep-set eyes were thoughtful.

Why now, at this late date, had she asked him? Was he a replacement for somebody who'd cried off? No – she must know dozens of socially gifted young toffs, who would fill that bill much better than he would. Like that rotter Carter.

So why? For there was certainly more to this invitation than met the eye. She didn't really want him to entertain this Australian cousin.

Hugh ran a thin hand through his rather long black hair. What was the matter with the confounded girl? Hot – cold, on – off, yes – no. She was really infuriating. He just didn't know why he bothered.

Yes, he did. He knew quite well.

Not that he had any real chance. Once or twice he'd thought there was a glimmer of hope. But they always seemed to end up bickering.

He wished now he'd refused the invitation. He had half a mind to call back and tell her he'd forgotten a prior engagement. There'd be no pleasure in the visit. The bucolic Australian cousin sounded utterly grim. That idiot film star would be preening himself all over the place. He'd seen a Rex Ransom film once. Never again. Gerry hadn't said who the other guests would be; no doubt they'd all be equally ghastly.

One thing held him back from cancelling. Curiosity. He had to find out why she'd invited him. Though he was going to hate every minute of it. The only consolation was that the fact she'd asked him certainly meant she wouldn't be seeing Carter for a few days.

CHAPTER FOUR

Thursday dawned bright, crisp and very cold, with a coating of frost silvering the lawns of Alderley and tracing fantastic opaque patterns on the windows. A thin layer of ice covered the lake.

In the house the atmosphere at breakfast was markedly strained. The Earl – nervous as a schoolboy at the prospect of meeting his idol – managed only one egg, two rashers of bacon and three slices of toast. Gerry, who, at the last minute, had been beset by Terrible Doubts as to the wisdom of inviting her two beaux at the same time, spoke hardly at all; while the Countess was feeling decidedly disgruntled at the prospect of entertaining eight people, all of whom had been more or less foisted upon her.

After breakfast the Earl decided to try and calm himself by spending half an hour with his beloved gun collection. On his way upstairs he encountered Merryweather.

He stopped. 'Ah – everything ready for the guests?'

'Quite ready, my lord.'

'Where you puttin' people?'

A close observer would have noticed a momentary expression of astonishment appear on the butler's impassive and august features, it being the first time in thirty years that Lord Burford had taken the remotest interest in domestic matters.

'You wish me to appraise you of the disposition of guests in relation to sleeping accommodation, my lord?'

'That's it.'

'Well, my lord, Mr Haggermeir is in the Cedar bedroom, Mr Ransom in the Grey, Mr Gilbert in the Blue—'

'Who's Mr Gilbert?'

'Mr Arlington Gilbert.'

'Oh, yes, of course. Go on.'

'Miss Bradshaw and her husband in the Oak, Mr Carter in the White next door, the secretary person in the Regency, and Mr Quartus in the Green.'

'No one in the Royal suite.'

'No, my lord. It is not usually occupied except by special guests.'

'But we've got a special guest! Mr Ransom.'

Merryweather closed his eyes. 'Your lordship is not suggesting we should accommodate an *actor* in the Royal Suite?'

'Not *an* actor, Merryweather – a Great Star. Why not?'

'May I ask, my lord, if this is also her ladyship's wish?'

'Not exactly. You think she'd object?'

'It's hardly for me to say, my lord. But I should recommend that your lordship consult with her before taking such a radical step.'

Lord Burford rubbed his chin. 'P'raps you're right. Very well, better leave it.'

He moved off. Merryweather breathed a sigh of relief.

Paul's manservant, Albert, brought him his early tea at six-thirty in his Park Lane flat. After drinking it, Paul rose, donned a track suit, and went for his usual run in the park. By the time he'd returned, glowing with health, and had shaved and showered, Albert had his breakfast ready. Paul sat down to eat it, saying, 'Better pack my traps now. And put my running kit in. May do a bit of cross-country training.'

By the time he'd finished breakfast, Albert had stowed the cases in the car. Paul gave him a few last minute instructions – he had decided not to take Albert with him on this occasion – and by eight o'clock was on the road. He'd be at Alderley comfortably before lunch. And then for a long, long weekend with Gerry.

'Happy days are here again,' Paul carolled lustily as he drove.

Hugh Quartus groaned thickly as the alarm clock clanged stridently a few inches from his ear. Without opening his eyes, he reached out an arm and knocked it from the table. It stopped. He lay still, trying to remember why he had set it. He usually slept till he woke. So there must be something important on this morning.

Then it came to him. Alderley. Oh, lor!

Hugh dragged himself out of bed, staggered to the washbasin, splashed tepid water over his face, shaved, and ran a comb through his hair. He made some tea, cut and ate a couple of thick slices of bread and jam, shoved some clothes and a few necessities into an old army kit-bag, and wrapped his only decent lounge suit in brown paper. Like it or lump it, they'd have to put up with one of their guests not wearing formal dress in the evenings.

Next he filled a Thermos flask with tea, dressed in two pairs of socks, thick corduroy trousers, three sweaters and his old, moth-eaten fur-lined flying jacket, and went down to the lock-up garage he rented.

He opened it and wheeled out his motorcycle and sidecar. He threw his luggage into the sidecar and took from it a scarf, goggles, cap and gauntlets. These donned, he was ready. Wrapped up though he was, it was going to be a fearfully cold trip. He was tempted, even at this stage, to go by train. But no; this way he'd have independence of movement. Without the bike, he'd be stuck in the heart of the country and utterly reliant on his hosts for transportation. Besides, he'd save a few shillings this way – always an important consideration.

The superbly tuned engine of the little motor-bike started at first kick. It really had been a bargain, this machine.

Hugh remembered he hadn't washed the breakfast things or made the bed. They'd be waiting for him when he got back.

Something else to look forward to.

It was a little after eleven o'clock when Merryweather threw open the big double doors of the morning room at Alderley and announced, 'Mr and Mrs Sebastian Everard.'

Thankful at last to know her cousin's surname, Lady Burford went forward to greet her.

The woman who led the way into the room was small, somewhat plump, had a round, good-natured face and blonde hair done in lots of small tight curls. She stopped, staring at Lady Burford, her head tilted to one side. There was something birdlike about her.

'Lavinia?'

'Cecily?'

'My dear, how lovely! You're looking wonderful.'

'And you, Cecily.'

They kissed. Lady Burford said, 'You remember George?'

'Why, of course.' Cecily turned and presented her cheek as the Earl stepped forward. He brushed it with his lips, a little uncertainly.

'Well, well, well,' he said, 'this is splendid. Splendid,' he added dogmatically, as though someone had contradicted him.

Cecily said, 'And this is my husband, Sebastian.'

Sebastian Everard was slight and thin, with a round, clean-shaven pink face and a bland expression. He smiled. 'How – how – how de do?' He spoke in an exaggerated drawl, offering a limp hand to the Earl and Countess. 'Jolly – jolly decent of you to ask us.'

'Delighted to have you,' Lord Burford said.

'Really? Oh, jolly good.' He gave an amiable titter, gazing round the room vaguely at the same time.

'Now, George,' Lady Burford said briskly, 'why don't you give, er, Sebastian a drink? Cecily and I have a lot to talk about. There'll be some coffee shortly and if I remember rightly that's what she'll prefer.' She led her cousin to a chair by the fireplace.

'Thank you, dear.' Cecily said. 'Now, there's so much I want to hear about you and George and Geraldine. And you must bring me up to date on twenty-five years of gossip. I want to know all about Lucy and the twins and Margaret and Reggie and Bobo and the Pearsons – and, oh, dozens of people.'

'My, that's a tall order.'

Lord Burford meanwhile had plucked at Sebastian's elbow. 'Come across here and let me pour you something.'

'What? Oh. Right. Jolly good.' He followed the Earl across to a sideboard where drinks were laid out. 'What'll you have?'

'Oh.' Sebastian frowned. 'Don't know, really.'

'Sherry?'

'Jolly good.'

Lord Burford poured and handed Sebastian a glass.

'Cheers.'

'Oh, yes, rather.'

They drank. There was a pause. Lord Burford cleared his throat. 'Chilly today.'

'Oh, rather.'

'Good drive down?'

'Jolly good.'

'Capital.' There was another silence. The Earl said, 'Er, I keep a few sheep.'

'Really? Oh, jolly good.' Sebastian peered out through the window, as though expecting to see them dotted about the lawn.

'Oh, not personally, of course. At the home farm. Have a good man running it. Must admit I find 'em rather irritatin' creatures. No offence, I hope?'

'No, no, not at all.'

'Always getting lost in the snow or caught in hedges, lambing at the most inconvenient time of the year. No doubt you feel quite different about 'em.'

'Well, I – I haven't given it a lot of thought, actually.'

'Really? You surprise me. I imagined it would be unavoidable.'

'No, never found it necessary. Partial – partial to the odd chop, don't you know. And useful for insomnia, eh, eh?'

'Countin' them jumping over a fence, you mean? Even that doesn't work with me. They always refuse to jump. Not that I'm often troubled by sleeplessness. Clear conscience, I suppose. How many thousand you got?'

The nearest thing so far to animation or surprise came over Sebastian's face. 'How – how – how many thousands?'

'Just roughly.'

'Oh.' He stared at his sherry glass. 'Don't know, really.'

'But you must count your stock sometimes.'

'Count? No. I get statements from the bank and my jolly old accountant keeps tabs on my position.'

Lord Burford's eye bulged. 'Your accountant counts your sheep for you?'

Sebastian blinked. 'Oh, no. Thought you meant money. I don't own any sheep.'

'You don't? You mean you ain't a sheep farmer?'

'Oh, no. Not at all. Never. Sorry.' He smiled.

'Great Scott! I could have sworn...' He turned and raised his voice a little. 'Lavinia, you said Sebastian here was a sheep farmer. He's nothin' of the sort.'

Cecily said gently, 'Oh, I'm sorry. I should have explained. It was Philip, my first husband, who was the sheep farmer. He died many years ago. Sebastian's not even an Australian. He was just visiting when we met. But then he decided to stay on.'

The entry of Gerry at that moment caused a welcome diversion. After introductions she said, 'Well, I suppose you know all about our expected VIP guest?'

'No, dear,' Cecily said. 'Who's that?'

'The great Rex Ransom, no less.'

'The film star? Really? How exciting. Did you hear that, Sebastian?'

'Oh, rather. Jolly good. When – when's he expected to arrive?'

'The train should be getting in to Alderley Halt in about five minutes. Hawkins has gone to meet it in the Rolls. Actually, there's quite a party of film people coming, isn't there, Daddy?'

Lord Burford nodded happily. 'Biggest thing to happen at Alderley since Queen Victoria stayed here in 1852.'

'Jolly good,' said Sebastian.

By the time Hugh reached Alderley village at about eleven-thirty and started on the final stage to the house he was stiff with cold. This last part of the journey did nothing to improve his mood. The estate was surrounded by a positive network of narrow lanes, and like all of them the one he had to follow wound irritatingly, several times approaching to within a mile of the house, which could be clearly glimpsed through the trees. Then the lane would suddenly turn away, without apparent reason, on another long detour.

Hugh's mind was filled with thoughts of blazing fires and hot coffee, and as bend followed bend he became more and more frustrated and began to push his machine ever faster.

At last he reached the final bend before the straight stretch of wider road that ran past the entrance to the drive leading up to the house. He twisted the throttle grip, leaning over so that the wheels of the sidecar actually left the ground.

One thing, however, which he had not allowed for was the heavy overnight frost that had resulted in icy roads. Until he'd reached the village he'd been travelling on main roads, on which grit had been laid. But this twisting, little-used lane had not been treated.

Suddenly Hugh felt the bike start to slip from under him. The next moment he found himself rolling over and over on the road. It seemed as though he was never going to stop. But eventually he did, and when his head had cleared he sat dizzily up.

After a few seconds he decided he wasn't hurt and got unsteadily to his feet. Suddenly he no longer felt cold. He walked over to his cycle and sidecar, which were apparently undamaged. Hugh tried to get the contraption upright. But it was heavy and his feet kept slipping on the still icy surface.

He was making another attempt when he heard

a car approaching from around the bend. It had the deep-throated roar of an expensive sports model. Hugh started to run towards the bend. But his feet went from under him again. By the time he'd scrambled up, a long, low scarlet drop-head tourer had appeared round the curve.

Hugh yelled and waved his arms. He saw the driver brake and the car start to skid. Hugh threw himself to one side, and in a graceful spin the sports car's nearside rear wheel went over the front wheel of the motorcycle.

Paul felt the bump and a horrible crunching clatter. Then the car had stopped and there was a great calm. He got hastily out and saw that the front wheel of the motorcycle was badly buckled. The driver, only his nose showing between goggles and scarf, was standing on the grassy shoulder, staring mutely at the wreckage.

Paul walked towards him. 'I say, old man, I'm most frightfully sorry—'

Without taking his eyes from his injured machine, the motorcyclist raised both arms skywards in a gesture of fury and shouted, 'You reckless imbecile!'

Paul said, 'Now, steady on. I only—'

'*You only*? You only wrecked my—' He looked at Paul for the first time and stopped short. '*You*?' he said.

Paul felt a sudden chill of alarm. He said, 'What?'

'Carter! What are you doing here?'

'I'm afraid I don't—'

The other suddenly tore off his goggles and scarf, and Paul's eyes widened. 'Quartus! Hullo. I didn't recognise you in that get-up.'

'I said, what are you doing here?' Hugh snapped. His face was white.

'I'm on my way to Alderley.'

'I gathered that, you fool. But just *why* are you on your way there?'

Paul frowned. 'I've been invited for the weekend.'

Hugh was breathing hard. 'By Geraldine?'

'Yes, of course.'

'The little beast!'

'Look here, don't you speak about Gerry like that.'

'What's it to you how I speak about Gerry?'

'I think a lot of her. I won't stand by and listen to her insulted.'

'Then don't stand by. Clear off. I'll stay here and insult her to my heart's content.'

Paul swallowed and managed to control himself. He said, 'I'm sorry about the bike.'

'So am I!'

'But I'm not really to blame—'

'Not to blame! I suppose you think my machine dived under your car – decided to commit suicide!'

'I came round the bend and it was in the middle of the road.'

'A driver should be prepared for obstructions in the road. He shouldn't drive so fast that he can't stop if—'

'Oh, for Pete's sake! Normally I could have stopped, but the road's icy—'

'The road's icy! He's telling me the road's icy! Why do you think I came off?'

'I wouldn't know,' Paul retorted. 'It could have been sheer incompetence – or, to judge from your manner, drunkenness. However, I have no wish to continue arguing. Although I admit no legal liability, I'm naturally prepared to pay for the repairs—'

'I don't want your confounded charity.'

'As you wish. But if you change your mind, the offer stands. Now, as the bike obviously can't be ridden, I suggest we drag it to the side of the road and then call up the local garage to come get it. I'll give you a lift to the house. Er, I suppose you are a guest there, too?'

'I was.'

'Was?'

'I wasn't looking forward to the weekend before. Now I doubt if I could stomach it.'

'Well, that's up to you. But you'll have to come to the house to use the phone. Hop in the car.'

'No, thanks.'

'But it's pretty well a mile—'

'That's my business.'

Paul shrugged. 'OK. What do I tell the Burfords?'

'Tell them to – Tell them what you like.'

'As you wish. So long.'

Paul walked to his car. Really, that chap was insufferable. What on earth did Gerry see in him?

He drove the last hundred yards, turned in past the lodge, and sped up the tree-lined drive to Alderley. Even his brush with Quartus couldn't take from him a delightfully pleasurable anticipation. His last visit had been in summer. He and Gerry had gone for long rambles in and outside the estate. He remembered his sense of pride when she'd presented him with a key to the small doors set into the walls that surrounded the park – a traditional mark of esteem in the family. This time there'd be few rambles, but plenty of time alone with her indoors; he'd make sure of that.

He pulled up before the impressive seventeenth century façade of the house, got out and started up the steps. As he did so, Gerry emerged from the front door. He grinned.

Gerry stopped, feeling the warm glow she always experienced when she saw those pleasantly rugged features, the deep blue eyes and the curly light-brown hair. He was so *nice*. She really liked him better than anyone else she knew. Why, oh why, could she never be quite sure she was in love with him?

He ran up the last few steps and kissed her. 'Hullo, my sweet.'

'Oh, Paul, it's good to see you! Thank you for coming at such short notice.'

'Try and keep me away.'

They went indoors as a footman emerged to unload Paul's luggage. As Paul was divesting himself of his overcoat in the hall, Gerry said, 'Paul, I have a confession to make. Hugh's coming for the weekend, too.'

'I don't think he is, actually.'

'What on earth do you mean?'

He explained what had happened.

'Oh, golly!' she said, when he'd finished. 'Where is he now?'

'As far as I know, still standing staring at his bike.'

'Why didn't you bring him to the house?'

'I tried, darling. He wouldn't come. He's very angry with me – and with you. And with the whole world.'

'But what's he going to do?'

'He wouldn't say. Honestly, darling, I did my best.'

'Oh, I'm sure you did, Paul. He's quite impossible sometimes.'

'Sometimes?'

She grinned. 'Now if *I* said that about a *girl*, you'd probably say "meow".'

'Sorry. All the same, Gerry, I think you might have told me he was going to be here.'

'I thought you wouldn't come if you knew.'

'I'm not scared of Quartus.'

'I know that, chump. But you know you can't stand him.'

'That's not true. I could get on all right with him if he gave me a chance. I admit I have been apprehensive about your interest in him, but I'm convinced now that it's merely a sisterly concern for the chap because he's a failure.'

'He's not a failure!'

'Oh, come off it! How many pictures does he sell?'

'Well, that's immaterial. I've got to do something. I can't just leave him down there. I must go and investigate.'

'Oh, send one of your countless minions.'

'No, no – *noblesse oblige* and all that rot.'

He sighed. 'OK, get your coat and I'll drive you back down.'

'I wouldn't hear of it. Go into the morning room and get some coffee. You must be frozen. Besides, you're needed in there. Our tame film star has arrived, together with his producer.'

'Rex Ransom? Great. I've been looking forward to meeting him. What's he like?'

'Very nice. No pretence to him at all. But the producer is very much out of his element. Daddy's been struck dumb with awe, and Mummy, who doesn't approve of them, is being frostily formal and polite. As the only others in there are Mummy's cousin Cecily, who hasn't been here for twenty-five years and keeps asking after people who are dead, and her idiot husband, who does nothing but grin inanely and say 'Jolly good,' the atmosphere is rather sticky. I've been doing my best to keep the conversational ball rolling. You can take over.'

'Oh, gosh, Gerry, it sounds frightfully grim.'

'It is. But to someone who's climbed Everest—'

'The Matterhorn.'

'—it will be child's play. So come on.'

Ten minutes later Gerry, driving her beloved Hispano Suisa towards the village, drew up by a lone figure, kit-bag over his shoulder, who was trudging along the road.

She leant over and opened the passenger door.

'Hop in.'

Hugh looked at her. 'Why?'

'I'll give you a lift to the station. There's a train to London in about ten minutes. You'll never catch it otherwise.'

He hesitated, then threw his kit-bag into the back and got in next to her. She drove on. He said, 'I won't be able to catch that train, anyway. I've got to stop at the garage about my bike.'

'I'll see to that.'

'No, thank you.'

'Well, there's not another train to town today.'

'Then I'll have to stay till tomorrow. I suppose there's a pub where I can get a room.'

'There's the *Rose & Crown,* but I doubt if they'll give you a room.'

'Why on earth not?'

'It's a highly respectable house. And they're very particular about who they take in. Of course, I could come and put in a good word for you.'

'Very funny.'

'Look, as it seems you've got to stay overnight in the area, why not come to the house? You needn't see Paul, or any of the guests. We'll put you up in the servants' quarters, if you like. You can eat with them and everything. I don't suppose they'll mind.'

'Again, no thanks.'

'*Why*, Hugh? What's the matter?'

'I don't like being made a fool of. Inviting me at the same time as Carter, without telling me, when you know how I feel about him?'

'I didn't tell *him* you were coming, either.'

'That makes things no better.'

Gerry was silent for a moment. She said, 'You're quite right. It was thoughtless. I'm sorry.'

He looked at her in surprise. 'My word, that must have taken some effort.'

'Don't rub it in.'

'Why did you do it, Gerry? You must have known we'd both be annoyed.'

'Paul's not annoyed.'

'Want to bet? He just doesn't show his feelings.'

'A trait you might well try to emulate.'

'Why?'

'It's a sign of good breeding.'

Hugh gave a snort. 'That's just the sort of talk that repels me about all your class.'

'In that case I can't think why you accepted the invitation in the first place.'

'Because I thought you wanted me here.'

'I did. I do.'

'But why? Why now – with Carter and all those other people? You must have realised I wouldn't exactly be the brightest company.'

'I – I wanted you to meet Rex Ransom.'

'*What?* You thought I'd want to meet that prancing purveyor of mindless mush!'

'There's not only him. There's Arlington Gilbert.'

'Who is Arlington Gilbert?'

'A writer. A creative person, like you.'

'Never heard of him. What's he write?'

'Film scripts mainly, I think.'

'For Ransom, I suppose?' Gerry didn't answer. 'Geraldine, this just won't do. You're up to something. I want to know your real motive for inviting me.'

'I don't admit there is one. But if there were, there'd be only one way you could find it: by staying for the weekend.'

'And have to watch you ogling and smooching with Carter all the time?'

'Ah! Now we come to the true reason you don't want to stay. You're jealous.'

'Of course I'm jealous! I'm in love with you.'

'Most of the time you behave as though you hate the sight of me.'

'I hate a lot of the trappings you surround yourself with – the privileges of rank and unearned wealth. I hate the inane conversation of your friends, the Philistine outlook on life of your whole circle.'

'I don't think I'm a Philistine.'

'No, I couldn't love you if you were. You've got a good brain. With a free hand I could mould you into something special.'

'What an utterly ghastly prospect,' she said.

They reached the village. Gerry said, 'Well, how about it? Coming back?'

There was a pause before he replied. 'Oh, all right. I suppose so.'

Gerry said, 'Thank you *so* much for the invitation, Geraldine. It's *awfully* kind of you. I really *do* appreciate it.'

Hugh said, 'Don't forget the garage.'

She drove on to Jenkins' Garage and pulled up in front. Hugh got out and disappeared into the workshop. Gerry sat and waited for him. But she could never sit doing nothing for long, and she suddenly grabbed a duster, got out and started vigorously – and rather unnecessarily – polishing the windshield. She was hardly conscious of the car that drew up alongside her, so she didn't raise her head when a voice nearby said sharply, 'Hey! You!' It was not a form of address she was accustomed to.

But then the voice repeated irritably, 'You! Girl! With the duster,' and she turned in surprise.

She saw a very small baby Austin car, driven by a very large man with long black hair. Sitting next to him was a severe-looking middle-aged woman. It was the man who had spoken, and now he did so again.

'Yes, you, girl. How do I get to old Lord Burford's place? Look lively. I haven't got all day.'

Gerry felt herself start to flush and she opened her mouth, prior to letting him know what she thought of him. Then she paused. Of course. This had to be Arlington Gilbert. She had had a full report of his appearance and conversation from her father. So she'd better watch her tongue.

Then an idea struck. She let a vacant expression come over her face and she strolled towards the Austin, wiping her nose with the back of her hand. In a broad west country accent she asked, 'What 'ee say?'

Gilbert said again, 'How do I reach Lord Burford's residence?'

Gerry leant up against the car. 'What 'ee wanna know for?'

Gilbert gave a bellow. 'It's no business of yours, but I happen to be spending the weekend there.'

With an exaggerated gasp, Gerry stepped hurriedly back from the car. He looked startled. 'What's the matter?'

Gerry made her eyes big. 'Do 'ee be gonna stay at the big 'ouse? Sleep there? Cor, mister, Oi wouldn't like to be 'ee. Nor 'ee, missus.'

The woman glared at her. 'Miss.'

Gilbert said sharply, 'What on earth do you mean?'

Gerry looked furtively over her shoulder, stepped right up to the car again and whispered, 'Things 'appen at big 'ouse.'

'What are you talking about? What sort of things?'

'Moighty queer things. They d'yu say folks bain't never

the soime again arter a noight at the big 'ouse. Those that leaves at all, that is.'

'I've never heard such utter balderdash!'

Gerry shrugged. 'All roight, mister, 'ave it your way. Only don't say 'ee ain't been warned.'

'Just tell me how to get there.'

At last Gerry told him. He gave a curt nod and thrust the car into gear again.

'One more word, mister,' Gerry said.

He glared at her. 'Well?'

'D'yu 'ee watch out for that there Lady Geraldine.'

'Watch out? What the deuce are you talking about, girl?'

'That's all I be gonna say. Just 'ee be careful, that's all.'

And Gerry turned away and went on with her polishing. Behind her she heard Gilbert give an exclamation of disgust and the car drive quickly away.

A few seconds later Hugh reappeared. 'All set?' she asked.

He nodded, 'They'll pick it up straight away.' He pointed after the disappearing Austin. 'Who was that?'

'A very remarkable man.'

'Oh? In what way?'

'He's even ruder than you are.'

In the Austin, Gilbert said, 'What a very odd young woman.'

Maude Fry said, 'And remarkably well-dressed for a garage hand.'

'Was she? I didn't notice. Probably her father's a smuggler.'

'Thirty miles from the sea?'

'Well, a coiner, or whatever branch of villainy is the most popular down here. What did you make of all that rigamarole?'

'About the big house? Bad hats in every old family. Legends grow up around them. Don't die out for generations.'

'I was really thinking of what she said about Lady Geraldine. Do you suppose she's insane, or something? Dabbles in black magic? Takes drugs?'

'I would guess nothing so dramatic. Probably she's just a man-eater – one of those depraved young women one reads about, around whom no male is safe.'

'I see.' Gilbert nodded slowly. 'Yes. That's quite possible.' He unconsciously raised a hand and patted his hair. 'I wonder if you're right. It'll be interesting to find out, won't it?'

Maude Fry sniffed.

CHAPTER FIVE

Arlington Gilbert and Maude Fry arrived at the house fifteen minutes later. Merryweather conducted them to the morning room. But before he could announce them, Gilbert marched past him into the room. Rather more slowly, Maude Fry followed him.

Just inside the door, Gilbert paused and stared round appraisingly. 'Yes,' he said with a decisive nod, 'this would be ideal for the proposal scene. Though all this Regency stuff will have to go. Make a note, Miss Fry.'

'Yes, Mr Gilbert.' Maude Fry took a pair of blue-tinted spectacles from her bag, put them on, got out a notebook, wrote in it, then put both glasses and book away.

Meanwhile, the Earl, seeing his wife begin to swell visibly, hurriedly stepped forward, holding out his hand. 'Ah, Arlington, how are you?'

Gilbert's eyebrows rose slightly. 'Tolerably well, thank you, er, George. Nice place you have here.'

It was Lord Burford's turn to look decidedly surprised. 'Oh, thanks. Let me introduce you.'

'Don't bother, George. I'll soon find out who everybody

is. Jupiter's teeth, though, I could do with some coffee! I'll help myself.' He strode across to where the coffee things were laid out.

The Earl rejoined Rex Ransom and Haggermeir, while Lady Burford, taking sudden pity on the rather lost-looking Maude Fry, went across and spoke to her.

Lord Burford lowered his voice. 'Strange feller, that,' he murmured to Rex. 'Called me by my first name.'

Rex said, 'Well, actually, you did call him by *his* first name.'

'I didn't. I called him Arlington.'

'That's right. Arlington Gilbert's his name.'

The Earl snapped his fingers in irritation. 'I keep thinking it's Gilbert Arlington. Dash it, it ought to be! Oh, drat – suppose I've got to keep it up now. It'll seem as if we're bosom friends.' He turned to Haggermeir. 'Do you know him well?'

'Not at all. But I made some inquiries after he called. He's quite well-known as a solid all-around writer. Had a couple of successful plays in the West End some years back and wrote quite a few film scripts. Hasn't done anything recently. Said to have made enough to live on and is working on a big epic novel.'

'And you'll be using him on *The King's Man*?'

'Looks like I may have no choice,' Haggermeir said grimly.

'I see. Still, I suppose if he can provide Mr Ransom with a good script we'll have to put up with him.'

'Surely,' Rex said, 'if you call him Arlington, you're going to call me Rex, aren't you?'

Lord Burford's face lit up. 'Really? May I? Oh, I say. I'm, er, George.'

Rex bowed. 'Glad to know you, George.'

* * *

By the time Gerry and Hugh arrived at Alderley the little party in the morning room had broken up, the guests having mostly retired to their rooms to unpack. Hugh went straight to his room and Gerry sought out her father.

'Did Gilbert arrive?' she asked.

'Arlington? 'Fraid so. Why?'

'Did he ask about me?'

'Yes, wanted to know when he'd be meeting you. Why?'

'What did you say?'

'Probably for drinks before lunch. Why?'

'Good. Mummy won't be there then, will she?'

'Doubt it. Why?'

'You'll see.'

'Look, what are you up to?'

'Never mind. Just don't be surprised at anything about me.'

'Ever thought of trying to make it in pictures?' Rex asked.

Paul laughed. 'Good heavens, no.'

'Why not think about it? You've got the looks and the physique.'

'For one thing, I can't act for toffee.'

'Don't let that stop you. It didn't stop me.'

'Oh, no false modesty, my dear chap,' Lord Burford said. 'You know you're one of the world's great actors.'

Rex gave an exaggerated start. 'Jumping Jehosophat! Hey, Cyrus.'

Nearby, Haggermeir, a dry martini in his hand, was conversing with Cecily. He looked up. 'Yeah?'

Rex said, 'Just say that again, will you, George – slowly and distinctly.'

'Certainly.' He did so.

'D'you hear that?' Rex asked triumphantly. '"One of the world's great actors." George, you've made a buddy for life. You're the only person – apart from my ma – ever to say that. And she doesn't say it too often. Just once in a while to try and convince herself.'

'Be careful, Lord Burford,' Haggermeir said, 'that's the way to wreck his career. If Rexy once gets it into his head he can act he'll want to start proving it. And *Hamlet's* box office poison.'

Lord Burford scratched his head. 'I don't understand. You mean *you* don't think he's a good actor?'

'Wa-all.' Haggermeir shrugged.

'But you amaze me, my dear fellow. To me he's every bit as good as Errol Flynn.'

'Can't hold a candle to Rin Tin Tin, though,' Rex said with a grin.

Quite perplexed by this, the Earl looked round the room. Cecily had moved away and was talking to Maude Fry, while Gilbert had cornered Sebastian and was holding forth on the iniquities of literary agents, emphasising his points with a series of prods to the chest, at every one of which Sebastian took a little step backwards. Standing alone, his face set in a scowl, was Hugh.

Lord Burford was wondering if he should go across and talk to him, though the young man's demeanour didn't suggest he'd welcome this. The Earl was just wishing Gerry would come in when the door opened and she entered.

Everyone glanced automatically towards her – and there was an abrupt silence.

Gerry had changed out of the tweed suit and brogues

she'd been wearing earlier and was now attired in a slinky, tight-fitting dress of black satin and very high-heeled shoes. Her face had been almost free of make-up before, but now her eyes were painted with mascara and her cheeks were rouged. Her hair was swept upwards to the top of her head. She was smoking a cigarette in a six-inch holder. She crossed the room in a sinuous, undulating walk.

Lord Burford closed his eyes, Paul coughed into a handkerchief and Hugh stared in horror.

Gerry made a straight line for Gilbert. He watched her approach with the fascination of a rabbit watching a snake. Gerry stopped in front of him, gave him a long, cool stare, slowly exhaled a lungful of smoke and said softly, 'Arlington Gilbert.'

She held out her hand in a regal gesture. Uncertain whether to shake it or kiss it, Gilbert compromised by taking it and giving a sort of half bow. 'At your service, Lady Geraldine.'

'I have long been an ardent admirer of your work, Mr Gilbert—'

Then, as he straightened up, gazing at her with a mixture of gratification, alarm, admiration and bewilderment, she broke off and said in a decidedly frosty voice, 'Mr Gilbert, you are looking at me as though I were something the cat had dragged through a hedge backwards. Why?'

Gilbert gave a start. 'I beg your pardon, Lady Geraldine. It's just that – there was a girl in the village earlier... Jupiter's teeth, it's incredible!'

'I see nothing incredible. There are many girls in the village.'

'But this one was – forgive me – the absolute image of you. In a bucolic way, of course.'

'But naturally.'

'I'm sorry…?'

'Mr Gilbert, my family has held sway over this district for hundreds of years. Until quite recently they virtually had powers of life and death over the peasantry. Even today there are hundreds of them dependent on this estate. My father is certainly the first lord of the manor of whom – unfortunately – the great majority of them are not absolutely terrified.'

For a moment Gilbert looked blank. Then comprehension dawned. 'I see. And you mean that your ancestors exercised this power, er, liberally?'

'Of course. You could no doubt find half a dozen girls in the vicinity who bear a resemblance to me.'

Gilbert chuckled. 'That sounds as though it would be a very worthwhile pursuit. But why did you use the word 'unfortunately' just now?'

Gerry took his arm and drew him to one side. She spoke softly. 'My father cares not a fig for power. If he did, the mere terror of our name would mean we could control these people as our forefathers did.' Her voice grew harsher. 'They could not get away with their present laziness and insolence.'

'Insolence? Well, I must admit that girl I mentioned was unusually cheeky.'

'Tell me: was she employed at the garage?'

'That's right.'

'Pah!' Gerry banged a nearby table with her fist. 'That hussy is one of the worst. And they say she is the one most like me in appearance. She no doubt made disparaging remarks about me. The things I'd like to do to that girl! Oh, for the power my great-great-grandmother had! Do you know what she did once to a serving wench who'd displeased her?'

Gilbert shook his head.

Gerry put her head close to his and whispered in his ear. As he listened, Gilbert's expression changed. He gave a gulp. Gerry drew back and gazed at him with satisfaction.

'And you'd, er, like to do the same to that garage girl?'

'Actually, I can think of some interesting refinements.'

Gilbert gave a sickly grin. 'I must say I'm sure your peasants don't appreciate just how lucky they are to be so free.'

'They'd better enjoy it while they can.'

'Oh, yes?'

'Yes. You see, I know of several ways in which our – or rather, *my* – dominance over them could be asserted as in old times. Absolutely reasserted – body *and* soul.'

For a moment Gerry's eyes shone with a fanatical light. Then suddenly this faded and she was giving Gilbert a warm smile. 'However, that's enough of me. Mr Gilbert, did I say how very great an admirer of your work I am? I do feel I'm going to become just as keen an admirer of you as a man. Do come and sit down and tell me all about yourself.'

And she put a hand on his and drew him unprotesting but bewildered across the room to a sofa.

Over lunch the atmosphere at Alderley grew considerably easier. Lord Burford, basking in the fact that he and Rex were now 'buddies,' had lost all his nervousness and was his usual self. Rex meanwhile concentrated on exerting all his considerable charm on Lady Burford, and in spite of herself the Countess could not help gradually softening under the impact.

The fact that Gerry was playing a hoax on Gilbert had also got round among the other guests, and everybody was waiting with anticipation for the next development. However, for the time being she contented herself with remaining largely silent and throwing him long and meaningful looks from under her lashes.

It was towards the close of the meal that Merryweather entered, bearing a silver salver on which was a telegram. He took it to Haggermeir.

As Haggermeir read it his eyebrows went up. 'What in tarnation...? This doesn't make sense. Lady Burford, it seems you may be having another guest shortly. I think you'd better read this.' He passed it to her.

Lady Burford picked up her lorgnette and read aloud, 'Invitation accepted. Arriving Alderley Thursday afternoon. Lorenzo.' She gazed at Haggermeir. 'Who is this person?'

'Search me.'

'You don't know a Mr Lorenzo?'

He shook his head. 'And if I did I'd certainly not invite him here without your permission.'

'How very strange,' Lady Burford said.

Gerry said, 'May I see?' She took the telegram. 'Handed in at a London post office. No address of sender. Quite a mystery.'

'Well, we certainly won't sit around waitin' for the

chap,' Lord Burford said. 'What d'you all want to do with yourselves this afternoon?'

'Well, I know what I want to do,' Rex answered, 'and that's to see your famous gun collection.'

Haggermeir nodded. 'Me, too.'

The Earl looked delighted. 'Oh, capital. Great pleasure. Anybody else? Arlington?'

Gilbert nodded condescendingly. 'I don't mind.'

'Sebastian?'

'Oh.' Sebastian looked doubtful. 'Guns? Will – will – will they be going off? Can't stand bangs, you know.'

'There is a firing range up there, and I may demonstrate one or two. But I'll give plenty of advance warning, so anyone who wants to leave can do so.'

'Oh, right. Jolly good.'

'Am I invited?' Cecily asked.

'Oh, of course, my dear. Didn't think you'd be interested. Ladies aren't very as a rule.'

'I can't say I am normally. But your collection *is* world famous, and I would like at least a glimpse of it.'

'Splendid. Any more for the Skylark? Hugh?'

'I don't like guns,' Hugh said shortly.

'Oh, as you wish, my boy. Paul – you saw it last time you were here.'

'Yes, but I didn't do it justice. I'd love to have another look.'

Hugh glowered at him, 'On the other hand,' he said loudly, 'I understand the craftsmanship on some of these old pistols is very fine. I'd like to see them from that point of view.'

Lord Burford looked pleased. 'That's everybody, then.'

He glanced round the table, counting on his fingers. 'No, that's wrong. Who did I leave out?'

'Me, I think, Lord Burford.' It was the quiet Maude Fry who spoke.

'Oh, I'm sorry, Miss Fry. You're very welcome, of course.'

'Thank you. Like Mrs Everard, I should be interested in at least a glimpse.'

It was therefore a party of eight which, half an hour later, Lord Burford led up to the first floor. At the top of the stairs he turned right. Halfway along the eastern corridor he opened a pair of double doors on the right and led the way through a long gallery, which ran most of the outer side of the wing. It was lined with painted portraits and was unfurnished, except for a number of sofas and upright chairs against the walls.

The Earl crossed the gallery to another door opposite. This was the entrance to the top floor of the eastern extension, the ballroom being beneath it. Lord Burford unlocked it with a key attached to his watch chain, saying as he did so, 'Live ammunition in here as well as the guns, so I always keep it locked.'

Immediately beyond the door was another one. The Earl unlocked this one also, then stood back and ushered his guests through.

They found themselves at the end of a long, delightfully proportioned room, with French doors leading onto a balustraded balcony at the end, beyond which the lake could be seen.

But the visitors noticed practically nothing except the hundreds of guns with which, apart from a clear path down the centre, the room was filled. Pistols were in display cases, rifles slung around the walls, while at the far end a number of cannon and other large guns were standing. One section of the room was partitioned off to form a firing range, and there was a large cupboard where Lord Burford kept ammunition and various accessories.

Except for Paul, the visitors each gave a little gasp as they entered. Then they just stood, staring round in amazed disbelief.

The years had given Lord Burford a great deal of experience in showing his collection. He knew well what interested people and had a fund of anecdotes concerning his exhibits, which – to their own surprise – kept even Sebastian, Hugh and the two women attentive. Two hours in fact passed quickly for everybody, and it was past four when they all trooped out, the Earl carefully locking up again.

They were making their way along the corridor when Cecily said, 'Oh, by the way, George, don't I remember something about a secret passage here?'

'Yes, I'll show you.'

He turned into the main corridor and opened the second door on the right. This was a room used for linen storage. As the others crowded in after him, Lord Burford crossed to the far wall, put his hands against one of the wooden panels, and pushed to the right. The panel slid sideways, revealing a large black square.

'There you are,' Lord Burford said. 'Comes out in the breakfast room downstairs. Anybody feel like going down through it? No takers?'

'Well, you know,' Cecily said, 'I really wouldn't mind. I

used to love stories about secret passages when I was a girl. Sebastian – shall we?'

'Oh,' Sebastian looked dubiously at the black hole in the wall. 'I hardly think so, precious. Awfully dark and dirty, what?'

'Dark,' the Earl said, 'but there are flashlights. And it's reasonably clean.'

'No – no – no, I'd much rather not, actually, if you don't mind,' Sebastian said. 'Spiders, you know, moths and things. Unpleasant generally.'

'Yes, I suppose you're right,' Cecily said, a little wistfully. 'I certainly wouldn't want to go on my own.'

'Madam, pray allow me to act as guide.' Paul stepped forward. 'I know this passage like the back of my hand. Been along it on at least – oh, one occasion.'

'Why, thank you,' Cecily said.

Paul stepped into the gap, reached for the shelf above his head and found the flashlight that was kept there. He switched it on. 'Very well, Mrs Everard, if we're to make camp by sundown, we'd better get moving.'

'Oh, right.' Cecily gave a giggle and stepped in.

'Mind the doors,' said Lord Burford, and he slid the panel across.

The Earl was waiting in the breakfast room when Paul and Cecily emerged into the light of day a few minutes later. 'Well, how was it? Rather borin', eh?'

Cecily blinked. 'Well, perhaps a little. But at least I can say I've been along a secret passage now.'

When Gerry came into the drawing room for tea she had transformed herself. She was wearing a simple jumper and skirt, sandals and bobby socks. All make-up had been removed and she had done her hair in two plaits tied with ribbon. She practically skipped about the room, prattling girlishly, and eating a great number of cream cakes, which she pronounced 'scrumptious.' Eventually she sat down by Gilbert and began plying him with questions about his work, such as didn't he find it terribly difficult spelling all those horrid long words?

Except for Maude Fry, everybody else – even the Countess – was now in on the joke and all behaved perfectly normally, making no comment on the transformation. Gilbert, however, was plainly utterly perplexed – and alarmed. At last, finding it increasingly hard to keep a straight face, Gerry retired to the window seat and curled up with a book entitled *The Most Popular Girl In The School*, which she'd brought in with her.

Gilbert immediately sidled over to Rex and tugged at his sleeve. 'What do you make of that?' he hissed.

'What?'

'Lady Geraldine. She was so different! You must have noticed.' He lowered his voice still further. 'I think she's a – a *schizophrenic*.'

Rex frowned sharply. 'Don't say anything, man.'

Gilbert's jaw dropped. 'You mean she is, *really*?'

Rex just put his fingers to his lips.

Gilbert walked shakily away and started whispering furiously to Maude Fry.

'Just been thinkin',' Lord Burford said. 'Haven't given you much time to start your inspection of the house, have we?'

'Oh, that's OK, Earl,' Haggermeir said. 'I wouldn't've missed your collection for the earth. Maybe, though, I could make a start after tea.'

'By all means. What exactly do you want to do?'

'Well, I'd just like your permission to wander all over the house. I want to measure the rooms and corridors, make rough sketches showing the positions and sizes of all the doors and windows, take some photos – all so I can figure out distances, camera angles, lighting and sound problems, decide which rooms could be used for the various scenes, and so on.'

'That's fine by me, old man. Go wherever you like.'

Before Haggermeir could reply, the conversation was interrupted by the entry of Merryweather, who approached them, said 'Excuse me, my lord,' and addressed Haggermeir. 'A visitor has arrived and is asking for you, sir.'

'Ah, is it our friend Lorenzo, by any chance?'

'That is the name, sir.'

Haggermeir said, 'I'll come out.'

Lord Burford said, 'No need, my dear chap. I'm sure we all want to see this mysterious stranger. Is this person presentable, Merryweather?'

'Eminently so, I should say, my lord.'

'Then let the stranger be presented.'

Merryweather bowed his head and withdrew. Half a minute passed and then he reappeared, to announce solemnly, 'Signorina Lorenzo.'

There was a stunned silence as a magnificent figure swept imperiously into the room. She was about thirty-five, tall, with long, jet-black hair, dark flashing eyes and a flawless complexion. Her features, bold and regular, were more striking than beautiful. She looked as though she might have a superb figure; however, at the moment, it was obscured by a sumptuous mink coat, which made the eyes of every woman present widen. On her head she wore a toque in matching fur.

She stood, regally surveying the room.

Rex muttered, 'Holy mackerel! It's *Laura* Lorenzo.'

Haggermeir stepped somewhat hesitantly forward. 'Signorina Lorenzo? This is, er, indeed a great...'

She eyed him up and down. 'Who are you?'

'Oh – sorry – I'm, er, Cyrus Haggermeir. I believe you—'

'Ah.' She gave a satisfied nod. 'You are Haggermeir. So, Meesta Producer, you want Laura Lorenzo, eh? Well, here she is. Perhaps you will have her – if you can sateesfy her. But it will cost you. Oh yes, it will cost you many dollars.'

For several seconds Haggermeir gazed at the woman, speechless. At last he managed to stammer, 'I – I see. Well, that's – that's certainly a most interesting...Do I – er, understand that you're offering me your services?'

'That is what I am here to talk about, is it not?'

'You are? I see. Well, in that case, perhaps...'

She said, 'Are you seek?'

'Seek? Oh, *sick*. No, I'm fine.'

'Then why you behave like an imbecile?'

Haggermeir's eyes bulged and Rex gave a snort of suppressed laughter. Laura bestowed on him a crushing glance – into which puzzled semi-recognition could be read – before turning back to Haggermeir. 'I have met many producers. Some have been peegs, others Pheelistines or creeminals. But never have I met one who was a fool.

Now, do you or do you not want me for your talkie.'

Haggermeir coughed. 'Gee, that'd be swell. I hadn't given the possibility any thought, but—'

'*You have not given the posseebility any thought*?' Laura positively screeched the words. 'Do you dare say that after you send me the telegram pleading with me to come here and talk about it?'

'I sent you no telegram.'

Laura froze. Then she spun on her heel and strode out of the room. As she did so she called loudly, 'Eloise! My handbag. Quickly!'

For seconds nobody spoke. There was a general letting out of breath. It was Lady Burford who found her tongue first. In a voice touched with ice, she asked of anybody who cared to answer, 'Who is that woman? She is, I take it, an actress of some sort?'

'Just about the best dramatic actress in Italy,' Rex said, 'perhaps in the whole of Europe.'

Hugh nodded firmly. 'Certainly among, the top half dozen. And she's actually considering signing with Haggermeir...' He gazed at the producer with an expression of incredulity.

'Must say I've never heard of her,' Lord Burford remarked.

Rex said, 'Well, she's not done any English-language pictures for years – not since she made her name. In the States you can only see her movies in little art houses in the big cities. But she's the darling of the highbrow critics. And most of the Hollywood moguls have been trying to sign her for years.'

At that moment Laura again sailed into the room. She

was carrying a telegram. This she thrust into Haggermeir's hand with a triumphant gesture. Haggermeir stared at it for a few seconds, then said, 'I know nothing of this.'

Laura scrutinised his features in silence for a moment, her own face darkening, her fingers twitching, her body almost seeming to pulsate before them. It was, as Gerry later remarked, like waiting for Vesuvius to erupt. Then she suddenly burst into a stream of impossibly rapid and passionate Italian. Her arms flailed, her eyes flashed. Vehemently she addressed the ceiling and each corner of the room in turn. There was clearly only one thing to do, and that was wait for her to run down. Gradually she did so, and then just stood, panting.

'So,' she said to Haggermeir, 'somebody play the – what you call – practical joke, yes?'

'It would seem so.'

'When I find him he will know what practical jokes really are.'

Paul said, 'May I see that telegram?'

Haggermeir passed it to him. 'Better read it out, son.'

Paul read aloud, 'Signorina Laura Lorenzo, Savoy Hotel, London, WC2. Offer starring role my next movie stop. Great English civil war extravaganza stop. Top payment stop. Cordially invite you come stay weekend Alderley to discuss stop. Cyrus S. Haggermeir.' He looked up. 'Handed in at Westchester post office five p.m. yesterday.'

'At that time I was still in London,' Haggermeir said.

Lord Burford said, ''Straodinary thing.'

Almost for the first time, Laura seemed to become aware of the other people in the room. She looked round at them vaguely. She said, 'I am sorry I will not have a chance to meet all you folks. But I go now.' She turned back to Haggermeir. 'Goodbye.' She started for the door.

Haggermeir said hastily, 'Now, hang on, signorina, please. The only reason I've never offered you a part is because I never figured you'd be interested. Can't we discuss it some more?'

She eyed him appraisingly. 'So, you do invite me to stay, after all?'

Haggermeir looked embarrassed. 'Well, I can hardly do that—'

She stiffened. 'May I ask why not?'

'Well, I'm only a guest here myself.'

She looked blank. 'Only a guest? I do not understand. Have you not taken this house? Rented it?'

'Good grief, no. I'm just staying with Lord and Lady Burford here.'

Laura's face was a study. She seemed quite disconcerted. She turned towards the Earl and Countess. 'Oh, Lord Burford, Lady Burford, I am so sorry. I took you all to be members of Signore Haggermeir's party – feelm people.'

'Well, I for one am flattered,' said the Earl. 'Just what sort of film person did you think I might be?'

'But an actor, of course.'

'Really?' Lord Burford preened himself. 'Hear that, Lavinia?'

'Yes, George. Signora, allow me to make some introductions.'

She went round the circle. Laura was now all charm, smiling bewitchingly at everybody. When Lady Burford came to Rex she said. 'And I'm sure I don't have to tell you who this is?'

Laura puckered her brow. 'The gentleman's face is familiar, but I regret I do not...'

Lord Burford interrupted. 'This is Rex Ransom!'

'Ah, yes, of course.' Laura held out her hand. 'Do forgeev me, but I have not seen any of your peectures – er, unfortunately.'

Rex shook hands and gave a stiff smile. 'That's quite OK. I haven't seen any of yours either.'

Lady Burford said hurriedly, 'Mr Hugh Quartus.'

Hugh said, 'While I, on the contrary, have seen all your films, Signorina Lorenzo. May I say it's an honour to meet one of the world's great actresses.' Then, in Italian, he added: 'This has made the weekend worthwhile.'

Laura looked delighted. 'Grazie, signore. Siete davvero troopo gentili.'

When Lady Burford had completed the introductions she said, 'Now I do hope that you'll stay for the weekend.'

'Unfortunately, that will not be possible. I must be on the set in Roma early Monday, and I go back to London first to see my English agent. I would like to stay two nights, but is vital I leave here by meed-day Saturday.'

'Then that's settled,' said the Countess. 'Now, will you excuse me?' She rang the bell, then went outside to meet Merryweather in the hall. 'Merryweather, Signorina Lorenzo will be staying two nights. Where do you suggest we put her?'

'Apart from the Royal suite, my lady, on the first floor the Spangled and Lilac rooms in the west wing, and the Dutch in the east are free.'

'Not the Royal Suite. And both the Dutch and the Lilac are rather small.'

'Yes, my lady, but on the other hand, the Spangled bedroom is where the – the' – he cleared his throat – 'the sudden death took place. It occurs to me that if Signorina Lorenzo should become cognisant of the fact it might disturb her.'

'Yes, quite right. Put her in the Dutch. And have a large fire lit and make sure the room's kept really warm. I imagine as an Italian she finds our winter rather hard to bear.'

CHAPTER SIX

Rex Ransom's brow puckered as he made his way to his bedroom to dress for dinner. He was worried. Had that telegram to Laura Lorenzo just been a hoax? Or was Haggermeir, in spite of his denial, responsible for it? Had he wanted to invite her, but not liked to ask the Burford's permission – or, more likely, not wanted him, Rex, to know he was after her for The King's Man? Either way, it seemed on the cards that she would sign. And Rex didn't like the idea at all.

For years his name had been the only one to appear above the title of his pictures. Laura Lorenzo, however, would certainly demand at least an equal billing – perhaps even top billing. Moreover, her first Hollywood picture would undoubtedly be something of an event. The top critics would attend press screenings in force. Haggermeir might even give it the full publicity treatment of a gala premier. Rex could see himself being reduced to the level of a supporting player.

His lips set tightly. He would not stand for it. He'd fight for his rights. And he had one trump card: Cyrus needed *his* cooperation to get this picture off the ground. It was *him* the Earl was a fan of. It was *his* charm that was going to win over the Countess.

As Rex reached his room on the corner of the main block and the west wing, he looked right and saw Haggermeir – camera round his neck, a tape measure and writing pad in his hands – leave an empty room at the end of the corridor. Rex was tempted to go and tackle him immediately. But then Haggermeir disappeared up the stairs to the next floor, and Rex opened the door of his room.

As he did so, he was hit by a blast of cold air. He switched on the light – and stopped.

Where the window had been was a gaping black hole. And the floor was littered with broken glass.

Rex stood hesitating, wondering what Emily Post would say was the correct thing to do under the circumstances. He shivered. Well, he couldn't pretend it hadn't happened. He'd freeze to death in here.

He went in search of his host.

Lord Burford stared round Rex's bedroom. He scratched his head. 'How very peculiar. I meantersay, if one of the maids had got careless and backed a broom through the window, you'd hardly expect her to do quite such a wholesale job. Likewise if small boys are trespassin' and started throwing stones.'

Rex said tentatively, 'I have heard of big birds – geese and suchlike – smashing into windows in the dark.'

The Earl looked impressed. 'That's a thought. You may – ah!' He bent down and picked something off the rug. It was a grey feather, two-inches long. 'Looks as if you may have hit the nail on the head, old man. Wonder if the creature killed itself. I'll send a servant to look outside in a moment. But what are we going to do with you? That's the problem. Of course!' He snapped his fingers. 'The Royal Suite.'

'Oh, I couldn't possibly—'

'Nonsense, Rex. We don't keep it exclusively for royalty. Besides, you've been a prince and a king in your time, so you ought to feel quite at home.'

'I've also been a pirate and a highwayman. All the same, I'm surely honoured.'

'Good. I'll arrange with Merryweather to have it made ready.'

Lord Burford smiled.

Dinner that evening was a great success. The food was a highly traditional English menu, most of it the actual produce of the estate; mushroom soup, grilled trout, roast beef and Yorkshire pudding, apple tart and cream and Cheddar cheese, with an excellent selection of wines.

But it was as a social gathering that the occasion turned out far better than could have been anticipated. This was due largely to the presence of Laura. She looked exquisite in an extra-tight sheath gown of black velvet, split over emerald satin; and although she didn't herself speak much, she seemed to act as a sort of catalyst on some of the others.

Lady Burford, for example had quite forgiven Laura's earlier behaviour on learning of the misconception she had been under; and was, in fact, secretly delighted to have a Serious Dramatic Actress added to the party. She had learnt that the highly respectable and respected magazine *The*

Londoner had recently devoted a long and fulsome article to Laura, who was clearly a fit person to be entertained at a house where Sarah Bernhardt had once stayed – and who would provide a most useful camouflage for the other film people; they could now be represented to friends as having been merely necessary appendages to Signorina Lorenzo. Consequently, the Countess was far happier with the house party than she had been.

Laura also brought out the best in Rex. Determined not to be outshone by her, he put all he had into making an impact, and compliments, jokes and anecdotes of the stars flowed from his lips throughout the meal.

The third person affected by Laura's presence was Hugh. It was obvious to everybody that he'd been deeply smitten by her, and to his delight, found himself sitting next to her. He talked animatedly to her all through dinner, mostly in Italian.

Gerry was rather irritated by his attentiveness, but she was honest enough to realise that she could have no real cause for complaint. Anything was better than the way he'd been behaving since his arrival.

Having run out of ideas for new characterisations, Gerry had decided just to be herself this evening. However, as this was a personality Gilbert had not previously seen, it was to him as much a new side of her as the others had been. Sitting opposite her, he stared at her with a fearful fascination.

It was during dessert, when Rex had just completed an amusing story concerning a backstage incident at the previous year's Oscar ceremony, that Lord Burford addressed the company at large.

'By the way, talking of prizegivings reminds me: wonderin' if you'd all care for a little jaunt tomorrow evening.'

'I'm game for anything,' Rex said. 'What do you have in mind?'

'Well, it may be a bit of a bore for you, Rex, but ever since the village learnt you were coming they've been agog, wonderin' if they were going to get a chance to see you.'

Rex grinned, 'I'm happy to display the old visage, sign a few autographs.'

'Actually, there's a little more to it than that. You see, each year about this time they hold a talent contest. Everybody turns out, and I usually act as one of the judges and present the prizes. Well, this year's contest is tomorrow night – seven o'clock – and I was wondering if you'd hand out the awards.'

'I don't want to steal your job.'

'I've done it dozens of times. No, it'll be a nice break for me, and a real thrill for the village.'

'Then I'll be glad to.'

'Oh, fine. As a matter of fact, the committee put the contest back a week when it first got round you were coming, in the hope you'd agree, and I said I'd do my best. Now, how about you, Haggermeir? Care to be one of the judges?'

'Me? Oh, I don't think so, thanks—'

Rex interrupted. 'Now, come on, Cyrus, you might discover a new Shirley Temple.'

'I'm afraid that's highly unlikely,' the Earl said. 'Most of 'em are pretty ghastly, actually, though there are usually two or three who aren't too bad.

'Well, I guess they couldn't be much more lousy than some of the screen tests I see every week. OK then.'

'Splendid. I'll telephone the chappie who's organising it in the morning and tell him to expect a couple of VIP guests.'

Gerry said, 'Daddy, don't forget we have more than just two VIP guests.' She inclined her head slightly towards Laura.

However, as she did so, Arlington Gilbert said, 'Thank you, Lady Geraldine, but I can think of no more revolting way to pass an evening than witnessing the cavorting and caterwauling of bucolic *brats*.'

Gerry bridled. 'Personally, I wouldn't miss it for the world. It can be the most spiffing fun. Paul, you'll come?'

'Certainly. Try anything once.'

'Hugh?'

'Thanks, but I'd rather not.'

Lord Burford, who'd got the gist of his daughter's hint, turned to Laura. 'Forgive me, signorina, for not including you. 'Fraid it just didn't occur to me that you...'

Rex said lightly, 'Oh, I can't imagine that such a distinguished and intellectual actress would find such an event at all amusing.'

Laura smiled at him sweetly. 'You are quite wrong, Mr Ransom.' She looked at the Earl. 'I should enjoy much watching the dear leetle bambini performing, and helping you judge them.'

Avoiding the eye of Rex, who was looking very slightly disgruntled at this, Lord Burford said, 'Well, we're going to have quite a party. Anybody else who'd like to join us, of course, will be more than welcome.'

Hugh said, 'Thank you, Lord Burford. I think I'll change my mind and come along.'

Now it was Paul's turn to look displeased. He said, 'Come with me in my car, Gerry?'

'Yes, of course.'

She glanced a little anxiously at Hugh. But he was looking at Laura.

When coffee was being served in the drawing room after dinner, Rex suddenly said, 'Do you know, George, what I've been looking forward to ever since I knew I was coming here: learning something of the history of Alderley and of your ancestors. There must be quite a few interesting stories in nearly three hundred years.'

'Oo, don't know about that. Pretty dull lot, actually. Most of 'em just hung around here, looking after the estate and collectin' things.'

'Surely, they can't *all* have been dull?'

'Well, there was the fifth Earl. He was very mechanical. Built a flying machine. Powered by gunpowder. Tried to take off from the roof of the east wing. People still fish bits of the machine out of the lake from time to time. And the Earl, for all I know. Then there's the business of the seventh Earl and the Westshire Declaration of Independence. Got the idea from the American colonists. Proclaimed the county an independent republic, with himself as president. Couldn't get anyone to take him seriously. So he went to London, bought up several tons of tea and dumped it in the East India dock. But nobody took any notice. He couldn't understand it. Said it had worked for the colonists. His wife came and took him home then.'

Cecily said, 'George, wasn't there a ghost at one time?'

'Oh, you mean Lady Elfreda.'

'That sounds interesting,' said Paul.

'Not especially. Daughter of the eighth Earl. Shut herself up in her room for the unrequited love of a dancin' master and swore never to eat again.'

'What happened?' Cecily asked. 'Did she die?'

'Oh, yes.'

'She starved herself to death for love?'

'Just the opposite. Kept it up for three days, then crept down in the night and stuffed herself with a rather doubtful game pie they'd been going to throw away. Died of food poisonin'. We still hear her voice sometimes. Calling for castor oil.'

'Wasn't your grandfather something of a character, sir?' Paul asked.

'Oh, old Aylwin. Well, I agree, you couldn't call him dull.'

'Tell us about him,' said Haggermeir.

'He wasn't exactly an admirable character.'

'So much the better,' said Rex.

The Earl collected his thoughts. 'Aylwin was a holy terror from the start. Always in scrapes – playing practical jokes, taking up dares. Got through dozens of nursemaids. No viciousness in him, mind. Just high-spirited, with a keen – if not very subtle – sense of humour. And apparently quite fearless. When he was eleven they sent him to Eton. There he was constantly in trouble for fighting, being out after hours, and was eventually expelled after being found playing cards for money in a public house. He came home for a few years, made life miserable for a succession of tutors, and was generally thoroughly pestilential throughout the neighbourhood. By the time he was eighteen he already had a county-wide reputation for drinking, gaming, wenching, fighting, and all kinds of wild stunts.

'Then, for the first time, he fell in love. The girl was a Lady Mary Carruthers, the daughter of a large landowner, with an estate ten miles away. She was as different from Aylwin as chalk from cheese – small, pretty, demure, shy – but he proposed after knowing her a week. And she accepted. However, her parents wouldn't hear of it. For one thing she was only sixteen, and although it would have been a very advantageous match for her, his reputation was just too bad for them.

'Aylwin, though, wasn't going to let that stand in his way. He asked Mary to run away with him. She agreed, and accompanied by Aylwin's manservant – a fellow called John – they eloped. They were making for Gretna Green in Scotland, to be married over the anvil as the saying went. 'Course, it wasn't long before Mary's parents found out what had happened, and her father and Aylwin's set off in pursuit – though not, I imagine, with much hope of catching them in time.

'But, by sheer luck, they did run them to earth, at an inn just short of the Scottish border. The youngsters gave way to the inevitable then. Explained that they'd been held up when the carriage had gone into a ditch.

'Aylwin and Mary were taken home in disgrace. But Mary's parents were so relieved to find that Aylwin had behaved as a perfect gentleman throughout, and her virtue was unblemished, that they didn't take the matter any further and a scandal was avoided.

'But Aylwin's father had by then taken just about all he could take of his son. He gave Aylwin five thousand guineas and told him to clear off. He never wanted to see him again.

'Aylwin didn't argue. He took the money and left, again with the faithful John in tow. He spent the next couple of years in London and Paris, until eventually he had just a few pounds left. With most of this he bought two tickets to America. He and John set sail in August, 1842.

'Now, he succeeded in winning about twenty pounds at cards on the voyage. It was the only money-making skill he had, and it seemed to him that his best course was to try and earn a living at it. After a few weeks in New York, though, he decided that he'd have a better chance of doing this out West.

'Aylwin took to the West like a duck to water. He loved the free and easy atmosphere, the opportunities for adventure and excitement. He was tough, knew how to use his fists, and was a first-rate horseman. As a result, he seems to have got on famously, and for the next six or seven years he roamed far and wide. Exactly how he kept himself all that time I don't know. He certainly made a living as a professional gambler for a spell; but he also went fur trapping, acted with a touring theatrical company, and had a few bouts as a professional prizefighter. He fought Indians, shot a man in a gunfight at Dodge City, and became a close friend of Kit Carson.

'Then in 1849 came the California gold rush. Aylwin was actually in Sacramento when the first strikes were made and was among the first at the gold diggings.

What's more, he made a strike. Not a fabulously rich one, but it made him money enough to live on for at least a couple of years. So, still accompanied by his servant John, he made his way to San Francisco for a holiday.

'Meanwhile, back here, his father had been in failing health for some time, and had been told by his doctor that he couldn't expect to live for more than another year. He wanted to see his son and patch up their quarrel before it was too late. Now, Aylwin had been writing tolerably frequently to his mother – care of her sister, so that the old man wouldn't hear of it – and consequently she at least knew that he was in San Francisco. So an employee of the family solicitor was sent to try and trace him. After several weeks he at last tracked Aylwin down.

'Aylwin, I imagine, had by then had about enough of the life he'd been leading. He knew his cash wouldn't last indefinitely and then it would be back to the old ways. However, he still had enough left to return home in some style, so his pride wouldn't suffer if he did go back. The short of it was that he arrived home early in 1852 and was quickly reconciled with his father. The old man died six mouths later, and Aylwin succeeded to the title as tenth Earl. That's just about the whole story.'

There was silence for a few seconds before Paul said, 'But what happened to him? What did he do for the rest of his life?'

'Nothing much. Ran the estate, became a pillar of the Tory party, took his seat in the House of Lords.'

'Whom did he marry?' Cecily asked.

'One guess.'

'Not Lady Mary?'

'The same. She'd waited for him and she was only twenty-eight or -nine when he came home. I think they were very happy. Had four children, my father being the eldest. Sorry if the end's a bit of an anticlimax.'

At that moment Merryweather entered. He approached the Earl. 'My lord, the window of the Grey bedroom has been boarded up.'

'Oh, fine.'

'No bird's body was discovered outside, but there were some more feathers.'

'I see.'

'And a thought has just occurred to me, my lord. The burglar alarm: I fear it will be impossible to turn it on. The contact will have been broken when the window was smashed. If the current is now switched on, the alarm bell will be automatically activated.'

'Lor', I suppose you're right. Oh, well, can't be helped.'

Merryweather departed and Lord Burford hastened to explain to his guests. 'Few years ago we had a very complex alarm system installed – too complex, really. Supposed to be foolproof, but it means that after it's switched on you can't open an outside door, or any window more than two inches, without setting it off. In fact, your bedroom windows have got stops fixed, though they can be forced easily enough in an emergency. However, as it would be pretty inconvenient if nobody could go outside during the evening without setting off the alarm, we don't usually switch the system on till the very last moment. Tonight, though, seems we won't be switching on at all.'

'Well, at least the burglars don't know,' said Gerry. 'That's the main thing.'

It was when the party was breaking up two hours later that Rex drew Lord Burford aside. 'In view of what's happened, I wonder: could you lock some money in your safe for me?'

'Of course – delighted. Go and get it now. I'll wait for you in my study.'

Three minutes later Rex entered the study to find Lord Burford ready with the safe open. He took a bulging billfold from his pocket and handed it to the Earl, who raised his eyebrows. 'Quite a bundle here, by the feel of it.'

'Something over two thousand pounds.'

'Great Scott! D'you always carry that much cash around with you?'

'Mostly. Psychological thing, I suppose. Makes me feel secure. Didn't always have a lot of dough. And I'm a country boy, raised not to trust banks. Don't mention it to Cyrus, will you? He thinks I'm crazy enough already.'

'Oh, shan't tell a soul.' Lord Burford put the billfold in the safe, closed the door and spun the combination knob. Together they left the room.

CHAPTER SEVEN

Cyrus Haggermeir looked at his watch, wound up his tape measure, left the room on the top floor of Alderley and made his way down to his bedroom. He went in – and stopped. Sitting in the room's only chair was Laura. In her hands was the script of The King's Man. She looked up with a smile.

'Do forgeev me, Meesta Haggermeir. I thought I would like to see the screenplay of the movie. I was going to ask to borrow it, but as you weren't here I deed not like to take it away.'

'Oh, that's OK.' He took his camera from around his neck and put it down.

'Will you be wanting this tonight, or may I take it to my room to feenish it?'

'You understand that's only the old silent version?'

'Of course, but the plot of the sound version will not be much deefferent, will it? Though naturally I understand that it will have to be, er – what you say – adapted to feet me.'

'Ah. Yeah.' Then he said a little awkwardly:

'Signorina, I, er – well, I'm not sure I can use you on this movie.'

She drew in her breath. 'What is it you say? *You* cannot use *me*?'

'Well, not – that is—'

She jumped to her feet, again breaking into a torrent of Italian.

Haggermeir held up both hands. 'Please, no, signorina. No understand Italiano.'

Eventually she ran out of breath and stood staring at him, her eyes flashing. 'Signore, you eensult me. Do you not know the big Hollywood men, they all – Goldwyn, De Mille, Warner, and Korda in England – they all want to sign up Laura Lorenzo. They go on their knees. They grovel in the dirt. But always I say no. Until now. I offer you my services. And you? *You* turn me down. I not forget this!'

Haggermeir ran his hands through his hair. 'Don't get me wrong, signorina. I'd be tickled pink to sign you up. It'd be a terrific feather in my cap. But for another movie, not for *The King's Man*. It's not your sort of picture. It's a crummy old story—'

'*Sciocchezze!* Nonsense! It is a fine story.'

'It is? You think so?'

'Of course.'

'Well, maybe for Rex. But there's no part in it that would suit you.'

'No part? You are mad. The part of Anne-Marie might have been written for me. It just needs to be – what you say – written up, made bigger. True, she is French, but she can be Italiano just as well. Call her Anna Maria. Where is the problem?'

'I'm not sure Arlington Gilbert would go along with that.'

'Geelbert? You let your writers deectate to you?'

'Not normally, but he's a touchy guy. Now, look, what I'd like to do is commission a screenplay from a really first-rate writer – S.N. Behrman, say, or Llllian Hellman – just for you.'

'Fine words, Meesta Producer, but disguising the seemple fact that you do not weesh to have me in your movie. Well, do not fear that you will have to. Do not imagine that you will ever get the opportunity.'

And she flung the script at his feet and swept from the room.

Gerry stood in her room, surveying herself in a full-length mirror. She gave a satisfied nod at what she saw. She was wearing a plain white sleeveless nightdress. She had combed out her hair, so that it fell straight to below her shoulders. She had applied a very pale, almost white, face powder and a bright scarlet lipstick, very thick. The effect was dramatic.

She opened her dressing table drawer and took from it a long-bladed carving knife, which she'd sneaked from the kitchen earlier, and practiced holding it in various positions, rubbing her thumb lightly along the blade. She rehearsed several different kinds of smiles. At last she felt ready.

She'd realised earlier that it was nearly time to abandon her hoax on Arlington Gilbert. However, she couldn't just let it fizzle out. It had to end with a bang. This last personality was going to be her *piece de résistance*. Afterwards she'd tell him the truth.

She opened the door and went outside. Brr, but it was cold. She must get this over as quickly as possible.

She turned right and hurried past the intervening bathroom to Gilbert's room. She paused outside, then gently turned the knob and pushed the door open an inch. No light showed, nor was there any verbal challenge. Gerry slipped in, silently closed the door behind her, and stood quite still, her heart beating fast.

She took a deep breath and stepped forward. The knife was held behind her back, ready to be brought forward at the crucial moment. What she was going to do after he saw it she didn't know. It would depend on his reactions.

When Gerry judged she was in the middle of the room she stopped. Then she spoke, softly and wheedlingly, in the voice of a little girl.

'Oh, Mr Gilbert.'

There was no reply. Gerry raised her voice. 'Mr Gilbert, would you like to play with me? I'm so lonely. Do wake up and play. I have a lovely toy here.'

But still there came no response.

Suddenly Gerry grasped the truth. She stumbled back to the door and switched on the light. The bed was empty.

She gave an exasperated exclamation. All for nothing. What a waste!

Then abruptly she realised how very relieved she was. She'd been behaving extremely childishly – not at all like a mature young woman with two prospective fiancés under her roof. So, back to her room quickly, before he returned.

But, she wondered, returned from where?

He hadn't just gone to the bathroom. It had a fanlight over the door and the light was out.

She looked round the room again and took in the fact that the bed had not been disturbed and that a pair of pyjamas were folded on the counterpane. It must be nearly forty minutes now since she'd seen him come in here, and it seemed he must have left again almost immediately. Perhaps he'd gone to talk to somebody. Haggermeir – about the script for the film, say?

Then Gerry saw something else. On the bedside table was glass. And in it was a set of false teeth.

She pondered. Surely no one would go to talk to somebody and leave his false teeth behind. He might have gone to the library to get a book. But he'd never have stayed all this time. So – where was he?

Gerry thought hard. She didn't trust Arlington Gilbert, and she found herself consumed by an intense urge to know just what he was doing. For Alderley contained many valuable things. The burglar alarm was out of action. And if Gilbert was light-fingered, tonight would present a fine opportunity for him to do some thieving, fake a forced entry and put the robbery down to some mythical burglar.

Gerry knew she had to try and find out what he was up to.

Hastily she returned to her room, donned a woollen dressing-gown, wiped her face free of make-up, put a flashlight in her pocket, and left again. She was still carrying the knife, which she intended to return to the kitchen. This time she turned left, went to the main stairs and started down. It was quite dark, but she didn't turn the lights on, just flicked her torch on and off occasionally. She knew the house intimately. Gilbert didn't. So the darkness would give her a big advantage. Besides, she didn't want to risk being seen herself, apparently spying on a guest.

It was just as she reached the bottom of the stairs that she heard the sound.

She couldn't be sure exactly what it was, for it was muffled. But she knew where it came from.

Her father's study.

Gerry stared towards the study door, which led directly off the hall. She felt a prickling up and down her spine, which had nothing to do with the cold.

What on earth could he want in there? Her father kept no valuables in the study. Only a few pounds in a cash box, family and estate papers, account books, correspondence. Of course, Gilbert might not know that.

Well, there could be no innocent reason for him – or anyone else – being in there. So there was no cause now for concealment.

Gerry marched to the study, paused for a moment, threw open the door and reached for the light switch just inside. She pressed.

But the room remained in darkness.

Only then did it occur to her that with the alarm out of action a real burglar could have got in. Her heart gave a lurch. But she'd shot her bolt. In a voice that quavered only slightly, she said:

'Who's in here?'

At that second a thin beam of light from a flashlight

pierced the darkness, hitting her full in the eyes.

Gerry groped frantically for her own flashlight. But before she could get it from her pocket she was aware that someone was coming towards her.

With a great effort she held her ground. In her right hand she was still gripping the carving knife. She raised it, holding it out in front of her like a sword, and said loudly, 'Keep back. I've got a knife.'

With her other hand she at last managed to get out her flashlight. She was fumbling desperately to switch it on, when it was wrenched from her grasp and fell to the floor.

Now very frightened indeed, Gerry slashed with the knife. She felt the blade make contact with something and heard the man give an exclamation of pain. But he drew back only momentarily, and the next instant he'd grabbed her wrist, forcing her to drop the knife. She opened her mouth to scream, but he must have anticipated this, for as she did so he released her wrist and clapped his hand over her mouth. She struggled furiously.

Then, unexpectedly, he pushed her to one side. She staggered, tripped, and sat down hard on the carpet. She drew her breath for a shout. Then she froze.

All was quiet – and there was complete darkness.

He'd turned off his flashlight. He was just standing silently, waiting to pounce as soon as he knew her exact position.

At that moment she heard another noise. But it wasn't in the room. It sounded like some sort of scuffle, maybe a fall or hurrying footsteps. It was from above, probably from the top of the stairs.

Gerry sat quite still, holding her breath.

* * *

Rex Ransom sat before the dying fire in the magnificent bedroom of the Royal Suite, sunk in gloomy forebodings. At last he stirred and gave a little groan. Keeping up his gay manner throughout the evening had really taken it out of him, and on coming to his room he had flopped down without even removing his evening jacket. Now he felt awful. He had let the room get cold, and he was stiff, uncomfortable and more depressed than ever. There was coming over him, too, that dreaded feeling of oppression, the sense of something pressing in on him. He had to do something about it quickly. He stood up, took off his coat and started to remove his cufflinks.

Three minutes later, stripped down to shorts and undershirt, Rex stared down at the two objects he was holding. How he hated them. Yet they were so necessary to him. He couldn't carry on without them.

At that second, to his alarm, he heard a slight sound from the next room.

The Royal Suite consisted of three connecting rooms: a sitting room, nearest to the grand staircase; next to it the bedroom; and then a dressing room. Rex had told Merryweather to have a fire lit only in the bedroom. It was from the sitting room that the noise had come.

There was nothing sinister about the sound – just a sharp tap, as though someone's foot had knocked against a piece of furniture. But why should anybody be in there, creeping about in the dark?

Rex swung round towards the adjoining door and saw to his consternation that it was open a couple of inches. He took a step towards it. Then he stopped. For there appeared through the crack a black-gloved hand.

Taken utterly aback, Rex stood momentarily transfixed as the hand, followed by a black-sleeved arm, moved like a deadly snake along the wall. Suddenly he came to his senses, gave a shout of anger and took two hurried steps towards the door. But he was too late. The hand had reached the light switch and the room plunged into darkness.

Rex stood motionless. In the blackness there was not much else he could do. In his best actor's voice he barked, 'Who is that? What are you doing here?'

There was no reply.

Rex backed a little towards the bed. Able to see nothing, dressed as he was and barefooted, he felt uncomfortably vulnerable. He spoke again, with a brash confidence he was far from feeling, 'OK, the joke's gone far enough. Clear off and I'll forget about it.'

He felt a rush of cold air hit him as with a creak the door opened wide. He heard footsteps approaching.

He shouted, 'I know who you are—'

Then a blinding light seemed to engulf him. Rex gave an exclamation and staggered back, dropping the objects he had been holding, as the room again went black.

For a second he flinched, waiting for an attack. But suddenly a sense of the indignity of his situation swept over him. Was this the way for the great Rex Ransom, dashing hero of thirty swashbuckling adventures to behave – skulking in a darkened room, waiting submissively to be set upon?

Never!

Rex gave an exclamation of rage and strode blindly forward, swinging random punches. For seconds he punched the air. Then one of his fists made contact with a face. It was a glancing blow, probably in the vicinity of the eye. But it gave him a surge of satisfaction, especially as it drew from his adversary a muffled gasp.

Rex gave a yell of triumph, 'One for all and all for one!'

The words were quite inappropriate, but they were the only ones he could think of. Then he realised that the intruder was retreating before him, making for the door. Since extinguishing his flashlight, he must be as blind as Rex himself. There was a chance of collaring him.

Rex kept moving forward. But then he heard the door to the sitting room slam, and a second later his outstretched fingers touched the door panels. He fumbled for the knob and pulled the door open. He heard somebody blundering across the sitting room, towards the corridor door. Rex groped for the light, but before he could get it on he heard that door in turn open and close.

About to go after him, Rex instead paused. He couldn't possibly go outside in this state, not at Alderley. He turned and went back into the bedroom, switching on the light. As he did so he thought he heard some sort of commotion from the corridor or landing outside. He grabbed for his dressing gown.

Gerry sat on the study floor. She had heard not a sound since the small rumpus from upstairs a minute before. Very quietly she let out her breath. He was gone; she was sure of it. Carefully she got to her feet, felt her way to the desk, groped for the reading lamp and switched on.

Apprehensively she peered round. The room seemed

in order. She'd been half expecting to see the safe door open and the desk drawers on the floor. But there was no sign at all of the intrusion, or of her titanic struggle with the intruder. Which was, in a way, rather irritating. She crossed to the window and examined it. It was intact and locked – virtual proof that it was no outsider she'd been dealing with.

The bulb from the centre of the room had been removed and was on the desk. Gerry fetched a chair to stand on and replaced it. Then she found her flashlight and left the study, switching off the light. She went to the kitchen, replaced the knife and made her way upstairs in the dark. For the moment she couldn't quite think what to do next. The obvious thing would be to rouse her father and take him to confront Gilbert. On the other hand, a scene of that sort would upset the Earl terribly. And Gilbert wouldn't try any more funny business tonight. Perhaps, then, it would be better to do nothing now and make a decision about her next move in the morning.

Gerry had nearly reached the top of the stairs when the light on the landing above her went on. She gave a start and blinked upwards, fearfully. Then she said, 'Mr Ransom!'

Rex gazed down at her, in obvious surprise. 'Lady Geraldine.'

She said, 'I – I thought I heard a noise.'

'Yes, so did I.'

He looked immaculate in an elegant mohair dressing gown, not a hair of his head out of place – and certainly not like someone who'd just got out of bed.

'It sounded like a sort of scuffle,' she said. 'But I expect it was just somebody stumbling in the dark.'

'Probably. Well, in that case I think I'll get back to bed. Good night, Lady Geraldine.'

'Good night, Mr Ransom.'

Rex returned to his room and at last got into bed. He lay on his back, staring up into the darkness. But it was a long time before he slept.

CHAPTER EIGHT

On Friday Alderley awoke to an even colder day. In addition; there was a strong north wind and the sky was a surly grey. The weather had none of the crisp, bracing quality of the Thursday.

Somehow this change seemed to be reflected in the atmosphere indoors. So, at least, it seemed to Lord Burford at breakfast. He was down early and had only just started his meal when to his great surprise the first person to join him was Gerry.

'Good gad!' he said. 'You all right?'

'Couldn't sleep.' She sat down and started buttering a piece of toast.

Her father looked astonished. 'No bacon and eggs?'

'No, I'm not hungry.' She spoke absently.

'Can't sleep and off your feed? You must be sickenin' for something.'

But Gerry wasn't listening. She was staring intently at the door, which was just opening. Then she visibly relaxed as Rex came in. He said good morning and sat down. There were dark circles under his eyes, and though he responded cheerfully to the Earl's remarks, his good humour was clearly forced. He too kept his eyes fixed on the door.

Sebastian and Cecily, Haggermeir, Paul and Hugh arrived during the next ten minutes and all seemed strangely preoccupied. Each was subjected to the closest scrutiny by Rex.

Then the door opened again and Gilbert entered. Lord Burford looked at him and gave an exclamation. 'My dear chap! What have you been doing to yourself?'

His words drowned Rex's quick intake of breath, and no one noticed the sudden expression of triumph in Gerry's eye. For down Gilbert's left cheek ran a long strip of bandage. And his right eye was a most magnificent shade of purple.

Gilbert said nonchalantly, 'Two quite separate mishaps. I walked into a cupboard door and then, while shaving with my old cut-throat, I slipped, and gashed myself. However, they say suffering is good for the creative artist.'

He went to the sideboard and helped himself to two large kippers.

Rex said, 'If you'll excuse me.' He stood up and strolled out. So now he knew. Gee, that punch he'd landed must have been harder than he'd realised. And thank heavens for it, for now he could act.

Gerry left the breakfast room a few minutes later and returned to her bedroom to think. The cut on Gilbert's cheek proved beyond doubt that it was him she'd slashed at in the study. But what was she going to do about it? She couldn't bring herself to tell her father. After so much apprehension, the Earl was now enormously enjoying the house party. To be told one of his guests was a crook would be to rekindle his fears of a repeat of that other disastrous weekend – and take away all his pleasure at the visit of Rex Ransom. What was more, without absolutely cast-iron proof, Lord Burford would certainly not just send Gilbert packing. He would merely worry. And if she told her mother, the Countess would undoubtedly go straight to the Earl.

Gerry was tempted to ask Paul's advice. But it seemed hardly fair to invite him to stay and then involve him in her problems.

No, she had to resolve the affair on her own. And really there was only one straightforward course: to confront Gilbert privately and give him the opportunity to make some excuse and leave. It would be a horrible task; bad enough at the best of times, but now complicated by her idiotic behaviour toward him the previous day. Whether or not she now revealed that she had been the girl at the garage, he'd have good grounds for putting round the story that Lady Geraldine Saunders was a candidate for the looney bin. And any accusation she made about his searching the study would just seem additional evidence of this.

However, there was no way out. Gilbert was up to no good, and had to be got rid of. At least he didn't, thank heaven, know about her nocturnal visit to his bedroom.

Gerry went downstairs again, deciding to wait outside the breakfast room and waylay Gilbert when he came out. She'd been there for five minutes when she saw Laura Lorenzo, who'd breakfasted in her room, descending the stairs.

Laura this morning was wearing a lettuce-green tweed jacket and corduroy trousers. She smiled charmingly. 'Ah, *buongiorno*, Lady Geraldine.'

'Good morning. I hope you slept well.'

'Oh, *si*, I did, *grazie*.'

'Sorry you've got such a pokey little room, right down at the end of the corridor.'

'Oh, that does not matter. It is a beautiful room. And such a lovely fire! For the first time since I arrive in England I am warm enough.'

Then over Gerry's shoulder she exclaimed. 'Signore Geelbert!'

Gerry swung round to see Gilbert emerging from the breakfast room. But before she could speak to him, Laura had swept past her. '*Scuzatemi*, Lady Geraldine. Signore Geelbert, a queeck word with you.'

'What? Oh, of course, pleasure.'

Laura took him by the arm. 'Perhaps we can go somewhere quiet.' She led him away.

'So, Signore Geelbert, that is quite definite?'

'Quite.'

'*Bene, bene*. I'm glad we understand each other. I just wanted to make quite sure. Now I must leave you. I have not long here and there is much that I must see to. Goodbye.' She went out.

Gerry saw Laura leave the small music room, where she'd been having her tête-à-tête with Gilbert, and walk off. She waited a moment and entered the room herself.

Arlington Gilbert was seated at a table near the window. He looked up as Gerry entered and his face took on an expression halfway between alarm and excitement. Gerry said, 'I want to speak to you, Mr Gilbert.'

He stood up. 'Oh?' His face now displayed a kind of apprehensive attentiveness, as though he was trying to work out which of Gerry's personalities was on display this morning. 'What about?'

'I think you know quite well.'

'I assure you, I—'

'Let's stop playing games. That cut on your face: you didn't get it shaving; I did it.'

He positively boggled at her. '*You*?'

'Oh, don't pretend you didn't know who it was!'

'I had no idea!'

'Well, now you do. And I want an explanation.'

'*You* want an explanation? Don't you owe me an explanation – and an apology?'

Gerry gave a gasp. 'Me apologise to you? What on earth for?'

'Well, do you normally go around attacking your guests in the middle of the night?'

'No – just defend myself when they sneak around in the dark and manhandle me.'

He gave a roar. 'I did not manhandle you! You ran into me.'

'I did nothing of the sort!' Then Gerry took a grip on herself. This was most undignified, and not at all as she had envisaged the conversation. More quietly she said, 'Who ran into whom is immaterial. What I want to know is what you were doing there.'

'I can't answer that.'

She said incredulously, 'You refuse to tell me?'

'I do.'

'But you had absolutely no right to be there!'

'*No right*? Jupiter's teeth, what sort of place is this? Alcatraz? Do you set a curfew, make certain areas off limits to your guests?'

'No, of course not! But we don't expect them to go snooping around in the dark.'

'I was not snooping!'

'Then why didn't you switch the light on?'

'Why didn't you?'

'You'd taken the bulb out!'

'I had not!' He said this with such vehemence that for a moment she couldn't manage to argue; after all there was no way to prove it.

Rather lamely she said, 'Well, somebody did.'

'Not me. And anyway, what were you doing spying on people in the middle of the night?'

'I wasn't spying.'

Suddenly his face cleared. 'Oh, I see?' He chuckled slyly. 'Date with one of the boyfriends, was it?'

'Certainly not!'

'Tell that to the marines.'

'I was looking for you, you fool!'

She could have bitten her tongue off as soon as the words were out, but simply stared dumbly at him.

Gilbert gave a start. 'Looking for me?'

'Yes, but—'

'Well, well, well,' he said slowly. 'I must say this puts a different complexion on things. And I won't say I'm not flattered. I am, of course, attractive to women, and I'm quite familiar with these sudden irresistible urges they get.'

Utterly speechless, Gerry just stood, her mouth open, the dozens of scathing words she wanted to utter stuck in her throat like a log jam on a river.

Gilbert continued thoughtfully, 'Now, I must try and work out just what happened, because it's all very confusing. I take it you went first to my room?'

Gerry gulped. 'I—'

He smiled. 'I can see you did. Don't be embarrassed – it's quite natural. You found my room empty, and, of course, were bitterly disappointed.' He took a step towards her. 'I'm terribly sorry, Geraldine, but I couldn't know you were coming. And now that I understand the situation, I don't mind telling you what I was doing. But one thing first: when we ran into each other, you must have realised you'd found the person you'd been seeking. Why then did you claw my face?'

At last, presented with a straight question, Gerry managed to reply. Through clenched teeth she hissed, 'I did not claw your face!'

'But my dear, you said—'

In a sudden bursting of frustration, anger and humiliation, Gerry yelled, 'I didn't claw your face. I did it with a carving knife!'

For seconds Gilbert didn't react at all; his face wore the same slightly pulled but patiently indulgent expression. Then it was as though something clicked. His jaw dropped.

He said hollowly, 'You came looking for me with a – a carving knife?'

'Yes! Now listen—'

But Gilbert had gone pale. Hurriedly he stepped back. He said, 'Keep away.'

Desperately Gerry shouted, 'You great imbecile, you don't understand—'

'Oh, yes, I do – only too well. I was warned about you, Lady Geraldine. I didn't know what the warning meant. But I do now. You're mad. Certifiable. You ought to be locked up!'

'Will you listen?' Gerry screeched. 'You've got it all wrong. I want to know what you were looking for. Either tell me or leave this house at once.'

'Well, I wasn't looking for a victim to stab! And don't worry, I'm going. Now. Nobody's safe with you around. It's monstrous that you're walking about free. The power of the aristocracy! Disgraceful! I shall show it up!'

And being careful to remain facing her, Gilbert sidled round her, backed to the door and went hurriedly out.

Gerry sank helplessly into a chair. She felt exhausted. Oh, crumbs, what a ghastly mess she'd made of that!

But at least he was going. To spread abroad heaven knew what sort of rumours about her. He'd make her out to be a maniac certainly – but whether on reflection he'd paint her as merely a nymphomaniac, or homicidal as well, she wasn't sure.

Suddenly Gerry's lips started to twitch. Then she gave a giggle. Next a chortle. Within seconds she was bent double in her chair, helpless with laughter.

Laura opened the door to the library and looked in. The only person inside was Paul, who was kneeling on the floor, peering under a chair.

She said, 'Oh, *mi scusi*.'

'It's all right.' Paul stood up. 'I was just looking for

my fountain pen. Thought I might have dropped it in here yesterday. But no luck. It's rather a nice one: gold, twenty-first birthday present from my godmother.'

'Ah, then it would be a peety to lose it.'

'Were you looking for somebody in particular?' he asked.

'It is no matter. I am seemply exploring this beautiful house.' She looked round her. 'Would it be eendeescreet of me, signore, were I to ask whether perhaps one day it will be your home?'

'Mine?'

'Forgeev me, but I got the impression that you and the Lady Geraldine were – were...'

'Oh, I see.' Paul grinned. 'Well, I'd certainly like to think we were. But I'm not banking on it.'

'Ah, you have a rival?'

'You could say that.'

'Signore Quartus, I think? And you hate each other, yes?'

'Great Scott, no!'

'But if you are both in love with the same woman...'

'That doesn't mean we hate each other. After all, we're not Latins, who—' He broke off, in confusion. 'I'm sorry, I didn't mean—'

Laura laughed, a rich appreciative laugh. 'Not crazy, hot-blooded Italianos? No, Signore Carter, you are certainly not that. You especially are very English, are you not? And so you stay in the same house as your rival, and you are very polite, and if the Lady Geraldine eventually chooses him you will smile and shake him by the hand and tell everyone what a frightfully decent chap he is. Right?'

Paul laughed. 'I sincerely hope the situation doesn't arise. But if it does, it wouldn't do any good to cut up rough. Just have to grin and bear it.'

'And suppose veectory should go to you. Will Signore Quartus also green and bear it?'

'I expect so. I mean, what else could he do?'

'Oh, quite a lot of theengs. You see, signore, you say you do not hate Hugh Quartus. But I look at his face once or twice last night, and I theenk very much he hate you.'

Paul felt decidedly embarrassed. 'I say, steady on.'

'You theenk perhaps that because I am an actress I seek the melodrama everywhere, eh?'

'Oh, I wouldn't presume to say such a thing.'

'Which means you do theenk it. Perhaps you are right.' Laura leant forward and helped herself to a cigarette from a box on a nearby table. 'Will you have one?'

She pushed the box towards Paul.

'No, thanks, I don't smoke.'

'Ah, no, of course not: you are an athlete, are you not? Deed I not hear it said that you competed for England at the Olympic games?'

'That's right.'

'And deed you ween a medal?'

'No, just missed out: I came fourth.'

'What was your event?'

'Three thousand meters steeplechase.'

'Steeplechase? Ah, yes, that is the one where they jump over the hurdles, yes?'

'That's it. But I shan't be doing much more serious competitive running.'

'I'm sure a boy so feet and active will not be content

to seet around and do nothing, though?'

'No, as a matter of fact, I'm very fond of climbing.'

'Indeed? But that is a very dangerous hobby, no?'

'It needn't be if you take reasonable precautions.'

'So you have never fallen?'

'Touch wood.' He tapped on the table with his knuckles.

'It would be a terrible death, I theenk.'

'I can think of worse. Very quick.'

'But eemagine those few seconds while you were actually in the air.'

'I'd rather not imagine them, thanks!'

'You have never known anyone fall to their death?'

'No, never.'

She stubbed out her cigarette half-smoked and stood up. 'I have to go. I do not have long here and I must make the most of the time. There are people I must speak to. *Scusatemi.*'

'Of course.' He stood up, too.

She smiled, crossed the room and opened the door. She was just going through when from outside a voice spoke, 'Oh, signorina, I've been looking for you. Can we talk privately? It's important.'

Paul remained standing after Laura had gone. For some reason he felt strangely uneasy. There seemed something in a way sinister about that woman. He gave a sudden shake of his shoulders. Oh, he was being ridiculous!

Now. His pen. Where could it be? He hadn't used it since he'd arrived. So, it must have fallen out of his pocket. And that could only happen when he was bending over. Had he had occasion to stoop at all since he'd been here?

Of course, the secret passage! The roof in there was very low in several places.

Paul went upstairs and a minute later was again making his way along the passage, carefully scrutinising the floor as he went. However, he met with no success, and by the time he'd reached ground level and knew he could be only yard from the end, he'd more or less given up hope.

Then by his feet he saw the slightest gleam. He knelt down. Yes, there it was. What a stroke of luck! The trouble was it had slipped down a deep crack between two bricks and looked as though it might be tricky to extract; if he knocked it, it could easily slip even further down. He felt in his pocket for something to hook the pen up with and brought out a comb. He was gingerly trying to slip the end of it under the pen clip when he gave a start that nearly made him lose them both.

From close beside him he heard a voice.

It took Paul a few seconds to realise what had happened. Having nearly reached the end of the passage he was now behind the breakfast room panelling. The person talking must be standing very near the wall.

It occurred to Paul he was eavesdropping. But for the moment there was no avoiding this. So precarious was his hold on the pen that he couldn't relax his concentration for a second, or he might lose it altogether. So he remained quiet, gradually drawing the pen out and listening with half an ear to the slightly muffled voice.

At last he got his fingers on the pen and lifted it clear of the crack. He was about to stand up and make his presence known by banging on the wall, when he heard some words that caused him to jerk his head up in utter amazement.

Paul remained frozen as the voice went on, saying incredible things. He knew listening like this was a caddish thing to do. But he couldn't help himself.

Occasionally the voice paused, the 'silences' occurring obviously as the other person in the room spoke. But Paul could hear nothing of this; plainly only the one speaker was near enough to the panelling to be audible.

For two or three minutes Paul remained where he knelt. Then the voice simply stopped in mid-sentence, though Paul couldn't tell whether the speaker had left the room or simply moved to the far side of it. He made his way to the end of the passage, slid back the panel, and peered cautiously into the breakfast room. It was empty.

CHAPTER NINE

After leaving Gerry, Arlington Gilbert hurried up to his room. He was breathing heavily. He threw open the door, burst in, and stopped. Standing by the mantelpiece was a grim-faced Rex Ransom.

Rex said, 'At last. I've been waiting to have a little chat with you. You know what about.'

'I assure you I don't.'

'Don't play the innocent with me. Just tell me what your little game is.'

'Game? Are you mad?'

Rex stepped forward menacingly. 'Listen, buster, I'm warning you: spill the beans, unless you want me to black your left eye like I blacked your right last night.'

Gilbert gave a start. 'You – you did that?'

'Who the blue blazes did you think it was?'

'Now, listen to me—'

'No, you listen. I've got a good mind to beat you to a pulp.'

'Do so, and I shall sue you for assault. Fine publicity for you. I can't see the Burfords agreeing to the movie being shot here after that sort of behaviour.'

Rex closed his eyes for a few seconds and got a grip on his temper. Then be said slowly, 'I just want to know what you were up to last night.'

Gilbert turned away. 'I refuse to discuss the matter.'

Rex was silent. He dared not push Gilbert too hard. He might just make things worse for himself. So it seemed the only course now was to play for time, in the desperate hope that his worst foreboding was not about to be realised.

He said, 'You may not be able to keep that attitude up for long. I advise you to think over what I've said. I'll give you until tomorrow morning to come clean.'

'I shan't be here tomorrow morning.'

'What do—'

'I'm leaving. *Now*.'

It was Rex's turn to give a start. 'Oh, no, you're not!'

Gilbert stared. 'What's that?'

'I'm not letting you out of my sight until I get to the bottom of this business.'

'You can't stop me leaving.'

'Yes, I can.'

'How?'

'If you leave this house, I shall use my considerable influence with Haggermeir to make sure you do not write the revised screenplay for *The King's Man*.'

'I've got the copyright.'

'Haggermeir's attorneys aren't at all sure you have. Apparently it's a moot point, legally. And if he cuts you out, could you afford to fight it through the courts?'

'That's a filthy trick.'

'So's whatever you're up to.'

Gilbert said slowly, 'If you want me to stay you'll have to arrange it with Geraldine.'

'Geraldine?'

'It's she who's given me the push.'

Rex's eyes narrowed. 'But why?'

'That is between her and me. However, if I'm to remain you'll have to convince her my presence is vital to the success of the movie – something like that.'

'All right, I'll speak with her. And if she agrees, you stay here. Understood?'

'Very well.'

Without another word, Rex left the room.

Haggermeir said, 'So that's the whole story. Satisfied?' Laura smiled. They were in his bedroom. She had been somewhat reluctant to go there, but with so many guests, and servants busy everywhere, it was hard to get privacy downstairs.

'And Signore Ransom does not know this?' she asked.

'Not likely!'

'He will be very angry, I theenk.'

'What of it? It's you I want. So, can you forget what I said last night and let me see your agent about a contract?'

She inhaled deeply on her cigarette. 'I theenk it may be arranged. It will have to be *very* remunerative.'

'I've already said it will be. I'll top any other offer that's made. Just so long as it's firmly agreed that we do have – have…'

'An understanding?'

'Yeah.'

'Very well. You've gotten yourself a deal, Meesta Producer.'

*   *   *

Sebastian Everard stood at the edge of the lake, his hands in his overcoat pockets, and stared at the dull grey water. After a few minutes he gave a shake of his head, turned and began to retrace his steps along the gravel path to the house. Shortly, he reached a point at which the path forked, one branch leading to the front of the house, another round to the side, ending eventually in the stable yard. Sebastian took the latter.

The Burford family these days kept only a few riding horses, and all the old stalls on one side of the yard had long ago been converted to provide covered parking space for half a dozen cars. Now Lord Burford's Rolls, Gerry's Hispano, Sebastian and Cecily's station wagon, Paul's red tourer and Gilbert's Austin Seven were standing side by side in a row in order of descending size, like a family group. Sebastian went to the station wagon, took a key from his pocket and opened the rear door. The luggage space was nearly filled with a number of bulky objects, all covered with a rug. Sebastian was about to pull the rug back when be heard a woman's footsteps behind him. He straightened and turned.

Maude Fry was approaching from the direction of the house. She was carrying a stamped and addressed envelope, and was in the act of putting on her glasses.

Sebastian said, 'Ah, good – good – good morning.'

She nodded stiffly. 'Good morning, Mr Everard.'

'You – you – you going out?'

'Yes, to the village. I have to mail a letter. I wonder if you'd mind helping me get my car out.'

'Your car?'

'Yes, the Austin is mine.'

'Oh. Thought – thought it was old Gilbert's.'

'No, his is being repaired. If you could just stand behind and guide me out. There's not a great deal of space and I don't want to scrape Mr Carter's car. Simply call out 'right' or 'left' as the case may be.'

'OK, then. Let me think. This is my right, isn't it?' He held up his left hand.

'On second thought, please don't bother.'

'No bother. Pleasure, and all that. Spot of point duty, eh? Quite exciting, really.'

Maude Fry said, 'What on earth's that?'

For some seconds they'd been conscious of a sound growing in volume, and now it had become very loud. The next moment a motorcycle combination came speeding through the archway at the end of the yard, closely followed by a small van bearing the name Jenkins' Garage. The two vehicles skidded to a halt in the centre of the yard.

The rider of the motorcycle, a lad of about eighteen, jumped off and came across to them. 'Name o' Quartus?'

'No, actually,' Sebastian said. 'Sort of know him, though.'

'Brought his motor-bike back.'

'Ah. Jolly good.'

'Tell him, will you?'

'Oh, right.'

'Ha. Here's the bill.' He handed Sebastian a manila envelope. 'Quite a machine he's got there.'

'Oh, has he?'

'I'll say. Really been souped up. Terrific turn o' speed. And acceleration. Oh, well, so long.'

He strolled jauntily over to the van, which had turned while they'd been talking, and jumped into the passenger seat. It drove off.

Immediately after leaving Haggermeir's room, Laura walked along the corridor to the east wing and opened the door of the picture gallery. She went in, looking interestedly around her.

'Hullo,' said a man's voice.

She turned to see Hugh. He was sitting on one of the sofas, a few yards to her right.

She smiled. 'Good morning.'

'Do you honestly think it's a good morning?' he asked in Italian. 'Can you really stand our weather at this time of year?'

'One puts up with what one has to.' She closed the door.

'But do you have to? Couldn't you at least have remained in a nice centrally heated London hotel?'

'I received an invitation from a producer. Naturally I came.'

'Tell me: you still believe Haggermeir sent that telegram?'

'Of course. Or had it sent.'

'But why should he lie?'

She shrugged. 'Maybe he did not want me to think he was too eager. Or perhaps he didn't want the Earl and Countess to know he had invited me without their permission.'

'Sly dog. May I ask an impertinent question?'

'If it's not my age.'

'No, it's this: Why should you, one of the world's great dramatic actresses, want to sign up with a man like him? He's got no reputation as a serious filmmaker.'

'I felt it was time to branch out, You see, I am not widely known outside Italy. As a result I've never made much money. I knew where the big money was to be earned – Hollywood. Yet for years I held back. I was nervous. My English wasn't good. But then I asked myself: If Garbo had stayed in Sweden, where would she be today? So I took English lessons. At last I thought I was ready. Then I received Haggermeir's telegram, while on a visit to England. I believe in fate. So I came to see him. He will, at least, make my face known to millions of people. Then again, he would love to please the intellectual critics. Now he will have a chance to do so, because they like me. He will not want to lose the opportunity. So he will be – amenable. I will be more likely to get my own way about all sorts of things than I would with a Zanuck, say.'

'Signorina Lorenzo, why do—'

'Call me Laura.'

'May I?' Hugh's pale face flushed with pleasure. 'My – my name's Hugh.'

'I know. You were saying?'

'Just – why do you tell me all this?'

'Perhaps because you're the only person here who speaks Italian. Also – well, I am always conscious of atmosphere. When I arrived yesterday there was only one person present whom I sensed was sympathetic, glad to see me. You. I was grateful.'

'I can't imagine anyone not being glad to see you,' he said simply.

She smiled. 'You're very sweet. But enough of me. Tell me about yourself. You are a painter, I know. What kind of paintings do you do? Very *avant garde*?'

'On the contrary. My specialty is portrait painting.'

'And you enjoy that?'

'I would if I could get some decent subjects. You should see some of the people I've had to paint.'

'Would you like to paint my portrait?'

Hugh gave a start. 'You?'

'Yes, me. Don't look so frightened. Am I so hideous?'

'Are you serious?'

'Perfectly. Oh, I would pay you a proper fee, of course.'

Dazedly Hugh said, 'I can't believe it. It would be absolutely wonderful!'

'Good. Then that's settled.'

He said eagerly, 'When do you want me to start? Now? Today?'

She looked surprised. 'You have your equipment with you?'

'No, but I can start on the preliminary pencil sketches.'

She said thoughtfully, 'I would like some time to sit and think. There are decisions I have to make. Or again, perhaps...Can you talk while you work?'

'Oh, yes.'

'Good. I may want to ask your advice, Hugh. I have a problem.'

'Well, if you think I can help...'

She gave a decisive nod. 'We'll start after lunch.'

He leant forward and took her hand. 'Laura—'

The door opened and Gerry came in. 'Hugh? I—' She stopped short. 'Oh.'

Hugh got hurriedly to his feet. 'Gerry. I, er, just came up to browse among the paintings.'

'Yes, I thought I'd find you here.' She looked at Laura. 'And you are an art lover, too, signorina?'

'But naturally, Lady Geraldine.'

'Did you want me for anything particular, Gerry?' Hugh asked.

'I wondered if you'd like to come riding this afternoon. If so, I must tell the groom to get the horses saddled up.'

'No, I'm sorry, I can't. Laura – Signorina Lorenzo – has asked me to paint her portrait. We're making a start after lunch.'

'I see.' Gerry looked a little taken aback.

Laura said, 'Oh, please, Hugh, do not let me keep you from going riding.'

'Oh, I can go riding any time. It's not often I get a chance to draw a beautiful woman.'

There was a pause. Then Gerry looked at her wrist watch and said brightly, 'Twelve o'clock. There'll be drinks in the morning room now, if anyone's interested.'

'I am. Very,' Hugh said.

Laura said, 'And I must go to my room and fix my hair, to be ready for my seetting. It looks awful today.'

'It looks much the same as it did yesterday to me,' Gerry said pleasantly.

They left the gallery together. In the corridor they saw Sebastian approaching his room. He came strolling towards them.

'Ah, er, Quartus. Been – been – been looking for you,

old man. Chappie just brought your jolly old motor-bike and thingummy back. Said to tell you. Said I would. Have.'

'Oh, fine.'

'And there was this.' Sebastian produced a crumpled manila envelope and handed it to Hugh. 'Jolly old bill – what?'

'Thanks.'

'Seemed quite impressed – garage chap. With the bike, I mean. Said it had a real turn of speed.'

'I believe so. I bought it from a chap who used it for competitions and made a number of modifications. Quite a genius with engines, I believe.'

'What's its top speed?' Gerry asked.

'I wouldn't know. What about those drinks you mentioned?' He started to walk away. Gerry followed him.

Sebastian gazed after them, a vacant expression on his face. Laura said, 'You are eenterested in motor-bikes, Signore Everard?'

'What? Oh, no fear. Frightfully dan-ger-oos, eh?'

'You do not like a leetle danger now and then?'

'Me? Not likely. Safety – safety first, that's my motto.'

'Signore Everard, we have met before, have we not?'

'What? Us? No, don't think so. Sure I'd have remembered. Don't meet many film stars, unfortunately.'

'But I have an excellent memory for faces, signore. You have been in Italy, I theenk?'

'Never at all. Sorry and all that. No offence.'

'But at one time you were in the limelight – the publeek eye?'

Did his eyes flicker slightly at that, she wondered, or was it just my imagination?

He answered after a couple of seconds. 'Me? Famous? Golly, no. Never done anything interesting. Just kept myself to myself.'

'You have a profession?'

'No fear! Don't need one, happy to say. Couldn't hold one down, I'm sure.'

'Have you never thought you would like to try?'

'Why?'

'Don't most men feel the need to achieve something, to make some contribution to society?'

He scratched his head. 'Did help the Fry woman back her car out earlier. 'Fraid she bashed the fender. Wasn't pleased. Best I leave things alone, really.'

'One of the other gentlemen – I cannot remember who, now – was saying you were an old friend of his, I theenk.'

'Me? No, never clapped the old peepers on any of 'em before yesterday. Ah, well, must go and have a snooze before lunch – make sure the old gastric system's fresh for the fray. Pip-pip.'

'You have a high performance machine and you've never bothered to try it flat out?' Gerry said incredulously as she and Hugh went downstairs.

He shook his head. 'Why should I? I've never been in that much of a hurry to get anywhere.'

'Haven't you any sense of excitement, adventure?'

'Not really. To get a cheap thrill out of speed for its own sake is simply juvenile.'

'Then why buy a hotted-up machine?'

'Because the owner was getting married and wanted a quick sale, because I needed a bike, and because it was obviously in first-class condition. Satisfied?'

Gerry said, 'You infuriate me. You know that?'

'Yes.'

'You're so dashed superior!'

'I can't help that.'

'Oh, go take a running jump at yourself!'

They went into the morning room. Lady Burford, Cecily and Rex were already there. Rex immediately came across to Gerry.

'Ah, Lady Geraldine, a word in your ear?'

'Of course.' They moved to one side.

'I've just discovered Gilbert's planning to leave, at your request,' he said. 'However, it's very important for this film that he does stay at least a little longer. He's reluctant to do so, but said he will if I clear it with you. I hate to interfere in private matters, but I have to ask if you'll relent. If it wasn't really important, I wouldn't impose.' He smiled persuasively.

Gerry hesitated. After all her efforts to get rid of Gilbert, this was annoying. On the other hand, he had probably learnt his lesson by now and would be too scared to try any more funny business. Moreover, she *would* rather like a chance to correct some of his misapprehensions about her.

So she gave in with good grace. 'Oh, if it's that vital, I certainly wouldn't insist on his leaving. Tell him it'll be all right.'

'Thank you. I really appreciate it.'

Just then Paul entered the room. She said, 'Oh, excuse me, Paul.'

He came across, looking a little preoccupied. 'Hullo?'

'Like to come riding this afternoon?'

'I don't think so, Gerry, thanks, I'm hopeless on a horse.'

'Come on! I'll put you on Sally. She's a lovely placid old mare.'

'I'd really rather not, Gerry. Actually, I thought I'd go for a long run. I'm entered for the English cross-country championships shortly and I must get some training in.'

'Oh, well, please yourself,' she said a little huffily.

Rex said tentatively, 'Lady Geraldine, I should love to go riding with you, if I may.'

She looked surprised. 'Do you ride?'

He smiled. 'You've obviously seen none of my movies.'

'Oh, I have. Only I always thought they used a double for the horseback scenes. I didn't know they let their stars actually *ride*.'

'Oh, yes, except for the stunt stuff. I've been riding since I was about three. I was raised on a farm.'

'Then I'd be delighted to take you riding. I can show you the estate.'

'Great. I only hope the snow doesn't start and prevent us.'

'I think you'll be all right,' Paul said. 'I was talking to the local weather forecaster, old Josh, earlier, and he says it'll come late tonight – a heavy fall – but not before. He's infallible, isn't he, Gerry?'

'Just about.'

At that moment Haggermeir entered. He had his camera around his neck and was carrying the inevitable tape measure and writing book.

Rex said, 'Been at it all morning, Cyrus?'

'Pretty well.'

Gerry said, 'Mr Haggermeir, you look as if you could do with a drink. What can I get you?'

'A Scotch on the rocks would be fine, Lady Geraldine. Thank you.'

'Mr Haggermeir, you'll soon have as good a knowledge of the interior of Alderley as the family.' It was Cecily who spoke, from a seat by the fire.

'I doubt that, ma'am.'

'What about some exterior shots, Cyrus?' Rex asked. 'Shouldn't you get a few to show folks back home?'

'What? Oh, yeah. I'll wander round outside tomorrow morning and snap off a roll. Carry on indoors this afternoon, though, if Lady Burford still doesn't object.'

'Not at all,' the Countess said.

Cecily cleared her throat. 'Excuse my asking, but isn't it unusual for the head of a studio to undertake this sort of work himself? I don't know much about movie-making, but don't you have designers and photographers and so on to handle that sort of thing?'

'Why, yes, that's right. But I figure I know every side of the business. I've acted and scripted and directed; I can light a set, operate a camera, do most everything except compose the music. So I couldn't send deputies to *Alderley*. Be kind've insulting not to come myself.'

Lady Burford bowed her head. 'Thank you, Mr Haggermeir. I appreciate that. And have you decided whether it will be possible to make your film here?'

'Oh, so far I'm thinking primarily in terms of building a replica—'

'That's what George told me. But please stop the pretence. You want to film here. That's really why Mr Ransom is here. He's been trying to soften me up.'

Rex grinned engagingly. 'All is discovered. But tell me, Countess, have I succeeded?'

'Hardly, Mr Ransom. Not in twenty-four hours.'

'So it's no go?'

'It's not actually for me to say, Mr Ransom. I'm not the battle-axe everyone seems to think. It's George's decision, ultimately.'

'He won't agree to anything that'll make you unhappy.'

'No, but I needn't be here when it happens. Promise your people won't do too much damage, and I won't, er – is "kick up a stink" the correct term?'

CHAPTER TEN

As lunch was finishing the Earl said, 'Oh, by the way, everybody, as the talent contest starts at seven, we're having a sort of high tea at five-thirty today instead of dinner. Then, after the contest, Sir James and Lady Needham, friends of ours, have asked us all back to their place for supper. I took the liberty of accepting provisionally, on behalf of everyone. Anybody else who wants to have second thoughts and come along will be most welcome.'

'Thank you, George. I think I'll take you up on that.' It was Gilbert who said this.

Trying to conceal his surprise, the Earl said, 'By all means, Arl – er, Gil – er, my dear chap. Delighted.'

Gerry looked at Gilbert pensively. Just what, she wondered, was the reason for this change of mind?

After lunch Rex made his way to the library for a smoke and read before setting out on his ride. He'd been there only a few minutes when Laura came in. He got to his feet.

Laura waved him down again, seated herself next to him, looked at him keenly and said, 'Signore Ransom, what is it that you have against me?'

'I have nothing against you.'

'Yet your manner, it has been hostile ever since I arrived.'

'I'm sorry you think that.'

'Why are you frightened of me?'

'Frightened? What in the world do you mean?'

'I have never done anything to harm you. We have never met before.' She paused. 'Have we?'

'Of course not!' He spoke sharply.

'Well, when in such circumstances one person is hostile to another, the usual reason is fear.'

'My, quite the little female Freud, aren't we?'

'Prego?'

'Skip it. No, signorina, I'm not frightened of you. If you feel I've been cool to you, I apologise. Let's put it down to the fact that I don't want the picture ruined. Oh, don't get me wrong: you're a fine actress. But completely unsuited to *The King's Man*. To accommodate you the story would have to be changed beyond recognition.'

Laura gave a quiet chuckle.

'Why do you laugh?'

'Oh, no reason. What you said: it struck me as funny.'

'I fail to see the joke.'

'Skeep it. But tell me, is it only that which concerns you? It could not be you are also afraid that I peench your thunder?'

'Steal my thunder?' Rex threw back his head and laughed. 'You're kidding. My fans are tremendously loyal. It's me they'll come to see. Your name will mean nothing to them.'

'Maybe not, when they arrive. But when they *leave*... You said I was a fine actress.'

'The finest actress on earth can be miscast.'

She nodded slowly. 'Ah, well. We shall see. Or perhaps not.'

'What does that mean?'

She just shrugged.

He said, 'I'm only concerned for the success of the picture.'

'So you say, signore. But I theenk there is something else. Something else that you are afraid of. And Signore Ransom, I eentend to find out what it is.'

Paul started on his training run in one direction just before two, and a few minutes later Gerry and Rex set out in the other direction on horseback. Laura commenced sitting for Hugh, Haggermeir again disappeared into the further recesses of Alderley, Gilbert and Maude Fry retired to do some work, Sebastian went to have another snooze, Cecily announced her intention of driving to the village to do a little shopping, and the Earl strolled off for a talk with Mr Briggs, who ran the home farm. Finding herself alone, Lady Burford seized the opportunity to go to her boudoir and write some letters.

It was four o'clock when there came a tap on Lady Burford's door. She called 'Come in.'

It was Maude Fry who entered. She said, 'I'm sorry to disturb you, Lady Burford, but could you spare a few minutes?'

'Yes, of course, Miss Fry.'

Maude Fry came somewhat hesitantly across the room.

The Countess asked her to sit down and she did so.

'Is there something I can do for you?' Lady Burford asked.

Maude Fry didn't answer for a few seconds. She was staring down at the carpet, looking decidedly embarrassed. Then she glanced up, and the light glinted on the blue-tinted spectacles that concealed her eyes as effectively as sunglasses. 'I wanted to apologise.'

'Er, for what, Miss Fry?'

'For being here. You see, I gather from certain things Mr Gilbert has just let drop that he foisted me on you, without warning or your permission. I really do feel extremely embarrassed.'

As she said these last words there was a sudden catch in her voice. It occurred to the Countess that this plain, competent and apparently self-possessed woman was in fact extremely shy. She said hastily, 'Oh, not at all. It's often assumed that a busy man will want to take a secretary wherever he goes.'

'But I am correct: he did simply announce he was bringing me – without even a by-your-leave?'

Lady Burford smiled. 'It was rather like that. But please don't worry. With eight other guests, one more makes no difference. Besides, nobody could possibly take exception to your presence in their home. Don't give the matter another thought.'

'You're very kind, but under the circumstances I cannot possibly remain.'

'But surely your leaving would inconvenience Mr Gilbert very much?'

'No doubt. But that does not concern me unduly. He

has treated me very badly in a number of ways.'

'You intend to leave his employment?'

'I do.'

'Well, far be it from me to try and dissuade you. But please accept that it is no wish of ours that you leave this house.'

'That's understood. Thank you very much. Now, if you'll excuse me, I must go and pack.'

'But you can't possibly leave *now*. You came in your own car, I believe. Very soon it'll be dark, and snow is forecast. To drive all the way to London this evening would be most unpleasant. Why not wait until the morning?'

'That's very kind of you, Lady Burford. I'd be tempted to accept, if I could be sure of not seeing Mr Gilbert again. We – rather had words.'

'Well, there's no reason why you should see him. Your rooms are at opposite ends of the house. He'll be going out with the others this evening, and I imagine that our party will not be back until quite late. I suggest you remain in your room until they've left. I'll have a tray sent along to you. Then, afterwards, perhaps you'll join Mr and Mrs Everard and me downstairs. Tell me, do you by any chance play bridge?'

'Why, yes, I play quite a lot.'

'Oh, excellent. Then we can make up a four. I must admit I've been wondering what to do with them. My cousin and I have virtually run out of "Do you remembers".'

Maude Fry said doubtfully, 'Mr Everard can play bridge?'

'It is rather surprising, isn't it? Apparently he had the rudiments drummed into him at an early age by a fanatical bridge-playing mother. It remains to be seen what standard he plays to; however, it will pass a couple of hours. So you will be doing me a favour.'

'In that case, Lady Burford, I shall be delighted to stay.'

The two horses thundered across the field under the lowering sky. Gerry's cheeks were aglow as the wind whipped them and she bent over her horse's head, urging him on. For a few seconds she managed to keep level with Rex Ransom's mount, but her eyes kept watering and at last she gave a laughing gasp. 'Whew, that's enough for me,' she said as she slowed her horse to a canter.

Rex reined in and waited for her. He grinned. 'You need goggles for galloping in this weather.'

'Yes, you do. Sorry it's been such a dismal afternoon. You haven't seen the estate at its best.'

'Oh, it's been great. I've thoroughly enjoyed myself. And this feller's got a real turn of speed.'

'You certainly got the best out of him, Rex.'

'How far are we from the house?'

'Less than a mile. Better walk them the rest of the way home.'

He said, 'Gerry, before we get back, there's something I want to ask you. It's a bit awkward, but it's about your requesting Gilbert to leave.'

'I've withdrawn that.'

'I know. Would you think it impertinent, though, if I asked why it happened?'

'Not impertinent, but I'd rather not say. Sorry.'

'That's OK. But would I be right in assuming you have been having trouble with him? I have a reason for asking.'

'It depends what you mean by trouble. It's not what a girl would normally mean by that. But, in a sense, yes.'

'I see. Well, you're not the only one.'

She stared. 'You mean you—? I don't follow. *You* wanted him to stay.'

'I know. It's a complicated situation. And rather worrying.'

'Do you want to talk about it?'

'I'd like to tell someone. Fact is, he's been prowling about my room.'

'Good heavens.'

'There's rather more to it than that, though. I'd like to tell you the whole story. I didn't know who to talk to before this afternoon, but in the last couple of hours I feel we've gotten to know each other. However, it'll take rather a long time to explain properly.'

'Well, we'll be home in a few minutes, but if we go off for a tête-à-tête after being out all the afternoon it'll look a bit odd. Then there'll be tea and changing and leaving for the village. Could we have a chat late tonight, after we get back?'

'Fine. Perhaps you could come to my personal sitting-room. I've not entertained anyone in it yet and I must do so before I leave.'

'OK, pardner,' Gerry said, 'you've got a date.'

Cecily turned into the drive on her return from the village and was surprised to see Laura Lorenzo waving her down. She stopped and Laura got in. Wearing a scarlet boxy top coat, she was nonetheless shivering. 'Grazie,' she said. 'A leeft back will be most welcome.'

'I'm surprised to see you out in this weather, signorina.'

'I have been seeting for Signore Quartus and I got rather steef. I decided I needed some exercise, but I did not realise how cold it was.'

'They say it'll be snowing by tonight.'

'Which will be an unusual experience for you, will it not?'

'Oh, yes. We don't get much in Australia. It'll be like old times.'

'When you and the Contessa were girls together, in those days you and she were very close, yes?'

'Well, fairly close.'

'It must be nice for you to meet her daughter.'

'Yes, Gerry's a lovely girl.'

'I understand, though, that in the past she has had rather a bad reputation?'

Cecily frowned. 'I don't think so.'

'Oh, *mi scusi*. Bad was the wrong word. Reckless, undisciplined perhaps?'

'Oh, I see what you mean. Yes, I believe she went through a rebellious phase, got in with a rather wild set. Her name was always appearing in the gossip columns.'

'*Ma perdio*, if her name appear in the gossip columns in Australia she must have been really notorious!'

'Oh, no. I have the English papers sent out to me.'

'Ah. But she appeared in court more than once, did she not?'

'I believe so.'

'Do you know what for?'

'Snatching a policeman's helmet and running off with it. And wading in the fountains in Trafalgar Square.'

'Oh.' Laura looked pensive. 'But of course as the daughter of a nobleman, nobody would charge her with anything more serious.'

Cecily said stiffly, 'That sort of thing does not happen in England.'

'You say you never see Lady Geraldine before yesterday. Your husband – he did not know her either?'

'Sebastian? Oh, no.'

Laura said suddenly, 'I have seen your husband before.'

'Oh? When?'

'Some years ago. But he seems not to want to talk about it.'

'He's rather shy with women, particularly film stars. So don't be offended.'

'I am not offended. But before I leave here, he will admit it. Oh, yes.'

After returning, showering and changing, Paul found Gerry in the drawing room with Merryweather, who had just brought her a pot of tea.

'Hullo,' she said. 'Want a cup?'

'Please.'

'Can I get you anything to eat, sir?' Merryweather asked.

'No, thanks. Not with high tea so close.'

'No doubt you are wise, sir,' Merryweather said. He sighed.

Gerry said, 'You don't approve of high tea, do you, Merry?'

'It is not a meal I recognise, your ladyship, though I acknowledge the need of it on occasions.'

'You coming along to the show, Merryweather?' Paul asked.

'Thank you, no, sir. I attended one year. The daughter of Hawkins the chauffeur was performing and I felt an obligation. It was an experience I would not wish to repeat.' He withdrew.

'Good ride?' Paul inquired.

'Yes, thank you. Rex is a fine horseman, and excellent company.'

'Oh, it's Rex now, is it?'

'Why not? If you choose to let us spend the afternoon together, while you go off on your own...'

'Oh, don't be like that, Gerry. I must do a certain amount of training. And I'm really not good on horseback. Besides, I wanted to think.' His face was troubled. She looked at him closely. 'Is anything wrong?'

'Well.' He stopped. 'I don't know what to do.'

'About what?'

'A conversation I overheard this morning.'

'What's the problem?'

'I can't decide whether I ought to take it further. You see, I was eavesdropping – quite accidentally, of course, and unavoidably.'

'Then I don't see how you can do anything about it.'

'Normally that's what I'd say. Except – what I heard was so *fantastic*.'

'Oh?' She looked intrigued.

'It's so unbelievable that I think the person may have been joking. But the words were spoken so seriously. And if they were true, then I can't help feeling that I ought to tell your father about it.'

'Why Daddy?'

'Because it means one of the people in this house is here under completely false pretences.'

'Oh. Then why don't you go to him – or her – and ask straight out?'

'Yes, I think I'm going to have to do that. But I feel such a fool. They're sure to deny it, or claim it was a joke, or that I misheard or misunderstood.'

'*Could* you have?'

'That's what I've been asking myself all afternoon. I just don't know.'

'Is it important you do something immediately?'

He looked thoughtful. 'I suppose not.'

'Then why not give it a few more hours? Maybe the truth will come to light without your having to do anything.'

His face lightened. 'Yes, perhaps you're right. Oh, Gerry, you always give such good advice! You've got so much common sense.'

'Don't be beastly! That's a horrible thing to say about me. Someone like Hugh's got common sense, not me.'

'Ah! So Quartus is horrible, is he?'

'I didn't mean it like that! In certain people common sense is all right.'

'Only 'all right'? Gerry, do I detect a slight change in your attitude toward friend Quartus?'

'You – you may. You're not to read anything into it, though.'

'But this must be the result of your having had a chance to study him at close quarters, and compare him with me.'

'Don't flatter yourself.'

'But I shall. I love to flatter myself. After all, nobody

else does. And you've got to admit I am much nicer than he is.'

'The conceit of the man!'

'No. I've been weighting myself up – and him. I *am* nicer than he is. Not that there's anything very exciting about niceness. I'm not as clever as he. In addition I'm lazy, rather selfish, and – at least where you're concerned – unscrupulous. Anything I can say to put you off him I will.'

'At least you're honest.'

'I try not to be, but with you I can't help myself.'

'The influence of a good woman,' she murmured.

'I know. It's awful. I've never experienced it before and it's ruining my life. Gerry, are you in love with Quartus?'

Gerry looked at him for a moment, then stood up, crossed to the window and stared out over the park. It was now nearly dark and the trees were gaunt grey skeletons against the only slightly lighter grey sky. She said, 'Snow any time now.'

Paul joined her at the window and gently turned her to face him. 'You didn't answer my question.'

'Am I in love with Hugh? I don't know.'

'Oh, sweetheart, you must!'

'I don't, honestly, Paul.'

'Well, do you love me?'

She nodded. 'Oh, yes!'

His face lit up. 'You do? But that's marvellous! Gerry, I don't know what to say. It's like a dream come—'

She interrupted. 'I love you, Paul. But I don't know if I'm *in love* with you, either.'

'Oh, that's splitting hairs!'

'It's not, really.'

'Well, then: you don't know if you're *in love* with Quartus. But do you love him?'

'Oh, no! Sometimes I hate him.'

Paul gave a mock groan of despair. 'Women! Ye gods! I'll never understand them.'

'Surely you never expected to, did you.'

'In my innocent youth I think I did.'

'I'm sorry, Paul. I've treated you badly. You *and* Hugh.'

'Oh, forget Hugh! He doesn't love you.'

'I think he does. In his own way.'

'A deuced funny way. I suppose he's still with Lorenzo, is he?'

'I imagine so.'

'At least I did spend the afternoon on my own, and not slobbering over another woman. If you ask me, he's got it bad.'

Gerry didn't answer.

CHAPTER ELEVEN

At six-thirty the male section of the party had assembled in the great hall.

Rex looked at his watch. 'Seems we're short a couple of ladies.' He'd been ready to leave before anyone else and had been waiting patiently in the drawing room for twenty minutes as the others trickled down.

'No, you're not.' Gerry spoke from the stairs.

The Earl looked up. 'Where's Miss Lorenzo?'

'Still in her room, I expect.'

'Someone better tell her we're ready to leave.'

'I'll go.'

Gerry retraced her steps to the top of the stairs, made her way to Laura's room and tapped on the door. '*Avanti.*'

Gerry went in. Laura, wearing her velvet evening gown and a matching cartwheel hat from which drooped an emerald feather, was seated at her dressing table, writing a letter. Without looking up, she said, 'Oh, Eloise, I—'

She raised her head and saw Gerry. 'Oh.' With a sudden, rather furtive movement, she closed her writing case. 'Lady Geraldine, *mi scusi*. I thought that would be my maid.'

Gerry smiled. 'Just to say that we're ready to leave.'

Laura glanced at a tiny jewelled wristwatch. 'It is later than I thought. I, er, was hoping to feenish a letter – just a reply to a fan – before we leave so I could post it in the veellage.'

'I'm afraid the last collection in the village was at six. We could have somebody take it to Westchester.'

'No, please, it does not matter.'

She opened a drawer, slipped the writing case inside and closed it. Then she crossed to the wardrobe, took out her magnificent mink coat and put it on. She and Gerry went downstairs.

A few minutes later the party left. The Countess and Cecily waved them off and went back inside.

'Well, my dear, we might as well start our bridge, don't you think?' Lady Burford said.

'Oh, so soon?'

'Not if you have something else—'

'No, no. I'll just go up and fetch Sebastian. He's having a nap.'

'Very well. Would you look in on Miss Fry, please, and bring her down? Tell her Mr Gilbert's left the house and we're ready to start our game.'

News of the personal appearance of Rex Ransom had obviously spread far and wide. The village hall was ablaze with light, and a crowd of about seventy people, ineffectually controlled by the village constable, was gathered outside. The Rolls drew up and a cheer broke out as Rex alighted. He grinned and waved. Autograph books were thrust into his hands, and as a photographer from the *Westshire Advertiser* popped flashbulbs, he made his way slowly up to the doors, the rest of the Alderley party following like a train of courtiers.

Across the entrance to the hall a banner, bearing the words WELCOME REX, had been hung, and Rex stood beneath it, waving to the crowd before finally going inside.

The hall was packed, and there was another great cheer as Rex was spotted and, with the rest of the party, made his way to reserved seats at the front. Shortly afterwards the entertainment commenced.

Sebastian Everard stared at his cards. 'Now, what did I say? Was it Two Clubs, Ah, yes – you said One Heart, didn't you, Lavinia? I nearly said One No Trump, though I hadn't quite got the count, and then you said One Heart, so I had to go Two Clubs. I always find it jolly difficult when one has two short suits.'

Lady Burford sighed. She wondered how soon she could put an end to this farce. Really, Sebastian might just as well lay his cards face up on the table. She looked apologetically at Maude Fry, who, from the expression on her face, would clearly rather be elsewhere. For a skilled player, this must seem an utter waste of time.

However, it wasn't long before there came a welcome diversion. Merryweather entered.

'Excuse me, my lady,' he said, 'a Miss Jemima Dove has just arrived.'

Lady Burford looked surprised. 'Jemima Dove? Who is she? And what does she want at this time on a Friday night?'

'I think, my lady, that she is expecting to stay. She has a suitcase.'

'Does the woman think this is a hotel?'

'She did ask me to tender her apologies for arriving at such an inconvenient hour.'

'Well, find out what she wants, Merryweather.'

'Yes, my lady. Naturally, I should have done so, only I assumed from the young lady's manner that she was someone you were expecting and had omitted to mention.'

He started back towards the door, but stopped when the Countess suddenly said, 'Oh, my goodness, I believe I am – expecting her, I mean. But not yet, surely.'

Cecily said, 'A guest arriving ahead of schedule?'

'Not exactly. I think she may be the woman who's coming to recatalogue the library. I've never met her; it was arranged through an agency. But I'm certain she wasn't due until the week after next. Merryweather, if she is the lady, show her in please. And send somebody to fetch the desk diary from my boudoir. I suppose you'd better have another bedroom prepared, as well – the Lilac, I think.'

'Yes, your ladyship.'

Merryweather withdrew, to return a minute later, accompanied by a small, fragile-looking girl. She had soft brown hair and big grey eyes behind large and strangely masculine-looking glasses. She was pretty, in a quiet, demure way. She had a slightly lost air.

The Countess said, 'Do come across to the fire, Miss Dove. I'm sure you're cold.'

Miss Dove crossed the room, 'Oh, thank you. Yes, I am. Lady Burford, I'm terribly sorry to arrive so late. It's the weather. The roads are terribly slippery and I got lost three times. I've been driving for hours.' She had a soft, rather musical voice.

The Countess said, 'You drove yourself? From where?'

'Cambridge.'

'My, my, you must be tired.'

'I am, rather. And I had hoped to start work before this. I do trust the delay hasn't inconvenienced you too much.'

'No, not at all.'

Just then Merryweather returned with the Countess's desk diary.

'Thank you, Merryweather.' Lady Burford flicked through the pages, then gave a nod. 'As I thought. Miss Dove, I haven't been inconvenienced, because – and you'll find out sooner or later – I wasn't expecting you until the week after next.'

Miss Dove's face fell. 'The week after next!'

'Yes; Monday the nineteenth.' She held out the diary for the girl to see.

When she looked up there was an expression of dismay on Jemima Dove's face. 'But I'm sure the agency said the ninth. Here, I wrote it down at the time.'

She delved into her handbag and drew out a small pocket diary. She found the date and handed it to the Countess. 'You see.'

'Yes, I see. Well, no doubt the agency is at fault. I shall get in touch with them on Monday. But in the meantime—'

'In the meantime, I must leave at once.' Jemima Dove was pink with embarrassment. 'I'm so terribly sorry. And thank you for being so kind.' She moved towards the door. 'I'll come back on the nineteenth, of course.'

'Don't be silly, child. I couldn't turn you out on a night like this. Besides, it's better to be early than late, and there's no reason why you can't stay and commence work as soon as you wish.'

'Oh, Lady Burford, are you sure? It won't be inconvenient?'

'Not at all. It's true we have a number of guests at the moment and they tend to wander in and out of the library, but if they don't disturb you, I'm certain you won't disturb them. Now, take your things off and let me perform some introductions.'

Jemima Dove shook hands shyly with Sebastian, Cecily and Maude Fry, and then said, 'I'm afraid I interrupted your card game. Please do carry on.'

'We had just finished a rubber,' Lady Burford said. She addressed the others. 'I don't know whether you want to continue...'

'Well, if you don't mind, I'd rather – rather like to pack up now,' Sebastian said. 'Always find bridge jolly exhausting.' He yawned. 'Fact is, think I'll have an early night, if no one minds. Pretty wearing sort of day all round, actually. 'Night, all.' He ambled from the room.

'I'm sorry about that,' Cecily said. 'I'm afraid Sebastian's not really a very good player. I rarely get the chance of a decent game.' She sounded quite sad. Then she looked at Jemima. 'You don't play, I suppose?'

'Bridge? Well, yes, I do.'

Cecily brightened. 'Really? Then perhaps we could have a proper game. What do you say, Lavinia?'

'By all means, if Miss Fry and Miss Dove would care to play.'

They both expressed their willingness, Maude Fry

adding, 'But I would like to slip up to my room for ten minutes first.'

Jemima said, 'I'll come with you and find my room. I'd like to freshen up.'

'It's on the right at the end of the west wing,' Lady Burford told her. 'The Lilac room. You'll find your things have been taken up.'

Jemima and Maude Fry left the room. At the top of the stairs, Jemima hesitated. 'West wing: now which way would that be?'

'To your left.'

'Are you near me?'

'No; I'm in the east wing, halfway along.'

'I see.'

They went their separate ways.

Maude Fry was the first to return to the drawing room, ten minutes later. It was a further five minutes before Jemima came in.

'Oh, I hope I haven't kept you waiting,' she said a little breathlessly. Then she saw that Lady Burford had had some refreshments sent in, and started to express her gratitude. Lady Burford stopped her – not, however, adding that Jemima's arrival was really a godsend. What she would have done with Cecily and Maude Fry for several more hours she just didn't know.

The children's talent contest was a great success. Most of the entrants rose to the occasion, and the committee had created so many classes of competition that the judges were able to make some sort of award to every entrant. Meanwhile Rex, handing out the prizes, was in top form

– radiating charm, good humour and an air of innocent enjoyment.

One person who, at the beginning, was plainly unhappy with this situation was Laura. She was clearly unused to taking a back seat. However, her striking looks quickly attracted attention, and after the Earl had quietly explained to the MC who she was, she was introduced to the audience and then assisted with the presentations. If Rex was not altogether pleased about this, he didn't show it.

The proceedings ended with more photographs and autograph signing, after which the Alderley group retired backstage for coffee with the committee and other village VIPs.

They eventually left at nine-thirty and arrived at the Needham's to find that quite a party had been arranged, with about twenty other guests, a huge supply of drink (at the sight of this, Arlington Gilbert, who'd been sunk in a morose gloom all the evening, immediately brightened) and piles of foodstuffs.

It was nearly half past twelve before the Alderley group finally got away. Gilbert had to be gently guided out to Lord Burford's Rolls.

As Gerry was climbing into Paul's car she felt the lightest of tickles on her forehead. She glanced up and felt several more. 'It's come at last,' she said.

Thick snowflakes were starting to fall.

She got in, shivering slightly and glancing a little wistfully at the Rolls, which was already sweeping down the drive. A convertible sports car was not the warmest form of transport on a winter's night.

* * *

Paul peered through the cloud of whirling snowflakes, which were being driven against his windshield. He swore softly.

Gerry, her eyes closed, sunk down in her seat, her hands in her pockets and her coat collar up, murmured, 'What's the matter?'

'I've lost the taillight of the Rolls.'

'Well, you know the way, don't you?'

'Hope so, but there's such a maze of winding lanes round here that I'm not too confident. Do you know where we are?'

'Of course I don't!'

'But this is your country.'

'I was asleep until woken by your foul language and the bitter cold. I don't even know how long we've been driving.' She peered into the gloom. 'There are three or four routes Hawkins could have taken. All these narrow country roads look exactly alike in the dark, particularly in a snow storm. If I could spot some landmark...'

'Oh, don't worry. I know roughly where we are.' Gerry closed her eyes again. Five or ten minutes passed. Then she sat up with a start as the car suddenly gave a sort of shudder. She said, 'Oh, no, I don't believe it!'

The engine cut out.

Between clenched teeth Gerry said, 'Paul, is that what I think it is?'

''Fraid so, old girl.'

'You're out of petrol! Honestly, of all the blithering idiots!'

Paul didn't reply as the car glided to a halt. He bent forward and peered at the fuel gauge. He muttered 'Knew I was low, but could have sworn I had enough to get back.'

'The important thing is: what do we do?'

'We could walk.'

'But you don't know how far it is.'

'Must be several miles.'

'Me walk several miles in these shoes in this weather? I'd have frostbite in a hundred yards!'

'Then you'll have to wait here, darling, while I go and get some petrol. Luckily, I've got an empty can.'

'But where will you go? Jenkins' won't be open.'

'I'll go the other way, to the main road. With any luck I can get a lift from a truck to that all-night filling station outside Westchester.'

'I don't fancy staying here alone.'

'But what's the alternative?'

'Can't we both just wait here? They're sure to come back for us when they realise.'

'Yes, but how long will that take them? And then they won't know exactly where we are. There've been several forks or crossroads since I last saw the Rolls, and I could have gone wrong at any of them. They could drive round for ages.'

'Oh, really, Paul. Of all the prize chumps, you take the cake!'

'I know, don't rub it in. Well, what about it: do I go?'

'How long will it take you?'

'Hard to say. Perhaps three quarters of an hour.'

'Well, all right, but be as quick as you can.'

'Oh, no, I'm going to stroll – enjoy the scenery, pick flowers.'

He took the key from the ignition, got out and went to

the back. Gerry heard the rumble seat open and a moment later slam shut.

He called, 'Chin up, sweetheart. I'll do my best.'

Then came the sound of his footsteps on the road for a few seconds. They gradually faded away and, but for the wind, all was silent. Gerry sat huddled down in the seat and shivered.

'Two Spades,' said Maude Fry.

'Pass,' said Cecily.

'Two Hearts,' said Lady Burford.

'Three Diamonds,' said Jemima Dove.

Maude Fry hesitated. Her face was flushed and she was breathing more heavily than usual. It was remarkable what a change had come over her since Sebastian had left and they'd started playing seriously. Not, thought the Countess, that she was a very good player. It was fortunate they were not playing for high stakes; Maude Fry would already have lost quite a lot of money.

Lady Burford's reflections were interrupted by the sound of tires outside. She said, 'Oh, they're back. Sooner than I expected.' She glanced at the clock. 'My word, it's nearly one! I had no idea.'

'Good gracious!' Cecily exclaimed. 'I've never known time to pass so quickly.'

Maude Fry got hurriedly to her feet. 'Oh, Lady Burford, do you mind if we stop now and add up tomorrow. I'm sorry to break off in the middle, but I did explain about Mr Gilbert.'

'Yes, of course.'

Jemima said, 'I'll come now, too, if nobody minds.'

They both said good night and left the room together.

Lady Burford and Cecily went out to the hall to welcome the others. They came in shivering and giving exclamations, the men removing their outer things and handing them to the footmen. Hugh especially looked particularly cold and hurried straight into the drawing room and across to the fire.

The Earl brushed some snowflakes from his hair. 'Brr – what a foul night!'

'I expect you'd all like something warming,' Lady Burford said.

It was Laura who answered first. 'Not for me, Lady Burford, thank you. If I may I will go up to my room in just a few meenutes. I am very tired and I have a slight headache. But may I make a telephone call first? I must ring my London agent at his home and tell him what time I arrive tomorrow.'

She smiled as she saw Lady Burford glance at the grandfather clock. 'Is all right. He keeps very late hours.'

'You know where the telephone room is?'

'Si, grazie.' Laura walked off.

Arlington Gilbert meanwhile was smiling benignly, swaying slightly as he did so. He said, 'Did I hear you talk about something warming? Does that mean rum, by any chance?'

Haggermeir said, 'You've had quite enough for tonight, feller.'

Gilbert raised his eyebrows. 'I have?'

'You have. It's bed for you, pronto. I'll see you up.'

He took Gilbert by the arm and led him to the stairs. Over his shoulder he said, 'I'll say good night, too, Lady Burford. Thanks for the outing, Earl.'

'Glad you came, my dear chap. 'Night.'

Haggermeir and Gilbert proceeded a little unsteadily up the stairs.

Lord Burford said, 'That fellow Arlington – much nicer when he's had one over the eight. Not that he seemed to me to drink all that much. All the same, we'd better keep him tanked up the rest of the time he's here.'

The Countess said, 'I take it the evening was a success?'

'Capital. Rex here was simply splendid. Great hit.'

Rex smiled. 'I enjoyed myself.'

'Fancy somethin' before you turn in?'

'No, really, thanks. Your friends the Needhams did us very well. I'll go straight to my room, if you don't mind.' He said good night all round and ran lightly up the stairs.

Cecily said, 'My turn now, I think. Good night, Lavinia. It's been a delightful day.'

'Good night, Cecily.'

They kissed and Cecily in her turn ascended the grand staircase.

Laura reappeared.

'Did you get through all right?' Lady Burford asked.

'I'm afraid not. The phone seems to be dead. Perhaps the lines are down.'

'Oh dear, how tiresome! I am sorry.'

'Is no matter. I can send a telegram from the veellage in the morning.' She gave an elegant little yawn. 'Well, if you do not mind I will go to bed now. *Buonanotte*.' She made her way up the stairs.

As she did so, Hugh emerged from the drawing room again. 'Gerry and Carter in yet?' he asked.

The Earl hook his head. 'No. Why?'

'I wonder what's happened to them. They were right behind us when we left the Needhams.'

The Countess looked alarmed. 'George, didn't you say the roads were difficult tonight?'

'Bit slippery.'

'Oh my, perhaps they've had an accident! Somebody must go and look for them.'

'Oh lor', Lavinia, let's give it a bit longer. I don't like to get Hawkins out again on what's almost certainly a wild goose chase. He's probably turned in already.'

'George, we're talking about your daughter.'

'You know I can't drive.'

'I'll go, Lady Burford,' said Hugh.

'Oh, would you, Hugh? I'd be so grateful.'

'That's all right. I want to know what he's up – I mean, I want to know what's happened to her.'

The Earl said, 'Thanks, my boy. You'll have to go and get the car keys from Hawkins.'

'Oh, I wouldn't risk driving the Rolls tonight – bit too big and heavy for me. Do you know where the keys to the Hispano are? Gerry's often let me drive that.'

'You'll probably find she's left them in the ignition. She nearly always does.'

'Oh, right.' He fetched his flying jacket, scarf and cap from the cloakroom and pulled on his gloves. 'Got a flashlight?'

'Should be one in that table drawer.'

Hugh found it and opened the front door.

'Be careful, Hugh,' Lady Burford said.

'Don't worry.'

He went out. The storm was worse than ever and only

the gale had so far prevented the snow forming a carpet underfoot. He stumbled to the stable yard, his mind full of black thoughts. He didn't for one moment believe there'd been an accident. Carter was up to some dirty business. Exactly what wasn't clear. But for him to disappear with Gerry at this time of night couldn't be chance. Hugh just hoped against hope that the little idiot hadn't let him persuade her to run away with him, or anything really drastic.

In the yard he made straight for the Hispano Suisa. To get to it he had to pass his motorcycle combination. The beam of his flashlight happened to fall momentarily on the sidecar. He noticed that it seemed to be leaning over at a strange angle. He directed the beam straight on to it. Then he stopped dead and gave an exclamation.

The motor-bike was gone.

Hugh stood, gazing blankly. The sidecar apparently hadn't been damaged. But the bike had been neatly detached. There was no sign of it.

Hugh's thoughts whirled. It didn't make sense. It had certainly been here just a few moments before they'd all left for the talent contest. He'd come out to fetch his scarf, which he'd left in the sidecar.

No one would come right up here just to pinch a motorcycle – or, if they did, be so insane as to stop and remove the sidecar first. It could only be some sort of hoax. But by whom?

However, this wasn't the time for speculation. He hurried on to the Hispano and opened the door. Yes, the ignition key was there. He got in and a minute later was on his way down the drive. Hugh gripped the wheel tightly and peered through the driving snow.

CHAPTER TWELVE

Gerry sat huddled in Paul's car. Her teeth were chattering. She'd never been so cold in her life. Surely, Paul ought to be back by now. She reluctantly drew her left hand from her pocket and squinted at the luminous dial of her wrist watch.

Oh no! He'd been gone less than twenty minutes. It seemed at least an hour. Why hadn't she been missed at home? Did she mean so little to her parents that they didn't even notice whether she was there or not?

There was a terrible draft in this car. She groped in the direction from which the wind was coming and gave a gasp of annoyance at finding the soft top of the car wasn't closed properly. There was a gap of at least an inch immediately above the windshield and the passenger door. She reached up and tried to close it. But it wouldn't budge. She leant to her right and felt above the driver's door. Here there was no gap. Obviously when Paul had last had the top down he'd closed it crookedly afterwards. The only thing to do was open it and re-close it – making sure it was straight.

Gerry jerked at the handle and the top flew back. Snow swept in. She heaved forward again. Nothing happened. She knelt on the seat and had another go. But it was hopeless. The top was well and truly jammed.

Gerry nearly wept. If there'd been a draft before, there was now a howling gale around and she was colder than ever. She threw herself back into the seat, staring dismally into the darkness. The next moment she stiffened. Lights – surely? Yes, a car was approaching. Slowly it drew closer.

Then Gerry knew a twinge of unease. It wasn't the Rolls – the lights were wrong. Suppose it wasn't from home at all? It might be – anybody.

The car came nearer still, and stopped about ten yards in front of her. Then a figure was suddenly silhouetted against the car's lights. It began walking towards her. She held her breath. The next moment a light was shining in her eyes and a voice was saying, 'Gerry? Are you all right?'

'Hugh! Oh, thank heavens!'

She opened the door and got stiffly out. 'Oh, Hugh, am I glad to see you! But what are you driving?'

'The Hispano.'

'Oh.' Of course, she'd never seen her own car approaching her in the dark, so it wasn't surprising she hadn't recognised it. 'How did you find me?' she asked.

'Followed the tracks of the Rolls until they got covered with snow. Then just kept straight on. But what happened?'

'It's Paul. He—'

Hugh grabbed her by the elbow. 'What's he done? Where is he?'

She pulled away. 'Hugh, please. It's ripping of you to have come for me, but this isn't the Old Bailey.'

'Gerry, has he hurt you? In any way?'

'Certainly not.'

'Then why's he run off?'

'He hasn't run off. He's gone to get petrol. We ran out.'

He gave a snort. 'Oh, come off it! Don't tell me you fell for that old chestnut.'

'It's true!'

'Gerry, for Pete's sake stop defending the rotter.'

'He's not a rotter!'

He grasped her roughly by the shoulders. 'Don't say you were in on it!'

'In on what?'

'This whole shoddy scheme. For the two of you to – to be alone. Where no one could see you.'

She gave a gasp. 'You're not serious! You don't honestly think we'd *choose* to stop – out here, in this!' She gestured to the elements.

'I think he'd do absolutely anything to get you. And I think you're so besotted with him that you'd let him.'

'Why, you utter beast!' And Gerry slapped him hard across the face.

He started shaking her, shouting to make himself heard above the wind. 'Gerry, come to your senses! The fellow's a cad. Give him up!'

Gerry's teeth were rattling so much that she couldn't speak. Then, when she was sure that if he continued any longer her head would fall off, there came the sound of hurrying footsteps, muffled by the snow, and then blessedly Paul's voice:

'Gerry? I've got the petrol. Didn't have to go to the garage. A truck driver let me siphon some out of his tank.

Gerry? What's happening? Who's that with you?'

Hugh let her go as Paul loomed up from the rear, carrying a can. 'What's going on?' he said urgently. 'Quartus!'

Hugh spun to face him. 'Right, Carter, I want a few words with you.'

Paul took in Gerry's distressed condition. He put down the can. 'What have you done to her?'

'Nothing, except give her a well-deserved shaking. The question is: What have I prevented you doing to her?'

Gerry stepped shakily towards Paul and fell into his arms. 'Oh, Paul, he's been saying horrible things about us: that we arranged all this so we could – could be alone.'

Paul drew his breath in sharply. 'You unmitigated bounder.'

'*You* call *me* a bounder?' Hugh shouted. The next moment, without any warning, he swung a wild right hook in the direction of Paul's head.

Paul easily evaded the blow, and Hugh's fist landed with a clunk against the windshield of the car. He gave a yelp of pain.

'Right,' Paul said grimly, 'if that's the way you want it.' He drew back his fist.

Gerry screamed, 'No, Paul!' and he stopped in mid-movement. 'No fighting, please!' she said imploringly. 'Let's get home before I freeze to death.'

He hesitated, then dropped his fist. 'Oh, all right. He's not worth it, anyway. I'll get the petrol in.'

He turned, and for the first time took in the appearance of his car. 'Why by all that's wonderful have you put the hood down?'

She stammered out an explanation.

He groaned. 'Stuck! Oh, marvellous! It's happened before. I'll never be able to put it right out here.'

'Well, I'm sorry,' she said tearfully. 'I didn't do it on purpose.'

Muttering to himself, Paul picked up the can and walked to the rear of the car. Gerry turned back to Hugh, who was nursing his knuckles.

'Is it bad?'

'What do you think?'

'It's your own fault.'

He jerked his head at the tourer. 'You going back in that?'

'I suppose so.'

'Why not come in the Hispano? At least you'll be dry.'

She looked longingly in the direction of the other car. 'No, I'd better go back with Paul. It is my fault the top's down, after all.'

'That's crazy reasoning—'

Paul came up. 'What's the matter now?'

'Hugh's suggesting I should go home in the Hispano,' she said. 'I say, let's all go in it.'

'I'm not leaving my car here,' Paul said. 'The inside would be sodden by the morning. You do what you like.'

'All right. Thanks. I'll go with Hugh. I'm so *cold*.'

'Is that settled?' Hugh asked irritably. 'Good. Then come on, Gerry. You drive. My hand's hurting.'

'All right, so long as *somebody* drives.'

They were about to move towards the Hispano, when suddenly and unexpectedly Paul gave a yell. 'Stop ordering her around!'

Hugh turned. 'What?'

'You heard, you insolent little twerp! "Do this, Do that." Do you think she's a scullery maid?'

Gerry said despairingly, 'Oh, Paul, it doesn't matter!'

'It matters to me. I won't have you spoken to like that by anybody, let alone this insufferable, jumped up pipsqueak.'

He stepped up to Hugh. 'You took a poke at me just now. Want to try again?'

'All right.'

Hugh jabbed out his fist. Paul effortlessly parried the blow. Gerry gave a yell and stepped forward.

'Stop it, both of you!'

But at that second Paul let fly with a left hook. It was a textbook punch, except for one thing. As he threw it his feet slipped on the icy road surface. He spun wildly, his arms flailed in the air, and his clenched fist caught Gerry square on the jaw.

Without a sound she collapsed on the road and lay still.

Paul stared at Gerry in abject dismay.

'You fool!' Hugh gasped.

Paul fell on his knees beside her and raised her head. Hugh shone his flashlight on her face. With immense relief in his voice Paul said, 'It's all right. She's breathing easily. She'll be round in a few minutes. Let's get her into the car.'

They lifted Gerry and manoeuvred her through the door of the Hispano and onto the passenger seat. Paul closed the door. 'Are you capable of driving this thing?'

'I'll manage.'

'OK.'

'Splendid,' Paul said ironically, 'then, follow me.'

It was less than five minutes later that Gerry gave a little groan and opened her eyes. 'What happened?' she said thickly.

'Carter socked you on the jaw.'

'Don't be silly,' she murmured.

'He did, I tell you. Unfortunately, I'm forced to admit it was a pure accident.'

She fingered her jaw. 'Ouch. Oh, I remember now. The clumsy oaf.' She started to sit up.

Hugh said, 'Keep your head down a bit. You'll be groggy for a while yet.'

She did as he advised. A few seconds later she said, 'Gosh, I'm colder than ever.'

'You'll have to put up with it a bit longer.'

'Where are we?'

'I don't know. I'm following Carter. But you were about four miles from home when I found you and we've done a mile or so since then. If only this snow would ease!'

'Paul will be frozen solid with the top down.'

'How sad,' said Hugh.

When Gerry eventually walked stiffly into the house she was blue with cold. Her mother fussed around, plying her with questions, as she made her way thankfully to the fireplace and sank down in the chair closest to it.

'Don't laugh,' she said, 'but Paul ran out of petrol.'

The Countess brought a cup of coffee across to her. 'Oh, thanks, Mummy. I need that.'

Her father asked, 'Where are the boys?'

'Just putting the cars away.'

At that moment Hugh came in. Lord Burford said, 'Ah, the good Samaritan. Come and have some coffee, Hugh.'

'No, thank you, Lord Burford. I'll go straight up. Just looked in to say good night.'

'Thank you very much, Hugh,' Gerry said.

'That's all right.'

He went out, closing the door. A minute later Paul entered. He avoided Gerry's eye, refused coffee, but accepted a whisky and stood chatting to Lord Burford while he drank it. Then he too said good night and left the room. The Earl followed him upstairs a couple of minutes later, after bolting the front door.

Gerry and her mother remained talking for a further ten minutes, until Gerry had thawed out a little; then they also made their way rather wearily upstairs.

After kissing her mother goodnight and going to her room, Gerry stood hesitating, trying to decide whether to have a bath. She did need one in order to warm up fully. On the other hand, it was very late – nearly ten past two – and she was extremely tired.

Golly, what a day it had been! First that row with Gilbert – Oh no! Thinking of Gilbert had made her recollect the appointment she'd had with Rex.

She wondered if he could conceivably still be waiting for her. It was surely unlikely. But, on the other hand, he might have been expecting her any minute for the last hour and not have liked to go to bed.

Gerry sighed. She'd have to go and knock on the door of his sitting room, just in case. If he had turned in, that wouldn't disturb him. She left her room again.

There was no reply to her tap on Rex's door and, relieved, she started to turn away. She'd done her duty.

Then suddenly the door was pulled open with great force and Rex stood in the doorway.

He was still wearing evening dress, minus the coat, and for a moment there was an utterly unfamiliar expression on his usual cheerful countenance. In that second Gerry saw the face of a worried, even frightened, man behind the actor's mask. Then he was smiling.

'Why, Gerry. This is an unexpected pleasure.'

She stared. 'Unexpected? You mean, you weren't waiting up for me?'

'No.' He looked blank. 'Should I have been?'

'We had an appointment. Granted I'm absurdly late.'

Recollection came into his eyes. 'Of course! Come right in.'

'Just for a few seconds.'

Gerry went in and he closed the door. She said, 'It's a bit late to talk tonight. I'm at fault, though not really to blame. Paul had car trouble. So could we have our discussion about Gilbert tomorrow?'

'Gilbert?' He looked dazed and his manner was so odd she wondered if he'd been drinking. 'I don't want to talk about Gilbert. You must have misunderstood me.'

'I did no such thing!' she said indignantly. 'You asked if I'd been having trouble with him, as you had been. He'd been prowling about your room, you were worried and wanted to tell me a story.'

'Oh, I must have been exaggerating – professional failing, to dramatise situations.' He gave a decidedly unconvincing smile. 'We had a few words about the script, but's all sorted out now.'

She gazed at him incredulously. He looked back, smiling stiffly, and there was silence.

At last she said, 'I see. Well, if you're sure there's nothing—'

'No, nothing,' he said sharply. 'Nothing at all.'

'Whatever you say.' She went towards the door.

'Good night, then.'

'Good night.'

Her hand touching the doorknob, on a sudden impulse she turned. 'Rex, are you all right?'

The eyes that met hers looked almost wild. Then, unexpectedly, he gave a harsh laugh. 'All right? Well, how would you feel if a career you'd spent all your adult life building up looked like it was over? Oh, yes, I feel just dandy!'

'I – I don't understand.'

'Well, I shouldn't try. I'm sure you've got your own problems. So why don't you go sleep on them?'

On the verge of demanding a fuller explanation, Gerry changed her mind. This wasn't the time. So she just said, 'Very well, if that's what you want. Good night again.'

This time she did go out, closing the door behind her. She made her way slowly back towards her room. What had happened to change him so? *Could* he have been drinking? There'd been no smell of it. If not, it really seemed he might be on the verge of a nervous breakdown.

She went into her room and sat down on the bed. Suddenly she felt wide awake. She decided to have a bath, after all. Perhaps a good soak would help her think. Her maid was long in bed, so Gerry left her room again to go and run the bath. Not wanting to disturb Gilbert, she decided not to use the next-door bathroom, but the one across the corridor.

She had just entered it when, in the distance – but definitely indoors – she heard an utterly unexpected but quite unmistakable sound.

It was a gunshot.

Gerry's heart gave a leap, and for seconds she stood quite still, as the report reverberated through the corridors.

Rex. Could it be? Had that been his meaning when he'd talked about his career being over?

Gerry ran from the bathroom and sprinted along the main corridor. She reached the door of the Royal Suite. But as she got there the conviction came to her that the shot had come from farther away. She ran to the corner and stared along the east wing. At the far end a shaft of light streaming into the corridor showed that a door on the left was open.

Gerry started to run again. She was conscious of doors opening beside and behind her, of voices calling – alarmed, questioning. Then she saw that the light came from the end room, Laura's room. She arrived in the doorway. She gazed fearfully through it, then hesitantly stepped inside. The heat from a huge fire in the grate hit her, but she was hardly conscious of it. Her legs turned to jelly.

Lying on her back in front of the fire, her beautiful eyes staring sightlessly at the ceiling, was Laura. Just visible on the breast of her evening gown, looking like a ruby brooch, was a small dark red stain.

And standing near her, staring down, an expression of blank horror in his eyes, was Paul. In his hand was a revolver.

CHAPTER THIRTEEN

At Gerry's cry Paul jerked his head towards her. For perhaps six or seven seconds they stood motionless, staring at each other, both quite unable to speak. Then Paul got out just two words:

'She's dead.'

Automatically Gerry gave a jerky nod. She was barely conscious of the footsteps outside, or of Hugh's voice in the doorway. 'What's up?'

Then he came into the room and stopped short. He didn't speak.

'Is anything wrong?' It was Maude Fry's voice, slightly alarmed. Then the older woman, too, had entered the room. She gave a gasp.

The next moment everybody seemed to be there. There was a buzzing of questions, exclamations, muted screams. And then suddenly everyone was silent. As if at a given signal all eyes turned to Paul.

For a few seconds he met them, unflinching and wide-eyed. He said, 'I just—' Then something in their faces seemed to hit him. His expression changed from one of uncomprehending horror to appalled realisation.

He gasped, 'You don't think I—?' He broke off, then shouted, 'I found her dead, I tell you!'

No one spoke. Seconds passed. Then Lord Burford stepped forward. There seemed a sudden new authority in his manner, as he held out his hand and said quietly, 'Better let me have that, my boy.'

Paul gazed at him blankly. Then his eyes followed the Earl's downwards and he seemed, almost for the first time, to become aware of the revolver in his hand. He looked up again and his expression altered once more. Suddenly he looked frightened. He took a step backwards, and as he did so he raised the gun.

'No,' he said.

There was an instantaneous ripple of movement among the others. Cecily gave a little scream. Gerry gasped, 'Paul!'

He spoke hoarsely. 'Listen, all of you. I didn't do it. The gun was on the floor.'

Lord Burford, the only one present who hadn't moved when Paul had raised the gun, said, 'We can talk about that later. Give it to me now.'

Paul hesitated. His gun hand dropped again. There was the slightest relaxing of tension in the room. Then a thought seemed to occur to Paul. He swallowed. 'Wait, just a minute.'

He looked quickly round the room and in a few strides crossed to the dressing-table. He picked up an inlaid mother-of-pearl jewel box and opened it. It was empty. He placed the gun inside, closed the box, locked it, removed the key, and handed the box to Lord Burford.

He said, 'My fingerprints are on that gun. But just possibly somebody else's – the killer's – are as well. They mustn't be smudged.'

With the pistol now safe, the Earl turned his attention to Laura Lorenzo. He knelt down by her and took her wrist, then looked up and shook his head. 'Dead, all right. Not that I doubted it, but must go through the formalities.' He got to his feet. Avoiding Paul's gaze, he said, 'Better try and get hold of a doctor, I suppose, all the same. And the police. I'll go and ring up. We'd better lock this room – not touch anything. Look, do you mind all, please, moving out?'

Desperately, Paul said, 'Listen, I beg you all. You've got to believe me. I didn't do this. I was walking along the corridor when I—'

Haggermeir interrupted him. 'I don't know what you want to say, son, but take my advice and don't say it.'

'But I'm innocent.'

'Innocent or guilty you're in a tight spot. I know a bit about the law. Don't say another word until you've spoken with an attorney.'

Gerry moved near Paul and took his arm. 'He's right, darling.'

Paul closed his eyes and breathed deeply. Then he said, 'OK, except for one thing. A few minutes ago the real murderer was in this house. By now he may have got away. Or he may still be in the building.' He looked round the assembled throng. 'Or he may even be in this room.'

Lord Burford said, 'Let's go outside.'

Everybody shuffled slowly out, several people

casting backward glances at the mortal remains of
Laura Lorenzo. Most of those present seemed anxious
to keep their distance from Paul. Only Gerry stayed
close to him, even tucking her arm through his.

The Earl let everybody leave, then removed the key from
the keyhole, closed the door and locked it. He addressed
Paul again, 'I've got to call the police. You'd better go
to your room and wait there. I don't want to have to do
anythin' undignified like locking you in, so will you give
me your word you won't try and do a bolt before they get
here?'

Paul licked his lips. Then to everyone's alarm he gave a
shout, 'I can't! I won't see the police!' He backed a few paces
down the corridor. There was sweat on his brow. 'They'll
arrest me. And I'm innocent. I've – I've got to get away.
Now.'

And before anyone could even attempt to stop him, he
turned and sprinted down the corridor.

Gerry screamed, 'Paul, no! Don't be a fool!'

She ran as fast as she could after him. But by the time
she'd reached the corner of the corridor he'd disappeared
down the stairs. She followed and caught sight of him,
scrabbling with the bolts of the great front door. Before
she'd got to the bottom of the stairs he'd heaved it open
and vanished into the storm.

Gerry ran across the hall and out through the
doorway. The driving snow was thicker than ever, and
seemed to have swallowed Paul up. She called his name
twice at the top of her voice, but the wind whipped the
words from her lips. She stood helplessly, staring into
the darkness.

Then, from the direction of the stable yard, she heard the familiar roar of the Hispano Suisa's engine. A few seconds later she saw the blaze of its headlights, and the next moment the car shot past her. As it did so, she heard Paul's voice, calling one word:

'Sorry.'

Then the car, sliding on the snowy surface, disappeared down the drive.

Forlornly, Gerry retraced her steps indoors, to meet the others, who'd descended in a body, in the hall. 'He's gone,' she said dully.

The Countess hurried forward and put an arm round her shoulder. 'Come and lie down, my dear.'

'I don't want to lie down, Mummy.' Then she burst out, 'Oh, the idiot – the stupid, stupid idiot! Why did he have to bolt? They'll never believe him now.' She gazed at her father. 'Will they?'

The Earl looked awkward. 'Well, er, couldn't say, my dear. Doubtful, I should think. No point in speculatin', though. I must go and phone them now, tell 'em exactly what's happened.'

'Daddy, you will tell them, won't you, that in spite of all the appearances, we don't believe he did it?'

Lord Burford avoided her eyes. 'Don't think I could actually do that, sweetheart.'

Gerry was white-faced. 'But – but you don't really think he killed her, do you?'

The Earl didn't answer. Gerry gave a gasp. 'I don't believe it!' She stared round the circle of faces. 'Tell him, somebody. Tell him Paul couldn't have done it.'

But the appeal got no response. Some eyes met hers

squarely. Others fell. But in none was there any sign of agreement.

Gerry burst into tears. She shouted, 'You're a lot of beasts!' Then she turned, ran across the hall, up the grand staircase and out of their sight.

Hugh took a couple of steps to go after her, but the Countess put a hand on his arm. 'Leave her alone for a while. She'll be all right.'

Lord Burford turned to his wife. 'While I phone the police, will you ring for Merryweather, Lavinia? Explain what's happened and let him tell the others, if he thinks fit.'

The Countess nodded grimly. 'He won't like it, you know, George; he won't like it at all. None of them will.'

'Can't say I'm absolutely overjoyed about it myself, Lavinia.' He started to move away.

Lady Burford said sharply, 'Oh, George, I've just remembered. You can't use the telephone. Signorina Lorenzo tried to make a call. The line's dead.'

The Earl gave a groan. 'Oh, of course, I remember. Gad, that's all we need. Well, then Hawkins will just have to drive to the village.'

He turned away a second time, only to bump into Jemima Dove, who'd been witnessing everything with large, frightened eyes. She gave a little squeak.

'Oh, sorry, my dear,' Lord Burford said absently. Then he stopped and looked at her. 'Who the deuce are you?'

Lady Burford said hurriedly, 'Oh, this is Miss Dove, George. In the anxiety about Geraldine earlier I forgot to tell you.' She made a hasty explanation.

'Well, sorry you've had such an inauspicious welcome to Alderley, Miss Dove,' Lord Burford said. 'Should explain: this sort of thing – murders and suchlike – doesn't happen here often. Only every few months.'

Merryweather entered the library, crossed to the hearth and coughed discreetly. Lord Burford abruptly stopped snoring. Merryweather coughed a second time and the Earl's eyes opened sleepily.

'Mm?' he said.

'Another police officer, my lord.'

'Oh.' The Earl sat up, rubbing his eyes. 'Expect he's got news. What time is it?'

'Ten a.m., my lord.'

'Any of the guests up yet?'

'No, my lord.'

'Good. Hope they keep out of the way as long as possible. All right, show him in.'

Merryweather went out. Lord Burford stood up, ran his fingers through his hair, and blew his nose.

Merryweather reappeared in the doorway. 'Inspector Wilkins, my lord.'

He stood aside and hesitantly into the room came a short, plump man with a drooping moustache and worried expression.

Lord Burford gave an exclamation. 'Wilkins.'

He held out his hand as the other came across the room and with a somewhat diffident air shook hands.

'Good morning, my lord,' he said in a deep and mournful voice. Then he added, 'Though, perhaps not.'

'Not?'

'Not good, my lord. Another melancholy occasion, I fear. However, not with some nostalgic appeal. I must admit. Quite like old times, as they say.'

'Yes, well, come and sit down, Wilkins. Merryweather, coffee, please.'

The Earl and Wilkins sat down as Merryweather went out. Lord Burford gave a huge yawn. 'Excuse me. Been up all night. Not strictly necessary, I suppose. But seemed a bit heartless, just to turn in. All the rest of the household stayed up till about five, too. Think they all felt the same. It was quite a night. Constant stream of people: first the village bobby; then those plain clothes men of yours – they were here for hours, taking statements from everybody; then your photographers and fingerprint men all over the place; doctor, ambulance men. And every time the door opened a howling gale sweeping through, snow coming in. Has it stopped?'

'Yes, my lord, a couple of hours ago. A slight thaw has already set in.'

'Thank heavens for that. Then there was the—' He broke off. 'Sorry. Wafflin' too much. Always do when I'm sleepy.'

'That's all right, my lord. Anyway you'll only have to put up with me and Sergeant Leather from now on.'

'Good. Sure if anyone can clear the business up quickly it's you. Not, of course, that it's going to present the problems of the last affair. Open and shut case, what? Just a question of catching Carter, really. Haven't done so yet, I suppose?'

'No, my lord, but it's only a matter of time.'

'You know he took my daughter's car? Oh, yes, of course, you're bound to.'

'Yes, my lord.'

At that moment Merryweather entered with coffee. When both he and Wilkins were gratefully sipping from steaming cups, Lord Burford said, 'Just how much *do* you know, Wilkins?'

'Well, my lord, I've seen all the officers who were first on the scene and I've had their reports. They were all very comprehensive.' He seemed to find this fact vaguely depressing.

'Ah, so you've got a pretty clear picture of what's been going on?'

'I couldn't really say that, my lord. Must admit I find it all rather confusing. So many people on the scene. All made statements. Just names to me, except Mr Ransom, of course. Difficult to get them all sorted out, as it were.'

'Well, I can explain exactly who everyone is, if you like.'

'No, my lord, please don't bother. Hardly think it's going to be relevant. Just a few points about events leading up to the incident, if you don't mind. As I understand it, you all – or most of you – went to some function in the village. Got home about one, all except Lady Geraldine and Carter.'

'That's right.'

'All the others, including Signorina Lorenzo, went straight up to bed, only she tried to make a phone call first, but was unable to on account of the telephone being out of order. Then Mr – er, Quarter, is it?'

'Quartus.'

'Ah, yes. He went out to see what had happened to Lady Geraldine and Carter, and found them out of petrol about four miles away. Carter got some petrol, however, and they all arrived home the same time, about one-fifty. Carter and Mr Quartus went up immediately, followed by yourself, and the Countess and Lady Geraldine ten minutes later. The shot was heard another ten or twelve minutes after that, at about two-twenty. Lady Geraldine, who hadn't retired, was first on the scene, and then everyone else in a sort of rush.'

'That's about it. And there he was, Wilkins, just standing by the body, holding the gun.'

'Yes, my lord, I think that part of it's clear enough. What I haven't got is much information about either Carter or the deceased lady herself. If you could just tell me what you know about them...'

'All I can tell you about Paul is that he seems just a nice, pleasant-mannered young chap. Don't know a lot about his background. He's comfortably off, athletic type – ran in the Olympics, climbs mountains, and so on. Gerry's known him a year or so. He's stayed here once before.'

'And would I be right – excuse me – in assuming that there is – er, was – something more than mere friendship between them?'

'Oh, he's in love with her all right.'

Wilkins coughed delicately. 'And Lady Geraldine? She, um, reciprocates?'

'Oh, I think so. That other boy, Hugh, was by way of being a rival.'

'That would be Mr Quartus – the young gentleman who went out on the errand of mercy last night?'

'That's right. Seemed quite anxious. Must say he and Paul both appeared to be in a bit of a temper when they did eventually get back. Unusual for Paul. Hugh, on the other hand, tends to be rather temperamental. But then, he's an artist. Where was I?'

'Saying Mr Quartus was by way of being a rival.'

'Oh, yes. And I think *was* is the operative word. I've seen Geraldine definitely swinging towards Paul over the past few days. She's terribly cut up about this, of course, swears he couldn't have done it. Trying to convince herself, I think.'

'Now, what can you tell me about the signorina, my lord?'

'Virtually nothing. Had never even heard of her until Thursday.'

'Yet you invited her for the weekend?'

'Didn't. Mystery about that.' He explained the full circumstances surrounding Laura's arrival, together with the reason for the visit of Haggermeir, Rex, and Gilbert.

When he'd finished, Wilkins rubbed his jaw thoughtfully. 'And this Mr Haggermeir denied all knowledge of the telegram?'

'Absolutely.'

'Interesting. Especially in view of what subsequently happened to the lady.'

'You're not suggesting Paul could have sent it, are you?' the Earl said suddenly. 'Sort of way of luring her down here, so he could kill her? That's ghastly. Would mean he planned the murder days in advance.'

'Seems highly unlikely my lord, but it would depend what his motive was. Any idea about that?'

'None at all. I've been assumin' it was some sort of brainstorm.'

'My men suggest robbery as the motive.'

'Robbery? But nothing's missing, is it?'

'Oh, yes, my lord. According to Signorina Lorenzo's maid, a very valuable mink coat, worth about two thousand pounds, has disappeared.'

'Disappeared? But how could it have? Paul didn't take it with him.'

'All we know, my lord, is that the lady was wearing it when she went upstairs after arriving home with your lordship at about one a.m. She wasn't wearing it when the body was discovered. It's not in her room, nor in her maid's room – she insisted on my men searching it. Their hypothesis is that Carter crept into Miss Lorenzo's room in the dark while she was asleep, and threw it out of the window to a confederate he'd previously arranged to have waiting outside. Then, before he could get out of the room, she awoke and he had to shoot her to silence her.'

'But she hadn't been to bed. She was dressed.'

'Well, the Countess told my men that before she went upstairs Miss Lorenzo told her that she had a headache. She might have lain down on the bed, meaning just to rest for a few minutes before getting ready to turn in properly – which, I imagine, is quite a procedure with a lady like that: lotions, creams, and so on – and then dropped off.'

'Seems extremely far-fetched to me.'

'Mm. Must admit it does to me, too, now I come to think about it.' Wilkins sounded surprised.

'Odd about the mink, though, I agree.'

Wilkins finished his coffee, put down his cup, reached into his pocket and brought out a grubby piece of folded paper. 'By the way, my lord, last time I was here I made a little sketch map of the first floor, showing which room every one occupied. I dug it out this morning. Could you just look over it with me and point out where everyone is accommodated?'

For the next few moments Wilkins scribbled in names on the plan at the Earl's instructions. Then he studied it for another minute before putting it away and saying,

'Now another point, my lord: the murder weapon.'

'I gave it to your men.'

'Yes, my lord, I've seen it. Had a job opening the box without forcing it – Carter took the key. I understand the gun came from your collection?'

This was a moment to which the Earl had not been looking forward.

'That's right. Recognised it immediately. Checked in there since, just to make sure. Afraid six rounds of ammo are missing, too.'

'Now, you always keep the collection room locked, as I remember, my lord. So presumably he broke in.'

'No. He got hold of a key.'

Wilkins looked reproachful 'Oh, my lord.'

'I know what you're going to say: I should have been careful with them. Well, I have been – especially careful since that other affair. There are two keys. One I keep always on my watch chain. Here it is.' The Earl lifted it for Wilkins to see.

'And the other?'

'That I keep in my study safe. But when I went to the gun room I found it in the lock. I looked in the safe – just to be certain somebody hadn't somehow got a third key made – but no. There was no key there.'

'The safe was locked?'

'Yes.'

'And the key to that?'

'It has a combination lock.'

'How many other people know the combination, my lord?'

'As far as I know – knew – only my wife and daughter.'

'Lady Geraldine, then, could have told Carter?'

'She could have. Don't see why she should.'

There was a knock on the library door. Lord Burford called, 'Come in,' and a tall, cheerful-looking young man entered.

'You remember Sergeant Leather, my lord?' Wilkins said.

'Yes, indeed. Good morning.'

'Good morning, my lord. Excuse me.' He spoke to Wilkins. 'Just had a message, sir, that Carter walked into Swindon police station an hour ago and gave himself up.'

'Did he indeed?'

'Said he'd been driving round in circles in a dither all night, trying to decide what to do. He's being taken to Westchester. And, my lord, they've arranged to have Lady Geraldine's car brought straight back here.

'Oh, fine.'

Wilkins looked at his watch. 'Better get along to the station shortly, I suppose. No rush, though. They won't be making much speed with the roads as they are. Radio in and tell them I'll be on my way soon, Jack.'

'Yes, sir.' Leather went out.

'Er, there wouldn't be any more coffee in that pot, would there, my lord?'

'Yes, of course. Help yourself.'

'Thank you, my lord.' Wilkins did so.

'You will be charging him, of course,' Lord Burford said.

'Well, I really mustn't announce that in advance, my lord, if you understand – not before I've even seen him. At least, I won't have to arrest him, thank goodness. That's a thing I hate doing.'

'A policeman who doesn't like making arrests? You must be unique.'

'I daresay, my lord. But handcuffing people, locking them in cells – it always depresses me. When I joined the force, I never saw myself out of the uniformed branch – perhaps a sergeant, at best. And in a peaceful place like Westshire, thought that poachers and the odd petty thief would be the extent of my contact with criminal types. But who could have anticipated the crime wave that's broken out among the English upper classes in recent years?'

'Crime wave? Put it as bad as that, do you?'

'Oh, my goodness, your lordship, yes. Never a week goes by without a nobleman being murdered in his library – oh, beg pardon, didn't mean to alarm you – or a don in his study, or an heiress in her bath. And where's it left me? Oh, I've made Chief Inspector, true—'

'Chief Inspector, now, eh? Congratulations.'

'Thank you, my lord. Could say you're responsible, in a way. It was your bit of bother here that finally got me promotion. But I can't honestly say I'm happy in my work. I'm out of my element. And I'm always scared the next case is going to stump me.'

'Oh, come on, Wilkins, you underestimate yourself. If

you could solve our last case you could solve anything.'

'I had a lot of luck, my lord.'

'Luck? Poppycock. I'll tell you something, Wilkins. I lunched at me club in town with Peter Wimsey a couple of months back.'

Wilkins eyes bulged. '*Lord* Peter Wimsey?'

'That's right. I told him all about that business – he'd been abroad at the time himself. He was most interested, and said it sounded as if you'd put in a first-rate bit of detection work. Said he hoped he'd run into you sometime; he'd enjoy swapping case stories with you.'

Wilkins was looking dazed. 'Really, my lord, that's quite a compliment. I don't know what to say.' With some reluctance he stood up. 'Better be making a move, I suppose.'

The Earl rose, too. 'Will you be coming back?'

'There may be a few more questions, my lord. It all depends, mainly on exactly what Carter's story is. I'll see you're kept informed of developments.'

CHAPTER FOURTEEN

The police constable unlocked the door and Wilkins went into the small, bare, windowless room, with its whitewashed walls and single light. The only furniture was a wooden table and three upright chairs. On one of these Paul was slumped. His hair was awry and his face haggard. A rough blanket was round his shoulders. A thick white china mug that had contained tea was on the table, and Paul was warming himself at an oil stove which was giving off a rather sickly smell.

Paul glanced up as Wilkins and the constable entered. There was a momentary flicker of hope in his eyes, which faded when he saw who they were and took in the expressions on their faces. For a few seconds Wilkins surveyed the young man without speaking. Then he pulled out a chair from the table and sat down heavily on in. The constable sat in the other chair and took out a notebook and pencil.

'I'm Detective Chief Inspector Wilkins.'

Paul looked up with sudden interest. 'Wilkins? I've heard about you from Lady Geraldine. You solved that other murder at Alderley.'

Wilkins didn't answer this. He took a packet of cigarettes and a box of matches from his pocket and lit up. Then he pushed the cigarettes across the table towards Paul. 'Want one?'

Paul shook his head. 'I don't,' he muttered.

'Oh, no, of course. You're an athlete, aren't you? Certainly helped you last night, didn't it?'

Paul looked at him sharply. 'What do you mean?'

'Getting away after the murder. They say you were off down the corridor like a scalded cat. No one had a chance to lay a finger on you. Why'd you do it?'

'Do what?'

'Run away.'

'Why do you think? A woman had been killed, almost certainly murdered. I'd been found standing by her body with a gun in my hand. The Earl was just going to call the police.'

'But you claimed to be innocent.'

'Never heard of an innocent man being convicted?'

'No.'

Paul stared. 'What do you mean?' he said again.

'I've never heard of an innocent man being convicted – not of murder, in this country, in modern times.'

'Well, let's say I didn't want to be the first.'

'All you did was make it much more likely that you will be. You made the case against yourself even blacker.'

'It couldn't have been any blacker than it was already.'

Wilkins considered this. 'Well, no, perhaps not,' he said unexpectedly. 'Do you want to make a statement?'

'What, now?'

'Yes. Shouldn't if I were you. See a lawyer first, that's my advice.'

Paul hesitated. 'But in that case, won't everybody assume I'm guilty?'

'Nearly everybody assumes that now.'

'*Nearly* everybody?'

'I'm told Lady Geraldine is convinced of your innocence.'

Paul's face lit up. 'Is she really? Still? Oh, bless her.' He took a deep breath. 'I'll make a statement.'

'Sure?'

'Sure. What's the point in keeping quiet? Even after I've seen a lawyer I can only tell the truth. So I might as well tell it now. What have I got to lose? So here goes. And I know all that stuff about everything I say being taken down and used in evidence, so don't bother. Now, this is what happened.

'To make everything clear I'll have to start at a point a bit earlier in the evening, when Gerry and I were on our way back from the party. I ran out of petrol – which is something I still can't understand, but that's by the way. I had to walk to the main road and wave down a truck to get some. When I arrived back at the car after being away twenty or twenty-five minutes, I found Quartus had turned up. We had a bit of a fight. First he tried to sock me, then I took a poke at him. But I slipped on the icy road and hit Gerry by mistake, knocked her out. We put her in her car. I drove home in my car, and he followed with her. We got home about ten to two.

'By then Gerry, naturally, wasn't too pleased with me. So I thought it would be better if I kept out of her way as much as possible until the following morning. I had a quick drink with the Earl and then went straight up. I was so cold and tired that when I got to my room I sat in the chair in front of the fire for about fifteen minutes, just getting warm. Then I decided to turn in. I took off my overcoat and left the room again, meaning to go to the bathroom. I went to the right, making for the one at the end of the main corridor, which I usually use. But as I did so I heard Lady Geraldine's voice coming from that direction. Well, as I explained, I didn't really want to see her again that night, so I returned to my room to wait until the coast was clear. Now, as a matter of fact, I'd forgotten about the other, smaller bathroom at the end of the wing – I don't think I'd ever been right to the end – but after five minutes or so I suddenly remembered hearing some reference to it once. So I left my room again and this time turned left.

'As you get to the end of the corridor the illumination isn't too good – the last light is about level with the door to the gallery. As a result, I particularly noticed a narrow beam of light being thrown across the corridor, which meant that Signorina Lorenzo's bedroom door was open an inch. But I thought nothing of that. Then, when I got a bit closer, I noticed a small object lying on the floor just outside the door. It wasn't until I was almost on top of it that I realised it was a revolver. I bent over it and thought I recognised it as being one of Lord Burford's. I couldn't think how it had got there, but naturally I didn't imagine there was anything wrong. However, I knew that the Earl was particular about keeping all his guns under lock and key, so I picked it up, meaning to return it to him immediately.

'Just then I heard a sound from Signorina Lorenzo's room, a sort of muffled groan. I hesitated a moment, then tapped on the door. There was no reply. I called out softly, just asking if she was all right. But still there was no answer. So I pushed the door open wide and stepped into the room. It was terribly hot in there, like a greenhouse. There was a huge fire in the hearth, and on the rug in front of it Signorina Lorenzo was lying.

'I started to move towards her. As I did so, someone gave me a tremendous shove in the back. It sent me staggering right across the room, nearly falling. At that moment I heard a gunshot in the doorway behind me. I managed to stop myself and spun round. But by then there was nobody there. For a few seconds I dithered – couldn't decide whether to run to the door or go to Signorina Lorenzo. At last I went to her and saw the bullet wound. I just stood there. I couldn't take it in properly. A few seconds later Lady Geraldine arrived. The rest you know. And that I swear is the truth.'

Wilkins dropped the stub of his cigarette on the floor, stepped on it, and with his toe flicked it out of sight under the table. 'What do you know about the lady's mink coat being missing?' he asked.

Paul looked bewildered. 'Missing? You mean stolen? It's the first I've heard of it.'

'Well, I assure you it is. And it provides a quite adequate motive for murder. If you'd decided to steal it – thrown it out of the window to a confederate, say – and the lady caught you in the act, you'd have had to silence her.'

'That's absolutely crazy! Why on earth should I want the woman's confounded coat?'

'It's worth two thousand pounds.'

'I don't need two thousand pounds.'

'So you say.'

'Check with my bank, my brokers. Get on to them now.' He broke off and looked at his watch. 'Well, it'll have to be Monday now, I suppose. They'll confirm what I say.'

Wilkins shrugged, 'If you say so, no doubt they will. But robbery isn't the only motive for murder.'

'But I didn't have any motive!' Paul said desperately. 'I'd never set eyes on the woman until two days ago. I talked to her for about ten minutes in the library on Friday morning, and apart from that I just made a few casual remarks to her, always with other people present. Check up as much as you like. Or do you think I'm just a homicidal sex maniac, or something?'

'Oh, no, this case doesn't bear the marks of that sort of crime.'

'Then please, please believe me. When I went through that bedroom door Laura Lorenzo was already dead.'

Wilkins regarded Paul silent for a few moments. Then, 'I believe you,' he said.

Paul sat motionless, his eyes fixed on Wilkins. It was as if for seconds be could not properly comprehend what had been said. Then his expression changed. Care was magically wiped from his face.

He slumped back in his chair. 'Oh, what a relief! But why? I mean, what...?'

'Oh, a number of reasons. Mainly because as things stand it's all too pat, too obvious. What's more, you, if I may say so, seem a highly intelligent young gentleman. I'm quite sure that if you were going to shoot somebody, you wouldn't be so careless as to let yourself be accidentally found standing over the body, holding a gun.'

For the first time in many hours, Paul grinned. 'Well, thanks.' He stood up suddenly. 'Can I go now?'

'Yes, sir. Do you want to go back to Alderley?'

'Well, I'd better collect my car and my other things. But I won't stay. Far too embarrassing, with all the rest of them no doubt still thinking I'm a murderer. No, I'll go back to London, until such time as you nail the real killer. Gosh, though, half an hour ago I never thought I'd be officially in the clear as quickly as this.'

'Now hold on,' Wilkins said. 'Don't get carried away. I don't say you're out of the woods yet.'

Paul froze. He stammered, 'But – but you said that, that you believe—'

'What I believe isn't really all that important, sir. As you said, there's a very strong case against you. To most people, including I strongly suspect my chief, and perhaps the Director of Public Prosecutions, it's likely to seem overwhelming. Then there's the question of public opinion. If no new evidence comes to light which either clears you or points to someone else, then I – or one of my colleagues – may be forced by circumstances to arrest and charge you.'

'And you said no innocent man gets convicted of murder?'

'I don't say you'll be convicted. But you may have to go through a very unpleasant couple of months before you're acquitted.'

Paul ran his fingers through his hair. 'This is ghastly. What on earth can I do?'

'Well, in the first place, sir, I suggest you go back to Alderley and stay there, rather than return to London.'

'But why?'

'For one thing, it'll look good from your point of view – the open act of an innocent man, not like someone with a guilty conscience running away. Secondly, if you were framed, you were framed by one of the guests in the house. I discount the servants – they've all been there donkey's years – and of course the family. On the other hand, I can't ask *them* to report or spy on their guests.'

'Is that what you want me to do?'

'I'd rather not put it in those words.'

'But, look, they're convinced I'm a killer. They're not likely to be friendly, or to allow me to pump them.'

'No, but you'll *be* there. You see, I want someone who can watch people, can gauge reactions – both to your return and to the realisation that the police aren't satisfied, that we're still investigating.'

Paul nodded thoughtfully. 'And as the person who was the victim of the frame-up, I'm the only one of the guests in the clear, the only one you can trust. Yes, I see.'

'*Officially* you're still a suspect, mind you, though just one of eight or nine. You've been released, pending further enquiries into the feasibility of your story and the possibility of somebody else's guilt. Though if you want to tell them that I personally believe you, you can. Will you do it?'

'I haven't got much choice, have I? You've as good as told me that if I don't help you spot the real killer I'll be re-arrested.'

'Put in that way, it sounds like blackmail, sir, but I assure you it isn't that. You're free to return to London, if you wish. It's just that I need all the help I can get to have any hope of cracking this case. We're dealing here with a very good brain.'

'But you will get him eventually?'

'I'd like to think so, Mr Carter. But without help, frankly I'm not sanguine, not sanguine at all.'

It was just after one when Paul got back to Alderley and, his heart in his mouth, mounted the steps to the big front door. As he approached it, it was opened from the inside and Gerry stood in the doorway. For about five seconds she just stared at him. Then she ran forward and threw herself into his arms.

'Oh, Paul,' she said. 'Oh, Paul.'

He clasped her to him. 'This makes it all worthwhile,' he murmured.

She drew back and looked up at him, bewilderment mixed with her pleasure. 'But why? I don't understand. What's happened? They said you'd given yourself up to the police.'

'I did. They let me go.'

She gave a gasp of delight. 'You mean they believe you?'

'Your Inspector Wilkins does.'

'Oh, good old Wilkins! I knew he wouldn't let me down!'

'I'm not completely in the clear yet, Gerry.'

Her face fell. 'What do you mean?'

'I'll tell you in a minute – inside. Listen, where is everybody? Having lunch?'

'Yes. I didn't want any.'

'So nobody else knows about my being free?'

'Not yet.'

'Well, I want to surprise them. But first I've got to clean up. Can I get up to my room without being seen?'

'I don't see why not.'

She turned, ventured just inside the front door, looked around the hall, then beckoned him. 'All clear.'

He went in and together they hurried upstairs and along the corridor to his bedroom. Once inside he gave a sigh of relief.

He said, 'First of all, sorry about pinching your car. It was a spur of the moment thing. It didn't seem a very good idea to take my own – not with the top stuck down, and less than a gallon of petrol in the tank.'

'Oh, that's all right, silly.'

'You got it back?'

'Yes, the police brought it. But forget the car. Explain what you meant about not being in the clear.'

He did so, ending by saying, 'So I thought if I could spring myself on them, while they were all together, and didn't even know I was here, it would be a good opportunity to gauge reactions.'

'You mean while they're at lunch?'

'Yes; have I got time?'

'I should think so. They've only just started.'

'Good. So what I want now is a quick wash, shave and change of clothes. Then will you go into the room with me and help watch their faces?'

She shook her head.

'You won't?' He looked amazed.

'Not *their* faces, Paul. There's only one face *I'm* going to be watching: Arlington Gilbert's.'

'You let him go?' the Chief Constable of Westshire, Colonel Melrose exclaimed incredulously.

'Er, yes sir,' Wilkins said.

'Are you out of your mind, man?'

Wilkins shuffled his feet like a schoolboy before his headmaster. The Chief Constable gazed at him helplessly, his honest, if not very intelligent, face displaying a combination of anger and bewilderment.

Colonel Melrose was popular with his men. Though a strict disciplinarian, he was basically kindly, scrupulously fair, backed them to the hilt when they did their best, and never used his position to fix his friends' speeding tickets. Moreover, he mostly left them alone to get on with their cases without interference. Occasionally, however, when people with whom he was personally acquainted were involved in criminal matters, he did feel obligated to take a closer interest in the investigation than usual. This, though, was not to help them get off lightly; rather in fact the opposite. He was determined to insure that none of his officers went easy on friends of the boss. As a long-time acquaintance of Lord Burford, it seemed he was going to make the latest Alderley murder one such case.

Wilkins sighed inwardly. Admirable though his chief was in the most ways, criminal investigation was not his forte. The lack of imagination, stubbornness and slight stupidity that had prevented him reaching the highest ranks of the army became all too obvious in such cases. Wilkins could see trouble looming on this one.

'I don't think I'm out of my mind, sir,' he answered.

'Then why the blue blazes did you do it? Here's a bloke, found standing over the woman's body, the murder weapon in his hand—'

Wilkins interrupted adroitly. 'That's been confirmed, has it, sir? I haven't seen the ballistics report.'

'Yes, I got a copy a few minutes ago. But surely, you didn't think the gun Carter was holding *wasn't* the murder weapon, did you?'

'Wouldn't be the first time something like that's happened at Alderley, sir.'

The Chief Constable fingered his moustache. 'No, point there. But Wilkins, this isn't a case like that one. It's open and shut, You can't let the chap go.'

'But I have, sir.'

'Then you can pick him up again.'

'I'd much rather not, sir, really.'

'But we'll be laughing-stocks – with the press, the other police forces. This case is going to get a shocking amount of publicity, once the papers hear about it. Italian actress, Olympic athlete, stately home. And to cap it all that blessed Yankee film star staying at the house at the time. We must get the killer charged and brought before the Magistrate quickly, so it becomes *sub judice*. There's no time to lose.'

'I'm aware of that, sir.'

'Then why don't you want to arrest the chap?'

'Because if I do, sir, I'm convinced I'll have to let him go again. And that *would* make us laughing-stocks.'

'But why should you have to?'

'Because sooner or later some new piece of evidence is going to turn up that would force me to.'

'But the shot, the gun in his hand...'

'I know all about that, sir. Carter says it was a frame-up.'

'You can't believe that.'

'I do, sir.'

'Great Scott.'

Colonel Melrose sat down suddenly, a blank expression on his face. After a few seconds he asked, 'Any evidence as to who might have been responsible for this – frame-up?'

'No evidence at all yet, sir.'

Colonel Melrose said quietly, 'I'm speechless, Wilkins.'

'I'm sorry about that, sir. But this is how I see it: frame-ups are very difficult things to arrange. There are too many imponderables, too much that can go wrong. They may hold for a while, but not for long. Sooner or later some fresh piece of information comes to light that blows the whole thing sky-high. That's what I expect to happen in this case.'

The Chief Constable sat silently for several moments. Then he said slowly, 'Do I take it, then, that you refuse to arrest Carter?'

Wilkins looked unhappy. 'Well, of course, sir, if you order me to...'

'I don't want to do that.'

Abruptly Colonel Melrose stood up again. 'How about a drink?'

'Oh, thank you, sir. I wouldn't say no to a Scotch and soda.'

Colonel Melrose crossed to a glass-doored cabinet and there was a clink of glasses for a few seconds. Then he came back, handed Wilkins a glass and raised his own. 'Well, bung-ho.'

'Down the hatch, sir.'

They both drank. When the Chief Constable spoke again it was with a confidential air. 'Wilkins, you've had a lot of these cases, haven't you – these involved, difficult murder cases, I mean?'

'Too many, sir.'

'Perhaps so. And I suppose one of the worst was that other business at Alderley, what?'

'It took a bit of unravelling.'

'Had some help there, didn't you?'

'Oh, yes, sir. I'm not trying to claim all the credit.'

'I didn't mean that. We all know the case wouldn't have been solved without you. Fact remains that the espionage element meant that that secret service fellow was *technically* in charge, if not openly. Nobody said as much, but he had direct links with the Prime Minister and could have taken over at any time if it looked as though you weren't up to it. Luckily he didn't have to. But the possibility was there.'

'Yes, sir, but I don't quite see—'

'What I'm driving at, Wilkins, is that if anything had gone wrong the ultimate responsibility wouldn't have been yours – or the responsibility of this force. It would have been his and his department's.'

'True, sir.'

'Well, I'm chewing over the possibility of somehow getting ourselves in the same situation again.'

'You mean ask the secret service to—'

'No, no, the Yard.'

'Call in Scotland Yard, sir?'

'Yes. How does the idea appeal to you? Don't take it as a criticism in any way, old man, but—'

'I don't, sir. I'd welcome it.'

The Chief Constable gave a slight start. 'You would?'

'Yes, sir, I've always wanted to work under a top Yard officer. The idea of just acting as a kind of glorified messenger boy and letting him do all the brainwork – why, it would be heaven. But you've always been dead against it.'

'I know I have. But I think there are special circumstances in this case. If we hand it over to them and they arrest this Carter chappie and then have to let him go, then it's no skin off our nose, what? On the other hand, if, as I suppose is possible, they agree with you that he's innocent, and then it turns out I'm right and he's not—'

'Our noses are still intact, sir. If I may say so, it's a fine idea, very subtle indeed.'

Colonel Melrose clapped his hands. 'Splendid, splendid!' He looked at his watch. 'I'll put through a call straight away and see if they can get somebody here by this evening. They have several men who specialise in these more bizarre mysteries, don't they – John Appleby, Roderick Alleyn, St. John Allgood. What's that name they've got for them up there?'

'The three Great A's, sir. If we can get one of them it'll be marvellous.'

'Yes, and with luck we'll have Car – er, somebody – charged before the story breaks publicly. If we don't, it's going to be grim, reporters all over us. Fortunate that phone at Alderley being out of order. Someone there would certainly have blabbed by now if not. As it is, the only people I've notified are the Italian Embassy. They won't make it public until her next of kin – whoever that may be – has been traced in Italy and informed. So we've got a day or two's breathing space, with luck.'

'I think perhaps we ought to notify her London agent as well, sir. Seems she was going to visit him today. According to Lady Burford's statement, Miss Lorenzo tried to phone him at one o'clock this morning to tell him what time she'd be arriving today. Of course, she couldn't get through, so presumably he won't be worrying yet at her not turning up. However, he obviously will start to get anxious before the day's out. We don't want him notifying the press of her disappearance, or anything like that.'

'Do you know where to contact him?'

'Yes, sir, we found his phone number in her address book.'

'Very well, put through a call. But be sure and tell him to keep it under his hat. Then grab a bite of lunch and get back to Alderley, keep the ball rolling until the Yard arrives.'

He gave Wilkins a clap on the shoulder. 'And thanks for being so accommodating. I won't forget it.'

CHAPTER FIFTEEN

Gerry looked at Paul. 'Ready?' He nodded, tight-lipped. She opened the door of the dining-room. Everybody looked towards her.

Lord Burford said, 'Oh, hullo, my dear. Change your mind about lunch?'

Gerry didn't answer. She said, 'Look who's here.'

She stood aside and Paul walked into the room. Any variation of reaction he might have been expecting from the assembled guests was not forthcoming. On every face, as he looked quickly from one to the other, he saw the same thing: blank astonishment. He let five seconds pass before saying quietly, 'Hullo.'

It was Lady Burford who first recovered herself. 'What – what are you doing here, Paul?'

'I was hoping, if I may, to have some lunch.'

'But we were told you were under – er, with the police.'

Gerry said, 'They let him go. Isn't it marvellous?' It was clear this reaction was not widely shared.

The Earl said, 'But why?'

'Inspector Wilkins believes my story,' Paul said.

From the lower end of the table Hugh uttered an exclamation. 'I don't believe it!'

Paul gave the slightest shrug. 'Ask him. I'm sure he'll be back later.'

'Come on, Paul,' Gerry said, 'let's sit down.'

They did so, Gerry first pulling the bell for Merryweather. There was a strained silence. It was broken by Paul himself.

'I'd like to repeat now the account I gave to Inspector Wilkins of just what happened last night, the account he believed. If anybody afterwards still disbelieves me, I can only say I don't really blame you. I probably wouldn't believe it in your shoes. However, it happens to be true and I hope before long you'll all know that for a fact.' He paused. 'As one of you does already.'

Wilkins arrived back at Alderley at two-thirty. He asked for Lord Burford, but was told by Merryweather that the Earl was lying down, as was the Countess.

'Perhaps you'd care to see Lady Geraldine, sir?' he said.

Wilkins looked pleased. 'Yes, I would, very much.'

'Then if you will kindly wait in the library I will find her.'

When Gerry entered the library a minute later, Paul was with her. She greeted Wilkins warmly. 'Mr Wilkins, I knew I could rely on you.'

'Very kind of your ladyship.'

'Any developments, Inspector?' Paul asked.

'Yes, sir. Very shortly the case will be out of my hands.'

Their faces fell. Gerry said, 'But why?'

'The Chief's called in the Yard, my lady.'

Gerry gave a gasp. 'Oh, no!'

'Now don't fret, my lady. They're sending one of their very best men, Chief Superintendent Allgood. You want the real killer nabbed, don't you?'

'Yes, of course.'

'With Mr Allgood here, he will be. He specialises in this sort of case.'

'I've heard of him,' Paul said. 'Quite a character, isn't he?'

'I'll say so, sir. He's a real lone wolf. Doesn't even have a sergeant to assist him – only his own valet, man called Chalky White. Ex-cat burglar. Mr Allgood saved his life years ago, climbed up a high building and brought him down after a drainpipe broke. Then persuaded the judge to give him a reduced sentence.'

'When will he be here?' Gerry asked.

'In an hour or two, my lady. As luck would have it, he's been investigating a case not far away – the murder of the Dean of Cheltenham. He finally cleared it up this morning – arrested the Bishop, as a matter of fact. After the Assistant Commissioner of Scotland Yard received Colonel Melrose's request, he sent instructions for Mr Allgood to come straight on here. It'll be an education to work under him. I'm really looking forward to it.'

'What do you want to do in the meantime?'

Wilkins scratched his nose. 'Well, nothing, really, my lady.'

'Wouldn't you like to question the guests?'

'No, I don't think so, thank you. Better leave that to Mr Allgood. Unless there's been any development since you got back, Mr Carter – any noticeable reaction from anybody which ought to be followed up immediately.'

Paul shook his head. 'Nothing.'

Wilkins shrugged. 'Didn't really expect a lot in the first instance, sir. Murderers don't often give away anything by their expressions. But continue to keep your eyes and ears open. I'm sure there's one person in this house very much on edge.'

Gerry said, 'You've convinced the murderer is here, then?'

'I'm afraid so, my lady. True, an outsider could have got in, the burglar alarm being out of action. But he'd have needed an inside accomplice: somebody who knew which room Miss Lorenzo was occupying, the location of a suitable gun in the collection room, where the ammo for it was kept, the fact that there was a spare key in his lordship's safe, and the combination of that safe. And that's the man I want, even if – which I doubt – it should turn out he brought someone in from outside actually to pull the trigger. Incidentally, that business of the safe is a bit of a poser in itself. His lordship thought that nobody but himself, her ladyship, and you, my lady, knew it. Now, could you by any chance have mentioned it to someone else?'

Gerry looked at him. She licked her lips. Then she shook her head.

'Sure, my lady?'

'Yes. Yes, of course.'

Quietly Paul said, 'Thanks, darling, but it's no good.'

'Paul!'

'Sweetheart, I'm convinced that Chief Inspector Wilkins is my best hope. We've got to tell him the complete truth.

What faith is he going to have in my innocence if he finds out later I've been lying to him?'

'There's no way he could have found out,' she said sulkily.

'Maybe not. But it'll be more comfortable if everything is open and above board. Fact is, Inspector, *I* know the combination of that safe.'

'But I virtually forced it on him,' Gerry put in.

'How come, your ladyship?'

'It was months ago. We were playing roulette at a place in London. Lord, I suppose that was illegal, too. Anyway, I was betting on the numbers of our birthdays. Paul was pulling my leg about being superstitious, and I said it must run in the family, because Daddy's birthday is on the, eleventh, Mummy's on the eighth, and mine on the twenty-third, so he'd had the combination of the safe made eleven right, eight left, twenty-three right.'

Wilkins nodded slowly. 'Was anybody else present at the time?'

'Of course. We were in a night club.'

Paul said: 'But there was nobody we knew standing close enough to have heard.'

'Oh, really, you are the most utter chump!' Gerry spoke exasperatedly. 'You seem to be going out of your way to paint as black a picture against yourself as possible.'

Wilkins raised a hand. 'With respect, your ladyship, Mr Carter is doing absolutely the right thing. I suppose you didn't mention the combination to anyone else, sir?'

Paul gave a sigh. 'It would be so easy, wouldn't it, to say yes? But, frankly, if a good friend happens to mention the combination of their safe, it's not the sort of thing one goes around blabbing to all and sundry. No, Mr Wilkins, to the best of my recollection I didn't mention it to a soul.'

'I still say somebody could have overheard me,' Gerry muttered.

'Apart from that, you've mentioned it to no one else, your ladyship?'

Reluctantly, she shook her head.

'Well, his lordship is certain neither he nor the Countess has told anybody else.'

'And it's so easy to remember, he's never written it down anywhere,' she said. 'Oh, dear, everything seems to make it worse for Paul than before. I suppose you have got to tell this Yard man, have you, Mr Wilkins?'

'Afraid so, my lady, but I'll also tell him Mr Carter freely volunteered the information. It'll count very much in his favour.'

'Thank heavens something will. In spite of your releasing him, I'm sure everyone's going to think he's guilty once the murder becomes public. Unless you and Scotland Yard can find the real killer first.'

'You just leave it to Mr Allgood, your ladyship.'

'Don't you want to do anything until he arrives?'

Wilkins looked doubtful. 'Suppose I ought to do *some*thing. Don't quite know what, though.' Then he brightened a little. 'Oh, I know. I'll interview the servants.'

'Is there any real point in that?' she asked. 'I'm sure they won't be able to tell you anything. They were all in bed at the time.'

'I agree, your ladyship. It's probably a waste of time, but it's something that's got to be done.'

'In all the hundreds of detective stories I've read,' Paul said, 'the Inspector always leaves that job to his sergeant.'

'No doubt, sir, but I've got to find something to do. And it's a nice, uncomplicated job, as a rule. Just right for me.'

The stable clock was striking four forty-five when a white Bentley swept up the now slush-covered drive of Alderley and skidded to a halt outside the great front door, with a fanfare on its horn. The driver – a dark, sharp-faced man, with a toothbrush moustache – jumped out and opened the rear door. The man who emerged was tall and broad-shouldered. The driver ran up the steps in front of him and rang the doorbell just a few seconds before it was opened by the imperturbable-as-ever figure of Merryweather. The tall man strode in without being invited.

He was wearing a stylish full-length vicuna motoring coat, a grey Homburg hat, grey suede gloves and grey spats. He had a large Roman nose, piercing dark eyes, and an upturned waxed moustache. He removed his hat to reveal curly black hair, saying as he did so, 'Allgood of the Yard. Kindly inform your master that I have arrived.'

Merryweather turned. 'Oh, here is his lordship, sir.'

The Earl bustled forward, Wilkins at his heels. 'Chief Superintendent Allgood?'

'St. John Allgood, yes. Of Scotland Yard.' He pulled off his gloves and held out his hand. 'How do you do, Burford? We haven't met, but I believe we have several mutual friends – Tubby Charrington, Pongo Smith-Smythe, Bertie Bassington.'

'Oh, yes, yes, of course. Delighted to meet you, my dear chap. How de do?'

Allgood snapped his fingers, and his driver hurried forward and helped to divest him of his coat. Under it Allgood was wearing a superbly cut grey pinstripe suit, with an Old Etonian tie. 'Understand you've been having a spot of bother here, Burford.'

'You could put it like that.'

'Ah, well, we'll soon clear that up.'

'I sincerely hope so. I don't know what you'd care to do first...?'

'First I must meet the local man and get the facts. I take it he's around somewhere.'

Wilkins, on whose face had appeared an expression closely resembling that on Lord Burford's when he had met Rex Ransom, cleared his throat nervously. 'That's me, sir.'

Allgood stared. 'You? Oh, I didn't realise. Don't exactly look the part, do you?' He chuckled, revealing a great many large and very white teeth. 'Wilkins, is that right?'

'Yes, sir.'

'Right. Where can we talk?'

'Well, his lordship has kindly given us the use of the small music room.'

'Excellent.' He turned back to the Earl. 'I'll talk to you in due course, Burford. And the rest of your household.'

'Oh, yes, of course. If there's anything you want...?'

'Yes, tea; China, please. And muffins.' He addressed his driver: 'Chalky, bring my cases in and take them up to my room.'

'Yes, guv.' Chalky hurried out.

Lord Burford looked a bit taken aback. 'Oh, er, you stayin'?'

Allgood turned slowly to face him again. 'I thought that was understood. It's the usual thing in cases like this. Much more convenient. Means the trouble gets cleared up far quicker. Only be for a couple of nights. Of course, if it's not possible, I suppose there's a hostelry of some sort in the village.'

'No, no, that'll be quite all right – pleasure and all that.'

'Good. What time do you dine?'

'Eight, as a rule.'

'Better make it a bit later tonight – nine, say. I'll dine in my room. Right, Williams, lead the way.'

In the music room Allgood threw himself down into the only comfortable arm chair and put his feet on a pouf. 'Very well, fire away, Chief Inspector,' he said.

'I'd like to say first, sir, what a privilege it's going to be to assist you on this case.'

'Yes, you should learn quite a lot. I must congratulate you, though.'

'What for, sir?'

'Knowing your limitations. I was told you were all in favour of your C.C. calling me in. It's refreshing to find a man who knows when he's out of his depth and it's time to call in the expert. It's disgraceful the way some of these provincials cling to cases they haven't got a dog's chance of solving. And you won't lose by your attitude. I have no intention of grabbing all the glory. I'll see you get full credit with everybody, just as though we were equal partners.

Now, tell me everything you know about this case. And I mean what you *know*. I want facts, and facts *only*.'

'Very good, sir.' Wilkins perched himself on the edge of an upright chair and took a deep breath. He had been mentally rehearsing this moment, and he was able to give a clear yet concise account of the events leading up to the murder. Then he picked up a briefcase from the floor and extracted from it a cardboard folder.

'As to the crime itself, sir, I have here a list of all the occupants of the house; a sketch map showing where everyone was sleeping; the reports of the officers who were first on the scene, including statements from Lord and Lady Burford and all their guests; ballistics and medical reports, etc. And a transcript of the statement made at the station this morning by Carter. Perhaps you'd better read them.'

Allgood snatched the folder from him and began casting his eyes over its contents at an enormous speed. While he was doing so a footman entered, wheeling a tea trolley. Without looking up, Allgood said, 'Thank you, my man, we can serve ourselves.'

The footman departed. 'Pour me a cup of tea, Wilton,' Allgood said. 'And butter me two muffins.'

'Oh, yes, sir.'

By the time Wilkins had completed this task and was wiping his fingers on his handkerchief, Allgood had come to the last page of the folder. He threw it down on the table, picked up a white linen napkin, shook it open, spread it on his knees, took the plate which Wilkins proffered him, and began devouring muffins hungrily.

'That's all right, as far as it goes,' he said. 'Now let's have your personal report.'

'Well, sir, first I had an interview with his lordship.'

'Tell me exactly what he said.'

Wilkins complied to the best of his ability. When he'd finished, Allgood said, 'Is that all you got out of him?'

'Just about, sir.'

'Hm. I'm sure that's not all he can tell us. Who else have you spoken to?'

'Well, Carter, of course. Lady Geraldine – though that wasn't a formal interview. And the servants.'

'The servants? Couldn't you have let your sergeant deal with them?'

'Well, sir—'

'Never mind. Tell me what you learnt from the servants.'

'Nothing of any great significance. I'm sure they're OK.'

'Of course they are! Once it was always the butler who did it, but not these days. That's very old hat.'

'For what it's worth, one of them – the third footman, William – confirms that the deceased did go straight up to her room last night. He was on a sort of patrol they've organised, since the burglar alarm is out of order at the moment. He came up the stairs at the far end of the eastern corridor at five past one, and she was just coming round the corner at the near end. They passed each other about halfway along. He looked back just before he turned into the main corridor, and saw her go into her room and close the door after her. That's all I got from the resident servants. I did have hopes of learning something about Signorina Lorenzo from her French maid, Eloise. But no luck. She'd only been with her mistress four weeks, and knew hardly anything of her private life. All she was really able to tell me is that nothing is missing, apart from that mink coat. She's struck up a friendship with Lady Geraldine's maid, a very reliable French girl called Marie, who's been with Lady Geraldine six years. They sat up very late chatting in Marie's room last night. Were together from about midnight till two-thirty, when they were told about the murder. Except, that is, for a few minutes at about twelve-thirty, when Eloise went along to her mistress's room to make the fire up. So she wasn't really much help at all.'

Wilkins paused for breath. Allgood swallowed his last portion of muffin. 'Well, go on, man.'

'Oh, right, sir. What else is there? Let me see. Ah, yes. I telephoned the signorina's London agent and told him what had happened. She'd been going to visit him at his home today.'

'What did he have to say?'

'He was naturally terribly shocked, but he couldn't tell me anything important. He hadn't seen her since she'd arrived in London on Wednesday. She booked into the Savoy and phoned him on Thursday morning, saying she was coming to Alderley to see Mr Cyrus Haggermeir, the film producer. She'd be back in London on Saturday and would call at his home and tell him all about it. The only odd thing is that late last night it seems she tried to phone him, only the line here was down. She told Lady Burford that she wanted to inform him what time she'd be arriving today, and she also mentioned that he kept late hours. Well, firstly, he says he told her that he'd be in all day today, and she could visit any time. Secondly, he does *not* keep late hours – he's invariably in bed by eleven. So it seems—'

'—that the ostensible reason for the phone call last night was false, that she had something important she wanted to tell him. Interesting.' Allgood sipped his tea ruminatively. Then he said, 'This mink coat: if nobody's left the house, and you reject the idea that Carter threw it out of the window to a confederate, it must be still here.

Have you had a search made for it?'

'No, sir.'

'What about that telegram, the one which brought Signorina Lorenzo here? Made any inquiries about that at the Post Office?'

'Not yet, sir.' Wilkins took a sip of tea, grimaced, and quickly put the cup down.

'Hm. What about the other guests? What can you tell me about them?'

'Very little, really, sir.'

'Just the ones you've interviewed.'

'I haven't actually interviewed any of them.'

'None of them?'

'No, sir.'

'I see.' Allgood was silent for a moment before saying, 'Wilkins, I'm baffled.'

'Are you, sir? I'm sorry. Still, I'm sure you won't be for long. You must have cracked tougher cases than this one.'

'No, man. Not by the case. By you.'

'Me, sir?'

'Yes. A murder is committed. A man is found standing by the body, a gun in his hand. He runs away, then later gives himself up. You interview him, and then release him. From those reports I just can't see why. I have to regard him as the chief suspect. But – all right. That was your privilege. What I can't understand is, having concluded Carter is innocent, you then do virtually nothing. You believe a murderer is at large, yet apart from a fifteen-minute interview with the Earl and five minutes with his daughter, you waste a couple of hours questioning the servants – something that a sergeant or constable could do quite well. You don't institute a search for the missing coat, make no inquiries about the telegram, and don't question the other people who were staying here. Surely you must realise that *if*, as you believe, Carter is innocent, he was cleverly framed – and plainly by one of the other guests. Yet you haven't spoken to any of them. Haven't exactly covered yourself with glory, have you?'

'Probably not, sir. But then I never expect to. As to the mink, well, Alderley's a big place. A fur coat would roll up very small, and I haven't had men here. An exhaustive search would take an age. Besides, if I might just explain my theory about that business, the matter of the telegram, and what you said about Carter being framed, I—'

'No, Wilkins, you may not. I don't want to be cluttered up with other people's theories. They're almost invariably wrong, and I'm quite capable of formulating my own. So I'm not interested in what you *think*. Only in what you know. Clear?'

'As you wish, sir. But about interviewing the guests. Frankly, I'm not very good at interrogating the gentry – uneasy, as it were. I knew you'd do that much better than I could.'

'Naturally. All the same...Oh well, perhaps you're wise not to attempt too much.' Allgood spoke in a more kindly tone. 'And I don't suppose any great harm's been done by the delay.'

'Very good of you to say so, sir.'

Allgood put down his empty cup and wiped his mouth. 'However, what I must do now is find out about all these people: what they're like, what their relationships are to each other, just what's been happening here for the past two days. I need an objective account of things.'

'Where will you get that, sir?'

'Well, I won't get a completely objective one, of course. But the nearest thing to one will certainly come from their host and hostess. I take it you have no grounds for suspecting either of them of complicity in this crime?'

'Oh, no, sir.' Wilkins sounded quite shocked.

'Well, we're agreed on something. Not that it would have been the first murder committed by either an Earl or a Countess, but certainly neither Lord nor Lady Burford would murder a guest under their own roof. So we can rely on their testimony. They may not tell us everything they know, of course. But they won't lie. We'll get the truth and nothing but the truth, though maybe not the whole truth.'

'You'll see Carter first, I expect, though, sir, as you consider him the chief suspect?'

'No. Before I tackle him I need more information, more background. Otherwise I'm not likely to get any more out of him than you did. So go and find the Earl, give him my compliments, and ask him to come along here, will you?'

'Very good, sir.' Wilkins left the room.

CHAPTER SIXTEEN

Lord Burford came into the room a minute or so later, accompanied by Wilkins.

'Ah, Burford, come in,' Allgood said.

'Er, what can I do for you?'

'Just sit down and tell us all about this house party.' He indicated the armchair, which he'd vacated in favour of an upright chair he'd placed behind the room's only table.

The Earl blinked. '*All* about it?'

'As much as you can remember: the reason for it, how this particular combination of guests came about, anything you can tell us about them – especially, of course, every conceivable thing you know of Laura Lorenzo – any unusual incidents, conversations, and so on. Anything at all.'

'Good gad. Could take hours.'

'No matter. That's why I'm here.'

'Don't quite know where to begin.'

'Suppose we start off by my asking questions?'

Immediately he began interrogating the Earl. Allgood's manner became quite different from what it had been until now. He was less formidable, gentler and quieter, drawing the Earl out bit by bit, seeming almost to mesmerise him into remembering details he thought he'd completely forgotten. After three quarters of an hour nothing of significance which had happened in Lord Burford's purview since his guests had arrived was not also known to Allgood and Wilkins. He left the room in somewhat of a daze, promising to ask the Countess to step in.

'Anything particularly strike you, sir?' Wilkins asked.

'A number of things. Chiefly that business of the broken window in Ransom's room. Had the effect of putting the alarm out of action, which meant the windows could be opened at night – more than the inch or two they could otherwise have been raised. If the mink *was* thrown out, that accident was highly convenient. It might, as you said, roll up small, but not small enough to go easily through that sort of gap.'

Just then Lady Burford entered.

With the Countess Allgood's style was again subtly different. Exquisitely polite, he was however rather more incisive: sharper and quicker in putting his questions. Lady Burford had entered the room determined to say the bare minimum she could get away with. Her attitude was that the crime was nothing to do with her. None of her family or relations was involved, and *she* had not invited Laura, nor any of the other guests (apart from her cousin Cecily and her husband), to Alderley. If a member of the house party, other than Paul, was guilty, then it was plainly one of the film people. She had had little to do with any of them and so could not help in any way.

In spite of this resolve, however, the Countess found

herself gradually revealing more and more. She was almost reduced to gossiping. The fact dismayed and astonished her. But such was Allgood's technique that she seemed unable to help herself, even relating conversations she had had with Cecily – not to mention those with Maude Fry and Jemima Dove. At last Allgood thanked her and she departed, looking more than a little shaken.

The Chief Superintendent sat with his brows furrowed, staring down at the table and drumming on it with his fingers. Then he looked up.

Wilkins said, 'Carter now, sir?' He sounded apprehensive.

Allgood smiled. 'Not just yet. I want to see the scene of the crime. Take me up.'

Wilkins led him up to the second floor, and Allgood made a quick but thorough examination of Laura's bedroom. He glanced in the bathroom opposite, and with the help of Wilkin's plan familiarised himself with who occupied each of the bedrooms. They then went back down to the music room and Allgood said, 'Right. Now for Carter.'

Paul came warily into the room. He was very pale. Allgood eyed him keenly from under his bushy eyebrows, his eyes seeming to burn into Paul. Paul gazed back unflinchingly.

'Sit down,' Allgood ordered curtly.

Paul did so. Allgood said, 'Now, Carter, I have to tell you that I have absolutely cast-iron proof that you shot Signorina Lorenzo.'

From his position behind Paul, Wilkins stared at Allgood in amazement. Paul drew in a quick, sharp breath – but didn't move.

'So,' Allgood went on, 'further denial is useless and will only make things worse for you. Far better to plead manslaughter, or even call it an accident. So tell the truth now and I promise the police won't press for a murder charge. You won't hang.'

Paul looked at him long and silently. 'You're bluffing,' he said.

'What do you mean?'

'About having cast-iron proof. There isn't any. There couldn't be. Because I didn't do it.'

Allgood was quite unabashed. 'All right. I was bluffing. But if you *did* do it, there *is* evidence – somewhere. And I'll get it. And you will hang. You've got one more chance now to change your mind. The promise stands. Understood?'

'Yes.'

'Well.'

'I'm changing nothing.'

'As you wish. Then give me your version of what happened.'

'I've already given it to Wilkins.'

'Now give it to me.'

'Well, in the first place, Gerry and I didn't get back from the party until nearly two a.m. last night. That was because I ran out of petrol.'

Allgood cut him short. 'No, no, start much earlier.'

'At what point?'

'At Signorina Lorenzo's arrival on Thursday afternoon.'

'Are you serious?'

'Perfectly. Recount to me everything you can

remember about what people said and did. Then tell me about the talk you mentioned to Wilkins, which you had with her on Friday morning, and go on to an account of the events of Friday evening – up until the time you left this party at Sir James Needham's.'

'Well, I'll do my best.'

Paul's account, though hesitant and somewhat abbreviated, was accurate in all essential respects. When he'd finished, Allgood gave a nod.

'Very good. Now you can revert to the point at which you were going to start earlier.'

This time Paul's narrative was virtually identical with that given to Wilkins at the police station. Then began one of the toughest and most searching interrogations Wilkins had ever heard. Drawing solely on memory, Allgood went over the whole of Paul's story, throwing question after question about every conceivable aspect of it, trying to make him slip up or contradict himself. Wilkins found his admiration for Allgood's technique growing every second.

At the end of twenty minutes Paul was sweating. But he hadn't budged from his story. It was a display as impressive as Allgood's own.

Eventually Allgood said, 'Now tell me about your relationship with the other people in this house.'

'What, all of them?'

'Start with your fellow guests.'

'Well, there isn't one – a relationship, I mean. I didn't know any of them except Hugh Quartus before Thursday, and my conversation with most of them has been limited to small talk. I've had a couple of yarns with Rex Ransom.'

'And what about Quartus?'

'I'd met him a few times.'

'And you don't get on?'

'Not really.'

'Was last night the first time you've come to blows?'

'We didn't come to blows.'

'That wasn't for want of trying, though, was it?'

'Well, nothing like it has ever happened before. We were just cold and tired and irritable. And I suppose he was a bit jealous.'

'Of you and Lady Geraldine?' Paul nodded. 'You're in love with her?'

'Yes.'

'And she with you?'

'I – I think so. I hope so.'

'And Quartus resents this?'

'Naturally. Wouldn't you?'

'Are you suggesting he resents it enough to try and frame you for murder?'

'Of course not! He wouldn't do a thing like that.'

'Yet you're saying somebody did.'

'The frame-up needn't have been set specifically for me – just for anyone who came along the corridor at the right time.'

'I see. Very well, Carter, that'll be all.'

'Aren't you going to charge me?'

'When I decide to charge you, you'll be the first to know.'

Paul got up a little uncertainly, threw a glance at Wilkins, crossed to the door, and went out. Wilkins looked at Allgood, who'd started writing busily, and cleared his throat.

'Well, sir?'

Allgood looked up. 'Well, what?'

'What do you think about Mr Carter? Was I right not to—?'

'My thoughts remain my own, Wilkins, until I've seen everybody. Next, I want to see—' He broke off as a knock came at the door and barked, 'Come.'

The door opened and Sergeant Leather came in. He addressed Wilkins. 'Sorry to interrupt, sir. I've been waiting outside for you to finish with Mr Carter.'

'What is it?' Allgood asked.

'I thought you'd want to see this straight away, sir.' He brought his hand from behind his back and for a split second Wilkins thought he was carrying the body of a drowned cat. Then he realised the truth. 'The mink!'

'Yes, sir. Sorry to roll it up like this, but I thought you mightn't want Mr Carter or anyone else to spot it before you saw it.'

'Where was it?' Allgood snapped.

'Outside, sir. Right underneath Miss Lorenzo's window. It's soaking wet. Must have been there since about the time of the murder. Thrown out of the window, if you ask me.'

'I don't,' Allgood said. 'Why wasn't it spotted before?'

'Covered in snow, sir. There's been quite a little drift there. The coat was spread out as though it had sort of floated down. It lay on the snow drift and then another layer formed on top of it. It's been thawing during the course of the day and gradually the coat was exposed.'

Wilkins nodded to himself in a satisfied way. 'I had a

kind of feeling it would turn up of its own accord sooner or later.'

Allgood glanced at him sharply before saying to Leather, 'You should have left it where it was.'

'I would have, sir. But one of the maids spotted it when she went to draw the curtains in one of the ground floor rooms. Slipped straight out, picked it up and brought it to me. I was having a spot of tea in the kitchen at the time.'

'Looked in the pockets?' Wilkins asked.

'Yes, sir, but there's nothing. There is something curious about it, though. Take a look.'

Leather gave a shake to the wet bundle of fur and the folds fell open. He held the coat by the shoulders and raised it high. 'See what I mean, sir?'

Allgood and Wilkins both stared.

In four different parts of the coat jagged holes had been cut.

Allgood's eyes narrowed. 'Extraordinary! Why the deuce...?' He stopped and was silent for a few seconds before saying, 'Lay it down on the floor.'

Leather did so. Allgood knelt down by it and examined the holes in turn. Each one was of a different shape, but all were about four or five inches across. Allgood remained kneeling, staring down at the coat without speaking for a full minute before suddenly getting to his feet, picking up the coat as he did so.

He said, 'I want to see where these holes come when the coat's being worn. Wilkins, it'll fit you better than the sergeant or me. Put it on.'

Wilkins took the coat gingerly. 'Bit wet, sir.'

'Only for a minute or so, man. You're not made of sugar!'

Leather helped Wilkins into the coat and he stood, looking rather absurd, as Allgood walked slowly round him.

Two of the holes were in the back: one up high in the left shoulder, the other about six inches from the bottom, in the centre. The third was also low down, in the front, while the fourth was in the left breast.

Leather said, 'Just sheer vandalism, do you think, sir? Someone venting their hatred?'

Allgood made an impatient gesture for him to be silent. His brow was furrowed in thought. Eventually he gave a shake of his head. 'It's no good. I'll need time to work it out. Get it off, Wilkins. All right, sergeant, take it away. But mind you keep it safe.'

'Right, sir.' Leather went to the door and opened it. Then he stopped. Gerry was standing outside.

She said, 'I want to see Mr Allgood.' She came into the room.

Allgood said, 'Ah, Lady Geraldine? What can I do for you?'

'I want to say I don't think it's fair, the way you're treating Paul. Mr Wilkins has cleared him once. Why can't you accept that – or at least tell him exactly where he stands? The suspense is killing him.'

'It wasn't suspense that killed Laura Lorenzo.'

'But Paul didn't do that.'

'You have evidence for that assertion?'

'No, but the idea's absurd. I know him.'

'Then who do you think did do it?'

'Arlington Gilbert.'

'Why him?'

She took a deep breath. 'I'll have to tell you rather a long story. It's a little embarrassing, I'm afraid. It all started with a silly and impulsive practical joke.'

'It's obvious what he was after in the study,' Gerry concluded, a few minutes later. 'The key to the gun room. I don't think he got it then. When I disturbed him the safe was definitely locked. Perhaps, though, he'd just been checking that the key actually was there, ready for the following night, and had already re-closed it. There'd have been lots of opportunities to go back on Friday and get it. Though don't ask me how he knew the combination.'

'And you say that on Friday morning Signorina Lorenzo seemed very anxious to speak to him?'

She nodded. 'And she stayed with him quite a long time.'

'Do you have any corroboration for any of this story?' Allgood asked.

She stiffened, 'No.'

'Pity.'

'I'm surprised you think it's necessary.' Her voice was cold.

'Corroboration is always useful if I'm going to question someone about alleged suspicious behaviour.'

'Oh, you are going to do that, then?' she said sarcastically.

'Naturally. But with nobody else involved, he has only to deny the whole thing.'

'Nobody else was involved in my encounter with him,

but he was mixed up in some other funny business.'

'What precisely?'

'You'll have to ask—' She broke off.

'Ask whom?'

She hesitated. 'I was going to say Rex Ransom. But it won't do any good. He'll probably deny it.'

'Why should he?'

'I don't know. But, well – I hate to say this, because I like him – but in the circumstances I suppose I've got to tell you. He really behaved very oddly.'

'Can you be a bit more specific?'

She recounted first Rex's request for her to let Gilbert stay on, then their conversation while out riding, and finally told about her visit to his suite the previous night.

'What time was this last conversation?' Allgood asked.

'About ten past two. I looked at my wrist watch just before I left my room.'

'And you left Ransom how long before you heard the shot?'

'About five minutes.'

'And then you ran the full length of the two corridors and found Carter holding the gun?'

'That's right.'

'Very well, Lady Geraldine, rest assured I shall look into all these matters. Now, is there any further information you wish to give me? Any other unusual incidents you can remember? Anything you learnt about the other guests that might be significant? Any interesting conversations?'

'No.'

'Anything you can tell me about Laura Lorenzo?'

'I don't think—' She stopped.

'You've thought of something?'

'It's very trivial.'

'I'll be the judge of that.'

'It's just that when I went to her room to tell her we were ready to leave, she was writing a letter. She put it out of sight in her writing case – rather furtively, I thought. And she was over-eager to tell me quite unnecessarily that it was a reply to a fan.'

'Which you don't believe?'

'No. Paul said it was probably just a love letter to a boyfriend back home, but I think it was to her agent in London. Then, when she discovered she'd missed the post, she decided to telephone him that night. But our phone was out of order. It must have been important.'

'What did she do with the letter?'

'Put it in the dressing-table drawer, still inside the writing case.'

When Gerry had left, Allgood said to Wilkins 'Your men went through the deceased's effects?'

'Yes, sir. There was no letter among them.'

'Then where is it?'

'Presumably the murderer took it, sir.'

'Possibly. Which would mean it was incriminating to him in some way. But let's not jump to conclusions. The lady might have burnt it herself. After all, if Lady Geraldine's right about it – and it seems a plausible theory – the signorina was expecting to see her agent before any letter could reach him. Why she should *bother* to burn it, I don't know. However, let's assume she did throw it on the fire when she got back—'

Allgood broke off in mid-sentence. Slowly he stood up.

The expression on his face had suddenly changed. It was as if a great light had dawned.

'Thought of something, sir?' Wilkins asked.

Allgood didn't answer. 'The fire in her room. It was a big one, wasn't it?'

'Yes, very big, by all accounts, sir. Several people mentioned how hot it was in there.'

Allgood strode across the room, jerked open the door and gave a yell. 'Sergeant!'

A rather alarmed-looking Leather arrived within seconds.

'Where's that fur coat?' Allgood barked.

'Locked in the car outside, sir, waiting to be taken to the station for—'

'Fetch it, quick!'

Leather hurried away. Allgood went to the piano, switched on a lamp that stood on it and took from an inside pocket a powerful magnifying glass. Leather arrived at a run, carrying the mink. Allgood positively snatched it from him and – holding it close up under the lamp and using the glass – carefully scrutinised the material round one of the holes. Wilkins saw that it was the one in the left breast.

Thirty seconds, then nearly a minute, passed. Allgood lowered the glass and raised his head. There was a strange gleam of triumph in his eyes. He addressed Leather.

'Sergeant, go and fetch Carter here immediately.'

'Yes, sir.'

Wilkins' face was suddenly pale. Quietly he said, 'Don't say – don't say you've found proof, sir.'

'Yes, Wilkins. I think I can say I have.'

Wilkins sat down slowly. 'Oh,' he said.

A minute later Leather returned, accompanied by an angry-looking Paul followed by Gerry. Allgood turned to face him. His expression was grim.

Gerry said, 'Look, how much more of this is he expected to put up with? It's disgraceful.'

'Please be quiet,' Allgood said.

He moved close to Paul, and unobtrusively Leather edged round to stand between Paul and the door.

Allgood spoke heavily. 'Paul Edward Carter, as you are aware, I am a police officer. I am inquiring into the murder of Laura Lorenzo. It is now my duty to—' He paused.

Then, utterly unexpectedly, he smiled. '– my *pleasant* duty to inform you that you are no longer suspected of the crime.' He held out his hand. 'Congratulations.'

At Allgood's words, Gerry gave a whoop of joy. Paul, however, said nothing. His face was white. He swallowed, then like an automaton slowly reached forward and took Allgood's hand.

'You mean that?' he said thickly.

'I do. You're a very lucky chap.'

The colour was slowly returning to Paul's face. He said, 'You're a cad, you know, to frighten me like that.'

'Sorry. Just my little joke. Couldn't resist it. If you want to sock me on the beak I shall quite understand.'

Paul managed a wan smile. 'It's tempting, but no. I'm just too grateful.' He turned to Gerry, who came up and took his arm. 'Well, sweetheart,' he said, 'looks as if the nightmare's over.'

She nodded happily. 'So Inspector Wilkins was right?'

'Yes, and I give him full credit for it,' Allgood said. 'Unfortunately' – he smiled – 'he was right for entirely the wrong reasons.' He crossed to Wilkins and put a hand on his shoulder. 'Wilkins, you have a natural flair for detective work. You're what I call an instinctive or intuitive detective. Take my advice: learn to reason, to use logic. I think in time you could become quite an effective investigator.'

'Thank you, sir,' Wilkins said.

Allgood redirected his attention to Paul. 'Want to apologise, old man, for putting you through all that cross-questioning. Unfortunately it was essential. By the way, understand you were at Eton. What years? Wondering if we overlapped?'

They moved to one side a little. Gerry looked closely at Wilkins. 'You all right, Mr Wilkins?'

'Oh, yes, my lady, thank you.'

'You don't look well.'

'I expect that's just reaction, as they say.'

Her face cleared. 'Oh, I see. *You* thought he was going to arrest Paul, too?'

'Yes, my lady, for a minute or two there I really did.'

'Which would have made you look a bit silly, I suppose. Well, he didn't. You've been vindicated. Congratulations.'

'They're not called for, my lady.'

'But you were right! Oh, you mean what he said about the wrong reasons? But the reasons aren't really important, are they? Besides, it's only a matter of opinion. I bet your reasons were just as valid as his. What were his reasons, anyway?'

'I'm not quite sure, my lady.'

'Well, I'll soon find out.' She turned back to Allgood. 'Chief Superintendent, may we know how you came to the conclusion that Paul was innocent?'

Allgood hesitated. 'Well, I suppose it won't do any harm. After all, if we let the story get around, it'll show the real killer what he's up against it. Well, it all swings on this.'

He picked up the mink for them to see and briefly ran through the circumstances of its discovery. Then he said, 'Let's see if Chief Inspector Wilkins can explain my reasoning.'

Wilkins blushed. 'Well, sir, you were examining the fur round that hole in the front. You found something. I would guess traces of blood?'

'Right. And plainly Laura Lorenzo's blood – though, of course, we'll have to get that confirmed by the lab. Now, what does that tell us?'

'That she was wearing it when she was murdered. The killer removed it from the body and threw it out of the window afterwards.'

'Precisely. There you are: you see, Wilkins, you can do it. Go on. What about the hole?'

'You mean, sir, that he cut the fur away just to remove the bullet hole?'

'Of course. And no doubt burnt it. It could only have been done after she was shot. Carter couldn't conceivably have done it in the time that elapsed between the shot being heard and Lady Geraldine arriving. Which means that, as Carter said, *that* shot was a blind, and she was really killed earlier. It's not this which proves Carter's innocence, of course, since he could easily have fired both shots himself. What really clears him – as the murderer must have realised at the last moment – is the mere fact that the lady was wearing the coat when she was killed; a fact given away by the existence of the bullet hole and the blood.'

Paul frowned. 'I'm sorry, and maybe I'm dense, but you'll have to explain that.'

Allgood was positively beaming by now. He said, 'Well, Wilkins, can you oblige the gentleman?'

'I'm afraid not, sir. It's got me beat.'

'Listen, in that bedroom there was a very big open fire. Several people commented on the heat in there, even with the door open. And we know that at about twelve-thirty the maid Eloise went in to make up the fire. Then, at about five past one, a footman saw Signorina Lorenzo enter the room and close the door after her. By then it must have been like an oven in there. Now, even granted that the lady was used to a warm climate and liked heat, it's inconceivable she would have kept her coat on for more than two or three minutes after going in. One of the very first things she would have done would be to take it off.'

Gerry said excitedly, 'Which means she must have been shot almost as soon as she went in!'

'Exactly, Lady Geraldine. Or before one-ten, at the latest, a time when Carter was still four miles from the house, stuck at the side of the road out of petrol – a fact vouched for by you, Lady Geraldine, and by Quartus.'

Wilkins was nodding slowly. Almost to himself, he said, 'Yes, I see. That's it. Very clever indeed.'

Allgood looked amused. 'Thank you, Chief Inspector,' he said, and there was irony in his voice. 'I assume you concur with my findings?'

'Oh, yes, sir. The murder was committed before ten past one, all right.'

'Most gratified.' Allgood gave him a mock bow.

'But what exactly happened?' Paul asked.

Allgood, now in high good humour, was eager to explain. 'The murderer got to the room before Signorina Lorenzo, and waited for her. He shot her almost as soon as she came in, took that letter – the one she'd been writing – from the drawer, and put the gun outside in the corridor. He had a second gun ready, to fire the alarm shot. He left the door open an inch and waited to give a groan as soon as he heard someone come along the corridor, stop and pick up the gun.'

'Someone?' Paul said. 'Not me specifically?'

'I don't think so. He couldn't have known you'd use that bathroom – though maybe, on the other hand, he didn't realise you usually went to the other one. I would say he just thought it inevitable that *somebody* – most likely you or Quartus or Miss Fry – would come along. But time passed and nobody did. You, Carter, had been delayed, and Quartus had gone out again to look for you. According to her statement, Miss Fry had entered her room before Signorina Lorenzo came upstairs, and didn't leave it again. We can imagine the murderer becoming more and more frantic as no one came, and then suddenly realising the point about the bullet hole in the coat giving away the actual time of death. His attempt at a frame-up was ruined, but his mind must have worked like lightning. There was a pair of scissors on the dressing-table, and it wouldn't have taken him more than a couple of minutes to cut the holes. No doubt he burnt the pieces he cut out. Then he threw the coat out the window.'

'Why?' Gerry asked.

'Well, the best way out of the coat problem would really be for it to disappear entirely. Perhaps he thought that if he got it out of the house temporarily, there was just a chance he might be able to dispose of it the following day. Failing that, however, then at least the holes would conceal the fact Laura Lorenzo was wearing it when she was shot. And they would have, had he not been a little bit careless in cutting round the bullet hole and left traces of blood. But, of course, he was working under great pressure.'

'Why cut four holes?'

'Camouflage, Lady Geraldine: to draw attention away from that particular hole, to disguise the reason for it.'

There was silence for a few seconds before Paul said, 'Isn't it odd that nobody heard the first shot?'

'I don't think it is,' Gerry said. 'The walls and doors here are so thick and solid that sound just doesn't carry. We found that out last time, didn't we, Mr Wilkins?'

'Yes, indeed, your ladyship. In addition, of course, the next door room is that of Mr Quartus, and he was out of it at the time.'

'There is another possibility,' Allgood said. 'He could have used a silencer. I must ask the Earl, if he owns a silencer for that gun, to check if it's still there.'

Paul said, 'That second gun – the one that fired the

alarm shot – you think that was the killer's own?'

'Well, there are no other guns missing from the collection, so it must have been. But obviously, it won't still be in his possession.'

'You mean he'll have hidden it in the house somewhere?' Paul said eagerly. 'Well, surely, if you search for it...'

'Oh, we will, in time. But it won't do a lot of good to find it, except to provide additional confirmation of your story. Plainly it won't be one that can be traced to the killer, since he could easily have stolen a second gun from the collection if he'd needed to. And he won't have been such a fool to have left his prints on it.'

Gerry was frowning. 'Where did that second bullet go? The window in Laura's room was closed, and so was the one at the end of the corridor. Or did he use a blank?'

'He might have, though I doubt it. If he brought blanks with him it would probably mean he'd planned the scheme before he arrived, which seems highly unlikely. No, remember the door of the bathroom is almost across the corridor from the bedroom, and the window in the bathroom is opposite the door. What's more, the window was open when I was up there a short while ago. Probably he opened it in advance. That wouldn't cause any comment, as people tend to open bathroom windows even in very cold weather, to let steam out. So all he would have had to do, after shoving Carter in the back, was stand in the corridor and fire his gun through the open bathroom door and out of the window. Then he could slip down the stairs, or actually into the bathroom itself, closing the door after him. A few seconds later he could quietly join the crowd which had gathered in the doorway. He could rely on nobody else looking anywhere but into the bedroom, though even if somebody did spot him coming out of the bathroom it would hardly cause any comment.'

Gerry gave a little shiver. 'He sounds awfully clever, doesn't he?'

'Yes, we're dealing with a very smart and ruthless criminal. However, one perhaps not quite as smart as he believes himself to be. Part of his scheme's gone wrong already. And he's one of a very small circle of suspects, some of whom will probably have alibis. So it shouldn't be too hard to root him out.'

She stared. 'You mean that?'

'Oh, yes. I expect to have him under lock and key by Monday. But if not, on Tuesday we'll start digging into the backgrounds of all the suspects – and Signorina Lorenzo – checking for past connections, possible motives, police records, and so on. The truth is bound to come out then.'

'I hope you're right,' she said. 'Incidentally, will you be starting your questioning tonight? Mummy was wondering about dinner.'

Allgood looked at his watch. 'I had meant to begin interviewing this evening, but all these developments have made it a bit late for that now. So tell them they can relax tonight, or at least the innocent ones can. I shall go to my room and spend a couple of hours in intense thought. I'll start my interrogations in the morning.'

'May I also tell them Paul is in the clear?'

'By all means.'

'And what you've discovered about the actual time of the murder, the mink and everything?'

'I don't see why not.'

She gave a grin. 'Spiffing. Come on, Paul, this is going to be fun.'

She took his hand, hurried him to the door and opened it. Then she stopped. Leaning up against the wall outside, his hands in his pockets, was Hugh.

She said, 'Oh, isn't it marvellous? Mr Allgood's completely cleared Paul of the murder.'

'Really?' He cocked an eye at Paul. 'Congratulations.'

'Thanks.'

Hugh sauntered into the room. Gerry said, 'She was killed much earlier than anybody thought – almost as soon as she got home. Paul was out with me then. So he's got an alibi.'

'I see. And that must mean I have, too.' He gazed coolly at Allgood. 'Is that right? Am I cleared, also?'

Allgood said, 'You're Quartus, correct?'

Hugh bowed his head.

'Let me see. You were downstairs, in full sight of the Earl and Countess when Signorina Lorenzo went up to her room. You left the house almost immediately, drove four miles, found Lady Geraldine and Carter, and brought her back with you, arriving here at about one-fifty. Is that right?'

'Hundred per cent.'

'Then, yes, Quartus, you're in the clear.'

Hugh nodded casually. 'Good.'

'That's wonderful!' Gerry said excitedly. 'Thank heavens Paul ran out of petrol!' She took Hugh's arm. 'Come on, we're going to tell the others.'

He shook his head. 'You go on. I want to talk to the law.'

'OK.' She and Paul left the room.

'I've been wanting to speak to one of you all day,' Hugh said, 'but thought I'd better wait until I was sent for. However, if I wait any longer it won't be worth bothering at all.'

'To do what?' Allgood asked a little coldly.

'To report a stolen motor-bike.'

CHAPTER SEVENTEEN

'A motorcycle?' Allgood looked annoyed. 'I am hardly the person and this is hardly the time to—'

'No? All right, I'll go and report it to the village bobby. Only as it was taken Friday night, shortly before the murder, I thought you might be interested.'

'Stolen from here?' Allgood was suddenly alert.

'Yes.' Hugh explained the circumstances.

'And the thief left the sidecar?' Allgood frowned. 'What an extraordinary thing. But I can't see any possible connection with the murder.'

Hugh said, 'The talk at first was of the motive being robbery and the fur coat being thrown out of the window to an accomplice. Although I see the coat's been found' – he nodded towards the piano, on which Allgood had put it down – 'it occurred to me that that might have been the original plan and they took my bike as a getaway vehicle.'

Allgood looked dubious. 'Well, it's a possibility, I suppose. Anyway, thank you for telling us.'

'I want it back, so put out an all-points bulletin, or whatever you call it, won't you? It's a jolly good machine.'

'That'll come under my jurisdiction, sir,' Wilkins said. 'I'll see to it.'

'Thanks.' Hugh went out.

Allgood sat silently thinking for a minute or so, until there came a knock at the door. It was Paul again.

Allgood said, 'Ah, Carter, how was Lady Geraldine's announcement received?'

'Oh, reasonably well. Everybody was very nice to me. The Earl apologised first, and then all the others – even though I'm far from certain they're all convinced. Particularly as it gradually sank in that if I'm innocent, they now understand they're all suspects. And when Gerry told them what you said about probing into their private affairs if the case wasn't solved by Monday, the atmosphere became a little strained.'

'Excellent! That should make all the innocent ones very eager to cooperate.'

'Lady Burford, of course, backed up by cousin Cecily, now maintains that the murder must have been committed by some passing tramp, who is now miles away. I think we're all going to pretend to go along with that, for the sake of normality. To admit openly that one of your companions is a murderer would make the situation intolerable. Why I came back, though, was to talk about silencers. Gerry told her father what you said. I offered to bring his reply. He has a dozen or more of the things. Seems he used to fit them to every pistol possible, so he could fire them without disturbing people too much. But since he's had that little shooting range put up, and the room is properly soundproofed, he's never bothered. They're all kept with the ammunition, and he couldn't possibly say if one is missing.'

Allgood nodded. 'I see. Well, it doesn't really matter. We know the shot was fired. Why it wasn't heard isn't vitally important.'

'Right. I'll tell him.' Paul started to turn away but hesitated.

Allgood eyed him keenly. 'There's something else, isn't there?'

Paul smiled. 'How did you know?'

'Why should *you* have brought the message about the silencers? It was a pretext. You wanted to see me again, and I would guess without Lady Geraldine being present.'

'Doesn't anybody ever fool you?'

'Not for long. Well, what is it?'

'It's a bit awkward, actually. But you said you wanted to be told of any unusual incidents.'

'You've remembered something?'

'I never really forgot it, but my own troubles sort of drove it from my mind. I'm not at all sure it's relevant.'

'Never mind.'

Paul collected his thoughts. 'Yesterday morning I discovered I'd lost my fountain pen.'

'And that's all I heard,' Paul concluded. 'Suddenly the voice just faded and there was silence. I waited for a couple of minutes, then opened the panel and stepped into the room. There was nobody there.'

Allgood shook his head. 'Remarkable.'

Wilkins said, 'Mr Carter, could you explain why you didn't tell us, or anybody else, any of this before?'

Paul wriggled uncomfortably. 'Well, dash it all, it was a bit tricky. I'd been eavesdropping. Quite unintentionally and all that, but it seemed hardly the done thing to take advantage of the situation.'

Allgood nodded sympathetically. 'Yes, one can understand that. But surely you couldn't have just ignored the matter altogether. You obviously had some sort of obligation to the family.'

'Of course. I didn't know what to do. I mentioned to Gerry that I'd heard something very odd, but not what it was. She advised me to wait. Then, as you can imagine, the murder put it out of my mind. When I did start to think about it again, I couldn't decide if it had anything to do with the murder.'

'Well, you can rely on me to look into it fully, Carter. Please don't say anything about the matter to anybody from now on.'

'Right. It's a weight off my mind.'

At that moment they heard the faint sound of the dinner gong. Paul said, 'I must go. An event unique in the annals of Alderley is about to take place: we're not dressing for dinner. Whether Merryweather will ever recover I don't know.' He went out.

'What do you make of that, sir?' Wilkins said.

'Well, assuming he's telling the truth, and I'm sure he is—'

'Yes, I agree, sir.'

Allgood frowned. '*If* I may finish, Chief Inspector.'

'Sorry, sir.'

'And if he heard and understood correctly, it opens up an entirely new aspect of the case. His allowing himself to be overheard by Carter like that suggests to me that our friend may be a little careless. After all, everyone knew of the existence of the passage, it seems. What's more, we know that the murderer can be careless, too. So it might be worthwhile having a search of his room.'

'Now, sir?'

'Yes, while everyone's in the dining-room. Wait here.'

He left the room. Wilkins thankfully lowered himself into the nearest chair and lit a cigarette.

It was ten minutes before Allgood reappeared. There was a gleam of triumph in his eyes. He opened his pocket book and extracted a piece of paper about four inches square. 'No incriminating documents, or anything of that kind – all been burnt, without doubt. But this escaped. It was down behind the coal scuttle.'

He held the piece of paper out for Wilkins to get a closer look. It was charred all round the edges and covered with writing in ink. Wilkins read this and nodded slowly.

'Suggestive, isn't it?' Allgood said.

'Yes, sir, but ambiguous.'

'Of course; there are only, what, forty words altogether?'

'Do you know whose writing it is, sir?'

'It'll have to be checked by an expert, of course. But there's no real doubt in my mind that it's Laura Lorenzo's. It means that that letter she was writing wasn't intended for her agent, after all. And it provides us with a real motive at last.'

'So do you intend to make an arrest now?'

'Good heavens, no. It's far from certain yet. There are lots of loose ends. I'm going to keep this in reserve, produce it at an opportune moment.' He put the piece of paper away again.

'Should be a most interesting moment, sir.' He coughed. 'Is that everything for tonight?'

'Want to knock off?'

'Well, it has been a long day.'

'That's all right. You toddle off home to your beans-on-toast and cocoa. See you in the morning.'

'Actually, sir, I was going to ask if you'll need me tomorrow.'

'Need you? No, of course I won't *need* you. If you've got another case in hand you have to deal with, by all means do so.'

'It's not that, sir. Matter of fact, it's my day off.'

Allgood looked as if he couldn't believe his cars. 'Day off? You're not serious.'

'Yes, sir. And as you said you don't actually need me, I thought I'd get my feet up for a bit – take it easy, you know.'

'Ye gods!' Allgood looked up at the ceiling in despair. 'You'd actually stay home, taking it easy when you could be here, assisting me in a murder inquiry?'

'Well, I don't get all that many days off, sir.'

'But what about what you called the privilege of assisting me – all you were going to learn?'

'I've seen you at work now, sir. I've assisted a bit. It'll give me something to talk about for the rest of my life. As to what I'd learn, well, you can't teach an old dog new tricks. I'd never be able to conduct a case like you do. I'll probably blunder on in my own way, whatever happens. Of course, Sergeant Leather will be here all day, to assist in any way you want. He wouldn't miss it for the world. But, then, he's ambitious.'

Allgood shook his head in disbelief. 'All right, you take it easy tomorrow. I'll solve your little murder for you, without your help.'

'Oh, thank you, sir. That's very kind of you. In that case I'll say good night – and good luck, sir.'

He went out. Allgood stared at the door as it closed after him. He gave a sigh. 'Pathetic,' he said to himself.

'I say, my boy, what's all this about a missing motorbike?' Lord Burford asked the question over coffee in the drawing-room later that evening.

Hugh shrugged. 'That's all there is about it, Lord Burford. My motorcycle's missing. From your stable yard.' Somewhat reluctantly he recounted the story to the room at large.

When he'd finished the Earl shook his head. 'Very odd. 'Course, we're insured against theft here, if you're not, so no need to worry from that point of view. Deuced annoying for you, all the same.'

Jemima Dove, who was sitting nearby, said, 'Er.'

The Earl glanced at her. 'Yes, my dear?'

She went a little pink. 'Well, this may sound silly, but I suppose it wouldn't be your motorcycle that's up in the picture gallery, would it, Mr Quartus?'

Everybody in the room turned to stare at Jemima, as though she were crazy. She gazed back out of big grey eyes, and her pinkness suddenly intensified.

It was Lord Burford who broke the silence. 'The picture gallery, Miss Dove? Do you – I mean, you quite, er…?'

She showed the first real sign of animation since her arrival. 'Yes, of course!'

'You're saying there's a motor-bike in the picture gallery?'

'Yes, down at the end. Nearly hidden behind a sofa.'

'But how did you come to know?'

'I – I was looking round there. I wanted to stay out of everybody's way as much as possible today. People kept using the library, and it was a bit boring in my room. I'm fond of pictures, so I decided to have a look in the gallery. I didn't see the motor-bike at first. It's not noticeable until you get quite close.'

'But you didn't say anything about it,' Hugh exclaimed.

'No. Why should I have? It was nothing to do with me.'

'But weren't you surprised to find a motor-bike in a picture gallery?'

'I thought it a little odd. But I decided there had to be some good reason for it.'

Hugh got to his feet. 'I'll go and take a look.'

Jemima jumped up, too. 'I'll come and show you.'

'Oh, there's no need.'

'I'd like to.' Her face was still very red, and it was obvious she only wanted an excuse to get out of the room. So he didn't argue and they went out together.

'Well, that's certainly my bike,' Hugh said. 'But what maniac brought it up here? And why the dickens didn't anyone else spot it?'

Almost apologetically Jemima said, 'Well, one doesn't really notice it unless one looks directly at the sofa. I didn't see it until I'd been in the room a few minutes. And I don't suppose many other people have been in here last night or today.'

'Well, better get it downstairs and back outside, I suppose.' He stepped towards the bike.

'Oh, do you think you should?' she said diffidently. 'I was wondering if this could possibly have anything to do with the murder.'

'It might have, I suppose, though I honestly can't see how. Why?'

'I was thinking perhaps – though I know nothing about these things, really – whether, if there is the possibility of a connection, the police would want to test it for fingerprints.'

He looked thoughtful. 'Hm, maybe you're right. Though I imagine most criminals know enough to use gloves these days. Still, I suppose it may be advisable not to touch it until we've spoken to the police. And it's probably better off here than anywhere.'

They turned to leave. Hugh's eye fell on a long, stout wooden plank, about fifteen feet by twelve inches, which was lying on the floor against the side wall. 'Wonder what that's doing here.'

'I wondered about that, too. I thought perhaps decorators. They put them between step ladders.'

'Possibly.' He glanced round. 'Not that it looks as if they've had decorators in here lately.'

'Perhaps they're coming soon and brought the plank in advance.'

'Perhaps.'

They walked to the door. 'Will you tell that policeman tonight?' she asked.

'No, our great detective apparently needs several hours of undisturbed meditation. Tomorrow will do.'

They were about to leave the gallery when Hugh

stopped. Jemima glanced at him curiously. He said, 'I knew there was some little thing wrong with that bike. The penny's just dropped. The petrol cap's not on properly.'

He walked back to the motor-bike. Jemima waited by the door until he rejoined her a minute later. 'Someone's put petrol in the tank,' he said.

'Really? How odd. I mean why, if they didn't intend to ride it away?'

'Your guess is as good as mine. Anyway, many thanks for finding it. Come on.'

They went out. Hugh closed the door and made to lock it. Then he paused. 'Oh, no key.'

'Is that important? It's been unlocked all day.'

'Agreed. But I would like to be able to assure old Allbad that the bike hasn't been tampered with since I found it. Look, sorry to bother you, but I wonder if you'd mind going and asking the Earl if he's got a key to this door. I'll wait here, just to be on the safe side.'

'Oh, yes, certainly.' She walked off.

It was ten minutes before Lord Burford came along the corridor, carrying a large key. 'Sorry to keep you waiting, Hugh. Had to find this.'

'That's all right. Before you lock up – it's none of our business, really, but Miss Dove and I were wondering about this.'

He went back into the gallery and pointed at the plank. The Earl stared. 'Great Scott! Where did that come from?'

'We thought about decorators – recently departed or imminent?'

'No, no plans that way at all. It's another mystery.

Oh, lor', I'm getting so fed up with them.'

They left the gallery again and Lord Burford locked the door and pocketed the key. Saying he wanted an early night, Hugh then went to his room, while the Earl rejoined his guests downstairs.

It turned out, however, that none of them was in the mood for sitting up very late. Nobody had got a lot of sleep the previous night, and mentally it had been an exhausting day for everyone. It was, therefore, almost as a group that the entire party shortly afterwards went upstairs. Paul remained very close to Gerry and walked with her to the door of her bedroom. She was just going in when he took her hand.

'Sweetheart, do me a favour: after Marie leaves, lock your doors.'

She gave him a startled look 'Why?'

'There's a murderer in the house, Gerry.'

'But he wouldn't want to kill me.'

'I expect that's what Laura thought. Will you, darling? Promise?'

'Oh, all right, you old fusspot, if it's going to keep you happy.'

'Thanks.' He gave her a kiss. 'And before Marie leaves make sure there's nobody hiding in there.'

'You know something,' she said, 'you couldn't be more protective if we were man and wife.'

'Gerry, darling, you know—'

She put a hand on his lips. 'Not tonight, Paul. Plenty of time for that when this is all over. Sweet dreams, darling.'

She went into her room and shut the door. Paul made his way to his own room with a song in his heart.

CHAPTER EIGHTEEN

At ten o'clock the following morning St. John Allgood seated himself behind the table in the small music room. He had moved it since the previous day. His back was now to the window, through which the light from a pale, wintry sun streamed in, waiting to strike straight in the face anyone sitting in the chair opposite him. On the table in front of him were the preliminary statements that had been taken from each of the guests the night of the murder.

Allgood addressed Leather, who was standing submissively by the door. 'Ladies first, I think. Go and tell Miss Fry I'd like to see her.'

Walking a little hesitantly, Maude Fry crossed the room, stumbling slightly as her foot caught the edge of the rug. She sat down, folded her hands placidly in her lap, and gazed at Allgood with a calm, uninquiring expression. Her eyes behind the blue-tinted glasses, were almost invisible, but she gave the impression of being prepared to sit there until kingdom come if it was required of her.

Leather sat down in the corner and unobtrusively picked up a notebook.

Allgood said, 'Miss Fry, how long have you worked for Mr Gilbert?'

'Only a matter of weeks. Before that I was personal secretary to Sir Charles Crenshaw, the company promoter. But he retired.'

'I see. That's a pity.'

'That Sir Charles retired?'

'I meant that you haven't been with Mr Gilbert very long. You can't know him all that well.'

'Quite well enough.' For the first time there was a note of emotion in her voice.

'Really? May I take it that he's not a very satisfactory employer?'

'You may. But I would prefer not to elaborate upon the subject.'

'Come, Miss Fry, that's hardly fair. It may mean that he works you too hard, that he fails to pay your salary on time, or that he makes improper advances.'

Maude Fry flushed slightly. 'Nothing like that. The work actually has been quite light. But he's insufferably rude to everybody, all the time – behaviour which, of course, tends always to rebound on the secretary – is invariably late for appointments and thoroughly disorganised. But the last straw was when he brought me here uninvited. It was a most invidious position, and one with which I was not prepared to put up.'

'Ah, yes, Lady Burford told me you'd been intending to leave on Saturday morning.'

'That is so, but naturally in the event I was unable to do so.'

'How did Gilbert react when you told him you were intending to leave his employ?'

'He wasn't pleased.'

'Why do you suppose he wanted you along in the first place?'

'To type the script of *The King's Man*.'

'But isn't it very early days for that? As I understand it, the film is only in a provisional planning stage: no contracts have been signed, no firm decision has been made about shooting here at Alderley. Would one normally start typing a screenplay without a lot more discussion and preparation?'

'Well, I have never worked in films before, but I can see his reason for that: he wants to establish himself at the earliest possible moment as the writer of the film – make himself one of the team from the start, so that there can be no question of the job being given to someone else.'

'I thought he had the copyright.'

'Apparently the position is legally a little uncertain. However, if he actually started the script and was able to supply Mr Haggermeir with some good material, as they call it, before he left here, then they'd be far less likely to drop him.'

'Quite astute.'

'Mr Gilbert is no fool. Of course, the murder has changed the situation for everybody.'

'Speaking of the murder, what can you tell me about it?'

'I can tell you virtually nothing. I think the only words I spoke to Signorina Lorenzo were "How do you do?" when we were introduced.'

'Did she speak much to Mr Gilbert?'

'They did have a private talk on Friday morning. I don't know what about. But then, she seems to have spent most of the day seeking out the various men and engaging them in conversation.'

'Is that so? Now, what about the night of the murder? Tell me just what you saw and heard, and what you did.'

'We'd been playing bridge – Lady Burford, Mrs Everard, Miss Dove, and I – until we heard the others arriving home. I was anxious not to see Mr Gilbert, and Miss Dove seemed eager to be out of the way before they came in, so we went up together. It was about one a.m. By ten past, I was in bed. I was very drowsy and fell asleep almost immediately. The shot woke me about an hour later. I got outside in time to see Lady Geraldine rush past, stop in the signorina's doorway, then go into the room. Mr Quartus emerged from his room and followed her. I joined them, and you know what I saw.'

'Can you tell me the order in which the other people arrived?'

She frowned. 'I'm afraid not. They just suddenly seemed to be all around me. And it's rather dim at that end of the corridor. Besides, I must admit I only really had eyes for what I saw in the bedroom.'

Allgood then questioned her about her activities since her arrival at Alderley. She gave painstakingly thorough replies. However, when he asked her about things said or done by the other guests, or any impressions or feelings she may have had about them, he might have been questioning somebody deaf, dumb and blind. He let her go, requesting her to ask Jemima Dove to come in.

* * *

Jemima sat on the edge of the chair, very pale in the harsh sunlight, her eyes flicking from Allgood to Leather as if she was fearful of a murderous attack being launched on her by one of them if she didn't keep a close watch on them. Allgood didn't speak, just gazed at her until eventually she let her eyes settle on him. Then at last she blurted out, 'I don't know anything.'

'Oh, I'm sure you do, Miss Dove.'

'But I don't honestly. I only arrived a little while before it all happened. I never even saw Miss Lorenzo alive.'

'We only have your word on that.'

'But it's the truth! I went upstairs before she and the others came in.'

'Which gave you a perfect opportunity to go to her room, wait for her, and shoot her. You could have then put the pistol outside, waited for Carter to come along, groaned to lure him in, pushed him in the back – it would have required no great strength – fired the alarm shot with a second gun, hidden in the bathroom for a minute or so, and then joined the others in the doorway.'

Jemima gave a squeak of dismay. 'But the gun, the murder weapon. When could I have got that? I mean, everybody's been saying that the murderer had to get the key to the collection room from the safe in Lord Burford's study first.'

'Are you saying you couldn't have done that?'

'Of course I am! Listen, no one could have got into the study while there were people about in the hall, could they?'

'No.'

'Well, from what's been said, after Miss Fry and I

went up, somebody was there all the time until at least
ten minutes after Miss Lorenzo went upstairs. I'd have
then had to come down, open the safe, take the key, go
to the gun room, open it, find and load the gun, and go to
Miss Lorenzo's room. By then she would have been in her
room at least a quarter of an hour. But according to Lady
Geraldine, you deduced from her still having her coat on
that she'd been shot two or three minutes at the most after
she went in.'

'That's correct. But what about when you first arrived?
You were left in the hall while the butler told Lady Burford
of your arrival. You might have had time to slip into the
study then.'

'Wrong!' she said triumphantly. 'I was only kept waiting
for about two minutes. And there was a footman there the
whole time. He was winding the clock.'

Allgood bowed his head and spread his hands. 'Miss
Dove, you have just cleared yourself of suspicion of murder.'

She fell back in the chair with a little gasp. 'Oh, my,
what a relief!' She looked at him, and was aware of a slight
smile playing round his mouth. She sat up again, suddenly
indignant. 'You'd worked all that out yourself, hadn't you?
You never suspected me at all.'

He drew back his lips, revealing his big teeth in a wolf-
like smile. 'Perhaps not.'

'Oh, Mr Allgood, I do think that's very unfair! Why put
me through all that?'

'Shall we say to stimulate you mentally, get you
thinking about that night and talking about it? I think I've
succeeded. Now tell me, what was the first you knew of
the murder?'

'I heard the shot. I was in bed, but not asleep. Then I heard other noises – voices, footsteps – and I thought I ought to go and see what was happening. I put on a dressing-gown and went outside. I walked along to the main corridor and saw a man making his way towards the east wing. So I followed him. It was Mr Gilbert, I think. When I reached the east wing I saw the crowd and joined them.'

'Everybody else was already there?'

'I think so, but they were mostly strangers and I wasn't really looking at them. And of course it was rather dark.'

'I see. Well, then, I think you can go. Unless there's anything else you want to tell me, anything you've seen or heard that strikes you in any way as odd or significant.'

She puckered her brow. 'No, I don't think so. Except the motor-bike in the gallery, of course. They told you about that?'

'Yes, the Earl mentioned it. Most intriguing. All right, Miss Dove, thank you. Ask Mrs Everard to join me, if you will?'

Cecily Everard was cool and calm and answered Allgood's questions crisply. She knew nothing of Laura Lorenzo, had never even heard of her before Thursday afternoon. She had spoken to her hardly at all, except for a few minutes when she'd been giving Laura a lift back up to the house. She related that conversation. Her knowledge of the other guests was no greater, only having engaged them in small talk. She had spent most of her time on Thursday and Friday talking over old times with her cousin. She had neither seen nor heard anything strange or unusual. As to the murder itself, she had not even heard the shot. Her husband had awakened her to tell her of it. They had gone outside, seen the Earl and Countess hurrying round the corner to the east wing, and followed. She thought that Mr Gilbert and Mr Haggermeir had arrived in the doorway just behind them, but hadn't really noticed.

Allgood let her go. He asked her to send her husband in.

Sebastian Everard was by far the most relaxed member of the house party whom Allgood had yet spoken to. He wandered vaguely into the room, smiled amiably and said, 'Colder again today, what?'

'Sit down, please, Everard.'

'Oh. All right. If you like.' He eyed the chair doubtfully. 'Mind if I move this a bit? Sun in the old peepers, you know.' He pulled the chair to one side, plumped himself down onto it, and took a bag of brightly coloured sweets from his pocket. He held them out to Allgood. 'Like one?'

'No, thank you.'

Sebastian turned to Leather. 'How about you?'

'No, thank you, sir.'

'Sure? They're very good.' He took one, unwrapped it, and popped it in his mouth. 'I can make one last over twenty minutes,' he said indistinctly.

Allgood decided on shock tactics. 'Everard,' he snapped, 'did you kill Laura Lorenzo?'

Sebastian slowly transferred the sweet to his cheek. 'You've got to ask that, have you? In the jolly old book of rules, sort of thing?'

'No, I—'

'Ah, your own idea, is it? Don't everybody say no, always?'

'Mostly, but—'

'Seems rather pointless, then, what?'

'Answer the question, sir!'

'Oh, sorry. Er, what was it again?'

'Did you kill—?'

'Oh, yes, of course. Well, as a matter of fact, the answer's no, actually. Sorry. Is that all?'

'No, it is not. How well did you know the deceased?'

'Who?'

'Miss Lorenzo.'

'Oh, her. Hardly at all, more's the pity. Quite a corker, what?'

'So you were attracted to her?'

'Who wouldn't be?'

'Was your wife aware of this?'

'Cec?' He frowned. Then his face cleared. 'Oh – see what you mean. I say, don't get me wrong; happily married man and all that. Fellow can look, though, can't he?'

'You contented yourself with looking?'

'Eh?'

'You didn't perhaps make advances to her, advances that were repelled?'

'Golly, no. Never have the nerve for anything like that. Nor the inclination, really. Such a drain, all that sort of thing. These married chaps who have a little bit of fluff on the side live on their nerves, if you ask me. Not worth the effort. All for the quiet life myself.'

'Do you know anything about the murder?'

Sebastian scratched his head. 'Been trying to make sense

of it, actually. Everyone seemed to think young Carter'd done it, then Gerry said he hadn't and Lavinia said it was a tramp, and Gerry said you'd said somebody'd cut up a fur coat because the room was too hot, and she was really shot through the bathroom window with two different guns, and the chap was going to get away on the motor-bike, but couldn't because the ignition key was locked in George's safe, so he hid it in the art gallery. I only heard one shot, though. I expect it was the Mafia.'

Allgood blinked. 'Mafia?'

'Yes, you know: Italians and Sicilians and all that.'

Allgood was silent. Clearly it would be an utter waste of time to try and get from Sebastian any coherent account of the events leading up to the murder, or ask if he'd seen or heard anything untoward. He sighed. 'All right, Everard,' he said. 'You can go.'

'Jolly good,' said Sebastian.

Allgood sat quietly thinking for ten minutes before sending Leather to fetch Hugh.

Hugh said, 'Look, I thought I was in the clear. My alibi—'

'It holds. But there are things I want to talk to you about. First, your motor-bike. The Earl gave me your message. Odd affair, I agree. However, I shan't bother to have it dusted for prints: there'll obviously be dozens of strange ones on it, impossible to check; in addition anybody here could have touched it quite innocently while it was parked outside, so their fingerprints on it would prove nothing.'

'As you wish. But there is a bit more you ought to

know. Somebody's put fuel in the tank. When I went out to check it after the garage chap brought it back Friday midday, I found it was practically dry – not more than a cupful in it. I was irritated that I hadn't told them at the garage to fill it up, or that they'd not had the sense to do so without being told. Now there's – well, not a lot, but a pint or two at least.'

'Which cars were parked nearest it on Friday?'

Hugh thought. 'Everard's on one side and Carter's on the other.'

Allgood nodded. 'And Carter ran out of petrol Friday night. He was surprised. He knew he didn't have much in, but had been sure he had enough to get back here.'

Understanding came into Hugh's eyes. 'You mean someone siphoned fuel from his tank and put it in mine? I see. But why? If they were going to steal the bike, yes. But why put petrol in, just to take it to the picture gallery? It doesn't make sense.'

'There's a lot that doesn't make sense so far, Quartus. But everything will soon. And you may be able to help. You had the room next to Laura Lorenzo's. I want you to think very carefully if you mightn't have seen or heard something that night which could help this investigation, something you may not have considered important at the time.'

'Do you think I haven't racked my brains about that? The answer's no. On Friday night I went straight up to my room after bringing Gerry home and threw myself down on the bed fully dressed. I was in a bit of a temper and wanted to think. I just lay in the dark, smoking. I heard nothing until the shot.'

'As you went along the corridor towards your room, did you happen to notice if Signorina Lorenzo's door was open?'

'No, I didn't. If it was, then the light was off in her room. I'd certainly have noticed if it hadn't been, as the corridor was rather dimly lit.'

'So you were unable to see if there was a gun on the floor?'

'Perhaps if I'd been looking for something there I might have seen it. But I wasn't.'

'What did you do after you heard the shot?'

'Went to the door and got it open just in time to see Gerry's back as she sprinted past. I joined her in the doorway of Laura's room.'

'Didn't it take you rather a long time to get your door open? Lady Geraldine ran the full length of two corridors while you merely crossed your room.'

'Well, I was scared.'

'Scared?'

'Yes, I admit it. Gunshots are no doubt an everyday part of your life, Allgood. They're not of mine. I did what I think most people would do if they heard a shot outside their door: sat tight and wondered if it was safe to investigate or if someone might take a potshot at me.'

'You definitely thought the shot had been fired with criminal intent and wasn't just an accident or horseplay?'

Hugh looked a little surprised. 'Yes, now you mention it, I did. My immediate assumption was that someone had been shot – deliberately.'

'Signorina Lorenzo?'

He nodded. 'I believe so.'

'Do you know why you assumed that?'

'Just because she was in the next room, I suppose. I know now the shot was actually fired in the corridor, but I didn't realise that at the time. It was just a shot, close at hand.'

'But Miss Fry's room was equally close at hand, and Carter's was only a short distance away.'

'What are you getting at?'

'Trying to find a reason for your instinctive assumption that it was Signorina Lorenzo who had been shot at. You see, I believe you had more to do with her than anybody else here.'

'Well, I speak Italian, you see.'

'Precisely. And I'm wondering if she said anything which might have subconsciously led you to believe she was in danger.'

'No, no, I'm sure she didn't.'

'What did you talk about?'

'Films, art. She asked me to paint her portrait. So you see, it wouldn't have really mattered if I hadn't had an alibi. I could have made quite a considerable sum, by my standards, for that painting – money I urgently need. I had every reason for wanting her alive. Apart from the fact that she was a beautiful woman, a great actress and a very charming lady.'

Hugh's voice was suddenly soft. He was silent for a few seconds. Then he looked hard at Allgood. 'You'll get him, won't you? I want that swine to hang.'

'Gerry,' Paul said, 'I've been thinking of that second pistol. I fancy, in spite of Allgood clearing me officially, that there are still people here who don't believe in that other gun. I'd love to find it and prove I wasn't making the whole thing up.'

'It would be rather fun.'

'Then let's have a go. Where would *you* hide a pistol here?'

'Oh, that's easy. Among the guns in Daddy's collection.'

'I thought of that. But I think it would have been too risky for the murderer to have gone back there. It would be obvious your father would go in to investigate the taking of the murder weapon. Where else?'

'Dozens of places.'

'Name one. Look, you're a murderer. You've got a gun in your possession which would point to you as the killer. What do you do with it? And remember, you don't know the house too well.'

She frowned. 'I suppose one place that springs to mind would be where the gun was hidden when we had our last murder here – how awful that sounds! – in the secret passage. Everybody here must know that story.'

'I say, that's an idea. All right, let's try there first.'

They went up to the linen room and Paul opened the panel. 'Do you want to look?' he asked.

'You bet.' She stepped into the passage, reached for the flashlight, switched it on and shone it round on the floor. Then she gave a gasp. 'It's here!'

'No!'

She bent down. 'Don't touch it,' he said. 'Prints.'

'I know! Got a pen, or something?'

He handed her his fountain pen and a moment later

she emerged with the pen inserted into the muzzle of an automatic pistol.

He gave a whistle. 'First time lucky! Congrats, darling.'

She looked modest. 'You started me on the chase.'

'But you thought where to look. Come on, let's take it to Allgood.'

'Thank you very much, Lady Geraldine,' Allgood said.

'That was extremely smart of you. And you, Carter.'

'It is *the* gun, I suppose,' Paul said.

'Oh, indubitably, I should say. One shot's been fired from it.'

'Does it tell you anything?' Gerry asked.

'Not just by looking at it, not even me. I'll have it checked for prints, of course, but it's a forlorn hope.'

'It's not a lot of use to you, then?'

'It confirms the hypothesis I'm working on.'

'And ought to convince everybody I *am* innocent, don't you think?' Paul said hopefully.

'All except the most bigoted, certainly. There's no conceivable way you could have planted this in the passage after the shot was heard. Now, if you'll excuse me, I must get on with my interrogations. Be so good as to tell Ransom I'm ready for him, will you?'

They found Rex in the library and passed on Allgood's message. He stood up. 'Oh, right. I suppose this is the time I ought to draw my sword, shout "Back, you villainous dogs!", and leap out of the window. Unfortunately, I didn't bring my sword with me.' He sauntered from the room.

Gerry wondered if he was aware of the beads of the sweat on his brow.

CHAPTER NINETEEN

'Sit down, Mr Ransom,' Allgood said.

'Thanks.' Rex sat.

Allgood pulled a sheet of paper towards him and picked up a pen. 'Your full name is Rex Ransom?'

'Yes.'

'And your age?'

'I refuse to answer on the grounds that it may incriminate me.'

'We have no fifth amendment over here, Mr Ransom. But I'll put "over twenty-one".'

'I'll settle for that.'

'Are you married?'

'Not at the moment.'

'And your occupation?'

Rex stared. 'You're kidding!'

'Oh, of course, I believe somebody did mention it. You're an actor, is that right?'

'As you know perfectly well, Mr Allgood. Do you have any more questions?'

'A few. How well did you know Laura Lorenzo?'

'Not at all. I only met her last Thursday.'

'Did you converse with her much?'

'Very little.'

'Isn't that rather surprising? Two film actors meet in a strange country, staying under the same roof with the likelihood of soon appearing together in a film, and they talk very little?'

'We didn't have a lot in common, I'm afraid. Her movies were – or had pretensions to being – intellectual. She tended to look down on my kind of picture.'

'You resented that?'

'Not at all. It's an attitude I'm used to. It means nothing. Most genuine intellectuals thoroughly enjoy my stuff.'

'In spite of her attitude toward your type of film, she was planning to take a part in one. Why, do you suppose?'

'I don't know, of course, but I guess she needed the money. I've no idea how well her recent pictures have done in Europe, but they've grossed zilch in the States.'

'But couldn't she have made more money with one of the bigger studios than with Haggermeir?'

'Maybe, but she'd turned them all down in the past, you know. And the moguls don't take kindly to rejection. She might have figured she'd get the brush-off if she went back to any of them now. Could be, too, she thought she'd carry more weight with Cyrus than with a Goldwyn or a Zanuck – get her own way easier, have the script adapted to her requirements, and so on.'

'That couldn't have been a pleasant prospect for you.'

Rex smiled. 'I think she would have found Cyrus a tougher proposition than she imagined. He's a mighty canny bird, knows exactly what the public wants and gives it to them.

I doubt Laura's ideas would have coincided with that. And while he might have liked the idea of the prestige he'd get from signing her, when it came to a choice between kudos with the critics and bucks at the box office he'd choose the latter every time. Which is why I doubted from the start she'd ever appear in this picture, and why I wasn't especially worried. Certainly not worried enough to murder her to prevent it.' He paused. 'Besides, I must be in the clear, anyway.'

'How do you make that out?'

'Well, she was killed between five and ten after one, right?'

'Yes.'

'And according to what Gerry told us, your theory is that the killer waited in Laura's room until Carter came along, and then the alarm shot was fired. Well, I was talking to Gerry in my sitting-room ten minutes before that shot was heard.'

Allgood shrugged. 'I may have been wrong about the murderer remaining in the room all the time. It could have been you. Say you couldn't stand the suspense of waiting any longer and crept out to see what was happening. Or perhaps suddenly realised you'd forgotten something – the second gun, say – and hurried back to your room to get it. While you were there Lady Geraldine knocked at your door. That would explain your odd manner when you were talking to her. As soon as she left, you ran silently back to Signorina Lorenzo's room, getting there just a minute or so before Carter left his room a second time and provided you with your fall guy.'

Rex said, 'Plausible, but completely untrue.'

'Oh, I'm not accusing you. I'm not accusing anybody

– yet. I'm just pointing out that you're not in the clear. Suppose you tell me exactly what you did see and hear?'

'Hardly anything. When we got home I went straight up to my room and stayed there. I was undressing later when I heard what sounded like a shot. I put on a robe and went outside. That's it.'

'That was surely over an hour after you first went up. What were you doing in the interim?'

'Just sitting, smoking. Reading a bit. Oh, and Gerry stopped by briefly.'

'Ah, yes. Now, can you explain your very odd manner at that time?'

'You said something about that just now. I don't know what you mean.'

'Oh, come, Ransom. Lady Geraldine's given me a full account of your conversation. She said you seemed embarrassed, dazed, that your speech was disjointed, and that when she asked if you were all right you laughed hysterically.'

'Aw, that's baloney. Frankly, I was embarrassed at her coming to my room like that, so late.'

'Really? That embarrassed *you*, a famous film star? Surely you must be used to girls doing that sort of thing.'

'Not English aristocrats. This was in her family home, and I was a guest of her father. Don't get me wrong: I don't think for a moment she was trying to snuggle up to me. It was just the look of the thing.'

'But you *had* arranged for her to call?'

'Yeah, but much earlier, immediately we got home. And it wasn't all that important.'

'It was about Arlington Gilbert, I believe?'

'I was just going to advise her not to take his ill manners too seriously, that he's a decent enough guy at heart.'

'But you told her he'd been prowling about your room.'

'Gilbert? No. Oh, wait a minute. What I think I did say was that he'd been *scowling* about my room: i.e., that it was a bigger and more central one than his. Presumably she misheard me.'

'Presumably. But you can imagine why she thought it was important to talk to you.'

'Yeah, of course. But I didn't realise that. I was just mighty anxious to get rid of her in case somebody saw her and got the wrong impression. I *did* laugh, because it suddenly struck me as funny: the idea of *me* trying to give the bum's rush to an attractive chick.'

Allgood asked him a few more questions, similar to those he had put to all the others, then said, 'Right, thank you, Ransom.'

'That's it?'

'Yes, you can go.'

'Thanks.' Rex got up and walked to the door.

Allgood said, 'Oh, by the way, Ransom.'

He stopped and turned. 'Yes?'

'You've starred in thirty-five pictures, the first being *The Rapier* and the most recent *Prince of Baghdad*. Your most successful was *The Fifth Musketeer,* co-starring Maureen Garland. My personal favourite, however, was *Swordsman of Sherwood*, directed by Larry Main, which also starred Veronica O'Brien, and for which the cinematographer, Herb Nelson, won an Oscar. Ask Gilbert to come in, please.'

* * *

Arlington Gilbert lounged into the room, a pipe in his mouth and his hands in his pockets. Superficially he looked relaxed, but whereas with Sebastian Everard this had seemed genuine, in Gilbert's case it looked definitely forced.

Allgood said, 'Ah, sit down, Gilbert.'

'I intend to.' He plumped himself down and gazed around.

'May I have your full name?'

'You'll find it at Somerset House, with all the other birth certificates, which will also give you my age. If you wish, that is, to waste your time on such irrelevancies.'

'I agree they are irrelevancies, but they help to put people at their ease.'

'I am always at my ease.'

'How fortunate. Where were you when the murder was committed?'

'I can't say. I don't know when the murder was committed.'

'Between five and ten past one.'

'At that time I was in my room.'

'In bed?'

'No.' He was silent.

'This isn't a film script, Gilbert. I suggest you stop trying to be funny.'

'Trying to be funny? Do you really think if I was trying to be funny I couldn't do better than that?'

'If you weren't in bed, where were you?'

'In the armchair.'

'Doing what?'

'Just about dropping off to sleep.'

'You were asleep in the chair?'

'Oh, well done, sir!'

'May I ask why?'

'You may.' Again he was silent, waiting.

Allgood breathed hard. 'Why?'

'Because I was a bit tipsy when we got home. Haggermeir took me to my room. When we got inside the whole place was swaying. I decided to sit down in the chair for a few minutes to get my bearings before undressing. That's all I remember before the shot woke me. Couldn't think what it was for a few seconds. Staggered across to the door, found I'd left it open a couple of inches, went outside, heard a bit of commotion, went along to see what was happening – last one on the scene, I think.'

'Apparently not. Miss Dove says she followed you.'

'Oh, did she? I didn't see her. Of course, I was unaware of her existence, then. Everybody I *knew* was there before me.'

'Of course, she didn't follow you all the way from your room. When she first saw you, you were already in the corridor.'

Gilbert shrugged. 'So?'

'So there's no witness to the fact that you were actually in your room when the shot was fired.'

'What of it? Have the others got witnesses?'

'No, but they were nearly all in their night attire. You were still fully dressed.'

'So was Quartus. And Carter, of course.'

'Yes, but they'd got in only twenty minutes before. You'd been in your room well over an hour.'

'I've explained that.'

'You were "tipsy", or so you claim. But Lord Burford said he was surprised by your condition when you arrived home. You didn't appear to drink all that much at the party, and you didn't seem tight at all.'

'It hit me when I went out into the cold night air.'

'But it passed off again quite quickly, apparently.'

'When I'd had an hour's sleep. Look, what precisely are you driving at?'

'Just this: a couple of minutes passed from the time Miss Dove heard the shot to the time she saw you. You could have murdered Laura Lorenzo, shoved Carter in the back, fired that shot, slipped down the stairs at the end of the corridor, and gone back up by the main staircase within a minute or so.'

'You buffoon,' Gilbert said distinctly.

'Now, wait a moment—'

'No, you wait. Do you honestly think that I, Arlington Gilbert, spent Friday night running about the corridors of this house, pushing people in the back, firing guns, committing murder? You're out of your mind.'

'Like it or not, Gilbert, you are a suspect.'

'Balderdash. I refuse point-blank to be a suspect. The idea is ludicrous. Why on earth should I shoot the woman? She was a virtual stranger to me.'

'Yet on Friday morning you had quite a long private conversation with her. According to Lady Geraldine, Signorina Lorenzo seemed very keen to speak to you alone.'

'Well, naturally. I'm a famous writer. She was hoping to play in one of my films. In those circumstances actresses are always all over one.'

'What did she specifically want?'

'For me to adapt the script so there would be a good part in it for her. Apparently Haggermeir had said I wouldn't be willing.'

'And were you?'

'Perfectly willing to consider it. I don't consider my work sacrosanct. I just won't have it butchered by fifth-rate hacks.'

'And is that all you talked about?'

'All? If you mean was that the sole subject of our conversation, the answer is yes. Now listen, Allgood. I'm not prepared to talk about my own movements and conversations any longer. I have given you a clear and truthful statement, which is all I am obligated to do. I came in here to offer you my assistance in solving this case. Do you want it or not?'

'What sort of assistance?'

'I know who committed the murder.'

'Who?'

'Lady Geraldine.'

Allgood showed no surprise. 'Really? You have evidence of that?'

'Not exactly. But the girl is a psychopathic schizophrenic.'

'Is she indeed? That's as may be. However, as it happens, we know she didn't commit this particular murder.'

Gilbert stood up. 'If that's your attitude, I refuse to stay in this room another minute. And I will answer no more questions. You, sir, are a pompous, incompetent ignoramus. Good day.'

Gilbert stalked from the room.

Allgood sat quite still. Then from Sergeant Leather's corner he heard a strange muffled, grunting sound. Allgood looked towards it suspiciously. But Leather's head was bent low over his notebook and though there seemed to be some kind of odd movement of his shoulders, the sound had now stopped.

Allgood realised he hadn't asked Gilbert for an explanation of his nocturnal visit to the Earl's study. But that would keep.

'George,' said the Countess, 'I'm worried about Geraldine.'

'Are you, Lavinia? She looks fit enough to me.'

'I don't mean that.' She lowered her voice. 'There's a murderer in this house, George.'

'There's always a murderer in this house, if you ask me.'

'Don't be flippant, George. Geraldine could be in danger.'

'How do you make that out?'

'Suppose this murderer is a maniac, a man who kills young women?'

'Don't think that's very likely. Men like that don't usually shoot their victims.'

'Perhaps they don't usually have access to guns. You have to admit it is possible. I must confess the danger hadn't occurred to me until she told me Paul insisted she lock her door last night. So he must think there's a risk. I think we should get her out of the house as soon as we can.'

'But the whole business may be cleared up tomorrow.'

'*May* is the operative word, George. Personally, I don't

think the police have the first idea who did it. It could drag on for a week or more yet. And I don't suppose they'll want the suspects to leave here until it's all over. I'd be much happier if Geraldine wasn't here.'

'Hm.' Lord Burford rubbed his chin. 'Maybe you're right, Lavinia. But she's not the only young woman in the house, remember.'

'I've spoken to Merryweather about the maids. I told him that if any of them wants to go home to her family until this affair is over she may do so, and that those who decide to remain should stay together as much as possible, do their work in pairs, and lock their doors at night. I don't think I can do more than that.'

'What about the little Dove?'

'Well, she's a free agent. She can leave any time she wishes, as far as I'm concerned. But that's a matter between her and the police. Whether they still consider her a suspect I don't know, but I cannot imagine they believe a woman did it. Either way, however, they have accepted Geraldine's alibi, and she's given them all the information she can. So I cannot see they can have any objection to her going away.'

The Earl looked dubious. 'Maybe not, but that doesn't mean *she* won't have an objection.'

'I want you to persuade her.'

'Oh, Lavinia, you know I can never persuade Gerry to do anything she doesn't want to. I could order her out of the house, I suppose, but it seems pretty drastic.'

'Maybe I could persuade her, sir.'

They turned. It was Paul, who had approached them without their hearing. He said, 'I'm sorry, I couldn't help overhearing the last part of your conversation. You'd like Gerry to go away?'

The Countess nodded.

'I think that's a very good idea,' he said.

'Why do you think you could persuade her, Paul?' Lady Burford asked.

'Well, I'm in the same position as she is with reference to the police. They've told me they've finished with me, and frankly I've been through quite a lot the last couple of days. *I'd* rather like to get away for a bit now. If I tell Gerry that, she might be willing to come away somewhere with me for a short while.'

He went a little red. 'Of course, I know in normal circumstances you wouldn't countenance her going off alone with a fellow, but naturally I'd take great care to see that the situation couldn't be misconstrued. I'm terribly fond of Gerry, and I wouldn't do – do...' He tailed off.

The ghost of a smile touched Lady Burford's lips. 'I'm quite well aware that you want to marry her, Paul.' His eyes widened. She went on, 'Also, that until this weekend it was very much a toss-up between yourself and Hugh. Now, however, I'd say you've got the field to yourself. It's remarkable what a little adversity can do for a young man's chances.'

He said, 'I say, Lady Burford, I'd really no idea that you – I mean...'

'Normally, although I trust her implicitly, I would, as you say discourage any plan of hers to go away alone with a young man. But the situation is not normal, and I do want her out of the house. I'm quite sure she'd refuse to go to one of her relatives, but an invitation from you might be a different matter. So if you can persuade her, I would consider it a personal favour.'

Paul's face lit up. 'I'll speak to her now.'

'I fancy you'll be unlucky,' the Earl said. 'She'll want to see this thing through to the end. Try, though, by all means.'

'Now, Mr Haggermeir,' Allgood said, 'you presumably know more about Signorina Lorenzo than anybody else here.'

'I doubt it.'

'But you had several long conversations with her.'

'Sure, but only about the picture, her contract, and so on.'

'You didn't touch on her personal life at all?'

'Nope. Never let an actor or actress start on their personal life or you get tied up for hours.'

'It must have been a blow to you when she died, though, all your plans being dashed?'

'Not so you'd notice. I was already figuring the broad was gonna be more trouble than she was worth. She was aiming to squeeze every cent she could out of me, for giving me the privilege of employing her! She figured on getting her own way with the script, not to mention billing, publicity, the whole caboodle.'

'You say she gave the impression she was doing you a favour by signing with you. Yet she came from London especially to see you. And I understand you didn't send that telegram yourself.'

'I sure didn't. She sent it, or had someone send it for her.'

'But why?'

'So she could come and talk turkey without seeming to be offering herself, make it look like she thought I'd made the first move.'

'Which would indicate that she was in fact eager to work for you. Again, why? If she was so much in demand, she didn't need to resort to such subterfuge.'

Haggermeir shrugged his beefy shoulders, 'I was available, and in England the same time as her. She'd said nix to most of the other studios in the past. I guess she figured that I'd be so hot to sign her I'd be a pushover when it came to the contract.'

'And you weren't?'

'Listen, pal, Cyrus S. Haggermeir wasn't born yesterday. No one hustles me into giving a contract I don't like. If Garbo herself was available I'd only sign her up on my terms.'

'You were eager to sign Laura up, though, at first.'

'Sure, tickled pink. *At first*. Then I got to thinking perhaps it wasn't such a lulu of an idea, after all. Oh, I hadn't turned her down. We were still talking. But there'd been no firm agreement, even a verbal one. Don't get to thinking the chick had gotten me tied into something I couldn't get out of without bumping her off.'

'Then why do you think she was killed?'

'When a good-looking dame gets croaked, ninety per cent of the time it's sex.'

'A crime of passion? It has none of the signs of that.'

'Well, you're the cop.'

'Then let me begin talking like one. Your movements on the night of the murder, please.'

'Got in about one, took Gilbert upstairs and left him at the door of his room. Went to my own room. In bed by about one-fifteen. Couldn't sleep. Read for a bit. Just dropping off and heard the shot. Went outside and saw the Earl and Countess hurrying towards the east wing. Followed them.'

Allgood questioned him for another ten minutes about himself and the other guests. But he learnt nothing new and let him go.

'How about it?' Paul said.

'Daddy's right in one way. Normally I would want to stick this out to the end. Or I would if I hadn't been through it all before. In a way it's exciting, as it was last time. Naturally I want to know who did it. But the end of it all last time was rather horrid. I certainly don't want to see anyone arrested for murder again. I'd just as soon find out afterwards who it was. So, OK, I'll come.'

'Oh, that's absolutely topping!' He gave her a kiss.

'Where shall we go?'

'Oh, anywhere. Let's talk about that later.' He looked at his watch. 'It's a bit too late to get away today now. First thing in the morning, all right?'

'Fine.'

He thought. 'I suppose I ought to clear it with the police first, just as a formality. I'll slip in and have a word with Allgood now.'

He made his way to the small music room. He arrived just as Haggermeir was leaving, tapped at the door, and went in. Allgood looked somewhat surprised to see him. Paul explained his mission.

'As far as I'm concerned,' Allgood said, 'you can both clear off whenever you like, though I'm sure Lady Burford's fears are quite groundless. It's no maniac we're dealing with.'

Paul smiled. 'Don't tell her, for heavens sake. She might change her mind.' He went out.

Allgood yawned and stretched. 'All right,' he said to Leather, 'that'll be all for today. I'm going to your police station shortly to send some telegrams and make some phone calls to various sources in London and elsewhere, have some inquiries set in motion. How long it'll take to get results I don't know, but certainly not before midday tomorrow. So you needn't return until then.'

'Very well, sir. Thank you.' Leather stood up and gathered his things together. 'Good night, sir,' he said as he went out.

Allgood raised an arm in a dismissive move but didn't speak.

Allgood returned to Alderley at eight o'clock and again had dinner served in his room. Then he slept for a couple of hours on his bed. At ten forty-five Chalky arrived with coffee and awoke him.

'Well, I've 'ad a kip, guv, as you suggested,' he said. 'What's the program?'

'I want you to take up position on the corner of the main corridor and the east wing,' Allgood told him. 'From there you can keep an eye on all the rooms except those in this corridor. There's a cupboard there you can slip into if you need to hide.'

'What about this corridor, guv?'

'I'll watch it from just inside the door. Move that chair across there, will you?'

Chalky complied. 'Expecting chummy to try something else, are you, guv?'

'I wouldn't be at all surprised, Chalky. We're reaching a crucial point in the investigation, and somebody – other than the killer – hasn't told us the full truth, I'm sure of it. It's probably for a quite innocent reason. But it could be vital, and they could come out with it any time. If the murderer knows this, tonight could be his last chance to stop that person talking.'

That night when they went upstairs Paul again took Gerry to the door of her room. They stood discussing their plans for the next day, then he kissed her good night. He waited until she'd gone in and he heard her talking to Marie, then made his way thoughtfully to his own room.

He was worried. Things had really worked out incredibly well, far better than he had ever hoped two nights ago. So in fact he oughtn't to have a care in the world. Nonetheless, something was wrong. The trouble was he couldn't put a finger on what it was. There was just this nagging sense of unease. If only he could think what was causing it.

He reached his room, opened the door and stepped inside, pushing it behind him and stretching out the other hand for the light switch at the same time. He pressed it down. But the room remained in darkness.

Paul swore mildly. The bulb must have blown. Now, where would they keep the spares?

At that second he gave a slight start, as immediately

behind him he heard a tiny sound. The next moment the room was dimly bathed in the cold glow of a flashlight.

Paul started to swing round, but be was too late. With a blaze of light, his head seemed to explode. He felt his legs turn to jelly under him. The floor lurched crazily beneath his feet. Then he was vaguely aware that his face was pressing against the carpet.

After this he knew no more.

CHAPTER TWENTY

It was eleven a.m. on Monday when Wilkins alighted from his little car outside Alderley. It was considerably colder again this morning, and all around the slush of the previous day had been transformed into treacherous patches of ice.

Wilkins was admitted to the house and went in search of Allgood. He found him, pale and weary-eyed, poring over his notes in the music room.

'Ah, Wilkins,' he said. 'Decided to give us the benefit of your cooperation today, have you? I trust you enjoyed your day of rest?' Then before Wilkins could answer he went on. 'They told you what happened here last night?'

'No details, sir. Just that Mr Carter's been attacked. How is he?'

'He's come round and he's going to be all right, though he'll have a nasty headache for a while yet. The doctor insists he stay in bed for a few more hours yet.'

'Do you have any clues, sir?'

'As yet, none. Strictly speaking, the only people in the whole house we can clear are Lady Geraldine and her maid. Carter had just left them in Lady Geraldine's room.'

'Might I know exactly what happened, sir?'

'You may well ask, Wilkins. I put Chalky on guard of the corner of the main corridor and the east wing. When he got to his post he noticed the door of Carter's room was open a little. He didn't think anything of it for a while, but after about fifteen minutes he decided to investigate. He found Carter unconscious on the floor. He fetched me, we sent for the doctor, roused the household, searched the place. But nothing. I must admit I never expected our friend to try anything so early in the night. I thought he'd wait until everybody had settled down. It was a very bold stroke that meant he was able to get back to his own room before Chalky or I had started our watches.'

'Any idea why Carter was the victim, sir?'

'Either he's been keeping something back – probably quite innocently, something of which he doesn't realise the full significance – or someone was searching his room and wanted a chance to search his person. But I went through his things while he was unconscious and it got me nowhere. I'm waiting to have another word with him as soon as he's up to it.'

A minute or two later a footman arrived to tell them they could see Paul. They went upstairs. Chalky White was seated on a chair outside Paul's bedroom. 'I'm taking no chances, you see,' Allgood said.

They went in. Paul was sitting up in bed. He looked pale but he summoned up a smile as they entered. 'Hullo, Allgood – Wilkins. Listen, tell this stubborn young lady there's no earthly reason why we can't start off on our trip this afternoon.' He indicated Geraldine, who was standing at the other side of the bed.

'There's every reason,' she said firmly. 'You're very lucky. The doctor said that if that blow had been a fraction harder or in a slightly different position you could be dead now.'

'But I'm not dead. I feel top-hole, apart from a bit of a headache.'

'Listen, you pig-headed chump, you are not leaving this house today. Tomorrow, if the doctor says so. And you're staying in bed until after lunch at least.'

'Feel up to answering a few questions?' Allgood asked.

'Sure,' Paul said, 'but I can't tell you anything. I've explained I didn't get a glimpse of the bloke.'

'Not about that. What I want to know is whether you've told me everything you can tell me about this whole business. Has there been anything you've seen or heard that's made you slightly puzzled? Anything, or any face, that's momentarily struck a chord in your memory?'

'I swear, nothing.'

'Very well. And are you absolutely certain you know nothing that I don't know about any of the other guests here? If so, I appreciate you may have had an honourable reason for not speaking out, and I won't hold it against you. Well?'

Paul looked at him. For a second it seemed to Allgood that his eyes flickered. Then he took a deep breath. 'I'm quite certain.'

Allgood made a gesture of resignation. 'All right. I won't press the point.'

'Is there anything else?'

'No.'

Gerry said, 'Good. In that case, I can start my reading?'

'Gerry, there's really no need for you to read to me.'

'It is my duty, Paul, and I intend to fulfil it. Now I have some detective stories, which I know you lap up. Ariadne Oliver's *Death of a Debutante*, *The Screaming Bone* by Annette de la Tour, Richard Eliot's *The Spider Bites Back*.'

'I've had enough of crime to last me a lifetime.'

'Then,' she said, 'it will have to be *Eric*, or *Little by Little*. Are you ready?'

Paul groaned.

Allgood and Wilkins went downstairs again. In the hall Allgood said, 'Oh, by the way, that telegram which supposedly brought Laura here. In the post office they think it was handed in by a small boy. Didn't know him. Probably given sixpence to do so. Now I must—'

He broke off as he saw a figure hurrying towards them.

It was Lord Burford and his face was excited. He said, 'Ah, I've been looking for you chaps. Got some information.' He looked round conspiratorially. 'Come into my study.'

When they were all seated in the study the Earl said, 'I know how the bounder got hold of the combination of the safe.'

Allgood sat up. 'Do you, by Jove?'

'I do. Ten minutes ago I had a telephone call.'

'Your phone's working again then?'

'Yes, just this morning. Seems a line was down near the edge of the estate. Anyway, the first call I got was from the manager of the company who made and installed the safe. Now, it seems that late Friday afternoon, after he'd left the office, they had a call from someone who claimed to be my secretary, and who said I'd lost the number of my safe and could they remind me of it.'

'They surely didn't just give it over the phone?'

'Hang on. He told me they've got a system in such cases, because they realise it's just the sort of trick a burglar might try. So what they do is hang up, look up the customer's number in the directory and call it themselves. If the customer answers and confirms that he has in fact just telephoned them—'

Allgood interrupted. '—they know the call was genuine and happily give him the combination of the safe.'

Lord Burford looked a little disgruntled at not being allowed to finish the story himself. 'Precisely.'

'And that's what happened in this case?'

'Yes. Same voice answered, confirmed the original query, took down the number and hung up.'

Allgood nodded admiringly. 'Very smart. Why did the manager phone you today, though?'

'He doesn't work Saturday mornings, and the first he knew about the incident was when his assistant told him about it this morning. Now the manager knew what the assistant didn't: that I have the family birthdays as the combination. He didn't see how I could forget those, so he called me up to check that everything was all right. Of course, I told him it was, but that we'd had a practical joker playing a few tricks lately and we'd like to find out who it was, so could his assistant describe the voice.'

'And?'

'All he could say was that the caller was an educatedsoundin' type, but spoke very softly, almost in a whisper. Couldn't even be quite sure of the sex. He thought it was a man, but it could have been a woman disguising her voice.'

'Did they say exactly what time the call was put through?'

'Near enough to five-fifteen.'

Allgood turned to Wilkins. 'Right. There's your job for the next few hours: find out if anybody was seen using the phone at that time.'

'My job, sir?'

'Yes. I'm going down to your station again for a while. I'm hoping for a number of important messages and I've arranged to receive them there. I should be back by mid-afternoon.' He started for the door.

Wilkins said, 'Sir, please, before you go, there is something I ought to say. You see, thinking about the case last night and having spoken to Leather on the phone and learnt much of what happened here yesterday, I came to the conclusion—'

'Wilkins, please.' Allgood raised both hands. 'I've told you repeatedly that I don't want to know. Your conclusions would just cloud the issue for me. Now, carry on with your assignment, there's a good fellow.'

Allgood hurried from the house.

Allgood arrived back at Alderley at three o'clock. He had a word with Chalky – who, with Paul now up and about, had been able to abandon his guard duty – and then went to the small music room. Here he found Wilkins, who'd been joined by Leather, waiting for him.

'Oh, there you are, sir,' Wilkins said wearily. 'No luck, I'm afraid. I've questioned everybody in the house. Nobody saw, or at least will admit to seeing, anyone on the phone at five-fifteen on Friday.'

'Oh, you needn't have bothered,' Allgood said airily. 'The case is solved.'

'You mean you know who did it sir?'

'I do. Took a bit longer than I expected, thanks to those nitwits in the criminal records office at the Yard, but I'm almost ready to make an arrest.'

'May we know of whom, sir?'

'You may.' He told them.

Wilkins listened, his eyes growing wider and wider. When Allgood had finished he said slowly, 'That's remarkable, sir. An amazing piece of deduction, if I may make so bold.'

'Elementary, my dear Wilkins.' Allgood rubbed his hands together. 'Now, I want everyone gathered on the landing at the top of the stairs right away. Arrange it, will you?'

Allgood looked round the ring of faces. They gazed back, some anxious, some curious, some impassive. Paul looked quite fit and remarkably cheerful, perhaps because Gerry was standing next to him, holding his hand.

Allgood said, 'I'm glad to say that the ordeal, for most of you, is almost over. But first I need everybody's help in conducting a little experiment. When the shot was fired on Friday night, you all, except Lady Geraldine – and Carter, of course – stated that you were in your rooms. I'd like you to go to them now, shut the door and do whatever you were doing at that time. If you were in bed, lie down on the bed. In a few minutes you will again hear a gunshot. Then I want you to re-enact what you did that night. Allow as much time as you think you took for getting out of bed, putting on dressing-gowns, slippers and so on. Then come out and make your way to the scene of the murder at the same speed as the other night. Will you all do that?'

There was a general nodding of heads. 'Go now then, please,' Allgood said, 'and be sure to close your doors.'

All those present except Gerry, Paul, Wilkins, Leather, and Allgood himself moved in the direction of their rooms. When they'd gone, Allgood said, 'Lady Geraldine, if you would kindly go and stand in the bathroom and when you hear the shot run as you did the other night.'

She nodded and walked away. Allgood went on, 'Wilkins, you wait here. Leather, you go to the corner of the main corridor and the west wing and remain there. Both make a mental note of everything you see.'

Leather moved off.

Paul said, 'What about me?'

'You come with me.' He strode in the direction of the east wing with Paul following meekly behind.

Allgood turned on the light in the east corridor and at the far end he drew the curtains across the window. Then he opened the door of Laura Lorenzo's room, turned on the light, and drew the curtains in there, too. 'Must get the lighting conditions as identical as possible,' he said.

'Do you want me to do what I did the other night?' Paul asked.

'That won't be necessary. I want you to play the part of the person who pushed you.'

He opened the bathroom door and looked inside. 'Good, the window is open.' He unbuttoned his jacket to reveal a shoulder holster, holding a 38-caliber revolver. He drew it and passed it to Paul. 'When I nod, stand in the middle of the corridor and fire that through the open bathroom door and out of the window. Then immediately step into the bathroom, close it all but a crack, and peer through. Whenever you think you can slip out without being noticed, do so, and join the crowd jostling in the doorway.'

'OK.'

Allgood took from one pocket his notebook and pencil, and from another pocket a stopwatch. Then he gave Paul a nod. Paul raised the pistol, took careful aim for the bathroom window, and squeezed the trigger. The report rang out, echoing through the corridor. Paul hastily stepped into the bathroom and pushed the door nearly to. At the same moment Allgood started the watch.

Within ten seconds Gerry appeared round the corner at the far end. She sprinted along the corridor. As she arrived Allgood said, 'All right, look into the room, see Carter and the body.' He glanced at the watch and made a jotting in the notebook.

Only a few seconds passed before Hugh's door opened and he joined Gerry, followed almost immediately by Maude Fry. Rex was the next to arrive; then the Earl and Countess, Sebastian and Cecily together, and Haggermeir. Allgood continued to make notes, all the while urging them into the doorway.

It was after Haggermeir's arrival that Paul opened the bathroom door wide, took a quick glance along the corridor and then, obviously unnoticed by the others, joined the gathering. It was a further thirty seconds before Gilbert arrived, followed at last by Jemima Dove.

Allgood stopped the watch and drew back the curtains. 'Thank you, ladies and gentlemen. Now, can anyone—' He broke off. 'No, we can't talk here; it's too crowded.' He addressed the Earl: 'Burford, do you think we might move into the gallery for a while? I don't want to go all the way downstairs again. There may be one or two other points I want to demonstrate up here at the scene of the crime.'

'Oh, of course. Gladly.' Lord Burford led the way to the gallery doors, saying as he did so, 'Still locked, actually, but think I've got the key here.'

He fumbled in his pocket, found the key, opened one of the huge double doors, and stood aside. The others trooped. As they were doing so, Chalky came along the corridor and whispered to Allgood for a few seconds. Allgood gave a satisfied nod. Then he and Chalky followed the Earl into the gallery and Chalky closed the door.

Allgood said, 'Those of you who'd care to sit, please do. We may be here some little time.'

Lord and Lady Burford, Cecily and Sebastian, Jemima Dove, Maude Fry, Gilbert, and Haggermeir moved to various of the sofas and upright chairs placed by the walls and sat down. Gerry, Paul, Rex, and Hugh remained on their feet, the latter ostentatiously strolling across to a Reynolds portrait of the fifth Earl and studying it lazily, his hands in his pockets and his back to Allgood. Wilkins and Leather took up position, sentry-like, at each side of the doors, with Chalky a little further along. Allgood moved to the centre of the room and surveyed his audience.

'This has been a quite interesting little case,' he said. 'Teasing, without being too baffling. It was complicated by a number of strange incidents which preceded the actual murder, and I intend to start by looking at those. First I'd like you to begin, Lady Geraldine, by telling everybody about your adventure Thursday night.'

Gerry looked a little aback, but collected her thoughts and gave a concise account of the struggle with the prowler in her father's study. When she'd finished and her parents and the others were still staring at her in amazement, Allgood said quietly, 'Lady Geraldine, do you know who the prowler was?'

She nodded.

'Tell us, please.'

She gulped, then said, 'It – it was Mr Gilbert.'

'What?' Gilbert leapt to his feet with a roar. 'That's a lie! I've never been near the study.'

She said doggedly, 'You admitted it to me Friday morning in the music room.'

'I did no such thing!'

'I told you it was I who scratched your face.'

His eyes bulged. 'That wasn't in the study. That was up here, near the top of the stairs.'

She gave a gasp. 'I never struggled with anybody there.'

'Well, I did. And I'm pretty sure it was a woman.'

'I suppose that was after you'd finished skulking about in Rex's room, was it?' she said bitingly.

Gilbert looked as thought he was going to burst. 'Skulking about *where*?'

'You heard what I said. And don't try to deny it. Rex told me about it.'

'Jupiter's teeth, it's a conspiracy!' Gilbert turned to Allgood. 'There's not a word of truth in any of this.'

Gerry said, 'I'm sorry, Rex, but I'll have to ask you to back me up.'

All eyes turned suddenly on Rex. He smiled a little nervously. 'Back you up?'

'Confirm what you said about Gilbert being in your room. I know the other night you said I'd misunderstood you, but we both know I didn't.'

Rex took out a cigarette case and lighter, lit up and inhaled deeply. He said, 'I'm sorry, Gerry, but Gilbert's never been in my room, as far as I know.'

Gerry gazed at him coldly. 'You're lying,' she said quietly. 'I thought when it came to the crunch you'd have more guts.'

Paul put his arm around her and addressed Allgood angrily, 'I don't know what's going on here, but Gerry's about the most truthful person I know. And she's certainly not crazy. I believe her implicitly.' Allgood just shrugged.

Gerry dashed a sudden tear from her eye. She said, 'I don't have to stay and put up with this. Take me out, Paul. Let's go away at once, after all. When we get back they'll all be gone.'

'Yes, of course, darling.' He started to lead her towards the door.

'Stop!'

The voice rang out like a whipcrack. It came from Rex. Under his tan his face was pale. He said, 'It's no good. I could never stand to see a woman cry. Sorry I let you down, Gerry.' He looked at Allgood. 'It's true. Gilbert was in my room Thursday night. We had a bit of a scrap.'

Gilbert raised both arms skywards and gave a howl of rage. 'It's a frame-up! I'll have you all in court! Slander! Libel! Defamation!' He pointed a finger at Allgood. 'You put them up to this, you – you – guttersnipe.'

'Kindly keep a civil tongue in your head, sir. If there's any conspiracy I'll get to the bottom of it. Now sit down and be quiet.'

Gilbert stared at him silently for a moment, then subsided, muttering, on to a sofa.

Allgood said, 'Ransom, why did you deny this just now?'

Rex inhaled deeply on his cigarette. 'Because – because I'm being blackmailed.'

'Blackmailed?'

'Yes, a photo was taken in my room Thursday night. I've since received a copy of it and a note demanding two thousand pounds for the negative. I was going to pay up. But I've changed my mind.' Suddenly his chin rose and his voice rang out proudly. 'In the immortal words of your Duke of Wellington, "Let them publish and be damned".' It was a beautifully delivered line.

'Hear, hear, sir. Well said.' This from the Earl. For a moment Gerry thought he was going to clap. Rex made him the slightest of bows.

'We'll look into this later,' Allgood said. 'But first tell me one thing, Ransom: what evidence do you have that the intruder was Gilbert?'

'I punched him in the eye. Gilbert had a shiner the next morning. He said he'd bumped into the closet door.'

'Was that true, Gilbert?' Allgood asked him. 'If not, I strongly advise you to tell the truth now, for your own sake.'

Gilbert hesitated, then shook his head. 'No, it wasn't. The man I struggled with near the top of the stairs did it.'

'The man? I thought you said it was a woman.'

Gilbert's eyes flickered. 'Both,' he said gruffly.

Allgood stared. 'Both?'

'Yes,' Gilbert snapped. 'First a man ran into me and blacked my eye and then a minute later a woman scratched my cheek.'

'Oh, for Pete's sake!' Rex gave a groan and looked at Allgood. 'You surely don't believe that, do you?'

'I neither believe it nor disbelieve it for the moment. But let's for the sake of argument suppose it's true. It means that apart from yourself and Lady Geraldine, another man and another woman were prowling about the house that night. Unlikely, but perhaps a little less unlikely if they weren't acting independently of each other, but were a couple, working together. Well, apart from the Earl and Countess, there was only one couple here.'

Allgood looked directly at Sebastian. 'Well, Mr Everard?'

Sebastian's mouth fell open. 'Me? Us? Walking about in the dark? Oh, no. Never. Both asleep. Cec and me. Sorry and all that.'

'You and who?'

'Cecily. My wife.'

'Ah, yes, of course.' Allgood suddenly swung round to face the Countess. 'Lady Burford, when did you last see your cousin, Cecily Bradshaw?'

'Before this weekend? Oh, twenty-five years ago, I should think.'

'You have not seen her this weekend, Lady Burford. I

regret to say that Cecily Bradshaw was killed eight years ago in a car crash, in Australia.'

Every eye in the room turned on the woman they'd known as Cecily. She'd gone deathly pale and didn't speak.

Allgood said, 'I should add that her second husband, Sebastian Everard, died in the same crash.'

He stepped across to where Sebastian and Cecily were sitting and looked down at them. 'If you have an explanation I would like to have it now.'

Sebastian stood up. Suddenly he looked different: less limp and languid, harder and tougher altogether. When he spoke his voice was different, too. The foppish drawl had gone completely.

'Yes, we're impostors. My name is Ned Turner. This is my wife, Mabel. And let me say first that this is absolutely nothing to do with her. I talked her into it, much against her will.'

'Talked her into what exactly?' Allgood asked in a silky soft voice. 'Into – murder?'

'No! We had nothing to do with that. I mean talked her into coming here and posing as Sebastian and Cecily Everard.'

In a bewildered voice, Lady Burford addressed his wife: 'But I don't understand. You knew everything about our family and the old days, people and places. And you look like Cecily.'

Mabel Turner nodded. 'That's the reason Cecily and I happened to meet in the first place. I was her understudy.'

'In Australia?' Gerry said.

'Yes, over twenty years ago. It was her first big part –

well, really the only big part she ever got. Unfortunately the play folded after about a month and we were both out of a job. Well, I'd been a singer and dancer before, and she'd been in the chorus, and we looked so much alike that we got up a sister act. We toured the music halls and vaudevilles all over Australia for a couple of years. As you can imagine, we got pretty close. In some of those little towns there was just nothing for respectable girls to do when we weren't performing but sit in the boarding house and talk. I was fascinated by Cecily's background. It was so different from my own, and I used to make her talk to me about it for hours. After a couple of years I knew as much about her family and friends as she did herself. Then she met and married a Philip Brown, a sheepfarmer, and gave up the stage. She'd told me so much about England that I decided to try my luck over here. Well, I didn't make the big time, but luckily I did meet Ned. We fell in love and got married. Cecily and I kept in touch, however, and I knew about Philip dying and about her marrying Sebastian three years later – though, of course, I never met him. Then eight years ago they were both killed. I doubted very much if any of her English relatives were aware of it, though, because I knew she'd had nothing to do with any of them for years. So when this – this business cropped up, I thought I'd stand a fair chance of getting away with it. And I did, until now.'

Lady Burford said, 'But getting away with what?'

'The silver, most likely,' Gilbert said.

Ned flushed. 'Nothing like that. We're not crooks. I talked Mabel into it because I wanted a chance to perform for Mr Haggermeir.'

Haggermeir sat up. 'Me? You're an actor?'

'No. I'm – I'm a stuntman.'

'Holy Moses.' Haggermeir looked baffled. 'Perform for me? I don't get it.'

'It's like this. I was one of the best stuntmen in Britain—'

'*The* best,' Mabel said quietly.

'Some people said so: cars, horses, planes, trains, falls, dives, anything. Then two and a half years ago I had my accident.'

Gilbert snapped his fingers. 'I remember. Some actress was badly injured.'

'What happened?' Gerry asked.

'It was a simple climbing job,' Ned said. 'The hero was supposed to shin up the outside of this building to rescue the heroine's cat, which was trapped on a ledge. The director wanted one shot of her on the ground, looking up at me – standing in for the hero, doing the climb. And when they were shooting that, I fell.'

'Were you hurt?' Lord Burford asked.

'Hardly at all. The lady cushioned my fall. I landed right on top of her. Her leg was broken. She was OK eventually, but the picture had to be scrapped. And I was black-listed.'

'Why did you fall?' Haggermeir asked him.

'They said I was drunk.'

'Were you?'

'No. Someone had smeared grease on one of my footholds. I knew who it was, but I couldn't prove it. It was wiped off before I could go and check. But the result was that I've never worked in films since, and never will in this country again.'

Rex said, 'How have you been earning your living?'

'Some circus and fairground work. But I hate it. I must get back into movies. I love them. They're my life. I thought my only chance was to get to Hollywood, where they probably wouldn't know of my trouble. I knew if I could get just one opportunity to prove what I could do I'd be OK. But we couldn't afford the fare. Then I read about Mr Haggermeir being over here and heard that he was actually going to stay with relatives of Cecily's, where Mabel could almost certainly wangle an invitation to stay if she could pass herself off as Cecily. It seemed too good an opportunity to miss.'

Haggermeir said, 'But how the heck were you figuring on giving me a performance?'

'I thought I might be able to pull off some spectacular stunt, which would impress you so much you'd want to give me a real chance in America. I spent the first two days here trying to work something out. Eventually I hit on something. And I have an apology to make.' He looked at Hugh, who had by now turned and was leaning against the wall. 'It was me who took your motor-bike. I'm very sorry.'

Hugh stared. 'But why on earth did you bring it up here?'

'The stunt I planned was to set myself on fire. I have a fireproof suit, crash helmet, and lots of other equipment in the car. Then I was going to ride the bike at full speed the whole length of the gun room, through the French windows, up a ramp formed by that plank, and leap off the balcony into the lake.'

There was a gasp in the room. The Earl said, 'But you'd kill yourself!'

'I don't think so, my lord. I've done similar stunts before. I carefully measured the distance and height and worked out the speed that would be necessary. I had to make the preparations on Friday. I played cards as badly as I could so the Countess and Miss Fry wouldn't want to go on playing with me for long, and as soon as Miss Dove fortuitously arrived I slipped outside and disconnected the bike from the sidecar. I put a little fuel in the tank, took the bike out to the road, and tested it. It's light, but it's got really tremendous acceleration. I brought it back and, while Mabel was making sure the other ladies were safely playing cards, I manhandled it up the back stairs and brought it in here. Naturally, I never imagined Mr Quartus would be going out again that night and would notice it was missing. Then I fetched the plank, which I'd discovered in the stables earlier. On Saturday morning I intended to ask his lordship to let me have the key to the gun room, so I could take another look at the collection on my own. If he insisted on coming with me, I was going to tell him the whole story. I think he's keen enough on movies, and a good enough sport, to have gone along with me. Then, when Mr Haggermeir went outside to photograph the exterior of the house, Mabel was going to go with him, give me a yell when he was in the right position, and make sure he watched. And that would have been it.'

'And good-bye to my motor-bike,' Hugh said dryly.

'No, it could have been brought up and without being too badly damaged. I would have paid for any repairs. I could just about afford that. But in the end, of course, the murder stopped everything.'

'Why play the idiot fop?' Gerry asked.

'I guess it was partly the name: Sebastian Everard *sounds* foppish. And I wanted to adopt a personality as different as possible from my own. I thought, too, that if I made myself a silly-ass type, without too much to say for himself, I could avoid serious conversations and be less likely to get caught out. Of course, I didn't anticipate having to keep it up all through a police murder investigation. Must admit, though, I did rather get caught up in the part.' He gave a weak and sheepish grin.

Mabel said, 'I really am terribly sorry. I feel awful. Of course, we'll leave as soon as Mr Allgood says we may.'

'Not so fast,' Allgood said. 'You two have admitted being here under false pretences. A murder has been committed. I have every right to detain you for further questioning.'

Ned went pale. He said, 'We know nothing about the murder. We told you the absolute truth about that. There's only one small point. Years ago, before she became a star, Laura did appear in a couple of films in this country. I worked on one of them. She didn't positively recognise me this time, but my face was obviously vaguely familiar to her. She was trying to remember where she'd seen me before and she went out of her way to talk to me. That's the only thing I didn't tell you, I swear.'

Allgood regarded him silently. At last he said, 'Very well. I believe you. Please don't leave yet, though.'

Ned gave a sigh of relief. He sat down beside Mabel, who was sobbing silently, and took her hand.

Allgood looked at Haggermeir. 'Tell me, if Turner had pulled off this stunt, would you have given him work?'

Haggermeir pursed his lips. 'Hard to say. Possibly. He'd have sure proved he knew his stuff. Trouble is, there are so many first-rate American stuntmen in Hollywood already.'

'How about the film you're making here, *The King's Man*? Couldn't you use him on that?'

'I, er, wouldn't like to commit myself at this stage.'

'Oh, come. I'm sure there'll be plenty of work for stuntmen in a Rex Ransom picture. If he proves his ability, can't you promise him work on *The King's Man* here and now?'

'Well, no, I'm sorry, at this stage I couldn't.'

'Is that because you have no intention of making *The King's Man*, and never have had?'

For long seconds Haggermeir just sat perfectly still, his eyes fixed on Allgood's face. Then: 'Don't know what you mean,' he said.

'Oh, I think you do, Haggermeir. The whole story of wanting to make a film here at Alderley was a ruse, a way of getting yourself an invitation to the house. You had your own private reason for wanting to spend a few days at Alderley.'

'Horsefeathers.'

'I don't think so. And I'm not the first to discover the truth, either.' He looked at Paul. 'Carter, I'd like you to recount the conversation which you inadvertently overheard in the breakfast room on Friday morning.'

At these words Haggermeir drew his breath in sharply.

Paul nodded. 'Very well.' He explained how he had happened to be in the secret passage and had suddenly heard the voice through the panels. Then he paused for a moment.

'The voice,' he said, 'was Mr Haggermeir's. He was saying he hadn't really come to Alderley to make a picture. That was merely an excuse to give him a chance to search the place. He said that just before she died his grandmother told him that as a young girl she'd been married in California to – to Lord Burford's grandfather, Aylwin Saunders.'

At this the Earl gave a gasp, Lady Burford's eyebrows nearly disappeared into her hairline, and Gerry gazed at Paul in amazement. Paul continued, 'Haggermeir said she'd told him that somewhere – probably here at Alderley – there was proof that he, Haggermeir, was in fact the rightful Earl of Burford.'

CHAPTER TWENTY-ONE

The Burford family seemed struck dumb by Paul's words. Nobody, in fact, said anything until St. John Allgood spoke quietly: 'Thank you, Carter. Well, Haggermeir, what do you have to say to that?'

Haggermeir got slowly to his feet. His face was grey but his expression was defiant. He said, 'Yeah, it's true, it's all true. And I guess I owe you an apology, Earl, for fooling you as I did. To tell you the truth, if I'd known you were going to turn out to be such a regular guy, and the Countess and your daughter such, well, such *ladies,* I guess I'd never have done things in this way. Though that don't mean I ain't still determined to get what's rightfully mine.'

'I suggest you explain just what you mean by that,' Allgood said.

'Ain't it obvious? My grandma – her name was Martha Haggermeir – met and fell for Aylwin Saunders in California in 1850, when she was eighteen. That was just before he'd struck it rich. He told her all about himself, and that one day he'd be the Earl of Burford. The next year, after he'd made his pile, they got married. It was all legal. The ceremony was performed by a fully qualified Baptist preacher named Jones in a little town called Last Straw. The witnesses were Aylwin's manservant and a girlfriend of grandma's. Aylwin took her to San Francisco and for a year or so they lived it up and spent money like water: on furs, jewellery, art objects, you name it. Now, among the things he bought her was a little Chinese casket. Grandma was examining it one day when quite accidentally she discovered it had a false bottom. More for fun than anything else, she put her marriage licence under the false bottom for safe keeping. Then she found she couldn't get it open again. She fiddled with it for ages, and decided eventually she'd have to take it back to the place where they'd bought it. She didn't say anything to Aylwin because at that time it seemed his manner to her was starting to change. She suspected he was tiring of her and he tended to snap her head off at the least excuse. He'd been very taken with the casket and had talked about using it as a cigar box. She was scared it might prove necessary to break it open to get the licence out and that he'd be angry with her.

'Well, it turned out she was right about his feelings for her, because shortly after he left her. One day there was an English visitor for him – that lawyer Lord Burford told us about, I guess – and the next Aylwin just went out and didn't come back. He wrote her a letter from New York a week or two later, saying he was sorry and was returning to England. To give the so-and-so what credit's due to him, he did leave her practically all the cash he had left, together with the jewellery and stuff they'd bought. In fact, about the only thing he took with him was—'

'The Chinese casket,' Gerry put in.

'Yes, Lady Geraldine.'

'What happened?'

'Well, Martha wasn't the sort to sit at home, sobbing herself into a decline. She was a tough little broad. She said good riddance to bad rubbish, raised all the dough she could on the jewellery and stuff, and opened a rooming house in San Francisco, calling herself Mrs Haggermeir and telling people she'd been recently widowed. Something she didn't discover until a month or so after Aylwin left, and which he obviously hadn't known either, was that she was expecting a baby. However, that didn't stop her running the house up to a week before my pa was born. That was on March 23rd, 1852. Incidentally, she gave him Saunders as a middle name.

'In no time grandma was back running the rooming house. It did well. She raised pa on her own. She let him believe his father was dead, though she always meant to tell him the truth one day. However, she kept putting it off. My ma and pa were married in 1881. I was born two years later, and also given the middle name Saunders. They both died of typhoid in 1886. That meant grandma had another boy to raise on her own. She did a pretty good job, too, except she could never make me go to school or get any sort of education. I got in with a pretty rough crowd, but that's by the way.

'Grandma was determined she wasn't going to die without anyone knowing the truth about her and Aylwin, and so when I turned twenty-one she told me the whole story. I guess it didn't really mean a lot to me at first, it was just a bit of a laugh to think I was descended from an

English lord. But as the years went by I thought about it more and more.

'Grandma died at the age of eighty-one in 1913, and soon after that I started to make inquiries. I went to Last Straw, but it was a ghost town by then. The Baptist church had collapsed and there was no way of tracing a Reverend Jones after over fifty years. No doubt the marriage had been registered somewhere, but who could say where? Probably in Sacramento, the state capital, but two-thirds of the city was destroyed by fire in 1852, and there were devastating floods in '53 and '61. So there wasn't anything more I could do. All the same, some years later, when I could afford it, I consulted lawyers. They told me that a genuine, duly witnessed marriage licence would be accepted as evidence by any court on earth.

'I checked up on the Burfords and learnt that Aylwin had succeeded to the title in 1854 and died in 1884. That meant that my pa had been the rightful Earl for two years, 1884 till he died, and now I was. I knew, too, that the only way I could ever prove it would be if I could get hold of that licence. I was pretty sure it would still be in the casket, but as it was likely the casket was somewhere in this house there didn't seem any way I could lay my hands on it. I couldn't invite myself here, and I sure wasn't gonna be invited.

'All the same, I couldn't forget about it. I kept tabs on the Burford family, even arranged for a clipping service to send me everything that appeared on them in the English press. I don't know really what I had in mind. I was just always hoping that something might turn up. Then a couple of months ago it did. A clipping landed on my desk about the Earl. He'd become a movie fan and he wanted to meet Rex Ransom, my number one star. As Turner said just now, it was too good an opportunity to miss. I needed a good excuse for coming here, and thought of the movie idea. I had to have a script, though, and I searched through a lot of old screenplays until I found a suitable one. But because, as you said, I'd never had any intention of actually shooting the movie, I didn't bother to check up on the copyright, as I'd normally have done. So Gilbert turning up kind of threw me.' He paused. 'I guess that's about it.'

Rex addressed the Earl and Countess: 'Lady Burford, George, I want you to understand I knew nothing about this. I'm as flabbergasted as you are.'

Lord Burford nodded abstractedly. 'All right, old man, understood.'

Gerry was still staring at Haggermeir. She said, 'And all the time you've been supposedly measuring and photographing the house, you've actually been searching for that Chinese casket?'

'Yeah.'

'Including my father's study, Thursday night?'

Haggermeir had the grace to look a little abashed. 'Sorry about that. Never figured on having to tangle with a lady. But I wanted to search the study as soon as I could, in case there wasn't a chance later. Thursday night I'd been working up on the top floor. I went back to my room to drop off my camera and found Laura waiting for me. We talked about the movie for a bit, and as soon as she left I went down to the study. I figured everybody'd be in bed. It was quite a shock when you burst in on me. I assure you

I used the least possible force, but naturally I couldn't let you identify me.'

'I cut your face,' Gerry said.

'No, my forearm. I was in my roiled shirtsleeves and I had my arm up. It was quite a nasty cut.'

'I hope you don't expect me to apologise.'

'Not at all.'

Gilbert said indignantly, 'It was you who blacked my eye.'

'Yeah. After getting away from Lady Geraldine, I high-tailed it right up the stairs. Somebody'd turned the lights off and I ran slap into you. Didn't know it was you, of course.'

'And you let me take the rap for searching the study! You're a bounder, sir!'

'Take the rap, baloney! No one was going to clap you in the jug.'

'My reputation could have been ruined.'

'Your reputation! A washed-up hack who hasn't written a screenplay in ten years. You're on your beam ends, so desperate to do *The King's Man* and scrounge a weekend's free board that you forced your way in here uninvited.'

Arlington Gilbert leapt to his feet without warning. He stepped up to Haggermeir. Then his fist shot out and caught Haggermeir squarely on the nose.

Haggermeir fell back for a moment, then launched himself at Gilbert, fists flailing. However, Leather grabbed him while Allgood stepped in front of Gilbert.

'That's enough,' Allgood snapped. 'This isn't a barroom.'

Haggermeir took out a handkerchief and clasped it to

his nose. With a great air of dignity, Gilbert folded his arms and took his seat again.

Rex looked at Haggermeir. 'For years I've lived in mortal fear of offending you, Cyrus. But that's over. You've used me to try and trick these folks. Well, no one makes a sucker out of me. I've made my last picture for you. I don't work for thieves.'

'Thief nothing,' Haggermeir snarled. 'I want what's rightfully mine. That casket was given to my grandma. Aylwin had no right to bring it to England. I still aim to get it back, and what's inside it. And I don't give up easy.'

'I'm afraid in this instance you're going to have to give up,' Lady Burford said quietly. 'You certainly will get no more chances to search the house. However, if it's any consolation, I have never seen such a casket as you describe. If it was here, you'd be more than welcome to it.'

'Thank you, Countess. I'll bear that in mind. Maybe I can't search myself any more, but there are other means. And I'm determined—'

Allgood interrupted. 'Just *how* determined? Are you determined enough to have killed?'

Haggermeir swung round on him. 'Listen, cop, don't try and pin a murder rap on me.'

'I don't need to pin it on you. This does it well enough.' He took a piece of paper from his pocket. 'This,' he said, 'is a photostat of a fragment of burnt paper I found in the fireplace of your room. It was badly charred around the edges, but what remains is quite incriminating enough.'

He looked round the room. 'You see, Carter wasn't the only person to discover why Haggermeir was really here. Laura Lorenzo also did. And she wrote him a note, telling him so and threatening to expose him.'

'It's a lie!' Haggermeir shouted, 'She didn't find out.'

'Just be quiet while I read this. Then, if you've got an explanation you can give it to us.'

He unfolded the paper. 'We've had the original of this checked against a specimen of Laura Lorenzo's handwriting. She definitely wrote it. This is what it says.' He read aloud:

'That the real reason...visit to Alderley is not...discuss making a movie...to expose a wicked...cruelly deceived a whole family...death at the age of...a young and innocent girl...married but he left her...having robbed her...valuable...'

Allgood looked up. 'It's easy enough to reconstruct the gist of the message. It no doubt read roughly like this:

'I know now that the real reason for your present visit to Alderley is not as you claim, to discuss making a movie. I think it my duty to expose a wicked trick, by which you have cruelly deceived a whole family. I know that before her death at the age of eighty-one your grandmother told you that as a young and innocent girl in America she had married but he left her to return to England, having robbed her of a valuable casket.'

Allgood paused. 'Well, I needn't continue with what obviously followed. The implication is plain. After Haggermeir received the note he—'

Haggermeir gave a yell. 'I didn't receive it, I tell you!'

'Yes, you did, and you burnt it. But you were careless, and one bit remained. Laura was a threat. If she exposed you all your hopes of acquiring the title – a thing which has become an obsession with you – would be shattered. You planned to kill her.'

Haggermeir's normally ruddy face was ashen. He whispered, 'No, it's not true.'

'It's no good. You were the only person in this house to have a motive.'

'I didn't kill the dame. I swear it. You gotta believe me.'

Allgood stared at him silently for fully five seconds, Then: 'I believe you,' he said.

A gasp went round the gallery. Haggermeir gazed at Allgood and buried his head in his hands.

Allgood said, 'Oh, everything else I've claimed is true. Haggermeir was the only person here with the motive. But *he* didn't kill her. Somebody else saved him the trouble.'

Lord Burford said bewilderedly. 'But it doesn't make sense. If nobody else had a motive...'

'I'll explain. This is one of those rare cases: a motiveless murder. And the explanation of that is simple. Laura Lorenzo was killed in error.'

'You mean the gun went off accidentally?' the Earl said.

'Oh, no. Murder was intended. But Laura was killed *in mistake for someone else*.'

'But in mistake for whom?'

'The only person she could have conceivably been mistaken for: your daughter, Lady Geraldine.'

Gerry's jaw dropped. '*Me?*'

'That's right.'

'But – but that's crazy! Who could possibly have mistaken Laura for me?'

'The one person in this room who had never seen either of you before last Friday night.'

Allgood turned and his finger shot out. 'There's the killer of Laura Lorenzo.'

He was pointing straight at Jemima Dove.

Jemima Dove had gone white. For a moment she didn't move. Then she made a sudden grab for a small handbag she had with her and which she'd put down beside her.

Allgood's voice rang out. 'Don't bother to go for your gun. The bullets have been removed from it by my man Chalky.'

Jemima froze. Then she seemed to relax and slumped back in her seat, her face expressionless.

Lady Burford said disbelievingly, 'Miss Dove, is this true?'

'She's not Miss Dove,' Allgood said. 'The real Jemima Dove is at present working in Cambridge. I've confirmed that beyond doubt. She's planning to start work on your library next week, as arranged. This young women is another impostor.'

Gerry said weakly, 'But why did she want to kill me?'

'The story starts about two years ago, when she fell in love, desperately in love. For a time the man she was in love with was quite captivated by her. But gradually he began to notice clear signs of mental instability in her. At the same time he fell truly in love with someone else, and he broke off the romance. The grief and humiliation drove the girl right over the edge into insanity. Love turned to hate, both for the man and for the woman *who'd* taken him from her. She determined to take revenge on them both.'

Allgood looked at Paul. 'Carter, for a long time I've felt that you were keeping something back. I'm sorry, but I'm afraid you can do so no longer. You were that man, weren't you?'

Paul hesitated. 'Er, no. Well, in a way, I mean yes, but...'

'Carter, we've found a number of people who'll testify to the fact that before you met Lady Geraldine you were involved in a romance with another girl.'

'Yes, that's true.' Paul turned to Gerry. 'I'm sorry, darling. It was never really all that serious, and as soon as I met you – well, she was just eclipsed.'

Gerry summoned up a shaky smile. 'That's all right, Paul. You never claimed I was your first love.'

Allgood said, 'And ever since this young woman arrived here, you've been concealing the fact that you knew her and knew she was an impostor. Though, of course, you did not know that she was also a murderess. Aren't I right, Carter?'

Paul's face was a picture of uncertainty and anxiety. Allgood said, 'Very well, I won't press you to answer. I admire your chivalry, and we don't need your evidence at this stage.'

Jemima Dove spoke harshly. 'You admitted yourself that I couldn't have stolen that pistol from the collection room.'

'Correct. And I was held up for some time by a preconceived idea: that the person who shot Laura must also have stolen the gun. What didn't occur to me at first was that two people were involved, working together.'

In a horrified whisper Gerry said, 'Somebody else wanted to kill me as well?'

'Yes, Lady Geraldine. And who hated Carter for exactly the same reason that this young woman hated you. As she had lost Carter to you, so he had lost you to Carter. Isn't that true, Quartus?'

Hugh was standing up, very stiff and very still. He was breathing heavily. He said quietly, 'You're mad.'

'No, Quartus, you're the one who's mad. You and your confederate. I don't know which of you planned it, but I would guess you, and I admit it was very clever: a way of taking revenge on the two people who'd humiliated you beyond endurance. Kill her, and frame him for the crime. It was all carefully worked out. On Friday evening you, Quartus, rang up the safe company and obtained the combination of Lord Burford's safe. Later you got the gun room key from it, took the pistol, loaded it, and left it in some prearranged place up here on this floor. After you'd gone out, your accomplice arrived, passing herself off as Miss Dove. Before the party returned she came upstairs. She picked up the gun and waited. One thing you hadn't told her about, however, was the arrival in the house of Laura Lorenzo. As far as she knew, there was only one *young* lady here. Granted Laura was a few years older than Lady Geraldine, but she was so skilfully made up that that wasn't really obvious.'

Allgood turned back to Jemima. 'You saw this attractive and glamorous young woman coming up the stairs, and you naturally assumed it was Lady Geraldine. You followed her to her room and shot her. You claimed to have been in your bedroom when the second shot, the alarm shot, was fired. But it would have been impossible for you to have heard the shot from there, at the farthest part of the house and with your door closed. Just now I asked you all to go into your rooms and shut the doors. But *you* didn't. My man Chalky was watching from my room opposite and he told me a few moments ago that you left your door ajar and stood just inside it. It was essential you hear this shot, and you knew you wouldn't if you obeyed my instructions. But to revert: after murdering Laura, you just waited for Carter to come along. But he'd been delayed. Meanwhile, you, Quartus, were becoming anxious that Lady Geraldine and Carter hadn't turned up. The plan could be ruined. Naturally, you didn't know your accomplice had already shot the wrong person.'

He looked at Jemima again. 'You, in the meantime, had realised the point about the bullet hole in the coat giving away the actual time of death. And – well, I've previously explained what happened then, and we all know the eventual outcome.'

Allgood paused and looked round at his audience. 'And so the mystery is solved and my job is over. Chief Inspector Wilkins will handle the formal charges. So now—'

He broke off, for a *most* unexpected sound had interrupted. It was laughter. And it was coming from the girl they'd known as Jemima Dove. Allgood stared at her in amazement. Then he barked, 'You may think this is all highly amusing, but perhaps—'

She broke in. 'I'm sorry, Mr Allgood. Yours was a marvellous effort, it really was. I'm filled with admiration.

Unfortunately for you, there's just not one word of truth in it.' She picked up her handbag. 'It's all right, I'm not getting my gun out – though incidentally I do have a permit for it.'

She reached into the bag and brought out a small folder of stiff cardboard. 'I *am* an impostor. My real name is Ann Davies. I'm an operative of the Tinkerton Detective Agency, as this will prove.' She handed him the folder and continued, 'I had never seen, or even heard of, Mr Carter or Mr Quartus until last Saturday. And I certainly didn't shoot Laura Lorenzo.'

Allgood was gazing at the identity card with an expression of utter disbelief. He looked up, stared blankly at her for several seconds, then suddenly swung round on Paul. 'Carter, this is the girl you knew, isn't it?'

Paul shook his head. 'No.'

Allgood gave what almost amounted to a screech of rage. 'You blithering idiot! Why didn't you say?'

Paul looked annoyed. 'I thought you didn't want me to say, that you wanted me to play along for a bit because you were laying some trap for her – or for somebody else. I didn't know what to say. Besides, you'd already accused her by then, so what difference did it make?'

Allgood's face was a study. He stammered, 'But – but she perfectly fits the description of your girlfriend, which your manservant gave a colleague of mine this morning.'

Paul looked amused. 'They've been talking to Albert?' He looked at Ann Davies appraisingly. 'Yes, I daresay she does. The colouring's the same, the height, the figure. But the girl I knew – her name was Jean Barnes, by the way – didn't look a bit like Miss Davies, really. As Albert, or any of my friends who knew her would confirm, if they saw Miss Davies. I haven't seen Jean for, oh, eighteen months. Last thing I heard she was in South Africa.'

Ann Davies bowed her head. 'Thank you, Mr Carter.'

Allgood rounded on her fiercely. 'All right, so you're not Jean Barnes. But you were here under a false name. And you wouldn't be the first private detective to commit murder.'

She shook her head. 'It won't do. If I'm not this Jean Barnes, where's my motive? And if Mr Quartus and I have never met before this weekend, which I know he'll confirm—'

Hugh nodded. 'Absolutely. You'll never trace any connection between us, Allgood, because there isn't one.'

'So,' Ann Davies said, 'who stole the gun? You've admitted I couldn't have.'

Allgood made a valiant attempt to recover. 'Then if you didn't come here to kill why are you here under a false identity? What are you up to?'

Ann stood up. She seemed quite a different person from the timid Jemima Dove – brisk, assured, decisive. She said crisply, 'I came here on the track of one of the world's most ruthless and efficient professional blackmailers.'

Rex Ransom looked up sharply.

'My firm was hired,' she continued, 'by a wealthy businessman who'd been blackmailed and was determined to see his persecutor brought to justice. He gave us virtually unlimited funds. I've been on the assignment for two years, always just one step behind the blackmailer. I've travelled thousands of miles. Four times I've traced victims who were unwilling to cooperate, seven times I've lost track of my quarry completely. I was on the verge of giving up. And then I got one more lead: the next job was going to be at Alderley this weekend. How I found out about Jemima Dove isn't important. What is important is that at last I've succeeded.' She looked straight at Arlington Gilbert. 'Is it true what Mr Haggermeir said earlier, that you're washed up and on your beam ends?'

Gilbert bridled. 'How dare you! Of course it's—'

But suddenly the piercing gaze she was directing on him seemed to make him think better of what he was saying. He stopped short and his eyes dropped. 'It's – it's true enough,' he muttered.

'In that case, how can you afford to employ a secretary?'

Gilbert seemed to come to a decision. He looked straight at her and spoke clearly. 'I can't.'

'You don't pay Miss Fry any salary, do you? In fact, *she* paid *you* to be allowed to accompany you here and pose as your secretary.'

This time he did hesitate, but only for a second before saying, 'Yes.'

'Would you be prepared to testify to that in a court?'

'I would.'

'Mr Ransom, are you prepared to give evidence and produce the photo and note that were left in your room?'

'You bet I am, honey.'

Ann Davies stepped across to Maude Fry and looked

down at her. 'And that, Miss Fry – or Miss Robinson, or Miss Harris, or Miss Clark – means that after two years I've got you cold.'

When Ann had first mentioned her name, Maude Fry had seemed to freeze. But now she at least reacted. She jumped to her feet. 'This is monstrous! I've never been so insulted in my life. I shall leave this house immediately. And I assure you, Miss, that you will be hearing from my lawyers.'

'Then in that case, you'd better sit down again and listen until I've finished. You'll then be able to tell them all I said about you, won't you?'

Maude Fry's lips tightened. 'Well, really! I most certainly shall. I have an excellent memory.'

'Good.' Ann looked at Allgood. 'This woman's usual technique, though not in this particular case, is to obtain a post as private secretary to some wealthy business or professional man. It's always somebody she's heard some whisper of scandal about, and she has quite a network of informers. She's a first-class secretary and quickly makes herself invaluable. A confidential secretary has wonderful opportunities to dig out her boss's secrets. Then, sooner or later, she strikes. She leaves his employ, her bank balance considerably fatter, and usually with a good reference to boot. She's been intelligent enough never to go back with fresh demands, and so her victims have never been driven to prosecute. This time, however, she changed her technique slightly. She'd plainly learnt something about Mr Ransom who, he'll excuse my saying, must be a very rich man. There was little chance, though, that he'd want a secretary: the studio handles all his correspondence, and so on. However, when she heard he was coming to Alderley she did the next best thing. She got herself ostensibly taken on by a man who was going to be a member of the same house party.'

'I didn't get my lead on her movements until last week – how doesn't matter – and then I had to find a way of getting into the house myself. It took some time. On top of that I was delayed by the road conditions on Friday, so I didn't arrive here until the party was well under way. I'd never seen my quarry face to face, but I'd been given enough descriptions of her to recognise her as Maude Fry as soon as I clapped eyes on her. I didn't know what the situation was: whether she'd started to apply the squeeze, or even who her victim was. It could have been any of the gentleman guests, or even the Earl.

'After I was introduced to Fry I was determined not to let her out of my sight more than I could help. When she left the room I went with her, but instead of going to my bedroom I waited a few seconds in the corridor and then followed her. I hid in this gallery and kept an eye on her door. It must have been after that that Mr Turner brought the motor-bike up. After a minute she left the room again, carrying a large envelope. She went into the Royal Suite, came out again almost immediately without the envelope, and went downstairs. I slipped in there myself. The envelope was propped up on the mantelpiece. I took it into the next-door bathroom and steamed it open. As I'd expected, it contained a photograph – which I did not, incidentally, look at – and an anonymous letter. This was cut from newspapers in the usual way and demanded two thousand pounds in cash for the negative. Otherwise copies would be sent to the press.'

'That's just about the amount of cash I have with me,' Rex said. 'How the heck did she know?'

'Oh, her research has always been excellent. She would probably have asked more, but that would have entailed a delay for you to get hold of the money.'

Ann addressed Allgood again. 'If Mr Ransom agreed to meet the demand, he was to come down the following morning wearing his watch on his right wrist. And he was then to leave the money in the roots of a certain specified tree in the park near the drive on Saturday morning. If he went out again in the evening he would find the negative in the same place. That way there need be no contact between blackmailer and victim, and Mr Ransom would not know who the blackmailer was. Fry, who had already prepared a reason for leaving the house on Saturday morning without causing suspicion, would simply slip back into the grounds later in the day and collect the cash.'

'But why do it this way?' Rex said. 'Why not wait until we'd both left here and she could have contacted me by post or phone? It would have been much less risky and, as you said, she could have squeezed me for even more money.'

'For the simple reason that she was in desperate need of the cash. She's made a great deal over the years, but she's gambled most of it away. She's in debt to several bookmakers, who are getting very nasty. She simply couldn't afford to wait. Of course, in the event, the murder meant she had no choice. One thing only puzzles me: why she didn't plant the envelope in Mr Ransom's room earlier on Friday. Before the party left for the village, I imagine, she was prevented by people constantly entering and leaving the other bedrooms all around, but I don't know why she didn't do it immediately after they all left.'

'I think I can tell you.' The words, unexpectedly, came from Mabel. 'I went to her room almost as soon as they'd gone and told her we were just going to start playing bridge. She more or less had to come straight down with Ned and me.'

'Thank you,' Ann said. 'Not that the delay really mattered. Mr Ransom would assume the envelope had been put there much earlier, while he was downstairs waiting to leave, and Mr Gilbert, as well as everybody else, was still upstairs, getting ready.'

Rex nodded grimly. 'That's just what I did figure. And all along it was *her* I tangled with in my room, not Gilbert at all. But I thought I blacked the intruder's eye.'

'You did,' Ann said. 'But it must have been a glancing blow and the bruising didn't show under these blue lenses. However—'

Suddenly her hand shot out and flicked the glasses from Maude Fry's face. 'You see? There's still a trace of a black eye there. She's been wearing these permanently since, and hasn't been seeing too well as a result – been tending to stumble over things. I fancy she only normally wears them for reading.'

'That's right,' Paul exclaimed. 'I remember her putting them on to write something almost as soon as she arrived and then taking them off again.'

Ann looked at Arlington Gilbert. 'It was after she left Mr Ransom's room on Thursday night that she cannoned into you.'

'I thought it was her,' he said in an unusually quiet voice. 'Until Lady Geraldine told me it was she who'd scratched me, that is. Even after that, when I'd had a chance to think about it, I decided Lady Geraldine had mistaken me for someone else. Because I became convinced it wasn't a knife I'd been scratched with. I couldn't prove it was Miss Fry, though.'

'I apologise for everything, Mr Gilbert,' Gerry said.

'But as a matter of interest, what were you doing walking about in the dark on Thursday night?'

'I'd been getting more and more worried about why Miss Fry had been willing to pay to accompany me here. She'd said she was hoping to wangle a job as Lady Burford's secretary, but I came not to believe that. I was determined to find out the truth. I knew she had a camera *and* a flash gun with her, and the most likely time to use that would be at night. I decided to keep a watch on her room. On Thursday night, I came along here and waited with the door open an inch. After about half an hour, however, there'd still been no movement from her room, and I realised I was being a bit of an ass and she might not stir all night. So I made my way back towards my room. But the lights had gone out, and just as I was groping across the landing somebody came blundering up the stairs and ran right into me. We struggled, and then he slugged me in the eye. So that bloody nose I gave you just now, Haggermeir, you had coming to you. I'd no sooner got to my feet, when almost the same thing happened again, only this time I got a scratched face instead. She must have gone into Ransom's room much earlier, before I'd ever started watching her room, and had been in there all the time.'

Ann nodded. 'The whole thing was well-planned. Even, I strongly suspect, to the extent of breaking the window in Mr Ransom's original bedroom.'

'She did that?' Rex exclaimed. 'But why?'

'She must have started snooping around as soon as she arrived and quickly realised it would be much easier to get a photo of you if you were occupying the Suite – three rooms with adjoining doors. If your first room was made uninhabitable, it was more than likely you'd be transferred to the Suite: his lordship wouldn't want you relegated to a room at the far end of one of the wings. I won't press that point, though. I can't prove it.'

During all this time St. John Allgood had obviously been making violent efforts to get his thoughts under control. Now at last he spoke again. 'This is all very well, but it's Friday night, not Thursday, that concerns me. You weren't in your room when that shot was fired.'

'I admit it,' Ann said. 'I'll tell you what happened. After reading the blackmail note I replaced it in its envelope and put it back where I'd found it. I wanted the victim to have the shock of finding it. Then a little later I'd go to him, tell him the truth, and ask him to come to the police with me. But at that time *I still didn't know who the victim was*. I had no way of telling who was occupying the Royal Suite. There was no time to go through the occupant's things and get a clue. I had to hurry back downstairs for the bridge game. I could have asked the Countess who was in there, but it might have looked a bit odd. So when we later heard the others returning I went upstairs again with Fry, hurried to my room and put a dressing-gown on over my clothes – I thought it would look more natural if I was up for any length of time – then took up position in that linen room opposite the Royal Suite. About five minutes later Mr Ransom came up and went into his rooms. I decided to give him about ten minutes fully to take in the situation, then go across, identify myself, tell him I knew who the blackmailer was, and ask for his cooperation. Eventually I left my hiding place and tapped on the bedroom door. There was no reply. I was surprised, and I suddenly thought with horror that perhaps he'd committed suicide. I went in. The room was empty. I crossed to the centre, looking fearfully round for a body. Then I saw the envelope where I'd left it – and heard Mr Ransom whistling in the next room. I realised he'd come in and gone straight through to his dressing-room without noticing the letter. The next moment I heard him coming towards the connecting door.

'In a flash it hit me that I'd made an awful blunder. If he came in and saw me there, he'd immediately assume he'd caught *me* in the act of planting the blackmail note. I was here under a false identity. I'd quite likely be accused of blackmail. I'd be able to clear myself eventually, but in the interim Fry would get away. It was vital he didn't find me there. There wasn't time to get to the door. I did the only thing I could think of – threw myself under the bed.'

Rex stared at her. 'When I found that envelope and opened it, you were under the bed? Good grief. I hope my language didn't shock you too much.'

'Oh, I've heard worse, Mr Ransom.' She addressed Allgood again. 'I stayed there for nearly an hour. I was more or less resigned to staying there all night. Then someone knocked on the door of the next room. It was

Lady Geraldine. While Mr Ransom was talking to her I at last managed to get out. I'd heard her say she'd only be staying for a few seconds, which meant I might not have time to get back to my own room before she re-emerged, and as I didn't want her to spot me in the corridor I slipped into the bathroom next door. I waited there until I heard Lady Geraldine leaving, gave it another minute or two to be on the safe side, and then started back towards the west wing. I decided it would now be better not to talk to Mr Ransom until the morning. However, I'd only got level with the stairs when Lady Geraldine emerged from her own room again. I'm afraid this time I slipped into Lady Burford's boudoir. I was waiting there with the door open an inch when I heard the shot. Everything else happened exactly as I told you, Mr Allgood. There are just a couple more points and then I'll shut up. While you were questioning Miss Fry yesterday, I took the opportunity to search her room. It was, incidentally, the first chance I'd had, though I'd been hanging around in here for hours, waiting for a clear moment. In a locked case under her bed – I'm good at picking locks – I discovered a full set of developing equipment. Unfortunately, I couldn't find the negative of that blackmail photo. For safety's sake, she no doubt went out on Friday and hid it somewhere in the area so that she could retrieve it after she had Mr Ransom's money.'

'She went out in her car on Friday morning carrying an envelope,' Ned said. 'She said she was going to mail a letter.'

'Thank you,' Ann said. 'I doubt very much if she did actually mail it. However, it's not important. So long as

Mr Ransom will prefer charges, we've got her where we want her.'

'Sugar,' Rex said, 'you've got yourself a deal.'

There was silence for several seconds. Everyone looked at Allgood. But he seemed incapable of speech. Eventually it was Lady Burford who spoke. 'Well, Miss Fry, have you nothing to say?'

Maude Fry burst into tears. 'I've never done anything like this before,' she sobbed. 'Whatever this girl says. It was a sudden temptation. I knew Mr Ransom had all that money, and – and...' She tailed off.

A look of pure self-satisfaction appeared on Ann Davies's face. She said, 'My case is proved, I think.' She sat down.

Suddenly Allgood shouted angrily at her. 'Why didn't you tell me all this before? It's disgraceful!'

'I'm sorry. I suppose I should have. But as I knew nothing about the murder, other than what I've told you, I didn't think it would matter.'

'You lied about where you were when the shot was fired.'

'Yes, but it made no difference. I told you the whole truth about what I'd seen and heard. Of course, if I'd known you were going to pick on me as your number one suspect, I'd have told you the truth about that too. But yesterday you informed me I was no longer under suspicion. If you'd put to me the point about my not being able to hear the shot from my room, instead of rushing in bull-headed with a public accusation, I'd have explained everything and you wouldn't have made such a fool of yourself.'

Gerry thought Allgood was going to burst, as his face slowly turned puce. It was the Earl who asked him the question in everybody's mind. Very gently, he said, 'Tell me, my dear chap, do you have any idea at all who killed Miss Lorenzo?'

'What? Of course I have. It was – it was – well, if it wasn't her, it was...' He gazed round desperately. 'It was him!' He pointed at Haggermeir. 'As I said first. Or them.' He indicated Ned and Mabel. 'Or possibly all of them. Yes, that's it. It's a conspiracy. They—' He stopped dead.

It was at that moment that Chief Inspector Wilkins cleared his throat.

CHAPTER TWENTY-TWO

Wilkins's intervention wasn't a particularly dramatic one. But it brought every eye in the room instantly round to him.

He stepped forward. 'I'm afraid Mr Allgood's rather got hold of the wrong end of the stick,' he said.

Lord Burford said, 'Wilkins, you mean you *do* know who killed Signorina Lorenzo?'

'Yes, my lord, I knew very early on in the investigation.' He turned his gaze mildly on Allgood. 'I did try to tell you, sir, but you weren't interested in my ideas only in facts. I gave you all the facts I knew. I really thought you'd make the same inferences from them that I had, but you didn't. So all I could do was play for time until I could get hold of the proof I needed.'

He addressed the room at large. 'Miss Lorenzo came to Alderley to try and identify a man who some years ago caused the death of a cousin of hers, a girl who was more like a sister, and robbed the family of some valuable jewellery. I learnt that the family still had a snapshot of this man. I arranged yesterday for an enlargement of it to be flown from Italy. Ever since then I've been waiting for it to arrive. It reached the Westchester police station a short time ago and was rushed straight here. A few minutes ago it was handed to me through the door by a constable. I don't think anybody noticed, as at that moment Mr Haggermeir and Mr Gilbert were engaged in their little fracas.'

Wilkins brought a glossy six-by-eight photo from behind his back and looked at it. 'As I said, it's only the enlargement of a snapshot, but I think it's quite identifiable.' Slowly he raised the photograph up for everyone in the room to see. The smiling face that confronted them was that of Paul Carter.

The first person to move was Paul. With one hand he caught Gerry by the arm and jerked her violently to him. The other hand flew inside his jacket and came out holding Allgood's revolver.

Only one man reacted as quickly. As the gun came up, Ned Turner threw himself at Paul, but he wasn't quite fast enough. The revolver barked. Ned fell to the floor, clutching at his leg. Mabel gave a cry and dropped to her knees beside him.

Paul shoved the muzzle of the gun against Gerry's head. 'If anyone moves, she dies.'

Halfway to his feet, Lord Burford froze. The Countess gave a strangled cry.

In a voice of disbelieving horror, Gerry gasped, 'Paul, are you out of your mind?'

'Shut up, you.' Then he snarled, 'Get against the far wall, all of you.'

'Do exactly as he says,' Wilkins ordered sharply.

The others began to back away to the wall adjoining the gun room, Ned being half carried by Rex and Haggermeir. When they were all lined up against it, Paul moved to the other door, pulling Gerry with him. Just inside it he stopped.

'I want some handcuffs.'

At a nod from Wilkins, Leather took a pair from his pocket. 'Slide them across the floor,' Paul snapped. Leather did so. They stopped near Gerry's feet. Paul gave her a jab with the gun. 'Put them on.'

He kept tight hold of her arm as she bent down, picked them up, and awkwardly manacled her wrists with them.

Paul addressed Wilkins. 'How many men have you got here?'

'None in the house. There's a man at the lodge.'

Paul gave a nod and looked at the Earl. 'Where will the servants be now?'

It was Lady Burford who answered. 'Probably all having their afternoon tea in the kitchen.'

'That's fine.' He gave Gerry a prod. 'OK, let's go.'

Rex said, 'If you want a hostage, why not take me? I'm not worth as much as Gerry, but I'm quite a valuable property.'

'Nothing doing, buddy.'

Allgood said hoarsely, 'Carter, you can't think you can get away with this.'

'Maybe not. But I'm certainly going to try. And remember this, all of you: if the police take me I'll hang. Well, can't hang twice, so I've got nothing to lose by killing again.'

He opened the massive door, pushed Gerry through, slipped quickly out after her, and pulled the door behind him. A second later they heard the tumblers slide across.

Wilkins swung round on the Earl. 'Is there a bell in here for the servants?' Lord Burford shook his head. 'Then we'll have to try and break the door down,' Wilkins said. 'Jack! And some of you help him.'

He hurried to the nearest window and looked out. 'No drainpipe, creeper, nothing. And a flat stone pavement underneath.'

Leather, Chalky, Arlington Gilbert, and Rex Ransom had begun throwing themselves against the door. Leather called, 'It's like a rock, sir.'

Hugh said quietly, 'Why not shoot the lock out?'

Lord Burford gave a gasp. 'Of course! The guns!' Groping on his watch-chain for the key, he hurried to the door of the collection room.

Haggermeir and Allgood meanwhile had lifted Ned onto one of the sofas and were attempting to staunch the flow of blood from his leg.

Lady Burford was sitting very still, erect and pale. Her eyes were closed and she appeared to be praying.

The Earl had by now disappeared into the collection room. Ann Davies followed him. She saw the French windows leading to the balcony at the far end and started to run towards them, calling, 'Perhaps there's a way down from the balcony.'

'There isn't,' Lord Burford said tersely, but Ann didn't stop.

The Earl strode rapidly to the part of the wall from which was slung a heavy modern hunting rifle. He snatched it down and half-ran to the ammunition cupboard again fumbling for keys, this time in his pocket.

Ann reached the far end, unbolted the windows, threw them open and stepped onto the balcony. She saw immediately that there was no possible means of climbing down. And below was the flat terrace outside the ground floor ballroom. Beyond that was the wide path that ran right round the house, a steep grass bank, and the lake.

Then, round the corner of the house, appeared Paul's car. The top was still down. He was at the wheel and Gerry was beside him. But he was going much too fast for the conditions, and Ann gave a gasp as the car skidded wildly on the icy surface. It slid to a halt, facing back in the direction it had come. Paul started to yank desperately at starter and gear.

Ann gave a yell into the room. 'Out here! He's getting away!'

Lord Burford, who'd loaded the rifle and was on his way back to the gallery, stopped, turned, and then ran down the room towards her.

By the time the Earl had joined Ann, Paul had got the car moving again, but the surface was as treacherous as a skating rink. The car was sliding from side to side, its wheels spinning furiously.

Ann gripped the Earl's arm. 'Can you shoot a tire out?'

He shook his head. 'Daren't risk it, with Gerry in the car.'

There was the sound of running footsteps, and they were joined on the balcony by Lady Burford, Hugh and Wilkins.

'Why's he come this way?' Hugh panted.

'He's avoiding the drive, and the policeman at the lodge,' the Earl muttered. 'He's going to take the track to the home farm. That'll lead him out onto a lane that runs directly to the main Westchester road.'

As he spoke, the wheels of the tourer seemed at least to find a dry patch. The car shot forward.

Just before the path reached a point opposite the watchers on the balcony, there was another bend in it. Hardly slowing at all to take it, Paul swung the wheel. At the same moment the car struck another patch of ice.

Its rear wheels skewed round, but the car continued in the same direction. It leapt from the path and over the bank, to land with an almighty splash in the lake.

The Countess gave a scream. The Earl dropped his rifle with a clatter on the floor. The car was slowly sinking beneath the water. They could see both Paul and Gerry struggling to extricate themselves.

In a matter of seconds Paul had got clear. He struck out strongly for the near bank. However, obviously realising that the steepness and slipperiness of it would make it almost impossible to climb unaided, he veered to his right and made for a point further away but where the bank was less steep. In his mouth, the trigger guard clamped between his teeth, was the revolver.

Lady Burford gave a cry. 'Gerry! Gerry, darling!'

Then they heard Gerry's voice. 'Help! I can't get out. The handcuffs – caught. Paul, help me!'

But Paul ignored the cries. He continued to swim for land.

The car was sinking even lower. The water was now only six inches below the top of the doors. 'When it gets to the top she'll sink in seconds,' Hugh whispered.

The Countess shouted, 'Oh, somebody do something!'

Lord Burford made a sudden lunge for the balustrade. Wilkins grabbed at him, and the Earl tried to shake him free.

'It's no good, sir. You'll break a leg at the very least.'

Suddenly Hugh gave a loud shout. 'I've got it!' He turned and sprinted down the room.

In the gallery the three men were still working on the door. But now they'd taken up Ned's plank and were about to start using it as a battering-ram. Hugh yelled to them, 'Take that to the balcony! Lean it against the balustrade! Make a ramp! Quick!'

They hesitated only a second, then turned and started to run, carrying the plank between them.

Hugh dashed towards the end of the gallery. As he did so he snapped over his shoulder, 'Allgood, help me with this sofa!'

Allgood, who was sitting slumped on a chair, a picture of defeat, jumped up and ran after him. 'What are you going to do?'

'Try Turner's idea.'

'*What?* Don't be a lunatic!'

'Stop arguing. Move it!'

From where he lay, Ned called, 'You'll never make it, man. You'll kill yourself.'

Hugh, with Allgood's help, was already heaving the sofa to one side. Over his shoulder he shouted, 'You were going to do it.'

'I'm a pro, and I'd have had a helmet and protective suit.'

'It's either this, or Gerry drowns.' He threw his leg over the saddle and kicked at the starter.

With a roar that reverberated like a dozen engines round the gallery, the motor burst into life. Hugh rode it to the centre of the room, turned it to face the door of the gun room, and backed it until the rear wheel was tight against the outer door. Beyond the far door of the gallery the collection room stretched ahead, a sort of passage running between the display cases. The other men had done their job. The plank was in position. It looked a tiny target, yet at the same time absurdly close.

Hugh closed his eyes, said a silent prayer, squeezed the clutch, engaged bottom gear, and twisted the throttle to give maxirevs. The engine howled.

Hugh opened his eyes, put all his weight on the saddle, pulled up on the handle-bars to give optimum grip under the rear wheel, and let out the clutch. The bike rocketed forward.

For the first time Hugh felt the full power of the machine's engine. Accelerating at an enormous rate, he shot across the gallery and into the gun room. As he tore along it he kept his gaze fixed on the ridiculously narrow plank. Two inches out and he'd tilt it and go crashing into the wall or the balustrade. Then his front wheel had hit it – dead centre.

There was a jolt, and for a split second he was climbing the steeply sloping ramp. The next second he felt a blast of cold air on his face, and he was flying. For a moment he saw everything laid out below him like an aerial photograph: the terrace, the path, the grassy bank, and the icy waters of the lake.

He wasn't aware of the moment he parted company with his bike. He just knew that suddenly he was sailing through the air like a bird. He felt an instant of wild, insane elation, and then he was plummeting feet first towards the lake.

Miraculously he managed to remain upright, and had the presence of mind to take a lungful of air. Then he was immersed in freezing blackness – sinking, sinking, sinking…

As Hugh hit the water every breath on the balcony was held. He'd landed seven yards from the car, in which Gerry was still struggling desperately to free herself. The water was now one inch from the top of the door. They waited, no one moving or making a sound. Seconds seemed like hours.

Then Hugh's head broke water. He stared, gasping, around him, spotted the car, and started a fast crawl towards it.

Lord Burford gave a gasp. 'By Jove, he's made it!'

But even while he spoke the car was continuing to sink. Then Hugh had reached it. He heaved the door open and water cascaded into the car. In seconds it had reached Gerry's shoulders. Hugh took a deep breath and once more disappeared beneath the surface.

Even though Gerry was straining upwards to the limit of her reach, the water had now got to her chin.

Then the horrified watchers saw her head suddenly vanish beneath the water like an angler's float. Lady Burford gave a little cry.

But the next moment they realised what had happened.

Hugh had grabbed her by the shoulders and pulled her down, as the only way of easing the tension on the handcuffs and releasing her.

Further nerve-racking seconds passed. But then the two heads, the dark and the red, appeared together, moving slowly but safely from the car as it finally sank beneath the water.

Just then a sight never before and never again to be seen at Alderley was observed: Merryweather appeared – running. He came around the corner of the house and threw himself down on the bank, exactly as Hugh and Gerry reached it. Ten seconds later, with his help, they were out of the water.

Gerry fell against Hugh and he put his arms around her. They stood locked together, the water dripping from them. The countess let out a long shuddering sigh. 'Thank heavens.'

Meanwhile, however, Paul had reached the other bank and had been desperately trying to scramble out. But although the bank here was less steep, it was very slippery, and he kept falling back. He took the gun from his mouth and threw it up onto the grass. Then he made one final effort and at last managed to heave himself up out of the water, at almost the same moment as Merryweather was helping the others ashore. Paul lay gasping for a few seconds, then dragged himself to his feet. He looked up and saw Hugh and Gerry together. Abruptly his expression changed to one of malice and rage. He bent, snatched up the revolver, and aimed it straight at them.

In the nick of time, Hugh saw the danger. As Paul

fired he threw himself flat, pulling Gerry down with him. Merryweather, too, dropped to the ground and the bullet passed harmlessly over them. Paul took aim a second time.

At that instant the Earl and Countess were deafened by a loud report from beside them. Paul fell as though poleaxed. He made an attempt to rise, then collapsed again and lay still.

Lord and Lady Burford swung round to see Wilkins in the act of lowering the Earl's rifle from his shoulder. He gazed at them. Suddenly he looked very tired. Then he seemed to collect himself.

'Oh, I beg your pardon, my lord. Do forgive me for using your gun without permission.'

Lord Burford let out his breath in a long gasp. He put his hand on Wilkins's shoulder. 'Any time, Wilkins, any time at all.'

The Countess drew herself up. 'Well, everything seems to be over. Oh, dear, that girl! Always in some sort of scrape. George, you really must have a serious talk with her.'

CHAPTER TWENTY-THREE

'Well, Wilkins,' St. John Allgood said in the small music room later, 'that all ended very satisfactorily.'

'I suppose so, sir.'

Two hours had passed. Two ambulances and a doctor had arrived and departed, as well as more policemen. The body of Paul Carter had been removed to the mortuary. Ned Turner had been taken to the nearest hospital, Mabel accompanying him. Maude Fry had been arrested and escorted by Sergeant Leather to the police station. Arlington Gilbert and Cyrus Haggermeir, both strangely subdued, had retired to their rooms. After a hot bath, a deeply shocked Geraldine had been given a sedative and sent to bed, and the Countess was still with her.

'Yes, indeed,' Allgood went on. 'Nasty things, murder trials. Unpleasant for all concerned. Always a chance, too, of the prisoner getting off on a technicality. If not, hanging. Messy business. So, in a way, good thing he had that gun of mine, after all, eh?' Allgood gave a short, forced laugh.

'Perhaps Lady Geraldine wouldn't think so, sir.'

'Maybe not. But all's well that ends well. Good shot of yours. Unfortunately, I was out of reach of a gun myself, watching from a gallery window. But I had every confidence in you.'

'Very good of you, sir.'

'Not at all. Had from the start, of course. And realised you'd had quite a bit longer to work on the case than I, and were probably close to cracking it. So let you get on with it. Put on a bit of a show, false accusations and all that, in order to distract attention from you and your investigations.'

'Thank you, sir.'

'I, er, suppose you'll be making a statement to the press?'

'No doubt, sir. And you needn't worry. I've no intention of grabbing all the glory. I'll see you get full credit, just as though we were equal partners.'

'Ah. Yes. Very good. Er, thank you.' He looked at his watch. 'Well, must be getting back to London. Heavy case load waiting. It's been a very, um, interesting investigation.'

'I'll make sure you get a copy of my report, sir. And that your Commissioner does, too.'

'Oh, I don't really think there's any need to trouble—'

'No trouble, sir. I'm sure my Chief will want one sent. They're old friends, I understand.'

'Oh, I see.' Allgood gave a sickly grin. 'That'll be something to look forward to, then. Now I really must leave. Chalky's waiting outside with the car. Bye, er, old man.'

He went hurriedly out. Wilkins shook his head and

gave a sigh. 'Three Great A's, indeed!' he said aloud. 'Reckon he coined that himself. He's not in the same class as Mr Appleby or Mr Alleyn.'

Just as Allgood departed, Merryweather entered. 'His lordship's compliments, sir, and would you care to join him in the library for some refreshment?'

'Ah, come in, my dear fellow.' Lord Burford got to his feet. 'Toddle over to the fire and sit down. We want a full explanation of this extraordinary business.'

'We', apart from the Earl himself, consisted of Rex, Hugh – a quite different Hugh, with a cheerful expression and a face flushed as a result of both a hot bath and the stream of thanks and compliments which had been showered upon him – and Ann.

'Very well, my lord, if you insist.' Wilkins sat down and stretched out his feet to the blazing fire.

The Earl pressed a glass of whisky into his hand. 'Now start talking.'

'Right, my lord. But let me say first that with both Carter and Miss Lorenzo dead, a great deal has to be surmised or inferred. The main outline's clear enough, but a lot of the minor details can only be guessed at.'

Ann said, 'But don't keep saying "I imagine" and "perhaps" and so on. Just give us the most likely outline, as though you actually *knew* all the facts.'

Wilkins collected his thoughts. 'I suppose the first thing to say is that Paul Carter was a professional villain of the nastiest sort. For years now he's been living by his wits, mostly off women. This case started about six years ago when he went to northern Italy to climb the Matterhorn.

While he was there he met a girl called Gina Foscari. She was a nice girl, and she invited him home to meet her parents. Mr and Mrs Foscari took to him as well, and asked him to stay. They were a pleasant, middle-class family, not especially well-off. Virtually their only valuable possessions were some jewels, which had been in the family for several generations, and which eventually would have been Gina's.

'I needn't go into the story in detail, but one day the girl and Carter just disappeared, together with the jewels. Two weeks later the girl's body was found. She'd fallen from the third floor balcony of a hotel where she and Carter had been staying as man and wife. There was no sign of Carter, nor of the jewels. It was never known whether he'd pushed Gina off, or simply abandoned her and she'd killed herself. Mr Foscari had to identify the body. The shock was too much for him. He had a heart attack and died a day or two later.

'Carter, of course, hadn't given the Foscaris his real name. Moreover, he'd told them he was American. Police inquiries were therefore directed across the Atlantic and were naturally unsuccessful.

'The relevance of all this is that Mr and Mrs Foscari were the uncle and aunt of Laura Lorenzo. She was very close to them, and had been to Gina. Her own parents were dead and she had no brothers or sisters, so it was a personal tragedy for her. Now, it so happened that she had met Carter briefly, having paid the Foscaris a flying visit while he was staying with them.'

Rex said, 'So when she turned up here, he recognised her.'

'Not at first, sir. She hadn't made her reputation in those days. She was just a fairly small-time actress, and it's probable she was introduced to him by her family name, Laura Lorenzo being a stage name. Also, I imagine she's changed her appearance – hair style and so on – quite a lot since then. On the other hand, however, she herself did have an excellent memory for faces.

'Years passed. Then six or eight weeks ago, *The Londoner* magazine carried a highly complimentary article on Miss Lorenzo. Her London agent sent her a copy. In the society pages there was a photograph of Carter and Lady Geraldine at a charity ball.'

'And she recognised him from that?' Ann said.

'Not positively, miss. If she had, I think she'd have notified the police immediately. My belief is that she wanted a chance to study him closely and at length, in order to be quite sure. Mr Haggermeir's visit here gave her the opportunity. She arranged for that phoney telegram to be sent to her and just turned up here, knowing she'd almost certainly be invited to stay. She knew there was a good chance Carter would be staying here as well; but if he wasn't, she could no doubt make friends with Lady Geraldine and meet Carter later through her. Well, at first she was lucky. He *had* been invited. Things, though, didn't go quite as she'd anticipated. She convinced herself that Carter was the man she was looking for, but she was put off by the fact that she also recognised Mr Turner, though wasn't able to place him. He denied knowing her, but she was certain. He was here under a false name and was therefore quite probably a villain. She must have asked herself if there could be any connection between him and Carter: had she years ago seen them together?

'Something else that bothered her was Mr Haggermeir's strange coolness. She'd expected him to be overjoyed at the prospect of signing her up. We know, of course, that her arrival embarrassed him intensely, because he actually had no intention of making a film here. Nevertheless, it must have been a blow to her ego. We must remember that she was first and foremost a professional actress. Although she came here to trace her cousin's killer, signing with Mr Haggermeir would probably be the necessary concomitant to that. It was going to be a big step to take. Hence her interest in the script, and in Mr Gilbert's attitude to adapting it, was quite genuine.

'I think it's possible that a further factor which unsettled her was uncertainty about Lady Geraldine: she didn't know if her ladyship was another of Carter's potential victims (in which case she ought to be warned against him); or if, on the other hand, she might conceivably be a partner in crime. According to Sergeant Leather, Mrs Turner told them yesterday that Miss Lorenzo questioned her quite closely about Lady Geraldine's past brushes with the law.

'As a result of all these doubts and questions, Miss Lorenzo dithered about what to do next. Then sometime on Saturday, probably around lunchtime, Carter recognised her. We can never know how – the odd giveaway word, the chance meeting of eyes. Perhaps, for all we know, she actually came out in the open: identified herself by her real name, and challenged Carter. But in whatever way it happened, she'd effectively signed her death warrant. He was playing for the biggest stakes of his life. For over a year he'd been exerting all his charm on Lady Geraldine, a lady who – begging your pardon, my lord – will one day inherit a huge fortune. And he believed he was on the point of winning her. Nothing, not the merest hint of a scandal, even if no crime could be proved against him, could be allowed to stand in his way. Whatever the risk, Miss Lorenzo had to be silenced.'

Wilkins drained his glass.

Lord Burford said, 'Well, that's all fascinating, Wilkins. But how did he do it, and when? How did he manage to convince you and Allgood that he was innocent?'

'He never convinced me, your lordship. I was careful never to say I thought him innocent – only, for example, that I believed him when he claimed that things weren't as they seemed, and that when he entered Miss Lorenzo's room a few minutes before he was found standing by the body, she was already dead. Actually, I was quite certain of his guilt within two minutes of the start of my first conversation with him.'

'Two minutes?' Rex exclaimed. 'You mean he gave himself away somehow?'

'Not in the sense you mean, sir.'

'But then how?'

Wilkins leant back in his chair. 'It's like this. I'm a simple sort of fellow. When I hear that a man's been found standing over a body with the murder weapon in his hand, my overwhelming instinct is that he's guilty. In fact, in the dozens of murder cases I've investigated, and the hundreds I've read about, I've never heard of one in which a person found in such a situation was innocent. Therefore I arrived here with a strong predisposition that Carter was the murderer. Of course, it was just possible that he'd been framed. But to be framed for a crime in such a way, a person would have to be very stupid or naive. Two minutes' conversation with him, however, showed me that he was neither, and I was then certain that he'd been found in that incriminating position only because he'd *wanted* to be. Great Scott, nobody planning a frame-up would arrange such a haphazard one as this one was supposed to be. A dozen things could have gone wrong. How could it be known that when Carter or anybody else came along the corridor and found the pistol on the floor that they'd be alone, that somebody else wouldn't be in the corridor at the same time? What certainty could there be that he'd actually pick up the gun and obligingly step into Miss Lorenzo's room, and then allow himself to be pushed in the back, without seeing the pusher? No, it's the stuff of mystery stories, not real life. And Carter, I found out, was a great fan of whodunits.

'Having come to this conclusion, I saw the case as fairly straightforward: my only job was to nail him. I doubted it would be possible to get cast-iron proof, so what I had to do was provide strong circumstantial evidence – firstly by showing how he could have done it and secondly by discovering a motive. That was why I perhaps seemed half-hearted in questioning the other guests. I knew none of them was guilty, just as I knew that the other strange incidents were either camouflage or completely irrelevant. They could be looked into eventually, if necessary, but they weren't of the first importance.'

Hugh asked, 'But if you were so sure of Carter's guilt, why did you want Scotland Yard called in?'

'It was really a question of my Chief Constable, sir.

Now he's a first-rate man, an officer and a gentleman. But to tell you the truth, he's not exactly very imaginative. I didn't think he'd believe for a moment in a man having framed himself. I didn't have the nerve to put it to him until I was able to make out a very good case for it. I needed time to do two things: first, to look into Carter's background and circumstances, and to a lesser extent into Miss Lorenzo's, to try and find some link between them; second, to work out just how Carter had done it. The delay caused by the calling in of the Yard gave me just the breathing space I needed. I was confident Mr Allgood would see the case in the same light as I did and play along with me. But,' Wilkins looked sad, 'he didn't, and I had to go my own way. At first my main worry that he might actually arrest Carter straightaway, which was the last thing I wanted. Fortunately, however, he came to the quite erroneous conclusion that Carter was innocent.'

'Why would it have been so bad if he had arrested Carter?' Lord Burford asked.

'Because we'd have had to release him again. I was sure that he had a trick up his sleeve. Evidence was about to turn up which was seemingly going to prove he was innocent. I'd expected, from the fact that the mink was missing, that this evidence might involve the coat. And I was right, though Carter also had two other pieces of back-up evidence, just to be on the safe side.'

The Earl stood up and started to replenish glasses.

'Well, no doubt I'm dense, but I don't see why he had to go to the trouble of framing himself at all. Why not just bump her off and have done with it?'

Ann said, 'I think I have a glimmering. Was it that

by being the first one to be suspected, albeit for false reasons, he could be the first one to be cleared?'

'That's it, Miss. You see, if we – the police – had arrived here and found a murdered woman and no leads to the identity of the killer, we would immediately have started checking up on all the guests, searching for a possible motive. We'd have looked into their backgrounds, sought a previous connection with Miss Lorenzo, investigated their financial situation, and so on. And it was vital to Carter that he not be put through such a probe. Firstly, although he'd made himself out to be well off, we'd have discovered that he was up to his ears in debt and was seriously overdrawn, which the bank had been pressing him about. It's true he did inherit quite a substantial sum from his grandfather, but he got through that years ago. We'd have immediately become suspicious, inquired into any sources of income he'd had, and who knows what we'd have turned up? He'd have been a major suspect, his movements would have been gone into minutely, and eventually – though it would have taken some time – we'd probably have discovered he was in northern Italy at the time Laura's cousin died.

'At all costs, he had to avoid that. He had to convince the police he was innocent. And the only way he could do that was to make it appear certain he'd been framed. Thereafter, everybody else in the house would be under suspicion and would have their backgrounds investigated – except, obviously, the victim of the frame-up.'

Lord Burford nodded slowly. 'I see...I think.'

Hugh said, 'Now, what I want to know most of all is how he did it. I thought he had an alibi for the time of the murder. Did Laura really die just after she entered her room, after all?'

'Yes, sir.'

Hugh banged the arm of his chair. 'But, Wilkins, he was out with Gerry then, four miles from here. I saw him.'

Wilkins gave a smile of deep satisfaction. 'There are two things which everybody overlooked: the geography of this area; and the fact that Carter was an Olympic three thousand meters steeplechaser.' He looked round. 'The point at which he supposedly ran out of petrol is indeed about four miles from here by road. In a straight line it's no more than a mile away.'

It was Rex's face which was the first to clear. 'For crying out loud, you mean he *ran it?*'

Wilkins beamed at him. 'Precisely, sir.'

Hugh said, 'Ye gods! So simple. But the petrol...'

'He had a full can in back of the car, sir. Of course, he didn't actually run out at that point, but he no doubt arranged things so that the tank was very low.'

'So Turner didn't siphon fuel from Carter's car into my motor-bike, after all?'

'No, sir, from his own car. Anyway, Carter walked back sixty yards towards the village, then climbed a gate into a field, left the can of fuel under a hedge, slipped into a pair of running shoes, and started off. There's a straight run of about three quarters of a mile across flat fields to the wall surrounding the park. He had a key to that door in the wall – I found it on a marked tab in his pocket – and then it was just another quarter mile to the house. He arrived just before the rest of the party got home. With a powerful flashlight it would have taken him no more than six or seven minutes all told. He scaled the drainpipe – remember he was a skilled climber – which took perhaps another minute. The lady arrived almost immediately. He shot her, stripped off her coat, and cut the fur partly away round the bullet hole – only being very careful, apparently, to mess up the job and leave some blood on the coat. Then he cut out the other holes and burnt the pieces. That was the trap he set for us.'

'Which Allgood fell into,' said Rex.

'Well, it was a very clever trick, sir; but I'm afraid when I said as much, Mr Allgood thought I was referring to him.'

'Next, Carter found the letter, which Lady Geraldine had, as she casually revealed to us, told him she'd seen Laura writing. He took her gun—'

'That was *her* pistol?' the Earl asked.

'Almost certainly, my lord. We found her prints, not on the gun itself – Carter wiped it – but on the cartridge clip. Where was I? Ah, yes. Carter went out of the window and down the drainpipe again, carrying the coat. He took a few seconds to make sure the coat was in a position where it would be covered with snow, then it was back to the car, stopping only to pick up the can of petrol and change into his ordinary shoes again. He could have done it all comfortably in twenty-five minutes, even if, as is a possibility, it was he who put the phone out of order, too. It wouldn't have taken him more than a couple of minutes to shin up a telegraph pole and pull down a wire; however, that might have been a lucky coincidence.'

Ann said, 'But what a chance he took! He could have

fallen, broken his ankle on his way back, anything.'

'Not too great a risk, considering the stakes he was playing for, miss. He was, of course, familiar with the estate from his rambles on his previous visit, and no doubt he planned the route carefully and examined it for obstacles and hidden pitfalls during his supposed training run that afternoon. And in fact, everything went perfectly for him until he got back to his car and found you there, Mr Quartus. That must have been quite a nasty shock.'

'Why?' Hugh asked.

'Firstly, I'm pretty sure he had you marked out as the fall guy, as they say in America. Now, though, you had an alibi. Secondly, you might have realised that the point at which you found them was only a mile from here.'

'Oh, there wasn't much likelihood of that. I'm not at a familiar with the area, and I just kept my eyes on the road one way and on Carter's taillight on the way back.'

Wilkins nodded. 'It must have been a great relief to him, and an added bonus, when you confirmed his car had been stranded four miles away. But before that, the real emergency arose when you hurt your hand and suggested Lady Geraldine drive home.'

Hugh frowned. 'I don't understand.'

'Well, sir, his scheme depended on Lady Geraldine not knowing exactly where they had stopped. If she did, she would be much more likely than you to realise how close she actually was to home, and later that Carter's alibi wasn't valid. So long as she remained slumped in her seat and didn't look out of the windows much he was safe. But if she drove home, it obviously wouldn't be very many minutes before she got her bearings. So he had to think quickly to stop that.'

Hugh gave a gasp. 'You mean he deliberately socked her on the jaw? He wasn't aiming for me?'

'That's my guess, sir.'

There was silence for several seconds before Rex and the Earl both started to ask a question together. Rex gestured to Lord Burford to proceed, and he said, 'I was only going to ask you when he took my gun.'

'Some time early on Friday evening, my lord, probably when you were dressing to go out. It would have been easy enough to slip unseen into the study first, to get the key. And he could be virtually certain you wouldn't be going into the gun room again that evening before you went out. Mr Ransom?'

'After we got home that night, how could Carter have been sure Laura would go straight upstairs, that she wouldn't have some refreshments first, say? Working on such a tight schedule, that could have botched his plan.'

'She must have made a prior arrangement to go straight up, sir.'

'An arrangement with Carter?'

'Yes. Perhaps she'd challenged him earlier and he'd claimed to have a full explanation for what had happened in Italy and begged to be allowed to give it to her before she took any further steps. She might have told him to come to her room immediately they got home that night – remember she had to leave here the following morning. That's only a guess, but I think it's indicated by her obvious wish to contact her agent that night before she went upstairs; and by the fact, as I discovered when I phoned the gentleman myself, that she gave a false reason to her ladyship for wanting to make the call and told a lie about his keeping late hours. So that call was for a private reason, and was obviously important. She wanted somebody, not a stranger but somebody she knew and trusted, to have the facts as to why she was really here.'

'As a sort of insurance, a lever to use against Carter?' Rex said.

'That's right, sir. She'd started to write a letter to her agent earlier, but had left it too late to catch the post. So instead, at the last moment, she tried to telephone him. But she was unsuccessful. She had no choice but to go up to her room all the same. Carter was waiting for her, and shot her.'

The Earl said, 'No wonder he was in such a hurry to get upstairs when he got back, knowing the body was up there all the time.'

'Yes, my lord. He just took a minute or two for a quick drink with you, which no doubt he badly needed. Then he had to go up and put Miss Lorenzo's gun in the secret passage, making sure you didn't see him when you went up. After that, he hurried to his own room, took his coat off, came out again, and then probably heard the voices of Lady Geraldine and Mr Ransom in the main corridor. That must have been a last minute stroke of luck for him – provided a plausible reason for his supposedly having gone to the far end of the corridor and found the gun on the floor.'

'Why put the gun in the passage?' Hugh asked.

'He must have wanted to be sure it would be found – though not by him. From what Leather tells me, Lady

Geraldine's account of its being found makes it pretty clear Carter led her on to look there. That gun, you see, was one of the other things that were apparently to prove his innocence. We were to believe it had been used to fire the alarm shot. One bullet had gone from it – no doubt he fired it in the air when he was a good way from the house on his return to the car – and, of course, as Carter hadn't had a chance to conceal it in the passage *after* the shot was heard, this would back up his story that the alarm shot had been fired by a second person.'

'So it was really fired from my revolver – which was also the murder weapon?' the Earl said.

'Yes, my lord. He must have put another bullet in the same chamber after the murder. And it was very important you didn't discover the fact that it was the same gun that had been used twice. That was why he was quick to lock the gun in a box. If you'd sniffed it you would have realised it had just been fired – which would have really spoilt his scheme.'

'I'd have certainly thought it confirmed that he had committed the murder a minute or so before. But isn't that what you said he *wanted* everyone to think?'

'Yes, my lord, but he only wanted it *thought* – not confirmed. If you had sniffed that gun, then later on, when it was known that the lady had been killed over an hour before, you would have remembered that the gun Carter had been holding had just been fired when you found the body. That would show that his story of the alarm shot having been fired by somebody else in the corridor, with another gun, was a lie. It was for the same sort of reason – though in reverse, as it were – that he left the body right in front of the fire: it had to be kept warm. Given the poor road conditions, and the telephone being out of order, he could be pretty sure the doctor wouldn't arrive soon enough to pinpoint the time of death with great accuracy. He wouldn't test exhaustively, anyway, time of death having already been established by a dozen witnesses. But if my lord, or anybody else, had touched the body and found it was cold, you would have immediately realised the lady must have died some time before.'

'And we would have thought, after all, that Carter was not guilty,' Hugh said. 'But isn't that what he wanted?'

'No, sir. With respect, you thinking him innocent would not be good enough. Carter had the sense to realise that when we – the police – arrived, it would make no difference to us if you all assured us he was innocent. We'd have to satisfy ourselves of that. We'd have suspected everybody equally and checked into Carter's history and possible motives as closely as everyone else's. He had to arrange things so that we cleared him. But he wanted to be our number one suspect at first, so that we'd concentrate on him. He knew we wouldn't be able to find out much about his financial position, say, until today, when the banks and so on opened, and that by then the fur coat would have come to light, the second gun found, and his story would have apparently been authenticated. He believed that he would then be crossed off our list of suspects at once, that we'd concentrate on finding out who had framed him and that inquiries about him wouldn't continue.'

'And if it hadn't been for you, Mr Wilkins, that's just how things would have worked out,' Ann said.

Rex said, 'You referred to three phoney clues Carter

had lined up that were supposed to clear him. You've only mentioned two: the mink and the second gun in the secret passage.'

'The third was more subtle. It was that phone call to the safe company. You see, Carter knew the combination because Lady Geraldine had told him. She urged him to keep quiet about his knowledge. But he couldn't have relied in advance on her doing that. Her knowledge that *he* knew might have made her suspicious. So by that phone call he gave the impression that somebody else had discovered the combination. Then he freely admitted his knowledge of it, in spite of Lady Geraldine's advice. It was a very smart move, making him appear thoroughly open and aboveboard. It was the one thing that, for a short time, did give me some small doubts about his guilt. Then Mr Allgood discovered the fragment of letter in Mr Haggermeir's fireplace, and that re-established my conviction.'

'Why?' the Earl asked simply.

'I couldn't believe it had actually been sent to Mr Haggermeir. Firstly, it seemed obvious to me that the person Mr Haggermeir had been talking to in the breakfast room was Miss Lorenzo herself – though it had never seemed to occur to Mr Allgood to ask who the other person in the room had been, no doubt because once he'd decided Mr Haggermeir was not the killer the matter wasn't relevant. But I've since checked with Mr Haggermeir and he confirms it. He'd had a row with the lady the previous night. He'd naturally been unable to offer her a part in *The King's Man*, and she'd taken this as an insult and been very annoyed. But he couldn't throw up the opportunity of signing her. He had to convince her that his reluctance to give her a part in the film was no personal slight. He decided the only way to do that was to take the big risk of telling her the full truth. Which he did on the Friday morning. They started their conversation in the breakfast room, and then when they were interrupted by a maid they moved upstairs to Mr Haggermeir's room. He offered to commission a film script especially for her, and promised to top any other offer she got from Hollywood provided she kept quiet about his real reason for being here.'

'So Carter told you the truth about that incident?' Hugh said.

'Yes, sir. He overheard it by chance, but later used it very cleverly.'

'What made you so sure that note wasn't written to Haggermeir?'

'Because if Mr Haggermeir had told Miss Lorenzo the facts, she wouldn't have written to him in those terms. She wouldn't have repeated in the letter things he'd already told her about his grandmother being deserted, and so on. She certainly wouldn't have bothered to mention the old lady's age when she died! She would have simply said something like, "the story you told me this morning convinces me it is my duty to expose," etc. Apart from that, though, I didn't believe Miss Lorenzo would have cared that much what Mr Haggermeir was up to. It was nothing to do with her. She certainly wouldn't have got so indignant as that fragment of letter sounded. Thirdly, if I was wrong and she *was* so concerned about what he was doing, why not tell your lordship or her ladyship the facts? As I said, after the Superintendent decided Mr

Haggermeir wasn't guilty of the murder, he didn't give much thought to these points. But I asked myself this: if the letter did not refer to Mr Haggermeir, whom did it refer to? I decided that the most feasible explanation was that Miss Lorenzo was writing about herself. And, in view of her attempted phone call later, it was a fair bet the letter had been meant for her agent. Now, when Lady Geraldine interrupted her, she thrust it into her writing case. But either because she felt guilty about the way she was deceiving Lady Geraldine, or because she was still suspicious of her, her manner was furtive. Lady Geraldine innocently and casually mentioned this to Carter. And incidentally, that was another point against him in my mind. The killer had known about that letter and where Miss Lorenzo had put it. It was overwhelmingly probable that Carter was the only person Lady Geraldine had mentioned the incident to; they had driven together to the village a few minutes after it had happened, and it was just the sort of thing one might naturally refer to. On the other hand, it was extremely unlikely Lady Geraldine would have gone round talking about it at the party later. Obviously, though, I didn't want to ask her straight out.

'Anyway, immediately she mentioned it Carter smelt danger. So later, after he'd killed Miss Lorenzo, he took the letter away with him. He read it and saw how, with judicious editing, it could be used to frame Mr Haggermeir. He carefully cut it to shape, charred the edges, and planted it in Mr Haggermeir's room. Then he told Mr Allgood and me about the conversation he'd heard. It was a fair bet we'd then search Mr Haggermeir's room.'

'But how do *you* reconstruct that letter?' Hugh asked.

Wilkins took out his notebook. 'I copied down the wording of that fragment in here. Now, let me see. Something like this:

'This is to state that the real reason for my present visit to Alderley is not, as I have said, to discuss making a movie, but to attempt to expose a wicked criminal who once cruelly deceived a whole family and caused the death at the age of eighteen of a young and innocent girl. He told her they would be married, but he left her, her reputation ruined, having robbed her of a valuable collection of jewellery.'

Wilkins closed his notebook. 'That would be the rough gist of it, anyway.'

Rex said, 'That's remarkable. But how did it lead you so quickly to the business of Laura's relatives? You said just now that in normal circumstances it would have taken a long time to trace Carter's connection with them. You did it in no time.'

'Well, given that the first part of that fragment referred to herself, the last part had to relate to people in her life. I've explained how I deduced that it had been intended for her agent. So yesterday, on my day off, I went up to London to visit him. Nice man, very helpful. Name of Cattin. He's only nominally her agent in this country, as she's never worked much over here. But they'd known each other many years, and she always looked upon him – as a sort of adviser and father confessor. So naturally he was eager to help in any way he could.

'I told him a good part of the story, though not my

suspicions of Carter, of course. I wanted to know if at any time of Miss Lorenzo's past life there'd been an incident concerning a family who'd been cruelly deceived, the death of a young girl, and the theft of some valuables. He told me yes, that she had talked about it years ago. But she'd never told him the name of the family and he was a bit hazy in his recollection of the details. However, he agreed to try and find out more. He spent much of yesterday afternoon on the telephone to Italy, speaking to various friends and relatives of Laura's. Eventually he pieced together the story, together with a description of the young man direct from Laura's aunt. It fitted Carter.

'Then Mr Cattin came with me to the Savoy hotel, where Miss Lorenzo had left her luggage, and we went through it together. We found a copy of the edition of *The Londoner* magazine containing the article on Miss Lorenzo and, on another page, the photo of Lady Geraldine and Carter. Mr Cattin explained how he'd sent it to Miss Lorenzo. But, of course, this wasn't anything remotely resembling proof. I asked Mr Cattin to do one more thing for me: try and find out from the aunt if by any chance she had a photo of the criminal. Well, it turned out she had a rather blurred snapshot, I was told. I then arranged with the Italian police to collect the negative from her and put it on the first flight to London. After that it was just a question of waiting.'

'By Jove,' the Earl said, 'and it only arrived in the nick of time. Allgood was really floundering.'

Wilkins cleared his throat. 'Well, actually, my lord, it arrived quite early this morning. Unfortunately, when

I saw it I realised what they'd meant by blurred. It was completely unrecognisable as Carter.'

They all stared. Rex said, 'But that photo you held out.'

'—was kindly supplied by the picture editor of *Athletics Weekly*. It was an unpublished photo taken just after Carter won the three thousand meters steeplechase at the British championships two years ago.'

The Earl slapped his knee and gave a roar of laughter. 'Wilkins, that's brilliant! You sly dog!'

'Thank you, my lord. I relied on the sudden shock breaking him down. These good-looking, charming, vain young criminals are almost always the quickest to show themselves up when things start to go wrong. And it worked. Unfortunately, what I didn't know, and what I don't think I could possibly have guessed, was that shortly before Mr Allgood had handed Carter a loaded revolver and not taken it back.'

Lord Burford said: 'Well, Wilkins, I must congratulate you and thank you for again gettin' us out of a very sticky situation. Rest assured, I shall write to the Chief Constable, praising your handling of the case in the highest terms.'

'Oh, no, my lord, please don't do that. The more commendations of that sort I get, the more cases of this sort I'll be assigned to. And I really don't like them. I'd much sooner be handling nice simple burglaries and car thefts.'

'Well, if you're quite sure...' The Earl broke off and called, 'Come in,' as there was a knock on the door.

It was Sergeant Leather. He came across the room. 'Excuse me, my lord.' He turned to Wilkins. 'Sorry to interrupt, sir, but you're wanted immediately.'

'What is it?'

'Murder, sir. At Meadowfield School.'

'Good gad,' Lord Burford exclaimed. 'I'm on the Board of Governors. Who's been murdered?'

'The matron, my lord. Found hanging in the gym, her hands tied behind her back.' He looked back at Wilkins. 'The odd thing is, sir, she was wearing a Red Indian headdress.'

Wilkins gave a groan and got to his feet. 'Oh dear, here we go again. I don't like school murders. So many people about, and all the teachers hate each other and lie like troopers all the time.'

Ann said, 'Oh, come now, Mr Wilkins. I'm sure you'll clear it up in no time.'

'I doubt it, Miss. I'm not sanguine, not sanguine at all.' He sighed. 'Well, goodbye, my lord – and everybody. Glad to have been of service. Lead the way, Jack.'

They started for the door. Suddenly Rex said, 'Hey, wait a moment, Wilkins. There's something you haven't explained.'

Wilkins stopped. 'Carry on, Jack. I'll join you in a jiffy.' As Leather went out he turned, asking, 'What's that, sir?'

'Who in the world clonked Carter on the head last night?'

Lord Burford said, 'My word, I'd completely forgotten about that.'

Wilkins said, 'Oh.' There was a pause.

'Don't you know?' Ann asked.

Wilkins hesitated. 'Yesterday, I understand, her ladyship put forward the suggestion that some passing tramp had gained access to the house. I think that's probably the explanation for the attack on Mr Carter.'

'A hobo?' Rex exclaimed. 'You've got to be kidding!'

'I suppose you'll be putting out a dragnet for him?' Ann said quietly.

'Oh, I don't think so, Miss. As a matter of fact, he did me a good turn.'

'What the deuce do you mean?' Lord Burford asked.

'Well, my lord, I was very anxious about Mr Allgood's decision to allow Carter to go away. Leather told me about it when I telephoned him after getting back from London yesterday evening. Let a criminal out of your sight and you might never see him again. If Carter had somehow spotted the fact that I was on to him – I didn't think he had, but I couldn't be sure – he might just disappear. But more important was Lady Geraldine's going with him. She's a smart young lady. It only needed him to make one tiny slip when they were discussing the case together and she might well jump to the truth. Then her life wouldn't be worth a brass farthing. So I started desperately trying to think up a way to prevent the trip. Do you know, I even went to the trouble of getting out my truncheon and driving up here last night? I don't quite remember what happened then. Think I must have fallen asleep in the car. Had rather a strange dream, might even have done a bit of sleepwalking. Anyway, when I woke up I just went home again. But when I heard this morning that Carter had been temporarily incapacitated I was mightily relieved, I can tell you. So you see why I say that this, er, tramp did me a good turn. Well, if that's everything, I must be going. Goodbye my lord, ladies and gentlemen.'

CHAPTER TWENTY-FOUR

'How is he?'

Mabel Turner paused outside her bedroom door at Alderley and turned to see that Cyrus Haggermeir had approached.

She said, 'Oh, he's going to be all right, thank you. They're keeping him in for a few days, that's all.'

'Swell. You just got back from the hospital?'

'Yes, I must pack our things and leave straight away. I'll stay in Westchester until Ned's released, though I saw Lady Burford just now and she asked me to stay on. I said no, of course, but I was very touched.'

'Well, I figure we were all impressed by his guts in jumping Carter.'

'That's what the Countess said. And they're not going to do or say anything about my impersonating Cecily. It's a great relief.'

'Can I come in a minute? I'd like to talk with you.'

She looked surprised. 'Yes, of course.'

They went into the room and she looked expectantly at him.

'Did you like him being a stuntman?' he asked.

She hesitated, then said, 'Frankly, no. It used to scare me stiff.'

'Ever try to persuade him to give it up?'

'Certainly not. He was a stuntman when I married him. I've no use for women who marry men with dangerous jobs and then try to make them change. It's thoroughly unfair.'

'All the same, you must have been relieved when he had to give it up?'

'In a way I was. But it made him so miserable.'

'But you wouldn't have wanted me to give him a job?'

'Oh, you're wrong, Mr Haggermeir. I would, for his sake. It's his one ambition to get back to work.'

'Well, I gotta warn you, I ain't going to.'

'I didn't think you would.'

'You see, I could find a couple of dozen guys in Hollywood who could have pulled off that motor-bike stunt. Even Quartus managed it. Chiefly, though, Ned's too old. It's a young man's job.'

She nodded resignedly. 'I know. I only hope I can persuade him to accept that and look for some other line of work. But I'm not hopeful. Movies are his life.'

'Do you mean movies are his life, or movie *stunting* is?'

'I don't think that he's crazy about stunting as such. But he just loves the film world. Stunting was the only way he was qualified to earn his living in it.'

'I don't think you're right there.'

'What do you mean?'

'Honey, what I saw from him over this weekend was a terrific acting job.'

She smiled. 'He thinks he overdid the characterisation.'

'Sure he did. He didn't have any direction. But he fooled a lot of people a long time, ad libbing the whole thing. I don't mind saying I'm impressed. I think he ought to take up acting.'

'At his age? With no experience? He'd never get parts.'

'I got a part for him.'

Mabel gave a jump. She whispered, 'What?'

'Now, it's a small one, but nice: English character in a movie that's scheduled to start shooting soon. Quite an important little role. We haven't been able to cast it. Couldn't find anybody just right. But it's Ned's if he wants it.'

Mabel's face was a study. 'Oh, Mr Haggermeir, I can't believe it!'

'Yeah, well, he's gotta prove himself. But if he handles it OK – and I don't see why he shouldn't – there's no reason he couldn't carve a niche for himself as a character actor. Other stuntmen, like George O'Brien, have made the switch. I'll pay his fare out of course, and yours.'

'I – I don't know what to say. You're so generous!'

'Don't say things like that! I want him for the part or I wouldn't be doing it. Here.' He reached into his pocket and took out an envelope. 'I wrote him a letter, laying it all out, before I knew I'd be seeing you again. Take it and show him. If he calls at my London office when he gets out, we'll fix all the details.' Then, as she started to stammer out her thanks, he added, 'OK, take it as said. I gotta go now. I'll be leaving here soon myself, but there's sumpin' I must do first and before that I gotta find Rex. So long.'

He went out. Mabel sank down on the bed and started to cry.

* * *

'You saved my life,' Gerry said.

'Yes,' Hugh said simply.

'It was incredibly brave, what you did.'

'I know.'

'You mustn't say that!'

'On the contrary, I must. For about the first time in my life I feel rather pleased with myself, and I shall no doubt keep talking about it for a very long time.'

'You're impossible!'

'No, I've *been* impossible. I know that. I've been a boor and a cad. I've behaved abominably, to you and everyone else. But you know why, don't you?'

'I think so. But tell me, all the same.'

'I could see myself losing you to Carter. And it was making me utterly wretched. I'm crazy about you, Gerry. You know that, don't you?'

She nodded silently. Her eyes were bright.

'At one time I thought I had a chance. Then you seemed to be leaning towards Carter and I got terrified. I was always certain he was a rotter. When you invited me here for the weekend again, I couldn't believe my good luck. But then I found out he was here, too, and I had to watch you getting closer and closer to him and farther away from me. It was the most miserable few days I've ever spent.'

'I never intended it like that. I meant to treat you both exactly the same. For the first day or two it was your own fault. You were such a bear.'

'I realise that.'

'And then, of course, it seemed Paul was going to be falsely charged with murder, and naturally I had to spring to his defence. Nitwit!'

'You weren't a nitwit. He had a lot of charm. In fact, I have to admit that, except when he was murdering people or robbing them, he was much nicer than I am. Anyway, now you have at least seen me at my worst.'

'That's nice to know.'

'So Gerry, will you marry me? I'll make an awful husband, but I do love you very much.'

'To distraction? I could never marry a man who didn't love me to distraction.'

'Positively to distraction.'

'Aren't you rather taking advantage of the fact that I'm grateful you saved my life?'

'Of course I am. Do you blame me?'

She said slowly, 'I'm a little scared of you, Hugh. I always have been. And you frequently infuriate me. Probably I shall often hate you. We'll no doubt have the most awful rows. But, well, I've never been one for a quiet life. So the answer's yes, without any doubts at all.'

He took her in his arms.

A minute or two later she said, 'You don't mind people saying you're marrying me for my money?'

'Not in the least. Do you?'

'Oh, of course not! I think it takes an awful lot of guts and character for a poor man to marry a rich girl and not let it make any difference. But I must admit I do worry a bit for your sake, about what people will say.'

'Let the oafs say what they like.' He kissed her again.

'Young man, don't you think it's time you stopped teasing my daughter?'

They sprang apart and spun round. It was the Countess, who'd entered the room silently and was gazing at them severely.

Gerry said, 'Mummy! I – er—' She took a deep breath. 'Hugh just asked me to marry him.'

'And clearly you had the surprising good sense to accept.'

Gerry stared. 'You approve?'

'I do. It's high time you were married. And you're obviously in love with each other, which is always an advantage.'

Gerry nodded vigorously. 'Yes, but I thought perhaps you'd raise objections to my marrying someone who – who...'

'Object to your marrying the only son of the Marquis of Gower? Why on earth should I? It's a most excellent match. His family owns five thousand acres in west Wales and a considerable amount of property in London.'

'*What?*' Gerry gaped. 'Hugh, is this true?'

''Fraid so. How did you know, Lady Burford?'

'Chiefly your name. Quartus was your mother's maiden name, wasn't it? She and I came out together in '05. Then again, you have her eyes. I haven't seen her for well over twenty years. How is she?'

'She's very well, thank you.'

Gerry said dazedly, 'But – but why didn't you tell me?'

'When we first met I didn't want it to look as if I were using my family position to get an unfair advantage with you over Carter. Oh, I knew it wouldn't make any difference to you, but I thought if I won *he* might think it had. I wanted to fight on equal terms without the privilege of rank. Besides, I'd put all that stuff behind me.'

'But why?'

'Because I was fed up with Society. All the trappings of the sort of life people like us lead was making me sick. Besides, I wanted to paint. Father wanted me to take over the running of the estate, so he could concentrate on his collection and his other hobbies. But I was convinced I had what it takes to make the grade as a serious artist. Father challenged me to prove it. Well, if I wanted to be a professional it was no good dabbling at it: I had to have a real incentive to get on. I'd never get anywhere if I could just stop painting whenever I felt like it, because I'm basically a very lazy person. If I was to succeed not just artistically, but commercially – I had to *need to* succeed. So I took just fifty pounds, went to London and started to paint. Father and I agreed that if I had not made the grade in six years I'd give up all my pretensions to art and go respectable again. I changed my name and cut myself off from all my old crowd. The last thing I wanted was a lot of chaps I'd been at Harrow with, and debs I'd taken to parties, finding out and buying my pictures or commissioning portraits, to help me.'

'But you pretended to be really poor.' Her voice was indignant.

'Pretended? *Pretended?* In six years I've sold forty-four pictures at an average price of a little over fifteen guineas a time. I've been living on about two pounds ten shillings a week! Unless I sell something else, I've got just twelve pounds four and sixpence to last me until the end of April.'

'Why April?'

'Because that's when the six years are up.'

'Oh, I see. And what are you going to do then?'

'What do you think? Give it all up, with great relief, go home to Wales and start running the estate.'

'I thought you hated Society and all the trappings.'

'Well, in spite of everything that's happened here, the last few days have made me realise that there is, after all, a great deal to be said for three square meals a day. I still don't approve of big houses and lots of servants, but I can happily learn to live with them again after six years of the other thing.'

'You're not going to be a great artist, after all?'

'Of course I'm not. I haven't got what it takes, and I've got it out of my system. But I do know a lot more about painting than I did. Moreover, I know what it *does* take to become a worthwhile artist. I can recognise talent in others now. So I intend to become a patron, do everything I can to support and encourage good young painters, and also start a collection. Collecting can be an art in itself, and my collection will become world-famous. I shall, in addition, write scathing criticisms of bad art. I shall use every ounce of pull that money, position, and powerful friends can give. I shall become the most influential, admired, and feared figure in British art. *That,* my lady, is what I'm going to do.'

Gerry couldn't speak. The Countess said, 'That sounds highly satisfactory. Be sure to repeat to George what you said about collecting being an art. That will put you very much in his good books.'

Hugh said, 'Heavens, I suppose I should speak to him,

ask for Gerry's hand and all that sort of thing.'

Lady Burford nodded. 'Yes, I think it's pleasant to keep up the old customs. I shall go and find George now and prime him, so you needn't be apprehensive that he'll refuse his permission, or anything ridiculous like that. Come along to the library in fifteen minutes. You'd better telephone your parents, Hugh, and then we can put the announcement in *The Times* immediately. A June wedding, I think. I don't approve of long engagements. Here, or in town, I wonder? I rather favour London; it's so much more accessible for most people. St. Margaret's, Westminster, I think, and the reception at Claridge's.' She went out.

Gerry grinned at Hugh. 'Satisfied?'

'Completely.'

'Me, too. Who'd have thought this time yesterday that everything could turn out so spiffingly so quickly.'

'Things have turned out pretty well for nearly everybody. Ned Turner's got a new job.'

'And Jemima, or Ann or whatever her name is, got her woman.'

'And Rex Ransom got a blackmailer off his back.'

'You know,' Gerry said, 'I've been meaning to ask you: what do you think she was blackmailing him for, on what grounds? What was he doing in that photograph she took?'

'There's only one thing I can think of,' Hugh said. 'I'm afraid it must be drugs.'

Her eyes grew big. 'You mean he's an addict? Surely not!'

'I agree he doesn't look it. But what else could it be? He was alone in the room. She must have got a snap of him giving himself an injection.'

'Nothing so dramatic.'

The voice came from the door, which the Countess had left open an inch or two. It was Rex.

Gerry and Hugh stared at him in horror as he came into the room. Gerry stammered, 'Rex, I – I'm terribly sorry. I didn't—' Then she stopped as she saw that he was smiling.

'It's OK,' he said. 'You wouldn't be human if you didn't speculate. And I'd probably think the same if it was someone else. Like to see the famous photograph?'

Hugh said, 'Certainly not! It's your business.'

'It's all right. I'd like you to look at it.' He reached into his pocket, took the photograph from it, and held it out to them. 'Here.'

Hugh took it and he and Gerry stared at it together. Expressions of bewilderment appeared on their faces.

The picture was of a man, wearing shorts and an undershirt. He was standing, holding a couple of strange, limp, shapeless objects in one hand. A large stomach bulged over the top of the shorts and he had a high domed, bald head.

Gerry said, 'But I don't understand. This isn't—' She broke off with a gasp. 'It is! It's you!'

Rex bowed. He raised a hand to his head, pulled at the thick blonde hair, and it came away to reveal a gleaming, egg-like pate. Hugh and Gerry goggled at him.

Rex jerked a finger at the photograph. 'The other object I am holding is, I regret to say, my girdle. I'd just taken it off.'

'All she was threatening to publish was this?' Hugh said incredulously.

'All? You're joking! Can't you imagine the effect that

could have on my career? The romantic, swashbuckling hero wears a wig and a girdle? I'd be a laughing stock. It'd finish me.'

Gerry said, 'Yes, I can see. Golly, no wonder your manner was so odd that night!'

'I was in a terrible state. I could see my whole world crumbling. When I first had the brush with the intruder I couldn't be sure what was behind it. It might be blackmail, or just a hoax. Even when I discovered – as I believed – that it was Gilbert, I still hoped he might just be a pathological snooper. I confronted him, but I couldn't accuse him straight out. If he hadn't thought of blackmail, I didn't want to let him realise there were grounds for it. But he was apparently scared, too. Then he said he was leaving and it seemed important to stop him. I thought it less likely he'd have the nerve to apply the squeeze while we were under the same roof. I used a little blackmail myself, threatened to see he didn't script *The King's Man*. I even made up a lot of hogwash about Cyrus's attorneys questioning the copyright situation. All I really knew was that Cyrus had mentioned he'd forgotten to check on who held the rights. Anyway, it seemed to work. He agreed to stay, if you okayed it, Gerry, and apparently climbed down. I decided that I'd either misjudged his motive or that he'd thought better of it. By that night I figured I was in the clear, which made the shock of finding that photo and the note in my room all the greater. I was in a real stew. Even if I paid and got the negative back, how could I be sure that dozens of prints hadn't already been made? I could see myself paying through the nose for years.'

Hugh frowned. 'But now you're quite prepared to

have the photo published. Why the change?'

'In the picture gallery earlier I suddenly got nauseous at the lie I was living. I decided to face up to what I am: middle-aged, fat and bald. I don't care who knows it. It's a tremendous relief.'

'But your acting career?' Gerry said.

'My acting career is finished. I'm getting out.'

'What will you do?'

'Something I've had a hankering to do for many years: direct. I've got a story all lined up, too. Arlington's going to do the screenplay.'

'Mr Gilbert?' Gerry exclaimed.

'Yeah. We've had a long talk. He's not at all a bad guy underneath the bluster. He started all that rudeness when he was successful, as a sort of gimmick. And he's had to keep it up so people wouldn't guess he'd fallen on hard times. Oh, and by the way, I've explained to him about you and your hoax, Gerry.'

'How did he take it?'

'He laughed. I think it was quite an effort, but he managed it eventually. Anyway, whatever his faults, he's a first-class screenwriter. I've spoken to Cyrus and he's willing to give us a chance.'

Hugh looked surprised. 'You've patched up your quarrel, then?'

'Heck, yes. That was nothing. We've both apologised and shaken hands. He even borrowed two hundred pounds from me, though I don't know what he wanted it for. He's quite enthusiastic about the story idea; particularly as he's gotten a sort of personal interest in it, as you have, too, Gerry.'

'Me? What *is* the story?'

Hugh said, 'Good heavens, it's not a murder mystery based on this weekend?'

'Not likely! Who'd believe it? No, I'm going to make a movie called *The Adventures of Aylwin Saunders*. And I've an old rival and buddy of mine in mind for the lead. I hear he's thinking of changing studios.'

Gerry whispered, 'Not – not...?'

'Yes,' Rex said. 'Errol Flynn. Who else?'

'Gower?' said the Earl. 'Yes, know him slightly. Eccentric, naturally, like all Welshmen. Collects coins. And he's fanatical, it seems. Can't see the appeal myself. And he gets these old crazes for things, jazz or breeding rabbits or something. They never last, apparently. Strange way to behave. Vague sort of fellow, too, terribly absentminded. Nice chap, though. Very amiable. Fine old family, of course.'

'So you approve, George? And you won't put any obstacles in their way?'

'Whose way?'

'Geraldine and Hugh.'

'Oh, no, course not. When did I ever put an obstacle in anyone's way? Gerry'll get engaged to whomever she wants, whatever I say. But I suppose she could have done worse. He can be an arrogant young puppy, but he's shown he's made of the right stuff. Only trouble is, I fancy he'll actually expect to marry her.'

'What on earth do you mean? Of course he expects to marry her.'

'She assured me that wasn't the idea at all. Still, if I

give him my permission to do either or both, that'll be all right, won't it?'

'I don't know what you're talking about, George.'

At that moment there came a tap on the door.

'Oh, he's a little soon,' Lady Burford said. 'I'll leave you.' She crossed to the door and opened it to find not Hugh, but Cyrus Haggermeir, on the other side. She said, 'Oh.'

'Sorry to interrupt, ma'am. Just wanted to say I'll be leaving shortly. Can I have a word first?'

The Earl raised his eyebrows. 'Yes, of course. Come in.'

Haggermeir did so, closing the door behind him. He said, 'I owe you both an apology.'

'Yes, you do,' Lady Burford said.

'Well, I make it here and now. I behaved badly. I admit it freely. And that's something Cyrus Haggermeir don't often do. I hope you'll accept the apology.'

The Earl cleared his throat. 'Well, that's very handsome. We'll say no more about it. Er, *bon voyage* and all that.'

'Thanks. But there's more. I ain't quite given up. I just been having a word with your butler.'

'With Merryweather?' the Countess said, surprised.

'Yeah. Told him I had reason to believe there may be something in this house that once belonged to my grandmother. I described the casket, told him that you knew nothing about it, but you'd said that if it is here I'd be more than welcome to it. I told him to put it round among the servants that there's a two hundred pound reward for anyone who finds it and brings it to me – either here and now or at my hotel. I'll be staying on a couple more weeks in England. I figured one of them might just have seen it around. Wanted to put you in the picture.'

The Earl said dryly, 'Suppose *I* offer four hundred to anyone who brings it to me?'

'Don't reckon you'd do that, Earl, not after the Countess said I could have it. Wouldn't be exactly, er, cricket, would it?'

'I'm not so sure I'd worry about that if I stood to lose the Earldom. However, I'm pretty confident I won't have to.' He chuckled.

Just then the door opened. It was Merryweather. He advanced towards them, bearing a silver salver. He said, 'Excuse me, my lady.'

Then they saw that resting on the salver was a small wooden box, brightly painted with an intricate design of Chinese dragons. It was about six inches by five, and four inches deep.

'Would this be the object you wanted, sir?' said Merryweather.

Haggermeir gave a cry of disbelief and sprang towards him. He snatched up the casket and turned it between his fingers. He whispered: 'It must be! It must be!' He opened the box and started desperately probing at the interior. The Earl and Countess watched with bated breath.

But nothing happened. Haggermeir started muttering angrily to himself. Then Merryweather gave a discreet cough.

'Might this be what you are searching for, sir? It was concealed in the false bottom.'

He took from his pocket a folded sheet of ancient,

yellowed paper, which he handed to Haggermeir.

Haggermeir gave a strangled gasp. With shaking fingers he unfolded the paper. For a moment he stood perfectly still, his eyes scanning it. Then he suddenly gave vent to a deafening howl.

'Yippee!'

His face alight with triumph, he brandished the paper. 'Got it, got it, got it! I was *right*!'

Lord Burford gave a gulp. 'That – that's it?'

'You bet your sweet life it is, Earl. Marriage licence: Aylwin Saunders to Martha Haggermeir, officiating minister Rev. P. Jones, solemnised at the Baptist Church of Last Straw, Calif., date 8th April, 1851. Take a look.'

He held it out for them to see. The Earl and Countess stared at it. Everything Haggermeir had read out was correct.

Lady Burford looked at her husband. 'George, what does it mean? Can it mean that – that...?'

The Earl sat down, a dazed expression on his face. 'I don't know, my dear. It certainly seems that my grandfather's marriage to my grandmother in 1852 was bigamous, and Haggermeir's father was Aylwin's eldest legitimate son and automatically succeeded to the Earldom. That means my father should never have had the title, and neither should I.'

Haggermeir nodded. 'That's about the size of it. Look, I know it's hard on you, but you gotta see the justice of it.'

'But George, surely you're not just going to accept this lying down?' Lady Burford was pale. 'You're going to fight?'

'Well, of course I'll see my solicitor. I honestly don't

know what the legal position is, or who decides things like this. Heralds' College? The Courts? I should imagine it's a pretty well unique situation. Of course I'll fight, if I'm told there's a chance.'

'Earl,' Haggermeir said, 'that's exactly what I'd expect you to say. It's what I'd say in your position. But do we have to fight?'

'You're suggesting we should just hand over everything to you and impoverish ourselves completely?' The Countess had regained a little colour and there was a gleam of battle in her eye.

Haggermeir gave a snort. 'I don't want to impoverish you!'

Lord Burford glanced at him sharply. 'You don't?'

'Heck, no! I don't want your money or your estates. Or your London house. Why should I? I got millions. I only want two things. Now, can't we come to an amicable agreement? If we fight it through the courts it could drag on for years and cost us both a fortune. Why make the lawyers rich?'

'Just what are the two things you want?' Lady Burford asked him grimly.

'First, the title. I wanta be the Earl of Burford. Can't you just see it: *The Lord Burford Picture Corporation*? And on the movie credits: *produced by Lord Burford*? That'd make Goldwyn and Warner and the other sit up, eh? Guess I'd have to give up my American citizenship, become a naturalised Britisher. Or perhaps I am legally British already. That's a minor point, though. Anyway, what about it?'

The Earl rubbed his chin. 'Well, I daresay I could live

without a title. Wouldn't make any difference to Gerry. Looks as if she's going to be Marchioness of Gower one day, anyway.'

'George, you can't just give away a title!' the Countess exclaimed.

Haggermeir said, 'But, Earl, if you stood up and admitted I was the rightful holder of it and you didn't want it, that'd be bound to make a difference.'

'I – I suppose it might,' the Earl said unhappily.

His wife was gazing at him in disbelief. 'George, you wouldn't do such a thing!'

'I don't know, Lavinia. Perhaps it would be the right thing to do, if Haggermeir's got justice on his side. I don't want to hang on to something that's not rightfully mine. Do you?'

Lady Burford didn't answer. She sat down very slowly beside her husband.

Haggermeir turned away and noticed that Merryweather was still present, his face as impassive as ever.

'Say, I was nearly forgetting.' He reached into his hip pocket, took out a thick wad of banknotes, and handed it to Merryweather. 'Here you are, pal. You sure earned this.'

'I am obliged, sir.' The money disappeared in a flash into Merryweather's waistcoat pocket.

The Earl regarded his butler sadly. 'Oh, Merryweather, what have you done to us?'

'I am exceedingly sorry, my lord. I did not realise until minutes ago just what the situation was. I would, of course, deeply regret causing the family any inconvenience.'

He bowed and silently melted from the room.

The Countess looked at Haggermeir. 'What was the second thing you wanted?'

Haggermeir took a deep breath. 'Alderley.'

The Earl and Countess looked blank. Lord Burford said, 'But you said you didn't want the estate.'

'I don't. Just the house. I aim to take it down brick by brick, ship it across the Atlantic, and rebuild it in Beverly Hills.'

Haggermeir's words seemed to strike both Lord and Lady Burford totally dumb. They sat motionless, their faces masks of utter horror.

Haggermeir went on hurriedly. 'It's technically feasible, I've checked into it. And I wouldn't leave you without a house here. I'd build you a swell modern one on the same site, all electric, air-conditioned, with a pool – everything. No one can say I'm not generous. Now, Earl, this isn't something the law would have to decide. The house is yours to do what you like with. So, whaddaya say?'

'Never!' Lord Burford jumped to his feet, his face red. 'You must be mad if you think I'd let you do such a thing. I'd sooner lose everything else than let Alderley be taken away. Good gad, it's been here nearly three hundred years. What you're suggesting would be vandalism.'

Lady Burford was staring at him in admiration. 'George, I never knew you cared so much.'

'May not talk about it much, Lavinia but I care!'

Haggermeir's face had hardened. 'Get this, Earl. I've been pretty easy in my demands so far. I was prepared to let you off light. But force me to go to the law and I'll go for everything: the title, the estates, everything you inherited. I'll ruin you.'

The Earl took a deep breath. 'Then you'd better try. If we lose everything, so be it. At least we'll go down fighting.'

Haggermeir shrugged. 'Sorry you're taking it like, this, Earl. It's not the way I wanted it.'

The silence that followed this was broken by the return of Merryweather. 'Excuse me, my lord,' he said, 'but I wonder if your lordship would care to look at this?' He held out his salver, which bore a folded piece of paper.

The Earl waved him away. 'Not now, Merryweather. I haven't time.'

'With great respect, I do urge that your lordship find time.'

The Earl snatched the paper up irritably. 'What is it?'

'If you will read it, my lord.'

The Earl unfolded the paper and glanced cursorily at it. His eyebrows went up. 'It's a marriage certificate. What the deuce? Gretna Green? Good gad!'

Lady Burford asked sharply: 'What's the matter, George?'

'It says "Aylwin Saunders to Mary Carruthers". I don't understand. They were married here at the parish church.'

Merryweather said softly, 'May I suggest you look at the date on the certificate, my lord?'

'Date? Where? Good heavens! It says 1839.'

'Let me see that!' Haggermeir stepped to the Earl's side and stared at the paper in his hand.

Lord Burford looked up blankly. 'Merryweather, I don't understand.'

'I can explain, my lord. The accepted story of the elopement of your lordship's grandfather is incorrect in one particular. When the young couple were found by their fathers, they were not still on their way to Scotland, but on their way *back*. They had reached Gretna Green and *had been married*. But Lady Mary was so nervous at the thought of her parents' reaction that she persuaded her husband to say nothing about it. However, the fact remains that when your lordship's grandfather went to America he was already legally married. His so-called marriage to Miss Haggermeir was bigamous, and the issue of it illegitimate. The later marriage ceremony he went through with Lady Mary in 1852 was in law quite superfluous.'

A look of delighted disbelief had come over the Earl's face 'So, my father was the rightful heir, all along?'

'Indubitably, my lord.'

It was now Haggermeir who, pale-faced, sat down suddenly in the nearest chair. He muttered, 'All these years...all these years...'

Lady Burford was on her feet again. With a surreptitious movement she dashed what looked suspiciously like a tear from her face. There was the merest catch in her voice when she said, 'We – we are really most grateful, Merryweather, most grateful. But you must explain how on earth you know all this, and where you obtained those certificates.'

Before Merryweather could reply, however, there was an interruption. A strange sound filled the room, a rumbling, gurgling sound as of a subterranean river. It was a noise that had not been heard anywhere for many years. Cyrus Haggermeir was laughing.

'My dear chap,' Lord Burford said, 'are you all right?'

Haggermeir nodded. He seemed to have difficulty in speaking. At last he said, 'Just seen the funny side of it.

Grandma married to a bigamist! Thank heavens she never knew.'

The Countess said, 'But this means you've lost. Don't you mind?'

Haggermeir wiped his eyes with his handkerchief. 'Reckon not.' He sounded quite surprised. 'Not now I know the truth. It was the thought that I'd been cheated out of what was rightfully mine that riled me. But now I know I wasn't. So it don't hurt any more. In fact, guess I'm kind of relieved. Didn't really want to give up my American citizenship, whatever I said.'

'Well, I must say, it shows a fine sportin' spirit,' the Earl said. He stuck out his hand. 'Will you shake, cousin?'

'Sure.' They shook hands.

'Don't ever let me hear anyone say Americans are poor losers,' Lord Burford said.

Haggermeir grinned. 'Maybe it's true as a rule. You see, we don't get a lot of practice at it.' He looked at Merryweather. 'Lady Burford asked you a question. I'd sure as eggs like to know the answer, too.'

'Both those documents and the casket were put in my possession very many years ago, sir, when I was little more than a boy.'

'But by whom, man?'

'The faithful servant John, sir. He also told me the story of the two marriages. He was a witness to both. The Gretna Green certificate was handed to him for safekeeping. He claimed his master had given him the Chinese casket as a present, but I consider it more likely he spied on your grandmother, saw her putting her licence in it, and deliberately expropriated the box without his master's knowledge before they returned to England. Why he retained the licences I cannot say. Probably he just hoped they would come in useful one day. He was of a conserving and secretive disposition. I was perplexed for many years to know what I should do with them. Eventually I decided to say nothing until such time as it seemed proper to speak.'

'But why in tarnation did he give 'em to you?' Haggermeir demanded.

'If you glance at the full name of the witness on one of the licences, sir, you will see that it is John Merryweather. My grandfather. Not an altogether estimable character. We have never spoken much of him in my family. Incidentally, sir, I feel that under the circumstances I should return this money to you.'

He held out the wad of notes.

Haggermeir hesitated. Then he chuckled. 'No, a bargain's a bargain. You earned it. You keep it. But thanks all the same.'

'Thank you, sir,' said Merryweather.

THE AFFAIR OF THE
THIRTY-NINE
CUFFLINKS

Relevant Section of the Family Tree of the Earls of Burford
(Only names in italics have any connection with the events related to this story)

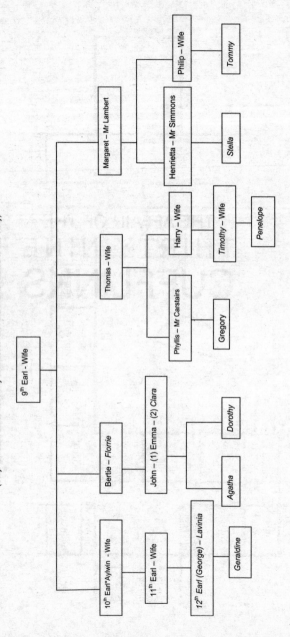

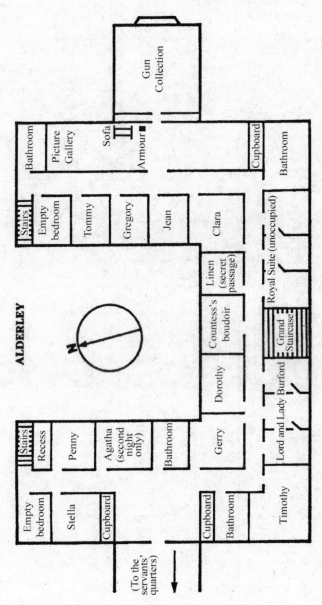

Plan of First Floor

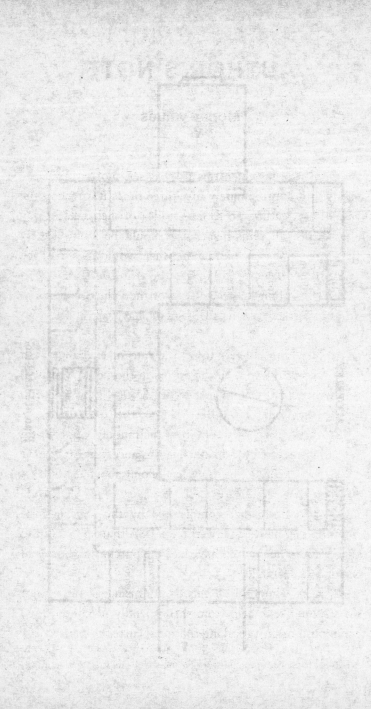

AUTHOR'S NOTE

Money values

At the period in which this story is set, money in Britain was worth approximately fifty-three times its value in the early 21st Century. So to get an idea of their present day equivalents, all sums mentioned should be multiplied by fifty-three. For example, £1,000 then would have had the purchasing power of £53,000 in the year 2001.

Those wishing to get an idea of the value of a sum in another currency, such as US dollars, have two choices:

1. They can convert using the rate of exchange as it was at the time of the events in the book. This will turn £1,000 into just under $5,000, and £53,000 into about $260,000.
2. Alternatively, they convert at the rate of exchange at a more recent time. In 2001, for instance, this would have made £53,000 the equivalent of only about $78,000.

The matter is further complicated by the fact that the inflation rate has been lower in the USA than in Britain, so that $5,000 then would have had the purchasing power of about $63,750 in 2001.*

Readers who find all this as confusing as the author does should seek help from their friendly neighbourhood economist, or any good international currency dealer.

*(Figures from Economic History Services website: http://eh.net/hmit)

CHAPTER ONE

'I want to make one thing absolutely plain,' said the Honourable Mrs Florence Saunders. 'After I'm dead, I will not come back.'

Jean Mackenzie, her companion, blinked. 'I don't quite...'

'You know perfectly well what I mean. I don't want you trying to get in touch with me at one of your séances. I'll have far more interesting things to do than potter around down here, spouting a lot of platitudes about peace and love. Understand?'

'Now, dear, you mustn't talk like this. It'll be many years yet—'

'Jean, don't talk nonsense. I'm ninety-six. It cannot possibly be *many* years. And I don't mind at all. My husband's dead. My only son is dead. I've had enough of this world now. I've repented of my sins and I'm ready to meet my Maker. So I want it made clear that there must be no long faces at my funeral. Let people enjoy themselves. I've taken one step in that direction already. Charlie Bradley has it in hand.' She chuckled richly.

Jean looked doubtful. She was a thin, nondescript woman of about fifty, invariably clad in a tweed skirt and twin-set. Mostly her face wore an expression of doubt, or sometimes of anxiety. Doubt was now dominant as she didn't know whether to take Florrie seriously. How could her solicitor ensure people enjoyed themselves at her funeral?

But then, Florrie had never been serious. Even the name. She should be called Florence, a properly dignified name for the widow of an Earl's son. Jean had never felt quite comfortable calling her by her first name at all. But from the time she had come to her, Mrs Saunders had been quite clear. 'Call me Florrie,' she had said. 'Everybody else does.'

It was her background, of course. Stage people were notoriously lax about such things. And although it must be seventy years since she had last trodden the boards, the music hall artiste, the old vaudevillian, was still there, struggling to get out.

Jean, though, wished she wouldn't talk about her death. For that made her think about what was going to happen to her when Florrie passed over. She had hardly any savings and it was many years before she would qualify for a small state pension. With no qualifications, she would have little chance of getting any job, except one as companion. And most paid companions were really no better than nurse and housemaid combined. But otherwise, what would she do? After twenty-three years in this lovely detached house, on the river, just outside London, it would be very hard to settle in some pokey bed-setter, even if she could afford the rent. Oh, if only she knew whether Florrie—

'Penny for 'em,' Florrie said suddenly.

Jean gave a slight start. 'I was just thinking what a remarkable life you've had,' she said, untruthfully. 'Tell me, would you change anything?'

Florrie shook her head firmly. 'I had a wonderful time on the halls. Never made the West End, but might have done, if I hadn't got married. And I certainly don't regret that. People thought I was just Bertie's little bit of fluff and I craftily trapped him into marriage. Not so. It was a love match, even though he was a good bit older than me. And I worked hard to make sure he'd never be ashamed of me. In a few months I could speak and dress so you wouldn't know the difference between me and a Duchess. And I gave him a son. John was the apple of his eye. May sound shocking, but I'm always grateful Bertie died when he did. He saw John happily married to a lovely girl like Emma, with two daughters of his own. Then he passed away, less than nine months later Emma died, eighteen months after that John remarried – and within a few months was killed himself. It was a – a terrible time.'

Her voice quavered and stopped. Jean wisely remained silent while Florrie collected herself. She had, of course, listened to all this many times before. Florrie would reminisce for hours. But it didn't bore Jean, who never tired of hearing about an early life so different from her own ultra-respectable middle-class upbringing.

Florrie was continuing now, talking almost to herself. 'Worst choice John ever made, marrying Clara. I can understand why he did it: he thought Agatha and Dorothy needed a mother. And Clara could really turn on the charm, when she needed to. I don't know why she cut herself and the girls off from me completely after John's death: jealousy, maybe, or snobbery. Yet I was always nice to her. I never let it show that she was a disappointment to me, after Emma. Then, when the girls are grown up, she suddenly realises I'm getting on, and she ought to make sure I don't get my own back by cutting them out of my will. So she brings them to see me, and fawns all over me, saying how fond she is of me. Lying cat. And Dorry just sits there, staring at the carpet and fiddling her thumbs, and Agatha is red in the face and fuming. Very painful. Only happened once, though.'

'Well, you did tell her you found three visitors rather tiring.'

'I was hinting it would be nice to see the girls on their own. But she wouldn't have that.'

'Still, you do see Agatha regularly now. I was amazed later on when I answered the door one day and there she was, in jodhpurs and all her motor-cycling outfit.'

'Yes, she's one of a kind, is Agatha. But imagine having to come secretly, so her stepmother doesn't find out! And Dorry so cowed she never comes at all and from what Agatha says is not much more than an unpaid skivvy.'

'Agatha seems to have made an independent life for herself.'

'As far as she could. She ought to get out of that house. But, of course, she's got no money. What they get under my will is going to make a difference, though.'

CHAPTER TWO

'You're not going to get away with it, you loathsome old woman,' said the voice on the phone.

Clara Saunders gasped and nearly dropped the receiver. She was about to slam it down, but some instinct stopped her. Managing with great self-control to keep her voice steady, she said coolly: 'Who is that?'

'Oh, this is nobody at all. Nobody of any importance.' The words were slightly slurred, the voice husky. It could have been a man or a woman.

'Obviously true. Equally obviously you're drunk.'

'Oh yes, I'm drunk. And you know why? Because you've ruined my life.'

'You're insane.'

'Don't play the injured innocent. You sent that piece to the paper about me, you bitch.'

Clara drew her breath in sharply. But she wasn't going to take this sort of thing lying down. 'How dare you speak to me like that, you uncouth, insolent creature!'

'Insolent? How can one be insolent to a slimy toad like you?'

'I am not going to stand here and listen to insults from a contemptible, cowardly drunk. And let me warn you that if you call again—'

'No, let *me* warn *you*, my fine lady, that you're not going to get away with it.' The voice got louder. 'You'll pay, yes, you'll pay. I'm going to get you. I'm—'

At this Clara did ring off. She stood quite still in the hall of the old, rambling house in Hampstead. Her heart was pounding and her legs felt weak. Never before had she been spoken to in that ghastly way. Old, indeed! She wasn't sixty yet. But she did feel she'd handled the person with considerable dignity.

Suddenly she needed to sit down. She turned, to make her way back into the drawing-room, then gave a jump. Standing just two feet from her was a young woman. Clara clasped her hand to her heart. 'Oh, Dorothy, don't creep up on me like that!'

'I didn't. I just came to answer the phone,' Dorothy Saunders said defensively. She was in her early thirties, painfully thin, with short, mousy brown hair, and a deathly pale complexion. She was wearing a drab brown dress, about ten years out of date, thick stockings and flat shoes. At the moment her eyes were big with alarm. 'Mother, who *was* that?'

'I don't know. Just some drunk.'

'He threatened you, didn't he?'

'Certainly not!'

'But I heard him say, "You'll pay, I'm going to get you."'

'He didn't know what he was saying. He was totally out of control.'

'It was terrible. It's the way Al Capone and those other Chicago gangsters talk to their enemies.'

'I'm pleased to say, I wouldn't know. And I don't know how you do.'

'Only from the talkies. It was one of *them*, wasn't it?'

'A gangster? Don't be ridiculous!'

'No – one of those people you've told the papers about.'

'I tell you I don't know who it was.'

'Aggie's always said something like this would happen – that one of them would try and get revenge.'

'Your sister is absurdly melodramatic sometimes.'

'But he did threaten you. Mother, you must tell the police.'

'No. What could they do? Besides, it was only empty bluster.'

'It might not be. And at least if he rings again you could tell him the police had been notified. It might just frighten him off.'

'Well, I'll think about it, if it'll keep you quiet. Now I don't want to hear another word on the subject. Go and do something useful. Clean the bathroom.'

'I cleaned it this morning.'

'Well, clean something else!'

And Clara strode into the drawing-room and slammed the door behind her.

CHAPTER THREE

'I wonder how many people will come to my funeral,' Florrie said reflectively.

Jean Mackenzie gave a tut. 'There you go again, dear. You really must not think about these things.'

'I like thinking about it. I want it to be a good one.'

'I'm sure it will be, if a funeral can ever be good. And no doubt there'll be lots of people there.'

'Hardly any family, though. All my generation long gone, and John's, too – all my nephews and nieces. Happened everywhere, of course. First the Great War, then the Spanish Flu.'

'But you've got lots of great nephews and nieces, and great-greats.'

'Four great nephews, one great niece and two great-great nieces. Yes, I expect they'll come. I think they're all in my will, aren't they? Let me have another look at it, will you, dear?'

Jean got to her feet and carefully navigated her way between the many stools, pouffes, chairs and occasional tables to the big Victorian bureau. She had no difficulty in locating the will, as this was a routine which was gone through at least once a week. Florrie knew quite well who was in her will and who would be coming to her funeral. But she enjoyed the little ritual, it helped pass the time and at her age such harmless whims could be indulged.

Jean glanced down at the envelope wistfully as she made her way back. If only she knew whether *she* was mentioned in it. She had never liked to ask; it would seem such bad form. And Florrie hadn't ever given the slightest hint. It would be so easy, she thought for the umpteenth time, just to come in one day, when Florrie was in bed, and look. But it wouldn't be right. The mere fact that Florrie gave her the opportunity would make it wrong to take advantage of it. Though it was such a temptation...

She handed the envelope to Florrie, who opened it.

'Now, let me see. Well, George and Lavinia will come. I'm sure of that. They've always kept in touch. Never any snobbery with the *real* aristocrats you know, the one's who've got aristocratic natures, not just a title.'

'Oh, I know. And that time we stayed at Alderley was so wonderful. I'll never forget it. Even now, when they visit, I can't believe I'm actually talking to the Earl and Countess of Burford. They treat me just as though I were, well, one of them.'

'That's precisely what I mean. And Geraldine's a lovely girl, such a live wire. So interesting, all she had to tell me about those terrible murders they had there. I do hope she'll be happy with that young man.' She gave a sigh. 'It must be lovely at Alderley now. I wonder what they're all doing at this moment. Keeping very busy I'm sure.'

* * *

The August sun beat upon the half-drawn curtains of the mellow, oak-panelled room. Through the open French windows wafted the smell of roses and the faint hum of bees. In a large, well-worn black leather easy chair an untidy-looking man with wispy grey hair, a pink complexion and a straggly moustache whistled softly and not unmusically as his chest rose and fell rhythmically. The *Times* crossword puzzle, half finished, was open on his lap. George Henry Aylwin Saunders, twelfth Earl of Burford, was enjoying his usual post-prandial snooze. It was a peaceful scene.

It did not long remain so, as the double doors were thrown open and a girl breezed into the room. She was in her mid-twenties, petite, red-haired, with a tip-tilted nose and deceptively innocent large hazel eyes. She seemed to ooze energy. 'Hello, Daddy,' she said loudly.

Lord Burford awoke suddenly and blinked pale blue eyes several times before focusing on the speaker. He gave a grunt. 'Oh. You've arrived.'

Lady Geraldine Saunders looked hurt. 'What happened to "My darling daughter! You're home at last! It's been so long!"'

'It seems about three hours. How's London?'

'Big. Noisy. But fun.'

'It's the noisiness – and the smelliness – that always strikes me most these days. Which is why I go up as little as possible. Is that *Peepshow*?' He pointed incredulously to a garishly coloured magazine she was holding.

'Yes. A little present for you.'

She held it out to him. Lord Burford took it gingerly and gazed at it with distaste. 'Why the deuce did you bring me this? It's an appallin' rag.'

'There's something in it that will interest you.'

The Earl read the caption to the picture on the cover: '"Shirley Temple: America's Little Sweetheart." You surely don't— ?'

'No, no – page twelve.'

The Earl reluctantly flicked through the pages and opened the magazine out. Then his eyes bulged. 'Good gad!'

A banner headline, across two pages, read:

IS ALDERLEY CURSED?

The rest of the pages consisted mainly of photographs, but there was a small block of text. The Earl read it.

```
Twelve months ago this week two
sensational murders were committed
at Alderley, the 17th-Century
Westshire home of the Earl and
Countess of Burford. Amazingly,
less than six months later, another,
completely unconnected murder took
place. Involving, among others, a
government minister, film stars,
American millionaires, European
aristocracy, foreign diplomats and
an Olympic athlete, with the murder
weapons valuable firearms from Lord
Burford's world-famous collection,
these crimes have led many people to
ask if an ancient gypsy's curse is
still exerting its malign influence
over the beautiful, stately home,
and if this could lead to further
tragedies. See the following pages
for the full astounding story.
```

The Earl looked up. 'This – this is preposterous!'

'I know.'

'It's absolute nonsense! It's ridiculous! It's – it's—' He groped for words.

'How about balderdash? That's a good strong word.'

'Claptrap,' said the Earl defiantly.

'Yes, claptrap's good, too.'

'This business about a curse, I mean. The eighth Earl turfed some gypsies off his land and one old woman swore at him a bit and told him he'd regret it.'

'And within twelve months he and his younger son were both dead.'

'The Earl had apoplexy – probably what they'd call a stroke today – and the boy most likely got pneumonia. There wasn't anything mysterious about it. Since then there's been nothin' out of the ordinary. Most of my ancestors died peacefully, usually at a ripe old age.'

'You don't have to convince me, Daddy. I'm not scared of any gypsy's curse.'

'And those murders didn't involve the family. The people just happened to be here. I shall complain to the editor.'

'I don't honestly think you've got any grounds. The story *has* appeared in a couple of books, after all.'

Lord Burford turned the page to reveal a page of text broken into many short paragraphs and headed THE ALDERLEY MURDERS: FULL STORY. 'You've read this?'

'Skimmed through it. Nothing that wasn't in the papers at the time. They seem to have got the facts right, and they don't libel anybody, so we'll just have to grin and bear it.'

'Bear it I may. Grin I will not.'

'The pictures aren't bad.'

'Didn't look at 'em.' He turned back the page. 'My word, they've really gone to town. That's your mother and me when she opened the County Show last month. Nice photo of you.'

'It's the one that was in *The Tatler*.'

'Oh yes. But they've put you in a line with all these other girls. "Beauties Involved in Murder." You, Jane Clifton, Anilese de la Roche, Laura Lorenzo, the little Dove – and Mabel Turner, for heaven's sake! This picture of her must be twenty years old, at least.'

'That "involved in" is a bit rich. You'd think they'd have had the decency to distinguish between the victims, the criminals and the innocent bystanders.'

'Well, *you* weren't a bystander, either time. You were gettin' mixed up in the investigations.'

Gerry nodded, a wistful expression on her face. 'You know, in spite of all the horrible things that happened, it was fun, wasn't it – looking back?'

'I look back as infrequently as I can. Reckon those weekends put twenty years on my life.'

'There's even a photo of Chief Inspector Wilkins – see.'

'Oh yes. "The Man Who Solved Both Cases." Looking as bewildered as ever. He came up trumps, though. Er, did you just get the one copy of this?'

'Two. Mummy's got the other.'

'Oh, you've shown her. How did she take it?'

'As you'd expect: phlegmatically.'

'Good. I was just thinkin', rubbish as it all is, might be

a good idea to get a few more copies. I can think of quite a few people who'd like to see it – some of the others who were here, apart from anybody else.'

'OK, I'll get another half dozen.'

'Better make it a dozen. So, what you doin' here? Row with the boyfriend?'

'Of course not! And he's my fiancé, not just my boyfriend; remember?'

'Thought you youngsters preferred these new-fangled terms. Anyway, why are you home?'

'I explained in my telegram. He's had to go away on family business. You know there was a death in his family – which is why we had to postpone the wedding. Well, it's led to a lot of legal and financial complications and he's had to go and help sort it all out. It was going to be lonely until he got back and I wanted a break.'

'Why didn't you go with him?'

'I felt I'd be in the way.'

'Lor, you've got sensitive all of a sudden. Anyway, it's nice to have you home, sweetheart. Place seems pretty empty sometimes, without you.'

Gerry looked surprised and pleased. 'Why, thank you Daddy. Anyway, I'm going to have a shower.' She started towards the door, then stopped and turned round. 'Oh, while I remember, I saw Great Aunt Florrie last week. She sent her love to you both.'

'Oh, good. Your mother and I called to see her for a couple of hours back in the spring. How is she?'

'Perky as ever. Apart from my wedding, all she wanted me to talk about was the murders – much to Miss Mackenzie's disapproval. I filled her in on all the undercover stuff that never came out publicly. I think I'll send her a copy of *Peepshow*. I'm sure she'll enjoy making Mackenzie read it to her.'

'Suppose I ought to read it – just to make quite sure they have got their facts right.'

'Oh, absolutely,' Gerry said.

She went out. The Earl buried his head in *Peepshow*.

CHAPTER FOUR

'Then there's Gregory,' said Florrie. 'He's certain to come when he learns he's in the will. Don't suppose his wife will bother, though. She's never been here.'

'That's Alexandra, isn't it?'

'Yes. Don't think it's much of a marriage. She's very politically ambitious, and I imagine the fact Gregory's not exactly had a dazzling career has been a disappointment to her.'

'But he's very respected as an MP, isn't he?'

'I believe so. I can't trust him, though. Maybe just because he's a politician. I don't believe a word one of them says. Frankly, I'd never be surprised to learn...'

She tailed off.

'To learn what, dear?'

'Oh, nothing,' said Florrie.

'Greggy, darling, I saw an absolutely too divine dress in Bond Street today.'

Gregory Carstairs, MP, who was pouring himself a gin and tonic at the time, gave a grunt. His companion, a sinuous dark-haired girl with pouting, scarlet lips, who was lounging artistically back on the sofa, displaying very long and shapely legs, clad in black stockings of the purest silk, went on: 'It's chiffon, the palest shade of blue, with these delicious little pleats...' She prattled away, but Gregory wasn't listening. He gazed out of the window over the roofs of St. John's Wood to the famous Father Time weather vane of Lord's Cricket Ground, just a few hundred yards away. Useful, at least in the summer. If anybody should happen to see him in the neighbourhood, it provided the perfect excuse. Watching cricket was something nobody objected to a Member of Parliament doing; it was almost expected.

He was a heavily built man of about fifty with closely cropped grizzled hair, a florid complexion, the beginnings of a double chin and a neatly trimmed moustache, which he fondly believed gave him a military appearance. He always refused to talk about his war experiences, leading many people to assume he must have had a good record. In fact, he had been rejected because of flat feet, and had spent the whole of 1914 to 1918 in a Whitehall office.

He turned round and surveyed the chicly furnished, ultra-modern sitting-room of the flat, with its sharp angles and chromium fittings. 'Strewth, but this place was costing him a fortune. How long would he be able to keep it up? Or Poppy, for that matter? He was going to have to do something about it. But what? Poppy was such a clinger. And she wouldn't forgive easily if he just dumped her. He had to keep her sweet. It wouldn't be so bad if it wasn't for that damned letter he'd written her. What a fool he'd been! Tipsy at the time, of course, and in those days he'd been really smitten by her, but that was no excuse. He had to get out of this entanglement soon. But how?

'...and it was only ten pounds – well, guineas, actually. It would really suit me.'

Gregory dragged himself back. 'I'm sure you'd look absolutely breathtaking in it, my sweet. We must certainly think about getting it for you, er, sometime.'

'Sometime?' There was a suspicious edge to her voice.

'Yes, Christmas perhaps.'

'*Christmas?*' This time the voice was an octave higher. 'But that's months and months away. And this is a summer dress!'

'But you've got dozens of summer dresses. And look so perfectly ravishing in all of them.'

Poppy gazed at him, a disconcertingly acute and appraising expression in her large violet eyes. 'Greggy, you're not getting hard up, are you?'

'Good lord, no! Whatever gave you that idea?'

'You haven't bought me anything nice for weeks and weeks.'

'Well, I am a bit short of the ready just now. But it's just a temporary thing. Hold up in funds, lots of expenses, have to take the old woman to Monte later this month, as I explained.'

'You've never taken *me* to Monte Carlo.'

'I know, my sweet, and I'd like nothing better, believe me. But we did have that weekend in Brighton a month ago.'

'That was no fun, not with you peering over your shoulder all the time, in a blue funk in case someone recognised you.'

'Well, I do have to be careful, sweetheart. I mean if we were seen together, it would cause the most awful scandal in my constituency. I've explained what a provincial backwater it is, and how narrow-minded they are there. Any hint of what they'd call impropriety could cost me my seat. Do you know what my majority was last time?'

'Five hundred and sixty-eight,' Poppy said in a bored voice.

'Oh. Then you can see how easily I could be kicked out.'

'Would it really matter if you were? You seem totally fed up with it half the time, and there's all these late-night sittings and asking questions you know the answers to already and having to write letters to all those silly little constituents. And you're never going to get into the Government, are you? You're always going to be a back-bencher.'

'I say, that's a bit below the belt. Besides, it's not true. One of the Whips was only saying to me a month ago that the Prime Minister's always got me very much in mind.' He straightened his shoulders and unconsciously straightened his tie. 'Anyway, it's a matter of duty. Family's got a long history of public service. Men from my background have a responsibility to serve this country.' He took hold of the lapel of his jacket with one hand and gazed out over the rooftops. His voice took on a more resonant tone. 'I often think, when I gaze at a view such as this, and look down at the people going peaceably, freely and unafraid about their business, how greatly blessed we are to live in a land like ours.'

He turned round and addressed her earnestly. 'Across a

mere twenty-six miles of water, storm clouds are gathering and tyranny is raising its vile head. Yet how often we in Britain tend to take our blessings for granted. It has been wisely said that the price of liberty is eternal vigilance. Such vigilance is the duty of us all, but particularly of those happy few of us called to serve in the front line of liberty's defence, in the Mother of Parliaments. We—'

Poppy raised her hand to her mouth and ostentatiously stifled a yawn. Gregory gave a blink and came back to earth. 'Well, you do see, don't you?'

'But do you really enjoy it, Greggy – all this defending liberty? Wouldn't you rather be spending your time with me?' The tone was wheedling.

'Well, of course I would, precious. You know that.'

'Then why don't you chuck it in? After all, you've done nearly twenty years of public service. You could get your divorce and never have to worry about who saw us. And it's not as though the salary is up to much. You told me once it only made up a teeny bit of what you earned.'

'Yes, but you don't understand. I'm on the Board of six companies, five of whom only want me because it looks good to have an MP on their letter heads. I'm an adviser to two business associations, simply because the idiots believe I can influence Government policy, or at least know what it's going to be. Then there's the odd bit of journalism. I'd lose all that if I gave up my seat. Besides, what would I do outside politics?'

Poppy gave a pout. 'So I suppose that means you'll be going off to your dreary old constituency more and more, does it?'

''Fraid so: make a few speeches, shake a few hands, kiss

a few babies. And don't worry – I mean the sort that guzzle milk, not the kind that quaff champers.' Gregory gave a forced chuckle.

'Will *she* be going with you?'

'Alex? Yes. She's dam' good at that sort of thing, I will say that. Worth a good few hundred votes.'

'I could do all that sort of thing.'

Gregory tried unsuccessfully to imagine Poppy earnestly discussing child welfare or old age pensions with the wife of his constituency party Chairman. But he wasn't forced to make a response, because she changed the subject.

'So, when you going next?'

'Tomorrow, actually.'

'How long for?'

'Rest of the week.'

'Oh, Greggy!'

'Frightfully sorry. But it can't be helped.'

Poppy gave a sigh. 'What about next week?'

'Not sure. Monday and Tuesday I've got speaking engagements. I'll phone you sometime Tuesday. Perhaps we can arrange something for Wednesday or later in the week.'

'I won't budge an inch from the phone, darling,' said Poppy.

CHAPTER FIVE

'Timothy will come, I'm sure,' Florrie said. 'I think he'd want to, but he'd come even if he didn't. Always does the right thing, does Timothy.'

'Such a distinguished-looking man, I always think. And a very clever barrister, I believe.'

'Oh, Timothy's all right. Terrible stick, though. How he came to have such a flibbertigibbet daughter as Penny I'll never know. She's a pretty little baggage, with no thought in her head apart from finding a husband.'

'So sad her mother dying as young as she did.'

'Yes. Can't have been easy for Timothy, bringing up a girl on his own. Still, he always seems completely in control of every situation.'

'Thank you, Mr Jackson,' said Timothy Saunders. 'I have no further questions. I'm sure his lordship and the jury will now know just how much weight to attach to your evidence.'

He sat down, as Jackson, looking decidedly shaken, hurriedly left the witness box. A cross-examination by one

of the sharpest forensic minds of the English bar left few
people unscathed.

Timothy's face showed no expression. It hardly ever
did. He felt no pleasure at having demolished one of
the opposition's most important witnesses: just the quiet
satisfaction of a professional at a job well done. He
gathered his papers together as the judge announced the
end of the day's proceedings. His junior counsel gave him
a sideways glance. It had been a ruthless performance, one
that made him feel slightly uncomfortable. But undeniably
effective. 'Nearly over, do you think?' he asked quietly.

Timothy nodded shortly. 'We can expect an offer in the
morning.'

He was a slim man of no more than average height,
with small, regular features, a neatly trimmed toothbrush
moustache, a pale complexion and thinning light brown
hair, concealed now under his barrister's wig. A man who
would never be noticed in a crowd, whom most people
would have difficulty in describing, even after spending
half an hour in his company. He recognised that it was
probably the constant experience of being unnoticed and
ignored when young that had driven him relentlessly on in
his determination to make an impact of some kind on the
world.

He strode rapidly back to his chambers. It was only
four thirty. Time for a full three hours' work on the
opinion he was preparing for Hargraves & Hargraves.
Not that there was any urgency. He could go home now.
But the house would be empty, apart from the servants,
tucked away in their quarters. Penelope would certainly be
out. What would he do? Read a law book? He sometimes

envied those men who had some all-consuming interest or hobby – gardening or golf or, like his distant relative, Lord Burford, gun-collecting. But he had never left time for things like that. And now he was surely not far away from achieving his life-long ambition: elevation to the Bench, leading, in all probability one day, to the position of Lord Chief Justice, and the opportunity not merely to practise law but actually to influence it, to change it. He knew that that was what his fellow lawyers expected. Even if none of them liked him very much, they all held him in the highest respect. And what was more important than respect?

Arriving back at his chambers, he sent his clerk home, poured himself a small glass of very dry sherry and sat down at his desk. He took out the case containing his pince-nez, thoroughly polished them with a clean linen handkerchief and put them on. He refolded the handkerchief and replaced it in his pocket, then opened his brief case, took out the papers – and saw It. His stomach gave a lurch. For a while he had managed to forget about It – this thing that clouded all his horizons, that threatened to shatter all his hopes for the future.

The Photograph.

Against his better judgement, he had to obey the impulse to look at it again. It was like the urge constantly to exert pressure on a painful tooth, just to see if it still hurt. His eyes gave the slightest flicker and his lips tightened momentarily – the closest he would ever come to wincing – and he hurriedly put it back in his case. He could not leave it in the office safe, as his clerk knew the combination, while Penelope knew that of the one at home. So he had been carrying it round with him. He ought really to deposit it at his bank. But then he would not be able to indulge the lacerating, but to him very necessary, urge constantly to stare at it, searching for some minute indication as to where or who... He knew when, but there was no clue, obviously, as to why. Was it a prelude to blackmail? If so, why was the demand delayed? Or was some enemy, someone he had destroyed in court, just playing with him, waiting to release it to the gutter press the moment his advancement was announced? The first he could put up with. And he would pay, unquestionably – provided he could think of some method to be sure he got the negative and all prints back; easier said than done, but it ought not to be beyond his wit. He just wished the demand would come tomorrow, so he knew where he was. But it was entirely out of his hands. And thinking about it at this time would serve absolutely no purpose.

With the strength of will and concentration that made him such a formidable lawyer, he thrust all thought of it from his mind, got out the Hargraves papers and commenced writing in a quick, neat hand. Every few seconds his eyelid twitched irritatingly, but Timothy ignored it.

CHAPTER SIX

'Now the one who I think's really going to miss me is Stella,' Florrie said.

'Oh, I'm sure she will. I do like Stella. And she's so smart and sophisticated.'

'I suppose working as a fashion journalist in New York for ten years does that for you.'

'I do enjoy her stories.'

'Yes, she's a wonderfully entertaining girl. I love her sense of humour. I'm sorry her magazine went broke, of course, but I am glad it brought her home.'

'But she seems to be doing just as well with this London magazine.'

'Don't suppose she earns as much, though. She's a very ambitious girl, and I wouldn't be surprised if she moved on fairly soon. Ah well, we'll see. Or at least you will.'

'She's the granddaughter of Margaret, your husband's younger sister, is that right?'

'I sometimes think you know my family better than I do. Yes. Margaret was pretty cool at first, but she came round in the end. We became quite good friends. And it's nice that her grandson keeps in touch, as well as her granddaughter.'

'Stella and Tommy are first cousins, aren't they?'

'Yes. I'm fond of Tommy – even though he's not the brainiest lad you could hope to find.'

'He's so charming, though. And funny. He really makes me smile with all those tales of his pranks.'

'Bit too funny and charming sometimes, perhaps, but his heart's in the right place.'

'He's such a good listener, too. He always seems really eager to hear the little stories I am able to tell him about communications with the Other Side.'

Florrie strongly suspected that Jean's little stories were secretly a source of great amusement to Tommy. But she said nothing.

The richly carpeted and gracefully appointed car showroom had the hush of a great cathedral. Here and there among the multi-coloured and glistening graven images, elegant and expensively attired young men, the priests of this secular religion, conversed in low and earnest tones with equally well-dressed but clearly timid acolytes. Occasionally a single word or phrase wafted, like a mantra, above the low hum: 'torque,' 'compression,' 'power-to-weight ratio.'

Tommy Lambert, an exceedingly tall and slim young man of twenty-three, with a pink complexion and a mop of unruly sandy-coloured hair, stood gazing out through the plate glass window at the sunlit bustle of London's Park Lane, his normally amiable expression replaced at this moment by one of profound gloom. No eager enquirers after truth had approached him that morning, perhaps sensing that he was as much a noviciate as they themselves. And no enquirers, to be promptly converted into cash-paying customers, meant no commission this week. And no commission meant no – what? Champagne cocktails? Tickets to the new Rodgers and Hart musical for himself and Ginny or Susie or Joanie? No afternoon at Epsom on Saturday? He could put up with that, though, if it wasn't for the other business. The day suddenly darkened as he thought of it again. What the deuce was he going to do? For the moment Benny seemed reasonably content with ten shillings a week. But that was just interest. It could only be a matter of weeks at the most before he demanded payment in full. And when he didn't get it he'd probably turn very nasty. Confound the fellow who'd given him that 'sure-fire' tip. Nothing seemed to have gone right since.

'Hello, Tommy,' said a soft and slightly breathless voice behind him.

Tommy spun round and his face lightened. 'Penny, old bean, what a surprise!'

The girl standing there was a few years younger than himself. She had bobbed, platinum blond hair, done in lots of tight curls, and enormous pale blue eyes, set wide apart. She was wearing a cream cotton suit with peak lapels and patch pockets, and perched slightly to the side of her head was a light green Tyrolean hat, decorated with a pheasant tail. She looked extremely fashionable and very pretty. She was smiling rather tentatively at him.

'How are you, Tommy?'

'Oh, spiffing, really, you know.'

'I saw you through the window. You were looking a bit in the dumps'

'Was I? Well, suppose I am, really.'

'Oh?' She stared at him sympathetically. 'Something wrong?'

'Nothing more than usual. It's just that I think that Lagonda might be exactly the car you're looking for, madam. Let me show it to you.' He ushered her towards a scarlet two-seater Tourer.

Penelope Saunders looked somewhat bewildered. 'I'm sorry, Tommy, I didn't really come in to buy a car.'

'I know, but the Lord High Sales Manager was approaching. Got to pretend you're a customer.' He stopped by the Lagonda. 'Look at the car, not me.'

'Oh, right. I thought I'd just pop in and see how you were getting on at the new job. Sort of cousinly interest.'

'Jolly decent of you. That is the trouble, really. I'm not much good at it. I've only sold three cars in four weeks.'

'Is that bad?'

'Well, they don't expect you to be a super salesman in a month, but I am starting to get some rather old-fashioned looks.'

'Oh, I am sorry. I was hoping this time you might have found something that really suited you. I mean, you've always been keen on cars, haven't you?'

'Keen on driving them, not selling them.'

Penny was staring intently at the sleek lines of the Lagonda. 'It is awfully pretty, isn't it? I wish I *could* buy it.'

'It's not all that expensive,' Tommy said hopefully.

'It is for me. Daddy keeps me most horribly hard up. My allowance is positively laughable. Only I don't laugh. You'd think he'd want me to have a good time.

But no. And it's always 'don't do this, don't do that.' He doesn't like me smoking in public. He won't even let me paint my toenails. And he thinks night clubs are dens of iniquity. He's like one of those Victorian fathers you read about.'

'Well, I suppose he is, really, isn't he? Victorian, I mean. How old is he?'

'Forty-six.'

'Well, there you are. He was born in the nineteenth century, so he *is* Victorian.'

'But he doesn't have to behave like it. It's the 1930s now.'

Tommy said: 'Get in the car – look as though you're really interested.'

He opened the driver's door and Penny got in. Tommy went round to the far side, gathering up a couple of brochures from a nearby stand on the way, and sat in the passenger seat. 'I'll pretend to be going through all this technical stuff with you.'

'It's really comfy,' Penny said, leaning back in the seat. 'You'd think he'd let me have a car, wouldn't you? I mean, just because I gave his Daimler the teeny-weeniest dent the only time he let me drive it, he uses that as an excuse – says he's frightened I'd have an accident. It's the money, really, I'm sure.'

'He must have oodles, too.'

'He's absolutely rolling. And it's not as though he's got anyone – or anything – else to spend it on.'

'So, what's he do with it?'

'Just invests it. I think he gives a lot to good causes, as well.'

'Well, I'm a good cause. Wouldn't slip a few quid to me, would he? I've got all sorts of ripping ideas that just need a bit of capital.'

'There's not a chance of that, darling.'

'He doesn't like me, does he?'

Penny wriggled awkwardly. 'It's not that he doesn't like you. But he doesn't really approve of you. Thinks you should have trained for some proper profession.'

'It's all very well for brainy geezers like him. Can you see me as a lawyer or doctor or architect or something?'

Penny tried for a moment and failed.

'I think I'll turn to crime,' Tommy said gloomily.

'Don't be silly.'

'I'm not being silly. I've seriously thought about it. Oh, not anything that would hurt anybody, but where would be the harm in pinching something from somebody who'd never miss it? Just to put me on my feet.'

'You mustn't say things like that. *I* know you're joking, but other people wouldn't – people who don't know how you're always kidding and playing pranks and practical jokes. That's something else which puts Daddy off you.'

'That's just fun! They never harm anyone.'

'I know that. I think some of them are screamingly funny. But Daddy's got no sense of humour at all.'

'I say, I brought off an absolutely terrific wheeze a couple of weeks ago. This old chum of mine was working for a company owned by an absolute bounder. Name of Hodge. Frightfully rich, and he and his wife are the most appalling snobs. Anyway, he had an application for a job from the son of some marquis or other, old Etonian, and all that, but totally useless. Old Hodge-podge, though, couldn't resist having a gen-you-ine aristocrat on his staff, so to make room for him, he sacked my pal. No excuse, no apology, just a month's salary and out on his ear.'

'How rotten.'

'As you can imagine, he was pretty browned off and wanted to get his own back. He asked me if I had any ideas. So I put the jolly old brain-box to work and made a few enquiries. These people have got a big place in Sussex, swimming pool, acres of grounds. And it's on a main road to the coast. I found out they were planning a big garden party for the next Saturday – lavish open-air buffet, marquee, and so on. Asking all the toffs of the county. So I went to a sign writer and got a lot of big placards done. The Saturday was a super day and my pal and I drove down. We got there just before the party started and we stuck these placards up about every fifty yards at the side of the road for the quarter of a mile leading to the house. They had things on them like 'Open Day,' 'No Charge,' 'Everybody Welcome,' 'Free Refreshments,' 'Beautiful Gardens,' 'Swimming Pool,' 'Bring the Kiddies.' And the ones nearest the house had big arrows, pointing through the gates. Then we beat it, pronto.'

'What happened?' Penny asked, wide-eyed.

'I found out all about it later, from a johnnie who was at the party. As you can imagine, on a beautiful Saturday, the roads were jam-packed with people on their way for an afternoon at the seaside, and within minutes cars started to roll in. The Hodges didn't realise what was happening at first, thought they were invited guests. The climax was when a charabanc, with about forty people on board, arrived. They twigged then, but it was too late.

There were already about twenty cars parked on the drive, people were helping themselves to grub and drinks from the buffet, kids were trampling all over the flower beds, changing into their bathing costumes in their cars and jumping in the swimming pool. Some people actually went in the house and started poking round all over the place, using the bathrooms, what have you. The butler was trying to get rid of them, which led to a lot of nasty arguments. And the most topping thing of all was that one of the real guests was an eccentric old baronet, who always dresses in the most disreputable togs and hardly ever shaves or has his hair cut. The butler thought he was one of the gate-crashers and forcibly ejected him. By which time, most of the toffs were pretty fed up, and started to leave, *en masse*. Hodge was running round in circles, trying to get *them* to stay and the intruders to leave, all at the same time. Mrs Hodge was having hysterics in her boudoir. I'm delighted to say that their great day was totally ruined. And serve them bally well right.'

Penny gave a sigh. 'Oh, Tommy, you're so clever! To think of that!'

Tommy endeavoured unsuccessfully to look modest. 'I do seem to have a flair for that sort of thing.' Then he became gloomy again. 'Good to have a flair for something, I suppose. Certainly haven't got one for selling cars.'

'What would you like to do?'

'Dunno, really. Used to think I'd like to be a reporter. Must be terrific fun, going round interviewing film stars and racing drivers. I'm not much of a writer, but that doesn't really matter; you just put down what they say. It was Stella getting her first job in that line that put the idea into my head. Incidentally, I hear she's back.'

'Stella who? Back from where?'

'Stella Simmons. Cousin Stella. Home from the US of A. A pal of mine ran into her. Seems she's working for some fashion mag, but I don't know which one and her number's not in the phone book, so I haven't been able to get in touch with her. I thought she might have given me a call, actually. I used to have quite a crush on her, when I was about thirteen.'

Penny gave an almost inaudible sniff. 'Really?'

'And she was jolly nice to me.'

'Really?' said Penny again. The temperature in the Lagonda had dropped a degree or two.

'Girls of that age haven't usually got much time for young lads.'

Penny frowned. 'What do you mean: 'that age'?'

'Well, she must have been twenty-three or more then.'

'Oh.' Penny's face cleared. 'Then she's quite old?'

'Mm, that was ten or eleven years ago.'

'I see.' The atmosphere was suddenly warmer again. 'She sounds very nice,' Penny said condescendingly.

'You never met her, then?'

'I've never even heard of her. And I don't understand. If she's your cousin and I'm your cousin, she must be my cousin, too, mustn't she?'

'You're not my cousin.'

'Don't be silly, Tommy, of course I am.'

'Not my full cousin – first cousin, nor even second. We're different generations.'

Penny looked quite blank. 'How do you mean?'

'Well, let me see. Your grandfather and my father were

first cousins. So I'm second cousin to your father. I think that makes you my second cousin once removed.'

'Removed where?'

'That's just what they call it. Means a generation younger.'

'I'm nothing like a generation younger than you, only three or four years.'

'That's got nothing to do with it. But if we were looking at the family tree, you'd be one level lower down.'

Penny was looking totally bewildered. 'I don't know anything about the family, really. Daddy never talks about them. So where does this Stella girl come in?'

'Ah, well, my father and her mother were brother and sister. So she *is* my first cousin. And you're her second cousin once removed, too, as well as mine. Aren't you a lucky girl?'

'Mummy had some first cousins. I used to call them Auntie or Uncle.'

'Oh, that's just an old convention. You needn't call me Uncle.'

'I wasn't going to,' Penny said blankly.

'We'd better get out. Can't sit here all day.'

'Tommy, you were joking, weren't you? About taking up crime.'

'What? Oh yes, of course. You know me. Here, take these.' He handed her the brochures. 'I'll give you my card. Look at it, say loudly: 'Thank you, Mr Lambert. I'm very interested in the car. I'll come back and see you when I've had a few days to think about it.''

'Say that again.'

Tommy did so, and Penny carefully repeated the words under her breath.

He got out, hurried round the car, opened the driver's door for her and with a flourish handed her his business card. 'Please don't hesitate to contact me, if you have any further questions, madam.'

Penny concentrated furiously. 'Thank you, Mr Carr,' she said in a loud voice. 'I'm very interested in you. I want to think about you for a few days and see you again.'

CHAPTER SEVEN

'I suppose Clara will let the girls come,' Florrie said.

'Surely she will! And come herself, I should hope.'

'Hypocrite if she does. But be criticised if she doesn't, I suppose. Unless she could claim pressure of work.'

'Work? What do you mean, dear?'

'I told you what Agatha told me about Clara's nasty little money-making scheme. I put in a guarded reference to it when I made those little changes to my will last month. Anyway, Agatha should be here again any day now. I must find out if it's still going on.'

Clara reached forward and took the rough-skinned hand of the plump young girl, who was sitting on the edge of the hard upright chair in the coldly furnished and immaculately tidy drawing-room, an expression of acute doubt on her pale, unattractive face. Clara's claw-like fingers tightened in what was meant to be a reassuring, clasp, but which only made the girl wince slightly. Clara hastily let go.

'Now, Martha,' she said gently. 'I know you're a good, loyal girl. But when you learn of some terrible deceit, you do have a duty to make sure the truth comes out. It's not right that your master should deceive your mistress in this way. Don't you think she should know about it?'

Martha nodded.

'Then can you tell her yourself?'

'Oh no, madam, I couldn't.'

'But she'll never find out unless somebody tells her. You tell me and I'll make sure she learns just what's been going on.'

Martha twisted her hands together. 'I don't know, I'm sure.'

'You came to me, remember, my dear, not the other way round. All you've told me so far is that your employer is deceiving his wife with another woman, but you haven't even told me his name. Why did you come, by the way? We've never met before, have we?'

'It was Lily suggested it, madam, Lily Watson. She was in service with Dr. and Mrs Forbes-King.'

'Ah yes, of course. And in that case, it was the mistress who was carrying on.'

'That's right, madam, and Lily said that after she told you about it, it all came out. They're divorced now, of course, and Lily had to look for another position, but she said that wasn't your fault.'

'Of course it wasn't. How can it ever be wrong to tell the truth? Now, I can see you're an honourable girl and you hate carryings-on. They go against everything your mother ever taught you, don't they?'

'Yes, madam.'

'And she was a good woman, wasn't she?'

'Oh yes, madam. She still is. She's still alive.'

'I'm so glad. The world can ill afford to lose women like your mother. Now I'm sure you want to be a credit to her – speak up fearlessly and uncover all this lying and deceit.'

'Oh yes, madam, but...' Martha ran her tongue round her lips. 'Lily did say as how you made it worth her while, like.'

'But of course. Virtue should always be rewarded.'

She opened her clasped left hand to reveal the crisp £5 which was folded in her palm. She made it crackle temptingly. 'Well.' Martha took a deep breath. 'The master is Mr Terence Leigh.'

Clara's eyebrows shot upwards. 'The novelist?'

'Yes, madam.'

'Really? Right, now tell me exactly what happened.'

'Well, it was Wednesday last week. That's me usual half-day – the mistress changed it this week. Anyway, the mistress had gone to visit her parents and wasn't expected back until late and the master was going to be working in his study. Now, he'd said he'd go out for a meal in the evening and told cook she could have the afternoon off, as well, which was very unusual. She went out about one. I went out about quarter past, and I noticed this big red and white American car parked a little down the road, with a lady sat in it. I didn't think nothing of it, really. I 'adn't gone very far when I found I'd left me purse behind, and I 'ad to go back. The car was still there, but the lady weren't in it. Well, I went in through the servants' door at the back and started up to me room. But when I was passing the main bedroom I heard voices coming from it.'

By now Clara's long, narrow nose seemed to be almost visibly quivering. 'What voices?'

'One was definitely the master, and the other a lady.'

'Could you hear what they were saying?'

'Just a few words. I heard the lady laughing, and then she gave a sort of little scream. And I heard her say: 'Terry, you're a wicked man, you know that?' And the master, he said: 'And you're absolutely wonderful, Marigold.''

'Marigold? Had you ever heard a mention of that name?'

'No, madam. And nobody ever calls the master Terry.'

'Go on.'

'Well, I would have liked to have seen who the lady was, if she was the one in the car, but they might be in there some time, and when they did come out, it wouldn't be likely I'd see her face, 'cos I'd have to keep out of sight myself, and anyway, it was me afternoon off, and I knew my friend would be waiting for me, so I just went on up, got me purse and scarpered. The car were gone, though, when I got back that night.'

'What did the lady in the car look like?'

'Real glamorous. Very blond hair, lots of make-up.'

Clara nodded to herself. 'Yes, it could be...' She fell silent for a few moments, then stood up. 'Well, thank you, Martha. You did quite right in coming to me.' The £5 note rapidly changed hands. 'Now, if at any time you have any further information, about this or any other matter, you know where to find me. And please pass the word among your friends.' She ushered the girl into the hall, opened the front door and practically shooed her out. Then she returned to the drawing-room.

What was the name of that girl in the new review? Marigold Green – that was it. She was blond. Clara grabbed up a copy of the *Evening News* and turned to the theatre page. Yes, *Keep Smiling* at the Star Theatre. Curtain up at eight. It was just ten past seven, so Marigold Green ought to be there now. It was worth a try.

She went into the hall, picked up the directory, found the Star Theatre's number and picked up the telephone receiver. As she did so the kitchen door opened and Dorothy came along the hall. Clara looked up irritably. 'Oh, go away, Dorothy. I told you I did not want to be disturbed.'

Dorothy gave a nervous jump, like a frightened filly. 'I'm sorry, Mother. I heard the girl go, so I thought—'

'Don't think so much. Just do as you're told. Go and do the ironing.'

'I've finished it.'

'Well, start getting the meal ready.'

'The joint is in the oven.'

'Are the potatoes done?'

'No, not yet.'

'Well, go and do them.'

'Very well, Mother.'

She started back to the kitchen. 'And scrape them, don't peel,' Clara called after her, and lifted the telephone receiver.

'Star stage door,' a rough Cockney voice answered, when she got through.

Clara adopted a gruff tone. 'Marigold Green, please.'

'Who wants her?'

'Terry.'

'Hang on.'

For a minute or so Clara heard distant snatches of conversation, footsteps and various bumps and bangs. Then a female voice, slightly breathless, came on the line. 'Terry, darling, you're not supposed to call me here.'

Clara rang off.

Her thin lips formed into a smile. That settled it. If only it could always be so easy. She put through another call. It was answered quickly.

'*News of the Week*.'

'Saucy Snippets column, please.'

A male voice spoke next. 'Saucy Snippets.'

'This is C. S.'

'Ah, dear lady, how nice to hear from you. It's been some time.' He had an exaggerated, plainly bogus upper-class accent.

'I have something for you.'

'Splendid.'

'One of the country's leading writers – married – is having an affair with a well-known young review artiste.'

'Excellent. What would we do without these people? Let me have the names.'

'Just a moment. How much?'

'Usual. Thirty.'

'No, I want forty. He's a very big name indeed. I can tell you exactly when and where they last met and what his wife was doing at the time.'

'Oo, I'm not sure about that.'

'I can easily go somewhere else. I came to you first.'

There was a pause before he said: 'Well, OK – provided he is as big as you say.'

Clara hesitated for a moment, remembering that awful phone call she had received. Suppose… But forty pounds was forty pounds. 'Terence Leigh,' she said.

There was a whistle.

'Big enough for you?'

'All right, it's a deal. Let's have the rest.'

'The girl is Marigold Green, who's in *Keep Smiling* at the Star.' She gave a summary of what Martha had told her.

'Is this one hundred per cent reliable?'

'Absolutely. If you want to confirm it yourself, find out what sort of car Marigold Green drives. I guarantee it's a big red and white American one. It was seen parked outside his house on Wednesday afternoon, by someone who couldn't possibly have known Marigold Green's car.'

'Sounds good. OK, if that checks out, I don't see any problems. You'll be paid within a few days.'

Clara rang off.

'And that's just about all my family' said Florrie. 'All the ones who matter, anyway.' She looked suddenly wistful. 'I do wish I could be there for the funeral. And for the reading of the will. There are going to be some surprises when it's read. I'd love to see the reactions.' She seemed to brighten. 'Perhaps I will. Perhaps, after all, I will come back, just to see my funeral and what happens after. And it wouldn't be because one of your mediums tries to conjure me, or whatever you call it. But because I choose to. I might even be able to cause a bit of a rumpus.'

CHAPTER EIGHT

The public hall was dingy, dusty and ill-lit. Nevertheless, the hundred or so seats were each occupied. The atmosphere was intense and all eyes were fixed on the man standing on a dais at the front. On the face of Jean Mackenzie, sitting in the third row, was an expression close to awe. Mr Hawthorne really was wonderful.

There was nothing in the appearance of the speaker to account for the effect he was having. He was insignificant-looking, with a receding chin and a few sparse hairs carefully spread across his scalp, and was wearing an ill-fitting suit. When he spoke it was with a pronounced London suburban accent. He was standing now with his eyes closed, making small clutching movements in the air with his hands.

'Now, I have a spirit here who wants to pass a message to a lady whose first name begins with – with, er, J. Jane? Joan?'

There was no response.

'Or perhaps Jean. Is there a Jean in the audience?'

Miss Mackenzie's heart missed a beat. She timidly raised her hand. 'My name is Jean.'

'The spirit is a woman who passed over at the age of about forty. Does that mean anything to you?'

'It could be my sister. She was forty-eight. Her name was Marion.'

'Marion, yes. I'm definitely getting the name Marion. Marion sends her love to you, Jean, and she has an important message for you. She says that you're going to be given a great opportunity. A chance that is vouchsafed to few. You must seize the moment when it comes. Be resolute. Do not be afraid.'

'I'm sorry, I don't understand. What sort of opportunity?'

'I cannot say. You will know when the time comes.'

'When will this be?'

'Soon. Very soon.'

'Will it be to do with the Message? The Work?'

'I'm sorry, the Spirit is fading. There is no more. Another appears. A man. He wishes to pass on a message to his daughter. Her name I think begins with S.'

But for once Jean Mackenzie was not listening. A message actually for her. It was thrilling. But what did Marion mean? 'A great opportunity.' It could mean so many things. And 'do not be afraid.' Afraid of what? It sounded rather frightening. She was not at all resolute, as Marion had very well known. It, whatever 'it' was, was going to be soon. How soon? Tomorrow? Next week? Next month?

Oh, dear, it was worrying. She almost wished Marion hadn't send her a message. But no, she shouldn't think that. She had been greatly privileged. So many others in the hall would be envying her. During the tea and biscuits afterwards she would be a centre of attention. A very unusual occurrence. She could at least make the most of that, while it lasted, before getting back to Florrie. With only Mrs Thomas, the housekeeper, for company, she would be getting bored and ready for a long chat. Probably about her funeral and her will again—

Then it suddenly hit Jean. Oh no. Surely Marion couldn't have meant that. Surely not.

CHAPTER NINE

Dorothy Saunders was engaged in her perennial task of scraping potatoes, when she heard the front door open and close. She hurried out to the hall. The young woman who had entered was tall and sturdily built and had a brown, weather-beaten face and untidy, short-cropped hair. She was wearing a fur-lined leather jacket and jodhpurs and carrying a motor-cycling helmet and goggles. She saw Dorothy and mouthed the words: 'Where is she?'

Dorothy pointed towards the drawing-room, then went back to the kitchen. The other followed her in and closed the door.

'Did you see Grandmamma, Aggie?' Dorothy asked, with as much eagerness as she ever showed about anything.

Agatha Saunders nodded. 'Yes, she seemed jolly bucked to see me, too.'

'How is she?'

'Well, frail, of course, but still got all her wits about her. She sent her love. And Mackenzie sent her regards.'

'Did Grandmamma like the chocolates?'

'Yes, she said they were her favourites. She was sorry she didn't have anything in return, but she said that both you and I can look forward to receiving something from her in the not too distant future.' She hoisted herself onto the table and lit a cigarette.

Dorothy frowned. 'What did she mean?' She started scraping potatoes again.

'That we're remembered in her will, I think.'

'Oh, we are, then. That's nice. Though I hope it's not for years yet, of course. I wonder how much.'

'Well, I shouldn't expect too much, petal. I doubt if she's all that well off. Anyway, it might be just things: ornaments, jewellery, paintings, stuff like that.'

'All the same, it's nice that she doesn't hold it against us that we didn't see her for all those years.'

'Well, I blame myself that I didn't think to go and see her long before ever Mother suddenly got it into her head that we should all go. I told Grandmamma that. She understood. 'It's water under the bridge,' she said. Anyway, I've kept in touch pretty regularly since then.'

'I haven't, though. Oh, Aggie, you're so lucky just to be able to jump on your motor-cycle and go all that way, whenever you feel like it.'

'I'll take you one day, I promise.'

'Did Grandmamma tell you anything more about Mummy and Daddy?'

'A bit, including a few things about Daddy when he was a boy. I'll tell you all about it later.'

'Oh, lovely. I'll come to your room tonight, when Mother's asleep.'

'What's she been doing today?'

'Well, there's been another girl here.'

Agatha gave a groan. 'Somebody's maid?'

'Looked like it.'

'Another little fool throwing her job away for a few quid, I suppose. That's two this week!' She banged on the table with her fist. 'It's not right, Dorry! How would she like it if her secrets were being offered for sale to the highest bidder?'

'She hasn't got any secrets.'

'She must have. Everybody has. You know that. She's never talked about her family. I've often thought there must be something there she's ashamed of.'

'Well, if there is, nobody knows it but her.'

'She couldn't be absolutely sure of that, though, could she?'

'What do you mean?'

'It ought to be possible to hint that one knew something. She just might give something away. Be fun to try, at least.'

'Oh, Aggie, don't cause any unpleasantness.'

'There's enough unpleasantness around as it is; a little more won't make any difference.'

She got down off the table and moved toward the door. 'I think I'll make a start now.'

'She may not have finished.'

'Too bad.'

'Aggie, the cigarette!'

'Oh.' Agatha turned, expertly flicked the stub into the sink and went out.

Clara was writing busily when Agatha entered the

room. She looked up crossly, then said: 'Oh, it's you. Where have you been?'

'Just riding.'

'You'll be getting yourself killed one of these days, careering round on that machine.'

'Which will solve a few problems for you, won't it, Stepmother?'

'Why do you call me that?' Clara asked sharply.

'I've decided to call you that in future. Because that's what you are. Dorry can call you Mother. I'll call you Mother in company. But my real mother is dead and I don't want ever to forget that.'

'I've been more of a mother to you than she ever was.'

'Only because she died,' Agatha shouted in a sudden temper.

'Keep your voice down!'

'Sorry.' Agatha looked abashed, but only for a second. 'I hear you've had another little visitor.'

'Er, yes. I did not invite her. She just showed up.'

'Seeking your advice, I suppose?'

'In a way.'

'And you told her just to dish the dirt to Auntie Clara and everything would be all right.'

'What a horrible expression!'

'Accurate, though. And which of your seedy journalistic friends did you peddle it to this time?'

'They are not my friends. Just people I do business with.'

'Some business. Breaking up marriages, ruining people's reputations, humiliating others, losing silly little maidservants their jobs.'

'I have never revealed a source. People sometimes guess who's been talking about their affairs, and they dismiss them. But if these servants are too stupid to foresee that possibility, it's not my fault. I only ever report the truth.'

'And that makes everything all right?'

'I have to supplement my income some way. Your father did not leave—'

'Don't blame Daddy for this. He'd turn in his grave if he knew what you were doing.'

'He did not leave us well off, Agatha.'

'That's what you always say. But you'll never tell us how much he actually left. And because there was no will ever found, we can't check up.'

'That is a private matter. But I assure you, financially it's been a very hard struggle.'

'Well, if you'd allowed Dorry and me to get jobs it wouldn't have been so hard. We could both have trained for something properly if you hadn't put your foot down. Just because you wanted a couple of unpaid housemaids.'

Clara sneered. 'And just what would you have trained for, my girl? Nursery governess?'

'Women are doing all sorts of jobs these days they've never done before – lawyers, doctors, even. I don't say I could have done that, but at least I could have gone to secretarial college and become a shorthand-typist.'

'People of our class do not become shorthand-typists.'

'Our class? What do you mean *our* class? Dorry and I are the great granddaughters of an Earl. What was your great grandfather? You always keep very quiet about that. And that's not the only thing you keep quiet about, is it?'

'What do you mean?' The question came just a bit too quickly.

'I think you know quite well what I mean.'

'I have absolutely no idea.'

'I see. Well, then, let's just leave it at that, shall we? For the moment.'

'You're a spiteful, ungrateful girl. Well, if you so despise me, you can leave any time you like.'

'You know I can't do that. I'm thirty-three and I've never had a job. Who'd employ me? Besides, this house was bought by my mother and father. I was born here. Why should I have to leave?'

'You don't have to. You're welcome to live here as long as you like. But while you do, I expect proper respect. Why can't you be more like your sister? Whatever her failings, she is always polite and obedient.'

'Because she's scared to death of you, that's why.'

'Nonsense.'

At that moment Dorothy put her head round the door. Clara rounded on her. 'Is the meal ready?'

'Not quite, but—'

'Don't come in here again until it is! Now go and finish.'

'Yes, Mother.' And Dorothy's head disappeared.

'I'll come and help, Dorry,' Agatha called. She walked to the door. Just inside it she turned and made a clumsy curtsy before going out.

A hit, a palpable hit, she thought with satisfaction.

CHAPTER TEN

It was a few days after Gerry's return, and she and her parents were at breakfast when Merryweather, Alderley's august and imperturbable butler, entered the room bearing a silver salver. He crossed to the Earl. 'A telegram, my lord,' he murmured.

'Ah.' Lord Burford swallowed a mouthful of bacon, laid down his knife and fork, tore open the envelope and read the enclosed message. 'Oh, dear,' he said. 'Oh, dear, dear.'

'What's the matter, George?' asked the Countess.

'Great Aunt Florrie's dead.'

'No? Oh, I *am* sorry. When?'

The Earl read from the telegram. '"Deeply regret inform you the Hon. Mrs Florence Saunders passed away peacefully in her sleep during night." Signed Mackenzie.'

'Miss Mackenzie will be terribly upset. She must have been with her for about twenty years.'

'At least that, Lavinia. Glad now we went to see her, back in the spring. And had 'em both to stay for a couple of weeks a few years ago. Probably the last time Florrie went away anywhere. I think Miss Mackenzie enjoyed it even more.' He looked at Gerry. 'And you said you went out to see her quite recently?'

'Yes, a couple of weeks ago. Florrie was very chirpy. Said she hoped she lived long enough to come to my wedding. Sad she didn't. You know, she was talking about her childhood in the East End. It suddenly hit me that at the period she was talking about, Dickens was writing about people like that. She might actually have met him! It made me realise just how old she was. Did you know her father drove a Hansom cab?'

'Oh yes.'

'How did Bertie's parents react to him marrying her?'

'Well, I don't think they were actually overjoyed, but mainly because she'd been on the Halls, which was considered highly disreputable. But Bertie's elder brother, Aylwin, my grandfather, took their side and did all he could to get her accepted in society. And as he was the heir to the title, that carried a lot of weight. Plus, of course, she apparently transformed herself remarkably quickly.'

The Countess said: 'When I first met her, it was quite impossible to tell she hadn't been born into the aristocracy.'

'But probably the most important factor in her being accepted was that it was impossible not to like her,' said the Earl.

'I thought she was terrific,' Gerry said. 'I'm really sorry she's gone. Still, she had a wonderful life, lived to be nearly a hundred and died peacefully in her sleep. What more could anyone want?'

'Not altogether wonderful,' said Lord Burford. 'Lost her husband, which was only to be expected; he was several years older than her. But to outlive your only son must be awful. And then John's first wife, Emma, died, too, and for years after that, she hardly ever saw her granddaughters, thanks to their stepmother.'

'You mean Clara cut them off from her entirely?'

'Yes. I think she was determined to keep them completely under her thumb and didn't want anybody else to have influence over them. Wasn't that it, Lavinia?'

'I'm sure it was. She loves to control people. Even when the girls had reached their teens and we invited them here in the summer once or twice Clara made it virtually impossible for us not to include her – instead of just enjoying the break and going off for a holiday on her own.'

There was a pause, which Merryweather, who was still standing impassively by, was quick to utilise. 'Will there be a reply, my lord?'

'Oh. Yes, suppose so. Let me see. Say "Very sorry to hear sad news." No, that sounds as though somebody's cat has died, or something. "Deeply saddened by tragic occurrence." No, dammit, that's what you'd say about a shipwreck. Oh, you decide, Merryweather, you're so good with words.'

'Thank you, my lord. I will endeavour to compose a suitable missive.' Merryweather glided from the room.

As the door closed behind him, Lady Burford said: 'Really, George, you leave too much to Merryweather these days. Surely you can compose your own telegrams.'

'He enjoys doin' things like that, so why not let him?'

'An excellent excuse for mental laziness.'

Gerry said hurriedly: 'So I've met Agatha and Dorothy, have I?'

'When you were little,' the Countess said, 'but they were eight or ten years older than you, so you wouldn't have had a lot to do with them.'

'I seem to remember the stepmother. A bony sort of person. Long, pointed nose. Rather like a witch. But very gushing.'

Lord Burford chuckled. 'Yes, that's Clara, to a tee: a gushing witch.'

'You've got to hand it to her in a way, though, haven't you?' Gerry said. 'I mean, you marry a widower with two kiddies, and then he kicks the bucket and you're left to bring them up on your own. It's quite a responsibility.'

'They were very polite, well-behaved children,' said the Countess. 'I will at least say that for Clara. Though I believe it was achieved more by fear than kindness. I'm quite certain they were afraid of her.'

'Is that why you dislike her so? I mean, it can't be just the long nose and the gushing manner.'

'I did not say I dislike her.'

'Oh, Mummy, it's as clear as daylight.'

Lady Burford hesitated, before saying reluctantly: 'Well, there are certain things. Things she's done.'

'What things?'

'Things that I – we – people think, well, dishonourable.'

Gerry's eyes were round. 'Crikey, this is fascinating. Spill the beans.'

The Countess hesitated. Lord Burford drained his coffee cup. 'We might as well tell her, Lavinia. Fact is, Clara has a big circle of friends, or at least acquaintances. People she's cultivated. She can be very winning, when she remembers not to overdo it. She's a very good listener and she's got a highly sympathetic manner. She gets people to tell her things. Things they wouldn't want known. And then she uses the information for her own ends – financial ends.'

'You don't mean blackmail?' Gerry said incredulously.

'No, no, no. At least, I don't think so. No, she sells it to the papers: the gossip columnists and the gutter press. Must have made quite a useful additional income, over the years.'

'Oh, is that all?' Gerry sounded quite disappointed. 'Well, I think that's rather enterprising of her.'

Her mother looked aghast. 'I hope you don't mean that, Geraldine.'

'Well, if a person's going to be so stupid as talk about their affairs to anybody they don't know they can trust, they've got only themselves to blame if it gets out. Of course, if it's something she's actually been told in confidence, I agree that is not quite-quite. But you don't know she's done that, do you?'

'Well, one thing I do know she's done is bribe servants for information about their employers.'

'Really? Mm, that I agree is going too far.' She gave a start. 'Golly, you don't mean – surely she didn't try to bribe Merry, did she?'

The nickname was one only ever used by Gerry, and went back to when, as a very little girl, she had been unable to pronounce 'Merryweather.' During one stage she had driven everyone nearly to distraction by wandering round the house chanting 'Merry'n'Gerry, Merry'n'Gerry' over and over again.

'I don't think even Clara would have had the nerve to try that,' said the Earl dryly.

'Would be lovely to see his reaction, though. Did Florrie know about what Clara was doing?'

'I'm pretty sure she did, aren't you, Lavinia?'

'Yes. From Agatha, I imagine. She didn't refer to it precisely, but she did mention something about Clara's 'activities' in a very grim voice the last time we were there.'

'I suppose the girls will do pretty well from Florrie's will, won't they?'

'I doubt Florrie'll leave much,' said the Earl. 'Great Uncle Bertie was never very practical and I remember being told made some pretty unwise investments. Florrie's had to live quite modestly. I mean, she only kept about three servants. There's the house, of course. Good area, but it's not all that big and a bit dilapidated. I'm not sure, though, that Clara would be too happy if the girls came into a lot of money. She still likes to keep 'em under her thumb, Dorothy especially, who didn't used to be much more than Clara's dogsbody. 'Course, we haven't had anything to do with them for years.'

'I doubt if things have changed,' said the Countess.

'Well, no doubt we'll see them at the funeral and maybe get some idea then.'

Late that afternoon the Earl was going over some accounts in his study when the telephone rang. He lifted the receiver.

'Burford.'

'Ah, my lord, I'm so glad to have caught you,' said a deep and somewhat fruity voice. 'My name is Bradley, Charles Bradley. I am the late Mrs Florence Saunders' solicitor and executor.'

'Indeed? How d'you do? And what can I do for you, Mr Bradley?'

'Firstly, I want to inform you that I have been told by Miss Mackenzie, Mrs Saunders' companion, that shortly before her death my client expressed a wish to be buried in the family plot at Alderley parish church.'

'Really? That's surprisin'. Always thought of her as very much a townee. Never showed much interest in Alderley that I can recall. It's not as though her husband's buried here; he was cremated, I seem to remember.'

'Yes, indeed, and I suppose his not having a grave elsewhere made her feel that somehow she would be closer to him there. You have no objection, I trust?'

'Good gad, no. She has a perfect right to be buried here. And at least it'll save me and my family a trip to town.'

'Of course, though it will not be so convenient for the other mourners. However, I understand there are frequent trains to Alderley Halt.'

'Yes, and they stop here if requested. That's an old right we have, going back to the days when the first railway company got permission to run the line through our land. And the church is only a hundred yards or two from the station. D'you expect many to come?'

'Impossible to say at this stage, but I should imagine a fair number. Although most of her contemporaries have passed on, she was held in high esteem. I imagine, however, that they will be mostly personal friends and relations, and it may perhaps be possible, at some later date, to arrange a memorial service in London, which members of Society and representatives of the various organisations and charitable institutions that she and her late husband, and indeed your family generally, have been associated with, might attend in order to pay their respects.'

Managing, with some difficulty, to hack his way through the dense undergrowth of this sentence, Lord Burford nodded absently, then, remembering that Bradley could not see him, said hastily: 'Yes, yes indeed.'

'There is one other thing, my lord. I have to inform you that you, Lady Burford and Lady Geraldine are beneficiaries under Mrs Saunders' will.'

'Oh, that was kind of her.'

'Now I have a great favour to ask you. To the best of my knowledge, the other major beneficiaries – nine in total – will be attending the funeral, and as it might present some difficulties for them all to be gathered at the same place at any other time, I am wondering if it would be convenient, after the funeral, for the reading of the will to be held, er—' Bradley hesitated.

The Earl came to his rescue. 'To be held here, you mean, at Alderley?'

'Precisely, my lord. I realise it is a great imposition.'

'Not at all. I see no problem.'

'That is a great relief to me, my lord. I do appreciate it.'

'Not at all. Glad to help. Nine other beneficiaries, you say? Possible to know who they are?'

'Of course. I have a list here, somewhere. Bear with me for a moment, if you please.' There was a few seconds' silence, punctuated by the sound of rustling paper, before Bradley came back. 'Here we are. Apart from yourselves, the principal beneficiaries, in alphabetical order, are Mr Gregory Carstairs, MP, Mr Thomas Lambert, Miss Jean

Mackenzie, Miss Agatha Saunders, Mrs Clara Saunders, Miss Dorothy Saunders, Miss Penelope Saunders, Mr Timothy Saunders, KC, and Miss Stella Simmons.'

The Earl, well aware that his wife and daughter would be interested in this information, was scribbling furiously.

'I see. Well, thank you, Bradley. We'll look forward to seeing them and you on – oh, I suppose the date hasn't been fixed yet?'

'Unfortunately not, my lord. I will, if I may, telephone you again as soon as I have finalised the details with your rector and the undertakers.'

The Earl said good-bye, rang off and went to find the Countess.

'Of course, we are going to have to invite them all back here.'

'*All* of them, Lavinia? Not just the beneficiaries?'

'No, all the mourners – all who come to the funeral.'

'But d'you think that's really necessary? There might be dozens of 'em.'

'It can't be helped, George. Most of these people will be coming from London, I imagine, though perhaps some from even farther afield. There's no decent restaurant or hotel for miles. The village has Miss Clatworthy's tea shop, which seats about a dozen, and *The Rose & Crown*, which is just a small public house. And we can't expect people to travel all this distance and then afterwards just to traipse back to the station and catch the first up train, without some proper refreshment. After all, she was your relative, and many of them will be coming as a mark of respect to the family.'

'Yes, of course, my dear, you're quite right. It's the least we can do. I'd better get Hawkins to have a word with Jenkins at the village garage about laying on some transport. Some taxis from Westchester – or perhaps a charabanc.'

'This will not be a factory outing, George.'

'Maybe you're right: not very suitable. Taxis, then. How many, I wonder...'

Gerry was scanning the list of beneficiaries. 'I've never heard of most of these people. Who are they? I mean, what relations are they to Aunt Florrie – and to us?'

'Well, actually, I'm not quite sure myself, offhand. I'm familiar with some of the names, and I know Timothy and Gregory slightly. But I can't place Thomas or Penelope or Stella. I'll try and work it out – go back through some old papers and photo albums and *Debrett*.'

'Don't bother on my account,' Gerry said. 'It's not all that important.'

'No, no, I want to do it. We're all going to be sittin' round a table together, and it could be embarrassing if I don't know who they are. Now, what was I going to do?'

'Taxis,' said the Countess.

'Ah yes. I was just tryin' to work out how many...' And the Earl wandered out, counting on his fingers.

The following morning there was a telegram from Bradley informing them that the funeral had been fixed for twelve noon on the Wednesday of the following week. 'That's really very convenient,' said Lord Burford. 'The last train to town from the Halt goes at four twenty-five. So if the service takes an hour, they can all come back here and have a bite at a civilised hour, then wander round the house and grounds for a bit, while those of us who're involved can listen to the will being read. Then we can have tea and get 'em back to the station in plenty of time.'

However, in the afternoon, there was another phone call from Bradley. 'Disaster, my lord,' he began dramatically.

'My word, that sounds serious. What's the trouble?'

'I spoke to your rector and then to the undertakers first thing this morning, sent the announcement to *The Times* and then wired or telephoned the legatees. No sooner had I completed everything, when I received notification that a very important court case, in which I am deeply involved, has been called for the morning of the day of the funeral. There is no way of obtaining a postponement and I simply have to be there.'

'I see. That's bad luck. So it means you won't be able to make it to the funeral.'

'Unfortunately, no.'

'Or be here for the reading of the will.'

'Well, I do not anticipate this case going on well into the afternoon. It is important, but not unduly complicated. So I am virtually certain that I could be there by 5 p.m. Unfortunately, as you are aware, by then it would be too late for the legatees to get back to London that night. It is really most unfortunate.'

'Yes, it is.' The Earl hesitated. 'No offence at all, my dear fellow, we would be delighted to meet you, and all that, but is it strictly necessary for you to be here in person? Is there nobody you could send in your place?'

'I'm afraid not. It really has to be a lawyer, as there

are always legal questions asked. But my partner, whom I could in theory ask to do it, will be on holiday next week. Then again, I am the executor of the will. There are numerous things which I can explain. People are frequently hurt or disappointed by the provisions of a will, and the executor can often smooth ruffled feathers, as it were, or explain and elaborate any conditions which might be attached to a bequest. It's really not satisfactory if the executor is not present.'

'Yes, I can see that. Well, I really don't know what to suggest.'

'Of course, and I hardly like to mention this, but if it were possible for the other beneficiaries to stay at Alderley overnight...' Bradley tailed away in a series of tentative little throat clearings.

Lord Burford did not reply for a moment. Eventually he said: 'Don't think that'll be possible, actually.'

'Oh. Then I'll just have to try and make other arrangements for some later date.'

They spoke for a few more seconds, then the Earl went to find the Countess.

'So naturally, Lavinia, I told him it wouldn't be possible. You agree, of course.'

'No, George, I do not. I think you should telephone Mr Bradley and tell him they are welcome to stay overnight.'

'But Lavinia, I don't *want* to have people staying here. After the last two house parties, we both agreed no more.'

'This wouldn't be a house party, George, it's nine guests for one night. By ten o'clock on Thursday morning they'll probably all be gone.'

'But the last two times we've had people here it's been disastrous.'

'This is quite different. These people are family, not spies and jewel thieves and blackmailers and film stars,' the Countess said, blithely grouping the four occupations in the same category. 'And when one occupies an historic house such as Alderley, where some of the most eminent men and women in the world have stayed, one cannot just shut its doors, because of a few unfortunate incidents.'

'I know you enjoy entertaining, Lavinia. And you do it jolly well.'

'I see it more as an obligation. And this will be a very good way of breaking the ice and getting back to normal again. After all, we do need to put an end to this stupid nonsense about a curse once and for all.'

'Yes, you're quite right, my dear, as usual. I'll telephone Bradley back and tell him we'll give 'em all a bed for the night.'

'I think perhaps you'd better make that nine beds, George, not just one.' It was unusual for the Countess to attempt a joke, however mild, and she looked quite pleased with herself.

'Oh, very good, Lavinia. Of course. Though it'll be ten, as I suppose Bradley himself will be staying as well. I'll go and put the call through now.'

'Ask Mr Bradley to tell them not to bring evening clothes. We will not dress for dinner that night. We do not want them all to have the bother of bringing large suitcases with them. This way most people should be able to manage with a small overnight bag. I'll have a word with Merryweather. I expect he'll be pleased. I'm sure he's missed all the organising.'

'Well, of course,' said Lord Burford, 'if I'd realised *that* I'd've arranged a house party months ago.'

He went out. Lady Burford considered. Ten people, most of whom she did not know. No couples, so ten bedrooms. Where would she put them? Ten very different people...

CHAPTER ELEVEN

The phone rang in Tommy's flat. He answered it in his usual way. 'What-ho.'

'Tommy, it's Penny.'

'Oh, hello, old girl. Nice to hear you. How's tricks?'

'OK. Tommy, did you hear about Great Aunt Florrie?'

'Yes. That's the one thing that's been helping me keep my pecker up.'

'Tommy!' The voice was reproachful.

'Oh, I don't mean her dying. I'm sorry she's gone, and all that, but, after all, she was about a hundred and fifty. It's just that apparently I'm remembered in her will.'

'Are you? So am I.'

'Really? You don't know what for, I suppose?'

'No.'

'Nor me. It's maddening. I mean, it might be only some old family heirloom, or something, but there's just a possibility it might be cash. Just a hundred smackers would be jolly useful.'

'Same here,' said Penny wistfully.

'Or even forty-seven,' he added unguardedly.

'Forty-seven? What a funny amount.'

'Oh, I meant fifty. Just saw forty-seven on – on a bus going past.'

'I see. So you're going to the funeral?'

'Gosh, yes, you couldn't keep me away. I've got two days off. A funeral's one thing they can't refuse it for. You?'

'Yes, me and Daddy.'

'And staying overnight?'

'Yes. I've never been there, have you?'

'Once, years ago. I'm really looking forward to it. I want to see where all the murders were committed.'

'Don't! Those are the last places I want to see.'

'They were the last places the people who were murdered wanted to see, but they were.' Tommy gave a subdued chortle.

Penny giggled. 'Tommy, you are awful!'

This had been so frequently said to Tommy that he had come to take it as a compliment. He smiled to himself.

'Anyway,' she said, 'you will be on your best behaviour, won't you?'

'What d'you mean?' he said indignantly.

'Don't do anything Daddy would disapprove of.'

He was about to say that that left very few things it was possible to do at all, but stopped himself in time.

'Butter won't melt in my mouth, Pen.'

'Good. So I'll see you there Wednesday, then.'

'You bet.'

''Bye, Tommy.'

'Toodle-pip.'

Penny rang off. She looked thoughtful. Surely, No. 47 buses didn't go past Tommy's flat.

* * *

'All right, all right,' Poppy muttered, as she hurried to answer the furiously ringing door bell. She opened the door with a cross expression on her face, which was instantly transformed when she saw the visitor.

'Greggy, darling, what a lovely surprise!'

Gregory cast a quick glance behind him before hurriedly stepping inside.

'Sorry about the bell, but I haven't got my key and I could hear someone coming up the stairs.'

'I didn't expect to see you today. You said you'd phone.'

'I know, but I had to see you.' He threw his hat onto the couch, crossed to the cocktail cabinet and poured himself a gin and tonic.

'What about?'

'Well, just to apologise, really. Fact is, I won't be able to see you for the next few days, after all.'

'Oh, Greggy, you promised!'

'I know and I'm frightfully sorry. But tomorrow I've got to go to a funeral. Old great aunt of mine just died, aged ninety-six.'

'But that'll only take a couple of hours!'

'No, it's down in Westshire, and I won't be back till Thursday.'

'Oh Greggy, do you have to go?'

'I want to.'

'Want to? But she's only a great aunt!'

'I know, but it seems I'm in her will.'

'For a lot?'

'I don't know. I don't even know how much she was worth. But I am hopeful. Anyway, they can't hold the reading until five o'clock for some reason, by which time the last train back will have left, so I'm going to have to stay overnight. The rest of Thursday I'll be catching up and then Friday evening Alex has invited a few quite important people round for drinks.'

'But if you're staying in a hotel, couldn't I come with you? Nobody's likely to recognise you down there. I'd love a trip out of town – no matter where. I get so bored sometimes.'

'I know, my sweet. But I'll be staying at Lord Burford's place.'

Poppy's eyes grew large. 'Alderley?'

'That's right. I told you he's a sort of cousin of mine.'

'But that's where they had all those murders. There were dozens of pictures of it in the papers at the time. Alderley's absolutely divine. Oh, you are so lucky! I'd give anything to stay there. Do you think one day…?'

'My dear, when we're married I'll wangle an invitation for us both. That's a promise.' One, he thought, he could safely make. 'Anyway,' he went on, 'we've got this evening.'

'Can we go out – do a West End show? You know, I've got this friend, who can always get tickets for anything.'

'That would be lovely,' he said enthusiastically. Then he looked doubtful. 'But perhaps it would be better if we stayed in. Or maybe a local cinema, eh? If we slip in before the second feature's finished, there shouldn't be too many people around.'

Poppy pouted.

* * *

Stella Simmons stared at her face in the mirror. She was quite pleased with what she saw. Not delighted. There was much room for improvement. But, on the whole, not bad. She looked, she thought, if not beautiful, at least attractive. And her training meant that she did know how to make the best of the face she had been born with. Her hair was good: thick, auburn, naturally curly and hanging loosely to her shoulders. Was that style a little too young now? Should she consider a more mature cut? Something to think about. Her brow and eyebrows were good, too, though the eyes were not as large or as deep as she would like – but eyes were something that you really could improve with make-up and false lashes. Her nose was on the large size, but at least straight; the mouth a trifle wide, but only a trifle, the jaw firm – but too square? No, on consideration, not really. She smiled mirthlessly at herself. Her teeth weren't absolutely straight and could do with a little cosmetic work, only she was such a coward when it came to dentists. And they were, at least, very white.

Yes, generally speaking, she would pass.

She got up from the dressing-table and looked at herself in a full-length mirror. She was wearing the smart black suit, which, together with a black straw hat, she had bought especially for the funeral. She was pleased with the cut and style. There was no reason why a funeral outfit had to be unfashionable. And, she, of all people, had to put on a good show: Florrie would have appreciated that.

She started to take the outfit off, thinking deeply as she did so. She wished she had known Florrie better. How many times had she seen her since arriving from America? Six? Seven? She certainly couldn't have hoped for a warmer welcome. Florrie had been genuinely delighted to see her. And her own stories about New York, the fashion scene there, and the Broadway shows had been a real hit with the old girl.

Everything Florrie had told her about the other relations had been useful, too, as they were, really, strangers to her. How would they receive her? The Earl and Countess and Geraldine sounded nice. She doubted there'd be any problems there. Clara, though, unless Florrie was exaggerating, which was possible, seemed to be a real witch.

She hung the suit in the closet. Now, who else would there be? Well, Jean Mackenzie, of course; she knew her quite well. And then the other relations. The second cousins: Gregory, the politician, and Timothy, the attorney. Timothy's daughter. And Tommy. Would he recognise her, she wondered? He was the only comparatively close relative among them and in his early teens had had, she fancied, quite an intense admiration for his older first cousin.

Anyway, this was a great chance to get to know them all. She had no close relatives, and kin were important, particularly to someone in her situation. After so many years in New York, she was making a fresh life for herself. Apart from a few colleagues on the magazine, she did not yet know many people in London. So it was going to be vital to create a good impression at Alderley. For some of these were important people and could be very useful to her, especially if she was to fulfil her ambition and break out from the fashion world into a wider sphere of journalism.

In fact, it suddenly occurred to her, this funeral might in itself be a way to start. There had been the usual formal obituaries of Florrie in the more serious papers, but no human interest stuff at all. After all, the old biddy had had quite a life. And her funeral was taking place within a mile or two of a house now famous or notorious for a series of lurid murders. The host and hostess on that occasion would be among the principal mourners. There must be a chance that some magazine or paper would be interested in a short piece. And Florrie herself would surely have approved of her taking advantage of their relationship, if it gave her a leg up.

The most important thing, though, was really to get to know these VIP relations.

'Nepotism for ever,' Stella said out loud.

Of course, it all depended on nobody in this country ever learning the real reason she had had to leave New York so suddenly. That would really be disastrous. But there was little danger of that.

Was there?

'No,' Clara said fiercely. 'We've had this argument before. The house cannot be left empty. Burglars always prefer unoccupied premises. Mrs Hopkins would be bound to tell her husband we were all going away, and he has some very disreputable friends.'

'If we had a maid or two, like everybody else I know, and didn't rely on just a cleaning woman, three times a week, the problem wouldn't arise,' said Agatha.

'A maid – or two, as you so vaguely put it – would be a totally unnecessary expense.'

'As long as you've got Dorry and me, you mean.'

'This is irrelevant. We do *not* have a maid. We do have Mrs Hopkins. And Mrs Hopkins has Mr Hopkins, and Mr Hopkins has friends. Which means you must stay home. Dorothy can accompany me.'

'I don't *want* to go,' Agatha said. 'I loathe funerals. In a way, I'll be very glad not to go. But it'll look most odd if I'm not there, especially considering that I am one of the beneficiaries.'

'We're *all* beneficiaries. I'll explain that one of us always has to remain behind and that you volunteered.'

'That's rich!'

'It will show you in a better light than if I explain how you objected to doing this one thing for me, just to set my mind at rest.'

'I've done it dozens of times for you – flitting around the house, turning lights on and off and playing gramophone records loudly until the early hours of the morning, but this is different.'

'I don't know that 'flit' is quite an apt word to describe your movements.' Clara eyed her large and somewhat ungainly stepdaughter meaningfully.

Agatha's already rather ruddy complexion took on an even deeper hue. 'That's damned unfair, Stepmother.'

'Do not use that sort of language in this house, Agatha! I won't have it.'

'Oh, please, don't quarrel!'

Dorothy spoke pleadingly, her hands clasped together, as if in prayer. Her face wore an imploring expression.

The words which had led to her speaking hardly merited the name quarrel, but to Dorothy even the slightest hint of what she always called "unpleasantness" was a major crisis, liable to lead to hysterics. Agatha immediately took a grip on herself and managed a forced smile. 'Don't worry, petal. No quarrel.'

She turned back to Clara. 'Why, for once, can't you stay behind and the two of us go?'

'I am not letting you take your sister away, even for one night. Heaven knows which of your godless and immoral ideas you might fill her head with.'

'That is totally absurd. Why don't you admit the real reason: that you're not prepared to forgo several hours of potentially very profitable gossip and prying and pumping, among some of the cream of society?'

This hit home and Clara could think of no better response than: 'That is unworthy of you, Agatha.'

Dorothy said desperately: 'Look, Mother, I don't want to go either. I dread having to meet all those people. Couldn't I stay home and Aggie go with you?'

'Wouldn't help,' said Agatha. 'It's the look of the thing I'm concerned about. We should both be there.'

'Besides,' Clara said, 'you know you'd be far too nervous to stay here on your own. Suppose some villain did break in? You'd be totally useless. He might murder you in your bed.'

'Whereas I'm expendable,' said Agatha.

'You know I did not mean that. But you are more capable of taking care of yourself.'

There was a sullen silence for a moment. It was broken by Agatha. 'You can't stop me going,' she said sullenly.

'No, I cannot physically stop you. But you would be unwise to go against me in this. It is my house you're living in, remember.'

'And you'd throw me out, just because I went to my grandmother's funeral?' Agatha sounded incredulous. 'This is unbelievable. I—'

'Please!' This time Dorothy's voice was almost a scream. 'Aggie, darling, do what Mother wants. Just once more. Please – for me.'

Agatha looked at her. She was plainly seething, but at last muttered: 'Oh, all right.'

'Oh, thank you.'

'That's more like it,' said Clara with a satisfied air. 'And if you like I'll tell everybody that you've got a bad cold or a sore throat or something. Would you prefer that?'

Agatha took a deep breath. 'Tell them what you bloody well like,' she said. And she strode from the room.

Clara gave a screech of horror.

CHAPTER TWELVE

'I've worked it all out,' said Lord Burford.

'What?' Gerry, sprawled inelegantly on the sofa, looked up from her copy of the new Edgar Wallace mystery.

'The family relationships you asked about.' He brandished a sheet of paper, covered with handwriting.

'Oh, you shouldn't have bothered. It wasn't all that important.'

'You asked about it and you're going to hear it. Make room.'

Gerry moved up about six inches and the Earl flopped down beside her. 'I've just concentrated on the people who are in the will and their immediate families, so this isn't complete, by any means.'

'What a bitter disappointment.'

'Just shut up and listen.' He cleared his throat. 'My great grandfather, the ninth Earl, had three boys and a girl. The eldest was Aylwin, my grandfather, who became the tenth Earl. You know all about him. The second son was Bertie and you also know about him.'

'Yes, and about Florrie and John and Emma and Clara

and Agatha and Dorothy and Old Uncle Tom Cobley and all.'

'Right. We can now proceed. The third brother, after Aylwin and Bertie, was Thomas. He had a daughter, Phyllis, and a son, Harry. Phyllis married a man called Carstairs and had a son, Gregory, and a daughter, whose name I've forgotten and who won't be here for the reading.'

'I thought you were only bothering with the ones who will be here.'

'Quite correct. My mistake. Forget Phyllis' daughter.'

'And I was just getting fond of her.'

'Gregory, an MP, is married to a woman called Alexandra but has no children. Harry had a son, Timothy, a KC, who is a widower and has one child, a daughter, Penelope, who will be here. Finally, Aylwin's, Bertie's and Thomas's younger sister, Margaret, married someone named Lambert and had a daughter, Henrietta, and a son, Philip. Henrietta married a Mr Simmons and had Stella, who lived a good number of years in America, working on some New York fashion magazine, but who's presumably home now. Philip had a son, Tommy. All those branches of the family tended to marry late, incidentally, which makes all the ages out of alignment with us; my father and I both married young, as you know. Is that all clear?'

'Oh, absolutely.' Gerry picked up her book again.

'Now,' said the Earl, deftly removing it from her hand and at the same time consulting his piece of paper, 'Bertie and Thomas being my great uncles, and Margaret my great aunt, means the following – I think I've got the terminology right: John, Phyllis, Harry, Henrietta and Philip were my first cousins once removed upwards, making their children, Agatha, Dorothy, Gregory, Timothy, Stella and Tommy my second cousins, and your second cousins once removed upwards, even though Tommy, at least, is probably a bit younger than you. Penelope is my second cousin once removed downwards, so of course your third cousin.'

'I feel so close to her already.'

'Clara, as will be obvious, being the second wife of my first cousin once removed upwards, is the second wife of your second cousin once removed upwards, or, in other words, your second cousin once removed upwards by marriage – meaning, I believe, that you can legitimately call her your second-cousin-once-removed-in-law.'

'Gosh, can I really? How exciting!'

He frowned. 'Or should that be twice removed? Anyway, as I said, there're lots of other relatives but they won't be here, so we can safely ignore them.'

'It's so nice to feel safe. To summarise, then, we can say that the people who are going to be staying here are a bunch of distant relations.'

'You could put it like that.'

'Rest assured, Daddy, that is how I shall think of them, now and always.'

'You have no sense of family history,' said Lord Burford.

He started to stand up, then froze in mid-movement. 'Oh, lor.'

'What's the matter. Hurt your back?'

'No.' He sank back down. 'Just remembered something. Gregory and Timothy aren't on speaking terms. They quarrelled years ago. They might have made it up, I suppose, but they're a stubborn couple of coves, so probably not.'

'What did they quarrel about?'

'Well, my memory's a bit shaky. It must have been shortly after Gregory first got into Parliament. Some little revolutionary magazine wrote something libellous about him: said he'd voted for a bill only because he stood to make money from it, or something like that. Gregory decided to sue them, and got Timothy to represent him. Stupid, really, much better to have simply ignored it. Anyway, the case had just started, when it fell apart. Gregory dropped the suit. I don't know exactly what happened, but I heard a rumour that Gregory had wanted Timothy to do something that Timothy thought unethical and after a big row refused to represent him any more.'

'Do you believe it?'

'I dunno. I don't say Gregory wouldn't do anything unethical; on the other hand, Timothy might well think something was unethical that nobody else would think was. He is a bit of a prig.'

'It's not a problem for us, though, is it?'

'No, but they ought to be kept apart. Rooms in different wings, so they don't keep running into each other, have to use the same bathroom, and so on.'

As he was speaking Lady Burford had entered. 'Ah, Lavinia, I was just telling Gerry about Gregory and Timothy. They must—'

'I heard, George, and it's all right. I remembered about the quarrel. Gregory is in the east corridor and Timothy the west. And they will be well apart at dinner.'

'You think of everything, my dear,' said the Earl.

CHAPTER THIRTEEN

The Wednesday of the funeral was a cloudless and bakingly hot day. 'Makes a change,' said the Earl. 'Practically always rains at the funerals I go to. Not the sort of day, though, you feel like getting togged out in a mornin' suit.' He ran a finger round inside his stiff wing collar.

Everything was ready for the guests, just nine rooms having eventually been prepared, after Bradley explained that he had friends living not far away, with whom he had arranged to spend the night. In the dining-room, the servants were busy laying out the buffet.

At eleven forty-five the Earl, the Countess and Geraldine set out in the Rolls on the short drive to the church, just the far side of the village. On the way they saw the smoke from the London train approaching in the distance. When Hawkins pulled up at the church, there were a number of cars already parked in the vicinity, together with eight taxis, brought in from the county town of Westchester by the efficient Harry Jenkins. The hearse, which had borne Florrie's coffin from London, was parked immediately outside the church. Twenty or so spectators, including a number of children, were standing around. For the sleepy village of Alderley, this ranked as quite a show. The village constable, P.C. Dobson, a stout, red-faced man whose uniform always seemed too small for him, self-importantly tried to appear to be keeping order.

They alighted from the Rolls. Some of the children cheered and Gerry gave them a cheery wave. Then she looked down the road in the direction of the station. 'Here they come,' she said.

Her parents followed her gaze. Quite a procession was approaching. All garbed totally in black, and looking, from a distance, like a disciplined army of beetles, they strode determinedly towards the church. As they drew closer, Lord Burford tried to count them. He made the number at least seventy. 'By Jove,' he muttered. 'Never thought there'd be so many.'

'There won't be enough taxis,' Gerry said.

'Then they'll just have to run a shuttle service.'

Fifteen minutes later everyone was seated in the little church, which had not been so full for many years, and the coffin had been brought in and placed in position. After the first hymn, 'Abide With Me,' and a prayer, the rector said: 'I did not have the pleasure of knowing the Honourable Mrs Florence Saunders, or Florrie, as I believe she insisted on being called by practically everybody, but I am assured that knowing her was indeed a pleasure. It is sad, though, if on occasions such as these, the priest has no recollections of the deceased, which can be passed on. I have, therefore, asked Mr Gregory Carstairs, MP, Mrs Saunders' great nephew, to deliver a eulogy.'

Lord Burford groaned under his breath. 'We'll be here for hours,' he muttered.

Gregory went forward and turned to face the congregation. 'Thank you, Mis—' he began, then quickly corrected it to 'Thank you, padre.'

Gerry stifled a giggle. 'He was just going to say 'Mr Speaker,'' she whispered to her mother.

'Ssh!'

The Earl had misjudged Gregory. One thing the MP could justly claim was to be a fluent speaker, and, when there were no votes at stake, when he tended to portentousness, a witty and interesting one. It was an ability that had given him the edge over his opponents at four general elections, and frequently in the House of Commons. Now he spoke entertainingly and at times quite movingly about Florrie, recounting several amusing anecdotes and referring to numerous kindly acts of hers. He went on for just twelve minutes before sitting down. A barely audible murmur of approval went round the church. Only Timothy remained stony-faced.

After this, the service proceeded in the usual fashion, ending with the interment in the Burford family's section of the churchyard.

As soon as he could decently do so, Lord Burford went across to Hawkins, who had been placed in charge of the transport arrangements. 'Everything under control?' he asked.

'I think so, my lord.' The chauffeur touched his cap. 'Harry and I made a rough count as people were going in, and we think we can get everybody there in two trips per car. He has a couple of cars in the garage we can use, as well as the taxis. Some people will have to wait, though.'

'Oh well, it won't be for long.'

Lady Burford and Gerry had already reached the Rolls, which Gerry on this occasion was to drive. The Earl hurried to catch them up. They had to get home before the first of the guests arrived. Two of the church's sidesmen had been deputed to usher the mourners to the taxis and within minutes the process was under way.

The Countess and Gerry had barely time to remove their hats and gloves before the first of the taxis rolled up. In it were Clara, Dorothy, Timothy and Gregory. The Earl felt a stab of annoyance with himself; he had forgotten to give instructions that Timothy and Gregory should be sent in different taxis. He also noticed that there was no sign of Agatha. The four alighted from the taxi and the Earl and Countess greeted them in the porch. After expressing the usual commiserations to the two women, the Earl asked: 'Er, Agatha comin' in one of the other cars, is she?'

'She isn't here, er—' Clara had obviously forgotten how she used to address him, and settled finally on 'Cousin George.' She ostentatiously dabbed at her eyes with a handkerchief as she spoke.

'Really? I didn't spot her at the church, but with so many people there... Anythin' wrong?'

'She woke up this morning with a severe sore throat. I suspect tonsillitis. We thought it would be highly unwise for her to attend. She is devastated, of course, isn't she Dorothy?'

'Yes.' Dorothy's eyes were cast down, her voice totally expressionless.

'So I should imagine. Poor girl.'

The occupants of the second taxi were approaching, so

the Earl and Countess had time only to shake hands briefly with Gregory and Timothy, who had been standing side by side studiously avoiding looking at each other. A footman had carried in the small cases that the overnight guests had brought. The Countess beckoned him across, spoke quietly to him for a few seconds; he nodded and then conducted the four upstairs.

The second group to arrive included a tall, thin young man, a blond girl, clinging firmly to his arm, and Miss Mackenzie. Gerry, who was standing a little apart, watching everything with keen enjoyment, saw Timothy, halfway up the stairs, turn and eye the boy with an expression of clear disapproval – of which he, however, seemed quite unaware. Miss Mackenzie was genuinely red-eyed, and Lady Burford devoted more time to her than any of the others. A second footman was still in the act of taking the bags from the second taxi, and the young man and the blonde stood waiting, gazing round them, seeming somewhat in awe of their surroundings.

The next car contained four people totally unknown to the Burfords. One of them was a young woman in her mid-thirties, wearing an extremely chic suit and hat. After shaking hands with Lord and Lady Burford she moved on a few feet and stopped, looking a little lost. Gerry approached her.

'Would you be Stella Simmons, by any chance?'

The young woman looked surprised and pleased. 'Why, yes.'

'I'm Geraldine Saunders.' Gerry held out her hand.

Stella took it firmly. 'It's a real pleasure to meet you,

Lady Geraldine. I've heard so much about you.' She had a very slight American accent.

'That sounds ominous.'

'How did you know who I was?'

'It was a guess. From your outfit. It's by far the smartest one here and I heard you were a fashion journalist.'

'Why, thank you. It's nice when someone notices. The magazine positively insists we always dress up to the nines when we're on public display. And it can be quite a bore. One day I swear I'm going to turn up at some do dressed like an old washerwoman.'

'I can imagine how you feel. But I'm glad you didn't do that today.'

'Oh, I couldn't do that at Alderley. Though I think Florrie might have liked the idea, don't you?'

'She probably would,' Gerry agreed.

'Stella?'

The tall young man had approached from behind her. She spun round and looked at him for a second or two, a puzzled expression on her face.

'Don't you know me, dear cousin?'

Her face cleared. 'Tommy?'

'The very same.'

'Oh, Tommy, I am sorry. But you were just a school kid when I saw you last. And now look at you! You're so tall!'

'And skinny. I'd have known you anywhere, Stella. You haven't changed a bit.'

'I'm sure I have but I love you for saying it. Here, give your old cousin a kiss.'

Tommy was nothing loath. After disengaging himself, he suddenly remembered his manners. 'Oh, this is another cousin, Penny Saunders.' He drew the blond girl forward.

Penny, whose suspicions had been immediately re-aroused when she had first laid eyes on the 'old' Stella at the church, had been looking at her wearing exactly the same expression that her father had worn when looking at Tommy; and her greeting was far less effusive than Tommy's had been. She shook hands with very stiff fingers, saying formally: 'Pleased to meet you.'

However, Stella smiled with the utmost warmth. 'So at last I meet the famous society beauty,' she said.

'Oh.' Penny clearly did not quite know how to react. 'Oh no, not really, it's nice of you to say so but—'

'You know something, Penny? You should be a mannequin.'

Penny's eyes widened. 'Do you really think so?'

'I sure do. You've got everything: looks, figure, poise.'

'Oh my, I never thought… It would be just wonderful. But Daddy'd never let me.'

'Ah, he must be Timothy, the great lawyer, is that right?'

'He is a lawyer, yes.'

'I do want to get to know everybody,' Stella said. 'I'm so out of touch with the family after nearly eleven years. Whether they'll want to know me is another matter, of course.'

'I can't imagine there'll be any doubt about that,' said Tommy.

'Thank you darling. Oh, you both know our hostess, Lady Geraldine, do you?'

'Actually, no,' Tommy said. 'Though I think we did meet when we were very small, Lady Geraldine.'

Penny said: 'I've wanted to meet you for many years, Lady Geraldine.'

Gerry smiled. 'I know – please don't say it – you've heard so much about me.'

They all shook hands. 'Now, two things,' Gerry said. 'First, I'm not the hostess. That's my mama. I'm really just a hanger-on here. Second, it's Gerry, OK? Now, I'm sure you'd all like to freshen up, so if you'll follow William, he'll show you your rooms, and then you can come down and have some grub.'

Meanwhile, in the doorway people were now arriving in a rush, with a queue already forming outside. The taxis were positively tearing off the second their passengers had alighted. 'Hawkins has certainly got 'em moving,' Lord Burford whispered to his wife during a rare free moment.

What he did not know was that there was keen competition between the drivers. Harry Jenkins had started a book on which of them would be the quickest to get to the house, unload his passengers and return to the church, and was carefully timing the cars with several stopwatches. With each of the drivers having bet on himself, there was no likelihood of any of the second wave of passengers having to wait a moment longer than necessary.

After the first dozen or so arrivals, Lord Burford gave up all attempts to work out who they were. Earlier, there had been some discussion about the possibility of having Merryweather take people's names at the door and formally announce them, but the Countess had considered that this would give the proceedings more the atmosphere of some grand reception or ball and was hardly suitable for a funeral. The Earl, however, had begun to wish that they had gone ahead with the plan – though he had eventually to admit to himself that in most cases it would not have made a great deal of difference, as even when the guests introduced themselves, the names usually meant as little to him as the faces did.

Eventually the last of the guests had been delivered and the Earl and Countess followed them to the dining-room, where the magnificent cold buffet was waiting. The taxi drivers, who were to remain and later convey all but the beneficiaries to the station, were conducted by Hawkins to the servants' dining-room, where an equally good spread was to be served.

Among the guests, quite a party atmosphere was already developing, which, Lord Burford had often noted, was usually the way when people relaxed after the strain and solemnity of a funeral service. He and the Countess separated and moved around, at last beginning to learn the identity of some of the guests. Gerry introduced Tommy, Penny and Stella to her parents and then drew her father aside.

'Who are the old girls?' She indicated with her head.

Six ladies, all clothed in long black dresses and black hats, with veils covering the top halves of their faces, were gathered together in one corner of the room, appearing somewhat ill at ease. Apart from their sizes, which ranged from tiny to quite large, they looked practically identical.

'Haven't the foggiest.'

'You should go and have a word with them, Daddy.'

'Me? That's your mother's job.'

'Mummy's got her hands full. Anyway, I'm sure they'd much rather talk to a man. Probably all old maids or widows.'

'But if I don't know who they are, what shall I call them?'

'Don't call them anything. See what they call you. That may give you a clue as to who they are.'

'Oh, very well.' Lord Burford made his way across to the group. 'How good of you all to come,' he said. 'I know my great aunt would greatly have appreciated it.'

Gerry watched him engage them in conversation for a few seconds, then turned away to survey the room. She was surprised to see that Miss Mackenzie, a glass of wine in one hand and a smoked salmon sandwich in the other, was talking animatedly to Tommy, who was listening closely and nodding, as if fascinated by what she had to tell him. Then he smiled, but shook his head firmly, as if regretfully turning down a pressing invitation.

Five minutes later the Earl returned. 'Well?' Gerry asked.

'None the wiser. One of them called me "George", two "Lord Burford", two "my lord", and the last one didn't call me anything. I'm not sure they know who each other are. They don't seem to be together, just sort of flocked – you know, birds of a feather. Anyway, I've split them up now.'

'There are two old gentlemen, near the fireplace, also looking rather lost, so—'

'No,' interrupted her father. 'I don't want to know who they are. I don't care. Let somebody else take care of 'em.'

CHAPTER FOURTEEN

About fifteen minutes later, Lady Burford approached Geraldine. 'Have you noticed Dorothy?'

'She's almost unnoticeable,' Gerry replied. 'I've never seen anybody who is so close to not being anything.'

'She hasn't left Clara's side for a second. And she's not spoken to anybody. But she can't take her eyes off you.'

'Really? I hadn't noticed. What excellent taste she must have.'

'Have a word with the poor girl, will you? I'll distract Clara.'

'OK.'

Lady Burford moved towards Clara, who quickly saw her coming and turned to meet her.

She took the Countess' hand. 'Lavinia, how very, very good of you it is to lay on all this. To open up your beautiful home to so many strangers is a really gracious act. The girls and I are so grateful. Without you, I just don't know what would have happened.'

'It's kind of you to say so.'

'No, it's not kind at all. How could I say less? You and

George are genuinely good people. I just wish there was some way we could repay you.'

In spite of herself, Lady Burford found herself softening. Clara was certainly capable of great charm. She told herself that it was flattery, of course – but remarkably effective flattery.

'Really, er, Clara' – she always found using her Christian name something of a struggle – there is really no need to think like that. We were very glad to do it. We were very fond of Florrie.'

'I know, and she was so fond of you and George and Geraldine. She always spoke of you with the utmost affection.'

The tactful thing to do would be return the compliment, but Lady Burford could not bring herself to utter this blatant lie. 'She spoke a lot of you, too,' she said.

If Clara noted the significance of the form of words, she did not show it. 'Thank you, too, so much for allowing us to stay overnight. Dorothy is really quite excited about it.'

Lady Burford was on the brink of answering with a phrase she had heard her daughter use: 'You could have fooled me.' But fortunately at that moment Clara suddenly realised that Dorothy was not at her shoulder. 'Where is she?' she said sharply and started to turn round.

Hastily, Lady Burford put her hand on Clara's. 'And tell me, how are you keeping?' she asked earnestly.

Gerry approached Dorothy with a broad smile. 'Hello, I'm Gerry Saunders.'

For a moment Dorothy looked terrified. Apart from

the merest smattering of powder her face was totally devoid of make-up, and she was wearing a dress that looked as though it could have belonged to her mother. Gerry suddenly felt very sorry for her.

Dorothy gulped. 'Y-Yes, I know. H-How do you do, Lady Geraldine?' She was gazing at her with something like awe.

'Oh, please call me Gerry, we are cousins of a sort, aren't we? And may I call you Dorothy – or is it Dorry? That's how Florrie always referred to you.'

'Well, Agatha calls me Dorry. Grandmamma must have picked it up from her. But nobody else does. Mother doesn't like it.'

'Then I'll call you Dorry, too, if I may. I think it's a very pretty name – much nicer than Dorothy.' Gerry actually had no strong feelings either way, but if Clara was anti-Dorry, then she was going to be for it.

'Really?' Dorothy's face showed its first sign of animation. 'Then I'll ask everybody to call me that in future.'

Gerry blinked. She had often thought it would be nice to live in a world where everybody instantly followed her lead and took her advice on all matters, but now she had met somebody who was, it seemed, prepared to do just that, she was not at all sure she liked it. But she smiled again and said: 'I was awfully sorry to hear about your grandmother's death. It must have been an awful blow for you.'

'Well, we knew she had to go sometime, of course, but it was a shock all the same. I – I just wish I'd known her better, but I didn't get to see her all that often.'

'I suppose with her living in Walton-on-Thames, and not getting out very often in recent years, and you living in – north London, is it?'

'Yes, Hampstead.'

'Then it can't have been easy. I'm sure Florrie understood. She was terribly fond of you and Agatha, you know. I last saw her about three weeks ago and she was talking about you all the time.'

This was a considerable exaggeration but, Gerry thought, a justifiable one under the circumstances.

Dorothy cast a somewhat furtive glance towards her stepmother, who was still being kept under tight rein by the Countess. Unnecessarily, in view of the babble in the room, she lowered her voice. 'Aggie saw her more than I did.'

'Did she?' Gerry was fascinated – not by the less-than-enthralling information that one sister had seen her grandmother more than the other, but by the fact that this had obviously to be kept from Clara.

'Yes, she used to go and see her every month or so. Usually on her motor bike.'

'Aggie has a motor bike? What make?'

'A Norton, 500 cc.'

'Gosh, I do envy her. I've always wanted a motor bike. I begged Mummy and Daddy for one years ago, but even Daddy put his foot down about that. I could get one now, of course, but I wouldn't want to worry them.'

'Aggie took me for a ride on the pillion of hers once. It was really exciting. Mother had gone to the dentist,' she added by way of explanation.

Gerry felt a surge of anger, but suppressed it. 'I'd like to meet Aggie,' she said. 'Sounds as though we might get on.'

'Oh, it would be lovely if we could all get together sometime!' But then she glanced again at Clara and added wistfully: 'Though I don't suppose it will be possible.'

'I don't see why not. Let's have a chat about it later and see if we can arrange something.'

'Oh, can we really?'

'What?'

'Have a chat tonight.'

'Certainly.'

'It'll have to be after Mother's gone to bed. She always retires early. I'll have to go up with her, but I'll sneak back down. If – if it won't be keeping you up.'

Gerry grinned. 'Far from it. I am definitely not one who always retires early.'

'No, that's what I thought – from what I've read.' Dorothy was by the moment becoming more animated and talking more easily. 'It's such a thrill for me to meet you, La— er, Gerry. I've wanted to for years. I've been such an admirer of yours. And even more since those murders, which you helped to solve.'

Gerry endeavoured to look modest. 'Oh, I didn't do much, really,' she said, not thinking it necessary to mention the fact that until the very end she had been as baffled as everybody else.

'But you were nearly killed!'

Gerry raised her chin and squared her shoulders. 'You have to be prepared for that sort of risk if you decide to get involved in murder investigations,' she said nobly.

'And your fiancé – though he wasn't your fiancé then – saved your life.'

Gerry's eyes went dreamy. 'Yes, he was incredible.'

'Perhaps you'd tell me all about it tonight, would you? There was so much that wasn't in the papers that I wanted to know.'

'Yes, of course.'

'Oh, I'll really look forward to it.'

Gerry said: 'And now I really must mingle for a bit. Have you had any lunch, yet?'

'No.'

'Well, go and get something now. You really look as though—' She broke off, about to say, eyeing Dorothy's figure, 'as though you need it.' But she amended it to: 'I'm sure you're hungry.'

She took Dorothy by the arm and led her across to the buffet. 'Now help yourself, and I'll see you later.'

She moved away to talk to somebody else. For once she really felt she'd made a hit. It was nice to have a fan.

Stella saw that Gregory, who was standing alone, moodily munching a sausage roll, was eyeing her. She strolled over to him. He brightened visibly as she approached. 'Hello, Gregory,' she said warmly. 'How nice to see you again.'

'Er, very nice to see you, too.'

'You haven't a clue who I am, have you?'

'I'm afraid not. But I'd very much like to.' He eyed her appreciatively from head to foot.

'I'm Stella.'

'Really. That's a lovely name.'

It was as if he were talking to a small girl, she thought. 'Which doesn't mean any more to you, I know. Stella Simmons, Henrietta's daughter.'

'Ah, of course! You're the girl who went to America.'

'And has come back again.'

'How splendid. I'm sure America's loss is England's gain.'

'Probably the other way round.'

'I'm certain that's not true. In fact, I was wondering at the service who the exceptionally attractive and smart young woman was.'

'And who was she?' Stella asked innocently.

'Why—' He broke off, with a chuckle. 'I didn't realise that she was my – what, second cousin?'

'I believe so.'

'Is that what the Americans call kissing cousins?'

'That depends on the cousins.'

'Well, it's delightful to meet you at last.'

'We did meet many years ago. At a wedding or a funeral, I can't quite remember which; I used to enjoy them both equally. I was only in my teens, then, and you'd just won your first election. I was thrilled to meet a famous Member of Parliament.'

'What a charming thing to say. But surely a teenage girl couldn't have really been excited to meet a boring politician? Not a patch on a crooner or film star, eh?'

'Oh, better for me. I've always been fascinated by politics.'

'Really? How very refreshing.' Gregory was becoming more and more interested and edging ever so gradually towards her.

'Of course, I'm rather out of touch with the British political scene.'

'You must be. So, whereabouts in America were you?'

'New York, for the past ten to eleven years.'

'Indeed? That must have been very interesting. And doing what, precisely?'

'Oh, I couldn't possibly tell you *precisely* what I've been doing. But I earned a fairly honest crust as a journalist.'

'And now?'

'Still a hack.'

'Oh.' An expression of wariness suddenly appeared in his eyes.

'On a fashion magazine,' Stella added quickly. 'I'm with *London Fashion Weekly* now.'

'I see.' He relaxed again. 'Not a subject I know a lot about. Know what I like to look at, mind. Pity hem lines are so low at the moment, I must say.'

Stella smiled. 'I'm sure a lot of men agree with you.'

'Then why don't you use your influence to get 'em raised a few inches, eh?'

'Oh, I've got no influence at all, Gregory. I just report. And I may not be doing that much longer.'

'And why would that be?'

'I'm hoping to spread my wings a bit.'

'I'd love to help you spread your wings, my dear.' The hand not holding the sausage roll started to stray in the direction of her waist. Then he obviously thought better of it and let his arm drop to his side again.

'And I'm sure you've had lots of experience at doing that.'

'I wouldn't put it quite that way.'

'Well, my aim is to move into another branch of journalism. Politics, say. I want to meet the people who really matter.'

'Indeed? Not many women political journalists around. In fact, I don't think there are any.'

'There has to be a first, doesn't there?'

'Now that's an attitude I like. You know, Stella, I think you and I are going to get on.'

'You know, Gregory, I was just thinking the very same thing.'

'So, if there's any way at all I can help you...'

'That's so kind of you. I would really be very grateful.' She looked at him from under half-closed lids. 'And I might well take you up on that offer. Perhaps we could get together sometime and have a proper chat.'

'I'd like nothing better.'

'I'll really look forward to it.'

She sensed it would be wise not to push her luck any further. 'I must talk to some other people now. And I'm sure there are dozens who want to speak to you. I'm so glad to have gotten to know you properly.'

'Likewise, likewise.'

She touched his hand briefly and moved away. Would he be any use at all? She had met many types like him in New York. Probably all talk and no action. Still, you never knew. It was another contact, anyway. And in one respect she strongly hoped he *would* be all talk and no action.

One down. Later, Timothy...

Gradually the dining-room emptied. Lady Burford had let everyone know that they were free to explore Alderley's public rooms and most did so, a few preferring to stroll in the gardens, now at their best. Gerry showed some people the secret passage, which had been much featured in the papers at the time of the two murder cases. It was like one of the old open days, which they had not held this year. After his previous misgivings, Lord Burford was now clearly enjoying being the genial host and the Countess congratulated herself on her idea. A number of ghosts should have been laid today.

She was not, though, entirely happy at having had a funeral turned into what had become quite a festive occasion, and said as much to Miss Mackenzie.

'Oh, Lady Burford, please don't think that. I assure you, this is just what she would have wanted.'

'Really?'

'Yes indeed. Shortly before she died she said to me that she didn't want any long faces at her funeral. "Let people enjoy themselves." Those were her very words.'

'Thank you, Miss Mackenzie. That certainly makes me feel better. And I think most people are.'

'I venture to say I believe Florrie is, too.'

'We must hope you're right. In a way, it is pleasant to be commemorating a peaceful, contented death, after all those terrible violent ones.'

Jean Mackenzie cleared her throat nervously. 'Forgive my asking, but have you, or anybody else, witnessed any kind of phenomena since they occurred?'

'I'm sorry?'

'Well, those who die violently, particularly those who have been murdered, frequently do not rest easily. Quite often they, er, walk, as the saying is.'

'You mean ghosts? Thankfully, no, nothing of that kind.'

'Oh.'

She seemed, the Countess thought, rather disappointed.

CHAPTER FIFTEEN

At three forty-five tea was served and shortly afterwards the taxis began taking those who were returning to town back to the station. By ten past four the last of them had departed, leaving just the eight beneficiaries remaining. With the reading of the will now imminent, these were all feeling various degrees of nervousness or expectation. Clara, Dorothy, Gregory, Timothy and Miss Mackenzie retired to their rooms; Penny, who had absolutely no interest in art, made Tommy, who had just as little, take her to look at the paintings in the gallery; and Gerry had a long chat with Stella, with whom she had struck up an immediate rapport. Later, they were joined by Tommy and Penny; the latter, seeming to have quite got over her initial distrust of Stella, questioned her eagerly about both life in New York and her opinions of the latest fashion trends.

At four forty Hawkins departed for the station to meet Mr Bradley. The train was on time, and it was shortly before five that Merryweather showed the solicitor into the drawing-room, where the Earl and Countess were waiting.

He did not look at all as the Earl had expected, being a

shortish man, nearly bald, with thick horn-rimmed glasses, and given to quick, rather bird-like movements. Lady Burford offered him tea, but he refused. 'Perhaps after the reading, if you would be so kind.'

'You'd like to start straight away?' the Earl asked.

'Whatever is convenient to you, my lord, but there seems little point in delaying. I expect the legatees will be anxious to hear their fates. And as it will be a somewhat unusual occasion in several respects, I admit I am anxious to get it over with.'

'Hm, that sounds interesting. Very well. I thought we'd go to the library. There's a table there we can sit around. If we did it in here, people would be scattered all over the room. You'd practically have to shout.'

'Splendid.'

Lord Burford rang the bell and when Merryweather answered, told him to ask the others to join them in the library. The Earl, the Countess and Bradley made their way there themselves. Lord Burford sat Bradley at the head of the table, and the solicitor opened his briefcase and extracted a sheaf of papers. Gerry and Stella were the first to arrive, followed quickly by Clara and Dorothy, Jean Mackenzie, Gregory, Timothy and finally Tommy and Penny. When they were all seated, Bradley looked round the ring of expectant faces and cleared his throat nervously. He seemed a little unhappy. 'Before I read the will, there is something quite unusual that must be done. My client made a specific request that the proceedings be opened in a particular manner – a highly, er, unconventional manner, but one she was very insistent upon. I had better read the actual words of her request.' He glanced down at the papers in front of him. '"I fear that there will have been much gloom and misery at my funeral and that at this moment everyone present is looking especially sombre. I wish to dispel that mood. So I request that before my will is read, everybody joins in singing *She'll Be Coming Round The Mountain*. I ask this because I have a firm hope that I may be doing that very thing – the mountain in question being Zion – just about then."'

Mr Bradley looked up at faces wearing expressions ranging from the blank to the aghast – and one face which bore a look of sheer delight.

'How absolutely topping!' Gerry exclaimed. 'Good for Aunt Florrie! That's what I want at my funeral. I shall put it in my will, too. In a few generations it'll become a family tradition.'

'I'm delighted you approve, Lady Geraldine. I don't know if anyone here feels capable of starting the piece in question. I have a made a note of the words.' He held up a sheet of writing paper. 'They are extremely simple, and I could make an effort, but if anybody else...' He petered out and looked hopefully around.

Now, much to her mother's disappointment, Gerry was not musical. As a little girl, she had gone through several piano teachers, who had left saddened and with their self-confidence badly shaken. There was, however, one good thing to be said of her singing voice: it was powerful. A friend of hers had once likened it to that of Ethel Merman. Greatly flattered by this comparison, Gerry had set about – mostly when driving her beloved Hispano-Suiza – perfecting what she believed was a first-rate impersonation of the young Broadway star. This she needed no encouragement to perform at parties, though she could not help noticing, and being rather hurt by the fact, that she was rarely asked to do an encore. Now, though, she suddenly realised that her big moment had come. 'Gladly,' she said happily. She took a deep breath, opened her mouth, and let them have it at the top of her voice.

'She'll be coming round the mountain, when she comes.'

She could not have hoped to make a greater impact. Everyone round the table gave a noticeable jump, Clara adding a startled 'Oh, my.'

'She'll be coming round the mountain, when she comes,' Gerry continued solo, then stopped. 'Come on. What's the matter with you? Can't you accede to an old lady's dying wish? Now let's start again. Follow me.' She raised her hands and began conducting as she recommenced.

Tommy, with a broad grin on his face, was the first to join in, followed quickly by Penny, and after a few seconds by Stella. The others opened and closed their mouths slowly, making vague humming and moaning noises.

The verse ended – after what to Lady Burford, at least, seemed an extremely long time. There was a sudden hush, which was broken by Mr Bradley. 'Well, thank you very much, Lady Ger—'

'Singing eye-yai-yippee-yippe-yai, yippe-yai,' Gerry bellowed. Lord Burford closed his eyes, as her supporting trio took up the refrain.

As the final 'yippe-yai' faded, Mr Bradley spoke hastily and firmly. 'That was most spirited and I'm sure would have pleased my client immensely. She would not, though, have expected more than one verse and one chorus,' (a murmured, 'Hear, hear' from the Earl) 'so I will now proceed with the reading of the will.' With a decided air of disdain, he dropped his copy of the lyrics into a nearby waste paper basket and immediately became more businesslike.

'We are here for the reading of the last will and testament of my late client, the Honourable Mrs Florence Saunders. If everyone is agreeable, I will omit the preamble, containing the various legal technicalities and provisos, appointment of and instructions to her executor, et cetera, and get straight to the bequests.'

Timothy looked slightly disapproving, but didn't speak. 'Jolly good idea,' said the Earl.

'The will is dated just five weeks before her death, but I perhaps should anticipate any questions by saying that only a few minor alterations to her earlier will were made at that time, and they were mostly in the nature of comments, rather than actual changes in the provisions. Very well, to proceed. There are very adequate bequests to her servants, of which she informed them some time before her death, and to various charities: The Variety Artistes' Benevolent Association, The National Society for the Prevention of Cruelty to Children and the Royal Society for the Prevention of Cruelty to Animals. I have, of course, copies of the will, for anyone wishing to see the full details.

'I should explain at the outset that most of the wording of this will is my client's own. Now to the principal bequests.' He began to read. '"To my dear great nephew, George, Twelfth Earl of Burford, I regret I am unable to leave the revolver with which Jesse James shot Billy the Kid or vice versa, which is no doubt what he would really like. But failing this, I give and bequeath the portrait of the Sixth Earl, painted by Sir Joshua Reynolds, given to my husband and me by his brother, the later Tenth Earl, on the occasion of our wedding, in the belief that Alderley is its proper home and where it will complement the portrait of the Fifth Earl by the same artist, which already hangs there."'

Lord Burford raised his eyebrows. 'My word, that is kind of her. I remember being told the story of that, but I had no idea she still had it.'

'It's been in storage,' Miss Mackenzie put in quietly.

'It will fill a gap in the gallery,' said the Countess.

Bradley resumed reading. '"To Lavinia, Countess of Burford, in recognition of her numerous kindnesses over many years, I give and bequeath my Georgian sterling silver tea service, which I hope will supplement the similar dinner service she already possesses."'

Lady Burford beamed. 'It certainly will. That is most generous.'

'"To my great-great niece, Lady Geraldine Saunders, who has always brought a sparkle into my life, I give and bequeath the diamond bracelet, which was my beloved husband's wedding present to me."'

Gerry's face lit up. 'She showed me that once. It's beautiful. Oh, thank you, Florrie, I'll treasure it always.'

Bradley continued: '"To my great nephew, Timothy Saunders, I give and bequeath the seventeen volumes of the first edition of the complete works of Charles Dickens, in the sincere hope that it will encourage him to read something other than law books."'

For the first time that day, Timothy's sculpted-like

features seemed briefly to soften. 'How splendid. I have always been meaning to read Dickens through from beginning to end, but to do it from the first edition of the collected works...more than I could have hoped.'

'"To my great-great niece, Penelope Saunders, I give and bequeath the pearl necklace which was my husband's gift to me on the occasion of our thirtieth wedding anniversary, trusting that the husband she is so ardently seeking, and whom I am sure she will find very soon, will wish to give her a gift she will value as much as mine when and if she reaches her thirtieth anniversary."'

For a split second Gerry thought that Penny looked a little disappointed, but she quickly covered it up. 'Pearls? Oo, I haven't got any pearls. That's lovely.' Her lack of any other reaction to the rather involved syntax of the paragraph suggested that she had not really grasped its meaning.

'You must take great care of them, Penelope,' said her father. 'Only wear them on very special occasions. They must be kept in the safe the rest of the time.'

'"To my great nephew, Gregory Carstairs,"' Bradley started, but at that point came to the end of the page and he paused for a moment. Gregory was staring at him rather in the manner of a dog hoping against hope that he was going to be taken for a walk.

Bradley continued from the next page. '"...knowing of his deep interest in political history, I give and bequeath the Chippendale desk, which has for many years occupied the study of my late husband, and which was previously owned by both William Pitt the Elder and the Younger, and whose wisdom will I hope, through it, be communicated to him."'

'Oh. Ah. Yes.' Gregory's words came like a series of little explosions. 'Most interesting. Great historical connections. I'm sure I'll be the envy of many of my colleagues. Capital.' But his face looked rather grim.

'"To Miss Jean Mackenzie,"' Bradley went on, '"in gratitude for many years' devoted friendship and loyalty, I give and bequeath the sum of two thousand five hundred pounds, free of duty, together with the furniture from the room which she has occupied in my house and ten other pieces of furniture of her choice."'

Jean Mackenzie gave a gasp. 'Oh, how generous! How very generous! I never imagined... It will ease so many worries.'

Stella, sitting next to her, patted her hand.

'The Testator adds two comments,' Bradley said. 'Firstly, "I am putting her on her honour to give none of this bequest to any medium or psychic and warn her that if she does so I will have a serious bone to pick with her when we next meet, which I trust will not be for many years yet."'

'How typical,' Jean Mackenzie said. 'Yes, indeed, I promise, Florrie.'

'Secondly, the Testator says: "Thank you for not peeking."'

Jean's mouth fell open. 'I – I – how did she know?'

'My client foresaw that question. I was to say to you: "By your face, when you handled the envelope."'

'Oh, what an amazing woman she was! I'm so glad now that I didn't. So glad.'

'"To my great nephew, Thomas Lambert, I give and bequeath—"' Bradley cleared his throat. He seemed decidedly embarrassed. Tommy was leaning forward expectantly. '"I give and bequeath precisely nothing. He is a worthless young scoundrel, who doesn't deserve a penny."'

There was a gasp round the table. Tommy's expression did not change, but his face drained of colour.

It was Penny who was the first to speak. 'Oh, Tommy, darling, how awful! I'm so, so sorry.' She put her hand on his. For practically the first time in his life Tommy was unable to speak. He just gulped and looked down at the table.

'My client's next words: "It's all right, Tommy, that was a practical joke – one that you richly deserved to have played on you."'

Tommy jerked his head up as Bradley continued. 'I should explain that the last three sentences are not part of the will, but which Mrs Saunders insisted I inserted at that point.' He held up a sheet of notepaper. 'I now revert to the will proper. "To my ever-entertaining great nephew, Thomas Lambert, I give and bequeath the sum of fifteen hundred pounds, free of duty, in the hope if not the expectation that he will use it wisely."'

Tommy gave his head a shake. His colour was returning. He managed a sickly grin. 'The old b— the old dear. She really got me, there. Suppose I did deserve it, though. I really get fifteen hundred quid?'

'Of course you do, silly,' Penny said. Bradley nodded.

'Gosh, that's hunky-dory.' He seemed already to have got over the shock. 'She needn't have worried. I've got some absolutely spiffing ideas.'

'"To my great niece, Stella Simmons,"' Bradley

continued, '"I give and bequeath the sum of fifteen hundred pounds, free of duty. It was a regret to me that I never visited the United States, but her most interesting letters over a number of years, and the stories she has entertained me with since her return, have made me feel that I really do know New York."'

Stella looked delighted. 'Oh, how swell of her! Unless this is a practical joke, too?'

'Most definitely not, Miss Simmons. I will continue. "To my daughter-in-law, Clara Saunders, I give and bequeath the sum of one hundred pounds, free of duty. I give and bequeath the remainder of my property—"' He broke off, for a strange sound had come from the direction of Clara. It was a sort of strangled squawking, like a person who had been gagged trying to call for help. Whereas Tommy had gone white, Clara's face had assumed a decided shade of puce. Her hands on the table had formed two bony fists and her eyes were bulging. Dorothy took her arm. 'Mother, it's all right,' she said urgently in a low voice. 'Calm down. There's more to come. Please, Mother.'

Clara raised one fist and for a moment Gerry thought she was going to hit Dorothy. But she merely brushed her hand off and, with what was clearly an immense effort of will, managed to get control of herself.

Bradley resumed hurriedly. '"I give and bequeath the remainder of my property jointly to my two beloved granddaughters, Agatha Saunders and Dorothy Saunders absolutely, feeling certain that in the event of their stepmother's present source of income ever proving inadequate, they will take care of her in whatever way they see fit." That is all, my lord, ladies and gentlemen. The will is correctly signed by the Testator and witnessed by my two clerks.'

He sat back and mopped his brow with his handkerchief. He seemed to have found the last ten minutes something of an ordeal.

Dorothy was looking dazed. 'That's – that's very nice,' she said. 'But, I'm afraid I don't understand: what does 'the remainder of my property' mean?'

'It comprises cash, shares, the house in Walton-upon-Thames and the rest of her personal possessions, not otherwise bequeathed. I calculate the total value to be in the vicinity of sixty-five thousand pounds.'

Dorothy's eyes grew so big that it looked as if they were going to take over all her face.

'By Jove!' muttered the Earl.

Gregory whistled softly and even Timothy looked startled.

Dorothy, who now looked on the verge of fainting, tried hard to speak. 'Six – six – sixty-five?'

'At a conservative estimate.'

'Congratulations, my dear,' said Lady Burford warmly. 'I am so pleased for you both.'

'Yes indeed,' added the Earl. 'I must admit I had no idea...'

'I doubt any of us had,' Timothy said dryly. 'Allow me to add my congratulations.'

All the rest then joined in, surrounding Dorothy, shaking her hand, or kissing her. The others had momentarily forgotten about Clara, who had not moved a muscle since Dorothy had last spoken to her. So it was a shock when she suddenly jumped to her feet, at the same moment shrieking at the top of her voice: 'It's a conspiracy!'

It was like a volcano erupting. She stood there, quivering, and Gerry would not have been surprised to see smoke coming out of her ears. Then she started to speak, loudly and so quickly it was difficult to follow her.

'How dare she! One hundred pounds! To her own daughter-in-law! The woman who brought up her granddaughters, single-handed! It's an insult! But I know what's behind it. Her mind was poisoned against me, by all of you. You've always hated me. And you made certain I wouldn't get what was rightfully mine. Well, you'll regret it, eminent ladies and gentlemen. I know things about all of you, that I've kept secret – some for years, some just for weeks. Things that would make your reputations mud. Well, don't think I'm going to keep quiet about them any more. You just wait! You'll soon regret what's happened today.'

And jostling aside those who were gathered round, Clara practically ran to the door and out of the room.

There was a stunned silence. It was broken by the sound of Dorothy sobbing. She looked tearfully round. 'I'm so sorry. I'm so terribly sorry.'

'You have nothing to apologise for, my dear,' Lady Burford told her firmly. 'You have done absolutely nothing wrong.'

'But for Mother to talk to you all like that...'

'Your *step*mother is plainly overwrought.' The Countess put a marked emphasis on the first syllable. 'Obviously she did not mean what she said.'

Dorothy got awkwardly to her feet. 'I'm very much afraid she did,' she said quietly. 'Will you excuse me, please? I must go to her.'

And stumbling slightly, she hurried from the room.

Gerry glanced round at the ring of faces. Was it her imagination, or did most of them at that moment look decidedly apprehensive?

'Poor girl,' Lady Burford said, as the door closed behind Dorothy.

'Not exactly poor, Mummy,' Gerry said. 'Half of sixty-five thousand, after all...'

'You know what I mean. Anyway, let us hope that the money will enable her and her sister to gain their independence now.'

'I am not at all sure that it will,' Timothy said. 'The woman seems to have a psychological hold over her. I know nothing about Agatha, but I fear Dorothy at least may have difficulty in breaking it. I would not be at all surprised if a good part of the estate found its way into Clara's hands before long.'

'Oh, that would be terrible.' The Countess looked at Bradley. 'Can nothing be done to prevent it?'

'I'm afraid not, my lady. Inevitably, in view of the fact that they are no longer young girls, the bequest was made to them absolutely, not in trust. They can do precisely as they wish.'

'Can you not put them in touch with a good financial adviser?'

'By all means, if I am asked to do so. But I am not the young ladies' legal representative.'

'I think you're worrying unnecessarily,' Gerry said. 'From what I gather, Agatha has a good head on her shoulders and is a lot tougher than Dorry. I think she'll take control now.'

'I'm just staggered by the size of the estate,' said the Earl. 'I was always under the impression that Florrie wasn't all that well off. I never liked to ask her, but I did tell her on a number of occasions that if there was ever any help of any kind I could give, she only had to ask. I imagine she knew what I meant.'

Miss Mackenzie cleared her throat in a ladylike manner. 'If I may say so, Lord Burford, I am sure she did know. Your kindness used to please her very much. But she never needed to take advantage of it.'

'I wonder where it all came from. I always understood that Great Uncle Bertie made some pretty disastrous investments.'

'I think Mrs Saunders – Florrie – would like me to explain. She would not want people to imagine that her late husband was financially incompetent. He did make some unwise investments, it is true, but apparently he also made some extremely shrewd ones. Moreover, she told me that he took out a very large life insurance policy soon after their marriage. So all in all she was well provided for. In addition, she herself had been investing, very cleverly, for a great many years. She seemed to have a real flair for it. Though, of course, even I did not know quite how big the estate was.'

Tommy gave a guffaw. 'I bet old Scary Clara would have been camping out on Florrie's doorstep for years, if she'd known just how much she was worth. Probably thought she was only going to leave a thousand or two, all told. Must admit I was hoping for a hundred quid at the most. Weren't you, Stella?'

'I had no idea what she was going to leave me. I'm just

very touched to be remembered at all. After all, I hadn't seen her for eleven years, until a few months ago. She looked at Bradley. 'What would fifteen hundred pounds be in dollars?'

'About seven thousand, five hundred.'

'How sweet of her.'

The Countess said: 'I think it's time for tea.'

When tea was over, Bradley had left and most of the guests had dispersed to their rooms or elsewhere, Dorothy reappeared. She handed the Countess a folded sheet of notepaper. 'From Mother.'

Lady Burford unfolded it and read:

My dear Lavinia,

Please let me offer my most sincere apologies for what must have seemed my extremely insulting words to you, Cousin George and Geraldine following the reading of the will. I wish to make it abundantly clear that it was not my intention for one moment to include you in the accusations which I made. Needless to say, I know nothing remotely detrimental about any of you, with whom I have always felt the closest friendship.

I regret that circumstances make it impossible for me to leave Alderley tonight. However, as it would be undoubtedly embarrassing for all concerned if I were to come down to dinner, I shall remain in my

room for the rest of the evening. Perhaps, if it is not
too inconvenient, a light meal might be served to me
here. You may, if you think it necessary, inform
your servants that I have an acute headache, which
is indeed true.

With repeated apologies, I remain, your friend,

Clara

Lady Burford looked up. 'Please tell your stepmother that
what she wishes can be easily arranged. I will also send some
tea up immediately. And ask her if she requires aspirin.'

'Oh, she has some, thank you. I'll tell her what you
said.' Dorothy scurried out again.

Lady Burford passed the note to her husband, who read
it. 'Well, at least she's got the decency to apologise to us,
but doesn't say she's sorry for causing the rumpus in the
first place. And you notice she doesn't withdraw a thing
she said about the others.'

'That's very noticeable. Do you suppose it's true,
George?'

'What, that she knows their guilty secrets? I've no idea.
Not likely, but I suppose it's possible she knows some.
But that they all conspired together is obviously nonsense.
However, I'm not going to worry about it. I reckon they're all
quite capable of looking after themselves. By the way, didn't
know Clara was your friend.' He passed the note back.

'It's news to me, too, George.'

* * *

Jean Mackenzie sat in her room and tried to think of her inheritance and what she would do with it. But a nasty, nagging little worry spoiled her full enjoyment of the prospect. It was those last words of Clara's. At first, she had not associated them with herself. But going over them again she had remembered that Clara had said 'I know things about all of you.' *All* of you. Could the woman possibly know the awful thing that she, Jean, had done? It didn't seem possible. Unless Florrie had said something to her on Clara's one relatively recent visit. But that was highly unlikely. Florrie had thoroughly disliked Clara and told her as little as possible. But it could have been Agatha – Florrie could have told *her* and Agatha could have passed it on in all innocence to Clara.

Suppose Clara did know what she had done, and why she had done it? It didn't bear thinking about. It would, in Clara's rather vulgar phrase, certainly make her reputation mud. It must not be allowed to happen. She had built that reputation – for probity, honesty, truthfulness – over many years. She could not lose it now.

How, though, could she stop Clara? Would offering her money work? Two hundred pounds, perhaps, or three? It would be a big lump out of her inheritance, but worth it if it silenced Clara for good. But could she be sure it would? Suppose Clara came back for more? That's what blackmailers did. She might bleed her dry. And anyway, how could she approach Clara in the first place? 'I'll give you two hundred pounds if you promise to keep quiet about' – when, perhaps, all the time, Clara did *not* know about it. Jean would be giving her the information.

Oh dear, why had she done that awful thing? She would

surely be punished. However, it was no good crying over spilt milk. The important thing was to decide what was she going to do now.

Jean thought deeply for several minutes and eventually came to a decision. She gave a firm nod. Yes, she was going to go ahead. She was not going to back out now. Whatever the cost.

CHAPTER SIXTEEN

The menu at dinner that evening was superb: chilled watercress soup, poached salmon, roast saddle of venison, with redcurrant jelly, and summer pudding, containing strawberries, raspberries and black cherries, served with cream. Nevertheless, the meal was a strained occasion. Perhaps it was the presence of Dorothy, who sat low in her chair, merely picking at her food, and when spoken to answered in monosyllables. Lady Burford had to resist a strong urge to order her to sit up straight and answer nicely when addressed. Of the others, Gregory seemed sunk in gloom, Stella distrait; Timothy at the best of times did not excel at light, dinner-table conversation, and Penny was preoccupied and apparently making valiant and unaccustomed efforts to think something through. Miss Mackenzie seemed decidedly nervous and was probably, the Countess thought, feeling rather out of place among a group of people who were all, however distantly, related to each other and all, as she would have described it, her social superiors.

Lady Burford, for whom hosting splendid dinner parties

was one of the joys of life, was disappointed. This occasion was perhaps not so very grand – no dress clothes, for one thing, and no especially distinguished guests – but it was, nevertheless, the first for six months, and she had hoped for better.

Only Lord Burford, Gerry and Tommy were in good form, the latter prattling away about various fantastic business plans for which he might use his newly acquired capital. His schemes became more and more wild, and Gerry, realising that without their contributions the atmosphere would resemble that of a morgue, played up to him, adding even more bizarre ideas. Among the projects they came up with were tortoise farming in North Wales, a speech training school for parrots and a company producing reconditioned pencils from the glued-together stubs of old ones.

When they eventually ran out of ideas, the Earl decided to make a contribution. 'I've got an idea.' They looked at him enquiringly.

'Collapsible and expanding cufflinks.'

Tommy stared blankly. 'Sorry and all that, but I don't quite get the jolly old joke.'

'I'm serious. I've got scores of cufflinks. Happened to mention once years ago that I was always not puttin' 'em in properly, so one fell out and I lost it, or else I kept breaking one of a pair, so I was always short. For ages after that I could practically guarantee gettin' a pair or two every birthday or Christmas. But I've never had a pair that it was easy to put in once you'd got your shirt on. I've never wanted a valet, and it takes me minutes sometimes, if somebody's not around to lend a hand. You want to invent some that are small enough to go through the holes easily, then when they're through, you just press a little button and they suddenly expand. You'd make a fortune.'

'I'll certainly bear that in mind,' Tommy said. He looked at Gerry. 'Make a note of that, Miss Jones.'

'Yes, sir.'

When the ladies retired at the end of the meal, things were little better in either room. Tommy was out of his element in the company of what he thought of as three old buffers. A glass of vintage port and a cigar did loosen Gregory's tongue somewhat, though Timothy remained aloof and as unbending as ever.

The Earl concentrated on Gregory. 'Congratulations on getting that Chippendale desk,' he said. 'I remember seeing it. Fine piece of work.'

'Is it? I've never seen it myself.'

'Yes, and in perfect condition, as I remember. Worth quite a bit, I imagine.'

Gregory's ears almost visibly pricked up. 'Really? Er, how much, I wonder.'

'I wouldn't know, my dear fellow. I'm not up in antique furniture. But you won't want to sell it, will you? I mean, tremendous historical interest, and all that, owned by both the Pitts; absolutely fitting that it should stay in the family *and* be owned by an MP, what?'

'Oh yes, yes, of course. I mean, no, I wouldn't want to sell it. Of course not.'

Timothy spoke for the first time. 'Nothing would induce me to sell my set of Dickens, no matter how short of money I was.'

'I am not short of money,' Gregory said angrily. 'I was

simply wondering about the value for insurance purposes. Those of us on fixed salaries have to think about these things, not being in a position to charge exorbitant fees for our work.'

'Perhaps those on fixed salaries should be careful to keep their non-essential expenses down to a minimum.'

'Just what do you—'

The Earl broke in hastily. 'Incidentally, wanted to say how much I appreciated your words at the funeral. Absolutely right, I thought: not too gloomy, but not too flippant either.'

'Oh, thank you. One does one's best.'

'Have some more port,' said the Earl. He refilled their glasses.

Tommy, having drunk nothing so good before, sipped it appreciatively. He was beginning to feel more at home. 'Must say, I do envy you fellows who can speak like that in public. I mean, if it's only a few people and everyone's feeling jolly I can chat away about anything.'

'We would never have known,' Timothy put in.

'No, I mean as long as I haven't got to talk about anything in particular, I'm fine.'

'You would clearly make a splendid Member of Parliament. They are expert at talking about nothing in particular for hours on end.'

'That from a lawyer!' Gregory sneered.

Lord Burford hastened to encourage Tommy; anything to keep the other two from getting at each other's throats. 'So what's your problem, exactly, my boy?'

Tommy, who had really said all he had wanted to, ploughed on. 'Well, I mean it's when it comes to talking seriously about a particular subject that I dry up. I mean, I was best man at a chum's wedding recently. Hundred guests and I was bally nervous. In the end it wasn't too bad, because I was able to spin 'em a few jokes. But you can't always do that, can you? I mean, you couldn't tell the one about the lighthouse keeper's daughter at a funeral, could you?'

'Oh, I don't know,' said Gregory, 'there are some people so totally without humour or warmth that they wouldn't recognise it as a joke at all.'

'Shall we join the ladies?' said Lord Burford.

In the drawing-room, talk was not quite so stilted, this being largely due to the fact that Penny and Stella now seemed to be the best of friends and chatted together quietly, except for the occasional burst of laughter. However, Dorothy and Jean Mackenzie both totally failed to respond to Lady Burford's attempts to engage them in conversation, so that she was forced to talk to her own daughter. She would actually have been grateful for the company of Clara, who, as she remembered, conversed extremely fluently. Usually it had just been gossip – sometimes quite scandalous – but nevertheless, the Countess had to admit, often rather interesting...

She was, therefore, relieved when the men eventually arrived, followed by Merryweather and a footman with coffee. After this, the atmosphere lightened as people moved into smaller groups or pairs.

Penny moved up to Tommy. He grinned at her. 'I say, this is all rather splendid, isn't it?'

'Mm. Tommy, I want to say something.'

'I'm all ears.'

'You mustn't be annoyed, but I don't think they're going to work.'

'What aren't?'

'Some of your ideas. The pencils, for instance. It would take an awfully long time to stick them together. And I don't think you'd find glue strong enough to hold them. They'd break up again when you pressed hard.'

Tommy just said: 'Ah.'

'And I don't think there are enough people who want to buy tortoises. The school for parrots could work, but it might take absolutely ages to teach just one to talk properly, and how much would people be willing to pay for the tuition?'

About to explain, Tommy wisely thought better of it. He just nodded thoughtfully. 'Yes, I think you're absolutely right, Penny. I tend to get carried away, you know, but I can see, now you've pointed it out, that they're all rather impractical schemes. Thanks very much. You've got quite a head for business, haven't you?'

Penny flushed a bright pink. 'Oh, do you really think so? It would be lovely if I had. It must be such fun to be a career woman, running your own company.'

'I don't know that it's always much fun, actually.'

'Oh, but it must be. Think of all that lovely money rolling in every week, and a private office and a secretary and letter headings and business cards with your name on: *Penelope Saunders, Managing Director*.' She gave a wistful sigh. 'You have got a bit of money now. You can try. I was hoping Florrie was going to leave me some, too, but all I've got is pearls.'

'They sound lovely, though.'

'But I'll hardly ever be able to wear them. They'll be shut up in Daddy's safe practically all the time. Of course, I might take them out sometimes, when he's away – I know the combination – but he doesn't go away very often and if I did it would be just my luck if they were stolen.'

'But they'd be insured, so you'd have the cash value then, which is what you want. It would the best thing that could happen.'

'Unless Daddy just invested the cash for me. In which case, I wouldn't see a penny.'

'But it would be your money. You'll be of age in a couple of years. You could do what you liked with it.'

'I wouldn't dare go against him. He'd probably cut off my allowance.' She looked thoroughly miserable.

Tommy tried to cheer her up. 'Tell you what, I'll steal them from his safe, sell them, and we'll split the proceeds.'

A beatific smile spread over Penny's face. 'Oh, Tommy, would you really do that for me?'

He was taken aback. The girl took everything you said perfectly seriously. Of course, given that she'd been brought up in a home without humour, it was hardly surprising. And in a way, he thought, it was kind of endearing. It made her seem so vulnerable. You felt you wanted to protect her. He said hastily: 'Of course I would. But I think we ought to leave it as a last resort. If your father ever found out, he'd never forgive you, and you wouldn't want to risk that.'

'I suppose not.' Penny sounded doubtful.

'Tell you what,' he said. 'I won't start my own business without consulting you. You can be my adviser. Then when I get it up and going you can come and work with me. We can be partners. Or I'll be Chairman and you can be Managing Director; you can have cards printed and everything. Though I can't promise you a secretary, yet.'

Penny almost jumped in the air with excitement. 'Oo, Tommy that'll be absolutely divine!'

'Yes, won't it?' said Tommy, wondering what he had let himself in for.

Timothy, sitting by himself on a large sofa, fastidiously sipping a cup of unsweetened black coffee, and looking disapprovingly at his daughter, as she talked to Tommy, glanced up as a shadow fell over him. It was Stella. 'May I sit down?'

'Please.' He made a gesture with his hand.

She did so. 'I wanted to have a word with you.'

'Oh? About what?'

The curtness with which he asked the question was not auspicious, but Stella carried on.

'I wanted first to congratulate you.'

'On what?'

'On Penny. She's such a lovely girl.'

'Oh, she's pretty enough, I dare say. But I cannot claim any credit for that.'

'I didn't only mean that. She has so much charm.'

'I'm afraid she doesn't get that from her father, either.'

'Well, there's one thing I'm sure she does get from him: she's smart.'

He raised his eyebrows. 'Are you serious?'

'Oh, she's not an intellectual. But she knows what she wants and my guess is she knows how to get it.'

'I must admit I am surprised by what you say. She seems to me to live in a fantasy world much of the time.'

'She day-dreams. What's the harm in that, at her age? She's also kind-hearted, totally without spite and devastatingly honest.'

'You've summed her up remarkably quickly.'

'Yes, but I've always been good at that, and we have to do it in my work. Sure, these are only my first impressions. Plainly you know her far better than I do.'

'Sometimes I feel I don't know her at all. But I appreciate very much what you say, and on consideration I think you're probably correct. Perhaps I do tend to dwell too much on the negative side of her personality. No doubt because I worry about her so.'

'That's only natural. But I think you've done a great job, raising her on your own. It must have been hard.'

'Well, her mother was there until she was nearly thirteen. It was terrible for Penelope, losing her then. I was proud of the way she handled it. But the past six years have not been easy. I knew nothing about teenage girls, really. Perhaps I've been too strict. She certainly thinks so. It's no secret that relations between us are somewhat strained at times. But girls of that age seem so vulnerable. One hears such terrible things. A few moments of recklessness and a life can be ruined. I've been so desperate to protect her that perhaps I've gone too far.'

After the first few moments of suspicion, he seemed now relieved to be talking; probably, Stella thought, he normally had no one to unburden himself to.

'I was the only one able even to try and take her mother's place,' he went on. 'It wasn't as though she had an older sister or any aunts. Both my wife and I were only children, and her relatives are scattered throughout the country.'

'You have at least one cousin, though, who is married, and living in London.'

'Gregory? We never meet except unavoidably, on occasions such as this. Besides, his wife, Alexandra, is extremely aloof and very politically minded – the only reason, I'm sure, she married Gregory. She would have no interest in Penelope at all.'

'I was chatting to Gregory this afternoon.'

'I noticed.' Timothy's manner was becoming slightly chillier again.

'He seemed very friendly.'

'Oh, I'm sure he did. You appeared to be getting on famously.'

'I was just making his acquaintance, really. Actually, I thought he might be able to help me. I'm hoping to make a career change. He's offered to lend a helping hand.'

'I should be very cautious of Gregory's helping hands.'

'Oh, I shall be extremely cautious of Gregory's hands: they may well want to help themselves.'

For the first time since she had first seen him, Timothy smiled. 'I can see that there are no flies on you – isn't that what they say in the United States?'

'Working as a journalist in New York City for nearly eleven years does help in that respect.'

'I'm sure. I just wish that Penelope had someone as sophisticated and worldly-wise as you that she could look to for advice and help.'

'Why can't she? I'd be delighted. Of course, we don't really move in the same circles.'

'I'm sure that can be rectified. Look, perhaps you would care to come to dinner in a week or two. I'll make sure Penny's there – oh, I'm sure she'll want to be, anyway.'

'That'd be swell. Thank you.'

'Excellent. I'll look forward to it.'

'And I have an idea. How old is she?'

'Nearly nineteen.'

'When's her birthday?'

'The first of October.'

'Why not throw her a party? Oh, I know not much is made of a nineteenth birthday, as a rule: people keep the big celebration for the twenty-first. But let this be an extra one – a sort of bonus. It'd be a thrill for her, I'm sure, and show her how much you care. I'd be pleased to help organise it, if you like.'

Timothy nodded. 'Yes, that is a very good idea. And I would certainly appreciate your help. I would not have the first idea how to set about it. In fact, you may find yourself doing more than merely *helping* to organise it, I'm afraid.'

'That's fine by me. I'll enjoy it.'

'The only trouble is that I suppose she'll want to invite Tommy. She's getting too close to that young whipper-snapper.'

'Oh, Tommy's all right.'

He said quickly: 'I'm so sorry. I'd forgotten he's quite a close relative of yours, isn't he? Do forgive me.'

'That's all right. He's only a first cousin. But I am fond of him. What have you got against him?'

'I'm sure he's quite without malice, but he just seems such a loafer, with absolutely no power of perseverance. He's had about a dozen jobs in the last four or five years.

He's never going to amount to anything. He's the last sort of friend Penelope needs.'

'He may just be one of those guys who takes a long time to find his niche. I'm sure he'll settle down – especially now he's got this money. I fancy he might pleasantly surprise everybody one day.'

'I sincerely hope you're right. Because the more I criticise him, the more vehemently Penelope defends him. So it seems I'm going to have to tolerate him.'

'I'm sure it's good tactics to try.'

'Anyway, er, Stella, I'm really very grateful for your interest, and your offer. If there's anything I can do...'

'You know, Timothy, I'm very glad you said that.'

'Indeed?' He looked slightly startled at the quickness and eagerness of her response. 'Well, by all means, feel free.'

'Now I know what you're thinking: first the offer to help and now the quid pro quo. But it's not that. I really do think Penny's a great kid, and I'll be glad to help her in any way I can. But I would like your assistance. If you say no, it won't make any difference as regards her. And no, to pre-empt your next suspicion, I am not looking for free legal advice. However, I do want to use you shamelessly to help further my career.'

'In what way?'

'Would you let me interview you?'

'I'm afraid I do not understand.'

'Well, as you may know, I'm a fashion journalist.'

'I am afraid that if you are seeking my opinions on the latest fashions, I have to tell you it is something I know nothing about, and care as little.'

'Well, we have one thing in common at least. While I know a lot about it, I'm coming to care about it as little as you do – or at least, writing about it professionally.'

'That must make life rather difficult.'

'Not really, just boring. Which is why I would like to break into a different branch of journalism, a more serious side. And I've been thinking that an interview with you, one of the country's foremost attorneys—' She broke off, with a laugh. 'Sorry – foremost barristers, might well appeal to one of the weekly or monthly magazines.'

'I find it hard to believe that any magazine would find me of interest. And I have to say that I deplore this modern tendency to build lawyers up as personalities, like film stars. Marshall Hall had a lot to answer for, great advocate though he was.'

The reference meant nothing to Stella. But she carried on. 'I'd place a bet that I could make your life sound a heck of a lot more interesting than you think it is. I mean, just your experiences of looking after a teenage daughter unaided would make a fascinating story. But of course I wouldn't write about that. I was thinking more about your cases.'

'No doubt of the more sensational ones?'

'Oh, of course. All the ones packed with jealousy, revenge, violence, blood, adultery.'

'I'm sorry. That was ungracious of me. Which ones would you really want to write about?

'The most interesting ones from a legal point of view. I'd also like to get your views about the law in general and the legal system – how you think it might be improved, for instance.'

Timothy took a sip of coffee before saying: 'Well, I certainly can see no objection to a serious piece of that nature. As a matter of fact, the editor of *The British Monthly* approached me some time ago, suggesting I wrote an article for him, along those very lines.'

'Oh, then it seems I'm redundant, if you intend to write such an article yourself.'

'Not at all, I turned him down. I just did not have the time. But I could certainly give you the facts and my opinions and you could write it up, if that is acceptable to you.'

'Acceptable? It would be terrific. I'd have a market for the piece ready and waiting.'

'I could get in touch with him, confirm that he is still interested and tell him the plan. You could then see him yourself and ascertain precisely what he requires in terms of length, general approach and so on.'

'That's better still. Timothy, I could kiss you!'

He looked away quickly and cleared his throat. She realised the last words had been a mistake. 'And you definitely would not write about me as a person?'

'Well, just a few basic details, perhaps. Give it a little human interest.'

'I have to say that I dislike human interest.'

'It does help sell papers.'

'I suppose so.'

'And it might be an idea to include a couple of anecdotes, just to lighten it a little. You must have had some amusing experiences in court.'

'None that seemed amusing at the time; embarrassing rather. Later one can smile.'

'Can you think of one in particular?'

'Well, perhaps, but I don't think it would—'

'Oh, I'd just love to hear it.'

'You may not find it at all amusing.'

'Try me.'

'Very well. It happened many years ago, when I was an inexperienced young barrister. It was a case, strangely enough, involving a will. It was hand-written, not drawn up by a solicitor, but perfectly legal – if it were genuine. In it, the Testator left all his property to his only son, who had lived some distance away, and it omitted any mention of his daughter, who had lived with him and looked after him for a number of years. I represented the daughter, whose contention was that the will was a forgery by her brother, who had slipped it among their father's papers on one of his infrequent visits. The matter seemed easy enough to resolve, so we sent the will, and a letter, known to have been written by the deceased, to a professional graphologist by the name of William Jones, who in a written report stated that in his view the will was definitely a forgery.

'Came the time for me to call my expert. I said: "My next witness is Mr William Jones." The usher put his head into the corridor, called out: "William Jones". A man entered and went into the witness box. I did what I normally did on such occasions, ran through his professional qualifications, prior to asking the first question – something along the lines of: "Mr Jones, you are a professional graphologist of many years experience, who has worked extensively with numerous police forces." He did not say anything, just looked a little bewildered, but I assumed that perhaps he hadn't often actually given evidence in court, and I carried on hurriedly: "Would you be so good as to look at these two documents and say whether in your opinion they were written by the same person?" I passed the will and the letter to the usher, who handed them to the witness. He gazed at the papers for quite a long time, and then said, in a broad west country accent: "Couldn't rightly say. They certainly look the same." I was totally flabbergasted. I said: "But Mr Jones, you have had the opportunity to study these documents at leisure and examine them under magnification, have you not?" "No," he said. "Never seen 'em before."

'Well, you can guess what's coming. This was not my William Jones. This William Jones had been waiting to give evidence as a witness to a traffic accident in another court. It transpired he had been too nervous to correct me when I listed his qualifications, imagining he would be guilty of contempt of court.'

'Oh, that's priceless. I love it. And I suppose at that very moment your Mr Jones was indignantly denying that he'd ever been anywhere near a road accident.' She threw back her head and laughed.

Seeming to find her amusement infectious, Timothy joined in. It was a strange and rarely heard sound, a sort of dry 'hih-hih-hih-hih,' all on the same note.

Standing not more than eight feet away, Penny spun her head and stared at him, an expression of astonishment on her face. She whispered: 'Tommy, Daddy's laughing!'

Tommy had followed her gaze. Penny went on: 'I haven't heard him laugh for years. Not since Mummy died.'

Tommy didn't reply, and Penny plucked at his sleeve. 'Tommy?'

He ignored her, took a few indecisive steps away from her towards Timothy and Stella. For a ghastly moment, Penny thought he was going to ask them not to make so much noise, but then he stopped and came back. He was wearing a strangely blank expression. 'Sorry. You were saying?'

She repeated the words. 'Oh. Well, good. That's fine.' He seemed as surprised as she was.

CHAPTER SEVENTEEN

At about twenty past ten, Dorothy slipped from the room, whispering to Lady Burford that she was going to say goodnight to her mother. She returned in about ten minutes and drew the Countess aside.

'Could – could I ask you a very big favour?'

'Of course, my dear.'

'Would you be very kind and look in on Mother? She really does want to apologise to you personally, but she's very anxious to avoid seeing anyone else, and wants to leave early in the morning. It would so ease her mind.'

About to remark that she felt no obligation to go out of her way to ease Clara's mind, Lady Burford took in Dorothy's wan and quite haggard face and relented. 'Very well. I'll go up now.'

'Oh, thank you so much.' Her gratitude was almost pitiable.

Lady Burford left the room. She came back in about seven or eight minutes. Dorothy immediately hurried across to her. 'Well?'

'We've talked quite freely. Your stepmother did say

some highly insulting things about members of George's – and your – family, and made some actual threats, which I told her frankly that I considered indefensible. She would not, however, apologise for that, and I believe she is truly convinced that some of them conspired against her. However, she has apologised handsomely for embarrassing George and me and Geraldine, as well as for any aspersions she seemed to have cast on us. I have accepted that apology and we left on relatively good terms.'

Dorothy gave a big sigh of relief. 'Oh, I'm so glad. Thank you.'

'I asked her if she wanted any refreshments and she requested a cup of cocoa and a couple of digestive biscuits, which I have arranged to be taken to her.'

'You're really so kind. I'm sure she'll sleep better now – oh, I don't mean because of the cocoa, but having spoken to you.'

The Countess smiled. 'You're a very loyal and dutiful daughter.'

It was shortly after this that the Earl made a short speech – one that he had delivered on a number of other occasions. 'Just a word about our burglar alarm. It's unique and we think foolproof. The one drawback is that while nobody can get in, no one can get out either, without setting it off. You'll find your bedroom windows will only open six inches. If you force them more than that – and, of course, you can do that quite easily in the event of a fire or some other emergency – or break the window or force an outside door, you'll trigger it. It can't be switched off but turns itself off automatically at six-thirty.'

It had been a long, tiring day for all of those present, and a stressful one for some, and few felt like staying up late that night. By eleven o'clock only the younger people were still downstairs. They chatted for another quarter of an hour, before Tommy, Stella and Penny all went upstairs together, the girls leaving him at the top of the staircase and making their way together to their rooms in the west corridor. Gerry, who of course, still felt wide awake, and Dorothy were left in sole possession of the drawing-room.

'Well,' Gerry asked, 'what's it feel like to be an heiress?'

'Wonderful – I think. I mean, I haven't really taken it in properly yet.'

Gerry stood up. 'Want a drink?'

'Oh, no thank you. I don't really drink alcohol very much.'

'Hot drink? Coffee, tea?'

'A cup of tea would be lovely.'

Gerry rang the bell, poured herself a glass of wine and sat down again.

Dorothy said: 'You're not going to bed yet?'

'No, it's much too early for me. I'm a real night owl.'

'Oh, good. I'm usually tucked up by this time, but I'm sure I couldn't sleep tonight.'

'I'm not surprised. It's been quite a day.'

A footman entered at that moment and Gerry ordered a pot of tea.

When he had departed, Gerry said: 'You phoned Agatha, I suppose?'

'No. I meant to immediately after the reading, but then that trouble with Mother put it right out of my head. By the time I remembered, it was too late, because she was going out for the whole evening, until quite late. I might phone her last thing, if that's all right.'

'Of course. She'll be over the moon, won't she?'

'I expect so. I mean, we were pretty sure we were going to get something, but nothing like this.'

'Got any plans?'

'Not really. It'll depend on what Mother says.'

Gerry felt a surge of exasperation. 'It's your money, Dorry – yours and Agatha's.'

'Oh, Aggie will probably be full of plans, when I tell her. She might even want to move into Grandmother's house. She'd like to be out of town, nearer the country. But I'm sure Mother wouldn't let me go with her, and she wouldn't want to move out of London. So I suppose I'll be staying in Hampstead.'

'You must tell her what you want to do, and then just do it.'

Dorothy looked doubtful. 'I don't know if I could.'

The tea arrived a few moments later. When she was sipping a very sweet and milky cup, Dorothy said shyly: 'Do you still feel like telling me about the murders?'

'Yes, of course, if you really want to hear it.'

'Oh, yes please!' She kicked off her shoes and tucked her feet up under her. 'This is such fun.'

It was amazing, Gerry thought, how much happier and more relaxed she was now Clara was not around.

'It's difficult to know where to start,' she said. 'You probably know most of the facts, from the papers. So why don't you just ask me questions?'

'All right.' Dorothy was eager. 'One thing I didn't

understand is what made you decide, that first night, to go on watch in the corridor after everybody supposedly had gone to bed?'

'Just a general uneasiness. As you know, we had two foreign diplomats here, an American millionaire, his wife and her fabulous diamond necklace, a notorious jewel thief was active, and we had one guest who had virtually gate-crashed under very suspicious circumstances. I was sure something fishy was going on, and I just had to try and find out...'

'And the very next day he proposed to you,' Dorothy said, with a sigh, a little over an hour later. 'And you said yes. It's so romantic.'

Gerry grinned. 'Well, I hardly felt I could turn him down, after he'd risked his life to save mine.'

'That's not the reason, though...?'

'No, no. I was quite certain by then. If he hadn't proposed, I probably should have.'

'When are you getting married?'

'I don't know. We would have been married by now, but the poor darling had a death in the family, and that led to a lot of complications, which he had to go and try to sort out. Which is why I'm here at the mo—'

She stopped short and both girls gave a start as from somewhere in the house came the sound of a loud crash. It had a sort of metallic ring to it, as if someone had dropped a heavy tool box. Although muffled by the thick drawing-room door, Gerry realised that the fact they could hear it at all must mean it had been very loud. She jumped to her feet. 'What on earth was that?'

She hurried to the door and pulled it open. Dorothy, after

thrusting her feet into her shoes, joined her. For a second, all was silent, then came the sound of a woman's voice. It was shouting, sounding more angry than afraid, and definitely came from upstairs, but from which wing it was impossible to tell. They could not make out the words.

Dorothy gasped: 'Oh, can that be Mother?'

'Let's go and find out,' Gerry said.

She ran across the hall and up the grand staircase, Dorothy at her shoulder. They had nearly reached the head of the stairs before the shouting stopped. At the top, Gerry turned towards the east corridor and passed a room on her left, which was used for the storage of linen and where the upstairs end of the secret passage emerged. The next room was the last before the corner which led to the east corridor. She made to hurry on, but Dorothy stopped by it. 'This is Mother's room.'

'Oh.' Gerry had not known which room had been allocated to Clara. 'I think the voice came from farther away.'

'Let me just check.' Dorothy tapped on the panel. There was no response and she opened the door an inch or two and gave a loud stage whisper. 'Mother? Are you all right?' There was still no reply, and she opened the door wider, groped for the light switch and clicked it on. Then she gave a muffled half gasp, half-scream and moved violently backwards, cannoning into Gerry.

Gerry stared past her into the room. The large double bed, sideways on to them in the centre of the wall on their right, was wildly dishevelled, the bedclothes half falling onto the floor. Clara was lying across the bed, her head hanging over the near side. Her face was nearly as white as the bed linen and her eyes, pointing fixedly at them, were totally lifeless.

CHAPTER EIGHTEEN

Dorothy buried her face in Gerry's shoulder. Her voice came in hoarse whispers. 'No. No. No.' Gerry wanted to scream herself, but she just raised her hand and robot-like patted Dorothy on the shoulder.

Then there was the patter of footsteps, and suddenly her father was beside them. Gerry had never been so pleased to see him.

'What the deuce is going on?'

Gerry just pointed into the room. He gazed past her and made a sharp intake of breath. Then he went into the room. He gingerly approached the bed, bent and took the wrist of Clara's left hand, which was hanging down, nearly touching the floor. He clasped it for a few seconds, then let it go and straightened up. He turned round, looked at Gerry and slowly shook his head.

That second the Countess arrived. 'What's wrong?'

Gerry said: 'It's Clara. She's dead. It looks as though she's been murdered.'

'Oh no! It can't be possible!'

'I'm afraid there's no mistake.' The Earl's face was

almost as white as the dead woman's. He muttered: 'I feared something like this.'

Dorothy was now sobbing uncontrollably, convulsions shaking her body.

Rapidly getting a grip on herself, Lady Burford said: 'Geraldine, take Dorothy to her room.'

'Yes, yes, of course.' She said gently: 'Come along Dorry,' and tried to lead her away. But Dorothy suddenly resisted. 'No. I must see her first, properly.'

She pulled away from Gerry and half-stumbled into the room. She crossed to the bed and stood looking down for ten seconds, while the others watched. Then she turned and came back. 'I – I think I would like to go and lie down now.'

'Come along, then.' Gerry put her arm round Dorothy's shoulder. 'Er, which is your room?'

Dorothy pointed to the left. 'The third on the right.'

'Oh, next door to me.' Gerry led her slowly along the corridor and opened the door of Dorothy's room. As she did so, she saw the door of the outside corner bedroom at the end of the corridor open and Timothy, dressing-gowned, emerging. She did not pause to explain the situation to him, but switched on the light, led Dorothy into the room and pushed the door closed behind them. Just inside, Dorothy suddenly resisted.

'What's the matter?'

'If Mother was – was murdered, the murderer's got to still be in the house, hasn't he?'

'Oh, I don't think—'

'But your burglar alarm. The Earl was saying earlier that no one can get out without setting it off.'

Gerry bit her lip. It was, of course, true.

'Suppose he's in here?' Dorothy said, fearfully.

'I'm sure he's not.'

'But why not? We must search. Will you look under the bed?'

'Of course.'

She walked across to the bed and knelt down, while Dorothy went to the large wardrobe, stopped and took a deep breath, before reaching for the knob. In spite of her airy manner, Gerry did feel a slight *frisson* of apprehension as she lifted the bedspread and lowered her head. Just suppose…? But all was clear. She stood up at the same moment as Dorothy, with obvious relief, firmly reclosed the wardrobe door.

'Nothing,' Gerry said, 'and there's nowhere else in here he could be.' The rest of the furniture consisted of a dressing-table and stool, a bedside table, one easy and one upright chair.

'I expect you think I'm terribly silly.'

'No, I should have thought of it.'

Dorothy sat on the bed, meticulously removed her shoes, then put her legs up and lay down.

'Can I get you some brandy?' Gerry asked.

'No, really, thank you.'

'Or just a glass of water?'

'Nothing at all just now, thank you.'

'I'll stay with you.'

'There's really no need.'

'I want to.'

'Well, if you're sure. You're very kind.'

Gerry sat down herself in the easy chair. Her mind

was in a whirl and she did not know what to say. Should she offer sympathy and commiserations? It hardly seemed adequate. Would apologies be more in order? Did any blame attach to her family? On two occasions they had had guests murdered under their roof. Now it had happened again. Was there anything she or her parents could have done to prevent it? Gerry closed her eyes. She suddenly felt very, very tired – something she was not at all used to.

Meanwhile, Lord Burford was explaining to a shocked Timothy what had occurred. Within a few seconds, they were joined by Gregory, Jean Mackenzie and finally by Tommy, to all of whom the situation had to be explained anew. Each of them, it seemed, had been woken by the crash and had got up to investigate.

'What the dickens caused that noise?' the Earl muttered. 'There's nothing in there' – he pointed into Clara's room— 'to account for it.'

'I can tell you that,' said Gregory. 'I was closest to it. Tremendous noise. The door of your art gallery's open, and I looked in. It was that old suit of armour you've got in there. It's fallen over – pieces scattered all over the place.'

Lord Burford looked totally bewildered. 'Why on earth should he have gone in there? There's no way out that way. And he surely couldn't have knocked it over accidentally.'

Before anyone could answer him they saw a sudden moving splash of colour at the far end of the main corridor. It was Stella and Penny, one in a sky-blue and the other a pink dressing-gown. They hurried towards the group, Stella calling out urgently: 'Have you caught him?'

The Earl stared at her. 'You saw him?'

'Yes, he was in my room.'

'In *your* room?' It was Timothy who reacted first. He looked really concerned. 'Did he attempt to harm you?'

'No. Something woke me, I opened my eyes and could just see the outline of a person poking about by the dresser. I yelled out something and he made a bee-line for the door.'

'Thank God. But what a terrifying experience for you!'

'It was all over too quick to be terrifying, really. I kept on shouting, he ran out and I lost sight of him. I jumped out of bed and ran to the door. I was still shouting at the top of my voice – I read once that if you surprise a burglar it's best to make as much noise as you can – but he'd disappeared. Then Penny emerged.'

Penny said: 'I didn't see him. I just came out to see what Stella was shouting about. We decided the best thing to do was wake Daddy. Then, when we got to his room, we saw you all. What *is* happening?'

The Earl put his hands to his head. 'Will somebody please tell them? I can't go through it all again.'

Timothy drew the two girls aside and started talking to them in a low voice. Penny gave a little scream. Stella remained silent, but her eyes widened in horror.

The Countess said urgently: 'George, we can't stand here all night like this. We must do something.'

'Yes, yes, of course. Losin' my grip a bit, I'm afraid. Just all too damn familiar. Doctor, first, I suppose, then the police. Lavinia, could you telephone them?'

'Of course.'

'I'll have to organise a search of the house. I'll rouse Merryweather, and he can wake the footmen. There are three of them, but it's still going to take some time.'

Gregory said: 'Well, you can count on me to help.'

'Yes, me too,' Tommy said eagerly.

'Oh, thank you. Well, William, Benjamin and Albert are all strapping lads, and even Merryweather's no weakling, so we should be able to handle him.'

Timothy turned away from the girls and was obviously about to speak. But before he could do so, Gregory addressed him directly.

'You'll probably be advised to keep out of it, dear cousin. I mean, *you're* not exactly a strapping lad, are you?'

Timothy's face remained expressionless but his complexion noticeably darkened. He moved towards Gregory and held out his hand. 'I appreciate your being so concerned for my safety.'

Clearly taken aback, Gregory hesitated for a second before taking the proffered hand.

Nobody afterwards could say precisely what happened next. With the speed of a striking cobra, Timothy pulled Gregory towards him, turned, put his left arm round Gregory's neck, bent his knees and drove back with his hips. The larger man's feet left the ground, he performed a graceful somersault in the air and the next second had landed on his back with a thump that shook the floor. Timothy said quietly: 'I have been practising ju-jitsu for a number of years, and am a 3rd Dan.'

As Gregory clambered awkwardly to his feet, the others gazed at Timothy speechlessly, the two girls with something like awe. 'Zowie!' Stella murmured under her breath, then softly to Penny: 'Did you know he could do that?'

Penny, wide-eyed, shook her head. She whispered: 'He goes to a gym twice a week, but I thought he just did physical jerks and things.'

'He's quite a guy, your pa.'

Meanwhile, as though nothing had happened, Timothy was addressing the Earl. 'Naturally, I will take part in the search. You are convinced, I take it, that this villain is still on the premises.'

'Um – what? Er...' He was uncertain whether or not to make any comment about what had happened, then decided it was better not to. 'Can't see any other explanation. I explained about our security system. Merryweather locked up at about ten thirty – he always reports to me as soon as he's done so – at which time the alarm automatically switches on. So the fellow must have got in before that. Now, we'd better search in pairs: each of us go with one of the servants. You three chaps better follow their leadin', as they all know the house like the backs of their hands. I don't suppose any of you ladies feel like goin' back to bed?' He looked in turn at Jean Mackenzie, Stella and Penny. There was a vigorous shaking of heads.

'Right, then, I suggest you all go downstairs with Lavinia. Stay together and you should be quite safe. Now I suppose I've got to wake Merryweather and tell him the news.'

CHAPTER NINETEEN

Gerry jumped to her feet as a light knock came at the door, and Dorothy opened her eyes. Gerry hurried to the door. 'Who is it?'

'Me.' It was the Earl's voice.

She opened the door. 'What's happening?' she asked.

He kept his voice low. 'We've just completed a search of the house. There's no sign of an intruder.'

Gerry's eyes widened. 'Are you sure?'

'Absolutely. We've looked in every room, every recess, in every cupboard, under every bed. Even the secret passage.'

'And he's certainly not in here.'

'That's what I was going to ask you. It suddenly occurred to me.'

'I checked under the bed and Dorry in the wardrobe. I suppose the alarm system *could* be faulty. I mean, nothing's absolutely infallible, so he could have got out.'

'Possible, I suppose. No doubt the police will check it.'

'You've called them?'

'Your mother will have done so by now.'

'Where is everybody?'

'Downstairs. I'm just going to join them. I need a drink. Er, you'll stay here, I suppose?'

Gerry was about to answer when Dorothy joined them in the doorway.

'How are you, my dear?' asked the Earl.

'All right, thank you.'

'Forgive my mentionin' it, but you haven't phoned your sister, have you?'

Dorothy shook her head. 'I explained to Gerry, she was going to a party this evening. I meant to phone about half-past twelve. I think she would have been back by that time. But then – it all happened. Er, what time is it?'

Lord Burford glanced at his watch. 'Just gone one thirty.'

'She's sure to be in bed by now.'

'But she'd want to be woken, wouldn't she?'

'She wouldn't hear the phone. It's in the hall, and neither Aggie nor I can hear it in our rooms. Mother's is the only bedroom it can be heard from. Of course, if you think I should try...'

'Well, it wouldn't do any harm, if you feel up to it.'

'Oh yes, I'll come down now.'

On the way downstairs, Gerry said: 'She'll have been wondering why you haven't phoned.'

'Yes, I expect so.'

'I wonder why she didn't call here.'

'I don't think she knows your number, actually.'

'Oh, and of course, we're ex-directory, so she couldn't get it from Enquiries. Stupid of me. And it's so easy, too: Alderley One.' She thought that to keep chatting away about trivialities might help a little to take the other girl's mind off the horror of the situation, but wasn't really hopeful.

She took Dorothy to the telephone room and waited outside while she made the call.

Lord Burford went to the drawing-room, where he found all the guests gathered. The women had been told about the result of the search, and everybody was looking rather grim as the full implications of this sank in.

Lord Burford crossed to the Countess. 'Did you get through all right?'

She nodded. 'Dr. Ingleby was out on a confinement, but his wife will notify him immediately he returns. I told her there was no great urgency, as there is nothing he can do. I also spoke to P.C. Dobson in the village – not going into any great detail. He was going to inform the County Police Headquarters in Westchester and then cycle here. I told him, too, that there was no hurry, as I knew you would want to complete the search before having to set off the alarm.'

'Quite right, my dear. Thank you.'

'And George – I'm so sorry. You were against this little house party from the start, I know. I talked you into it. And your worst fears have been realised. I feel very much to blame. But who could have anticipated that something like this could happen, again?'

'No need to blame yourself, Lavinia. I went along. Heaven help me, I went along.'

Dorothy came out of the telephone room in about three minutes. 'No reply.'

'Well, at least you can tell her you tried. What do you

want to do now? Come into the drawing-room with the others?'

'No, I think I'd like to go back up to my room.'

'Come on, then.'

'No, Gerry, there's no need for you to come with me.'

'Oh, but I don't mind, honestly.'

'No, really, you've been marvellous, but I would like to be on my own for a while.'

'If you're certain. Do you want anything?'

'A cup of tea would be nice.'

'All right, I'll have some sent up.'

'Thank you very much.'

'Oh, and don't be startled if you hear an alarm bell shortly. We'll be opening the door to let the doctor and police in.'

'Of course.'

Dorothy ascended the stairs. Gerry watched her until she disappeared from sight, then pulled the cord of the nearest bell. Merryweather arrived within seconds. He was fully dressed and as immaculate as ever.

'Merry, will you have some tea sent up to Miss Dorothy, please?'

'Certainly, my lady.' He started to turn away.

'And Merry, thank you. For taking all this so wonderfully in your stride, I mean. Please thank all the servants. I'm so sorry you're having to go through it all again.'

'That is quite all right, your ladyship. I, for one, am becoming quite accustomed to these occurrences.'

Gerry joined the others in the drawing-room. For the next ten minutes, conversation was virtually non-existent. When one had said how terrible it was and how inexplicable three or four times, there seemed nothing more to say.

At last there came the sound of the doorbell. The Earl heaved himself to his feet. 'That'll be Ingleby or Dobson.'

He went out to the great hall, where Merryweather was approaching the front doors. He unlocked and unbolted them, and pulled one open. Immediately a deafeningly loud clanging shattered the silence.

It was Dobson who was standing in the porch.

'Come in, Constable,' Lord Burford shouted above the din.

'Thank you, my lord.' He removed his helmet, carefully and unnecessarily wiped his feet and entered.

The Earl went up to him and spoke loudly into his ear. 'Come into the morning-room. Won't be so loud in there. It is morning, after all.'

He led the way and when he had shut the door behind them the noise was considerably muffled. 'What did my wife tell you, exactly?'

'Just that a lady had been found dead, my lord, and that it looked as though foul play might be involved.'

'I think that's pretty definite. Her name is Mrs Clara Saunders. She's a distant cousin of mine.'

Dobson took out his notebook and slowly wrote down the name. 'She would have been one of the mourners at the funeral, my lord?'

'Yes, she was the dead lady's daughter-in-law. D'you want me to go on?'

'I don't think there's much point, my lord. Better to wait until the CID arrive and give them all the details.'

'So, what do you want to do?'

'I had better inspect the remains, my lord. There is not much else that I can do.'

'Very well, I'll take you up.'

They had just reached Clara's room when the alarm bell blessedly fell silent.

The Earl opened the door. 'Nobody's touched anything, other, obviously, than the knob and the light switch.'

Dobson went into the room, looked down at Clara's body for a quarter of a minute and then came out. He took out a pocket watch, glanced at it, put it away and wrote in his notebook, saying as he did so: '*Viewed remains of victim at 2:10 a.m.* Right, my lord, I'll just wait here until CID arrive.'

'You don't happen to know who the investigating officer's going to be, do you?'

'It'll depend who's available, my lord.'

'Yes, of course. I do hope it's—' He broke off. 'Never mind.'

He went downstairs again.

CHAPTER TWENTY

It was just twelve minutes later when they heard the sound of car tyres on the gravel outside. Again the Earl went into the Great Hall. But this time when Merryweather opened the doors two men were standing there. The first was rather plump, had a drooping black moustache and a melancholy expression. He was wearing a raincoat and black bowler hat. With him was a tall, strongly built, brown-skinned young man.

Lord Burford gave a sigh of relief. 'Wilkins! I'm so glad it's you.'

Detective Chief-Inspector Wilkins came in, removing his bowler hat. 'Why, thank you, my lord. That is extremely gratifying.' He had a surprisingly deep and somewhat mournful voice, and did not sound in the least gratified. 'It's not often people are pleased to see me. And I must say this is like coming home, if I may make so bold.'

They shook hands. The Earl looked at the younger man. 'Detective-Sergeant Leather, isn't it? How are you?'

'Well, my lord, thank you.'

He turned back to Wilkins. 'How much have you been told?'

'Very little, my lord. Just that there has been another regrettable incident here. Murder, I believe.'

'Yes.'

Wilkins made a tutting sound. 'Dear, dear. Most unfortunate. Well, I can't say that I'm surprised.'

The Earl stared at him in astonishment. 'You're not? You mean you expected us to have another murder?'

'I wouldn't go that far, my lord. But twice I have been called to investigate murders here. You know the old saying, "Never two without three."'

'Bit superstitious, isn't it?'

'I am superstitious, my lord, I admit it. But I don't think that particular saying is superstitious. Two unusual occurrences in the same place, or involving the same person or persons, might well suggest some underlying cause leading to a third.'

'The only underlyin' cause I can think of is that blasted gypsy's curse. I'm startin' to think there might be somethin' in it. Otherwise, it's such an incredible coincidence.'

'Perhaps not, my lord. Let's wait and see.' He lowered his voice. 'And may I ask, my lord, do you have any film stars here this time?'

'No, nobody like that.'

'Or oil millionaires?'

'No, just relatives. One of them's an MP.'

'Really?' He seemed to perk up a little.

'Thinkin' of your memoirs, were you?'

He was amazed to see the Chief Inspector actually blush, but before he could reply two more men appeared in the doorway. One was carrying a small case and the other a camera and a large accessory bag.

'Perhaps my fingerprint man and photographer could be shown the deceased, my lord?'

'Yes, of course. Oh, and one of the other guests reported an intruder in her room, lurking by the dressing-table. I don't know whether he'll want to check in there as well.'

'Yes, indeed, my lord.'

'Merryweather, will you take these gentlemen to the scene of the crime, and also show them where Miss Simmons' room is. And if I'm not here when the doctor arrives, take him straight up. I'll speak to him afterwards.'

'My lord. Please follow me, officers.'

He started towards the grand staircase, the two policemen at his heels.

'You're not going up to see the body, Wilkins?'

'Not yet, my lord. I don't like looking at bodies. I find it so depressing, so I always put it off as long as possible. I suppose I'll have to take a peek sometime.' He sighed. 'Not that it'll tell me anything. I would prefer it if you could list the *dramatis personae*, as it were, and give me an account of the events of the day.'

The Earl led the way, to the morning-room, they sat down and Leather produced a notebook and pencil.

The Earl ran his fingers through his hair. 'Difficult to decide where to start. You know we had a funeral here yesterday?'

'Yes, my lord. So a melancholy day on two counts.'

'Well, the funeral wasn't too melancholy, actually. Quite a nice funeral, as funerals go. It was a great aunt of mine. The – the victim was a Mrs Clara Saunders, the daughter-in-law of my great aunt.'

Wilkins had rested his elbow on the table, with the

palm of his hand supporting his chin. He closed his eyes and might have been asleep. The Earl eyed him doubtfully for a second before continuing.

Twenty-five minutes later the Earl sat back. 'I think that's all I can tell you at the moment. Sorry, if it was a bit incoherent, but I don't think I left out anything of importance.'

Wilkins opened his eyes. 'Not at all, my lord. It was extremely clear and comprehensive. Let me just see if I've got the names of your guests correct: Miss Dorothy Saunders, stepdaughter of the deceased; Mr Timothy Saunders, KC; Miss Penelope Saunders, his daughter; Mr Gregory Carstairs, MP; Mr Tommy Lambert; Miss Stella Simmons; and Miss Jean Mackenzie, companion to your great aunt. All of these people, with the exception of the latter, being relatives of your great aunt, and indeed of your good self.'

Wilkins had made no notes or consulted Leather, and Lord Burford looked impressed. 'That's it. Very distant relatives, of course.'

'And some relatives can never be distant enough, can they? But all of these were beneficiaries under your great aunt's will. Now tell me, this unpleasant contretemps at the reading of the will, when Mrs Saunders made these threats: do you think they were genuine? I mean, did she really know damaging facts about the other beneficiaries, and was she serious when she made her threat about exposing them?'

The Earl sighed. 'I honestly don't know, Wilkins. It may have been just pique. And, of course, Clara was a great forager-out and collector of secrets. But I can't believe she knew somethin' damaging about each of them.

One, perhaps, or maybe two. But if she did, then yes, I think she would have made sure the facts got known. I'm sure, though, that her accusation of some conspiracy between them to get her cut out of the will is absolute nonsense. Most of them barely know each other, as far as I can gather. Anyway, I'm certain none of them knew my great aunt was going to leave enough for it to make it worth anyone's while to try and cut Clara out.'

'Now, about this search you made, my lord. You are absolutely certain no one could have been concealed in the house.'

'Quite certain.' He told Wilkins all about the search.

'And he couldn't have sort of dodged from one place to another, as you were searching?'

'We thought of that. We did it in a pretty systematic way. After we searched every room, Merryweather or I – he's got the only other set of keys – locked the doors that are lockable and one of the other searchers stuck sticky tape across the doors that aren't, so no one could get in to hide there without moving it, and obviously couldn't replace it after he was in. After we'd finished, we went back and checked every door. There were eight of us, and it took nearly an hour.'

'That sounds like almost military efficiency. And it certainly seems conclusive. However, you do realise the implications of it, I'm sure.'

'Only too well, Wilkins. Unless somehow the alarm was circumvented, or faulty, the murderer's one of my guests.'

'And which of them do you fancy, my lord?'

Lord Burford jerked his head up. 'You're asking *me*?'

'You're the nearest thing I have to an expert witness, my lord. You know them all, at least to a certain extent.'

'Not well enough to commit myself on that score – especially after the other times, when all my early ideas were totally wrong. Anyway, how d'you know it wasn't me?'

'Oh no, my lord. One of the things Chief Superintendent Allgood got right last time was that you'd never murder one of your guests at Alderley. Wouldn't be the done thing, would it?'

'Is murder ever the done thing?'

'Some of your peers have thought so, my lord. And not only in the distant past.'

'Just as long as you can clear it up for us quickly. You did wonders the other times.'

'Oh, I had great deal of luck, my lord. Can't expect that to continue. I'm not sanguine, not sanguine at all.'

At that moment Merryweather entered. 'Dr. Ingleby has completed his examination, my lord, and would like a word with Mr Wilkins.'

'Show him in, Merryweather. Oh – unless you want to speak to him alone, Wilkins?'

'No, no, my lord, that will be quite all right.'

Dr. Ingleby was tall, in his thirties, with a mass of ginger hair. He had been the Alderley medical attendant for a number of years and was also the assistant police surgeon.

Lord Burford stood up and shook hands with him. 'Sorry to have had to drag you out, Ingleby.'

'All part of the job.'

'What can you tell us, doctor?' Wilkins asked.

'There'll have to be a post-mortem, of course, but cause of death almost certainly suffocation; there are small haemorrhages of the upper eyelids, blue lips and fingertips, slight contusions around the mouth – usual signs. It was very probably done with the pillow from the bed. There are what seem to be marks of her teeth on it.'

'Would it have required considerable strength?'

Ingleby shook his head. 'Not provided she was taken by surprise, asleep or just lying down. The murderer would have been able to throw their whole weight on top of her. She clearly put up quite a struggle and got her head over the side of the bed, but that wouldn't have prevented the assailant keeping the pillow clapped over her mouth.'

'And the time of death, Doctor?'

'Between eleven thirty and twelve thirty, with perhaps ten minutes' leeway either way.'

'It was about half twelve when we found the body,' Lord Burford said.

'Did you touch her?' Ingleby asked.

'Just felt for a pulse.'

'Did you notice if the skin was cold?'

'Hard to say. I just took her wrist between my thumb and forefinger. I'd say it felt fairly cold. But not icy, if you know what I mean.'

'That's not a lot of use in narrowing the time of death further, then.'

'But not before eleven twenty, doctor?' Wilkins said.

'Better say eleven fifteen, to be on the safe side. Look, I must go. I'll let you have my report.'

'Thank you, doctor,' Wilkins said.

'Would you care for a drink, or a coffee, Ingleby?' the Earl asked.

'Not just now, thank you. Good night.' He went out, then put his head back round the door. 'I didn't step on any of the cufflinks,' he said, then went out again.

CHAPTER TWENTY-ONE

The Earl and Wilkins stared at each other. 'What did he say?' asked the Earl.

'That he didn't step on any of the cufflinks.'

'What on earth did he mean?'

'I was just going to ask you that, my lord. You didn't see any?'

'No, but I only really looked at Clara.'

'Well, I suppose we'd better go up and take a look-see.'

'D'you want me to come along?'

'It might be helpful, my lord.'

They went out and up the stairs. The photographer and the fingerprint man were standing outside the door of Clara's room, talking to Dobson.

'Finished, lads?' Wilkins asked.

The fingerprint man answered. 'Yes, guv. Didn't take long. Hardly any dabs. The butler explained all the bedrooms were dusted and polished before the guests moved in. Three sets altogether, all women's by the look. One set in here and in the other room, nearly all on movable things – ornaments and the like. Obviously the maid's. She must have moved them to dust and polish and then put them back after. Then there are the dead lady's prints in here, and another's in the other room, no doubt the occupant's. Killer probably wore gloves.'

'You'll have to take the maid's and Miss Simmons' prints, just to confirm it, but tomorrow'll be soon enough.'

He stepped into the room and stood silently looking down at the body of Clara. Then he went close to the bed and turned round, to get a better view of her face. 'A sad lady, I should imagine, my lord.'

'I never thought of her like that, Wilkins, but you could just be right.'

Wilkins gave a little shiver. 'I hate murder. Never get used to it.' He picked up the top pillow from the bed and handed it to the fingerprint man. 'Take this with you, when you go. It could be the murder weapon. Doctor said something queer about cufflinks.'

'Oh yes, they're all over the place. You can't really see them from this side of the bed – except that one.' He pointed to a small square of gold touching the leg of the bed near the skirting board. 'But if you go round...'

Wilkins did so. 'My, my,' he said, 'how very rum. Come and look, my lord.'

The Earl, who had remained in the doorway, joined him. 'Great Scot,' he muttered. There were cufflinks everywhere. Most of them were on the floor, but there were two on the chair, one on the bedside table, and three on the dressing-table.

'Did you count them?' Wilkins asked the fingerprint man.

'Only roughly, guv. We spotted about thirty. That's without moving anything, or making a proper search. I didn't dust them – would have taken far too long.'

'Quite right. Any ideas, my lord?'

'Well, they're mine. At least, some of them are. I recognise that one, and that one, and one of those on the dressing-table. Which means they're probably all mine.'

'*All* of them? Really? How remarkable.' Then light seemed to dawn. 'Oh, I see, collect cufflinks, do you, my lord, as well as firearms?'

'No. Well, not purposely. I get given 'em, and never throw any away. Stupid, really. There are a lot of single ones, which have lost their partners.'

'Where would they normally be kept?

'In a little box in my dressing-room – the other side of the corridor, just beyond the stairs.'

'Well, perhaps your lordship would be so kind as to take Smithson here and let him dust the box for prints.'

'Oh yes, of course. Come along, my dear feller.' He went out and Leather took the opportunity to enter the room.

'What d'you make of it, Jack?'

'To me, sir, it looks as if he's deliberately placed them away from the door, so that they can't be seen unless you come right in – except for that one by the leg of the bed.'

'Well, some of them *can* be seen.' Wilkins went back to the doorway. 'Those three on the dressing-table, for instance.'

'Yes, but they're not noticeable. I mean, if you just glanced into the room, you wouldn't remark on them.'

'True. I reckon there's a simpler explanation, though.'

'What's that?'

Wilkins made the movement of an underarm throw.

'Oh, you mean he chucked them in?'

'Yes, from the doorway. Threw them quite hard and most of them cleared the bed. Probably in a hurry.'

'But why do it at all?'

'You tell me.'

Leather's brow furrowed. 'Some sort of symbolic act?'

'Symbolic of what?'

'Let me see. Links. Things linked together. A broken link. Many links, joining two people, now scattered, or thrown away. Or cuffs. Handcuffs. Restraint. Captivity. He's saying to the dead woman: all links between us have been discarded, you hold me in captivity no longer. On the other hand, of course, he's thrown them at her, or surrounded her with them. So perhaps he's saying the links binding us will always be there. You can never get away from me, even in death.'

Wilkins pulled at his ear. 'Bit of a contradiction there, isn't there?'

'Yes, well, either could be true. It's only a theory.'

'Well, let's make another one on the same lines. A cuff can mean a sort of slap on the head. Links are seaside golf courses. So we could surmise that the deceased lady once hit somebody on a golf course, and this was an act of revenge.'

Leather grinned. 'OK, my effort was a bit far-fetched.'

'I've got nothing against far-fetched theories. I've had a few that turned out to be right.'

At that moment the Earl and Smithson returned. 'Box quite empty,' the Earl said.

'No dabs at all, guv,' Smithson added. 'Been wiped clean.'

'That would mean they were definitely taken by the murderer, wouldn't it, sir?' said Leather. 'Because he obviously expected us to be called in. Someone who'd just done it for a prank wouldn't have anticipated the box being dusted for prints.'

'Yes, good point, lad.'

Leather obviously felt that he'd redeemed himself after his theorising, and looked pleased.

Smithson said: 'The only other unusual thing is that postcard, guv, on the bedside table.'

Wilkins moved over and looked down at the white card. On it were written in big block capitals the words IN MEMORY OF MISS DORA LETHBRIDGE.

'This been dusted, too?'

'Yes. Nothing.'

Wilkins picked it up and turned it over. The back was blank. 'Would your lordship have ever heard of a Miss Dora Lethbridge?'

'No, not that I can recall.'

'Oh well.' Wilkins put the card in his pocket.

There was silence. Everybody was looking at Wilkins, who suddenly seemed to be far away and was staring moodily at the carpet. Then he came to himself and rubbed his hands together. 'Right, so what shall we do now?' He looked round, hopefully.

It wasn't quite clear to whom the question was addressed. After a few seconds, Lord Burford took it upon himself to answer. 'That's rather up to you, my dear fellow.'

'Yes. Yes, I suppose it is.' He looked depressed. Then he brightened. 'Oh yes, the armour. Better take a look at that, I suppose.'

'Lord, I'd forgotten all about that. Come along. I think it was Albert and young Tommy who checked in there during the search.'

He led the way round the corner into the east corridor, the others following, like a retinue of attendants. The art gallery was half way along on the right.

Wilkins said: 'I see there's an open fanlight over the doors. Accounts for the crash being heard so far afield.'

'Yes, we were told years ago that it was a good idea to keep a flow of air through, particularly in the hot weather; helps stop the pictures getting warped or the paint cracking, or something. We keep the windows open a couple of inches, as well. I ought to lock the gallery at nights, really, but we've got so reliant on our alarm system that I don't usually bother. And, of course, the windows are barred.' As he had been speaking, he had torn a length of brown sticky tape from the crack between the doors, thrown them open and turned on the lights. Now he stopped short. 'Good lord.'

He went in and the others followed him. They saw that the component pieces of the armour were strewn across the room for a distance of about ten feet. The wooden frame to which they had been attached was lying near to the small plinth on which the assembled suit had stood, just to the left of the doors that led to the gun collection.

The Earl crossed the gallery, the others behind him, and looked at the wreckage more closely. 'The impact on landing seems to have snapped the cord that was attaching the parts to the frame. Wouldn't have expected that. Could have perished, I suppose. Must admit I haven't had the thing apart in donkey's years.' He scratched his head and looked around. 'None of it makes sense. If he came in here just to hide, he might have crossed to try and get in the gun-room, tried the doors and found them locked. But then why would he go to the left? You can clearly see that the windows are barred, so he couldn't have been looking for a way out.'

'Might he have been thinking of trying to hide behind the sofa?' Leather suggested.

The piece of furniture in question, one of several chairs of various kinds placed around the room, for the benefit of people wanting to sit and study the paintings, was against the wall to the left of the plinth.

'Might conceal him from anyone in the right of the room,' Lord Burford said, 'but he could still be seen from the doorway.'

'I'm not so sure, my lord. Smithy, go and crouch down to the left of it.'

With an inaudible mutter under his breath, Smithson went across and did as Leather instructed. Leather backed to the doorway. 'Can you make yourself smaller?'

Smithson shuffled back and to his left and bent his head. 'That's about it, Sarge.'

'No, I can't see him from here now,' Leather said. 'So it would conceal him from anyone just glancing in. Pretty useless sort of hiding place, though. OK, Smithy.'

Smithson scrambled to his feet and came back to the centre of the room. 'Perhaps he was groping about in the dark, and just cannoned into it,' he suggested.

'But it looks as though it was knocked over with real force,' said the Earl. 'It obviously fell straight forward: there are no pieces to the side, so he didn't cannon into it from the right. And look at the way the pieces are scattered. If it had just toppled over gently, you'd expect them more or less to stay where they fell.'

'Might have slid, my lord,' Leather said. 'The parquet blocks are very smooth and shiny.'

'Mm.' The Earl nodded. 'Maybe you're right, Sergeant. I suppose that is the only logical explanation.'

'Look at this, sarge,' said the photographer. He'd wandered a little to the right and was pointing to the floor a few feet from the inner wall. The others, apart from Wilkins, joined him. Scattered around were a number of small pieces of shattered glass.

Leather crouched down for a closer inspection. 'Looks like a broken wine glass.'

'Shall I take a photo?'

'Might as well.'

'Well, what do you think of it all, Wilkins?' asked the Earl.

The Chief Inspector, who had apparently rapidly lost interest in their conversation and was paying more attention to a painting of some horses by Stubbs than to anything else, seemed to pull himself back with an effort.

'I don't, my lord.'

'Don't what?'

'Think. About this. It's another rum thing, like the cufflinks. There'll probably be a third. But I don't reckon this one's going to help us catch the murderer, so I'm not going to waste my time racking my brains about it for now.'

'Prints, sir?' Leather suggested. Smithson gave a low groan.

'I heard that, Smithy,' Leather said.

Wilkins shook his head. 'It'd take ages, all probably to no avail. After all, any one of the guests might have come in here, quite innocently, and touched the armour, during the afternoon. Quite right to suggest it, though, Jack. But better take a couple of shots,' he added, to the photographer, 'just for the record.'

When the man had done so, Wilkins addressed him and Smithson. 'OK, you lads can clear off.'

'Right, guv. Goodnight.' They started to move away.

'I think,' Wilkins added. They froze in mid-movement. Wilkins concentrated for a moment, then he said, 'Yes, all right, go and get a bit of kip.'

They hastily departed, before he changed his mind again.

The Earl, Wilkins, Dobson and Leather followed them, Lord Burford this time locking the gallery doors. Then they made their way back to the main corridor. When they reached Clara's room, Wilkins said: 'Dobson, you can collect those damned cufflinks. Try and make sure you get them all. When you've done that, you can vamoose, too.'

'Right, Chief Inspector.'

'What about prints on them, sir?' Leather suggested.

'They're so small you'd never get more than a tiny section of the print. Still, better be on the safe side, I suppose. Pick them up with tweezers, Dobson. I've got some here, somewhere.' He started to search through his pockets. 'Put them in a bag and give it to me or the sergeant. We won't bother to dust them yet, but we can if we need to later on. It'll mean, though, that Smithson'll have to take everyone's prints tomorrow, while he's here, just in case we do need them for elimination.'

He found the tweezers and handed them to the constable.

'I haven't got a bag, sir.'

'Oh drat it. I should have got one from Smithson. Chase after him, Jack.'

'Why not just put 'em back in the box?' Lord Burford suggested.

'Good idea, my lord.'

'I'll get it.' The Earl hurried off.

'We can't do much more here now,' Wilkins said. 'But I suppose we'd better put the poor lady to rights. Come on, Jack.'

They laid Clara straight in the bed, crossed her hands on her breast and covered her with the sheet. As they finished, the Earl returned and handed Dobson the box. Then the Earl, Wilkins and Leather went out, leaving Dobson to his task.

'Now, my lord, I suppose I'd better come down and have a word with your guests.' The prospect seemed to depress him still further.

They went down the staircase. In the great hall, Wilkins paused before a large gilt mirror and carefully straightened his tie and smoothed down his hair. Lord Burford opened the double doors to the drawing-room and entered, Wilkins and Leather on his heels. Everyone looked at them.

The Earl said: 'Detective Chief Inspector Wilkins would like a word. Wilkins, you remember my wife.'

Wilkins went forward and bowed over the Countess'

proffered hand. 'Yes, indeed. How do you do, my lady?'

'Chief Inspector. I am pleased it is you. We are relying on you.'

'And my daughter.'

'Lady Geraldine.'

Gerry smiled up at him. 'Hello again, Mr Wilkins. We can't go on meeting like this.'

The Earl introduced him to the others. When he got to Stella, Wilkins said: 'Ah, you're the lady who found an intruder in her room.'

Stella nodded.

'Must have been very frightening.'

'Surprisingly, not really. I was angry, more than scared.'

'Nothing taken?'

'Not that I could see. There wasn't much of my stuff there, anyway: hairbrush and comb, make-up, sponge bag, things like that. Nothing remotely valuable.'

'And that was just about the same time as the crash?'

'I think so. I wasn't conscious of actually hearing the crash, but it has to have been that which woke me.'

'I heard it,' Penny put in. 'But I'm a very light sleeper. It was hardly any time after when Stella started shouting.'

'It must have been within eight or ten seconds,' Gerry added. 'Dorry and I heard the crash, rushed to the door, and heard Stella start to shout almost at once.'

Lord Burford moved on. 'Miss Mackenzie, friend of my great aunt.'

Jean Mackenzie took a deep breath. 'Chief Inspector, I—' She stopped, then said quietly: 'How do you do?'

The Earl completed the introductions, then said: 'Right,

Chief Inspector, if there's anything you want to say, the floor's yours.'

Wilkins cleared his throat. 'Just to confirm, ladies and gentlemen, that there seems no doubt Mrs Saunders was indeed murdered.'

There was little reaction to this until after a few seconds Stella spoke: 'And by one of us, right?'

There was a gasp from the Countess. Gerry though shot an admiring glance at Stella. Miss Mackenzie gave a little cry of dismay.

Gregory said: 'I say, steady on.'

Timothy said: 'A perfectly logical deduction.'

Penny uttered a reproachful wail. 'Daddy!'

Tommy assumed a sepulchral voice. 'So who done it? Who done the foul deed?' He fell on his knees in front of Wilkins and held up clasped hands. 'I am innocent, Inspector, I swear I am innocent. Have mercy. Think of my two wives and ten helpless children.'

'Oh, stop playing the fool, man!' Timothy snapped irritably. 'This is serious.'

'Yes, I know. Sorry.' Tommy sat back down, looking a little embarrassed.

Wilkins said: 'There is at least the possibility that the alarm system is faulty and that an intruder did manage to escape without setting it off. We cannot get an expert to check it until tomorrow. There's not much point in doing anything further tonight, so as far as I'm concerned you can all go to bed now, unless there is anything any of you wish to tell me tonight.'

He looked round. Miss Mackenzie opened her mouth as if to speak, then obviously changed her mind and closed it again. The others shook their heads. 'Very well. I will, of course, be wanting to speak to you all later in the day. I trust there will be no problem for anyone in remaining here?'

There was a general shaking of heads. 'It's confoundedly inconvenient,' Timothy said, 'but it is plainly unavoidable.'

'And I'm afraid we're going to have to take your fingerprints tomorrow, for the purposes of elimination. They will, of course, be destroyed when the case is closed. Good night.'

Wilkins backed towards the door, giving little nods of the head to everybody in turn, as if exiting from the presence of royalty. He went out. Leather, who had remained just inside the door, followed him. Lord Burford went out after them.

'That's a remarkable young lady, my lord,' Wilkins said.

'Miss Simmons?'

'Yes. Just coming out like that with what everybody was thinking.'

'She's a journalist. They tend to like things out in the open. Sorry about young Tommy.'

'Think nothing of it, my lord. Everybody reacts in a different way when they're frightened. That's Mr Lambert's way.'

'Oh, by the way, you haven't seen Dorothy – the stepdaughter. She's still in her room.'

'That'll keep till the morning.'

'Good, good. Doubt if she's really up to it tonight. Oh, and it's just occurred to me: we've got no burglar alarm for the rest of the night. If one of those people is the killer, they could easily do a bunk.'

'Oh, I hope they do, my lord, I really hope they do. Make my job a lot simpler. Easy to catch someone you know is guilty. Much easier than finding out who the guilty party is.'

'But don't I remember your saying something last time along the lines of "If you let a criminal out of your sight you might never see him again."'

'A *criminal*, yes – a professional criminal. They've often made contingency plans to disappear in an emergency: money, false papers, clothes, stored somewhere safe. But none of these suspects are professionals in that sense; they'd all have the dickens of a job just to vanish without trace.'

At that moment they saw Dobson descending the stairs. He was carrying the cufflink box carefully in both hands, came across and presented them to Wilkins like a votive offering.

'Thanks. Get them all?'

'I think so, sir. Can't be dead sure, of course, but I looked under the bed, behind the dressing-table, everywhere else I could think of.'

'Good man.' He turned back to the Earl. 'We'll have to hang onto these, I'm afraid, just in case there *are* prints on them. Don't know how you'll manage tomorrow. I could lend you mine. Not such good quality, I'm sure, but—'

'Much obliged, my dear chap, but at the moment I don't feel I ever want to see another cufflink. I'll be happy to wear my sleeves rolled all day tomorrow.'

'Very well, my lord. I don't think there's much more

we can do now. We will return in the morning. I expect it would be convenient if we were not too early. About ten thirty, say.'

'Oh, that's decent of you. I expect everyone will appreciate that.'

'The ambulance will be coming to collect the body, so I'll tell them to leave it until about then, too. Well, goodnight, my lord.'

'Goodnight, Wilkins, Sergeant, Constable.'

Merryweather showed them out, closed and locked the doors. He turned round, with an almost indiscernible sigh.

'Merryweather, we'll put everything back a bit tomorrow morning. Breakfast about nine thirty be early enough. Tell the servants they can all sleep in a bit longer.'

'Thank you, my lord. They will welcome that. I, however, will be rising at my usual hour.'

'I'm sure you will, Merryweather, I'm sure you will. G'night.'

The Earl returned to the drawing-room and explained the situation to the others. Slowly they trooped upstairs to their rooms. But it was a long time before anyone slept.

CHAPTER TWENTY-TWO

Dorothy crept almost furtively down the grand staircase. It was just gone seven a.m., but there was no sign of life and Alderley was enveloped in silence. It made Dorothy feel she must not on any account disturb the stillness. She reached the bottom and made her way along the short corridor that led to the telephone room. She reached it, turned the knob and pushed. The door didn't move. She pushed harder, but it was definitely locked.

Dorothy stood there irresolutely. It was vital she phoned Agatha now. It couldn't possibly be delayed any longer. She wondered if the room was always locked at night. But why? It seemed most odd.

Eventually, Dorothy returned to the great hall. Should she just go back to her room and wait there until she heard people moving about? Or wait down here? Or walk to the village and find a telephone kiosk? Dorothy's life was a series of such uncertainties, tiny in themselves but a never-ending source of worry for her.

Then she gave a terrific start as a voice behind her said quietly: 'Can I be of assistance, miss?'

She spun round. 'Oh! Mist— er, Merryweather. You startled me.'

'I do beg your pardon, miss. I did not realise you had not heard me approaching.'

'You walk so quietly.'

'I know, miss, and I realise that on occasions it can be a fault, but seem unable to correct it. Lady Geraldine has remarked amusingly that I should go to evening classes and take clumping lessons.'

'Please don't apologise. Normally, I would have thought nothing of it. But I am rather on edge.'

'Perfectly understandable, miss, in view of the shocking occurrence. May I take this opportunity of offering my most sincere condolences?'

'Thank you. Thank you very much. Er, I need to make a phone call.'

'I will show you where the telephone is, miss.'

'No, I know where it is. I've just been there. But the door seems to be locked.'

Merryweather's right eyebrow rose about an eighth of an inch. 'How very strange. I have never known it to be so before. If you will kindly follow me I will investigate.'

He led her back to the telephone room, turned the doorknob and pushed. The door opened.

Dorothy gave a gasp. 'It *was* locked! I swear it.'

Merryweather crossed to the phone and felt the receiver and mouthpiece. Then he put his hand on the base and nodded. 'I would say the contraption has definitely been used within the last few minutes, miss. The earpiece and mouthpiece are very slightly warmer than the rest.'

'Oh, Mr Merryweather, how clever! I should never have

thought of that. But I wonder why they locked themselves in. And where did they go?'

'There is a back staircase at the far end of the corridor, which leads to the first floor, miss.'

'Of course, I remember seeing it. Well, I can call my sister now. Thank you.'

'And may I get you some tea, miss?'

'Yes, please, thank you.'

'Breakfast has been put back today, owing to the unusual – or perhaps I should not use that particular adjective – owing to the unfortunate circumstances, and the kitchen staff are not up yet. However, I would be happy to prepare something for you myself.'

'That's very kind, but no thank you. Tea will be splendid.'

Merryweather gave a slight bow and withdrew. Dorothy went to the telephone.

Needless to say, Gerry was the first of the others down, though it was ten o'clock when she breezed into the breakfast room and began helping herself to devilled kidneys from the heated sideboard. She was feeling excited and, probably alone among the occupants of Alderley, greatly looking forward to what lay ahead. During the last two cases she had made pretty much a prize idiot of herself, totally failing to spot the murderers; and, worse, nearly getting herself killed and having to be rescued. She was determined that this time she really was going to solve the case. She was just starting her breakfast when Merryweather entered.

'Good morning, your ladyship.'

'Morning, Merry. Seems I'm the first for once.'

'Not quite, my lady. Miss Dorothy was down at seven a.m. She telephoned her sister, and asked me to inform you that Miss Agatha said she would set out on her motor cycle as early as possible, and hopes to be here at approximately eleven o'clock.'

'Oh, good. She'll be able to look after Miss Dorothy and leave me free to pursue my enquiries. Where is Dorothy now?'

'After partaking of a cup of tea, she returned to her bedroom. She had not slept previously, but suddenly became somnolent and decided to try and obtain some repose before Miss Agatha and Detective Chief Inspector Wilkins arrive.'

'Thanks, Merry.' She gave a little cough. 'Got a bit of a sore throat this morning. Miss Agatha's supposed to have tonsillitis. Hope I haven't picked it via Miss Dorry.'

'I tend to doubt that one could so rapidly contract it via a third person, not herself showing symptoms, my lady. May I suggest you may have strained it yesterday during your full-throated rendering of *She'll Be Coming Round the Mountain*?'

'You heard that?'

'Yes, my lady, I happened to be on the terrace outside at the time – I had occasion to go out to speak to MacDonald about some flowers – and the library window was open.'

She gave him a quizzical look. 'I see. Very convenient. It was a dying wish of Great Aunt Florence, by the way.'

'I surmised something of that nature.'

'Is there anything that happens in Alderley that you don't know about, Merry?'

'I do my best to avoid that state of affairs, my lady. In the interests of the Family.'

'So, perhaps you know who murdered Mrs Saunders?'

'Unfortunately I do not. However, apropos of that, there was one rather unusual incident this morning, which might be of interest to you if you are concerning yourself with the elucidation of the mystery.'

'You bet. Tell me.' Gerry was all ears.

He explained about the locked door of the telephone room and how he had deduced that the telephone had recently been used.

'Well done, Merry!' she said when he'd finished. 'You're obviously a natural detective. I can see I'm going to have to get you to help me on this case. After all, Bunter, Lord Peter Wimsey's man, often assists him in his investigations.'

'I am slightly acquainted with Mr Bunter, my lady; an admirable man, but I fear I do not share either his ability at or enthusiasm for ratiocination and criminology.'

'Where's your spirit of adventure?'

'I have none, your ladyship.'

He went out. Gerry pondered. Why should one of the guests not want it known they had made a phone call? After all, most of them would be likely to have people they would need to notify of their delayed return. So why try to conceal the fact?

The Earl and Countess were the next down, followed at few-minute intervals by the guests. If the atmosphere at dinner the previous evening had been strained, the tension this morning was almost palpable, with no one in the mood for talking.

At about twenty-five past ten, the ambulance, which

was to convey Clara's body to the mortuary, arrived. There was some discussion as to whether Dorothy should be awakened to witness the departure, but in the end it was decided it would be better if she were not. Everyone else gathered in the great hall and there was a solemn silence as the stretcher was carried downstairs and outside. Only Miss Mackenzie showed any sign of emotion, dabbing at her eyes with a handkerchief, but Gerry suspected this was a matter of form for her, rather than genuine feeling.

After this, nobody seemed quite to know what to do. People wandered from room to room, sitting down, flicking through magazines or books or just staring into space. Others went outside and mooched round, looking at the flower beds or just staring up at the house. It was as though everyone had retreated into a private world. Gerry had planned to engage each of them in turn in conversation and question them so subtly that they would not even realise that they were being interrogated; but their attitudes made this impossible. It was as if the spectre of the return of Wilkins hung like the sword of Damocles over the entire household, she said to herself, enjoying the mixed metaphor.

At last, at about ten forty, a police car rolled up the drive and stopped in front of the house. Wilkins and Leather alighted. Merryweather admitted them and showed them into the morning-room, where the family were waiting.

'Good morning, your lordship, your ladyship, your ladyship,' Wilkins began, sounding rather liked a cracked gramophone record. He looked more cheerful this morning. 'First of all, let me apologise for being late, but there were many things to attend to. Now, while Mr Merryweather is here, could you tell me who it was who served the deceased lady refreshments in her room last night? It seems she must have been the last person, apart from the murderer, to see Mrs Saunders alive.'

'It was the maid Janet, Chief Inspector,' Merryweather said.

'I'd like Sergeant Leather to have a word with her, if that is agreeable to you, my lady.'

'Of course,' said the Countess. 'I trust she is in no way a suspect, Mr Wilkins.'

'Oh, by no means, your ladyship. And it is highly unlikely she will be able to tell us anything useful, but we have to go through the form. And perhaps afterwards the Sergeant could briefly speak to the other servants, just on the off-chance that one of them heard or saw something.'

'Arrange that, will you, please, Merryweather?'

'Yes, my lady. And will you be requiring coffee?'

'Well, I for one only finished breakfast about twenty minutes ago,' said the Earl. 'And I imagine you'll be wanting to make a start straight away with your investigations, eh, Wilkins?'

'Actually, my lord, a cup of coffee would be most welcome.'

'Oh, then, of course. I suppose we'll all have some. Help to get us back to the normal timetable, I suppose, at least.'

Merryweather and Leather went out. 'Better take the weight off your feet, Wilkins,' said the Earl.

'Thank you, my lord.' He sat down in a deep leather easy chair and gave a sigh.

'Tell me,' Gerry said, 'why do you rule out any of the servants being involved?'

'I asked Mr Merryweather when I arrived whether any of them were new, and he said no, that they'd all been with you for at least three or four years, many much longer. They're all local people. I just cannot imagine one of them suddenly deciding to murder one of your guests. In fact, I have never come across a country house case in which any of the servants was guilty. It's true that some years ago there did seem to be a spate of cases all over the country, and in the United States, too, I believe, in which the butler turned out to be the villain, but that trend is long past.'

'Oh, talking of butlers, Merryweather was telling me he did a piece of detection this morning.' She narrated the story of the locked door.

Wilkins nodded. 'Interesting,' he said, not sounding remotely interested.

'Why would somebody do that, do you suppose?'

'Someone having a private conversation and didn't want to be interrupted, I imagine. Probably didn't hear somebody trying the door, finished their call and went back up to their room via the back staircase.'

'Oh,' Gerry said, feeling rather crushed. 'Is that all?'

Just then William, the footman, entered with the coffee. When they were all sipping from steaming cups, Wilkins said: 'Oh, by the way, my lord, you may be interested to know that there were thirty-nine of your cufflinks in the room.'

'Good lord, never knew I had that many. Still, quite an evocative number, what?'

'Ah yes, your lordship is doubtless referring to the Church of England's Thirty-Nine Articles of Religion.'

The Earl looked a little awkward. 'No, actually, I

was thinking of *The Thirty-nine Steps*. You know, John Buchan.'

'Oh, of course. I'm afraid I read very little crime fiction or thrillers.'

'Too much of a busman's holiday?' Gerry asked.

'That's about it, Lady Geraldine.'

'So, what do you like to read?'

Wilkins leaned back. 'Well, I have very catholic tastes, but if I had to choose one author, I suppose it would be Dostoevsky – even though his perhaps greatest work is called *Crime and Punishment*.'

Gerry looked impressed. 'Golly. I'm afraid I've never read anything of his.'

'Oh, you should, Lady Geraldine. Amazing man: such insight, such power. I've read everything he wrote, I believe.'

'In translation, I suppose?' she said dryly, feeling a little irritated.

Wilkins smiled. 'I'm afraid so. I do try it in the original from time to time, but every other page I come across a word I don't know and have to stop and look it up, which does slow you down.'

They all stared at him in amazement. The Earl said: 'You read Russian?'

'Not very well, my lord.'

'So you speak it, too, then?'

'After a fashion. Enough to get by.'

''Pon my soul. You show me up. I only speak a little French.'

'I certainly found French easier to master,' Wilkins said.

'Well, I must say, you're full of surprises, Wilkins.' Lord Burford took out his pocket watch and glanced at it meaningfully. 'Expect you'll be wanting to get on with your enquiries.'

'I'm in no hurry, my lord.'

'Oh, I was just thinkin' the guests will be gettin' a bit anxious.'

'That's just it, Daddy, don't you see?' Gerry said. 'Mr Wilkins is deliberately keeping them waiting, simply to get them nervous.'

'Oh.' Lord Burford's jaw dropped a little. 'I see. Is that really it, Wilkins?'

'I'm afraid Lady Geraldine is wise to me, my lord. The longer you keep people waiting, the more on edge they get, and the more on edge they are, the more likely they are to slip up, let something out they didn't mean to.'

'But they may not all have anything *to* let slip out.'

'Oh, my lord…' Wilkins shook his head reproachfully.

'Everyone's got something to hide, isn't that so, Mr Wilkins?' Gerry said.

'Almost invariably, Lady Geraldine. And there is something I want to ask you.'

'Oh dear. I'm petrified now.'

'No cause to be. It's just that from what his lordship was telling me last night, you were with Miss Dorothy for an hour before the discovery of the body.'

'More than an hour.'

'And she didn't leave you even for five minutes?'

'Not for five seconds. I know what you're getting at, but it's out of the question. Mummy came down from talking to Clara. Dorothy was there then and she remained in the drawing-room until we heard the crash and rushed up to see what it was. I was at her shoulder the moment she first saw the body. She's absolutely in the clear. Anybody else might have killed Clara: Mummy, Daddy—'

'Really, Geraldine!' This from the Countess.

'She's right, my dear,' said the Earl.

Gerry continued. 'Even Merryweather might have gone against the trend and done it. Dorothy definitely didn't. Of course, I realise you can't take my word for that.'

'Oh, I think I can, Lady Geraldine.'

'But she and I might have conspired to do the murder together. After all, Clara did at first claim to know some appalling secret about *everybody* in the room. Perhaps I held her down, while Dorry killed her.'

'Oh no.'

'Why not?'

'Two against one? Wouldn't be sporting.'

'Ah yes, the code of the Burfords.' Gerry leaned back and lit a cigarette. 'So, tell me, how would I murder someone?'

Wilkins considered. 'With a gun: quick, clean and totally unambiguous. Probably in front of a number of witnesses. And not at Alderley, unless it was absolutely unavoidable.'

'Yes, I think you're right. Though not even in Westshire. I wouldn't want to be in your jurisdiction.'

'I appreciate that, Lady Geraldine.'

He turned to the Countess. 'Now, your ladyship, I wonder if you could kindly tell me just what was said between you and Mrs Saunders when you visited her in her room?'

Lady Burford thought for a moment, and, without adding any significant details, gave a slightly fuller account of the scene than the one she had given to Dorothy the previous evening.

'Thank you, your ladyship,' Wilkins said, when she had finished. 'And did you get the impression that she'd been speaking the truth when she claimed to know discreditable secrets about all the other beneficiaries?'

'I really wouldn't like to say, Mr Wilkins. She sounded convincing and she did make a point of finding out things about people.' She shot a meaningful glance at the Earl.

He gave a sigh. 'Yes, you'll have to know, Wilkins, that for some years Clara had been supplementing her income in a rather unsavoury fashion.' He briefly explained about Clara's dealings with newspapers.

Wilkins nodded thoughtfully. 'I see. Yes, quite unpleasant. Apart from that, I take it there is nothing any of you can tell me that might throw some light on this affair?'

The Earl shook his head. The Countess said: 'I honestly don't think so. And naturally I have thought about it a great deal last night and this morning.'

'Lady Geraldine?'

'You don't know how I'd love to say yes, Mr Wilkins.'

'Now, there's just one more thing.' He reached into his inside pocket and brought out a somewhat grubby-looking piece of paper. 'I've still got the little sketch map I made at the time of the egg cosy affair, showing which bedrooms were occupied by each person. The next time I rubbed out the names and filled the new ones in. Now I've rubbed those out, and I would be grateful if you could fill them in with the present names.' He held it out.

'You do it, my dear,' said Lord Burford.

'Certainly.' She took it. 'Does someone have a pencil?'

Wilkins handed her one and she started to write.

'It's a very rough plan,' Wilkins said. 'I'm sure the proportions are wrong and I haven't bothered with all the windows, and so on. But it's adequate for my purpose.'

Lady Burford finished writing and handed it and the pencil back. Wilkins perused the plan. 'Might I ask if there is any sort of order of precedence, as it were, in the allocation of rooms on occasions such as this?'

'Not really. Normally we will put members of the same family in adjoining rooms, but I decided to abandon the tradition in the case of Mrs Saunders and her stepdaughters – a small symbolic act. The only other factor is that as it is slightly more convenient to be near the centre, we tend to put the older people there, and the younger ones towards the ends of the corridors. I made an exception this time in the case of Agatha and Dorothy. It somehow seemed more fitting that, as principal mourners, they should be closer to the centre.'

Wilkins nodded. 'I see, though, that Mr Gregory Carstairs was given a room half way along the east corridor.'

The Countess gave a sigh. 'There was a slight problem. Mr Carstairs and Mr Timothy Saunders are not on good terms, so it was thought advisable to keep them as far apart as possible. Originally, in order to be more even-handed and not to give rise to suspicions of favouritism, I had intended to put Timothy in a corresponding room in the west corridor – the first one on the right, beyond the bathroom – with Miss Penelope in the room beyond, and Miss Agatha in the slightly larger corner bedroom, next to our suite. But when Miss Agatha did not turn up, it seemed rather absurd to leave that room empty, and I told the footman to put Timothy in there. That left the room originally allocated to him empty. I could have moved Miss Penelope into it. But I decided to leave her opposite Miss Simmons, as it occurred to me that two young women, spending a night in a room towards the end of a long corridor in a house which has recently acquired a somewhat notorious reputation, might both feel slightly more comfortable knowing that the room directly opposite was occupied.' The Countess looked rather pleased with herself for this involved explanation.

Wilkins made a sympathetic clucking sound. 'Who would have thought it would be so complicated? Rather like the allocation of beats to constables, which I had to deal with when I was in the uniformed branch. Certain routes are very much more popular than others, and some of the lads can get quite disgruntled if they're put on the less favoured ones too often. It requires a fair amount of diplomacy. Police constables can be as touchy as prima donnas sometimes.'

'So can barristers and Members of Parliament, believe me, Wilkins,' said Lord Burford.

CHAPTER TWENTY-THREE

Wilkins got to his feet. 'Better get a move on, I suppose. And if I could kindly be informed when Miss Dorothy wakes, or her sister arrives...'

'I'll let you know,' said Gerry.

'Thank you. Now, is there a room where I could interview the witnesses? We used the small music room last time, if that would be convenient.'

'By all means,' said the Earl. 'Can't imagine anyone's goin' to want to play the piano today.'

'I'll take you,' Gerry said.

They went out. 'I remember where it is, Lady Geraldine,' Wilkins said, 'but if you could lend me one of your servants to fetch each of the witnesses when I'm ready for them.'

'I'll do it.'

'Are you sure?'

'Yes, I'd like to. Who do you want to see first?'

'Miss Mackenzie, please.'

'Really? Why her? In my book, she's the least likely – sorry. Nothing to do with me.'

'Miss Mackenzie has something she badly wants to tell

me. She nearly came out with it twice last night, in the drawing-room, but couldn't quite bring herself to. I think she will this morning.'

'OK, I'll fetch her.'

She hurried away, meeting Sergeant Leather in the great hall. 'He's in the music room,' she said, pointing.

'Well?' Wilkins asked when Leather entered.

'I've spoken to all the servants, sir. Started with Janet, but, as you thought, she couldn't tell me anything. She took Mrs Saunders cocoa and biscuits in her room at around quarter to eleven. The lady was sitting in a chair, reading. Looked quite normal, no sign of fright or agitation. Janet just put down the tray, said goodnight and left. She wasn't in the room fifteen seconds. And none of the others saw or heard anything. Most of them were in bed by then, and all were by the time the body was discovered. Albert, the footman, says he and young Lambert both went right into the gallery and had a good look round. He's willing to swear that then there was nobody hidden behind the sofa or anywhere else.'

'Well done, Jack. Did they give you coffee?'

'Yes, and a very nice slice of rich fruit cake.'

'Oh, I didn't get any of that.'

'Something to be said for life below stairs. Oh, and Smithy's arrived. He's started fingerprinting the servants.'

The door opened and Gerry entered. 'I've brought Miss Mackenzie.'

Jean Mackenzie, looking even more anxious than usual, came in, her eyes darting around the room, as if expecting to see some assailant waiting to pounce.

'And she says she would like me to sit in, if that's all right with you,' Gerry added.

'Certainly, Lady Geraldine. Please sit down, Miss Mackenzie.'

'Oh, thank you.'

As she was doing so, Wilkins looked at Gerry, put his finger to his lips and then pointed at her. Gerry grinned and gave a nod.

The others sat down, Leather taking out a shorthand notebook and pencil.

'So, Miss Mackenzie, what do you want to tell me?' Wilkins asked.

She gave a gulp. 'I have a confession to make.'

'I see. Confession to what, exactly?'

'I have done something terrible. Really wicked.'

'Really? So, why did you kill Mrs Saunders?'

She gave a shriek of horror. 'Kill? I didn't kill her.'

'Oh, I do beg your pardon, miss. When you said you'd done something really wicked, I assumed it had to be murder.'

'Well, it wasn't quite as bad as that, but the fact is I told a lie. And Mr Bradley passed it on – in all good faith, I must emphasise – to Lord and Lady Burford. I do not think Florrie would have minded. She had no strong feelings either way. And I have been worrying in case she had said as much to Agatha, and that Agatha passed it on to Clara, so she would know I had lied. But I only did it because it did seem to be the Great Opportunity that I had been promised. Marion had said I would recognise it when it came. Well, of course, I had been wishing so strongly for just such a chance, and it seemed quite amazing that the opportunity should have presented itself in this way. I had thought at first that it was something quite different that was being suggested, but I soon decided that that would have involved spying in a quite underhand way, so it couldn't be that. I should, though, have realised that when it actually came it would never involve telling a lie, either. And the terrible thing is that if I had not sinned in this way, Mrs Saunders – Mrs Clara Saunders, that is, not Mrs Florence Saunders – would be alive today.'

All of this was said at a breathless pace and Leather's pencil had been flying across the paper. Wilkins waited for a moment for him to catch up, before asking: 'But what precisely was this lie?'

'Oh, didn't I mention that? It's this. I told Mr Bradley that Florrie had expressed a wish to be buried at Alderley. She hadn't. She hadn't said anything about where she wanted to be buried.'

'And you said that because you believed this was the great opportunity you'd been told about? Why were you so sure of that?'

'Don't you see that even before last night there had been three murders here in the past twelve months? It is a well-known fact that souls who are murdered are often restless – unquiet. They are unable to Pass On. They remain confined to the site of their murder. They sometimes Walk. Of course, one would need to be a Sensitive actually to be aware of them. I'm sure, for instance, that were Mr Hawthorne here, he would experience a Manifestation. I, to my great sadness, am not a Sensitive, but for so long I had been desperately wishing for a chance to come here and try an experiment, though it seemed totally impossible. Then Marion told me I was going to be given a great opportunity. A chance that is vouchsafed to few. "You must seize the moment when it comes," she said. "Be resolute. Do not be afraid."'

Wilkins broke in. 'Just for the sergeant's record, could you tell us Marion's surname?'

'The same as mine, Mackenzie. She never married.'

'So how did your – ' he paused momentarily before guessing ' – sister know about this great opportunity?'

'Well, they do, don't they? Know things, I mean, that we don't.'

'Who do?'

'Yes, I'm afraid that may well be true.'

Wilkins took a deep breath. 'What may be true?'

'That there was a hoodoo on my whole enterprise.'

'No, I mean who know things that we don't?'

'Those who are no longer in the body.'

Light dawned in Wilkins' eyes. He nodded sapiently. 'Yes, I suppose they do. When did your sister die, Miss Mackenzie?'

'We prefer not to use that word, Mr Wilkins. My sister passed on nearly eight years ago. And in all that time she has never communicated before, which was what made it so exciting.'

'And this was at a séance with Mr Hawthorne, the medium?'

'A public meeting, really. He's truly wonderful. And the message was so direct: from Marion, for Jean. I couldn't think what it could mean, though I puzzled about it for days. Then Florrie passed on and that of course put it out of my head. But when I was talking to Mr Bradley, he actually asked me if Florrie had ever said anything about where she wanted to be buried. And it suddenly hit me. If the funeral were held at Alderley, I felt sure, knowing how kind and hospitable they are, that the Earl and Countess would invite the mourners back to the house, and there just might be a chance, even if we were only here for an hour or so. So that's when I told my lie. Then we were actually invited to stay here overnight. It seemed to be working out so wonderfully and I honestly believed that I would be able to achieve a really important Communication with the Unquiet Spirits – or at least one of them.'

'But what exactly were you planning to do? You said yourself that you're not a sensitive.'

'No, but I had the next best thing: a ouija board. I've had really remarkable results with it in the past.'

'But you didn't actually go ahead with your plan?'

'Oh, but I did. Last night.'

'You did? When?'

'After everybody, except Lady Geraldine and Dorry, had gone to bed.'

'In your room?'

'No, no. I wanted to get as close as possible to the actual site of one of the murders, and I knew that one had taken place in the room which houses the gun collection. Of course, I couldn't get in there, but the art gallery is very close to it. I went in there yesterday before the reading of the will, and I felt a definite coldness about half way along to the right as you go in – often a sign of a spirit's presence. And, remarkably, I'd actually been allocated a room across the corridor, which made everything very easy. It really seemed as though it were all part of some great Plan.'

Wilkins stared at her. 'You were actually in the picture gallery last night? What time?'

'It was just a minute or two before twelve when I went in.'

'So it was you who knocked the suit of armour over?'

'Oh dear me, no. But I was there when it happened. It was terrible, really terrible—'

'Miss Mackenzie, just tell me precisely what you did and what occurred.'

'I took my ouija board and a small glass, to use with it as a sort of pointer, into the gallery. Do you know how it is done?'

'I think so. You upturn the glass on the board, put your finger on the bottom, and it's supposed to move about of its own accord and point to the various letters.'

'Exactly. I went to the cold spot and sat down on one of the upright chairs. I said a short prayer, that I would be protected from any evil forces, and then waited, trying to prepare myself mentally. I must admit I found it difficult to start. I was a little nervous, being alone, and so close to where a murder had been committed. It must have been about fifteen or twenty minutes before I felt ready. At first I put the ouija board on my lap, but it kept sliding about. So I put it on the chair and knelt down by it. I put the glass on it, rested my fingers on the glass and said: "Is there anyone there?" And then...'

Miss Mackenzie, who seemed to be quite enjoying herself now, paused dramatically. 'Suddenly, without any warning whatsoever, the suit of armour just fell over. It made the most dreadful noise you can imagine. I literally jumped out of my skin. But I knew immediately what had happened. And it could hardly have been worse.'

'What do you mean?'

'I had obviously raised an evil spirit or a poltergeist. It is something I have heard of happening, but it had never happened to me. I have to admit I was absolutely terrified. I grabbed the board and the glass and positively ran to the door. I dropped the glass, but couldn't stop to pick up the pieces. I did turn the light off as I went out, but I left the door open. When I got back to my room I was shaking like a leaf, positively like a leaf. I realised, of course, that this was a punishment for me, and a warning that no good can ever come of telling lies. Very shortly, I heard footsteps and voices outside. I would have stayed in my room, but, frankly, I felt the need of human company, so I went out, and then learned the terrible news.'

Wilkins rubbed his chin. 'Did you hear Miss Simmons shouting?'

'Yes, as I crossed the corridor, though I did not know it was her. I thought perhaps that somebody else was experiencing poltergeist phenomena, but it seems not. I just pray that there will be no recurrence here and that the manifestation was aimed solely at me, not at the house.'

She turned to Gerry. 'Lady Geraldine, I can only offer my most heartfelt apologies. I shamelessly took advantage of your parents' known generosity and I feel most terribly guilty.'

'Miss Mackenzie, please don't reproach yourself too much. I think you're jolly plucky to have come out with it all like this. If you hadn't, no one would have ever known. And it was very suitable to have the funeral here. It was right that Florrie should have been buried at Alderley, as I know my parents both felt eventually.'

'But I'm responsible for the murder. Clara wouldn't have been here if it hadn't been for me.'

'You mustn't think that, Miss Mackenzie,' said Wilkins. 'This crime would have been committed somewhere. It arose out of that scene at the reading of the will – which would have occurred wherever the reading had taken place. What Mrs Saunders said frightened somebody very much. And that led directly to her death.'

'You do make me feel a little better, Mr Wilkins. Thank you.'

'Just one or two questions. Did you tell anyone in advance of your plans to hold a séance?'

'Yes, I told Tommy. He's always been most interested in psychic matters. I even invited him to take part with me, but he refused. I think he was a little nervous – and quite rightly, as it transpired. I have been warned that ouija boards are dangerous things, but I foolishly ignored the warnings.'

'And you told him afterwards what had occurred?'

'Yes, earlier this morning. He was very concerned.'

'Is there anything else you can tell us about last night?'

'No, nothing. I retired to my room quite early and stayed there, reading, until I went to the art gallery.'

'Finally, have you ever heard the name Miss Dora Lethbridge?'

'No, never.'

'Then that will be all for now. We may ask you to sign a statement later.'

'Very well.' She stood up.

'If you go with Sergeant Leather, he'll take you to our fingerprint man.'

'It's all right,' Gerry said, 'I'll take her. And afterwards, a glass of sherry, eh, Miss Mackenzie?'

'Well, it is a little early for me, but it does sound very tempting. Tell me, Lady Geraldine, is your rector here an experienced exorcist?'

'I really wouldn't know.'

'It might be advisable to find out. If not, I know a very good man.' Her voice faded as they went out. Then Gerry put her head back round the door. 'Who do you want to see next?'

'Who would *you* see next?'

She thought. 'Tommy, I think – see if he confirms her story.'

'Then Mr Lambert it'll be.'

'OK.' This time she finally disappeared, closing the door.

Leather had put down his pencil with relief.

'Blimey, what a load of double-Dutch! I couldn't make any sense of it when she started, could you?'

'Not a lot, but we got there at the end.'

'But wouldn't it have been quicker just to say you didn't know what she was talking about and ask her to spell it all out in words of one syllable? Instead of going all round the houses, trying to find out who Marion was without actually asking her, for instance.'

'Oo, you don't ever want to let them know there are things you don't understand, Jack, unless it absolutely can't be helped. Things you don't *know*, yes, but you've got to let them see you take in everything they tell you right away. Besides, I'm a detective. I'm supposed to deduce things. Anyway, we're not in any hurry. This is a very nice place to conduct an investigation. And with luck they'll give us a very nice lunch.'

Leather was flexing his fingers. 'I'll be getting writer's cramp if they all go on at that rate.'

'Get it all?'

'No. Not all the psychic claptrap, but enough, I think.'

'You don't believe in poltergeists, then, Jack?'

'No fear. You don't, surely?' He took out a penknife and started sharpening his pencil.

'Dunno. Some pretty astute people have vouched for 'em. I've read some very weird accounts. And if it wasn't a poltergeist, how do you account for the armour toppling over like it did?'

'Could have been badly positioned on its plinth. Someone might have touched it yesterday afternoon, pushed it another half inch, so it was just on the verge of falling. Could have happened the first time anybody came in, opened and closed the door, caused a draught. Something like that.'

'Mm. Maybe. Can't see it's got any connection with the murder, either way.'

There came a cheerful-sounding, rhythmic tap-a-tap-tap on the door.

'Come in.'

It opened and Tommy entered. 'What-ho. Wanted to see me?'

'Yes, come in, Mr Lambert.'

With a not very successful attempt at nonchalance, Tommy strolled over to the table, sat down and leaned back. 'Mind if I smoke?'

'Not at all, sir.'

He took out a pack of Gold Flake, extracted and lit one. 'Oh, sorry, have one?'

'No thank you, sir.'

Tommy proffered the pack to Leather, who shook his head.

'So I'm in for the jolly old third degree, am I?'

'Hardly that, sir. Just a few questions.'

'Fire away.'

'Let's get a secondary matter out of the way before we start discussing the actual murder. We've been talking to Miss Mackenzie and we seem to have an eye-witness account of the armour falling over. I understand she told you about it.'

'Yes. Quite spooky, eh?'

'Keen on psychic research, are you, Mr Lambert?'

'What? No, not really. Just showed a friendly interest, you know.'

'So much so that she told you about her plans beforehand, even invited you to join her.'

'That's right. Not really my cup of tea, though.'

'So you were in bed when the crash occurred, were you?'

'Actually, not exactly, no.'

'Not exactly? Oh, you mean you were half in and half out, or sitting on the edge, prior to getting in?'

'No. Actually, when I say not exactly, I actually mean not at all, if you see what I mean.'

'Not really, sir, you'll have to bear with me. So, where were you – er, actually?'

'I was in the art gallery, act— as a matter of fact.'

'What, at the same time as Miss Mackenzie?'

'That's right.'

'But she said she was on her own, that she'd asked you to take part but you'd refused.'

'She didn't know I was there. I was sort of hiding.'

'Sort of hiding where?'

'The far side of that sofa, to the left of the armour.'

Leather looked up, an expression of deep satisfaction on his face, then quickly returned to his notebook.

'And she didn't see you?' Wilkins said incredulously. 'I wouldn't have thought that sofa would have been big enough to conceal you, you being so tall.'

'Well, I had to curl up into a pretty tight ball and keep absolutely still. I dare say if she'd looked straight in my direction she might have spotted me, and obviously she would have if she'd turned to the left when she came in. But she'd told me earlier about something she called a cold spot towards the other end and that was where she was going to set up the thingamy board. So I thought there was a fair chance she wouldn't see me.'

'But what was the point?'

Tommy's embarrassment was becoming visibly more acute by the second. He took a nervous pull on the cigarette. 'Look, this is bally awkward. I know it sounds awful, but the whole thing was a practical joke. On her, Miss Mackenzie. The truth is that I – I was responsible for the crash. I made the armour topple over.'

'Is that so? I think you'd better tell us the whole story, Mr Lambert.'

'OK. Well, as I say, as soon as Mackenzie told me about her plan, I thought it would be a lark to give her a bit of a shock. I'd had a look in the gallery in the afternoon and

I'd seen the armour and noticed the sofa and it occurred to me that if the armour came crashing down just when she was in the middle of her spook-hunt it might really give her something to think about, don't you know. Now I know it sounds dashed unkind, might have given her a heart attack, or anything, and I feel pretty ashamed of myself now. Anyway, what happened was that after I'd gone to my room at about twenty past eleven or so, I undressed, put on my pyjamas and dressing gown, and had a read and a smoke for half an hour or so. Then at about quarter to twelve, I got a length of string, went to the gallery and tied one end of it round the armour. I played the string out until it reached the far end of the sofa. Then I went back to the door, turned the lights out, made my way over to the sofa again, with the help of my lighter, and crouched down beside it. Then I just waited. After about quarter of an hour or so, Mackenzie came in, messed around for a bit and then started her "Is there anybody there?" rigmarole. I thought that would be a good time to give her an answer, so I just gave the string a tug – and the armour went crashing down. It made an enormous noise, even made me jump. I heard Mackenzie give a shriek and go scuttling out. I waited just long enough to grab up the string and then hared it back to my room. That's about it, really. Sorry and all that.'

Wilkins eyed him. 'You must have realised you were going to wake up the household.'

'Not really. First of all, I didn't realise quite what a big bang it was going to make. But the floor's very hard, and that gallery's a big place with nothing much in it, so there's a sort of echo. What's more, I knew how thick the walls and doors are here, but I didn't see the open fanlight over the door, which let the sound carry much farther. Oh, I thought it'd probably wake up Gregory the Great, who's got the room between Mackenzie and me, but that didn't bother me too much.'

'Did you hear Miss Simmons shouting as you ran back to your room?'

'Yes – at least, I thought it was her – and I wondered what was up.'

'It didn't occur to you to investigate?'

'For a second, yes. But she didn't sound frightened, just jolly ratty, as though she was having a big row. I had a girlfriend once, who used to go on at me just like that sometimes. So I thought better to leave well alone. Anyway, I stayed just inside the door of my room, keeping it open a crack, and very soon after that I heard voices and general commotion, so I joined the throng outside Clara's room and found out she'd been croaked. Jolly upsetting.'

He stubbed out his cigarette.

'Why didn't you tell us all this before, sir?'

'Well, it's pretty shaming. I was hoping it wouldn't need to come out at all. After all, it's got nothing to do with the murder. I did tell you as soon as you asked.'

'Yes, and I want to thank you for being so frank with us now, Mr Lambert. And talking of the murder, how well did you know the deceased?'

'Not at all. Yesterday was the first time we'd met. And we didn't exchange more than a dozen words.'

'Yet yesterday at the reading, she said that she knew things about everybody there that would make their reputations mud, if they came out. She withdrew it later as regards the Earl and Countess and Lady Geraldine, but specifically refused to do so for the guests. So what do you reckon she knew about you?'

'Nothing, I'm sure.'

'Got a clear conscience, have you, Mr Lambert?'

'Well, not exactly. I mean there are things I wouldn't want shouted from the rooftops, obviously. But nothing that would make my reputation mud. Certainly nothing it'd be worth committing a murder to keep dark. I haven't got a criminal record, or anything.'

'Three speeding tickets in the last five years. And fined two pounds for being drunk and disorderly in the West End on New Year's Eve.'

'Ah. Yes, of course. You looked me up. But that is all, honestly. And they'd hardly make my reputation mud, or be worth Clara's while to spread around.'

'So you think she was bluffing?'

'Must have been, in my case.'

'Did you see her yesterday, after the scene in the library?'

'No, not for a second.'

'Did you hear or see anything in any way suspicious or odd?'

'Not a thing. And I've really been racking my brains – what there are of them.'

'Ever heard of a Miss Dora Lethbridge?'

Tommy shook his head.

'Well, I don't think we need keep you any longer, for now, Mr Lambert.' Wilkins repeated what he had said to Miss Mackenzie about a statement and fingerprints.

'Yes, of course. Only too glad to help in any way

possible. And, by the way, does Mackenzie have to know – about what I did, I mean? Can you just let her go on thinking it was a poltergeist?'

'We'll see, Mr Lambert. I won't reveal it unless it becomes necessary.'

'Thanks.'

'Perhaps you'd kindly ask Miss Simmons to step in next.'

'Righty-ho.'

CHAPTER TWENTY-FOUR

Stella was the first person to enter the room with an air of complete confidence. She sat down, folded her hands on the table and smiled at Wilkins enquiringly.

'Miss Simmons, I'd like to talk first about this intruder in your room last night. You can give no description of any kind?'

She shook her head. 'I was half asleep. It was almost totally dark. I was just aware of a presence, a kind of even blacker patch against the surrounding blackness, by the dresser. I think he'd most likely been using a flashlight or a match to see. I got the impression of a light going out just a split second after I opened my eyes. He probably put it out when he heard the crash, realising I might wake up.'

'I see. When you awoke, he, or she, was by the dressing-table—'

Stella interrupted. 'She? You think it could have been a woman?'

'Can you be sure it wasn't?'

She looked thoughtful. 'No, I suppose not. I assumed it was a man. But if it was a woman, who could it have been? Let's see, Gerry and Dorry were downstairs, Miss Mackenzie was in the picture gallery – oh, she's told us all about it now – and Clara was dead. That only leaves the Countess, which is surely absurd, and—' She broke off.

'And Miss Penelope Saunders. You did say the intruder had vanished by the time you got to the door. Miss Saunders' room was right across the corridor from yours. And according to Lord Burford's account, you told everybody that she appeared almost immediately after you looked out.'

'But that's screwy. Why on earth should Penny have been poking about in my room?'

'Why should anybody have been poking about in your room? Do we have to suppose they meant you harm of some kind?'

'You're not saying he was going to kill *me*, too?' She sounded incredulous.

'So you think your intruder was the person who killed Mrs Saunders?'

'Search me. But if not, it means that two people were up to no good last night.'

'For Alderley, that's nothing, I can assure you, miss. But when I wondered whether the intruder meant to harm you, I was thinking of something not quite so drastic.'

'You mean one of the guys was after my virtue? Come off it!'

'Is it beyond the bounds of possibility?'

'I'd say yes. And I speak as someone not without experience. Tommy would be far too scared. I'd bet my bottom dollar that Timothy'd be absolutely horrified at the very idea. Gregory'd probably try it on if the time and place, and the woman, were right. He's quite a masher. But he's an MP, for Pete's sake! – and holding on by the skin of his teeth. He'd never risk the scandal. He'd be finished if it got out.'

'He might have thought there was no likelihood of a scandal: that you'd welcome it.'

For the first time, she looked doubtful. 'Well, I guess I did flirt with him a mite. But only for my own ends, though keep that under your hat.'

'He couldn't have known your real reason.'

'Well, if that *was* his motive, why would he have been messing around by the dresser?' She shook her head decisively. 'No, I'm sure that's not it. Think again, Mr Wilkins.'

'Well, you're the expert, Miss Simmons. So we're no nearer an explanation. You said there was nothing worth stealing there, and nothing *was* stolen.'

'Oh, but there was.'

'Eh?' For the first time, Wilkins looked surprised. 'But you said last night—'

'I know. I only discovered it this morning. I didn't have a chance to tell you before.'

'So what was it?'

'A tube of toothpaste,' Stella said.

'A tube of toothpaste?' Wilkins looked totally bemused.

'Yes, and I can give you a description. About six inches long by an inch wide. White, with blue lettering. Answers to the rather unfortunate name of Dentigleam. Value, hard to assess, as about half the paste had been used but, at an estimate, perhaps sixpence. I haven't decided yet whether to put in an insurance claim.'

'Are you absolutely sure about this, Miss Simmons?'

'Well it may have been slightly less than six inches long, and—'

Wilkins flapped his hands, and she stopped. 'I mean, could you have just mislaid it?'

'No,' she said firmly. 'It was in a little draw-string toilet bag, with my toothbrush. I used it last night and left it on the dresser afterwards, rather than put it in my case, because I knew I'd be using it in the morning. When I went to get it this morning, the bag was open, the toothbrush was there, but the paste was gone.'

Wilkins shook his head. 'Rum. Most rum. It's not as though anybody could have mistaken it for something else, even in the dark. A tube of toothpaste doesn't feel like anything except a tube of toothpaste. However, again it doesn't seem to have anything obviously to do with the murder of Mrs Saunders. So let's move on to that. How well did you know her?'

'I met her yesterday for the first time. We chatted, mainly about Florrie, for a few minutes in the afternoon. That's it. I'd heard about her, from Florrie, who saw her as the original wicked stepmother. I admit I thought she might be prejudiced, but after Clara's performance yesterday, I could believe anything of her.'

'So when she said she knew something damaging about all of the other beneficiaries, what did you think she knew about you?'

'Nothing. I've been in the country for less than six months. I doubt Clara even knew of my existence. She couldn't know any of my guilty secrets.'

'So you do have some guilty secrets?'

'That would be telling. No, my bet is that all that baloney, knowing things about all of us, was camouflage and she really had one of two people in mind.'

'And which two would they be?'

'You're the detective, Detective.'

'Oh, I'm never too proud to ask for help, miss.'

'No, I'm not saying: wouldn't be quite cricket, what? Anyway, it's only a hunch.'

'I take it that yesterday was the first time you'd met any of the others?'

'Apart from Jean Mackenzie and Tommy, yes. Tommy's my first cousin and I knew him quite well years ago, though he was only a kid then. Oh, and I met Gregory once, when I was in my teens.'

'You must have felt a bit of an outsider.'

'Not really. I'd kept in touch with Florrie by mail for years. When I came to...came home, one of the first things I did after I'd gotten settled in was look her up. She was as sharp as a needle and had a fantastic memory, and she filled me in on dozens of relatives. Also, of course, I'd read all about the earlier Alderley murders – they got pretty wide coverage in the New York papers, what with several big-shot Americans being mixed up in them, and there was quite a lot of stuff about the Earl and Countess and Gerry. So, all in all, I knew who I'd be meeting and just how we were related.'

'So what can you tell us about last night?'

'Zilch. I didn't see Clara after the time she blew her top. I went up to bed at the same time as Tommy and Penny. I went to my room, undressed, took off my make-up, brushed my hair, put on my robe, went to the bathroom, washed my face and hands, brushed my teeth and so on, returned to my room and got straight into bed. It had been a long day and I was asleep in five minutes. The rest you know.'

Wilkins nodded absently. He looked depressed again. Stella seemed to feel responsible for this. 'Sorry,' she said.

'That's all right, miss. I didn't really expect anything else. Oh, one more thing: does the name Miss Dora Lethbridge mean anything to you?'

'Not a thing.'

'Thank you. Would you ask Miss Saunders to come along next, please?'

'Sure.'

She went out.

CHAPTER TWENTY-FIVE

Tommy was sitting on the terrace gloomily going over in his mind his decidedly embarrassing interview with Wilkins, when he saw Lord Burford come round the corner of the house. The Earl was carrying what Tommy at first took to be a bunch of flowers, but then saw that there were no blooms on them; it just seemed to be a mass of greenery. Next Tommy noticed that he was wearing a pair of brown kid gloves. For the middle of August this seemed extremely odd. Tommy kept his eyes fixed on the Earl as he got closer and a few seconds later was able to make out that what his host was carrying was a large bunch of nettles. Tommy stared at him in amazement, and at that moment Lord Burford looked up and saw him. He stopped short. 'Ah,' he said.

'Nettles,' Tommy said, intelligently.

The Earl glanced down at them, as though until that moment he had been unaware of their existence. 'Oh yes, yes.'

'I thought so. I mean, can hardly mistake them, can you?'

'Suppose not. Make, er, excellent, er, soup – yes, soup, that's it.'

'Really? Never tried it.'

'Oh, you should. Very nutritious. I'm just going to give 'em to Cook.'

'Give 'em a cook? Yourself?'

'No, no – give 'em *to* Cook – our cook, Mrs Baldwin, to make into soup. Or something.'

'Oh, right.'

Lord Burford hurried off, moving more quickly than Tommy had yet seen him. He blinked. Very weird. He wondered if the strain was getting to the old boy. Perhaps he should say something. But to whom? Not the Countess. He couldn't face that. Gerry, perhaps. But it would need tact. Well, he had plenty of that. He got to his feet

Tommy found Gerry in the morning-room, writing furiously in a notepad. He sat down near her.

'Another lovely day, what?' he said brightly.

She nodded absently. 'Mm.'

'Eat a lot of nettle soup, do you?'

Gerry gave a little start. '*What* did you say?'

'Or should I say drink? Nettle soup. Like it, do you? Your family, I mean?'

'Nettle soup? Certainly not. Why the dickens should you ask such a thing?'

'Your papa. He says it's very good. Nutritious and all that sort of thing.'

'Probably just something he's read. I don't believe he's ever tasted it in his life, unless it was in France during the war.'

'Well, you're going to be having some soon, apparently.'

'What on earth are you talking about?'

'He's just picked a big bunch of nettles, to give to your cook.'

'Tommy, stop pulling my leg.'

'I'm not, cross my heart and all that rot.'

Gerry stared at him in bewilderment. 'But it doesn't make sense. He never takes the remotest interest in anything like that. Just eats what's put in front of him. Mrs Baldwin will probably give her notice in if he starts taking her peculiar things to cook.'

'I did wonder if it was all getting on top of him, you know. All these murders. Quite natural.'

'When was this?'

'Just a few minutes ago.'

She stood up. 'Then let's hope I can stop him before he gets to the kitchens. And, Tommy, if you *are* ribbing me...'

'Gerry, if I wanted to, I could do a darn sight better than this.'

'Yes, I imagine you could. Sorry. And, Tommy, keep your trap shut, OK?'

'Oh, absolutely.'

Gerry sped off.

There came a very timid knock on the door of the small music room. This time Wilkins got up and opened it. 'Ah, Miss Saunders. Do come in. Would you care to sit down?' He might have been a particularly unctuous head waiter welcoming an old and valued customer.

Penny sat down. She looked terrified. She said: 'I didn't do it.'

'Didn't you? I'm very pleased to hear it.'

She stood up again. 'Can I go now?'

'Just a few questions, if you don't mind.'

'Oh.' She sat down again.

'So, who do you think did do it?' Wilkins asked.

'Gregory.' The answer came immediately.

'Really? Why's that?'

'Because of what Clara said. She was going to expose him.'

'She threatened to expose lots of people. I mean, why do *you* think it was Mr Carstairs?'

'He's a horrid man. Daddy hates him.'

'I see.'

'And he's a Conservative.'

'Is that bad?'

'Daddy's a Liberal, and he says the Conservatives are' – she screwed up her eyes and concentrated hard – 'reactionary relics.'

'Set a lot of store by your father's opinions, do you, Miss Saunders?'

'No!' Penny looked quite indignant. 'I mean, not on important things like nail polish and cigarettes and night clubs. But he does know an awful lot about politics and things. And it was yummy when he threw Gregory down last night. Stella was really impressed.'

'It didn't upset you too much, then, this murder?'

'No. I think it's thrilling. It's not as though anyone nice was murdered. She was a horrid woman. And she was awfully old, so she'd have probably died soon anyway.'

'No doubt. So Gregory murdering Clara was just about the best thing that could have happened?'

'Well, I don't know about the *best* thing. But pretty good.'

'But tell me, do you have any evidence that Gregory did it? Because, you see, we haven't, and we really need some.'

'You can't just arrest him, then?'

'Not without evidence.'

'It seems so silly, when we know he did it.'

'That's the law.'

'I'll tell Daddy it ought to be changed.'

'Yes, you do that, Miss Saunders. But you didn't see anything?'

'I could say I did, if you like. Or would that be cheating?'

'Yes, that would definitely be cheating.'

'Well, then, no, I didn't see anything at all.'

'In that case, we needn't keep you any longer.'

'Really?' She looked disappointed.

'I thought you wanted to leave.'

'I did, but I didn't realise it was going to be such fun. Can I ask a question first?'

'Oh, I've just got one more first: have you ever heard the name Dora Lethbridge – Miss Dora Lethbridge?'

'I don't think so, no.'

'Right, ask your question now.'

'Do you think *Peepshow* might do another piece about this murder and put my photo in, as one of the Beauties Involved in Murder?'

'I don't see how they can fail to, Miss Saunders.'

An expression of deep happiness came over Penny's face and she gave a little sigh, before getting up and starting for the door. Then she stopped and turned. 'And it's OK if I tell everyone you know Gregory killed her, is it?'

Wilkins gave a start. 'No! Definitely not, Miss Saunders.'

'But I thought—' She stopped and a look of sudden understanding came into her eyes. 'Oh, I see! You think if he knows we know, he might get away.'

'Yes. That's it. And heaven knows who else he might kill in the process. You, your father, Tommy.'

'Oh, golly, I never thought of that. All right, I won't breathe a word.'

'Thank you, Miss Saunders. Could you kindly ask your father if he could join us, please.'

'OK.' She looked at Leather, who was still writing rapidly in his notebook. 'You're very good at that, aren't you?'

Leather looked up. 'Pretty good, I reckon, miss.'

'Do you think you might like to be a secretary, one day? To a career woman, running her own company?'

'I don't think so, miss. I'm very happy in the police force.'

'That's a shame. If you change your mind, let me know.'

'I'll do that.'

She smiled at them both radiantly and went out.

'Talk about dumb blondes!' Leather exclaimed, as the door closed behind her.

'Likeable, though.'

'She's jolly pretty, I'll say that.'

'I thought you would, Jack.'

CHAPTER TWENTY-SIX

Gerry went first to the kitchens. There was no sign of the Earl. She engaged Mrs Baldwin in conversation for a few minutes, on the pretext of seeking her advice about the menu for an imaginary proposed dinner party in her London flat. She cast surreptitious glances around, but nowhere was there any sign of nettles, nor did Mrs Baldwin seem in any way bemused or disgruntled, so presumably the Earl had been delayed *en route*.

She thanked the cook and made her way to her father's study. She tapped on the door.

There was a couple of seconds' pause before her father's voice called: 'Who is it?'

Gerry raised her eyebrows. That was an unusual response, for a start. 'Me.'

'Oh, hang on.'

This time there was a full half minute's delay before he called: 'Come in.'

Gerry opened the door and peered somewhat apprehensively into the room. The Earl was seated at his desk, which was covered by an open copy of *The Times*.

He had quite a guilty expression on his face as he stared enquiringly at her. 'Er, what is it, my dear?'

'Daddy, what is this nonsense about nettle soup?'

'Oh. Well, supposed to be quite nice and good for one. Thought we might try it sometime.'

'Tommy said you were going to take some nettles to Mrs Baldwin.'

'Haven't got round to that yet.'

'Thank heavens. She'd have thought you were absolutely doollally.'

'Don't see why. Traditional British dish. We ought to keep up these old customs.'

'But why bring the stuff in here? That is it, isn't it?' She reached out and removed the newspaper. A big pile of already somewhat wilted nettles nearly covered the desk top. There were also two kid gloves and a pair of scissors. Gerry stared. Many of the leaves had already been cut from the stalks and themselves further cut into small pieces. 'Why, by all that's wonderful, are you cutting them up?'

'Er, just thought I'd save Cook the trouble. Get them ready for the pot. Didn't want her or one of the maids gettin' stung. I had to wear my gloves.'

Gerry took a deep breath. 'Daddy, promise me one thing: don't take these to the kitchen. Mrs Baldwin really wouldn't appreciate it. You know she can be as temperamental as any French chef and she might well be insulted.'

'Oh, if that's what you think. I'll forget all about it.'

'That would be a very good idea.'

'Run along now, my dear. I've got a lot of things to do this morning.'

Gerry refrained from asking what they were. She left the room with a baffled expression on her face.

Timothy came into the room without knocking, walked quickly to the empty chair and sat down.

'I'm sorry to have kept you waiting, sir,' Wilkins said.

'I imagined at first it was some kind of psychological ploy.' (Wilkins looked hurt.) 'Then after you asked to see Miss Mackenzie first, I decided you were taking us in the order of the degree of suspicion that is attached to us, working upwards. However, if that is the case, I fail to understand why you saw Lambert before my daughter. I cannot imagine that you consider Penelope a suspect in this case.'

'Everyone is a suspect, Mr Saunders. Some, of course, are more, er' – he hesitated – 'more suspectable than others.' He frowned, as though unhappy with the word, before continuing. 'No, actually, we saw Miss Mackenzie first because she obviously had something she wanted to tell us. I understand you now know what that was.'

Timothy nodded. 'Highly bizarre.'

'We saw Mr Lambert next, as Miss Mackenzie informed us she had told him in advance of her plan, and we wanted his confirmation of that. Miss Simmons was possibly the only person actually to have seen the murderer, so it seemed sensible to talk to her next. In fact, it turned out she saw nothing. Then I spoke to Miss Penelope, as I imagined she might be nervous. Though that also turns out to have been wrong.'

'I regret to say she seems to be quite enjoying the situation.'

'Ah well, sir, the exuberance of youth, as they say. What a wonderful thing it is.'

'I must say I never felt especially exuberant as a youth. May we get on now?'

'Of course, sir. Well, I don't intend to start questioning the best cross-examiner in the country. So I'll just leave it to you to tell me anything you think may be relevant, though I may have one or two points to clarify when you've finished.'

Timothy bowed his head slightly. 'Thank you, Chief Inspector, I appreciate the courtesy. I had best begin by saying that Mrs Saunders' statement at the reading of the will regarding having damaging information about each of us was, in my case, totally incorrect. I do not say my life is an open book – no man's is – but that she possessed knowledge which, as she put it, could ruin my reputation is simply not conceivable. I therefore had no motive for killing her. As to the crime itself, I can offer nothing of value. I retired to my room a minute or two before eleven. The next thing I can tell you is hearing the sound of the crash. I looked at the luminous dial of my watch. It was precisely 12:28.'

Wilkins interrupted. 'How accurate is your watch?'

'Extremely accurate. I correct it every morning by the chimes of Big Ben on the wireless, and it is never more than thirty seconds out.'

'Thank you, sir. Please carry on.'

'There is little more to tell. I wondered whether I should go and investigate but decided that it was no concern of mine. A minute or two later, I heard raised voices and then did go to the door and look out. I saw a small group of people outside the room occupied by Clara. I joined them and learned what had occurred. Shortly afterwards, I assisted in the search of the house, accompanied by one of the footmen. When that was completed I went downstairs and gathered with everybody else in the drawing-room. I remained there until you came and spoke to us.'

'I understand that before the search there was a little altercation between you and Mr Carstairs, just outside Mrs Saunders' room.'

For the first time, Timothy looked a trifle discomposed. 'Yes. I regret that now very much. It was most unseemly. He made a disparaging remark about my physical ability to handle myself in the event of some ruffian being discovered on the premises, and I could not resist showing him that I am more than capable. I am a third Dan in ju-jitsu, and am perhaps unduly proud of the fact. I should, of course, have ignored his sneers. I did apologise to the Earl afterwards.'

'But not to Mr Carstairs.'

'Er, no.'

'It seems quite widely known that you and he are not on good terms.'

'That is so. But before you ask, it arose from something that took place fifteen or sixteen years ago, and which Clara could not possibly have known about. It can have no conceivable bearing on her murder, so I do not intend to talk about it. If Gregory should prove less reticent, then I shall, of course, give my side of the story.'

'That's fair enough, sir. Just how well did you know Mrs Saunders?'

'Hardly at all. I had met her only once, at her husband's funeral.'

'And the young ladies?'

'The same. I feel guilty about not having kept in touch with them. Our fathers were very close friends, and, of course, my father was John's solicitor for many years and his executor. I had intended to use this opportunity to reacquaint myself with them, offer them any help or advice I can give. The trouble is that now they have come into such a large sum of money, they will assume that is the reason for my new-found concern for them.'

'Oh, I'm sure they wouldn't think that, sir.'

'I am a lawyer, Chief Inspector. People always think the worst of us. As I am sure that you, as a police officer, do.'

'That usually depends on whether they're prosecuting or defending, sir. But to revert, there's nothing else you want to tell us about the events of last night?'

There was a perceptible pause. Wilkins looked at him and Leather glanced up from his notebook. Timothy's eyelid gave a twitch. At last he said: 'There is nothing else I can tell you.'

'I see, sir. So just one more question: do you know the name Miss Dora Lethbridge?'

'Ah, my daughter mentioned you asked her that. To the best of my recollection, I have never known anyone of that name.'

'Then that's all, sir. Thank you.'

Timothy stood up, gave another stiff little bow of the head and left the room.

'You let him off pretty lightly, didn't you?' Leather asked.

'For the moment.'

'But there was obviously something he was on the verge of telling us.'

'I know. I asked him if he *wanted* to tell us anything, and as you say, he plainly did. But he didn't know if he *should*. He decided not. I could have pressed him. But when a man like that makes up his mind there's no budging him. We'll get it out of him sooner or later, if we need to. Interesting answer he gave to the last question, too.'

'About the mysterious Dora? I didn't spot anything.'

'Read the question and answer.'

Leather consulted his notebook. '"Do you know the name Miss Dora Lethbridge?" "My daughter mentioned you asked her that. To the best of my recollection, I have never known anyone of that name."'

'I didn't ask him if he'd ever *known* a Dora Lethbridge, but if he knew the *name*.'

'Think that means anything?'

'I think when anyone uses language as carefully as Saunders, KC, it nearly always means something.'

'Want me to go and fetch Gregory the Great?'

'Yes, and make sure you treat him with all the deference and respect that befits a Member of Parliament.'

CHAPTER TWENTY-SEVEN

Gerry was feeling a bit disgruntled. Sitting in on the interview with Jean Mackenzie had been fine, but Tommy, Stella and Penny had all politely rejected her offer to accompany them during their interrogations. So her own investigation had come to a dead-end. Now she had the distraction of her father's odd behaviour. Perhaps she ought to tell her mother about it, just so that she could be on the watch for any other eccentricities.

She found the Countess in the morning-room, and was about to give an account of the Earl's behaviour when Merryweather entered.

'Bates has been on the telephone from the lodge, my lady. Miss Agatha Saunders has just arrived on her motor-cycle.'

'Oh, thank you, Merryweather. Tell his lordship, will you; he is in his study, I believe. And show Miss Saunders straight in here.'

The butler bowed and withdrew. 'You were saying, dear?' the Countess asked.

'Nothing important. It'll keep.'

The Earl joined them, looking, Gerry had to admit, quite normal, if a bit pre-occupied. She and her mother both noticed something that looked strangely like a grey sock protruding from his side pocket, but before either of them could say anything, Merryweather returned. 'Miss Saunders, my lady.'

Agatha positively strode into the room. She was wearing a fur-lined leather jacket, over a scarlet sweater, and jodhpurs. Her face was red from the wind. Lord Burford went forward and took her hand. 'Hello, my dear. So sorry about all this. You have our deepest sympathy. It's shockin'. Feel terribly guilty.'

'No, Cousin George, you mustn't, please. Nobody could possibly blame you.'

'Nice of you to say so. You remember Lavinia and Geraldine?'

'Yes, of course. How are you, Cousin Lavinia? And you, Geraldine?'

They kissed. 'We're very well. More important is how you are, Agatha?' the Countess asked.

'Oh, I'm OK. In a bit of a daze, still. Can't take it all in. All that money, and now our stepmother murdered. It's unbelievable.'

'Is your throat better?'

'There was never anything wrong with my throat, Cousin Lavinia. That was my stepmother's little story, to account for my not being here. She won't have us all leaving the house at the same time. I'm sorry. But, tell me: how's Dorry?'

'She was devastated last night,' Gerry said. 'I stayed with her for some time, until she told me she wanted to be alone. We haven't actually seen her this morning. After she phoned you, she went back to bed. She told our butler that she'd been awake all night.'

'I looked in on her about half an hour ago,' Lady Burford said. 'She was fast asleep. No doubt quite exhausted emotionally and physically.'

'I'm not surprised. I'm amazed she didn't go completely to pieces.'

'How much did she tell you?'

'Well, just a brief outline, really. I'll get all the details from her later. But I'm not going to disturb her yet.'

'Will you have some coffee?' the Earl asked.

'Cousin George, that would be an absolute life-saver.'

Gerry rang the bell.

'Do sit down,' said Lady Burford.

'Thank you.' She slipped off her leather jacket, sank into a chair and dropped the jacket on the floor. 'Forgive the clobber, by the way. Only practical outfit for motor-cycling. I have bought some more suitable stuff, and I'll change shortly, if I may.' She leaned back and hitched her left leg up, resting the ankle on her right knee, in a very masculine way. Unlike her sister, she seemed totally at ease and relaxed.

'You will be staying, I take it?' the Countess asked.

'If that's OK.'

'Of course. We invited you and expected you yesterday, so we had had a room prepared. In the event I gave it to Timothy, but the one I had in mind for him is free.'

'Thanks very much. I appreciate it, and I'd like to stay as long as Dorry does. I suppose exactly how long that is will depend on the police. They are here, are they? I saw a

Wolseley outside that looked as though it might be a police car.'

Gerry nodded. 'They've been interviewing everybody.'

At that moment, Merryweather entered with coffee. 'Ah, you anticipated us,' Lord Burford said.

When the butler had left, Agatha uncrossed her legs, sat up, groped in the pocket of her jacket on the floor and produced a packet of cheroots. 'May I?'

'By all means,' the Countess replied, hiding her surprise admirably.

'What are those like?' Gerry asked.

'Try one.' Agatha proffered the packet.

'Oh, thanks.' Gerry took one, casting an amused glance at her mother. She knew the Countess could not protest, without tacitly criticising their guest. Agatha lit it for her. Gerry drew on it, and concealed a grimace. 'Interesting,' she said.

'An acquired taste.' Agatha looked at the Earl. 'So, what do the police think, do you know?'

'They've said nothing yet.'

'But it does have to have been one of the household?'

'Seems so. They've cleared the servants. They know it wasn't Dorry or Gerry. And it seems they don't suspect Lavinia or me.'

'I should hope not. And I'm sure it wasn't Miss Mackenzie. I've got to know her quite well, and I can't imagine a more unlikely murderess.'

'Seems she's responsible for the funeral takin' place here at all,' the Earl said. He recounted Miss Mackenzie's story, which she had confessed after emerging from her interview.

Agatha shook her head. 'Who'd have thought it? Still, she'd have hardly admitted that if she *had* been the murderer, would she? So that just leaves the relatives, doesn't it? Gregory Carstairs, Timothy Saunders, Penelope Saunders, Tommy Lambert and Stella Simmons. Is that right?'

Gerry nodded. 'Do you know any of them?'

'Not really. I seem to remember Timothy from Daddy's funeral, but I knew virtually nothing about the others before I started visiting Grandmamma. She loved to talk about all her relations, and I was glad to hear it, because we've never had much to do with the family. Which is why I cannot conceive why any of them could have had a motive for killing my stepmother. Though Dorry was a bit incoherent on the phone, she did say something about Mother threatening them all in some way. Could you tell me about that?'

'Well, that was a bit embarrassin', actually,' Lord Burford said. He ran briefly through what had occurred, while underplaying the degree of Clara's anger and malevolence; she would, he thought, hear about that soon enough from Dorothy.

When he'd finished, Agatha stubbed out her cheroot. 'Sorry about that. It's typical of Mother, I'm afraid. *De mortuis*, and all that, but she did have a fearsome temper and didn't take kindly to being slighted. Now, could you tell me just what happened last night, please? As I said, I only got a very sketchy account from Dorry on the phone.'

Gerry took it upon herself to do this. When she had finished, Agatha was silent for half a minute, before saying: 'Poor Mother. Still, I suppose it's a better way to go than some long, lingering death.' She looked round at them. 'Perhaps you think I'm not showing enough filial emotion. Well, I'm not going to be hypocritical about it and pretend a grief I don't really feel. Mother and I were at loggerheads for years. She's not here to put her side of it, so I won't say much. She fed and clothed us well, when we were kids, and brought us up to be reasonably civilised human beings. And there was never any physical cruelty. But I don't think she ever loved us. And she – dammit all, I'm sorry, but I've got to say it – she used Dorry as an unpaid drudge. She tried to do the same to me. But I'm not as sensitive as Dorry and I stood up to her and managed, to a certain extent, to live my own life. Dorry would never have done that. But now with this money, she may be able to make something of herself.'

She suddenly seemed embarrassed by this outburst, coughed, gathered her jacket and got to her feet. 'And, if it's all right, I'd like to go upstairs and change and freshen up now. And then I'll see Dorry. I can find my own way, if you tell me where my room is.'

'Second door on the right in the left hand corridor,' the Countess said.

'Thanks. And, I'm sorry, for all that. Very bad form, I know.'

And Agatha hurried out. 'Quite a character, what?' said the Earl.

'An unusual one, certainly,' said the Countess. 'I shudder to think what my mother would have said to me if I'd sat like that, even when I was Agatha's age.'

'She's much more interesting than Dorry,' said Gerry. 'And she's got no pretence about her at all.'

'I'm of the generation that considers there's a lot to be said for a little pretence sometimes.'

'You don't like her.'

'Oh, I don't say that. She's just not the type of young woman to whom I am accustomed.'

Gerry stood up. 'Well, must see how the investigation's going.' She went out.

'George, what's that sticking out of your pocket?' the Countess asked.

The Earl looked down and hastily poked the grey shapeless object out of sight. 'Oh, nothing.'

'Of course it's something. It looks like a sock.'

'Yes, it is. You know, when I'm trampin' round the estate I sometimes get my feet wet. Messing around by the lake, or crossing a ditch or something. Deuced uncomfortable. Thought if I carried a spare pair of socks with me, it would save having to trudge back to the house to change every time.'

'But – but it hasn't rained for two weeks at least. The ditches must be quite dry. And why would you step into the lake?'

'Well, it's not for now especially. But if I get into the habit of keeping a pair in my pocket, they'll be there when I need them.'

Lady Burford blinked.

'Anyway, must go and, er, look over the accounts.' And he made off in the direction of his study.

The Countess stared after him.

CHAPTER TWENTY-EIGHT

Leather opened the door, stood back and Gregory strode in. He started talking as soon as he crossed the threshold. 'I must say at the outset, Chief Inspector, that I do not take kindly to being kept waiting so long.' He sat down and folded his arms.

'Oh, but, sir, you must understand that in every case of this sort, we choose one witness whom we recognise as being the most important and reliable one. We always leave this person until after we have spoken to everybody else, so that we can use his testimony as a kind of benchmark by which to judge what the others have told us. You, as an MP, were the obvious one on this occasion.'

Unexpectedly, Gregory laughed. 'Nice try, Wilkins. A load of codswallop, but a nice try. You left me till last because I'm your number one suspect; that's it, isn't it?' It seemed to Wilkins that he was actually quite gratified at the idea of being Number One.

'No, no, sir. I must confess that I do talk codswallop from time to time, but I assure you I don't at this stage consider you any more suspect than several other people.

I'd like to know indeed why you think that I should.'

'Because of my position. Who, as much as a Member of Parliament, is susceptible to being ruined by the merest rumour of scandal, no matter how unfounded? A paid companion? A motor salesman? A fashion journalist? An eighteen-year-old flapper?'

'Perhaps a King's Counsel, sir.'

'Not to the same extent. The press don't care about his private life, nor do his clients. It's not like an MP, with his constituents and his party whips breathing down his neck. As long as the KC doesn't breach professional ethics, or actually commit a crime, he needn't worry.'

'So you think Mrs Saunders may have been in a position to cause you embarrassment in this way, sir?'

'Yes, if her claim became public knowledge, it would be enough to set tongues wagging. Even though what she said was a total fabrication. In fact, her murder puts me in a worse position. If she hadn't been killed, I could have laughed it off, and if people looked as though they might be taking it seriously I could have issued a writ, and she would have been forced to eat her words. I can't do that now. Which is why, whatever it seems like on the surface, it is absurd that I should be considered a suspect at all.'

'I can certainly see the strength of that argument, sir. But, tell me, why do you think Mrs Saunders should have made that claim?'

'I haven't the foggiest. You'd do better to ask her stepdaughters. She claimed we were all in a conspiracy to do her out of her inheritance and deliberately slandered her to Florrie. It's ludicrous. I hardly know the others. It's years since I've seen George, Lavinia or Timothy. I've met

Miss Mackenzie briefly when calling on my great aunt. Oh, and apparently I met Stella when she was in her teens, but I have no recollection of it. I barely knew of the existence of Penelope or young Lambert.'

'And what can you tell us about last night, Mr Carstairs?'

'Nothing, really. Went up at almost exactly eleven. Woken around twelve-thirty by the commotion. Got up, learned what had happened. Joined in the search. Went downstairs and waited for you.'

'Do you have any reason at all, off the record, to suspect any one of your fellow guests of the crime?'

As with Timothy, there was a very slight hesitation before the reply came. 'No.'

'Are you familiar with the name Miss Dora Lethbridge?'

'Never heard of her.'

'Well, thank you, Mr Carstairs. I think that's all I need from you now.'

Gregory stood up. 'Look, how much longer are we going to have to stay here? I really need to get back to town.'

'I can't keep you here, Mr Saunders, if you decide to leave, but I would much prefer it if everybody remained one more night.'

'You think you might clear this up by tomorrow?'

'Put it like this: if we don't, it could drag on for a long time, perhaps weeks. Plainly, I couldn't expect everybody to stay that long, so one more day would be the maximum I would ask people to remain. If one person left today, it would probably mean others would want to follow his example.'

'Very well, I won't rock the boat.'

'Thank you, sir.'

Gregory went out.

Gerry saw her father leaving the morning-room and remembered she hadn't told her mother about the nettles. She decided she'd better get it over with and went back in, but before she could say anything the Countess forestalled her. 'Oh, Geraldine, good, I wanted to talk to you. I may be worrying quite unnecessarily, but I have to tell somebody. I'm rather concerned about your father.'

Gerry was suddenly alert. 'What do you mean?'

'Well, he's behaving very oddly.'

'Why, what's he done now?' She spoke sharply.

'"Now"? You mean you've noticed something, too?'

'Well, perhaps.'

'Tell me, please,' said the Countess.

'If you'll tell me.'

'Very well. But you first.'

Five minutes later Lady Burford said: 'Of course, your father has always been a trifle eccentric. And after all, some people do enjoy nettle soup, I believe, and carrying a spare pair of socks in one's pocket could be regarded as quite a practical idea. Nonetheless...'

'Putting them together,' Gerry said. 'And at this time, with policemen in the house and all of our guests under a cloud.'

'Precisely. He is terribly upset by what's happened. In a way, it's worse than the other times because these people are all members of the family. Quite distant relatives, they may be, but they do all have Saunders blood, and some of them actually carry the name. Your father is totally without any personal pride or conceit, but he *is* immensely proud of the family, and now it seems one of its members is a murderer. I'm wondering if the blow has just been too much for him. And it's all my fault, really. I virtually insisted on having them here.'

'Mummy, you mustn't think that. Daddy did fully agree eventually. No one could have foreseen what happened. And I think we are probably over-reacting. It could be he's just trying to take his mind off things. He does get these sudden crazes. Remember how he became an avid film fan, virtually overnight?'

'Cutting up stinging nettles in one's study, and deciding always to carry a spare of socks in one's pocket in the middle of the summer hardly fall into the same category. And if he wants to take his mind off things, why doesn't he go up and play around with his guns? That's what he's always done in the past when he's wanted to relax.'

'Well, there's nothing we can do about it now. Unless you think you ought to call Dr. Ingleby to come and see him?'

'Oh no. Not for the time being, anyway. No, we'll just have to keep a close eye on him – both of us. And hope the guests don't notice anything.'

'Tommy already has.'

Before they could say any more there was a tap on the door and Agatha and Dorothy came in. Agatha was now dressed, the Countess was relieved to note, in a very suitable tweed skirt and dark grey twin-set. Dorothy, who looked even paler than before beside Agatha's rubicund features, was still dressed in her funeral garb. Gerry remembered her promise to Wilkins and after a brief word hurried out.

CHAPTER TWENTY-NINE

As Gregory went out, Gerry came in. 'Just to let you know, Agatha Saunders has arrived and Dorry's up. They're both in the morning-room with Mummy, if you want to see them.'

'I do indeed.'

'Will you want me there when you talk to them, sir?' Leather asked. 'If not, I'd like to go through my shorthand notes, check everything's readable, while what people said is fresh in my mind.'

'That's OK, Jack, I won't need a note of what the Misses Saunders say.'

He and Gerry went out, to find Merryweather waiting to inform him that he was wanted on the telephone.

'Ah. Probably the result of the PM. I'll join you in a few moments, Lady Geraldine,' he said, and trotted off.

Having come off the phone, Wilkins was waylaid by Smithson, who told him he had finished the fingerprinting. Wilkins sent him back to Westchester and then went to the morning-room. The Countess introduced him to Agatha and Dorothy, who were sitting close together on the sofa.

Wilkins offered his sympathies. 'I'm very sorry not to have had an opportunity to pay my respects earlier, Miss Dorothy,' he said, 'but it didn't seem necessary to disturb you.'

Dorothy gave a nervous little smile. 'That's quite all right.'

'First of all I have to tell you that the post-mortem has confirmed that your stepmother was suffocated.'

Dorothy screwed up her face in horror and gave a shudder. Agatha squeezed her hand. Her face was grim. 'And you've no idea by whom?'

'Not yet, miss, no.'

'But by one of the people in the house.'

'Unless we find that the alarm system was faulty, I'm afraid so.'

The Countess interrupted. 'Oh, I'm sorry, Mr Wilkins, I should have mentioned that a man came by earlier and checked it. He said it's working perfectly and there's no sign of it's being tampered with.'

'Thank you, my lady. It's what we expected, really.' He looked at Dorothy. 'I'm not going to make you relive the horrors of last night, miss. I've had a full account of what happened from Lady Geraldine, which I'm sure is completely accurate. But I would like to ask both of you about the accusations which your stepmother made yesterday. What do you think was behind them?'

They looked at each other. Dorothy spoke first. 'She was terribly upset. She felt Florrie had slighted her in front of her relations.'

'As, of course, she had,' Agatha said. 'Dorry's told me what she said in the will about Mother's income proving inadequate, and that she'd made a few changes in it recently. I reckon that could have been one of them. I told Grandmamma about Mother's little enterprise some months ago. I must say, though, I wish Grandmamma could have been a bit more diplomatic, tried to say *something* just a little nice about Mother and perhaps left her some token, a piece of jewellery, or something. Not that perhaps she deserved it, as she'd no doubt provoked and upset Florrie after Daddy died. We never saw our grandmother when we were children. But it would have avoided what sounds to have been a dreadful scene, and spared poor Dorry the embarrassment.'

'Do you think she really believed there'd been a conspiracy?'

Dorothy nodded. 'I followed her up to her room and she was adamant that was what had happened. I didn't believe it, but I didn't argue.'

'Your mother, though, must have made herself some enemies.'

'Well, she did get a threatening phone call a few weeks ago.' Dorothy said.

'Really? Tell me about that.'

'It was somebody drunk and very abusive. He said she'd ruined his life and that he'd make her pay. I persuaded her to tell the police, but, of course, there was nothing they could do.'

'You think killing her might have been an act of revenge, Mr Wilkins?' Agatha asked.

'Oh, I doubt it, miss. No, I think the significance of her having enemies is that people the lady has exposed, like that caller, would often know whom they had to blame, would be extremely bitter and no doubt make this very clear to their friends. As a result, quite a lot of people – perhaps some of them in this house – would have got to know that when she threatened to expose somebody, she was genuinely capable of doing so. It wasn't just empty words. So this claim of knowing damaging things about her relatives: was that true?'

The young women again glanced at each other. Then Dorothy gave a little nod, as if prompting Agatha to answer.

She seemed to weigh her words before speaking. 'She was only really interested in people well-known or wealthy or of high social standing. So the only two guests here whom she might have targeted are Timothy and Gregory. She may have discovered something about one or both of them, but I've never heard her mention either of them in any context. So my guess is that it was a shot in the dark. She thought there was a fair chance one or both of them might have secrets in their lives, so she just let fly. I think she included the others, just because she was so angry with everybody, and also didn't want anyone to think she just had those two in mind. That is, as much as she had time to *think* about what she was saying at all.'

'I'm sure that's an extremely perspicacious analysis, Miss Agatha,' Wilkins said.

'Sounds spot on to me,' said Gerry. 'And surely the important thing is not what Clara knew or didn't know, but what somebody *feared* she knew.' She saw all eyes on her and smiled a little sheepishly. 'Sorry, Mr Wilkins. There I go again.'

'No, you're quite right, Lady Geraldine. Which is why,

if we don't clear it up quickly, it could take weeks – because it will be necessary to investigate each of the suspects exhaustively to try and discover if any of them do have a really big and clanking skeleton in their cupboard.'

'Well, just as long as you do get him,' Agatha said. 'I may not have been at all close to my stepmother, but that doesn't mean I want to see the swine who held a pillow over her face escape justice, especially if he – or she – did it to cover up something shady in their own life.'

'Well, I'll certainly do my best, miss. Now, there is just one more question, before we leave. Do either of you know of a Miss Dora Lethbridge?'

As one, they nodded. Agatha said: 'She was our stepmother's mother – our stepgrandmother, I suppose you'd call her.'

'We never knew her,' Dorothy added. 'She died before our stepmother married Daddy.'

'I see. The answer so near at hand all the time. Was Lethbridge her maiden or married name?'

'Both,' said Agatha. 'Apparently she married a second cousin or something, also called Lethbridge.'

'You don't happen to know the date of her death, do you?'

They both shook their heads.

'Or her birthday?'

The reaction was the same. 'What's your interest in her, Chief Inspector?' Agatha asked.

'It's this, Miss Agatha.' Wilkins produced a wad of papers from his inside pocket, ruffled through them and handed a card to Agatha. 'That was found in your stepmother's bedroom. I was wondering if she was planning to insert it in one of those In Memoriam columns some papers carry. People mark the anniversary of someone's death, or their birthday. If her mother was born or died this month, or next, it would be an indication that might be what she was planning.'

Agatha stared at the card. 'I don't remember her ever doing anything like that, do you, Dorry?'

'No. But that's not to say she never did. I never read through those columns, so I wouldn't have seen it, if she had.'

'And I suppose it's possible – if there was a particularly important anniversary coming up. Would it have been Dora's hundredth birthday soon?'

'She couldn't have been that old.'

'Fiftieth anniversary of her death? No, that doesn't seem right, either. Anyway, why would she have been writing it here? Though I suppose it might have just occurred to her, and it was something to do. She must have been pretty bored, staying in her room alone all that time.'

Dorothy held out her hand. 'Give it me, a moment.'

Agatha did so and Dorothy studied it closely. 'I don't think this is Mother's writing.'

'Are you sure, miss?' Wilkins asked.

'Not absolutely. It's difficult when something's all in capitals. But she always wrote an 'E' with a very short middle bar. There are' – she counted – 'three 'Es' here, and in each of them all the bars are the same length. See?'

She passed the card back. Agatha nodded. 'Yes, I see. But I never studied her writing all that closely, so I wouldn't know.' She returned it to Wilkins. 'I'm sure we could find out the dates Dora was born and died, if we went through Mother's papers.'

'Maybe we'll have to ask you to do that. But it's probably of no importance. It's just one of those little points one likes to clear up.' He got to his feet.

'You said you're leaving us now, Mr Wilkins?' the Countess asked.

'Only briefly, my lady. The sergeant and I are just going to slip down to the village and get a bite to eat at the pub.'

'Oh, please stay and have something here.'

'Oh, that's very kind. An offer I didn't expect.'

'I don't suppose you'll want to sit down with all the suspects – might be somewhat embarrassing. But if you don't mind lunching in the breakfast-room...'

'I think I can speak on behalf of Sergeant Leather when I say that will cause us no qualms at all, my lady.'

'He's been in his study an hour now,' said the Countess to Gerry later, 'supposedly looking over the accounts. But he only did it a week or so ago. And now with a murder investigation going on here!' She stood up. 'I've got to know what he's up to.'

'What are you going to do?' Gerry asked.

'Just walk straight in as though I didn't know he was in there. Tell him I was looking for some writing paper or envelopes, or something.'

'He might have locked himself in.'

'I hope not. He's never done that. It would mean he wants to keep whatever he's doing a secret.'

Lady Burford left the room and marched resolutely to her husband's study. Outside, she paused and listened.

All was silent within. She took a deep breath, turned the knob, threw open the door and marched into the room.

The Earl, sitting at his desk, spun round with a start and stared at her, a positively guilty expression on his face.

'Oh, George, I'm sorry, I didn't know you were still here. Do you have any envelopes? I seem to have run...' Her voice tailed off as she took in the contents of the desk. Two half-empty bottles of ink, one blue, one red, stood each side of a small bowl, which contained a purplish liquid.

With a great effort of will, the Countess suppressed any sign of surprise. 'What are you doing?' she asked casually.

'Doing? Oh, nothin' much. Just been makin' some purple ink. Mixed red and blue.'

'I see. Any particular reason?'

'Not really. Just thought it would be a change. Gets a bit boring, always using blue for everything.'

'I suppose it does. But couldn't you have bought a bottle?'

'Not likely to have any in the village shop. Would have meant sendin' someone into Westchester.'

'Was it so important to have some now?'

'No, no. But had the red ink. So thought, might as well, you know.'

'Of course.' The Countess was running her eyes rapidly over the other things on the desk.

'What was it you wanted? Oh yes, envelopes.' The Earl opened a drawer, withdrew half a dozen envelopes and handed them to her. 'That enough?'

'Oh yes, plenty, thank you. I'll, er, leave you to it, then. Try not to spill any.'

'No, I'll be careful.'

The Countess went out.

'Purple ink,' said Gerry. 'It's the sort of thing he'd usually think was rather vulgar.'

'Well, of course, it is. But that's the least of my worries. There was something else extremely odd.'

'What?'

'A thin strip of paper, with writing on it – big block capitals.'

'Saying what?'

'I couldn't tell. It was backwards.'

'Backwards?'

'Yes. Mirror writing. I didn't have time to work it out. For a moment I thought it was Russian, or some other language, but then I did recognise the word 'all' – 'LLA,' with the 'Ls' the wrong way round.'

'Anything else?'

'Not really. Well, there was a candle on the desk, which was a little unusual.'

'But why should he want it there at the same time as he was mixing the ink?'

The Countess shook her head helplessly.

'Well, all we can do is just keep an eye on him.'

'One of us can't always be with him, not with all these guests here.'

'Talking of guests, I think I'll enlist Tommy's help.'

'What do you mean?'

'Well, in spite of all outward appearances to the

contrary, I believe he might be quite a reliable sort of cove. And as he knows something about it already, I think to take him into our confidence to a certain extent, and ask him to help keep an unobtrusive eye on Daddy, might make him even less inclined to gossip about either the nettles or anything else he may notice that's odd.'

'You know him better than I do, so I'll leave it to you. But it's true I knew a number of young men like Tommy before the war. Quite vacuous on the surface. But a lot of them ended up leading battalions and winning medals.'

CHAPTER THIRTY

Wilkins leaned back in his chair, with a sigh. 'Well, that was very nice.'

He and Leather had just finished lunch, which had consisted of cold tongue, salad and new potatoes, with cold apple tart and cream for sweet. 'Told you, didn't I?'

Leather, who had been hoping for something with chips and tomato ketchup, finished up his coffee. 'Yes, it was OK. Could have done with a pint of bitter, though. So, what do we do now?'

'Well, we've finished here for the moment. Have to go and check up on a lot of things, but can't leave straight away, or it'll look as if we just hung on to get a free lunch.'

'Which, of course, we didn't.'

'What I really need to do is just sit and think. There never seems to be the time.'

At that moment, Gerry entered. 'Your HQ just phoned again, Mr Wilkins. I took it. They said it wasn't important to speak to you, but to warn you that the early edition of the London *Evening News* is splashing the murder all over its front page. So we can expect swarms of reporters outside the gates very soon, I suppose. Heaven knows how they found out so quickly.'

'Oh, I think I can guess, Lady Geraldine. I think you can, too, if you put your mind to it.'

She furrowed her brow. 'I don't think…'

'Your own personal mystery,' Wilkins prompted.

She gave a start. 'The early morning phone call! But who could it have been?'

'You should be able to work that out, too, if you're the detective I think you are.'

Light dawned. 'Of course! Right, I'm going to ask her, straight out. She's on the terrace, I believe.'

'I'll be right behind you, Lady Geraldine.'

Lord Burford dipped the paint brush in the purple ink and ran it down the length of the candle. Most of it immediately ran off, back into the bowl. 'Dammit,' said the Earl. It was being harder than he'd anticipated. The ink did not stick easily to the wax. After a couple more attempts, he took the candle by the wick, lowered it into the bowl and twirled it around before drawing it out. This time some ink at least stayed in place. He held it suspended over the bowl, spinning it round and blowing on it gently, until it had dried, then lowered it back into the ink and repeated the procedure. It took quite a long time, but eventually he laid the candle down on the desk and surveyed it proudly. Definitely a purple candle. Just what he'd wanted.

Then a little doubt began to niggle. It wasn't *really* a purple candle: just a white candle, inked to look purple. Suppose they could tell the difference? Oh, well, it couldn't be helped. It would have to do for now. He could always get a real purple candle later on. He took the strip of paper, with the mirror writing, wound it round the candle and held it in place with a small rubber band.

One more job nearly completed. Now he'd better knock off for a while and go and see how Wilkins was getting on.

'All right,' Stella said. 'It was me. I called a guy I know on the *News* early this morning. It was the chance of a huge scoop. But where's the harm? You couldn't have kept the lid on this much longer. Today or tomorrow you'd have had to issue a press statement. I just got in first by a few hours. And I didn't reveal the names of any of the guests, only that several well-known people were staying here. I didn't even give the name of the victim. I simply said a woman had been found dead, believed to have been suffocated, that the police were treating it as a case of homicide and that Detective Chief Inspector Wilkins of the Westshire police department was in charge of the investigation. Oh, and I did mention that a lot of cufflinks had been found scattered round the body. I thought that would give it a bizarre touch to hang the story on. If you'd asked us to keep quiet about it, I would have. But you didn't.'

'I take your point, Miss Simmons,' Wilkins said. 'I should have done so. But, as you say, no real harm done, I suppose. No more phone calls, or telegrams, though, OK?'

'Understood, Mr Wilkins.'

He made his way back indoors, leaving Stella and Gerry alone. 'Gerry, I'm sorry,' Stella said. 'But I don't think I've done anything to embarrass you or your parents. And look at it from my angle. I'm desperately trying to break into mainstream journalism. I've given the *News* an exclusive and several hours' lead over the *Standard* and the *Star*. They'll be cock-a-hoop. It's bound to put me in good with them. Now honestly, in my shoes, wouldn't you have done the same?'

Gerry, who was incapable of staying angry or feeling resentment for long, hesitated for a second, then smiled. 'Probably.'

'Oh, thanks for taking it like that. It's swell of you. I know there'll be reporters arriving. But it's not like a town house. They won't be able to get past the gates. So they won't bother anybody. Tell me, you've been helping the cops, I know: do you have any ideas yet as to who might have done it?'

'Nothing concrete. There is something at the back of my mind – something somebody said, or didn't say, or did, or didn't do – that at the time momentarily made me think "That's odd." But for the life of me I can't remember now what it was.'

'You don't think it could have been Timothy, do you?'

'It *could* have been. Theoretically, it could have been practically anybody.'

'But he seems such a non-violent type.' She looked thoughtful. 'Of course, there was the way he threw Gregory.'

'Yes, those quiet, repressed people can sometimes snap, if they're provoked.'

'You think he's repressed? You know, I think he's just shy and – outside the courtroom – rather unsure of himself.'

'You may be right. I haven't seen a lot of him.'

'Things aren't easy between him and Penny, apparently. She thinks he's too strict. 'No secret relations are strained,' as he put it. And that's probably an understatement. So one can understand it if he's a bit on edge.'

'Must be difficult,' Gerry said.

'I do hope it's not him. I kinda like the guy.'

'I fancy it's reciprocated.'

'Do you? Honestly? Why?'

'Oh, just the way he was talking to you last night. He lightened up a lot. He actually laughed.'

'Which I don't suppose anybody's done since,' Stella said.

'OK, Jack,' Wilkins said. 'We've done a bit more work since lunch, so we've justified staying on. We can go now. Let's tell his lordship.'

They found the Earl in the drawing-room. 'We've done all we can do here for the moment, my lord,' Wilkins said, 'and we're leaving now.'

'So when will you be back?'

'Difficult to say. There's lots to do and we're a bit short of time. However, I believe you can help me.'

'Certainly. What do you want?'

'Two things, actually. Sergeant Leather has to go up to London now.' (Leather, to whom this was news, concealed his surprise admirably.) 'And he needs to get on the earliest possible train. If we drive back to Westchester, the first one he could catch would be the two fifty-five, which wouldn't give him enough time in town to get everything done today. However, the twelve forty-five express will be leaving Westchester in about five minutes, which means it will pass through Alderley Halt at about five to one.'

'D'you want me to have it stopped?'

'If you please. What is the procedure?'

'Oh, I just phone the chappie at the Halt – he seems to be station master, ticket collector and signalman rolled into one – and he signals it to stop. There's plenty of time. What was the second thing?'

'You can tell me something about one of your guests; oh, nothing confidential, a matter of public record, but a thing it might take some time to find out.'

'By all means. Anythin' to speed things up. What d'you want to know?'

Wilkins told him. The Earl thought for a moment, before giving him the information he wanted.

'Thank you, my lord. That's a great help. And it all means that we'll be back tomorrow morning, if everything works out.'

'Really? Oh, that'll be splendid. Do you think you may be making an arrest then?'

Wilkins sucked air in through his teeth. 'Well, *if* our enquiries turn out as I hope, I shall then need to speak to several people here again, and give them a chance to change their earlier statements.'

'You think *several* people lied to you?'

'At least three, quite possibly more. Once we've got them out of the way, I think I may be making an arrest. But if we draw blank in the next twenty-four hours, then I'm not sanguine, not sanguine at all.'

'Well, I'm not surprised, Wilkins. I mean, there are so many mysteries, aren't there? That business of the cufflinks—'

'Oh, I know the explanation of that.'

'You do? 'Pon my soul. What about the Dora Lethbridge card?'

'I believe so, my lord.'

'The stolen toothpaste?'

'I have an idea about that and hope to confirm it today.'

'And the armour crashing down?'

'Yes.'

'Then what the deuce is it you don't know?'

'Who killed Mrs Saunders, my lord.'

CHAPTER THIRTY-ONE

'I'm wondering,' Stella said, shortly after lunch, 'whether it would be possible for Penny and me to get a ride into Westchester? If we're going to be here another twenty-four hours, we both need to buy a few things.'

'Of course,' Lady Burford said. 'I should have thought of it myself. You must be thoroughly tired of those clothes.'

'Well, they are starting to get a little crumpled, to say the least.'

'I'll have Hawkins bring the car round straight away.'

'Thanks very much. A shopping trip in a chauffeur-driven Rolls will be quite a treat in itself.'

'Forgive my asking, but how are you both placed for cash?'

'Well, we're a bit short. I'm hoping I can find a store which will take a cheque.'

'Don't worry about that. We have accounts at the two main stores, Harper's and Dawson's. Charge everything to us and settle up later, whenever it's convenient. Tell Penny the same. I'll telephone the two managers and instruct them.'

'That's terrific. Thank you very much.'

'It's the least we can do, considering the situation we've been at least partly responsible for putting you in. I wonder if anybody else would like to go. I don't imagine Agatha and Dorothy will want to leave here, but perhaps one or more of the men...'

Stella grimaced inwardly. A shopping trip with Gregory in tow was not what she had had in mind. She needn't have worried, however, as only Tommy, on hearing of Lady Burford's offer, decided to accompany the girls, though Timothy instructed Penny to buy him a shirt, plus some socks and handkerchiefs, while at the last moment Gregory requested Tommy to do the same for him.

The shoppers returned at half past four, loaded with packages. They reported – to the obvious delight of Penny – that they had been snapped on entering and leaving by the half a dozen photographers already gathered outside the main gates. The three then retired to their rooms to change. Stella emerged in a very plain light grey silk dress, of the kind which Gerry thought would be suitable for almost any occasion; while Penny had one in pale blue linen; both also had new shoes. Tommy sported a smart navy blazer and a pair of Oxford bags. Almost immediately Gerry cornered him.

'Yes, of course,' said Tommy. 'Glad to help. But what exactly d'you want me to do?'

'Just keep your eyes open and let me know if you see him do anything unusual. Or if anybody else mentions seeing anything. But don't let them know you're particularly interested.'

'Do my best. Where is your papa now?'

'He's gone back to his study. He's been there ages. I wish I knew what he was up to.'

'Can't you find some excuse just to go in and see?'

'I don't want him to know I'm checking up on him. There's a sort of unwritten rule nobody disturbs him when he's in his study, except for something really important. Mummy and I have broken it twice already today and I don't want to do it again. It's his sort of sanctum.'

'I've never had a sanctum,' said Tommy. 'Nobody's ever felt they mustn't disturb me.'

After Gerry had left him he sat thoughtfully for a few minutes. Would he be justified? Under normal circumstances, obviously not. Still, Gerry was clearly worried, and if the old boy *was* going off his rocker, somebody ought to know. He'd do it. He went outside.

Slowly, hands in pockets, he strolled round the side of the house. He gazed around him casually, kicked aimlessly at the turf and generally tried to give the impression of someone bored out of his wits. As he passed each window, he glanced quickly inside. He wasn't sure which room was Lord Burford's study. The first two clearly weren't, but as he passed the third he clearly saw the Earl, sideways on to him, seated at his desk.

Tommy stopped and stood for a few seconds, staring out over the park, then turned and looked up at the house, as though admiring the architecture. Slowly, he let his gaze drop, until he was looking straight into the study. The Earl was plainly engrossed in whatever it was he was doing and quite oblivious to being observed. Tommy, though, was unable to make out what was so engaging his attention.

He strolled on a few paces, glanced around to make sure the coast was clear, then moved up close to the wall of the house, bent his knees and in a crouching position moved a couple of feet, until he was beneath the right corner of the window. The Earl had been facing to Tommy's left as he had looked in, so viewing from this side of the window should mean he would be out of Lord Burford's line of sight, even should he happen to glance out.

Very slowly Tommy raised himself until he had a clear view into the room. The Earl was obviously working on something small, yet his movements were quite quick; it did not look as though he was repairing anything. A crumpled white handkerchief was lying on the desk, partly obscuring his hands.

Then the Earl gave his hand an irritated shake, sucked his finger, picked up the handkerchief and dabbed at his fingertip with it. Tommy could see that there were several small spots of what looked like blood on it. Lord Burford threw the handkerchief down again, this time in a slightly different position, giving Tommy a clear view of his hands.

For two minutes Tommy watched him in amazement, then moved clear of the window, straightened up, made his way back indoors and went in search of Gerry.

'He's bending pins,' Tommy said simply.

'He's doing *what*?'

'Bending pins in half and putting them in a little glass jar. He must have done about a dozen while I watched. He kept pricking his fingers, but he didn't stop.'

'Oh, lor.' Gerry looked really worried now.

'Probably a perfectly logical explanation,' Tommy said, encouragingly.

'Such as?'

'Well' – he groped for words – 'I know: people make models out of things, don't they? You know, Taj Mahal out of matchsticks, and so on. Might be possible to do the same sort of thing with pins.'

'Thanks for trying to help, Tommy, but do you really think…?'

'Perhaps not. So, what are you going to do?'

'There's nothing really I can do, short of calling the doctor, which Mummy's totally against.'

'Are you going to tell her?'

'I'm not sure. I'll think about it.'

'Well, if there's anything else you want me to do, just say the word.'

He went out.

Gerry sighed. She'd really had hopes of solving this mystery single-handed, but her father's odd behaviour meant she had not been able to spend as long on the case as she had hoped. He had told her about Wilkins' progress report. It was certainly impressive. But – he had not yet identified the murderer. Which meant she still had time. It was just gone five. Nearly three hours till dinner. She must put that period to good use. She stood up and left the room.

Lord Burford furrowed his brow. That, surely, was just about all he could do here. Only two more jobs, but very simple ones. He opened the drawer of his desk, took out a ball of string and a pair of scissors and cut off two pieces of string each about a foot long. He took from the drawer two small glass jars, both nearly full of bent pins, and a pair of grey socks, bulging like miniature Christmas stockings. These he put in his pocket. He struck a match, applied it to the bottom of the candle for a second, placed the candle in the centre of an ashtray and lit it. Then he left his study, locking the door behind him.

Gerry found Agatha and Dorothy sitting on the terrace, where Stella had been earlier. They were talking quietly, heads close together, but looked up as she approached and both smiled.

'May I join you?' Gerry asked.

'Please do,' Agatha said.

Gerry sat down. 'I've been feeling guilty that I've hardly spoken to either of you today. But I didn't really know what to say. How are you bearing up?'

They glanced at each other and Agatha answered. 'I'm OK. It was much worse for Dorry than for me, of course. I'm shocked, obviously, but, as I said earlier, I'm not going to feign any great grief. And to be brutally frank – which I feel I can be with you, Gerry, as I couldn't with many people – I have to say I think it was one of the best things that could have happened for Dorry. Though not the manner of it, of course.'

Dorothy looked distressed. 'You shouldn't say things like that, Aggie.'

'I don't see why not. It's a relief from servitude, petal.'

'I don't feel it like that.' She looked at Gerry. 'I'm sure you, and everybody else, got a very bad impression of Mother yesterday. And I'm not going to pretend she was always easy. But she'd had a very difficult life. I'm sure she loved Daddy and then to lose him like that so soon after the marriage was a terrible thing for her. And she was left with us: two little girls whom she'd really hardly got to know. She could have washed her hands of us. She had no real obligation. She could have sent us to grandmother—'

'Wish she damn well had,' put in Agatha.

Dorothy ploughed on. 'She could have sent us to a home. But no, she took us on. She brought us up on her own. She sent us to good schools. She protected us. Money was always tight but she worked very hard. I didn't like all the things she did. But she did them because she had to and we never went short. Yes, she did become embittered, but I think she had cause. And I'll always be grateful to her.'

Gerry felt a surge of guilt for all the uncharitable thoughts she had harboured about Clara. Someone who could engender such loyalty could not have been all bad. It made her more determined than ever to solve the case.

'I think that's wonderful,' she said. 'So there's certainly no doubt that you want this murderer caught, even though he or she might well be a relation?'

'Well, of course there isn't.' Dorothy looked quite shocked.

'And don't get me wrong,' Agatha added. 'I didn't feel so well-disposed to our stepmother as Dorry did, but she didn't deserve to be murdered. So I don't want the bastard to get away with it.' She bit her lip. 'Sorry.'

Gerry grinned. 'Don't apologise. I've heard much worse. The reason I asked was that it occurred to me that if Clara *had* given any sort of hint that she knew something bad about one of the others, you might have been reluctant to tell Chief Inspector Wilkins about it. I'd be the same myself. I'd hate to make the police suspicious of someone, just on the basis of a casual word. But if there *was* anything, you could safely tell me. I'd promise not to pass it on to Wilkins, until I could find something additional to back it up. But it might just be the lead I'm looking for.'

'Gerry,' Agatha said, 'if there was anything, we'd tell you like a shot. But she certainly said nothing at all to me.'

'Nor to me,' Dorothy said. 'She was interested to know who the other beneficiaries were – we all were. And we discussed them. But all Mother said was things like Timothy was obviously very well off and it was a waste to leave him anything, and that Gregory probably wasn't short of cash either and she'd be interested in seeing what Stella was like. Things like that. And naturally we speculated on what we might get.'

'I told Wilkins what I thought,' Agatha said. 'You were both there. Mother was bluffing. Only purely by chance, with somebody there she hit home. He believed the threat was genuine. And that meant Mother had to die.'

Next, Gerry went in search of Gregory. She eventually tracked him down in the billiard room, where he was knocking balls around the table in an aimless manner. He glanced up as she entered and put down his cue.

'Looks pretty heartless, I expect,' he said.

'Not at all. We've all got to take our minds off things somehow.'

'Just wish it worked.'

'Must be getting you down,'

'Being chief suspect?'

'Oh, not *chief* suspect – just one of half a dozen.'

'I'm under no illusions. Looking at the others, I've got to admit that I'*d* probably think I'd done it – if I didn't know I hadn't.'

'Well, it's good you can joke about it.'

'Must maintain the old stiff upper lip. Sure you feel safe being alone in a room with me? Don't think the other girls do. Stella was as nice as pie yesterday, but she's decidedly keeping her distance today.'

Gerry didn't think it tactful to explain that, from what Stella had said to her, it was not the fear that Gregory was a *murderer* that was influencing Stella. She hoisted herself up onto the table. Gregory offered her a cigarette and lit it for her.

'Yes,' she said. 'It must be very nasty.'

'I don't honestly believe they're going to try and pin it on me. But if Wilkins doesn't clear this up in a day or two, they're going to keep digging and digging – talking to my friends and colleagues, local party members, and so on. What I dread is that they'll never get proof and it'll just be left as an unsolved crime. The details are bound to leak out, and if just a few hundred people in my constituency decide I did it, my political career will be over come the next general election.'

Gerry drew on her cigarette thoughtfully. 'The only consolation I can offer is that, for all appearances to the contrary, Chief Inspector Wilkins is very smart. I'm sure he'll get to the truth. That is, if I don't first.'

'Doing a bit of private detective work, are you?'

'Trying to.'

'I didn't realise this was what they call a grilling.'

'Oh, don't think of it like that. I am speaking to everybody, but I don't expect anybody to break down and confess, or slip up and give themselves away. I'm just trying to find out what people are thinking, or anything they might know. So if there's anything at all that *you* know that you didn't mention to Wilkins, you could tell me in strict confidence.'

Gregory crossed to the mantelpiece, collected an ashtray, came back and put it on the edge of the table. 'What sort of thing?'

'Any strange or odd behaviour, even if it apparently had nothing to do with the crime.'

'Well, to be frank, just a few minutes ago I did see your father burying some small items outside, each side of the porch. Nothing to do with me, of course, but seemed rather, er, unusual.'

It was all Gerry could do not to over-react. Somehow she managed to give a little smile. 'Oh, that. Yes, it must have seemed odd. I can't explain now, but I assure you it's absolutely nothing to do with the murder. Feel free to tell Wilkins, if you like.'

'No, no, take your word for it, of course. Anyway, neither you nor your parents are suspects.'

'So did you see any of the suspects acting suspiciously?'

Gregory flicked some ash off his cigarette and carefully smoothed off the remaining loose ash against the inside of the ashtray. 'Oh yes,' he said.

Gerry gave a start. 'You did?'

'Most decidedly.'

'What? Who?'

'I can't tell you.'

'But why—'

'Because I have absolutely no confirmation, no witnesses. It would be just this person's word against mine. And if I was to tell the police about it, the person could quite easily claim to have seen *me* acting suspiciously.'

'Yes, but if you got your story in first, you'd have the advantage. If this other person did invent something about you, Wilkins would ask why they hadn't mentioned it before. They'd have a job to explain that.'

'Not really. They could easily put it down to a reluctance to, er, sneak, as we used to call it as kids.'

'Yes, I can see that, but I wasn't suggesting you tell the police at this stage: just tell me. I give you my word—'

'Naturally, I accept that without question, but I just cannot tell you, Geraldine. I'm sorry.'

'As you wish. But this thing, whatever it was, it does give you definite grounds for suspecting someone?'

'No.'

'But you just said—'

'Not grounds for suspicion. Knowledge. I know who killed Clara, Geraldine, know beyond all reasonable doubt. And as things stand at present, there's not a damn thing I can do about it.'

CHAPTER THIRTY-TWO

Gerry found Timothy in the library. He was sitting extremely tidily, feet together, hands folded, reading a very thick book. He closed it when she approached and started to rise.

'Please don't get up,' Gerry said. She sat in a chair opposite him, seeing with slight surprise that the book was one she had never seen before on ancient folklore and superstitions. He noticed her glancing at it. 'It was on the table,' he explained. 'Just caught my eye. Quite interesting. Amazing what they believed in those days. Still do, apparently.'

'Oh, there are some strange old customs still practised around here.'

She realised as she said it that it was not the best form of words, given their present circumstances. 'And I don't just mean murder,' she added, making it worse.

He smiled frostily.

'I realise what a terrible situation for you this is,' she said.

'It is not pleasant. One must hope that it doesn't

continue too long. And although I know that Wilkins is an experienced officer, his manner does not inspire confidence.'

'You shouldn't take too much notice of that. He's good. He does seem to be pretty baffled this time, though, I must admit.'

'An alarming fact.'

'Not for the murderer, though.'

'No, indeed. The thought that he might get away with it is truly horrifying.' Then he flushed slightly. 'Oh, I realise you may think I am in fact hoping that the murderer does escape; in other words that I am myself he. And assuring you that I am not would plainly be quite pointless. Obviously, I am one of the chief suspects. Believe it or not, I have even found myself considering which of my fellow-counsel I might brief to defend me, if the worst should come to the worst.'

'Did you choose somebody?'

'I could think of no one as capable as myself.'

On the surface, the words suggested a breathtaking arrogance. But in fact they came across as a balanced, impassionate judgement.

'However,' he continued, 'I cannot really believe it will come to that. In fact, to me it is truly bizarre that anyone could even imagine me capable of murder.'

Gerry decided on shock tactics. 'I can imagine it,' she said calmly.

There was no immediate display of indignation. Only his eyelid twitched rapidly three times. 'Really? I admit to feeling disappointment. Under what circumstances, may I ask?'

'To protect Penny.'

'Oh, I see. Well, yes, perhaps. I suppose most parents would kill to save their child's life.'

'Or even perhaps to protect her reputation.'

'Ah, I understand which way your mind is working: that it was Penelope who had some guilty secret, which Clara was going to expose.'

'No, my mind's not working that way at all. I'm just trying to think how a policeman's mind might work.'

'I cannot conceive of any police officer believing she could be guilty of anything which would make such a course necessary.'

'Again, I can – just. A road accident, perhaps. Say she knocked down and killed someone. It may not have been her fault, but she panicked, and drove on.'

'She doesn't own a car.'

'She could have borrowed one. Suppose the accident was seen by someone who recognised her, and who also knew about Clara's little enterprise, and passed it on to her. Penny could go to prison for quite a long time. You would be desperate to prevent that.'

'I would certainly do all in my power legitimately to prevent it. But most decidedly not murder.'

Gerry gazed at him. 'No,' she said at last, 'I don't believe you would.'

'Perhaps you think the less of me for it – consider that I should be prepared to kill in those circumstances.'

'Not to kill just anybody. But perhaps to kill a person like that in such a situation might be legitimate.'

'I cannot agree with you. However, we seem to have moved a long way from reality. Unless you believe some such course of events did actually take place.'

'Good lord, no. I'm just pointing out how to someone like Chief Inspector Wilkins, with his experience, almost anything is possible.'

'I take your point and I can see the logic of what you say. Nonetheless, I simply should not be a suspect. You see, I know—' He stopped.

'Know what?'

'It's nothing.'

Suddenly Gerry knew what had been on his lips. 'You were going to say you know who did kill Clara, weren't you?'

For the first time since she had met him, she saw him really startled. 'What – what – ?' he began, then took a deep breath. He obviously realised it was too late to deny it. 'How did you know?'

Gerry couldn't answer this. Had it been intuition? Telepathy? Or merely the more prosaic fact that Gregory had said almost exactly the same thing? Resisting the temptation to reply 'I have my methods,' she just gave an enigmatic little smile. 'Do you want to tell me about it – in confidence?'

'I'd like nothing better than to tell somebody, but I can't.'

'Because you have no evidence.'

'Yes.'

'And if you were to say what you know, the person you accuse might well fabricate a story about you.'

He stared at her. 'This is remarkable. I can almost believe you have psychic powers.'

'Nothing like that. It's simply logic. But you could tell

me – not the police – and be sure it wouldn't get back to that person. It might just help me to get to the bottom of this affair.'

He shook his head firmly. 'If I tell anybody, it will be the police. I might have to do so eventually. But in the meantime it would be unfair to burden you with knowledge which you were honour bound to keep to yourself.'

There was obviously no point in arguing with him. 'OK. Don't forget, though, that if this person has killed once, they'll have no compunction about killing again. Having this knowledge, you yourself could well be in danger.'

'That had not occurred to me, I must admit. But thank you. I shall be on my guard now. And I think you know I am well able to take care of myself.'

Gerry's brain had been in a whirl after she left Gregory; it was in a positive turmoil after she left Timothy. That they should both have come up with almost identical stories was incredible. Was one of them lying? Were they both lying? It was hardly possible to imagine that each had seen the other behaving suspiciously. So had they both independently seen a third person doing so?

Her cogitations were interrupted by Tommy. He wasted no time in preliminaries. 'Something else to report.'

She felt a stab of alarm. 'What?'

'Nothing much, this time. He was just walking round the courtyard, tying knots in a piece of string, lots of them.'

'When was this?'

'About twenty minutes ago. I saw him out of my window. And he seemed to be talking to himself. At least, his lips were moving. I couldn't hear anything. He could have been singing, I suppose.'

'If Daddy's walking round the courtyard, singing to himself, when we've just had another murder in the house, things are really serious.'

'Perhaps he was singing a hymn. You know, sort of private requiem, in memory of Clara.'

'I'd much rather he was talking to himself,' Gerry said.

'You didn't make me look too good in front of Geraldine, you know,' Agatha said.

Dorothy stared at her. 'What do you mean?'

'Well, here I've been telling everybody how badly she treated you, and then you come out with all that about how grateful you are to her, and how much you'll miss her. Makes me seem a pretty unfeeling bitch.'

'Oh, Aggie, I'm sorry. I didn't mean to. It's just that when someone dies you've got to think of their good points, haven't you? And she did have some.'

'How you can say that the way she treated you, I just can't understand. If she did have some good points, they weren't very obvious to me.'

'But there's no need to come out with it. Not here. It's just not the done thing.'

'Well, I've never been the one for doing the done thing, as you know. I believe in honesty.'

'Absolutely agree with you,' said a cheerful voice.

They both looked up sharply. It was Tommy, who'd approached without their being aware of him. 'Sorry. Wasn't eavesdropping. Couldn't help hearing what you said about honesty, though, and about not doing the done thing. I'm dead against doing the done thing. Positively an undone thing chap.'

He cleared his throat a little awkwardly. 'I just wanted to say one thing. Pretty pointless, really, sort of thing everybody'd say, but just wanted you to know, er, I didn't do it. Honestly.'

'Never thought you did,' Agatha said, gruffly.

'Dunno why. Could have done.'

'Anyone can see at first glance you could never be a killer.'

'Really?' Tommy looked a little disappointed. 'Bit too wishy-washy, eh?'

Agatha hastened to reassure him. 'Oh, I don't say you couldn't kill if it was necessary, in a war, say. But I can't imagine your murdering a woman.'

'Ah.' He seemed happier. 'No, no, jolly well couldn't. Anyway, we all know who did it, don't we?'

'I don't,' Agatha said. 'I only got here today and I hardly know the others, so I'm not prepared to speculate.'

'I am. Well, it's a process of elimination. Couldn't possibly be either of the girls or old Mackenzie. Timothy's far too cautious. No, it's got to be Gregory the Great. He's absolutely the type. Can't you just see him creeping into the room at night—'

'YOU INSUFFERABLE YOUNG BOUNDER!'

Tommy gave a start and spun round. Gregory was standing about eight feet away. His face was crimson and he was quivering with rage. 'How dare you! How dare you blacken my name like that! I'll sue! I'll take every penny of that inheritance of yours. I'll ruin you. But first I'm going to thrash the living daylights out of you.' He tore off his jacket and advanced on Tommy, his fists clenched.

Dorothy gave a scream and Agatha jumped to her feet. Tommy backed hastily away. His face had gone the colour of partly melted snow. He stammered.

'I say, frightfully sorry and all that. Only joking, you know.'

'Joking? You can joke about a thing like this?' He continued to advance and Tommy continued to retreat, holding his hands up in front of him.

'Stop backing away, you young coward. Stop and fight like a man.'

Tommy started to babble something, but nobody heard him because at that moment there was a further intervention. A small blue, pink and gold blur appeared, seemingly out of nowhere, and flung itself on Gregory. It was Penny. Like an avenging fury, she beat at his chest with both fists and tried to scratch his face. 'Leave him alone, you beast!' she screamed.

Taken unaware by the onslaught, Gregory was forced to back away, but eventually he managed to grab her wrists.

'Whoa, whoa,' he said, as if trying to calm an overexcited filly.

Penny squirmed and struggled unavailingly. 'You bully!' she shouted at the top of her voice. 'You – you Conservative!'

Agatha was standing indecisively, obviously quite at a loss to know how to react to all this. Dorothy had her hands clasped to her head and was rocking back and forth in her chair, making little moaning noises.

Tommy at last seemed to realise his situation: that he

was being protected by an eighteen-year-old girl. He drew a deep breath and stepped forward. 'It's all right, Penny, old thing,' he said in an unnaturally low voice. 'Thanks, but I can handle this.' He took her gently by the upper arm. The back of his hand against her side could feel her body trembling violently. 'Let her go, please,' he said to Gregory. 'She won't hurt you now.'

Somewhat dubiously, Gregory released Penny's wrists. Tommy gently drew her aside. Then he slowly removed his blazer, folded it and handed it to her. 'Will you hold this, please?'

He deliberately turned back his shirt cuffs and faced Gregory. 'I'm not a violent bloke. But if this is your way of settling differences, I'm willing.'

He clenched his fists and took up an exaggerated pose, left arm extended and bent upwards at the elbow, his fist level with his forehead, the other lower down; plainly a stance remembered from school boxing lessons. 'Come on, then,' he said,

If he was hoping the MP would back down at this stage, he was disappointed. 'Right,' said Gregory and moved forward. Tommy stood his ground and at that moment an ear-piercing shriek rent the air. It came from Dorothy.

'Stop it, stop it, stop it,' she wailed. 'I can't stand it! My mother was murdered yesterday. Have you no sense of respect? None of you?'

Agatha went to her and put an arm round her shoulder. She looked at the others. 'She's right, you know.'

Gregory slowly lowered his fists. 'Sorry. Sorry, my dear. Lost my head. Bad form, in front of you and all that. Forgive me.' He glared at Tommy. 'Count yourself very lucky we're in the presence of ladies. I'm just sorry the days of duelling are over. I advise you to keep out of my way the rest of the time we're here.' He looked at Penny. 'And as for you, young lady, your father should give you a damn good spanking. Still, like father, like daughter, I suppose.' He made a stiff bow to Dorothy and Agatha, picked up his jacket and strode off towards the house.

In a most unladylike gesture, Penny poked out her tongue at the retreating figure.

Tommy looked at the sisters. 'My apologies as well.'

'Me, too,' Penny added.

Tommy offered his arm. 'Shall we go and see if someone will give us a drink?'

'Oo yes, that would be lovely.'

She tucked her arm in his and they strolled off.

It occurred to Agatha that in death her stepmother was capable of stirring up almost as much trouble as when she was alive. But she kept the thought to herself.

'You were wonderful, Tommy,' Penny said, 'standing up to him like that.'

'Well, thanks to you, got to admit. Couldn't let a girl fight my battles for me. I say, it was jolly sporting of you to stick up for me like that. Thanks awfully.'

'I hate him,' she said simply.

'Gosh, I wish duelling was still carried on, too. I bet I could make rings round him with a sword.'

'Of course you could, Tommy. Or with a pistol.'

He stopped, turned and looked at her. 'Er, there's something I've got to say, old girl.'

'What, Tommy?' Her voice and expression were eager.

'There's something you don't know about me. Fact is, that, well – I'm a Conservative, too.'

Her eyes widened and he hastened to reassure her. 'Oh, I don't mean I'm a member of the party, or anything like that. But I do vote for them. Well, I did once. Well, last time. Well, the only time I've voted, actually.'

Penny blinked. 'I see,' she said slowly, clearly perplexed. 'So, you think they're all right, do you?'

'Well, yes, not bad.'

'Not reactionary relics?'

'Not especially.'

She furrowed her brows in a deep frown. This was obviously a totally new concept, which took some grasping. 'Are you going to do it again?'

'Probably. Haven't really given it a lot of thought yet. Couple of years to go, after all.'

She looked relieved. Two years was an eternity. 'Yes, of course. That's all right then. And I think it's very brave of you to tell me, Tommy. You didn't have to. You could have kept quiet about it and I'd never have known.'

He smiled modestly. It seemed that nothing he could do was wrong. It was a rather pleasant feeling.

CHAPTER THIRTY-THREE

Gerry turned away from the window, to which she had hurried when she first heard Gregory's shout of rage and from which she had watched everything that went on. A completely new thought had come to her. Earlier, she had suggested to Timothy that he would be willing to kill to protect Penny. But she had just seen Penny, faced with a perceived threat to someone she cared for, turn in total fury and abandon on the source of that threat – even though the most damage Gregory had been likely to inflict on Tommy was a black eye. How would she have reacted had the threat been much worse, either to Tommy – or to her father?

If Timothy did have a guilty secret, it was quite possible Penny knew about it. If Tommy had one, she was at least more likely than anyone else present to know about it. And if she truly believed Clara had been about to make it public...

Gerry had not until now seriously considered Penelope as a suspect. But there was a remorseless single-mindedness about the girl which made Gerry realise that this had been a mistake.

But which of them would she kill for? Her devotion to Tommy was plain. But what could *he* have done that was so terrible that it had to be covered up at all costs? She came back to her earlier idea about a road accident. A hit and run. Tommy driving – and Penny with him. That was quite feasible. If someone had been killed and Tommy was proved to have been the driver, he would go to prison for a very long time. And for someone like Tommy to be shut up in Dartmoor or somewhere like it for many years would almost be as bad as a death sentence. (Of course, this line of thought put Tommy himself very much back in the picture as a serious suspect; but for the moment, she was concentrating on Penny.)

The trouble was that she just could not see Tommy being so carefree if he had something like that hanging over him. Even with Clara out of the way, there was always the possibility that the hit and run would come to light. Surely any decent person would feel a terrible guilt for the rest of their life: Gerry knew she would. And she still felt Tommy was basically a decent person.

No, of the two men in Penny's life, Timothy was by far the more likely to have something on his conscience – something that he might, in a weak moment, have confided to his daughter. Some professional indiscretion. Jury tampering or the bribing of a witness. Or more likely something not quite so blatant, some breach of the legal rules that the ordinary person might not think was too bad, but which would put a lawyer beyond the pale in the profession. Failing to disclose evidence – something like that.

One important thing to discover was just how much

Penny cared for her father's welfare, how far she would be willing to go to protect him. If things were as difficult between them as Stella had said, it might be that she wouldn't care too much if he did come some kind of cropper.

Perhaps she could devise some sort of test to discover just how devoted a daughter Penny really was.

Gerry spent ten minutes in intense thought and at last came up with an idea. She would need two accomplices. Yes, Stella for one, and her mother would do for the other; she would only have to sit and listen. Now, what was the name of that book, and where was it? If she couldn't find it she was sunk – she had actually to have it in her hands at the time. Another fifteen minutes was spent unsuccessfully scouring first her room and then the library. Eventually, she found her mother writing a letter in her boudoir and asked her if she had seen it.

'Oh yes, I'm reading it at the moment,' said the Countess. 'It's by the side of my bed.'

'Oh, terrific! Could you please bring it to the drawing-room straight away?'

'Am I to know why?'

'Eventually, Mummy, but it would take too long to explain now. I've got to find Stella.' She rushed off. Lady Burford gave a little shrug to herself and made her way to her bedroom.

Gerry located Stella in her room, also busily writing. She could not help noticing that the page was headed 'My Ordeal as a Murder Suspect.'

'I want you to do something for me,' Gerry said. 'It's important. Could you bring Penny to the drawing-room in about five or ten minutes?'

'I guess so. Why?'

'It's a long story. Don't let her know I asked you to do it, come into the room without speaking, but do make enough noise for me to know you've arrived. Cough or something. And whatever you hear me saying, don't react at all.'

'But what reason do I give her?'

'Oh, you'll think of something.' She scurried towards the door again.

'Where is she?' Stella asked.

'I don't know,' Gerry called, as she vanished, 'but she can't be far away.'

When Gerry got to the drawing-room, she found Lady Burford sitting meekly on the sofa, the book on her lap. Gerry grabbed it. 'Wonderful! Now I must find a good passage.' She sat down next to her mother and for two or three minutes she flicked frantically through the pages. At last she exclaimed: 'Ah, that'll do. Page one-seven-five.' She closed the book.

'Now what?'

'Tell me the plot of the book.'

'But you've read it.'

'Never mind.'

'I haven't finished it.'

'That doesn't matter. Just talk. And don't stop when you hear somebody coming in.'

'Well, it's rather a hackneyed story. It's about this young girl, Isobel, who is left an orphan when her parents are killed in a rail crash and goes to live with an uncle and aunt, who live in this big, gloomy house in the middle of the Yorkshire Moors.'

The Countess ploughed on until Gerry's sharp ears heard the click of the doorknob, followed by a rather theatrical cough. 'Stop in five seconds,' she whispered.

'Well, the girl doesn't know what to do. But then she has a surprise.' Lady Burford stopped.

Gerry said loudly: 'Oh, Timothy's a totally despicable character. Thoroughly deceitful and slimy.'

There was a few seconds' silence in the room. It was broken, deafeningly, by Penny's voice. 'I heard that!'

They both turned. 'Oh, Penny—' Gerry began, but got no further.

Penny was staring at her, an expression of pure loathing on her face. 'How dare you speak about my father like that! He's a wonderful man! He's – he's practically a saint. You're the despicable one, talking about him like that behind his back. I hate you, I hate you!' There were tears in her eyes.

Gerry jumped to her feet. 'I wasn't talking about your father.'

'Don't lie to me, you sly cat! I heard you say Timothy.'

'I was talking about a character in a book! This book.' She held it out.

'I – I don't believe you.'

'I'll show you.' She opened it and quickly found page one hundred and seventy-five. She handed it to Penny. 'There you are: read the second paragraph.'

Penny took it doubtfully and read aloud: '"I can't stand Timothy," said Isobel. "You're not alone," Frank replied. "In fact, I don't know anyone who's got a good word to say for him."'

'There you are, you see,' Gerry said. 'I read it some

time ago and Mummy's half way through it. We were just talking about it. I said despicable *character*, not *person* or *man*.'

'Oh,' Penny said blankly. The anger had drained from her face. 'I'm sorry. I – I really thought...'

'Of course you did. I'd have thought the same. But I'd never talk about your father like that. I don't really know him. But I do know he's got a fine reputation.'

'Yes, yes, he has.'

'It's just a very weird, unfortunate coincidence. Come on, let me get you a glass of sherry.' She moved with Penny to the far side of the room.

Stella came forward to join the Countess. 'Do you have any idea what that was about?' she asked.

'Absolutely none, my dear. But one gets used to that, living with Geraldine.'

'I think I'm beginning to get an inkling,' Stella said.

'I don't intend even to try and understand.' She frowned suddenly.

'Something wrong?'

'Not really. I just didn't know Frank felt like that about Timothy. I thought they got on rather well.'

CHAPTER THIRTY-FOUR

When Gerry went up to change for dinner, she was feeling very pleased with herself. She had proved one thing beyond doubt: however strained things had been between Penny and Timothy, in reality she idolised him. If looks could have killed, Gerry thought, she would be dead by now, simply for appearing to say something derogatory about him. If she had represented actual danger, would those looks have been converted into action? She was beginning to think it was very possible. The trouble was that her experiment hadn't really got her any further forward. No matter how sure she was that Penny would kill to protect her father, she still couldn't say that she actually had.

Nor had she yet remembered what it was that had struck her as somehow wrong. She'd heard that hidden memories were sometimes recalled in dreams. Before she went to sleep tonight, she must will herself to remember.

She had spoken now to practically everybody – well, with one exception. She hadn't had any really long conversation with Tommy since the murder. She couldn't think it would do any good, and didn't even know what she would ask him. But she supposed that for the sake of completeness she ought at least to go through the motions. There was still about forty-five minutes before dinner. He might be in his room.

She left her own room, went to the east corridor and tapped on his door. There was a cheerful call of 'Come in.'

He was lying on the bed, smoking and reading a new P.G. Wodehouse novel. He could almost be a character in it himself, she thought. There was definitely a touch of the Wooster about him.

He sat up when he saw her and swung long legs onto the floor. 'Hello, Gerry. This is an unexpected pleasure. Take a pew.' He indicated the room's only chair.

'Thanks.' She dropped into it.

'Gasper?'

'Oh yes, please.'

He gave her one and lit it. 'Nothing else to report, by the way.'

'Oh, good. But I didn't want to talk about that now. Tommy, do me a big favour.'

'What's that?'

'Confess to the murder of Clara.'

He grinned. 'Like to oblige, and all that, but just wouldn't be true, and well, second George Washington, me.'

'You think it was Gregory, don't you?'

'Ah, you heard about our little fracas?'

'Saw it through the window. Heard quite a lot. You stood up to him well.'

'Eventually. In a bit of a funk, actually. Bad show all round, of course. Should have kept my mouth shut.'

'Did you have any particular reason for accusing him?'

Tommy wriggled awkwardly. 'Not really, I suppose. Just seems more the type than anyone else.'

'Tommy, do you know anything at all that you didn't tell the police? Anything you could tell me, in confidence.'

There was just a split-second pause before he answered. 'No, not a thing.'

It was enough for Gerry. She sat up and looked at him sharply. 'You do, don't you?'

'No, no, honour bright.'

'Tommy, second George Washington, remember?'

He had gone a little pink. 'Nothing at all about the murder, truly.'

'But something else?'

'Well, perhaps. It's just that, well, I'm pretty sure, no, I know, actually, that someone here's been telling whoppers. But please don't ask me who.'

'I wouldn't tell anybody.'

'It would put you in an impossible position.'

'I could go to the person and ask them straight out.'

'And how would you tell them you knew about it?'

'I wouldn't tell them.'

'They'd know it came from me.'

'Would that matter?'

'It would to me.'

'But we're dealing with murder here.'

'It's got nothing to do with the murder. I'm sure of it. When that's cleared up I'm going to tackle this person myself. But to do it now would only muddy the waters.'

'And suppose the murder isn't cleared up?'

'Then I might have to tackle them anyway. But it will be. Gosh, it's not twenty-four hours yet. Give the rozzers a chance.' He was silent for a moment. 'I'll tell you what. Let me sleep on it. Then in the morning, if I feel up to it, I'll ask the person about it. And if they can't give me a satisfactory explanation, I'll tell you and you can tell Wilkins, if you like.'

'Oh, that would be marvellous. But couldn't you do it tonight?'

'Rather not. It's going to be dashed embarrassing and I want time to work out what I'm going to say. And, er, afterwards, if I am satisfied everything's OK, then that'll be OK with you, OK?'

'OK,' said Gerry.

On their way down to dinner, Timothy and Tommy met at the top of the stairs. Tommy gave a brief nod and started to hurry on down, but paused, with a slight tinge of alarm, when Timothy said: 'Oh, a word.'

'Er, yes?'

'Penelope's been telling me about what happened outside earlier. How you accused Gregory to his face of being the murderer and stood up to him and refused to withdraw when he wanted to resort to fisticuffs.'

'Well...' Tommy began, but got no further.

'I just wanted to say, congratulations. Showed a lot of courage, moral and physical.'

'Oh.' Tommy was taken aback. Penny had obviously been shamelessly exaggerating. Perhaps he ought to put Timothy right as to what had really happened. But, no. One shouldn't contradict a lady. Not the act of a gentleman. So he just smiled self-deprecatingly. 'It was nothing, really,' he said.

* * *

Gerry woke with a start. For a moment she thought there was somebody in the room. But no. What—

Then it came to her. She remembered what it was that had been wrong. It had worked. She had concentrated on the problem before going to sleep, and it had worked. She sat up and turned on the light. What did it mean? It couldn't really be significant, after all. Could it? She thought hard.

The next moment she knew. She knew who had killed Clara. It had to be. It was the only answer. For seconds she couldn't take it in. There was still no way of getting proof. Except – except that one other person had to know. Somebody had been covering up. Could she somehow persuade that person to tell the truth? Obviously it wouldn't be easy. But she had to try. She looked at the bedside clock. Ten past four. She couldn't go back to sleep, not tonight, with this new knowledge. No, she had to act now and use all her powers to force an admission. She got out of bed, put on her slippers and dressing-gown and left the room.

CHAPTER THIRTY-FIVE

'Wonder what time Wilkins'll be here?' Lord Burford said moodily.

He was picking at his bacon and eggs and for once *The Times* lay unopened beside him. It was 8 a.m.

'Extremely soon, I hope,' said the Countess.

''Course, he may just tell us he's drawn a blank.'

'Well, at least he'll have to let them all leave and we can get back to something like normal.'

'I sometimes think nothin' is ever going to be normal again.'

At that moment the door of the breakfast-room was thrown violently open and they both turned towards it. A dark, pretty girl rushed across the room towards them. It was Gerry's maid.

'Marie, what on earth—' Lady Burford began.

'Oh, milord, milady, it is the Lady Geraldine. I cannot wake her! She is so still and white! Please, you must come.'

They leapt to their feet. Lady Burford gasped: 'Oh no!' and then followed the Earl, as he ran out of the room.

The Earl charged into Gerry's bedroom and ran across to the bed. Gerry was lying perfectly still on her back, only her head showing above the bedclothes. He put his hand on her forehead, then pulled back the sheets and grabbed at her wrist.

'Is she – is she…' The Countess, behind him, could not finish.

'I can't feel a pulse. Looking-glass, quickly!'

Marie ran to the dressing-table, grabbed a mirror and handed it to him. He sat on the edge of the bed and held it close to Gerry's mouth for a few seconds, then peered at it. 'She's breathing.'

'Oh, thank God.'

The Earl swung round to Marie. 'Find Mr Merryweather, tell him what's happened and to send Hawkins for Dr. Ingleby at once. Hurry.'

Marie rushed from the room. 'And just pray he's not out,' Lord Burford muttered.

'George, can you tell what's wrong?' The Countess was wringing her hands.

He shook his head. 'Sorry, my dear.'

'Is there anything we can do?'

'I can't think of anything. If we tried to force some brandy down her, or something, it might be absolutely the wrong thing.'

'She's – she's still breathing?'

He again put the mirror to Gerry's lips. 'Yes. But it's so shallow. Her chest's not moving at all.'

The Countess fell on her knees beside the bed and took Geraldine's hand in hers. She closed her eyes and her lips started to move silently. With a restless, jerky movement, Lord Burford stood up.

A voice spoke from the doorway. 'Can we help at all?'

It was Stella. She and Penny were standing close together, their faces horror-struck.

The Earl answered. 'Oh. No, don't think so, my dear, thank you. You can tell the others what's happened.'

'Yes, of course. Come on, Penny.'

They went but a moment later there was the sound of hurrying footsteps and Merryweather appeared. 'Hawkins is on his way, my lord. I instructed Marie to wait outside and bring the doctor straight up.'

'Good, good.'

The butler gazed past him at the wax-like figure on the bed. 'Oh, my lord, this is terrible. But she must be all right, she must.'

'It's out of our hands, Merryweather.'

'May I remain, my lord?'

'Of course.'

Merryweather sat down on an upright chair and fell silent. The Earl took out some cigarettes and lit one with fingers that trembled only slightly.

It was only a little over twenty minutes, though seeming to those in the room like twenty hours, before they again heard hasty footsteps along the corridor and Marie's voice saying: 'In there, Doctor.'

Ingleby appeared in the doorway and strode across to the bed. The Countess and Merryweather got to their feet. Lord Burford said: 'We just found her like this, Ingleby, she was fine last night.'

'Yes, her maid told me.'

He opened his bag and began his examination. He looked in her eyes with a small torch, took her pulse and blood pressure and then pulled back the bedclothes, put his hand under the crook of her leg, raised it and struck it sharply just below the knee with the side of his hand. To her parents' inexperienced eyes, there seemed a momentary delay before the lower part of her leg kicked up. Next, Ingleby gently turned her onto her face and closely scrutinised the back of her head.

At last he looked up. 'Well, I can tell you what's wrong with her.'

The Earl and Countess stared at him apprehensively.

'She's been knocked unconscious.'

'*What?*'

'There's a big lump on the back of her head.'

'You – mean somebody just crept into the room and hit her?'

'I can't say whether they crept into the room, but she's certainly been hit with some heavy object.' He turned her over again onto her back.

'The murderer,' Lord Burford whispered. 'She's been going round questionin' everyone, hoping to solve the case before Wilkins. Oh, why couldn't she have left well alone!'

'Will she be all right?' Lady Burford asked fearfully.

Ominously, it seemed to them, Ingleby avoided a direct answer. 'I would ideally like to get her head x-rayed, but I think it's probably safer not to move her, at least for the time being.'

'But she will regain consciousness?' Lord Burford said.

'Prognosis is notoriously difficult in the case of head injuries. She will either recover spontaneously, or—' He stopped.

'Or what, doctor?'

'Sink deeper into a coma.'

'And – and if that happens?'

'It could be days, or weeks.'

'Or longer?'

'It's possible.'

'You're saying she could be in a coma, for months, or years.'

'Let's not think that far ahead. Twenty-four hours will tell. If she has not come round by then, I will have her removed to hospital and get some x-rays taken. We should then learn more about the extent of the damage and be able to make a more accurate forecast.'

'Is there nothing you can do now?'

'I'm afraid not. It's just a question of waiting and keeping her under observation.'

The Countess sank down slowly on the bed. 'Oh, dear Lord.'

'I'm very sorry I can't be more helpful. But I can say that in the majority of head injury cases the patients do recover spontaneously.' He glanced at his watch. 'I wish I could stay longer. But unfortunately I have another emergency awaiting me. I will look in again later. If Hawkins could take me home to collect my car...'

The Earl shook his head. 'Have Hawkins take you wherever you need to go for the rest of the morning. We won't be needing him.'

'Oh, that's extremely kind. Thank you. Just keep her comfortable and warm.' He hurried out. Merryweather unobtrusively followed him.

The Earl and Countess looked at one another. Her lips trembled. 'Oh, George.'

He put his arm around her shoulder. 'Bear up, my dear. She'll be all right. Gerry's a Saunders. She'll pull through.'

'She put the wind up somebody,' Stella said. 'She must have been getting close to cracking it, and the murderer realised that and decided to silence her before it was too late. No doubt thought he'd killed her.'

'*He*?' Tommy queried.

'OK, I know we're none of us in the clear.'

Penny gave a gasp. 'You don't think the police would suspect me, do you?'

'That cop suspects everybody. If the Archbishop of Canterbury was here, he'd be a suspect in Wilkins' eyes. And I figure we're all capable of violence.'

'Oh crumbs. Do you think he'll hear about yesterday – me and Gregory?'

'Afraid so, honey. Sorry and all that.'

The three of them were in the morning-room. Tommy, seeing Penny was distressed, quickly changed the subject. 'Talking of Gregory the Great, he's conspicuous by his absence this morning. Don't suppose he's done a bunk, do you?'

'No, I saw him from my window, mooching about down by the lake,' Stella said. 'Must realise he's still the number one suspect and wants to keep out of the way.'

'And where's your father?' Tommy asked Penny.

'He's in the library, catching up on some paper work. He says he knows he's a suspect, too. It's idiotic! If everybody knew him like I do, they'd never think for a second he could do anything like that.'

'Who else is missing?' Tommy said. 'Oh, Mackenzie. Anybody seen her today?'

The girls shook their heads. 'I wonder if anybody has?' Stella said. 'Gosh, I hope she's all right. If she'd seen the attack on Gerry, and the murderer saw her, she could have been attacked, too. I think I'll go and check.'

She left the room, went upstairs, made her way to the east corridor and tapped on Jean Mackenzie's door. She was relieved when she heard her voice call 'Come in.'

Miss Mackenzie was sitting in a chair by the window. There was a book on her lap but it was closed. She looked alarmed when she saw Stella. 'Is there any news?' Stella saw that for the third time in two days her eyes were red.

'No, not yet. You know what happened, then?'

'Yes, Geraldine's maid told me.'

'We wondered if you were all right. Is something wrong?'

'Oh, Stella, I feel so guilty.'

'What about?'

'What's happened to Geraldine. It's all my fault.'

'How on earth do you figure that?'

'You all know about the lie I told – that Florrie had asked to be buried at Alderley. It came about as a result of what I now see was my obsession with mediums and séances and that sort of thing. I'm giving all that up. However, it's too late to undo the damage I have done. At first I blamed myself for Clara's death, but the Inspector assured me that after she'd made that threat at the reading, she would have been murdered wherever it had taken place. But that's not the case with this wicked attack on

Geraldine. It wouldn't have happened if the reading had taken place somewhere else.'

Stella went across to her and took her hand. 'Look,' she said, 'Gerry was thoroughly enjoying herself. She knew there was danger involved. Dorry was telling me the afternoon of the funeral how Gerry had been saying to her that you have to be prepared for that sort of risk if you get involved in murder investigations. She herself would be the very last one to blame you.'

'You're very kind, my dear, but if that lovely girl – if she...she...dies, I'll never forgive myself.'

'This brooding all on your own is not good,' Stella said. She drew Miss Mackenzie to her feet. 'Now come on down to the morning-room. There's only Penny and Tommy there, and you know how you say he always cheers you up.'

'Oh, really, I don't think so.'

'I insist. And you can talk to us about Florrie. You knew her better than anyone, and she must have told you some wonderful stories over the years. I know I'd love to hear some.'

And she led the older woman, still protesting a little, from the room.

CHAPTER THIRTY-SIX

Nearly three hours had passed, during which Gerry had not stirred. The Earl and Countess had hardly spoken or moved, except when three times Lord Burford again put the mirror to Gerry's lips, afterwards giving his wife a brief reassuring nod. Then, a little after eleven, there came a light tap on the door.

It was Merryweather. 'No change, my lord?'

'Not yet.'

'Chief Inspector Wilkins is here, my lord.'

'Oh, I can't see him now.'

'He wishes to come in, my lord. He says it is important.'

'What? Oh, very well.'

Wilkins entered the room almost on tip-toe. He bowed his head stiffly to the Earl and Countess.

''Morning, Wilkins,' said the Earl. ''Fraid I can't talk about the case now.'

'No, of course, my lord. This is appalling, really appalling. I can't say how shocked I am.' He gazed down at Gerry, shaking his head slowly. Then he looked up. 'I've been given the details by Mr Merryweather and Marie. I understand you think the attacker came in here during the night and did this?'

'Seems obvious.'

'With respect, my lord, I think not.'

'Eh? What d'you mean?'

'May I ask if anyone has touched Lady Geraldine's bedroom slippers this morning?'

The Earl looked down at them. They were placed neatly side by side, close to the bed. 'No. Why d'you ask?'

'They're the wrong way round, my lord. Right on the left and left on the right. If Lady Geraldine had just lifted her feet out of them as she got into bed, they could not have got in that position. Which indicates to me that she was lifted into the bed. Either the slippers fell off, or the attacker snatched them off and let them drop, and then afterwards straightened them, without realising that they were in the wrong positions relative to each other.'

'Good gad.'

Lady Burford spoke for the first time. 'He's right, George. Something has been worrying me as wrong ever since we've been sitting here. Her dressing-gown.' She pointed to where it was draped on a hanger suspended from a hook on the back of the door. 'She never hung it up at night – just laid it across the bottom of the bed. And during the day it was always hung in the cupboard.'

Lord Burford said slowly: 'So she was up in the night.'

'Yes, my lord. Elsewhere in the house. About her investigations, no doubt.'

'And actually identified the murderer?'

'We can't say that for sure. It's possible she uncovered a

secret that someone other than the killer of Mrs Saunders might have been desperate to prevent coming to light. Now, forgive me but I must get on. My investigations are complete and when I arrived I took the liberty of asking Mr Merryweather to gather all the guests in the drawing-room. I must join them.'

'You've solved the case?'

'Let's just say I have logical and coherent explanations for everything that occurred, though at this stage I cannot be certain there are not equally logical alternative ones. And the attack on Lady Geraldine is an additional complication, which I cannot as yet fit in. Anyway, my lord, I felt it only right to tell you of my plans. I don't suppose under the circumstances you yourself will want to be there.'

'Not really, Wilkins, not really. Not at all sure I can face up to it.'

'I hate to ask you, my lord, but I really do need you there, just for part of the time. There'll probably be something I want you to do.'

'I see. Well, suppose I ought to be there, really. But I don't like leaving you here on your own, Lavinia.'

'Go, George,' said the Countess. 'Ask Marie to join me. I'm sure she would like to. I'll let you know the moment there's any change.'

'Very well. What is it you want me to do, Wilkins?'

'I'll explain on the way down, my lord.'

'Come along, then.'

He started to move to the door, then suddenly stopped and turned. 'Lavinia, it's no good, I've got to tell you. I'm partly to blame for this.'

'George, what do you mean?'

'I could have prevented it, but for my laziness and stupidity. I can't explain now, but I had to get it off my chest.'

He made for the door again, inside which Wilkins was standing waiting for him. As the Earl passed him he muttered something, almost under his breath. Wilkins raised his eyebrows, gave a little shake of the head and then made to follow him. But the Countess called after him. 'Mr Wilkins!'

He came back. 'Yes, my lady?'

'What did my husband say as he passed you?'

'I think he was just talking to himself, really, not to me at all.'

'But what did he say?'

Wilkins looked decidedly embarrassed. 'It was rather odd.'

'Mr Wilkins, please.'

'He said, "Should have had a real purple candle. Rosemary, too."'

Wilkins caught up with the Earl on the stairs. 'All I want you to do, my lord, is, if you are shown a pair of cufflinks, to identify them as your own.'

'Even if they're not?'

'Oh, they will be. So say they are, even if you don't actually recognise them.'

'Very well.'

Merryweather was standing outside the drawing-room, as though on sentry duty. He opened the doors as the Earl, Wilkins and Leather, who had been waiting in the hall, approached and went in. Like those of spectators at a tennis match, eight pairs of eyes swung towards them in unison. Gregory was standing by the huge fireplace and Tommy half sitting on and half leaning against a table just inside the window. The rest were seated, Timothy and Penny on one sofa, Agatha and Dorothy on another, Stella in an easy chair and Miss Mackenzie, as if in penance and recognition of her own perceived lower social status, in a hard upright chair against the wall.

Timothy got to his feet as they entered. 'George, is there any news?'

'No, no change.'

'Penelope and I are appallingly shocked, needless to say. You do both have our heartfelt sympathy and prayers.' He sat down again.

'Thank you,' said the Earl, gruffly. 'Appreciate it.'

'I'm sure that goes for every one of us,' said Gregory.

'Absolutely,' added Tommy. Gregory shot him an angry glance, as if he objected to having Tommy agree with him.

'I guess not quite *every* one,' Stella said dryly.

Miss Mackenzie gave a shocked gasp and there was no one who did not look embarrassed.

It was Wilkins who broke the silence. 'A very perceptive comment, Miss Simmons. Lady Geraldine was certainly attacked by somebody at present in this house. Needless to say, I rule out the servants.'

He moved to the centre of the room. There was a sudden air of authority about him that had been totally absent before. Leather and the Earl remained standing just inside the door.

'I'm sorry to have to ask you all to come together, like this,' Wilkins said. 'But there are questions I need to ask most of you, and I want everyone else to hear the answers. We need some interplay, some cross-fertilisation, as it were. I'm hoping one person may be able to add something to another's answer or comment, or possibly refute it.'

He paused, before continuing. 'According to Dr. Ingleby, Mrs Saunders died after eleven fifteen and we know she must have been killed before twelve thirty. That, obviously, is the key period. There were, apart from the murder itself, a number of very strange incidents during that time. I'd like to look at those in turn. The most obvious of them was the armour falling over. Miss Mackenzie, who was present, was totally unable to account for it.'

He swung suddenly on Tommy. 'However, you were able to give me a perfectly logical explanation of it, Mr Lambert.'

Tommy gave a start. His mouth opened. 'Uuuhhh,' he said.

'Perhaps you'd be so good as to share that explanation with everybody now, sir.'

At last Tommy found his voice. 'I say, Wilkins, this is jolly unsporting. I told you that in confidence.'

'I promised it wouldn't be revealed unless it became necessary, sir. It is necessary now. Perhaps you'd prefer it if I recounted it.'

'Well, if you must, I suppose,' Tommy said grumpily. He lit a cigarette.

Wilkins addressed the room at large. 'Mr Lambert explained that he was responsible. He had decided to play a practical joke on Miss Mackenzie, tied a piece of string round the armour, hid behind the sofa, and when she commenced her session with the ouija board, pulled the armour over.'

Jean Mackenzie stared at Tommy in horror. 'Tommy! I can't believe you did such a thing! You frightened me out of my wits.'

He was red-faced. 'I know, and I'm awfully sorry. It was an idiotic thing to do. It was just meant to be a prank, but it was quite out of place, I see that now. I didn't mean to scare you so much. Do forgive me.'

'I'm not at all sure that I can,' she said stiffly. 'I'm gravely disappointed in you.'

'It was a pretty mean sort of trick, wasn't it, Mr Lambert?' Wilkins said. 'Rather uncharacteristic of you.'

'All right, don't rub it in.'

'Very well. Anyway, that's one of the mysteries solved. Now to turn – oh.' He broke off. 'One small point first: where did you get the string?'

Tommy looked blank. 'Eh?'

'The string you used to topple the armour: where did you get it?'

'Oh. I usually carry some with me, you know.'

'I see. So there's a ball of string in your case now, is there?'

'No, no, not a ball. I just carry a length, you know, a few yards. Never know when it might come in useful.'

'So you still have it, do you?'

'No, think I left it in the gallery, actually.'

'No, you didn't, Mr Lambert. You said you only stayed long enough to gather up the string, before hurrying back to your room. Presumably you thrust it in your dressing-gown pocket.'

'Suppose I must have.'

'And no doubt it's still there.'

'Er, no. I remember now. I threw it away.'

'When?'

'Can't quite remember.'

'Why did you throw it away, if you always carry a length, in case it comes in useful?'

'Well, I realised that if it was found it might give the game away: you'd realise what it had been used for.'

'So you must have thrown it away before you told the Sergeant and me the story yesterday morning. You had nothing to conceal from us after that time.'

'That's right. It was early yesterday.'

'Where did you put it?'

'Oh. Jolly good question. Waste basket, I suppose.'

'Which one? Where?'

'Sorry. Shocking memory, you know.'

'Oh well, we can always ask the servants. I'm sure any of the maids would remember finding several yards of string in one of the waste baskets.'

'Oh, I remember now. Actually, I burnt it.'

'You did what?'

'Set fire to it with my lighter. In my room. And scattered the ashes out of the window.'

'Let me get this straight, sir. Because you feared that if we found a length of string in your possession we would immediately realise it had been used to pull the armour over, early yesterday morning you burnt it, threw the ashes out of the window – and completely forgot having done so until this moment.'

Tommy grinned weakly.

Wilkins gave a sudden shout, which caused everyone in the room to give a start. 'Oh, come on, Mr Lambert! Let's stop this farce, shall we? You no more pulled that armour over than I did. For one thing, with your height, you'd never conceal yourself properly behind that sofa. Smithson, who's four or five inches shorter than you, could only just manage it. Again, the armour fell straight forward, away from the wall. If your story was true, it would have toppled sideways, no doubt hitting the sofa. And don't say you rearranged the pieces before you left the gallery, because you've already said all you did was gather up the string, the non-existent string, I should say.'

'Oh, steady on. Why would I confess to a mean trick like that, if I hadn't done it?'

'For a very good reason, Mr Lambert. The armour fell at almost exactly the same time that Miss Simmons woke to find an intruder in her room. You realised that claiming responsibility for the armour incident would give you a perfect alibi.'

'But why should I need an alibi?'

'You didn't, no more than anybody else in the house. Just to say you were asleep in bed would have been perfectly natural, and I couldn't reasonably have expected anything else. Unless, that is, you had reason to think that you could fall under particular suspicion, that perhaps Miss Simmons had caught a glimpse of the intruder and might mention that he looked like you. After all, your appearance, even in silhouette, is highly distinctive: you're very tall and thin and no one else here looks remotely like you. The previous night, Miss Simmons had said she'd not seen the intruder. But suppose she was playing safe and was just waiting to tell me privately the next morning that she had seen you? So you needed a stronger story, apparent proof that you were nowhere near her room at that time. Miss Mackenzie's experience with the armour was a godsend to you and you quickly saw how you could use it to your advantage. Now, Mr Lambert, I'm going to give you one last chance: tell the truth. If you didn't kill Mrs Saunders and attack Lady Geraldine you have nothing to fear. But if you keep up this ridiculous story, then I shall have to assume the worst.'

Tommy licked his lips. Then he sighed and shrugged. 'OK, you're right. No, I didn't topple the armour. It was me in Stella's room.'

Only two people reacted, and in very different ways. Jean Mackenzie beamed. 'Oh, Tommy, I'm so glad.' He gave her a sheepish smile.

Stella, on the other hand, looked decidedly frosty. 'And perhaps you'd explain just what you were doing there, Tommy. And why in tarnation did you steal my toothpaste?'

'I didn't mean to steal it, Stella. I only meant to look at it. But I'd just got my hand on it when you woke up and I ran out still holding it.'

She stared at him in bemusement. 'You wanted to look at my toothpaste? Are you loco, or something?'

'Yes, I'm sure we'd all be interested to know just what fascination Miss Simmons' tube of Dentigleam held for you, Mr Lambert,' Wilkins said.

'I – I really only wanted to know whether she used toothpaste at all.'

'Oh, so my teeth looked dirty, did they? Well, have a

good look. Do they look dirty now?' She bared them at him in a mirthless smile.

'No, no, they're fine,' he said hastily. 'Very white. But, well, they're not perfect. They're not a hundred per cent straight.'

'Oh, I'm so sorry if they offend you!'

'What I mean is they're obviously natural.'

'Well, of course they're natural!'

'But they shouldn't be, should they, Mr Lambert?' Wilkins said quietly.

Tommy shot him a surprised glance. 'No,' he said. 'You see, my cousin, Stella Simmons, had all her teeth extracted after rheumatic fever, when she was in her teens. She wore false ones always, after that. And if your teeth are natural, it means you're not Stella at all.'

CHAPTER THIRTY-SEVEN

For a good five seconds, she said nothing and showed absolutely no emotion. Then at last she gave Tommy a very small smile. 'So, maybe you're not loco,' she said. 'Perhaps you'd better finish your story before I say anything.'

Wilkins realised she was giving herself a little time to think, but he didn't intervene.

'OK. Well, I was only a little kid when Stella had her teeth out, but when I heard about it I was fascinated. I'd never known anybody young who had false ones. They were something for grandparents. I longed to ask her to take them out and show me, but when I mentioned this to my mother she was horrified and told me I was on no account ever to mention them to Stella. I'd more or less forgotten about it, but then, after dinner, the first night, she laughed and I saw her teeth properly for the first time. And then it all came back to me. I was shaken. They looked so obviously natural, and all the false teeth I've seen have been absolutely perfect – too perfect. You can nearly always spot them. It occurred to me that perhaps in America now they're deliberately making them a bit crooked, just to make them look natural. But one thing I do know is that ordinary toothpaste is no good for false teeth; it doesn't get them white. People use special denture cleaner. I thought if Stella was using one of those, it would show that her teeth were false and everything was OK. But if she was using ordinary toothpaste – well, it wouldn't *prove* her teeth were natural, but it would be a pretty strong indication. And, well, that's it, really.'

'Didn't it occur to you just to ask me straight out?' she asked.

'Yes, but I funked it at first. Thought there might be some perfectly normal explanation, and that I'd make myself look the most awful idiot. But after I'd found you *were* using ordinary toothpaste, I made up my mind to tackle you. And I would have done if it hadn't been for the murder. I mean, someone had crept into a woman's room at night and suffocated her. How could I admit to anybody that same night I'd crept into another woman's room and then run out when she'd woken up? It would look as though I was a homicidal maniac, hunting for another victim. Besides, you'd have either denied you were an impostor, in which case I'd be pretty sure you were lying, or admitted it. Whatever, I'd be almost bound to tell Mr Wilkins, and it would obviously make you the number one suspect. And I didn't want that to happen because I was quite sure you weren't the murderer.'

She raised her eyebrows. 'I'm flattered. What made you so sure?'

'You were fast asleep when I went into your room. I could tell from your breathing and the way you suddenly woke up. I couldn't believe that anyone, except a hired assassin or a gangster, could murder someone and then go fast asleep. Even if they were absolutely without conscience, they'd surely lie awake for hours, thinking about it, wondering if they'd left a clue or something. Anyway, I decided just to keep mum for the time being and see how things panned out. Anyway, that's just about bally well all.' He turned to Wilkins. 'Sorry and all that, Chief Inspector. But I didn't really lead you astray, you know. I knew I was innocent and that Stella was, so I just stopped you being distracted by red herrings.'

'Very considerate of you, sir, I'm sure. Anyway, I think it's high time we heard from Miss – whatever her name is.'

'It's Julie Osborne,' said the girl they'd known as Stella. 'I'm an actress, and American born and bred. I come from a little town in the Midwest that nobody'll have ever heard of so I won't name. I always loved amateur dramatics and usually played leads in our little local society. About twelve years ago, I went to New York, to try and make it as a pro. After a couple of years living on bread and cheese, I started to get pretty regular work. Nothing big time, but I got by. Then about four years ago I was invited to a party by a guy who said there was someone he wanted me to meet. I hoped it was going to be some big-shot producer, but no such luck. It was Stella. This guy thought we were remarkably alike and wanted to see us side by side. Well, it was true. I mean, we weren't doubles, but we were the same height, same figures, same colouring and so on. Naturally, we got talking and found we had a lot in common. We were roughly the same age, we were both orphans, with no brothers or sisters and our only relatives various uncles, aunts and cousins, to whom we weren't particularly close. We'd both come to the Big Apple to try and make our fortunes, she as a journalist, me as an actress.

'We hit if off, and after a few months decided to share an apartment. We were different in many ways: different opinions, different tastes. But on the whole we got on OK, and it was convenient. The landlady was a bit short-sighted and often couldn't tell which of us was which. Stella used to talk a lot about her aristocratic relations in England. She was mighty proud of them, bit too proud sometimes, to be quite frank. But I got to know quite a lot about them over three or four years. The only one she kept in touch with, though, was her Great Aunt Florrie. She used to write her regularly, telling her all about life in New York, and she let on she hoped to inherit some money from her one day. I was interested in Florrie, seeing that, like me, she'd been on the stage and had come from a pretty poor background, and I got Stella to tell me all about her. Oh, I should also mention that we were listening to some lawyer talking on the radio one day about how important it was that everyone should make a will, even if they didn't have much to leave. So just for fun, really, we made wills in each other's favour.'

It seemed to Wilkins that this was a well-prepared and rehearsed statement, one she had been expecting to have to make at some time. She continued.

'Then last fall, two things happened at about the same time. Stella's magazine folded and she found herself out of a job, and I broke up with a guy I'd been dating for about six months. Also, for some time I hadn't been doing too well professionally. Parts had been getting very thin on the ground. We both had the blues pretty bad and to try and cheer ourselves up we decided to drive down to Atlantic City for a short vacation. About half way there, we took a little diversion, to have a look at the scenery. We were on this dirt road, and Stella was driving. It was her car – I didn't have one. We rounded a bend and suddenly there was this truck, coming towards us, much too fast in the centre of the road. Stella had to swerve violently. She lost control and we hit a tree. She was killed outright. How these things happen I don't know, but I just had a few cuts and bruises. I was in hysterics, of course. The truck didn't stop but luckily a guy on a motor bike was about fifty yards behind us, had seen the whole thing, knew we weren't to blame for the accident and that I hadn't been driving. He checked that I was all right, then rode on to call the cops and an ambulance at the first phone box.

'Well, I'm not proud of what I did next, but I'm not too ashamed, either. I was at a dead end, professionally and personally. I had nothing to keep me in America. I saw a chance for a fresh start in a new country – a country where I would have a number of influential and wealthy – quote – "relatives" and a new profession. I know a lot about fashion, quite as much as Stella did, and I could use her very good references. I can write – I've had a few pieces in a New York theatrical magazine – so I was pretty confident I could hold down a similar job in this country. So I simply switched purses with her. There was a lake nearby, and I put everything with my name on it in my case, weighed it down with a couple of rocks and threw it in the lake. When the police arrived I gave my name as Stella Simmons and told them I didn't know the dead woman's name, that she was a hitch-hiker I'd picked up, and when I'd got drowsy she'd offered to take the wheel and I'd let her. It was a bit unlikely, perhaps, but they had the biker's evidence that the truck driver was wholly to blame for the accident and that I hadn't even been driving, so they had no reason to doubt me or hold me.

'Anyway, when I eventually got home I kept out of the landlady's way – we often didn't see her for days on end. During the next couple of days, I scoured all the papers, to make sure the accident wasn't reported: 'Mystery Woman Killed. Journalist Escapes in Fatal Car Crash,' type of thing, but it had happened out of town, out of state, even, and there was nothing.

'I spent time practising Stella's handwriting and signature, and learning to imitate her voice – luckily, she'd once made a recording of it in one of those booths. When I thought I'd got the voice right, I made a recording of myself, and played the two records one after the other. It was OK. I spoke to the landlady, keeping my distance, identified myself as Stella, and told her that Julie had decided to move out and wouldn't be returning, and gave a week's notice for myself. Then I phoned every one of Stella's friends I could think of – I had her address book – identified myself as her and told them that as I had lost my job I was returning to England straight away. None of them questioned that I was Stella. Afterwards, I called a lot of my own friends, telling *them* that I was going west to try and make it in Hollywood.

'Stella had kept dozens of clippings from the papers about the two earlier murder cases you had here and there was a lot in them about Alderley and the Earl and

Countess and Geraldine and I went over those again and again, more or less memorising them.

'I also spent a long time in front of the mirror, trying to make myself up to look as much like Stella as possible. My nose is a bit bigger than hers, and my mouth a bit wider, but on the whole it was a pretty good likeness. I was aware my teeth weren't perfect – that doesn't really matter if you're just a stage actress and not in movies. I couldn't really remember how Stella's teeth were. She didn't show them a lot. Strangely enough, even though we shared a bathroom for nearly four years, I never knew she wore dentures. I guess she must have been pretty self-conscious about it. Anyway, as soon I'd got the likeness as good as I could I went to Stella's bank, drew out all the money – three hundred and seventy odd bucks – and closed the account. That was the most nerve-racking part, but they didn't question it. Unfortunately, of course, I had to leave my own money in my checking account, but that was less than a hundred dollars and I had drawn out some cash to take on the vacation. I gave most of Stella's clothes to the Salvation Army, but sold a few quite nice pieces of jewellery she had. A few days later I sailed for England, using Stella's passport – I don't have one of my own.'

Julie was now clearly enjoying telling her story, and had her audience riveted. She paused to light a cigarette and then continued.

'I went straight to London, got myself a room, and started job-hunting. *London Fashion Weekly* was the second paper I applied to. Luckily, the woman who interviewed me there had subscribed to Stella's old New

York magazine for years and was familiar with her work. She offered me a job straight away.

'As soon as I got settled in, I went to see Great Aunt Florrie. She accepted me without question and was really thrilled to see me. I visited her regularly after that. I was nervous at first in case I slipped up over anything, but it was OK. I knew a fair bit about the family from listening to Stella. And Florrie, like me, had read all there was to read about the Alderley murders, as well as hearing about them from Gerry, and she loved to talk about them. In addition, of course, having supposedly been out of the country for nearly eleven years, I could legitimately ask about all the other members of the family, so I was soon pretty well primed for when I did meet any of them. Most of the time, though, I just talked to her about New York. She really loved hearing about it. I'll never feel guilty about deceiving her in that way. I gave her a lot of pleasure during those last six months or so of her life, and she never knew that Stella was dead, which would have upset her terribly. I grew really fond of her. She was a great old girl, and I shed a few tears when she died.'

She stubbed out her cigarette. 'That's about it, Mr Wilkins. I want to apologise to everybody – especially to you, Tommy. It's rotten for you to have to learn about Stella's death in this way. You were the one person I was really nervous about meeting, which is why I never contacted you after I arrived in England. I was sure relieved after the funeral when you said you would have recognised me anywhere. That really sealed my credentials.'

Tommy gave a wry grin. 'I hadn't seen Stella since I was

about thirteen, and you do look awfully like I remember her.'

'Anyway, thanks for not snitching on me – until you had to. Well, Detective, am I under arrest?'

'No, Miss Osborne. Not yet.'

'That sounds ominous.'

'Well, you've committed a number of crimes, miss, both here and in the United States. It'll obviously be necessary for us to notify the authorities there.'

'I don't think they're likely to seek my extradition. After all, what did I do? I gave a false name to the cops, told them I didn't know the name of the dead woman, and – quote – "stole" some money and jewellery of Stella's, which would have all come to me under her will, anyway.'

'That's as may be. But there is the little matter of attempting to obtain money by false pretences in this country.'

'Oh, you mean my inheritance. Well, actually, I think not.' She picked up her handbag from the floor, reached into it and took out a folded sheet of paper, which she handed to Wilkins. 'That's a copy of a letter I sent to Mr Bradley, immediately I got his wire notifying me that I was a legatee under Florrie's will – he has the original, of course.'

Wilkins took it and read it. Stella looked round the room. 'In it, I tell him in confidence that I will not accept anything that I am bequeathed in Florrie's will. I add that I want, nonetheless, to attend the funeral and the reading.'

Wilkins handed the letter back to her. 'Yes, that's roughly what it says. However, as I understand, you said nothing at the reading about refusing the bequest.'

'No, why should I have? I didn't figure it was anybody else's business. But I said nothing about accepting it, either. I never mentioned anything about having plans for the money. And I think Mr Bradley will confirm that I asked him what fifteen hundred pounds *would be* in dollars – not how much it *was* or *will be*, which points to it being of just academic interest.'

'Very subtle, Miss Osborne. But then again, there's nothing legally binding in that letter. You could have easily changed your mind – if you hadn't been found out.'

Timothy spoke. 'What Miss Osborne may or may not have done or intended to do in a hypothetical situation is itself hypothetical and therefore irrelevant. It is my opinion that the existence of that letter would make it virtually impossible to succeed in a charge of attempting to obtain money by false pretences. If such a charge were brought, I would positively relish the chance to defend her against it.'

Julie's face lit up. 'Why, thank you, Timothy. I really appreciate that.'

'Well, it won't be my decision,' Wilkins said. 'And I'm not really concerned. I should warn you, though, miss, that there is no getting away from the fact that you did enter the country under a false name, using somebody else's passport. Even if no other charges are brought, you are very likely to be deported.'

'We would fight such a move most vigorously,' Timothy said, and, except perhaps the Earl, who clearly was not really taking in the proceedings, nobody present missed the use of the plural pronoun. 'But even if we should lose,' Timothy continued, 'Stella – er, Julie – er, Miss Osborne could always marry a British subject and so obtain British citizenship, meaning she could not be deported. I feel it quite probable that that could be arranged, in fact, I can guarantee it, if she so wishes it.' He went very red, took out his handkerchief and blew his nose vigorously.

Penny was gazing at him in amazement. She gave his hand a squeeze. He gave hers a hurried and somewhat awkward pat.

'Timothy, I don't know what to say.' Julie spoke dazedly.

'Good,' said Wilkins, 'and I suggest you don't try to think of anything. I am investigating a murder and I would like to get on with that.'

'OK,' Julie said. 'Just one thing: I am in the clear, as regards the murder, I take it?'

Wilkins regarded her coolly. 'Whatever gave you that idea, Miss Osborne?'

She went white. 'But, but after what Tommy said about my being asleep...'

'Why should I believe Mr Lambert? He's lied from the start. You could have cooked the whole story up between you.'

'Oh, I say!' said Tommy.

Wilkins ignored this. 'Anyway, we've cleared up the business of the stolen toothpaste. I now want to turn to the matter of the 'Dora Lethbridge' card, or I should say the '*Miss* Dora Lethbridge' card, because that 'Miss' is important.'

He turned to the two sisters. 'Miss Agatha, Miss Dorothy, perhaps you wondered why I asked for you to be present this morning, as I realise it must all be painful for you. The reason was that I am going to divulge something that cannot be kept secret, concerning your stepmother, something which I don't believe you know. I had meant to talk to you privately before convening this little gathering, but the attack on Lady Geraldine disrupted my plans, and I decided the best thing I could do was make sure that at least you did not hear it *after* everybody else.'

Agatha answered. 'Very considerate of you, Mr Wilkins. I'm intrigued, must admit.'

Wilkins addressed the room at large again. 'The reason for that card, with its use of the word 'Miss,' was to indicate the writer's knowledge that Dora Lethbridge, Clara Saunders' mother, had always been 'Miss' Lethbridge, to the end of her life. In other words, she had never married. That, of course, means that Clara Saunders was illegitimate.'

'I don't believe it!' Agatha exclaimed. Dorothy gave a little gasp.

'I'm sorry, but I can assure you it's true,' Wilkins said. 'Sergeant Leather visited Somerset House in London yesterday and saw her birth certificate. The space for the father's name is blank. I'm quite certain no copy of that birth certificate will be found among Mrs Saunders' papers, that she destroyed it many years ago. The story of her mother marrying a cousin of the same surname as herself was obviously invented by Mrs Saunders to account for the fact that her mother's maiden name, which she might have to give on occasions and which might appear on various documents that other people would see, was the same as her own maiden name.'

'She would have been absolutely horrified at the

thought of that coming out,' Agatha said.

'Precisely,' Wilkins said. 'It made her extremely vulnerable. When she saw that card, I'm sure she would have realised its significance: that somebody else in the house knew of her shameful – as she would have thought it – secret and that it was a coded warning not to reveal somebody else's secret or the same thing could happen to her.

'I asked myself who of those present could conceivably know the secret. I felt sure her step-daughters didn't, as I could not imagine her being able to exercise such control over their lives – particularly over Miss Dorothy's life – if she had known they were in a position to make it known more widely.'

'She certainly couldn't,' Agatha said. 'Golly, I wish I had known. I wouldn't have let on, of course, but she wasn't to know that. And I could certainly have put a stop to her money-making enterprises.'

'So,' Wilkins said, 'who could have known? Perhaps his lordship, but that was unlikely and even if he had, I feel sure he would have kept it absolutely confidential. I considered each of the other beneficiaries, but could think of no way in which any of them could have found out about it. With one exception.' He looked at Timothy.

'Mr Saunders, your late father was Mr John Saunders' solicitor and executor. No doubt he had access to many family papers and was privy to many family secrets. Some things he may have discovered perfectly properly but inadvertently and, while not divulging them, thought it necessary, as a lawyer, to keep a written record of them. Illegitimacy, with all the legal ramifications that has, would certainly be such a thing. You, I take it, would have been responsible for going through your father's papers after his death and would certainly have come across any such record. All of which means that you are the only person here who could have known that Mrs Clara Saunders was illegitimate – and so written that card. I should warn you that, although it is written in block capitals, we have obtained a photostat copy of a passport application you filled out a few years ago, also in block letters, and the lettering is identical, as I'm sure a graphologist would confirm.'

CHAPTER THIRTY-EIGHT

Timothy's eyelid twitched twice, but he did not hesitate before answering. 'Very well, Chief Inspector. Your deduction is quite correct. I found out about Clara's illegitimacy in precisely the way you assumed. And I did write that card. It was, as you say, a warning to Clara about what might happen if she was to reveal other people's secrets. You may consider it to have been a cowardly act, and it is true, I could have spoken to her face to face. But that would have been less effective; she could be virtually certain that I would be honour bound not to reveal anything learnt in the course of my professional duties, or by my father in his. So it wouldn't matter too much to her that *I* knew. However, there are others here about whom she could feel no such confidence. So I considered it wiser to leave her uncertain about the identity of the writer of the card, thus hoping to ensure she would keep quiet about *any* secrets she might have.'

'And that was just a gesture of goodwill, was it, sir: a wish to save your fellow beneficiaries any possible embarrassment?'

This time Timothy did hesitate for a moment before saying: 'No, not entirely. I did have occasion to believe it possible – well, it was no more than a suspicion, really – that Clara possessed something which I did not wish seen by anybody else. It concerned no crime, and the exact nature of it is irrelevant, so I am not prepared to say what it was.'

'You don't need to, sir.'

'Thank—' Timothy began.

'It was this, I imagine,' Wilkins said. He reached into his pocket, brought out what was clearly a six by four inch photograph and, very carefully, so that no one else, not even Penny, could glimpse it, held it out for him to see.

Timothy positively blanched. 'May – may I ask where you obtained that?'

'It was in Mrs Saunders' handbag,' Wilkins said, putting the photo back in his pocket. 'So in fact your suspicion of her was quite correct. I suggest it was far more than mere suspicion. You knew she possessed this photograph and presented a real threat to you.'

'No, she did not possess that photograph, at least, not for any length of time.'

'I beg your pardon, sir?'

'I believe that to be a photo which was locked in my briefcase, in my bedroom here. There is a slight mark in the top left-hand corner. If I am correct, the date I received it, 10th July, is written in pencil on the back.'

'Yes, that's correct, sir. May I ask why you were carrying it with you?'

'Because I feel happier when I know where it is. But I hadn't checked on it since I arrived here at Alderley.'

'So what you are suggesting, Mr Saunders, is that some time on the day of the funeral, after her outburst at the will-reading, probably while you were having dinner, Mrs Saunders – oh, I can't go on using the name 'Saunders' all the time, it's too confusing. I'll use first names from now on. Where was I? Oh yes: you say Mrs Clara went into your room, searched it, found some means of picking the lock on your briefcase and abstracted the picture.'

Timothy nodded. 'And if that is what happened, she must have lighted upon it purely by chance; there was no way she could have known it was there. The fact, then, that she took it, means that she did not previously have a copy – she would not have needed another. Which in turn means that she could not have used it to ruin my reputation and that when she made her threat at the will-reading she was not threatening *me*, after all.'

'But you *believed* she was, sir, that's the important point. And when you went up to your room that night, you discovered the photo was missing. Perhaps the briefcase had been moved or left open. You knew Mrs Clara had had the run of the first floor for several hours that evening, while the rest of you were downstairs, and that she was virtually the only person who could have taken it. You decided to confront her. You went to her room and demanded it back. She refused, you lost your temper and killed her. Then you panicked. You didn't dare stay long enough to search for the picture among her things and you hurried back to your room. That's what happened, isn't it?'

'No! Nothing like that.' Timothy shook his head vigorously. He took out his handkerchief and dabbed at his lips. He cleared his throat. 'I'll tell you what did happen. I went upstairs at about 11 p.m. and straight to my bedroom. I undressed and then went to the bathroom next door. As I was leaving it, I saw someone coming out of Clara's room. I was surprised, but at that moment not unduly so. They didn't see me, just turned away and went round the corner into the east corridor.'

'And that would have been around ten or fifteen minutes past eleven, sir?'

'Yes.'

'Please carry on.'

'When I returned to my room, I found that somehow what I had seen had unsettled me. It seemed to me in retrospect that there had been something hasty and rather furtive about that person's movements. I wondered if the purpose of the visit could be something to do with Clara's threat. That caused me to start worrying whether she had had me in mind when she made it. I tried to read but I couldn't concentrate. I wasn't able to get Clara's words out of my mind. It was then I thought of a warning message. I always carry a little writing case with me and I keep a few postcards in it, as well as writing paper and envelopes. I spent some minutes composing a suitable form of words and then made my way to her room.'

'What time was this, sir?'

'I cannot be precisely sure. Probably between eleven forty-five and eleven fifty.'

'Carry on.'

'I meant just to push the card under her door. But the door fits very tightly and it wouldn't go under. There was no light coming through the keyhole, so I decided to risk going in. I left the door open behind me an inch or two, which gave me just enough light to see the position of the bed and not to bump into anything. I crept across to the bed and put the card on the bedside table. Everything was absolutely silent. I suddenly realised it was too silent. I have exceptionally sharp hearing and I should have been able to hear her breathing, but I couldn't. I became alarmed. I took a chance and switched the bedside lamp on. I saw Clara, just as you saw her later, Chief Inspector: lying across the bed, plainly dead, almost certainly murdered, and obviously by the person I had seen leaving the room. It was a frightful shock and I have to admit I did panic. I should, of course, have raised the alarm immediately, but my only thought was that I might be suspected. After all, what reason could I give for having gone to her room, after she was asleep? So I decided to return to my own room to try and think what I should do. I opened the door very cautiously – and actually saw the same person as before going down the stairs. I waited until the coast was clear, and hurried to my room. Then I remembered the card, which in my confusion I had left on the bedside table. It would serve no purpose now Clara was dead, might mislead the police, and – most important from my point of view – would almost certainly have my fingerprints on it.'

'There were no prints on it,' Wilkins said.

'No, later I remembered that before I went into Clara's room I noticed that the card had got quite dusty and dirty from my efforts to force it under the door. So I gave it a wipe all over with my handkerchief. Thereafter, I must have only held it by the edges, though I wasn't conscious of doing that. I knew I had to get it back, and I was also trying desperately to think of some way of directing suspicion onto the person to whom it belonged. But I had absolutely no proof of what I had seen earlier and if I mentioned it to you, it could easily seem that I was simply attempting to divert suspicion from myself. Moreover, I would have to explain why I was up. It occurred to me that if I could put something belonging to that person in Clara's bedroom, that might point the police in the right direction. George's talk about cufflinks at dinner gave me the idea. If, while that person was still downstairs, I could obtain one of his cufflinks and leave it by the body, that might do the trick. This person—'

Wilkins interrupted. 'Mr Saunders, this constant talk of a person is nonsensical. Concealing things doesn't do your credibility any good. Now, tell me who it was you saw.'

'Very well. It was Gregory.'

Wilkins looked across to where the MP was standing by the fireplace, but he didn't react in any way.

'Carry on, Mr Saunders,' Wilkins said.

'There is little more. I took a chance. I went to his room. It was still empty. I took a cufflink and left it in Clara's bedroom. I should point out that everything I did was intended to further the ends of justice.'

Gregory came forward slowly. 'No doubt my learned cousin expects me to splutter a lot of indignant denials. But why should I? Yes, I looked in to see Clara on my way to bed. To tell you the truth, I felt a bit sorry for her. She'd been bitterly disappointed and humiliated by the will and on top of that had made a complete fool of herself. She'd been stuck alone in her room all the evening, and I just wanted to show her that as far as I was concerned there were no hard feelings. I think she was grateful. We chatted for about five minutes. When I left her, she was perfectly well and I think a little more cheerful. The idea that there was something hurried or furtive about my movements is the fantasy of an over-active imagination.'

'What did you talk about?'

'I commiserated with her, said I didn't think Florrie meant to insult her, but was relying on the girls to see she was all right – nonsense, of course, but one has to say something – and that Florrie was very old and getting perhaps a little eccentric, and that she mustn't take it to heart. She thanked me, congratulated me on my few words at the funeral, said how kind Lavinia had been, and so on.'

'Her threats at the reading weren't mentioned?'

'No, I thought it was well to stay clear of them. As I was leaving, she did say she was very sorry about everything. A bit ambiguous, but that must have been what she was referring to.'

'And this was at about ten or fifteen minutes past eleven?'

'I suppose so. I couldn't say precisely.'

'Why didn't you mention this before?'

'Suppose I should have done. But I thought about it carefully and decided that it was quite irrelevant to your investigation. So I asked myself, why complicate things? Might look suspicious if I said I'd been to her room.'

'Not nearly as suspicious as keeping silent about it, sir.'

'I can't see it as suspicious. I went into her room while she was still up. I left openly, without even looking round to see if I'd been observed. I didn't creep into her room in the dark, for the purpose of leaving a frightening anonymous note, and then run like a scared rabbit back to my room and sit quaking in my shoes, without telling anyone, when I found her murdered – which is what Timothy says he did. He then goes on to say, simply on the grounds of seeing me leave her room half an hour earlier, that I was 'obviously' the murderer. This from a reputedly top rank barrister. Let's all hope to heaven he never sits on the bench. He'd be another Judge Jeffries! Worse, in fact: at least Jeffries never actually killed anyone with his own hands.'

'How dare you!'

Timothy positively bellowed the words. He jumped to his feet and strode towards Gregory, who took a hasty step backwards. Leather quickly and silently strode across the room, until he was standing a foot or two behind Timothy. Wilkins reached into his pocket, produced a boiled sweet, unwrapped it, popped it in his mouth, folded his arms and watched interestedly.

'You murderer!' Timothy shouted, seemingly totally out of control. 'You did kill her, you blackguard! She knew all about your kept woman in St. John's Wood. She was going to tell the papers. You went to her room to try and threaten or bribe her out of it, and when you couldn't you killed her.'

Gregory's face took on the colour of ripe beetroot. 'Liar!' he yelled. 'It was your drunken orgy she was going to tell about.'

'*Drunken orgy?* What the devil do you mean?'

'What else does that photo show?'

Timothy's eyes bulged. 'How do you know what that picture shows? It was you – you sent it!'

He started to make a lunge at Gregory. But Leather was

quicker. In a flash his right arm had gone round Timothy's neck and his left under Timothy's arm and he had the lapels of his jacket in a firm grip. Timothy made a series of convulsive movements, desperately trying to break the hold, but without success. 'Give it up, sir,' Leather said quietly. 'I'm a fourth Dan.'

Timothy tapped the back of Leather's hand, and Leather immediately released him

Timothy coughed, then swung round to Wilkins. 'Ask him. Ask him how he knows about that photo.'

'No,' Gregory positively snarled. 'Ask him why he's so desperate to pin the murder on me.'

The next second they were shouting at each other again. Hardly a clear word could be picked out.

Wilkins raised his hands. 'Gentlemen, please.'

They ignored him. 'Please, please,' he repeated, but there was no effect.

Wilkins took a deep breath. 'SHUT UP!'

His low, resonant voice filled the room. Gregory and Timothy both gave a start and at last fell silent.

'Thank you,' Wilkins said. 'I would remind you, gentlemen, that we are all guests of Lord Burford, whose daughter is at this moment lying unconscious upstairs, perhaps fighting for her life. Is this appropriate behaviour?'

They both had the grace to look guilty.

Timothy spoke first. 'No, it is not and I'm sorry. I rarely lose control, but the situation is somewhat exceptional.'

'I apologise, too,' Gregory said. 'My only excuse is that it is hard to remain calm when you can see the possibility of being charged with murder.'

'Very well,' Wilkins said. 'Let's see if we can get to the bottom of what did happen that night. Mr Carstairs, Mr Timothy has said he planted one cufflink in Mrs Clara's room. I suppose it was you who planted the other thirty-eight?'

'Don't know what you're talking about, Wilkins.'

'Then let me make it simpler. When did you first notice one of your cufflinks was missing?'

'None of my cufflinks is missing. Only brought one pair with me and I'm wearing them. See.' He pulled down his shirt cuffs to reveal a pair of gold links.

'I wonder if you would show those to Lord Burford, sir.'

Apparently with some reluctance, Gregory crossed to the Earl and held out his wrists. Lord Burford peered at the links. 'Why, those are mine. Recognise them anywhere. But do hang on to them, by all means. Now, please all excuse me. I must get back to Gerry.' He hurried out of the room.

'Seems pretty conclusive, sir,' Wilkins said. 'But before you comment, I want to say one thing to both you and Mr Timothy. You've both concealed things and hindered my investigation. If you hadn't done so, the case might have been solved before this. And I warn you that if there are any more lies or concealments I shall have no hesitation in charging you with obstructing the course of justice, which would do neither of your careers any good. Now, the full truth, if you please, sir.'

'All right.' Gregory seemed suddenly to have shrunk an inch or two. He sat down on the arm of an easy chair and ran his fingers through his rather sparse hair. 'I went upstairs about a minute after Timothy and stopped in to see Clara, exactly as I told you, and afterwards went on to my room. I got all ready for bed but I couldn't settle down and after about fifteen minutes I decided to go and help myself to a drink. I put on my dressing-gown and went downstairs. Geraldine and Dorothy were in the drawing-room but I didn't feel correctly attired to join them. I knew there were some drinks kept in the billiard-room, so I went there and had a Scotch and soda – well, two to be quite accurate – and smoked a cigarette. I stayed down there about fifteen or twenty minutes, and then started back upstairs. I had nearly reached the top when I saw Timothy in the act of closing Clara's door. He had his back to me and hadn't seen me. There were dim lights in the hall and in the corridor, but nothing on the stairs, so I retreated half a dozen steps, until I was more or less in shadow. The next second I saw him practically run across the top of the staircase, going towards his room. I imagined he'd been trying to persuade her to keep quiet about whatever it was she knew about him. Well, I wanted another word with her myself—'

Wilkins interrupted. 'Why, sir?'

'What?'

'You'd had a reasonably pleasant conversation with her earlier, parted on good terms, so why did you want to see her again? Was it because *your* attempt to persuade her to keep quiet had failed and you wanted another go?'

Gregory hesitated. 'Not exactly. I hadn't tried to persuade her to keep quiet earlier, but I admit I did try to pump her. She was like a clam, though. I don't believe now she knew anything at all, but at that time I was convinced she did, and I decided it would be worth one more try to find out what, and what she intended to do. I had assumed she'd be asleep, but now it seemed clear she wasn't. I tapped on her door but there was no reply. That surprised me, because it was less than a minute since Timothy had left. I knocked a bit louder and when there was still no answer I opened the door. The light was out and I began to think this was rum. I turned on the light and, well, you know what I saw. I needn't bother to tell you my emotions. I closed the door behind me but apart from that just stood there, more or less rooted to the spot, trying to think, for five or ten minutes. It was plain Timothy had killed her – or else why wouldn't he have raised the alarm immediately? I was going to do so myself, but then I wondered if somebody might have seen me going in there earlier. I had absolutely no proof that I had left Clara alive and well, or that Timothy had been in there after me. What was more, as an MP, I would obviously be by far the most likely person to want to cover up any so-called guilty secret. But I just couldn't concentrate, with Clara lying on the bed like that, staring up at me. I had to go back to my room, to work out what to do.

'Almost as soon as I got there, I noticed something. When I'm staying in a place for just the one night, I don't usually bother to put my clothes away overnight. I'd brought a clean collar for the next day, of course, but no spare shirt, and I'd thrown it over the back of a chair. My tie, this black tie, had been on top of it. Now it was on the floor. Somebody'd been in there. I had a look round, to see if anything was missing – and at once noticed that one of my cufflinks, which I'd left half in the cuffs, ready for the next day, was gone.

'I realised in a flash what had happened. When I had seen Timothy leaving Clara's room, he had not at that moment killed her. He must have done it *earlier*, and then tried to think of a way to divert suspicion. He'd no doubt seen me going downstairs, slipped into my room, pinched one of my cufflinks and hidden it in Clara's room. When I saw him leaving, he'd just done that.'

'This is the most—' Timothy began, but Wilkins silenced him. 'Mr Saunders, please, I'll come back to you in a moment. Let Mr Carstairs finish.' Timothy gave a resigned shrug and sat down again on the sofa.

'For minutes I just couldn't think what to do at all,' Gregory continued. 'I couldn't go back and look for it. It might take half an hour, or I might never find it. But I couldn't let the police find one cufflink, my cufflink, in Clara's room. Then it came to me. If I could camouflage my link with lots of others, it wouldn't be recognised, wouldn't stand out. I remembered what George had been saying at dinner about having a good many pairs. So I went to his dressing-room and took them all – and gave the box a wipe over with my handkerchief. I kept the pair I'm wearing for myself, went back to Clara's room, opened the door and just threw them in. No doubt you think I've misled you, Chief Inspector, but I would say I was unmisleading you, even though it was confusing for you. If you had found that one cufflink by Clara's body, you would have been convinced I was the murderer. All I was doing was getting myself out of what I believe nowadays is called a frame-up. Well, that's just about it.'

'I don't think so, sir.'

'I'm sorry?'

'Didn't you attempt to do a little framing yourself?'

'What do you mean?'

'The photograph. Mrs Clara never stole that from Mr Timothy's room. She would have had no earthly reason to think he would be carrying anything compromising with him. Anyway, while she may not have been averse to a little bribery, I don't believe she was actually a thief. What do you say, ladies?' He looked at the sisters.

Dorothy shook her head. 'No. Mother would never have done that.'

'I agree,' Agatha said. 'Everyone knows I was under no illusions about her, but she wasn't a criminal, for heaven's sake. Besides, I think she would have been far too afraid of being caught.'

'She knew she'd behaved very badly earlier,' Dorothy added, 'and she would never do anything that would make people think even worse of her, if it ever came to light.'

'Thank you. My thinking exactly. No, you're the only one who could have done that, Mr Carstairs. Now please remember what I said: I want the full truth.'

'All right. Yes, I did.'

'Why, you unmitigated cad!' Timothy shouted.

'Tit for tat, Timothy, tit for tat.' He looked at Wilkins. 'You must remember, Chief Inspector, that I saw him leaving Clara's room, and then discovered he had tried to frame me for the crime. I knew I had to put the police back on the right track. It was after I'd taken the cufflinks that it occurred to me to plant something of *his* in Clara's room. But it seemed impossible, as he was still in his room. But just as I was leaving George's dressing-room, I saw a shaft of light appear in the corridor from Timothy's door opening, and I dodged back in. I kept the door open a fraction of an inch, and watched him go past. I peered after him and saw that he went down the staircase. I guessed that, like me, he needed a drink. I knew that would give me a few minutes, so I hurried into his room. I couldn't see anything at first that would be suitable, on the dressing-table or bedside table. I had a quick rummage through his overnight bag, but there was nothing there, either. Then I saw his briefcase.'

'And you forced the lock,' Timothy interrupted angrily.

'No, it was unlocked.'

'It wasn't – oh.' Timothy stopped short. For the first time he looked a little awkward. 'I must have forgotten to lock it after I took my writing-case out. And later I had other things on my mind.'

'Such as murder,' Gregory sneered.

'Mr Carstairs, please!' Wilkins said exasperatedly. 'Just carry on with your story.

'I had a rummage through the briefcase. And, no, I did not look at any of the papers in there. They were of no interest. I was looking for something like a fountain pen or propelling pencil, something that might easily fall out of a breast pocket if you were bending over somebody suffocating them with a cushion. But then I saw the corner of a photograph. I took it out and looked at it. I could hardly believe my luck. I hurried back to Clara's room and put it in her handbag. In my haste, I forgot the cufflinks, which were in my pocket, until I'd got back to the door. So, as I said, I chucked them from the doorway then went back to my room. It had only been about seven or eight minutes from the time I left it. And that, Wilkins, is the truth, the whole truth and nothing but the truth.'

'Thank you, sir. Mr Saunders, do you have any comments?

'At this time just one. When he saw me as he was coming up the stairs, I had not in fact been *in* Clara's room at that time. I had intended, as well as leaving the cufflink there, to retrieve the postcard, but as I was opening the door, I heard a slight sound from the east corridor, which could have been another door opening or closing. No doubt it was Miss Mackenzie, on her way to the art gallery, but I didn't know that then. So all I had time to do was throw the cufflink in blindly, before practically running back to my own room. When I got there, I suffered a quite severe attack of palpitations and had to sit down for five or ten minutes. Then I did decide I needed a drink, went downstairs and had a brandy, and then returned to my room, where I remained until I heard the commotion.'

'And that is everything you have to tell us, Mr Saunders?'

'Yes, but I do have a request.'

'And what would that be?'

'Perhaps this is not the best time, in the middle of your interviews, but I feel it may be the last opportunity, the last time we are all together. I would like you to show that photograph to everyone else.'

Wilkins raised his eyebrows. 'Are you sure, sir.'

'Quite sure. I do not want everybody indulging in much fruitless speculation as to its nature.'

'As you wish.' Wilkins looked round the room, then took a few steps towards Julie and held it out to her.

There was a marked apprehension in her eyes as she

took it and glanced down at it. Then her face changed. However, anyone who had expected an exclamation of disgust or horror was surprised.

She looked up. 'Is this it? Is this all?' she asked blankly.

'All?' echoed Timothy.

'But it's totally innocuous!'

She looked at it again. It showed Timothy lolling back in a chair. He was in evening dress, with his collar askew, and was wearing a barrister's wig sideways. He was holding an upturned champagne bottle to his mouth. On his lap, her arm around his neck, was an extremely attractive brunette.

'Yes,' Julie said, 'I think everybody should see this.' She handed it back to Wilkins.

He took it round the circle. Miss Mackenzie frowned with slight distaste, Agatha and Dorothy showed no emotion. Tommy started to give a grin, which he quickly stifled before handing it back.

Timothy meanwhile was talking, very quickly. 'I want to explain what happened, though I don't expect every one here will believe me. A few weeks ago, I went to a one-day legal conference in Oxford. It was to carry on into the evening, and I'd arranged to stay the night in my old college. After the events had finished, I was persuaded, somewhat against my better judgment, to go out for a drink with a few others to some club. It seemed a perfectly respectable place. I had one drink. And that is all I remember until I woke up in bed at home the next morning. How I got there from Oxford I have no idea. I must have let myself in, because none of the servants did; they were extremely surprised the next morning to find me home. They had heard nothing, perhaps not surprising as they sleep on the top floor, but neither had Penelope, whose bedroom is next to mine.'

'Some dirty rat slipped you a Mickey,' Julie said.

Timothy stared at her. 'I beg your pardon?'

'A Mickey Finn. A drink spiked with some fast-acting sedative.'

'Ah. Is that what they are called? Yes, no doubt. The photo arrived in the post a couple of days later. You will have seen that my eyes are closed. I realise it could be assumed that I was blinking, due to the flash. Actually, I was asleep or unconscious at the time. How it was arranged for my arm to be up, holding the bottle, I cannot explain. I was extremely perturbed. But I did not like to ask any of the fellows who were there what had happened, because I did not wish them to be aware of my ignorance. I was half-expecting some kind of blackmail demand, but there has been nothing. It has nonetheless caused me severe disquiet.'

Wilkins was looking at the picture again. 'I think the business of your arm and the bottle can be easily explained. Someone crouching down behind the chair, holding your arm aloft. A piece of thread attached to the bottle and it being dangled by someone standing on a chair, so that your hand was actually merely resting against it. I daresay if the picture was enlarged sufficiently the thread might become visible.'

'Do you really think so? I must certainly try that. It would prove, wouldn't it, that the whole thing was a frame-up. That would be wonderful...' His voice tailed away. Then he looked at Julie. 'You said it was quite innocuous.

No doubt in theatrical or journalistic circles that would be the case. But imagine if a copy of that were sent to the Lord Chancellor, when he was considering my possible elevation to the bench. Or, almost worse, if it appeared on the front page of some scandal sheet immediately after my appointment was announced.'

'I can almost see the headline,' Tommy put in. "Sober as a Judge."

'I can imagine worse than that,' Timothy said.

CHAPTER THIRTY-NINE

'Right,' Wilkins said, 'having got that little diversion out of the way, let me just run through your combined testimony. Mr Carstairs visited Mrs Clara, stayed about five or ten minutes and then went to his room. Mr Timothy saw him leaving. Some time later, he himself went to her room and put the postcard beside the bed before discovering the body. When leaving, to return to his own room, he saw Mr Carstairs going downstairs. Shortly afterward, he abstracted Mr Carstairs' cufflink from *his* room, returned to Mrs Clara's room, was alarmed by a sound, threw the cufflink in and hurried back to his room, where he remained. Mr Carstairs, on his way upstairs, saw him, went to Mrs Clara's room himself, saw the body, and after another ten minutes, returned to his own room, when he discovered his cufflink missing. He made his way to the Earl's dressing-room, took all the cufflinks he found there and was about to leave when became aware of Mr Timothy going downstairs. He went to Mr Timothy's room, found the photo, went back to Mrs Clara's room, put the photo in her bag and scattered the cufflinks, before finally returning to his own room. Is that it?'

'Congratulations, Chief Inspector,' said Timothy, 'a remarkably accurate summary of my movements.'

'And of mine,' said Gregory. 'So what does it tell you?'

'It tells me that, rather surprisingly, you're in total agreement. Neither of your accounts contradicts the other's. Only your assumptions differ. Nothing in Mr Timothy's account proves his own innocence or Mr Carstairs' guilt. And vice versa.'

He scratched his head. 'It's all very confusing. I think I'm going to have to move away from what happened in the night, to the following morning. Several quite noteworthy things occurred then, though you are probably not aware of them. The timing of them is important. And I need some help in working that out.' He took a notebook from his pocket and opened it. 'Miss Osborne, you were first down, I think.'

'I believe so.'

'What time would that have been?'

She screwed up her eyes. 'Let me see. A few minutes before seven.'

'And you went immediately and phoned your friend on the *Evening News*.'

'Uh-huh.'

'How long did the call take?'

'Well, they were a minute or two finding him, but when he came on I was able to give him the gist of the story in about four minutes.'

'So six minutes would be a fair estimate?'

'I guess so.'

'You didn't hear Miss Dorothy trying the door?'

'No.'

'And afterwards you returned to your room by the back stairs?'

'Yes, it was quicker.'

'And then it would have been five, six, seven minutes past the hour?'

'Around that.'

'Thank you. That's very helpful.' He made a brief entry in his notebook and then turned to Dorothy. 'Miss Dorothy, what time did you come down?'

'Just a minute or two after seven.'

'And you also went straight to the telephone room, found the door locked, returned to the great hall, and told Mr Merryweather about it.'

'Yes.'

'So it would have been about ten past by the time you eventually got through to her?'

'I suppose so.'

'And how long did your call last?'

'Oh, I really couldn't say.'

'Well, let's try to work it out. You told her first, of course, about your stepmother – that she was dead, murdered, almost certainly by one of the guests.'

'Yes.'

'And no doubt she had a number of questions.'

'Yes.'

'Did you mention Mrs Clara's outburst at the will-reading.'

'Just briefly, an outline.'

'So all that would have taken three minutes, at the very least, I should imagine.'

'I should think so.'

'And, naturally, you then told her about your inheritance.'

'Of course.'

'The money and the house, how much it was all worth?'

'Does that seem terribly heartless?'

'Not at all, miss. But it would have taken another minute or two. And then you asked her to come and she said she'd be here as soon as possible.'

'That's right.'

'Does that agree with your recollection, Miss Agatha?'

'Pretty well.'

'So that means we can say the call took a minimum of five minutes, probably longer. Are we agreed on that?'

They both nodded.

'That's very strange,' Wilkins said.

'What do you mean?' Agatha asked.

'Well, according to the telephone people, there were two calls put from here at about that time, both to London. The first one lasted approximately six and a half minutes – Miss Osborne's to the *Evening News*. The second call lasted precisely eleven seconds. Perhaps you could explain just how you managed to impart all that information in just eleven seconds, Miss Dorothy.'

The room had been quiet before Wilkins' last question. Suddenly it seemed even quieter, the silence to become almost palpable. It was as though everyone had stopped breathing.

It was Agatha who broke it. 'Oh, must be some mistake.'

'I don't think so, miss. I saw the supervisor, looked at their records. They don't get things like that wrong; and after all, they were bang on as regards Miss Osborne's call. No, the call took only eleven seconds because you *already knew everything that had happened*. You were here at the time. And you killed your stepmother.'

CHAPTER FORTY

'That's – that's absurd!' Agatha exclaimed. 'Everybody knows I wasn't here. The house was searched from top to bottom.'

'Yes, but Miss Dorothy's room was searched only by her and Lady Geraldine. Lady Geraldine told her father that she looked under the bed, while Miss Dorothy looked in the wardrobe. You were concealed in that wardrobe, as Miss Dorothy knew – and so made sure that only she looked in there. You'd been there since the afternoon. That morning you had ridden to Alderley Village, changed somewhere into a long black dress and a hat with a veil, attended the funeral and come back here with all the other guests. There were no doubt a number of ladies dressed in exactly the same way. You were totally anonymous. Everyone had free time in the afternoon to explore the house. At some stage, Miss Dorothy had whispered to you the location of her room. You simply slipped in there and got in the wardrobe, which is a very capacious one. There you remained – Miss Dorothy no doubt supplying you with refreshment from time to time – until late that night, when you went to your stepmother's room and smothered her. You believed all the other occupants of the house, except for Lady Geraldine and your sister, downstairs, were in bed. You couldn't have known that Miss Mackenzie, Mr Lambert, Mr Carstairs and Mr Timothy were all up and about on their various adventures, and you were amazingly lucky not to have run into any of them, particularly Mr Carstairs or Mr Timothy. After the murder, you returned to the wardrobe. Following the discovery of the body, your sister looked in on you briefly, with Lady Geraldine actually in the room. Later, they both left and then Miss Dorothy returned alone.

'When PC Dobson arrived and the alarm was set off, you were able to leave the room, Miss Dorothy no doubt leading the way, to make sure the coast was clear, go down the back stairs and exit the house by one of the side doors or French windows. You returned to your motorcycle, changed your clothes again and rode home, arriving probably just in time to take Miss Dorothy's call and almost immediately start on the return journey.'

Agatha regarded him coolly for a few seconds before replying. 'You're a clever little bugger, Wilkins, aren't you? Well, I could deny it all, but I don't suppose it'd do any good in the long run.'

'I must warn you, miss, that—'

'Oh, you can skip all that about anything I say being given in evidence. Yes, it's all true. I set out on my bike on Wednesday morning, shortly after our stepmother and Dorry left by train. I stopped in the woods just outside the estate, changed my clobber, and walked to the church. When we got here after the service, I tagged on to a bunch of old girls, none of whom I knew from Adam. Cousin George even came and spoke to us at one time. It was a devilish long wait in that wardrobe. I didn't get out of it until about half past ten. Then I went to the door, opened it an inch and stood waiting, just inside it, with the light off. I had to know when people had gone to bed. Of course, it was far from certain, even then, that I'd be able to go through with it. If people had drifted up to bed, one at a time, over a period of an hour or so, I just wouldn't have had the time. Luckily, everyone except Dorry and Gerry came up in the space of about thirty minutes. I could only go by listening, and couldn't be absolutely sure they were all up. I just waited until it got quite quiet, but it was still quite a risk. Of course, if I'd known how many people were still up and scurrying around I'd never have chanced it. Also, if Gerry had wanted to turn in a bit earlier, I'd have had to scrap the whole thing, because Dorry had to be with her every second until the body was found.

'Afterwards, I went straight back to the wardrobe. The armour crashing over was a shock. I couldn't think what it could be. Hadn't anticipated that, of course, but it was lucky in a way, because it meant the body was discovered a bit sooner, so I was able to get out of the house much earlier than otherwise.

'You're absolutely right about what happened afterwards. I have a key, which belonged to Daddy, to the doors in the outer wall of the estate, so that was no problem. I had to go home, because it would have been thoroughly unnatural if I hadn't come here – so there had to be a record of a call put through from here to our house; otherwise, how would I have learnt what had happened? I was just bloody stupid not to have told Dorry to stay on the line a bit longer. Reckon it was my only mistake. And I want to make it absolutely clear that this was entirely my idea and I forced Dorry to help me, blackmailed her, in fact.'

'Blackmailed her?'

'Yes, for her own good. You see, she's got a secret, too. Oh, nothing too terrible, but our stepmother had been using it against her for years, in order to keep Dorry her virtual slave. Just this once, I used it, too. Because I knew that as long as our stepmother was alive, Dorry would never be free. It's ironic that if we'd only known about our stepmother's secret, she could never have treated Dorry as she did: if *she'd* talked, *we* could have talked. Grandmamma's money might have made a difference, too, but probably not: Dorry would never have broken away. Which is why I decided to go ahead, even after I learned about the inheritance. Anyway, as I say, I started planning it a long time ago. Oh, and by the way, that threatening phone call Stepmother received: Dorry didn't know it at the time, but it was me on the line.'

'What was the purpose of that?'

'There were two, one quite legitimate. First, I hoped it might scare her into giving up her little game altogether. But, looking ahead, I also thought it might be a good idea to implant the idea that she had an enemy who had threatened her, and have the police officially notified of it. A waste of time, as it turned out: it didn't stop her, and you quickly quashed the idea that she'd been murdered in revenge by one of her victims.'

'So it was part of a long-term plan? Tell me more about that.'

'Stepmother often used to go away and take Dorry with her, both as a sort of messenger and maid, and leave me behind. So when I started thinking about it, I decided the best way would be to follow them on my bike one of these times, do the job and come back. There were several trips when for various reasons it turned out not to be possible. But Grandmamma's funeral was perfect. I remembered a lot about the house from when we came here as kids, and there were pictures and floor plans in the papers at the times of the other crimes, so it was all quite easy to work out. Naturally, I had no intention of coming to the funeral *as myself*, but when Clara told me I had to stay behind I argued with her, just so she wouldn't think I was up to anything.'

'Now, what about the attack on Lady Geraldine?'

'I'm really sorry about that. I like Gerry. It was purely a spur of the moment thing. I was in Dorry's room, talking, when Gerry came to the door, saying about how she knew who the murderer was and accusing Dorry of knowing as well, and covering up. I was behind the door. I just panicked, snatched up a bronze statuette and hit her. Thought I'd killed her, actually. Should have done a bunk as soon as I knew she was still alive, but that would have meant saying good-bye to the money, so took a gamble.'

'A gamble that she'd die. You hoped she would.'

'No! Just a gamble that she wouldn't remember what had happened. Anyway, that's immaterial now, isn't it? I suppose you'll want me to "accompany you to the station", as they say in books?'

'Both of you.'

Dorothy, who had sat as though frozen and totally

expressionless since Wilkins' last question to her, gave a little strangled cry. 'Don't worry, petal,' Agatha said, 'it won't be for long, for you.'

He formally cautioned and put them both under arrest, and he and Leather led them outside, Dorothy sobbing silently.

In the hall, Agatha said: 'Mind if I have my leather jacket? Rather fond of it. It's in the cloaks cupboard.'

Leather went to the cupboard and came back carrying the coat. 'Thanks.' She started to put it on. 'Bit hot for it, today, but easier than carrying it. Oh, must make sure I've got my cheroots.' She put her hand in the pocket. The next moment a small snub-nosed automatic was pointing straight at Wilkins.

Dorothy gave a gasp of horror. 'Aggie!'

Leather took a step towards Agatha. Wilkins said sharply: 'No, Jack,' and he froze.

'Right,' Agatha said calmly, 'let's all go outside. You two stay close together.'

They slowly made their way out onto the gravel forecourt in front of the house. A police car was parked there, a uniformed constable standing near it. He gave a start when he saw what was happening. 'You, over here,' Agatha called.

'Do as she says,' Wilkins told him and he joined them.

Agatha's motor-cycle was standing where she had left it the previous day. She backed towards it, still keeping the pistol trained on Wilkins.

'This is useless, Miss Agatha,' he said. 'You haven't got a chance.'

'Well, I haven't got a chance any other way. And I don't relish the prospect of being hanged.'

'It may not come to that.'

'Oh, just life imprisonment? Not a tempting alternative, thanks all the same. Now, lie down on the ground, all three of you.'

Slowly, they did so. Agatha mounted the motor bike. She looked at Dorothy, who was wringing her hands. 'Aggie, don't do this, please.'

'No choice, petal. Sorry to leave you in the lurch, but you'll be all right. Get a good lawyer, you can afford one now. Put all the blame on Aggie.'

She started the engine, thrust the pistol in her pocket, gave a wave and roared off, sending a shower of gravel into the air.

Wilkins, Leather and the constable scrambled to their feet. Wilkins pointed at Dorothy. 'Keep an eye on her,' he ordered the constable. 'She's under arrest. Come on, Jack.' They ran to the car, Leather jumping behind the wheel.

By the time they had got moving, Agatha was already two hundred yards down the drive and in a few more seconds was out of sight. 'Whew, she's going at a lick,' Leather muttered. 'Still, the gates are closed. She'll have to stop for the lodge-keeper to open them.' He put his foot down hard.

It was about fifteen seconds before they heard the sound of the crash.

Half a minute later, they skidded to a halt near the heavy wrought-iron gates and jumped out. The motor-cycle lay on its side, the front wheel buckled, the handle-bars askew. Agatha lay motionless a few feet from it. The lodge-keeper, Bates, was standing, gazing down at her in absolute horror. He looked up as they approached. 'I – I heard the bike coming and came out to open up. She had to have seen they were closed. But she didn't try to stop. She must have been doing sixty or seventy when she hit them. If I'd been just a bit quicker...' He buried his head in his hands.

'It's not your fault,' Wilkins said. 'She knew what she was doing. Go and phone for an ambulance, there's a good chap.'

'What? Oh, right.' Bates half stumbled into the lodge.

Wilkins knelt down and felt Agatha's pulse. Then he looked up and shook his head.

'Suicide, you think?' Leather asked.

'Yes, she preferred this to the rope. And who can blame her?' He reached into the pocket of Agatha's jacket and drew out the pistol. He got to his feet and put the muzzle of the gun to his head.

'Don't—' Leather began, in alarm.

Wilkins pulled the trigger. There was a barely audible click.

Leather gave a gasp. 'Unloaded, all the time! How did you know?'

Wilkins put his hand into his side pocket, took it out and displayed several small cartridges.

'You took them out?'

'Yes, had a rummage through the pockets of her jacket as soon as I arrived. Just a precaution, really, but after the last case here I certainly wasn't going to arrest anyone without making sure first they weren't armed.'

'So you knew then that Agatha was the murderer?'

'No, no. I thought she was the most likely, but I had no

proof. And several of the others had questions to answer, things to explain. Let's say I would have been surprised if it hadn't been Agatha, but not flabbergasted.'

'But when you found the gun in her pocket...?'

'Could have been quite innocent. She was a woman who roamed around on a motor-cycle, on her own. Quite natural if she felt she needed some protection. Daresay she had a permit for it.'

'But we could have stopped her getting away!'

'I know, Jack.'

'You wanted her to make a run for it?'

'She obviously couldn't get far and I thought there was a good chance she'd end it like this. I hate sending someone to the gallows, and I've never sent a woman. Would haunt me always, if I did. Not that I feel sorry for her, mind. Would have done. Clara was a real monster, and killing her seems to have been a totally unselfish crime, done solely for Dorry's sake. But the attack on Geraldine changed everything. Agatha Saunders was a dangerous woman and if she'd got away with this one, killing would always have been an option for her when anyone posed any kind of threat, or even inconvenience, eventually. So it's better she's gone like this.' He reloaded the automatic. 'Not a word about this, eh?'

'No, of course not.'

Wilkins put the gun in his pocket. 'Now we've got to go and tell Dorry.'

'I should never have gone along with it,' Dorothy said tearfully. 'It was very, very wrong of me. But Aggie was always so forceful. It was all her doing, really. She planned every bit of it. And I am weak. I've always found it easier just to do as I'm told. And I suppose even up to the last minute I didn't really believe in my heart that she would go through with it. When I opened Mother's door that night and saw her lying dead, it was terrible. But, of course, it was too late, then. I had to protect Aggie. But I swear I never, never knew she was going to hit Gerry. That was the most awful shock. So although I don't know what I'll do without Aggie, I am glad in a way it's ended as it has. Though I suppose I'll have to go to prison. But, it won't be for long, will it?'

'That's not for me to say, miss.'

'Oh dear, I don't think I could stand it for very long. You want me to come with you, now?'

'Go with Sergeant Leather, miss. I've got a few things to clear up here. Send a car for me, Jack.' Leather gave a nod.

'Do we have to go past the – the crash?' Dorothy asked.

Leather shook his head. 'No, miss, there's a track that leads to the Home Farm and then out onto the road. You'll be taking that route.'

'Thank you.'

Wilkins watched silently as Leather led Dorothy to the car, put her inside and got in next to her. The car moved off. Wilkins watched until it was out of sight, then turned and went back indoors. Merryweather was still standing outside the drawing-room.

'Are they all still in there?'

'Yes, Mr Wilkins. I did not know whether you had finished with them, so I took the liberty of saying you wished them to remain for the time being. I hope that was correct.'

'Yes, thank you. I must tell them what's happened.'

He opened the door and went in.

Five minutes later, Wilkins said: 'So the case is closed, and you are all free to go. You'll be pleased to know I've decided not to bring any charges of obstructing the police, concealing evidence, or anything of that nature.'

'I for one am very grateful, Chief Inspector,' said Timothy. 'And I would like once again to tender my apologies for my behaviour.'

A quiet murmur of assent went round the room.

'What about me?' Julie asked.

'I won't be detaining you, miss, but I'm putting you on your honour not to leave your present address in London. No doubt you'll be hearing from the Metropolitan Police in due course.'

'Of course. Thank you.'

'One more thing I want to say to you all. A lot of secrets came to light in this room earlier. Nobody will hear about them from me or Jack Leather. And I think you'll all be wise to bear in mind that if one secret leaks out, others are likely to, as well. So I suggest you keep your traps shut.'

The doors behind him burst open and the Earl came rushing in. His face was an expression of pure joy. Merryweather, his face wreathed in smiles, was just behind him. 'She's come round!' the Earl positively shouted. 'Gerry's come round!'

CHAPTER FORTY-ONE

Wilkins said, 'Oh, my lord, that's wonderful news.'

Timothy said: 'Splendid, splendid.'

Gregory said: 'Attagirl!'

Tommy said: 'Absolutely ripping!'

Julie said: 'Oh, that's swell.'

Penny said: 'How lovely!'

Miss Mackenzie said: 'Praise the Lord!'

'Thank you, thank you, all. She just suddenly opened her eyes, saw her mother, said, 'Hello, Mummy, what time is it?' and went straight back to sleep. But she was breathing normally, after that. Ingleby arrived a few minutes later. He's left some tablets for her but he says he thinks she'll be fine.' He looked round. 'Where are Agatha and Dorothy? I must tell them.'

'There's something you need to know, my lord,' said Wilkins.

Having brought the Earl up to date and said his good-byes, Wilkins left the room. He found Gregory waiting for him. The MP was looking a little embarrassed. 'Oh, Wilkins, just wanted to congratulate you. Terrible business, really tragic. But you handled it superbly. And thanks for what you said about everybody keeping quiet about anything that came out. Save me a bit of embarrassment, I must admit. Actually, I've realised the young lady's not much more than a gold-digger, so I'll be severing my connection with her – if I can just think of a way without putting her back up, which might be tricky.'

'I don't see why it should be, sir.'

'Er, how d'you mean?'

'Well, if she's a gold-digger, no doubt she believes you're very well off. You need to disabuse her of that belief.'

'Easier said than done. Only last week, she asked me if I was hard up, and I assured her I wasn't.'

'Why did you do that? Would have seemed an obvious way out.'

'I know. Pride, I suppose. Anyway, she'll never believe me if I plead poverty now.'

'Then you've got to convince her.'

'Yes, but how?' He seemed to be hanging on Wilkins' words.

'Well, I've never been in such a situation, but if I were you I should leave a bill unpaid.'

'I'm sorry, I don't...'

'A small bill, from some big company or organisation, who won't miss it. Ignore all their follow up demands, until they write threatening legal action, or better still, until you actually get a summons. Pay it immediately then – apologise, urgent constituency business, family bereavement, etc. But keep the letter. Take it with you next time you visit the young woman, and leave it somewhere about the flat, where it could have fallen from your pocket. When she finds it and sees you're being sued a few pounds, you won't have to convince her you're hard up. She'll either confront you, when you can admit it, or more likely you'll find she'll be severing her connection with you pretty quickly.'

'Wilkins, that's brilliant! I'll do it. Thanks very much. Anyway, must go and pack. Good-bye.'

He shook hands hurriedly and ran up the stairs. Wilkins looked after him. If Leather had been here, he thought, he'd have asked why his chief had bothered to help get Gregory Carstairs off the hook. But you never knew when it might be useful to have an MP in your debt.

Wilkins noticed that Timothy and Julie were standing in the porch, chatting quietly. 'Nor a KC, if it comes to that,' he said under his breath, and went over to them. 'Miss Osborne, I'll make a bargain with you.'

'What's that?'

'Give me your word that first thing next week you will go to Scotland Yard and confess to having entered the country illegally, and I'll forget to include it in my report to my Chief Constable. It should help.'

Her face lit up. 'Oh yes, of course I promise. That's terrific. I don't know how to thank you.'

'You have my word, too, Wilkins,' Timothy said. 'I'll go with her. It's much appreciated.'

'Mr Wilkins,' Julie said. 'Do explain one thing. Why did you question me so about my call to the *Evening News*? I've been racking my brains to think why it was important.'

'It wasn't important. I did it to get the Misses Saunders

off guard. If I'd just turned on them suddenly and started asking about their conversation, they'd have certainly realised I was on to something. And it only needed them to say that Dorry had just gabbled out a few words and then rung off, and I'd have been sunk, because I didn't have a bit of concrete evidence. But as I questioned you first, they weren't wary when I started on them. It seemed simply routine. Also, it gave the impression that I didn't know how long your call had lasted, so it didn't occur to them that I'd know how long *they* had talked.'

'I see. Gee, there's an awful lot to this detective business, isn't there? Tell me, when did you first suspect I wasn't really Stella?'

'From the start it occurred to me that your speech was almost totally American in vocabulary, phraseology and accent. Granted Stella Simmons had lived in New York for nearly eleven years and would obviously have picked up many Americanisms, but I couldn't think she'd have lost all her Britishness. I also noticed that when we talked, you used the words "When I came to" – and then changed it to "When I came home". I guessed what you'd been about to say was "When I came to England". I think the clincher was when you referred to the Westshire "Police Department", rather than "Police Force" or "Constabulary". Yesterday I went to the village in Worcestershire, where Stella had been brought up – I got the name of it from the Earl – and saw the local doctor, who's been in practice there for over twenty years. He remembers the family well. I was still puzzled by the business of the toothpaste, though I thought it must be something to do with proving or disproving your authenticity. When I asked the doctor about Stella's teeth, he told me they'd all been extracted when she was in her teens. He recalled it clearly, because she had been so upset. Then everything fell into place.'

'You could have accused me outright of being an impostor on the terrace yesterday. I might have admitted it.'

'Or you might have denied it, and it could have taken weeks or months to prove it either way. Until I had the doctor's testimony – and for all I knew, he might have been dead – there'd have been only Mr Lambert's word that Stella had ever had her teeth extracted; it would be virtually impossible to find the dentist who had done it after all this time. No, I wanted to get all the business of the toothpaste and the postcard and the cufflinks and the armour out of the way at the start. Besides, it's a bit of an idiosyncrasy of mine that I like to find things out for myself, rather than being told them. It gets on Jack's nerves sometimes.'

'I bet you're a dab hand at crossword puzzles, aren't you?'

'I must admit it gets the day off to a good start if I can complete *The Times* one over breakfast.'

Timothy blinked. 'You *finish* it – over *breakfast*?'

'Not always, sir. Only mostly. Well, I'd better go out and wait for my car. Hope if we meet again it's under pleasanter circumstances. Good-bye.'

He strolled out into the sunlight. He found Penny already there, staring thoughtfully out over the park, and went across to her. 'Leaving now, miss?'

'Yes, there's a train at two thirty. Hawkins is taking us. He thinks he can squeeze us all in.'

'Your father and Mr Carstairs won't like that very much.'

She smiled absently.

'Answer me a question, Miss Saunders, or two actually.'

'What?'

'Why did you arrange to have that photo taken of your father?'

Penny went crimson. 'I – I didn't – what – how?'

'How did I know? Well, as Miss Osborne pointed out, the picture was so bland. Anyone really wanting to damage him would have made it a lot more compromising. No blackmail demand followed it. Then again, someone, probably two people, brought him home and put him to bed. Your father seems to have imagined he got home under his own steam, but that's very unlikely. It was obviously the early hours of the morning. And you can't draw up in a car or taxi, let yourself into a house, carry an unconscious man upstairs, undress him and put him to bed without making a fair bit of noise. You said you're a very light sleeper; so why didn't you, in the room next to his, wake up? Also, when I was showing the picture round earlier you kept your head down and looked thoroughly unhappy and didn't ask to see the picture, even after Miss Osborne said it was quite innocuous. That confirmed my earlier suspicion that you'd seen it before.'

Penny gave a sigh that seemed to come from the depths of her soul. 'I never intended to blackmail him, of course. He wasn't even supposed to see the picture. The silly chumps were just supposed to give it to me. Only they couldn't resist sending him a print. I was mad with them.'

'One of the silly chumps being Mr Lambert?'

'Crumbs, no. He knew nothing about it. It was a couple of young lawyers, who loved the idea of playing a trick on a top KC. When I suggested it to them, they jumped at it. There wasn't supposed to be a girl in the picture, though. That was their idea. And I didn't know they were going to drug him. They're keen photographers, and I simply asked if they could fake a picture that made him look drunk. That was all.'

'And what was your reason?'

'To have a sort of bargaining counter, to keep by me. He's so strict. And he disapproves of Tommy and he'll never agree to my marrying him. I just wanted something I could use if it really came to a deadlock. But it was a stupid idea, and I'd never have gone through with it. I've destroyed the negative already. And I'd no idea he'd been worrying about it, all these weeks. I thought he would have just thrown the photo in the waste-paper basket and forgotten about it. I've been feeling awful for the last hour. And he's sure to go on worrying.'

'Then let's see if I can put his mind at rest. Tell you what, I'll write to him in a week or two, saying I've discovered who was responsible, that I cannot give him the name, but that the negative and all the prints have been destroyed and I guarantee he'll hear no more about it.'

'Oh, that's wonderful! He'll think you tracked down the criminal and somehow frightened him off. He'll be awfully grateful.'

'Oh yes, I suppose he will.'

'But why aren't you going to tell him it was me?'

'I feel very kindly disposed towards you, Miss Saunders. Apart from Miss Mackenzie, you're the only one of the guests who didn't tell me a single lie.'

'Really? Oo, I must tell Daddy that.'

'And I suggest you think of some other way of persuading him to be a bit less strict.'

'Well, actually, I've got high hopes of Julie. He seems really keen on her, and he doesn't mind she's not Stella. We're good chums already and I think she'll soften him up.'

'I hope you're right, and I wish you every happiness. By the way, I didn't know you and Mr Lambert wanted to get married.'

'No, Tommy doesn't know yet, either. But he will soon. Oh, what was the other thing you wanted to ask?'

'Just why you pretend to be the typical dumb blonde of fiction and the films, when in your own way you're obviously a very smart young lady.'

'Well, Tommy'd never marry anyone cleverer than himself. And though he's absolutely adorable, he hasn't got the world's greatest brainbox. So I've got to be pretty dumb, for the time being.'

At that moment, the adorable one emerged from the house, carrying a small overnight bag, just as a police car rolled up.

'My transport,' Wilkins said. 'Back to the station and a lot of paperwork, I'm afraid. Well, good luck, Miss Saunders.'

'Thank you for everything, Mr Wilkins. You were wonderful.' She stepped forward and kissed him lightly on the cheek.

Wilkins reddened a little, gave an awkward little bow and hurried to the car. Penny waved as it moved off.

Tommy came across to her. 'New boyfriend, Penny?'

'Oh, he's sweet, Tommy, don't you think?'

'Well, not exactly the word I'd use, not after the way he put me through it.'

'It was your own fault, you silly boy, telling all those fibs about playing a practical joke on Miss Mackenzie and pulling down the armour.'

'I know. But everything's OK now. I've apologised to Gregory for what I said and he's promised not to sue me for slander. And I've thought of an absolutely spiffing idea for a company. It'll be called Get Your Own Back, Ltd. It's really up my street. What happens is that if anyone's had an absolutely rotten deal from somebody, their boss, say, or a boyfriend or a girlfriend, they come to me and I pull a prank on the culprit, just like I did to the Hodges. Then if the client's happy, he or she pays me: ten, twenty quid, perhaps even fifty for a really super wheeze. He's got to pay, because he knows that if he doesn't I'll do the same sort of thing to him. Of course, I'd have to make absolutely sure first that the client is in the right. And I wouldn't do anything to really hurt anybody, just give 'em a very uncomfortable and embarrassing time. It really fits my talents. What d'you think?'

'Tommy, it's terrific. It could really work.'

'And I wouldn't need much capital to get started. It'd hardly eat into my fifteen hundred quid at all.'

'Don't you mean fourteen hundred and fifty three?'

'Oh. You guessed. Forty-seven?'

'Mm. Is it a bookie?'

'Yes. I put fifty quid, which I didn't have – over the phone – on this absolute cert. It came in fourth. I've been horribly worried. But it's all right, you needn't lecture me. I've learnt my lesson.'

'Good.'

'So we're in business?'

'Well, I'm sorry, Tommy, but I really don't think I can be the Managing Director.'

Tommy hid his relief. 'That's OK. Be a – a consultant. That's it. All you'll have to do is just keep your eyes and ears open and when you hear anybody moaning about how badly someone's treated them, just point them in my direction. I'll pay you commission. Then when I come up with a wheeze I'll run through it with you and you can tell me if there are any flaws, or suggest refinements, and so on.'

'Oh, that sounds perfect.'

'Topping! I'll put your name on the letter heading. I'll even get you some cards. 'GET YOUR OWN BACK, LTD. Miss Penelope Saunders, Special Consultant."

'*Special* Consultant? Oo, that's even better. Tommy, this is so exciting.'

'I think I can come up with a better name.'

They turned round. It was Julie, who had approached, unheard.

'What's that?' Tommy asked.

'"Get Even, Ltd." That's what we say in the States. It's shorter and snappier.'

Tommy nodded thoughtfully. 'Yes, I think you're right. Penny, your first consultation. What do you think?'

'Mm. I like it.'

'That's settled, then. Oh, and I've got something for you, Julie.'

He put his hand into his pocket and took out a crumpled tube of toothpaste. 'This is yours. I put it in a vase in one of the empty rooms and just retrieved it.'

She threw up her hands in mock delight. 'I'm overcome! I thought I would never see it again. I've been devastated.' She clasped it to her breast. 'But it's come home! I shall keep it always, as a souvenir. Tommy, you've done the decent thing.'

'One tries to, don't you know.'

'But seriously, Tommy, I want to apologise again, for impersonating Stella. I know you were very fond of her. I don't mind about the others but I feel fooling you was pretty mean.'

'No, it's all right. I was fond of her a long time ago. But I'm not sure she was all that fond of me. I mean, she never wrote – just Christmas cards. Not even birthday cards, even though I sent her one regularly for years. And I'm beginning to think all those letters to Florrie were for only one reason, really.'

'Well, I have to say she never showed much affection for her. She was always saying things like, "Oh lord, I suppose I've got to write to Florrie again this week. Crashing bore." It used to kind of rile me, sometimes.'

'Well, I don't blame you for what you did. I think it took a lot of spunk.'

'That sure makes me feel better. Timothy actually said that while he could not approve of what I did, it demonstrated considerable initiative. I guess I'm pretty lucky all round.'

'Guess we all are,' said Tommy.

* * *

Jean Mackenzie took a last look around the room, then, carrying her small suitcase, made her way towards the stairs. She had just reached them when she saw the Countess leaving Gerry's room. She hurried across to her.

'Oh, Lady Burford, any further change?'

'No, she's still sleeping very peacefully and normally.'

'How wonderful. A real answer to prayer.'

'Yes, indeed.'

'I have been feeling so guilty, having in a way been responsible for bringing Agatha to this house.'

'Please don't think like that. Only Agatha was responsible.'

'I still find it so hard to believe that she should do such terrible things. She was a strange girl in some ways, and most outspoken in her language. But I was nonetheless fond of her. It must have been some inherited – oh, inherited from her mother's family, of course – some kink of the brain, perhaps, for which she could not really be blamed.'

'I find it difficult to think like that, I must admit.'

'Oh, naturally, naturally. We cannot know, of course. We must simply commit her to God's infinite mercy.'

'Yes, well, we all need that.'

'I would like to thank you for your great kindness, and for making me feel so much at home here, in spite of the unusual circumstances.'

'Not at all. It's been a pleasure having you. We are all grateful for your kindness to Florrie over many years.'

'Thank you.' She went slightly pink. 'Would you consider me terribly impertinent if I offered a small piece of advice?'

'Not at all.'

'Please don't think I've been spying, but I spent a lot of time yesterday simply sitting, staring out of the window. And I saw Lord Burford twice, once carrying a large bunch of nettles, and later burying some small items each side of the porch. It was obvious, of course, what he was attempting.' She broke off and frowned before saying thoughtfully: 'I wonder if he tried bent pins or nails, as well.'

For a moment Lady Burford was at a loss for words. Here was somebody who seemed to find her husband's behaviour not at all odd. She had to try and find out more. 'I wouldn't know. But, er…he did mix blue and red ink to make purple.'

'Purple ink? I don't quite… Oh, wait. Yes, I think I see. He had some candles, no doubt.'

This woman was miraculous, thought Lady Burford. 'Well, one candle. And later, after Geraldine was attacked, he did say it should have been a real purple candle.'

Miss Mackenzie nodded sapiently. 'He's right, of course. But I honestly don't think it would have made any difference. Do tell him that. It may set his mind at rest.'

The Countess moistened her lips. 'He – he also said Rosemary should have been here. But we don't know anyone called Rosemary. At least, I certainly don't. I keep asking myself, if George does, why he should never have mentioned her?'

Miss Mackenzie smiled. 'Oh, I shouldn't be concerned about that. I'm sure he was not thinking of any female friend. But the advice I wanted to give was that these things are not really a good idea. Far better to have a word with your rector.'

The Countess had considered the possibility of consulting the doctor, but the idea of consulting the rector had not entered her mind. But she gave nothing away. 'Yes, I'm sure you're right. I'll tell George. Thank you.' She suddenly felt very indebted to Miss Mackenzie and groped around in her mind for some way to show it. 'By the way,' she said, not without a slight qualm, 'I'm sorry your experiment was spoiled. If at some time you would like to come and try again, we would have no objection.'

'Oh, that is very kind of you, Lady Burford. But no, thank you all the same. I shall never touch a ouija board again. In fact, I'm giving up all that sort of thing. I realise I have been very gullible. I shall always be interested in psychic research, but I won't let it take the place of true religion in future.'

'I'm sure that's a wise decision.'

'And now I really must go. The car will be coming round. Thank you again, and good-bye.'

'I'll come down with you,' said the Countess.

They descended the stairs. A moment later, Timothy came out of his room and started towards the stairs himself. As he did so, Gregory appeared around the corner of the east corridor. They saw each other at the same time, both slackened their stride for a second, then continued to advance. At the top of the stairs they stopped. Both spoke together.

'Look—'

'I—'

'You first,' said Timothy.

'Well, just wanted to say, very sorry. For my suspicions

and the way I acted. Idiotic, really, but sort of lost my head. Frankly, in a blue funk, to tell you the truth.'

Timothy gave a quick nod. 'I know. I have never behaved in that way before. Quite irrational. But it was a unique situation. So I apologise, too.'

'Perhaps we should, er, bury the hatchet. After all, it's many years since it all started and we're not getting any younger.'

'Yes, I agree. Let bygones be bygones.'

'I had nothing to do with that photo being taken, by the way.'

'No, I realised afterwards that you couldn't have.'

'Might I ask, what you said about St. John's Wood: how did you know…?'

'Oh, I was lunching at my club one day – the Reform. There were some chaps talking at the next table. Couldn't help overhearing them. One of them seemed to be an MP and he was telling them about one of his colleagues who was paying the rent for "a little bit of fluff", as he put it, in St. John's Wood. In the next few minutes it came out that the man he was talking about was a Tory, married, had a small majority, and sat for a strongly non-conformist West Country rural constituency. I realised all of it applied to you. I have to admit that later I browsed through *Who's Who* and a couple of parliamentary reference books, and found that you were the only one who fitted the bill.'

'I see. No idea anybody knew. Actually, I'm going to end it – or rather, I've thought up quite a subtle way to make sure she does. It's been pretty nerve-racking. And, after all, I do like Alex. Wouldn't want to lose her.'

They went down the stairs and outside.

CHAPTER FORTY-TWO

It was Saturday morning and Wilkins was in his office, working on his report, when his phone rang and he was told, by an impressed girl on the switchboard, that there was a call for him from the Earl of Burford.

'Ah, Wilkins,' said the Earl, when he got through, 'sorry to bother you again, but wonderin' if you could come out to Alderley some time today.'

'Oh, my lord, not another – ?'

'Great Scot, no! Nothing wrong. It's Geraldine. She wants a chat with you: to compare notes, as she puts it. She's got to stay in bed for a couple of days and she's not a good patient, is bored stiff and frankly is driving everyone crazy. She's been nagging me to phone you.'

'My lord, I'll be delighted. I've been hoping for a word with Lady Geraldine myself.'

'Splendid. Come around four, if that's all right.'

Gerry was sitting up in bed, wearing a pink bed jacket. Apart from the fact that a bandage completely enveloped her head above the eyebrows (in spite of Dr. Ingleby assuring her it was not necessary, she had insisted upon this), she looked quite ridiculously healthy.

Wilkins went across to the bed. He was carrying a large bunch of red roses.

'Oh, are those for me?' Gerry asked, unnecessarily. She took them, held them to her nose and breathed in deeply. 'How lovely! Thanks awfully.'

'Rather superfluous, I'm afraid,' Wilkins said, looking round the room. There were about eight large vases, all filled with flowers of every conceivable colour.

'Oh, you can never have too many flowers. Marie, put them in water, please. And we'd like some tea in about half an hour.' She handed the roses to the maid, who left the room.

'Sit down,' Gerry said, pointing to a chair, and Wilkins did so.

'How are you feeling, Lady Geraldine?'

'Terrific. It's barmy, making me stay in bed, but Ingleby's a bit of an old woman. Up tomorrow, though, thank heavens. But let's not talk about me. I've got absolutely millions of questions. I've only had a second-hand account of things.'

'From his lordship?'

'No, he didn't take it all in, by any means. Actually, from Merryweather, who was outside the door throughout and just happened not to have closed it properly. But there's a lot to be filled in. So, please.'

'Well, first of all I've got to admit that at the beginning I made a bad mistake. I briefly considered the possibility that Dorothy had done it, but as soon as you gave her a cast-iron alibi, I decided that the murder had to have arisen out of the scene at the will-reading: that Mrs Clara's threat had frightened someone, who decided she had to be silenced before she could spill the beans. In fact, the murder had been planned well in advance and Mrs Clara's outburst had nothing to do with it. But it was a big stroke of luck for the girls, because for a while it stopped me looking for any other motive. I kept questioning them about whether their stepmother had ever mentioned having some dirt on any of the other guests. And I'll say this for them. They could have taken advantage of the situation to try and divert suspicion on one of the others: said yes, Clara had mentioned knowing something disreputable about Timothy or Gregory. But they didn't.'

'When did you first realise your mistake?'

'I don't think there was one moment. But one thing about Dorry puzzled me from the start: why she hadn't phoned her sister earlier? I mean, they'd inherited a large fortune, which was going to transform their lives. The first thing she'd want to do would be call her sister and tell her. OK, immediately after she learned about it, she was distracted by Clara's tantrum, and had to go up and try and calm her down. But even when she'd done that it couldn't have been much more than six o'clock at the latest. Agatha was (supposedly) going to a party in the evening, but Dorry had an hour or two in which she could have at least tried to get in touch with her. But she didn't. The same thing applies at the end of the evening: you can't be sure what time a person is going to get home after a party, but in such a situation I'd certainly ring them at about eleven or half past – and keep trying. But she stayed with you – as, of course, she had to – all the time. It did sow the seed in my mind that perhaps she wasn't being entirely above board with me.'

'Yes, I thought it was odd. But nothing more than that, of course, at that stage.'

'There was something else: Agatha referred to the killer having held a pillow over her stepmother's face. As far as I could discover, she had never been told it was a pillow. Of course, it's a reasonable assumption, but it could just as easily have been a cushion or a towel or something. I decided at the time it was probably just a lucky guess. I was still working on the belief that the murderer was one of the other beneficiaries. After I'd interviewed them, I knew that most of them had lied to me, the possible exceptions being Miss Mackenzie and Penelope. But I was sure that all of them were capable of having done it. I was already fairly certain, from the way she spoke, that Stella was an impostor. I didn't believe Tommy's story about the armour for a moment and the fact that it gave him an alibi for the time of Stella's intruder made me virtually sure that that was him. He was the only one who'd known her at all well years previously and I wondered if he had spotted she was a fake and was trying to prove it. The stealing of the toothpaste clearly suggested something to do with her teeth, but that's as far as I was able to take it. I'd marked Timothy down as the likely source of the postcard, as soon as I learnt who Dora Lethbridge was. It occurred to me that the use of the word "Miss" was meant to indicate she had never been married, and there was a subtlety about that which suggested a lawyer to me. I couldn't think, though, that he'd leave the card *and* scatter the cufflinks, so that left Gregory as the likely culprit as regards them.

Anyway, that was the position when we left here yesterday lunchtime.'

'So what did you do the rest of the day? What were those enquiries you were pursuing elsewhere?'

'I sent Jack up to London. First of all he went to Somerset House and obtained a copy of Clara's birth certificate, which showed that she was almost certainly illegitimate. I also wanted to see what Timothy's block lettering was like, and I thought the best source would be some official form he had filled out. I phoned the Passport Office, asked them to look him up and ten minutes later they rang back to say that he had made an application for a passport a few years previously. I asked them to do a photostat of it and informed them that my sergeant would pick it up. I'd told Jack to phone after he'd finished at Somerset House and I left instructions at headquarters for them to tell him to go and get the photostat. Then I went up to Worcestershire.'

He told her what he had told Julie the previous day. He went on: 'By then I'd confirmed many of my suspicions and theories but I still didn't know for sure who the murderer was. I'd ruled out Miss Mackenzie and Penelope, and almost, but not quite, ruled out Tommy and Stella. That left Timothy and Gregory. All the time, though, at the back of my mind those two little facts about the sisters – the delayed phone call and Agatha's knowing about the pillow – must have been nagging away. I woke up thinking about them yesterday morning. It was the phone call that worried me most. I was on my way to work, asking myself, "Why didn't she call earlier?" And then it suddenly hit me. There was a possible reason – that Dorry had already spoken to her sister, face to face. Which would mean Agatha had been in the house all along. I realised how she could have got in unobserved and where she could have hidden.'

Gerry gave a grimace. 'Actually in the room with me! And I didn't have a clue.'

'No way you could have, Lady Geraldine. Anyway, that left the question of the early morning phone call – obviously necessary because there had to be a record of a call to their home: it would be unthinkable that Dorry wouldn't phone her *eventually*. And, of course, Agatha had had to go home after the murder, in order to answer it.'

'It also gave her a sort of alibi, didn't it? I bet that if you'd made enquiries in Hampstead, you'd have found a neighbour or postman or milkman who saw her leaving in a hurry on her motor-bike early that morning.'

'More than likely. But this all meant that the call could have been very brief – just long enough for Dorry to tell her that nothing untoward had happened since Agatha had left and that she could start back straight away. I wondered if it was possible that they had slipped up and forgotten to make the call long enough. I turned round and went straight to the telephone exchange. They showed me their records, and there it was: call from Alderley 1 to their Hampstead number, starting at 7.09 a.m., lasting for 11 seconds.'

'And that's when you knew Agatha was guilty.'

'Not knew. She was now obviously a very strong suspect, but so were Timothy and Gregory. That's why I needed them all present when we went through the events of the night, as that might show up some blatant discrepancies in someone's story which would clearly point to his guilt. But actually it didn't. When I finally got Timothy and Gregory, as well as Tommy, to tell the whole truth, their accounts dovetailed remarkably well. And that was when I knew.'

'Marvellous,' Gerry said. 'But you say you didn't work out how Agatha could have done it until you were actually on your way to work yesterday morning. What time was that?'

'Oh, around eight-fifteen, I suppose. Why do you ask?'

Gerry looked smug. 'Because that means I beat you to it, by about four hours.'

'Really? Congratulations, Lady Geraldine.'

'You see, Aggie made one other mistake. I didn't spot it at the time, though I knew there was *something*. About four o'clock, I woke up and remembered what it was. When she first arrived, Aggie spent about a quarter of an hour with us. Then she said she'd like to go up to her room and asked which one it was. Mummy told her. She said that after she'd freshened up she'd go and see Dorry. *But she didn't ask which was Dorry's room.* Of course, she could have asked one of the servants, but the natural thing would have been to ask the location of both rooms at the same time. I wondered if Dorry could have told her when they spoke on the phone. But it was inconceivable to me that, with everything else on her mind, she would have mentioned that. Can you imagine it? "Oh, Aggie, Mother's been murdered, and we've come into sixty-five thousand pounds, and I've got a nice room, almost opposite the top of the stairs"? I thought to myself that the obvious explanation for Aggie's not asking where Dorry's room was, was that she already knew. And then, just like you, everything came to me in a flash. All those unidentified ladies in black veils at the funeral, free to roam the house during the afternoon. So easy just to stay behind when everyone else had left. Only where I was stupid was at first it didn't occur to me that Dorry had been in it from the start. I imagined she'd only discovered afterwards what Aggie had done, and had simply been covering up for her. I just had to go and see Dorry at once and confront her. But before I'd got out more than a few words – wham. After that, as they say, I knew no more.'

'Well, you did very well, Lady Geraldine. You've got the natural makings of a detective. I'm just sorry you weren't in at the dénouement.'

'No, no, it was horrible seeing people being arrested the other times and I would have hated to see it happen to Aggie and Dorry. You know, for a while earlier today I found myself feeling quite sorry for Dorothy and worrying about her.'

'Oh, I shouldn't worry too much about that young woman.'

Something about his tone made Gerry glance at him sharply. 'Are you thinking what I'm thinking, Mr Wilkins?'

'What would that be, Lady Geraldine?'

'Well, she seems such a natural victim, a pushover for anyone who wants to use her or manipulate her. And apparently being virtually blackmailed by Clara over this guilty secret – and I suppose we've all got a pretty good idea of what that must have been. But I can't help remembering that hour or two when she and I were together downstairs. She seemed really happy, and totally engrossed by all I had to tell her about the other cases. And yet she knew that at that very time her sister was murdering their stepmother.'

'She says she never believed Aggie would go through with it.'

'But she knew Aggie was *planning* it, and at the very least there was a chance she'd do it. Even when we first met here, after the funeral, she virtually arranged that she and I should stay down and have a chat after everyone else had gone to bed. And when the time came, she made sure she was with me every second. Yet, she didn't seem even slightly anxious. And later, going on about how she would always be grateful to Clara. Aggie at least wasn't a hypocrite. But Dorry could have stopped the murder, as soon as she knew about the inheritance, which was obviously going to change everything – just told Agatha it was off, and Agatha could have walked out of the house, pretending to be one of the funeral guests, who had lost count of the time. Again, when I knocked on Dorry's door and called out that I had to speak to her about the murder, Aggie must have got an inkling I was on to something and gone behind the door immediately. Didn't Dorry wonder why? Didn't she see her pick up the statuette? No, I'm sure she knew just what Aggie was going to do. Then, helping Agatha carry me in here, putting me to bed and leaving me, without attempting to let anybody know. I could have died in those four hours before Marie found me unconscious.'

Wilkins nodded. 'And then she let Agatha take all the blame, and after she's killed she's only really concerned about what's going to happen to her, and she wouldn't get a long sentence, would she? No doubt within a few months she'll have a cell to herself, she'll be a trusty with all sorts of privileges, and all the wardresses will be saying what a pity it is that such a nice, ladylike, gentle person should have to be there.'

'And I suppose in a year or two she'll be out. With sixty-five thousand pounds in the bank – plus interest.'

'Oh, I wouldn't be so sure of that. When it comes to trial, I'll emphasise all the points we've just made, as I'm sure the prosecutor will. Miss Dorry could be in for quite a shock. She won't do life, of course. I don't say she deserves to. I don't believe she planned the murder – that *was* sister Aggie's work. But she's not the used innocent she pretends. I reckon about eight years would be satisfactory, from my point of view.'

'I just hope you're right,' Gerry said, fingering the back of her head.

CHAPTER FORTY-THREE

'Well, Wilkins, we have to thank you yet again,' said Lord Burford, when the Chief Inspector was saying his good-byes.

'We are greatly in your debt,' added the Countess.

'Not at all, your ladyship. Very pleased to have been of service. A complex case. But its occurrence here not such a coincidence as your lordship at first assumed.'

'How d'you mean?'

'Agatha had decided to kill her stepmother whenever the opportunity arose. The funeral provided the first such opportunity. And the funeral would not have taken place here had it not been for the earlier crimes. It was those murders that made Miss Mackenzie so eager to conduct her experiment here and tell her little fib about your great aunt's wishes. So the location of this crime resulted directly from the earlier ones. It was a simple matter of cause and effect.'

The Earl nodded. 'Yes, I see. Good point.'

'And I have to say that in one respect this was the most satisfying case I have ever handled.'

'Really? What respect was that?'

'For the first time in my life I was able to tell both a Member of Parliament and a King's Counsel to shut up.' A quite dreamy expression came over his face. 'It was a moment I shall long remember and cherish.'

Lord Burford chuckled. 'So shall I, Wilkins, so shall I.'

When Wilkins had left, the Countess said: 'George, it's wonderful about Geraldine, but it's almost as good that you seem quite your old self, too. I was so worried about you.'

'Worried about *me*? Why?'

'Well, you were behaving extremely oddly: picking bunches of nettles, carrying spare socks around with you, making purple ink, burying things outside.'

'Oh. That. Yes. I see.' He looked decidedly embarrassed.

'What were you up, to, George?'

He coughed. 'Well, suppose I can tell you now. Fact is, I was trying to break the curse.'

'What curse?'

'That old gypsy's curse. Thought perhaps all these dreadful things happenin' here, might be something in it, after all. Found this old book about folklore in the library. Lots in it about black magic. Full of ways you can undo or nullify curses and hexes. Some of 'em quite disgustin', actually. But some of the others didn't seem it would do any harm to try. One of them was to take a lot of nettles, cut them up into small pieces and stuff them into things they call poppets – sort of effigies, made of cloth. Best I could do was a pair of old socks. Then you bury them one each side of the porch. Another was to put a lot of bent pins or nails into glass jars and bury them as well. Then there was one where you take a purple candle, write "All blocks are now removed" in reverse on a strip of paper, fold it round the candle and then let it burn out. Only I didn't have a purple candle, so I dipped an ordinary one in purple ink. Then some say you've got to rub oil of rosemary on it, and I didn't have any of that, either.'

Lady Burford gave a slight start. 'Rosemary?'

'Yes. Why?'

'Nothing. Go on.' She gave an almost imperceptible sigh of relief.

'So all in all I wasn't too sure of that one. The last one was simpler: you just tie a length of twine in dozens of knots and say, "Tie and bind, tie and bind, No harm comes to me or mine" and bury that. Anyway, I buried two of each, a poppet of nettles, a jar of bent pins and a length of knotted twine, one each side of the porch. Then, of course, Gerry was attacked, so it didn't seem any of it had worked and I thought it was because I hadn't done it properly. But then she got better, so perhaps there was something in it, after all. What do you think?'

'What do I think? George, it's pagan!'

'But a curse is pagan, isn't it? So why not fight fire with fire?'

'Well, you worried Gerry and you worried me. And you had young Tommy thinking you were out of your mind. We must make sure he learns what was really going on. And Miss Mackenzie saw some of the things you were doing, and guessed what it was about. She seems to be something of an expert. I told her that you'd said it should have been a real purple candle and she said to tell you that you were quite right, but it probably wouldn't have made any difference.'

'Really? Well, glad of that, anyway.'

'She suggested we have a word with the rector. I didn't know what she meant at the time, but I do now. If you really believe Alderley is cursed, we could ask him to come and perform, well, not an exorcism, it's not haunted, after all, but a blessing or a service of cleansing. But I'm sure he'll be willing to arrange something. That will be the Christian thing to do.'

'Yes, fine idea, Lavinia. Will you speak to him? More in your line than mine.'

'Yes, I'll see him after church tomorrow. Now something else. That armour is still scattered all over the picture gallery.'

'Oh, I know. There just hasn't been time to clear it up so far.' He looked at his watch. 'I'll go up and make a start on it now.'

'You'll do it yourself? Isn't it quite a complicated job?'

'I'm sure there's nobody else here who can do it. And I'm darned if I'm going to call in somebody from a museum, or something. No, I know a bit about armour. I think I can manage all right.' He went out.

The Countess leaned back in her chair and gave a sigh. So all was explained. But what had George been thinking of? Nettles, bent pins, purple candles. Really, if it wasn't so ridiculous, it would be quite funny. In fact...

The Countess smiled. Her lips twitched. She gave a little chuckle. The chuckle turned into a laugh. The laugh became louder. Lady Burford laughed as she had not done for years.

* * *

In the gallery, the Earl stared at the various components of the suit of armour, trying to recall just what would be the best way to set about putting them together. Doing it on his own could take quite a time. He was going to need some help. He went out and made his way back along the corridor, towards the main staircase. But before he reached it, he saw his butler coming towards him, stopped and waited until Merryweather reached him.

'I've just been looking at that armour,' the Earl said. 'I'm going to start puttin' it back together.'

'Strangely enough, my lord, I was looking at it only ten minutes ago, and was intending to remind your lordship of the situation.'

'I'll need a hand, though. So if William or Benjamin aren't doin' anything vital at the moment, send one of them along to the gallery, will you?'

'I shall be very happy to assist your lordship.'

'Really? It'll mean some crawlin' about the floor, you know.'

'Quite within my capabilities, my lord.'

'Well, if you're sure, come along then.'

He turned and began to retrace his steps towards the gallery, Merryweather accompanying him. A thought struck the Earl. 'You know, we never did find out what caused it to fall over. That young scallywag Tommy confessed to it. But seems he didn't, after all. So, who did?'

The merest ghost of a smile appeared momentarily on the butler's august features. 'Perhaps Miss Mackenzie's original belief was correct after all and it was indeed a poltergeist, my lord.'

The Earl chuckled. 'Don't believe in 'em.'

They had reached the double doors of the gallery. About to go in, Lord Burford suddenly stopped dead, causing Merryweather very nearly to bump into him. Both men stared into the room. In a strangled whisper the Earl uttered just two words. 'Good gad.'

The suit of armour was standing on its plinth, intact and perfectly reassembled.

Long seconds passed. At last, Lord Burford gulped. He seemed to have difficulty in speaking. 'Not – not two minutes ago that was all over the floor. There was an hour's work to put it back...'

His normally pink complexion had become very pale. He turned and gazed at Merryweather uncomprehending-ly.

The butler's face, by way of contrast to his employer's, had gone a dingy grey. He stared at the suit of armour. 'There – there seems to be a piece of paper stuck under the visor, my lord.'

'What? Oh, so there is.' The Earl looked around, then, somewhat hesitantly, crossed the gallery, lifted the visor and gingerly extracted a sheet of crumpled note paper bearing a dozen or so lines of writing. He stared down at it and his eyes bulged. Merryweather gazed at him expectantly. Lord Burford looked up at him, his face a blank mask. 'It's the words of *Comin' Round The Mountain*. Bradley's notes. He threw this away. How the deuce...?'

Merryweather gulped. 'You think possibly the Honourable Mrs Florence Saunders, my lord...?' His voice, too, tailed away.

'Great Aunt Florrie? You think *Florrie* knocked the armour over – just for Miss Mackenzie's benefit? And put it back again? But, good gad, she's dead. It's not possible. Is it? Is it possible?'

With a sharp click, that sounded like a gunshot in the stillness, the visor of the suit of armour fell shut.

The Earl gave a convulsive start, Merryweather a slightly more controlled one. For a full ten seconds neither of them spoke. It was the butler who found his voice first. 'My lord, may I suggest we retire downstairs immediately and that you allow me to fetch you a stiff whisky and soda?'

At last the Earl pulled himself together. 'Merryweather, you may indeed. And for once, you're going to join me.'

'Thank you, my lord,' said Merryweather.

ABOUT THE AUTHOR

JAMES ANDERSON was born in Swindon but lived in or near to Cardiff most of his life. He took a degree in History at the University of Reading and worked as a salesman, copywriter and freelance journalist before writing his first novel. He went on to have fourteen novels and one play published before his death in 2007.